I0582420

RED,

WHITE

AND

GREEN

Red, White And Green

Copyright © Joe Lane

First Edition

ISBN: 978-1-7392187-1-3

All rights reserved. No part of this publication may be reproduced or transmitted in any form or by any means, electronic or mechanical, including photography, recording, or any information storage or retrieval system without permission in writing from Joe Lane. The book is sold subject to the condition that it shall not, by way of trade or otherwise, be lent, copied, altered, resold or otherwise circulated without Joe Lane's prior consent in any form of binding or cover other than that in which is published and without similar a condition, including this condition, being imposed on any subsequent publisher.

This book is a work of fiction. Any references to real people, events, organisations or places are used fictitiously. All other names, characters, organisations, places and events, incidents and all dialogue are the products of the author's imagination and should not be construed as real. Any further resemblance to any actual persons, living or dead, places or actual events is entirely coincidental.

Design & publishing services provided by JM Agency

www.jm.agency

RED, WHITE AND GREEN

Joseph Lane

For Liam Deasey and the people of Kerry and Cork.

— 01 —

Exiled

The young man walked; slowly at first, then quickening, as his mind filled with rage and loneliness demanded greater effort from his body. Rage created and fuelled by the memory of two families and a way of life destroyed by a savage act of violence. Loneliness by longing for loved ones lost forever. His face was buffeted by rain, wind, and the stale odours of the vast city. Sad, strained, deep blue eyes exposed a tortured soul and lonely heart. For an instant he thought of living in peace surrounded by family, friends and laughter in the beautiful west Cork countryside where he grew up. Now he just existed in a cell as a cynical and bitter inmate serving a self-imposed sentence while searching for answers to many questions. How could the man who had brought despair and destruction with one act of brutality be so cruel, so ruthless, and so stupid? Why? Maybe, just emptiness. Anything, other than the bitterness, the hatred and the anger. As he walked on through the capital of the British Empire a year after the end of the Great War, he saw a man working; in a way that he knew was wrong and could put right. Certainty briefly returned. He stopped and began to speak.

Peter Wilde had always wanted to be a painter, and his art master had encouraged his liking for the art form. Unfortunately, the man paying the school fees, Wilde's banker father, was adamant that he take up a profession. Wilde chose architecture – which might allow the aesthete in him to covertly develop. Wilde senior snorted,

"It will have to do. I would have preferred law. Always busy in the law courts. Good money too."

Peter Wide had qualified at the age of twenty-six and by 1914 had a small practice renovating Victorian and Edwardian buildings which gave him a comfortable living and a three story house in Belgravia. During the Great War, the firm maintained munitions factories - something Wilde loathed, but it kept his business viable and vexed Wilde senior. Now, in 1919, Wilde was again renovating houses for clients with old money and those who became wealthy thanks to the Great War. One such self-made man had demanded a recent site meeting.

"Your workmen are not up to standard, and you are eight weeks behind the agreed schedule. Rectify both, or I'll see you in court."

Wilde watched as the client drove away, then turned and heard the foreman carpenter at the front of the house shouting.

"Fuck off Paddy, and do it now."

Wilde groaned inwardly, then heard.

"You're not fitting that window properly. I'm a carpenter; I know I'm right."

"You'll be fucking flat out if I come down, you Irish bastard," the foreman yelled.

"Well, maybe, but that won't fix that window."

The aggressor, now halfway down the steps, slowed on seeing the Irishman's coat open to reveal sturdy legs, a powerful torso, muscular arms and a strong neck. Wilde intervened,

"What are you doing? You're supposed to be working!"

"I ain't taking shit like that from some bloody Paddy."

The man on the pavement spoke.

"All I'm saying is that the window isn't being fitted right. That's all."

Wilde looked at the unknown man.

"What do you mean?" "Speak up!"

The young man hesitated, thinking.

'Jesus!' 'They'll probably have me locked up just because I'm Irish'. He spoke.

"I don't want any trouble. I'll be on my way."

Wilde insisted,

"Come up here, will you?"

He continued.

"What are we doing wrong?"

"Well, I don't know about you, but *he* is fitting those counter-weights at the wrong height. Any trained carpenter would know that. That's a box sash window."

Wilde asked.

"Show me your hands would you?"

As the Irishman did so, the foreman cut in,

"If you know what's good for you, Paddy, you'll fuck off now."

Wilde saw the young man was visibly nervous and reassured him.

"Just ignore him; nothing will happen to you."

The architect looked at the man's hands, seeing both were hard and calloused.

"What's your name, and where did you work?"

"My name is Connor Cork, and I served my time with a builder in West Cork," he replied. The foreman shouted.

"I'm not working with him. Take it or leave it."

The architect looked at the window and made a decision.

"I'll leave it. Finish now. I'll pay you for today. Now go."

The foreman threw his hammer down as he grabbed his coat. Wilde counted out some cash but before handing it over, demanded,

"I want the keys to this building, and just remember, if anything is stolen or there is any damage to the site, the police will know where to look first."

Cork stayed silent, sensing the sacked man was looking for trouble. The tall, blonde man's reaction to the foreman's rant was similar.

"I never wanted to work for one of your sort anyhow. Good fuckin' riddance." Wilde ignored the insults, watched him disappear, then turned to see a man about six feet tall with thick, brown, wavy hair, an open face and deep blue eyes, which showed tiredness and pain. Just like so many other young men he had seen because of the Great War.

"Well, I hope you are as good as you say you are. Be here tomorrow at eight."

Connor Cork lay on his bed, recalling the events of the morning. Since leaving home, he'd no interest in work. Suddenly he had a job. Then he laughed harshly, thinking of the sacked man.

'If that's the best carpenter they have in London then they're in trouble.'

Connor was on site early. His new employer, an elegant man with longish blonde hair, a slightly tanned face and dark brown eyes, instructed:

"Right! You can start with that window at the front."

The window was refitted by lunchtime. For the rest of the week, his boss said nothing other than to give the Irishman jobs which, when finished, were meticulously checked. Friday night came, and as Connor packed away his tools, Wilde approached;

"Can you work tomorrow and maybe Sunday? The job is way behind, and there are problems."

"What problems? There's nothing wrong with my work."

The taller man replied,

"The client is very demanding, so I am checking everybody's work. Now, are you willing to work this weekend?"

Connor had nothing else to do except sit in that horrible room.

"I'll work whenever you want me to. But if you have any questions about my work, you say it to me."

Slowly the job started to take shape. Wilde was impressed by Connor and asked him to work the coming weekend. The Cork man demanded,

"How many problems can there be on one job?"

"The problem, my quick-tempered Irish friend, is the client. He wants everything perfect, and he wants it yesterday."

"Well, he's entitled to be asking for perfection, but 'yesterday', is a little unreasonable. Tell me, is he a good payer Mr Wilde?"

Wilde laughed as he answered the very perceptive question.

"Yes, he is a good payer. Probably the only reason I am still on the job."

Cork spoke,

"Well, in that case, we'd better keep him happy. Good payers are few and far between."

The client made an unannounced visit and was pleasantly surprised. He began talking to Connor. Wilde watched, and saw that the man seemed impressed. When leaving he turned to Wilde;

"You've done well to get this job right. I have bought another two properties in Kensington. The work is similar to what you've done here. The job's yours if the price is right. You've got a good man there," motioning toward Cork.

"He told me that there are always problems with renovation work, but these lovely buildings are worth it. I asked him if he would work for me if I gave the job to another firm, but he said he's happy with you."

Then he handed Wilde an envelope.

"These are the tender documents - I'll expect your prices within a month. Good day, Mr Wilde."

As the men worked more closely, they began to relax. Wilde asked the young West Cork man for his opinion on various problems on site and then decided to put his young carpenter to the test.

"Tell me, Mr Cork, how you feel about this type of renovation work. Is it something you would be interested in doing long term?"

Connor suppressed a laugh as he thought, 'Jesus! As if I had a choice.'

"It's interesting work. The thing with renovating old buildings is that you will always have problems. The clients don't know how tricky this work can be." Wilde rolled out some papers on the desk.

"I want you to work this weekend but not with the tools. I need your help in pricing two houses in Kensington. We'll go over first thing in the morning and do the survey. I need the tenders finished by Monday."

Connor nodded his head.

"Ok, Mr Wilde. I'll see you here at eight o'clock."

Wilde smiled. "Good!"

The weekend went quickly, as Connor demonstrated his extensive knowledge of general building methods. By Sunday evening, the tenders were completed. Wilde was delighted.

"Tell me, Connor, where did you learn so much about building houses?"

Connor wanted to talk about his home, but the memories were raw. So he talked of his apprenticeship - nothing more. Wilde sensed the man was opening up slowly but did not push. He had seen enough over the previous month to realise that this young man was too good to lose.

"Connor, I want to offer you the foreman carpenter's job when we open these sites."

Cork almost snapped,

"We haven't got them yet, Mr Wilde."

"Will you please stop being so pessimistic, Connor?" Wilde replied.

"It's not pessimism; it's realism," Cork retorted, then said in a less ardent voice;

"I'm sorry. It's just that I haven't had too much to be optimistic about recently."

Wilde took a different tack.

"How are your digs?"

"Bloody awful, if I'm being honest. Just one room - it's depressing. Sorry, I'm very short-tempered; it's not your fault."

In a flash of inspiration, the architect suggested;

"Don't worry about it. Listen! I know a few property owners around London. I'll ask around for available rooms, but you've got to do something for me. Connor, we need more tradesmen. You get me some good men and I'll find a good place for you to live. How does that sound?" Connor, though uncertain, answered;

"Right! I'll start looking for tradesmen."

Wilde enthused,

"And I'll start looking for rooms. Goodnight, Connor. See you tomorrow."

The client called at the site the following week and informed Wilde his tenders had been successful. When told, Connor's earlier uncertainty hardened. He did not know anyone in London, let alone tradesmen. Later he remembered where he could meet other Irish people. The Holy Roman Catholic Church - the salvation (or the curse) of the Irish wherever they went. That Sunday, Connor went to a Catholic church in Cricklewood, North London. After mass he asked the curate - a Kerryman - if he knew of any men looking for work. The priest pointed out a member of the local GAA club who quickly gathered footballers who were after jobs. Connor arranged for three men to meet Wilde on Monday. After a brief walk around the site and a few questions, all three, two carpenters and a bricklayer, were taken on. Connor learned something that weekend, and the GAA would, in time, become a regular source of labour.

In the middle of all this activity, Connor suddenly realised that he was enjoying work again. Wilde kept his part of the bargain, arranging for him to look at a sitting room with a bedroom, kitchen and bathroom in a house in Dollis Hill, North London. The rent was high but, with foreman's pay and being a non-drinker, affordable. He moved in within days. What Wilde didn't tell his foreman was that a friend of his owned the house and that he had guaranteed Connor as a responsible tenant.

Every Friday afternoon, Wilde and Connor would meet to go over the week's work. These talks were increasingly relaxed, but their private lives were hardly touched on. Though Wilde tried to encourage him, the young Cork man never talked of his family or life in Ireland. The foreman never asked about Wilde's private life. The men almost knew what not to ask. Wilde commented on how pleased he was with the other Irishmen working for him - all were very good tradesmen. Connor had been mulling over a question for a number of weeks, and finally, he felt he had to ask his boss.

"Mr Wilde, something has been on my mind. Why did you take me on that morning when we first met? I mean, you're an Englishman, and I'm Irish. Why did you take my side against the man you sacked who was English?"

Wilde spoke.

"Connor, it was obvious to me that you knew what you were talking about. Anyway, his work was shoddy. I took a chance and it worked out - your being Irish didn't come into it. Don't believe all you hear about the English - not all of us eat babies. Now I'm going home. I'll see you Monday."

Wilde closed the front door of his home, poured a large whiskey, and sat in a very large, gull wing chair; Connor's question came to mind. There were many reasons for giving the Irishman the job. Among them was that Wilde had seen in him the scared, haunted look that was on the faces of so many young men in London since the end of 'the war to end all wars.'

Wilde thought about the spacious drawing room and the rest of the house in which he lived a life separate to that of 'Peter Wilde Architect' – an intensely private life. He was deeply suspicious of the reasons for the Great War. Some former schoolmates were now senior civil servants and were regular visitors to his home. Wilde loved to entertain – being a good cook and naturally generous. Occasionally, due to overindulgence in the excellent wines and spirits provided, the guests would let slip snippets of gossip from their respective government ministries. One outburst, in particular, was an admission of fear in the establishment of rebellion by certain sections of the population unless social conditions improved in Britain. Over one hundred thousand troops had been kept in Britain during the War to counter any such action. Wilde laughed cynically when he thought of Lloyd George's 'A Fit Land for Heroes' speech.

Again, his gaze wandered around the room. It was very tasteful. The entire house was very tasteful - but it was empty. Peter Wilde was a reasonably successful man but desperately lonely. Seeing a similar loneliness in Cork's eyes was another reason for employing him. As for his former schoolmates, uncaring or not, he could not escape the fact they were a reliable source of good quality, well-paying work. Wilde had tried to assess what the Great War had cost his generation. A terrifying measure had been provided at a school reunion held in late 1918, where it was revealed that only twelve of the original class of twenty-six boys had survived the 'War to end all Wars.' He shuddered and reached for the whiskey decanter.

As Connor was opening the door of his flat, a quiet, gentle voice called him. The elderly grey-haired lady who owned the house next door approached. Connor had done a few small repair jobs for her.

"Excuse me, Mr Cork, my son is home from hospital but needs to attend the doctor just round the corner. He's very nervous of falling over. Would you ever just walk him there and back until he gets a bit stronger? Hopefully, just once a week until we know more from the doctor." Placing her hand on his forearm, and in an almost tiny voice, she finished;

"All these wars should be stopped. Fighting never got anyone anywhere. He's had a rough time, you see, but he's alive - there are so many mothers without their sons. God help them!"

Connor's heart went out to Mrs Saunders.

"I'll walk him round whenever you want me to; please don't worry, leave it to me."

Connor couldn't refuse. The lady had described one such woman. His mother! The following evening, Con accompanied a broad-shouldered man about six feet two inches with light-brownish hair and pale skin. At first they were silent, but as the ex-soldier gained a little confidence, he spoke;

"This is good of you, Connor; I shouldn't need help for too long. They told me in the hospital I was healing well."

Steven Saunders explained before the war had been a barrister's clerk in the City of London.

"The 'Chambers' have been very good, keeping my job open for me until I get sorted out." Then he became serious, criticizing the Government about the treatment of returning servicemen. Con listened, afraid to say too much until he found out where the man had been wounded. It could well have been Ireland - maybe even Cork!

Saunders continued,

"I got this leg in Belgium; they gave me a medal because I brought a wounded officer back from no man's land. That's where we should put the politicians, Connor, out there in no man's land and leave them there."

At this point they had reached the surgery. Steven Saunders introduced himself, Connor standing nearby, listened and thought he picked up a Kerry accent from the receptionist. The examination didn't take long, and on the way home, he told Connor that the doctor had confirmed he wanted to see him once a week, then asked;

"Is that alright with you, Connor? I don't want to be a nuisance, mate, what with you out working all day."

Connor assured Saunders,

"It's no problem. We'll manage until you get a bit stronger."

Connor found Saunders to be an intelligent man with a great sense of humour, a little mischievous but good-natured and relaxed as he told him about his background. Steven Saunders explained how his experiences in the trenches had made him think about his life.

"Connor, we went to war to help smaller nations but look at us now, tied up in wars all over the world. If the colonies in the Empire want to be independent, then they should be allowed to go their own way. That includes Ireland - and I'm not saying that because we're mates. I mean it Connor. I swear Britain has more troops overseas now than we had during the bloody war."

Connor didn't reply, but his view of the average Englishman was changing almost daily, thanks to his friend Steven Saunders. Yet, one evening, in the surgery, he could have happily strangled him. As Saunders approached the desk to confirm his appointment for the following week, Connor heard;

"Next week again, please, Mary. How are you? What part of Ireland are you from, love?"

Connor heard, "I'm from Kerry, Mr Saunders."

"'Ere Connor, this lovely girl's from Kerry. That's near Cork ain't it? Come over and say hello."

Connor, a little embarrassed when approaching the desk, shot his neighbour a dirty look. Saunders burst out laughing.

"What you looking at me like that for? All I said was, 'say hello'."

Connor did and was greeted by a smile and an equally charming reply.

"Hello, Connor. How are you? Mr Saunders has been telling the doctor and me how kind you have been to him and his mother."

Connor managed to talk to the girl during every appointment. Then one evening, as Saunders' treatment was coming to an end, he asked her.

"Would you like to go out for an evening? We'll do whatever you want to do."

The woman didn't hesitate.

"That sounds nice, thank you. We'll go dancing on Saturday."

It was the first time Mary made a decision for them as a couple, and Connor felt it would not be the last. The date was a success for, although Connor had spent most of his adolescent years working, his mother did ensure that her boy could dance. Mary Clifford was tall, slim and elegant with auburn hair and blue eyes. She, like so many other young Irish people, had come to London looking for work. That date was followed by another, and within a few weeks, they were seeing each other twice and sometimes three times a week. Connor realised he had shut himself away from everything he had known and held dear. Mary Clifford was an Irishwoman, and he'd forgotten just how much he needed Irish people. Mary was raised in a small fishing village in Southwest Kerry. Her parent's marriage had been a match. Her father, a fisherman and farmer, was ten years older than his wife and their daughter had mostly happy memories of growing up.

Mary was uncertain, but she felt that wanted to get to know this man. At first shy, he soon began to talk about his home and family. He was hard working and very gentle, yet she felt something was being held back. Occasionally he was silent as if thinking of somewhere or someone else. At those times, Connor's eyes would become sad and a little angry. Mary would only feel right when she knew the secret that was deep inside this man's heart. One night, before he saw her into her house, she asked;

"Connor, why did you leave home?"

Connor was in love with Mary Clifford and was terrified he would lose her. So, he told her everything about his home and family and why he had left West Cork and Ireland forever. In doing so, he broke down in tears. Mary put her arms around her fine Cork man, all doubt now gone. That evening, they talked about marriage and forgot the time as they both trod on the new path of a life together. Now aware of Connor's past, his wife-to-be made a few things clear.

"Connor, my family has never had anything to do with politics or fighting. You must tell me now, are you finished with the people that caused the terrible things? I must know this Connor." Connor spoke openly of his hatred for the British. But how working for Peter Wilde and becoming friends with Steven Saunders had forced him to think again about the British and the English in particular. Then he added;

"Mary, I have left all of that behind me. I promise you - all of it. Mary, there is only one important thing in my life now: you and, God willing, our children. I want them to grow up with open minds - no blind allegiance to a lost cause. There is just one thing I must ask of you. Never tell anyone about what happened in Cork. Please - that is all I ask of you." Mary Clifford hugged her young man. That night the couple set a date for their wedding. Connor went to sleep one of the most relieved and happy men in London.

Peter Wilde noticed another side to Connor. He was relaxed and outgoing, running and handling the workforce with firmness and humour. Wilde wondered what had brought on this change. The answer was quickly provided by a brightly coloured envelope with his name handwritten amongst the office post. Connor heard his name called and was greeted by an exultant Wilde.

"I will be delighted to attend your wedding. Now, what do you and your fiancé want for a wedding present?"

Connor spluttered,

"Mr Wilde, I haven't a clue. I'll ask Mary. Can I tell you tomorrow?"

Wilde put his hand on Connor's shoulder, laughing,

"Connor, from now on, you call me Peter. Tomorrow will do nicely."

Peter Wilde thoroughly enjoyed the wedding. He watched the new Mrs Cork, an elegant attractive woman, confidently welcome her guests and knew Connor had found happiness. Steven Saunders took great pleasure in telling everyone repeatedly how he had introduced the couple.

1920 passed, and the business grew along with the men's friendship. Mary told Connor he was to be a father. Steven Saunders and his mother called to express their delight for the newly married couple. Mary encouraged Mrs Saunders to call more often. During one visit she expressed her concern about her son returning to work saying,

"Mary, we have enough to live on from the rental income, and I know Peter is still not over the war..." A few days later, Steven called to see Connor and, clearly upset, explained.

"Connor, it's all the people in the city. I feel like I'm back in the trenches - men everywhere - no room to move. It's all the noise, like shells and smoke. The nightmares are almost real. I woke up screaming the other night; one of the tenants nearly went for the police". He paused and his face lightened.

"I talked it over with mum, and we think we've found a way. We want to talk to you and Mary. Can we call over tomorrow night?"

The Corks sat in silence as Mrs Saunders proposed that they move into the flat currently occupied by Steven and herself. Mary knew the flat made up the entire ground floor with three bedrooms. Much larger than where they lived now. Mrs Saunders had a number of conditions. That any repairs to the house were done by Connor and the tenants' rents collected by Mary. A figure for the rent was mentioned, and the Corks would get first offer on the house should Mrs Saunders decide to sell. She finished with;

The rental income would allow her and her son to move to the country where Steven would be better off - lots of room and peace and quiet.

Mary Cork took the lead.

"Mrs Saunders, can we have a little time to think about this?"

Mrs Saunders agreed. One month later, the Cork family moved into their new home.

Patrick William Cork was born healthy and strong in February 1921. As an only child he was lavished with attention by his ecstatic parents. Before his fifth birthday, he was told there would be another baby in the house.

"Good, that will give me someone to play with in the evenings," then went to sit on his dad's lap as he did most nights. The boy remembered just one time when he had was unable to do so.

In 1922, Connor Cork's mother had died, and he returned to Ireland for her funeral. He spent a little time with his beloved sisters; both were happily married and lived away from West Cork. The War of Independence had finished, bringing British rule to an end in twenty-six counties of Ireland. Connor never went near his home town; there were too many unknowns and bad memories. A civil war was raging as many people refused to accept the terms of the treaty with Great Britain. One of the leaders of the Pro-Treaty side was a man called Michael Collins, a Cork man. Just after their mother's funeral, news spread that Collins had been killed in an ambush. Connor returned to England, all thoughts of the land of his birth gone forever. His only loyalty now was to his family and his employer.

Connor Cork was now in charge of 'hiring' labour. He made his attitude toward politics clear to every man joining the company; "Politics stops at the site gate. During working hours, keep your opinions to yourself, and we'll all get along."

A Donegal man challenged his right to 'free speech' - as he put it. The foreman's reply was instant.

"Don't talk to me about free speech. Did Michael Collins get free speech? There's work here for anyone who wants it - but on my terms. If you don't like it - there's the gate. This is nothing to do with the British. These are my rules."

The challenger sensed the Cork man was not to be argued with and for reasons that were not up for debate.

Mary Cork made Peter Wilde welcome; he was invited to dinner almost monthly, not because he was her husband's employer. She felt he was lonely, enjoyed his company, and was pleased with how relaxed he was in her home. Peter sensed that Mary knew his secret but never felt threatened. Connor enjoyed seeing him outside work.

The second son of the Corks was born almost five years to the day after his brother, a fine healthy boy named Christopher. As the child approached six weeks of age, his parents discussed the christening.

"Who will we ask to be his godfather? Is there anyone you had in mind Connor?" Mary continued, "I was thinking of Peter Wilde."

Connor was at first surprised, but as he thought it over, the idea grew on him. Wilde accepted immediately, hoping he managed to conceal his shock and delight at the gesture made by the Corks. Not a particularly religious man, he took a great interest in his godson - Christopher Peter - and took immense pleasure, when visiting, in putting the baby to bed.

When he was five, Patrick Cork went to school, and developed a thirst for knowledge and a love of reading which was to stay with him all his life. At home his brother was the baby until a third child arrived - a little girl called Rachel. His daddy was always home every evening and his mummy was warm, gentle and loving. Patrick Cork didn't have a care in the world. At school, the boy was gregarious. His school report described an above-average boy with a quick mind and an appetite for learning and sport. At home, Mary made sure the family ate together. At an early age her eldest son began asking an eclectic array of questions which his parents gainfully answered. At seven years old, Patrick announced he would walk to and from school with his friends. The first sign of a lifelong independent streak. The questions continued, some about Ireland. No attempt was made to hide the dark side of Anglo-Irish history. Of evictions and the 'Black and Tans', and Connor told his eldest son of the Civil War. Patrick noted that British history taught at school hardly mentioned Ireland. During the winters, which limited sport, the library became Patrick's second home and the questions increased. Connor, though tired, would answer as father and son grew to adore each other. Connor was a marvellous father. One evening, in particular, Rachel was unsettled, had cried all day and seemed determined to carry on through the night. Connor took the child into the living room, giving his wife the luxury of a night's sleep.

The neighbourhood in which they lived was safe and pleasant. Mary's family was happy, healthy and secure.

Social conditions in Britain were changing after the Great Depression, and the General Strike highlighted society's problems. Peter Wilde was a shrewd business-man, and a full order book ensured his employees were unaffected. Connor was now senior foreman for all sites and undergoing training in producing budgets and project management. As the business grew, Wilde took silent pleasure in further vexing his father.

The Saunders had settled in a small village near the South Coast and were in touch by regular letter. Then one letter read that Steven would visit, the first call in five years. The Corks were pleased to see him looking so well. Saunders was amazed by how much the children had grown and delighted at the condition of the house. After dinner, he got to the point.

"Connor, Mary: Mum and I have built a nice little business in the village of Shoreham. We run a small guest house which is attached to riding stables. Up until now, we've been renting the place, but now we've got the chance to buy it - the whole lot. I've met a lovely lady, who Mum is very fond of, who runs the stables and wants to help with the guest house. Mum wants to retire, so it seems to have worked out well."

Connor asked,

"How are you, Steven? How are the nightmares and such?"

Saunders smiled.

"Connor, Mary, I haven't had one in the last two years - that's why I'm asking this lady to marry me. She knows about the war and all that, and I think she has a lot to do with the improvement in me. I feel so relaxed and content."

Mary reached out, taking Steven's hand.

"Steven, we're delighted for you and your mother."

Saunders stood up as he said,

"Mum and I want you to have the house. I know exactly how much we need to buy the business and have a little to spare. The sitting tenants will affect the price, but I think it's a fair one."

He then handed a sheet of paper to Mary Cork.

Peter Wilde was having lunch with his bank manager - an old school friend. "Well, Peter, things are going very well. The order book looks good and your personal and company accounts look even better. What do you plan for the future?"

Wilde mulled the question over as he savoured the excellent wine.

"The problem I have is that we are beginning to lose men. As the economy picks up, the rates paid to skilled men are increasing. This in itself is not an insurmountable problem, but I am concerned about losing Connor Cork. He's become my right arm. I want to diversify, to find other markets and customers. To do that I need him to run the business on a daily basis."

The banker didn't offer any solutions as he poured more of the Chateauneuf-du-Pape, merely saying, "Well, if you need any money, you know where to come. Cheers old boy."

Connor went to the Friday meeting where he and Peter talked about the turnover of tradesmen.

"Peter, I know we are losing some men, but there seems to be a good number of skilled men in town. We'll find more, don't worry. Tradesmen are independent-minded people. They move on when they feel like it - except for the married men, of course." Wilde picked up Cork's drift.

"I want to talk with you before you go. Listen Connor. I want to expand the client base, to diversify the business. To do this, I need you to run the business day to day. Are you willing to do that?"

Connor thought, 'I might as well tell the man'.

"Peter, the Saunders' have given Mary, and me first offer on the house in Dollis Hill. I need some advice on how to get a mortgage. Can you help me there? We have a good amount saved for the deposit."

Wilde stood and closed the office door.

"Connor, there is something I want to put to you. Of course, I'll help you with the mortgage - I can't see any problems. I was going to speak to you and Mary about my plans later on, but things have moved faster than I thought. If you are willing to take my offer as the manager of my building company, then I will arrange a mortgage and will, if necessary, guarantee the loan."

Wilde was concerned at the shock on Connor's face but relaxed as the look changed to a smile.

"I would be easier in my mind if Mary and I had talked about this, but I really can't see her disagreeing. Of course, I'll stay. We work well together."

It was Wilde's turn to smile as Con handed him a sheet of paper with details of the house.

"That's what the Saunders' are asking for the house, and all of the tenants will stay, which Mary's very happy about."

Wilde remained silent whilst reading the sheet of paper and then commented.

"That is a very fair price, Connor, and the property is freehold. The tenants will be a valuable source of income. I'll start on Monday. I estimate that we can have the whole thing sorted out in a month or two at the latest. You and your wife and family belong in that house, and you'll be happy there. It's a very good investment."

The men stood up and shook hands. Con went home to tell his wife that she was soon to become a householder. Peter Wilde sat in his drawing room, a mixture of relief and satisfaction in his mind. The first thing he would do on Monday morning would be to call his friend the banker and keep him to his word. Then a knock came at the door, and his guest for the evening smiled and entered.

"You were right to accept it. We belong in this house, and the children love it here. We'll manage the mortgage."

Mary Cork handed her husband another cup of tea. Their eldest boy had just gone to bed. His fourteenth birthday was approaching. At school, his form teacher spoke of Patrick developing well but with a lot more to come. The following evening he sat with his parents to talk about what to do for a living. The discussion finished with Patrick saying he'd like to be a carpenter. When asked why, his logic was unshakeable.

"Mum, a tradesman is always going to be in demand. Nearly all carpenters become foremen and more. The skill allows you to be independent - to go wherever you want, whenever you want. You'll never be out of work as a carpenter. Now all I need is an apprenticeship."

Patrick went to bed, and his parents talked. Mary felt the common sense shown by her son was impressive but believed he would need much more of an intellectual challenge as he grew. His father hoped he had not influenced his son too much, remembering his habit of saying how useful a trade was to a man. Both agreed that their son was growing up and would soon be making his own decisions.

Mary was delighted with how her son and husband talked. Her childhood had been happy, but she remembered with sorrow the fearful rows between her father and brother. Connor and Patrick were the opposite, very good friends, as well as father and son.

Mary had many gifts, but a singing voice was not among them. The Cork men could and did sing. One favourite song was the anthem of all Cork people, 'The Banks of My Own Lovely Lee', which Patrick knew by his twelfth birthday and would never forget. On an evening when Peter Wilde came to dinner, having tucked his Godson in bed, he sat with a glass of Brandy and asked.

"Mary, may I briefly talk about business?"

His hostess nodded. Wilde explained about pre-cast concrete, which, he believed, would revolutionise parts of the building industry and allow his company to expand.

"I intend to train an apprentice who will become the charge hand carpenter at a plant to be built for the manufacture of numerous types of pre-cast concrete products. Do you think Patrick would be interested in this position?" Mary replied.

"Peter, we will have to talk to Patrick about this. He is a bright boy and might want to do something else."

Wilde nodded.

"I am fully aware of that, Mary, but the offer is there if he wants to pursue a career in the construction industry. Please don't think I am looking for an answer straight away."

A week later, Patrick and his parents listened to Peter Wilde as he explained how the training would take four years. The first spent on a large site and the rest with Wilde's company. As Patrick and Wilde discussed the job, his mother knew her son's mind was made up. Two weeks later, Patrick Cork began his working life.

He started on a large housing estate site. At first, Patrick found the –all male environment unnerving but soon settled. On site were all nationalities, all with an opinion. Patrick found the lunch breaks great fun as he listened to his workmates talk about their backgrounds and homelands. The language and humour were coarse. Occasionally, if those arguing were hot-headed, things got heated but never violent. He felt proud that he was amongst working men. The site taught him other things. That not everybody was like his father; some men were hard-working - others were just lazy.

As planned, Patrick joined Wilde's company, and during the next two years, learned his trade. He also came to realise his father was a very capable man.

Patrick's seventeenth birthday neared, and in Britain, rumours were rife about the King and his American friend. During dinner Mary asked her eldest son what he thought. Patrick's experiences at work made him appreciate many things especially his parents. He began.

"Mum, I think the man is a disgrace. How can he walk away from his responsibilities? His place is on the throne - a man in his position has no right to be so selfish. If he is that weak, then we are better off without him."

His father picked out one point.

"When you say 'we,' Pat, do you mean the English, the British or the Empire?" Patrick carried on forcefully.

"Dad, I mean the people in this country, living and working here, trying to earn a wage and raise a family. They don't walk away from their responsibilities. You don't, mum doesn't, and Mr Wilde doesn't. It's not a question of nationalities; it's about each person's responsibility to do what is necessary to get things done."

Mary silently appreciated the compliment in her son's answer. Connor said nothing. His son's opinion of the King's abdication was based upon his experience in life and practical objectivity. Connor saw a man of six feet in height, broad-shouldered and slim in the hips, with his grandfather's wavy thick light brown hair and the Cork neck. Hard work had filled him out, and look more mature. Connor relaxed as he appreciated how well his son was growing into a man; there would be no repeat of the stupidity that had brought ruination to his generation of the family. There would be no blind allegiance to a cause or flag of any colour. Patrick Cork would make up his own mind, and his father was delighted about that.

Some days later, the newspapers ended their unofficial embargo and had front page headlines demanding the government tell the British people what was happening.

As Connor entered the site office, Peter Wilde, clearly upset, threw down a copy of the Daily Express.

"This is a bad business, Connor, a very bad business. This weak man is jeopardising the one institution that holds the Empire together. I wish to God he would just go and allow his brother to take over."

Connor asked, "What do you mean, Peter?"

Wilde began.

"Connor, We live in a constitutional monarchy with many political parties. We blame politicians and civil servants for our problems but never the Royal Family. Now this stupid, selfish man is endangering the stability that the Crown brings to British Society".

Connor had never seen Peter so passionate as he listened to a totally different view of the British Royal family from his own, which was, they were the figurehead of the forceful occupation of his homeland. It added to his increasing realisation that the world was a far bigger place than Ireland. In time, much to Peter Wilde's relief, the man in question abdicated - his brother assuming the throne. Connor was pleased for Peter Wilde.

In their area of North London, the local general store was Paxton's. The owner had watched the Cork children grow up and had good time for them. Patrick was in his third year at work and, due to overtime, was late returning books to the library. He was hurrying in the shop when Mr Paxton asked.

"Why are you in so much of a rush?"

Patrick explained the situation. Paxton smiled.

"Patrick, leave them in here, and I'll get my daughter to run them over - she spends half her life in the place anyway."

With that, Patrick's friendship with Mr Paxton grew and with his daughter began.

Her name was Barbara. They began seeing each other, eventually as more than just friends. Barbara Paxton was a well-built young woman with naturally blonde hair, blue eyes, and a lovely smile lit up by perfect, white teeth. She was about five feet six inches tall. Their dates were spent dancing - a skill Patrick had learned from his mother - and discussing the political and economic issues of the day. They found each other stimulating intellectually and physically. Barbara was a very forthright young woman with confirmed views on many subjects. Patrick disagreed with a number of her opinions and said so. They were walking home one night after a heated discussion on the current British Prime Minister's policy of appeasement. Barbara was a committed pacifist and, as such, believed that Neville Chamberlain was right. Patrick was well versed on the subject and quoted a man called Churchill who warned of impending disaster if too much leeway was given to the Nazi party in Germany. The ensuing silent impasse was broken when surprisingly, Barbara said,

"Pat, kiss me."

Their first kiss lasted for quite some time as their tongues entwined, lips parted. Barbara whispered,

"I know your mother taught you to dance; who taught you to kiss?"

Pat didn't know whether he was being complimented or criticised, so he replied flippantly,

"I read a lot."

Barbara laughed deliciously.

"You must give me the book."

Leaning again to kiss her he quipped.

"No, in this case, practical demonstrations are far more beneficial."

Pat had just turned eighteen. Barbara was just a few weeks younger. They became bolder in their physical relationship and decided to be lovers, which happened on a bank holiday weekend when her parents were away. After some nervous and awkward fumbling with a condom, they relaxed and found sex very easy and satisfying. They had sex regularly, agreeing that, whilst they were very close, marriage was not on the agenda. Lying in each other's arms, Barbara talked of her plans.

"Pat, we are lovers, but only dear friends, and that's all. I have more important things to do with my life than marriage and children - at least for the time being anyway."

Her independent, single-minded point of view actually attracted him to her as much as anything else. Patrick discovered he was drawn to strong, independent women and would all his life. He agreed with his dear friend. The idea of being in love with Barbara had never once crossed his mind.

Another strong-minded woman came to Pat's mind, one who need not know too much about him and Barbara. Later, as he sat in the kitchen, his mother looked at him as she handed him a mug of tea. Her eyes were as kind as ever. Revealing no sign that she knew of her son's earlier activities, All he could say was,

"No one makes a cup of tea like you, Mum."

Later on that day, he thought about his life. He was about to qualify as a carpenter, and Peter Wilde had set up a site for the new production company. He was satisfied with life so far though a cautionary thought nagged him about the dark forces spreading on the continent of Europe.

02

Choosing Colours

"**M**y God, Connor, they've gone and done it again! Those bloody Germans! The prime minister's been on the radio. We're at war again. Not the Kaiser this time, but that bastard Hitler. Christ, I've got two boys, both old enough to fight. I didn't raise those lads to go to war, not after the last lot."

Connor had worked with George Bailey for five years and had never seen him so upset. Now he stood beside his workmate, both terrified fathers, as the rugged cockney continued.

"Connor, I'm going home. My missus will be hysterical. Her nerves aren't good at best."

Cork told the rest of the men to come back tomorrow. Suddenly the site was empty, and Connor felt very alone.

Mary had listened to the radio in her kitchen, almost paralysed with fear as a flood of bewilderment and dread swept over her; then, her husband came through the door. They hugged and sat in silence. Slowly words began to form into sentences, which helped to relieve the terror they both felt and led them to discuss what was best for the family. Mary wondered where the safest place to be during the war was. Connor answered her question by suggesting she take the children to Ireland.

Clutching at any solution she readily agreed. Connor felt slightly relieved and then his wife, with a mother's bravery, spoke of the person they both feared for most.

"Connor, what will Pat do? He is a man now. He was born in this country - will he fight?"

Connor remained silent, his mind filled with countless reasons why their son should not fight - all originating in Ireland. How could he ask Pat not to do what he had done as a young man? Fight for the land of his birth.

Patrick had been thinking about joining up, knowing that doing so would terrify his parents. The reason for enlisting was simple. He was an Englishman, and England was at war. Walking home, Patrick desperately searched for a way to tell his parents. As the family sat down to supper, his father once again solved the problem. Connor asked everyone to listen.

"When I first came to this country, I hated the English in every way possible. Then, as I worked with Englishmen, I found they were no different to me. They had the same problems, fears, opinions, and dreams. I'd been told how bad things were for the Irish in England. I moved here during the War of Independence and was afraid of how the people in London would react. There was some hostility but no violence. I was treated as any other working man. The people your mother and I worked with and lived amongst got on with their lives and did not trouble us or other Irish people. In fact, most people didn't care about where you came from. I soon realised the working people here were just the same as anywhere. Most of what I had heard about this country in Ireland was just lies told by men who blamed everything on the British and called themselves fighters for Irish freedom.

When Michael Collins was killed, I realised that the Irish freedom fighters were only interested in freedom in Ireland if it was on their terms. Irish freedom is a myth. Collins was shot during a gunfight that took place because he disagreed with other men in Ireland. Your mother and I have lived and raised our family in this country and have enjoyed freedom and prosperity. Pat, you are our first-born son. You have an English accent, and in most respects, this is your country. The British did not start this war - in fact they have done everything to avoid it. From what I have read of this man Hitler and his kind, it would be better to put a stop to them now. If you feel you have to risk your life defending the land of your birth, then you have our full support." Mary Cork walked around the table and kissed her first-born son. Then - as any mother did every day – she made sure her family had enough to eat. That night she cried herself to sleep as her husband lay awake, feeling utterly defeated.

Patrick Cork told Peter Wilde his decision. His employer listened with an impassive face then shook Pat's hand as he left. Then he broke down in tears, his voice a tormented whisper.

"It's all going to happen again. Every mistake we made before, every mortal sin committed, we will commit again."

Peter Wilde contacted two people - an engineer in Portsmouth and his solicitor, who he asked to change his last Will and Testament.

Mary Cork's mind reeled, her son was going to war, and the life she and her husband had built for their family was in mortal danger. Then her immense common sense came to the fore. Pat was going to fight, and there was nothing she could do about that. Her eldest boy was an intelligent, adaptable man. She sensed he would cope.

The other children, however, had to be protected. Christopher was coming up to his twelfth birthday, and Rachel was nearly nine. There were rumours of plans to evacuate children. Not her babies - of that, she was certain. Then there was her husband. He, she knew, would not go to Ireland under any circumstances. He would stay in London with all the inherent dangers. These issues were uppermost in her mind as the year drew to a close.

Patrick William Cork entered the recruiting office of the Irish Guards. His details were recorded; he underwent a preliminary medical and was told to go back to work and wait for his call-up papers.

Connor felt angry at the politicians. Another war so soon. Then pondered: How Michael Collins might have confronted Hitler. Slowly his anger was replaced by logic. With time and thought, the Cork family would find answers. In the meantime, there was a business to run. The next day, as he sat down in the site office, Wilde came in and, unusually, closed the door.

"Do you remember when we first met all those years ago, Connor?"

Connor nodded.

"We have known each other a long time, and I trust you implicitly. There are a number of things I need to tell you." He paused and opened a folder.

"I have sold the business to a man called Peter English, and everything will be moving to Portsmouth. One of the non-negotiable conditions of the sale is that he employs you and as many of the men as will move. There must be a job for Patrick after the war." Connor sat in disbelief. Wilde's words were like hammer blows.

"Connor, I am going to live in America. I think many people, my father included, will say that the war is my reason for going, but it is not. When you started to work for me, it was at the end of the Great War - 'the war to end all wars!' Well, as we now know, it wasn't. I can't face another war, watching fine young men killed or condemned to lingering deaths."

Again, he paused, his voice softened.

"I have had the good fortune to know men such as you, men who have become my friends, who have helped me run my business and have never asked any questions about my private life. But there are other men in my life, Connor, men that I wanted sexually. Connor, my dear friend, I have fallen in love with an American, an architect. We are going to his home in California as soon as possible. We have more than enough money to live comfortably."

Connor managed to splutter a garbled question,

"Do you have to go so far? Couldn't you stay a bit closer, and I mean Peter, California, that's about six thousand miles away, why not Ireland? No one would take any notice of you and your friend there. Jesus, Peter! California! Why so far?"

Wilde insisted that his mind was made up. Connor looked at his friend, resigned to his decision.

"When do you go, Peter?"

Wilde laid out papers from the folder. His plan was to be settled in California within twelve months and stressed that he would be leaving only when satisfied that all was in order with the men and the new owner. They stood up and, for the first time since they had met, Connor Cork hugged his boss in a fierce embrace. He left the office and went straight home where, standing in the kitchen, he exclaimed,

"Mary, Peter is homosexual!"

Despite all her worries, Mary managed to laugh.

"Connor, did you not see that in the man in all the years you have known each other?"

Her husband demanded,

"Mary, are you telling me you knew?"

And was duly informed,

"A woman has a way of knowing these things."

Then, possibly still in shock, he told his wife of Peter Wilde's plans. She asked.

"I'm delighted for him, aren't you?" Connor shrugged agreement.

Again, Mary Cork was exceedingly grateful to Peter Wilde. His plans had made her decision much easier. She'd read of Hitler's forces bombing civilians in Spain, convincing her Nazis were capable of anything. With Connor out of London and Patrick in the army, she would be free to take the younger children to Kerry. Now there was only one terror for her, saying goodbye to her son when he went to war.

For Patrick there was one more person to tell, and that did not go well. Barbara was now an out-spoken pacifist and just kept repeating that there was no justification for any war and stormed off.

Patrick William Cork received his call up papers, reported to the Irish Guard's barracks and, having passed a strict medical, was classified as A1 fit for active service.

Patrick entered fourteen weeks of basic training as part of a platoon commanded by Sergeant Greenwood. Short, stocky and exceedingly fit with steely, grey hair. He had been in the army since before anyone could remember and had seen action in the Great War. Greenwood trained men strictly by the book. His religion was the British Army, and his Bible was King's Regulations. He started training with the words,

"I have no intention of allowing anyone to die for king and country unless I give them permission to do so."

Basic training was designed to adapt men from a comfortable civilian life to a disciplined, ordered and, occasionally, chaotic military regime. Patrick's construction background made the male-only environment easier to deal with, unlike some of the other recruits, all perfect strangers. Soon all were bound by one cause - to survive basic training.

The recruits quickly came to the conclusion that the common enemy were the NCOs. However, as the weeks went by, Patrick realised that, compared to other platoon NCOs, Greenwood was almost human. Training moved from endless route marches and square bashing to weapons training and infantry tactics. Patrick began to see the point of the rigorous programme. The blind discipline, which at first infuriated him, was wholly necessary. Thanks to the route marches and exercise regime, he was fitter than he had ever been. It was now obvious that most of the NCO instructors were clever men who were trying to get everybody as prepared as possible. Their demeanour and language were just shock tactics as they knew the time allotted for basic training was, cruelly, too short. Greenwood noted that Pat and two other men were helping other platoon members who were struggling with training. He checked the three men's files and all were well educated compared to some recruits. As a result Pat and the other men were promoted to Lance Corporal as the basic training ended.

The men paraded for the last time as Platoon 'A' Light Infantry. Lance Corporal Cork, would join the Irish Guards. The other NCOs were posted to the Green Howards and a new unit, the Parachute Regiment. Twenty-two men stood. Sergeant Greenwood addressed them. His voice was respectful.

"Are you all paying attention, as I have no intention of repeating myself?"

The platoon replied.

"Yes, Sergeant Greenwood."

"Good. Now, listen, my lads. From now on, you are on your own. You are the best bunch of men I have had through here in years, but if you tell anyone, I said that I will have you all on charges of aiding and abetting the enemy. Now, as I have told you. There are four things you must never forget,"

"One - never volunteer for anything.

Two - never trust anyone or anything but your rifle.

Three - do not make close friends because they could be dead within seconds.

And finally, always say the Soldiers' Prayer, which is?"

The platoon sang out,

"Please, God, not while I'm on duty."

He finished with the mandatory,

"Any questions?"

A soldier asked,

"What if you don't believe in God, Sergeant?"

Greenwood replied in a fatalistic tone.

"Son, I was in the last lot. Believe me. You will believe in a God before long!" The soldiers were dismissed. Sergeant Greenwood had one more piece of business with 'A' platoon and had ordered the gate guards to have three men report to him before leaving the camp.

Lance Corporals Cork, Simpson and Beck waited outside the mess. Greenwood watched with amusement as the three highly confident young men hesitated - they had learned the army way of thinking. No one but non-commissioned officers went into the NCOs' mess. They had yet to realise they were just that. Finally, he sent a mess orderly for them. Once inside, they were greeted as equals by all and relaxed. The matter at hand was of personal interest to Greenwood.

A soldier had been reported as injured - this happened all the time in a large camp. What puzzled the sergeant was the nature of the injury; the man had burns to his penis and testicles. The three men in front of him had satisfied the investigating officer that his injuries had not been caused by 'A' platoon. Greenwood suspected this was not quite the case and he intended to discover what had really happened to Private Peter Godwin.

Godwin had been in the army for ten years, had been stationed at Sutton Coldfield for two years, and had made a tidy niche for himself in the administration section of the camp postal service. He also ran errands for officers who were busy elsewhere. To carry out these errands, he held a pass which allowed him off camp most evenings, during which he enjoyed the local pubs. Where Godwin would loudly and drunkenly inform the clientele that he had no intention of dying for any king or country. The publicans reported this to the local police, who reported to the camp security officer. Due to his drunken antics, Godwin was regularly passed over for promotion. He vented his frustration by making trouble for the conscripts. Personal hygiene was drilled into the men. Inspections were rigorous. Godwin would use the fire buckets in 'A' platoon's hut to relieve himself when returning to the camp after a beer binge. To his satisfaction, the platoon members were punished with fatigues, extra duties and cancellation of weekend passes. Then, one night, Private Godwin was found unconscious, his genitals exposed and burned. On a personal level, Greenwood could not have cared less about Godwin. Over the years, he had seen a number of soldiers and officers like him; he called them 'uniform hangers'. However, Godwin's current condition intrigued him. He raised his glass to the young NCOs before him.

"We are all NCOs now, and I need not tell you that what is said in here goes no further."

They nodded as one.

"So, what happened to that obnoxious little man, Godwin?"

They looked at each other; then Patrick Cork began to explain. During the next two hours, a lot of beer was drunk, and the full story of Godwin was revealed. Wishing his former charges, 'good luck', the sergeant reported to the camp security officer. One end of a cable had been attached to the fire bucket in the hut where Godwin urinated. The other end had been connected to a power supply. Godwin's urine in the bucket completed the circuit, and he got two hundred and forty volts for his trouble. The evidence was removed and nobody was any the wiser except for Godwin. Both soldiers laughed out loud. The captain in charge of security asked the veteran sergeant,

"What do you want to do?"

Greenwood shook his head to signify 'nothing', as he wrote in a file headed, 'Training Injuries'. The open page referred to Godwin. The Sergeant wrote, 'Accidental injury. No further action'.

Fourteen weeks was a long time to be away; Patrick was going home to see his family and maybe Barbara. Did he want to see her sort things out, or was it just to have sex? Barbara wouldn't be fooled on that score, being too worldly to believe love was the reason. Both knew that whatever was between them was good - but not love. He remembered the good times, how practical Barbara was, particularly before sex. Demanding he use a condom.

"Pat, my darling, you can never be too careful."

Her insistence gave him considerable expertise in self-control and concentration, which, when applied during radio training, earned a commendation. Pat did not explain how such concentration had been achieved.

The carriage was full of cigarette smoke. 'Christ, all that smoking will kill them and me' crossed his mind. He saw all ranks and services; they were so young and all laughing - some were undoubtedly close friends. Sergeant Greenwood's words echoed. 'Don't make friends! They could be dead within seconds.' In solitude aboard a crowded train, he assessed the situation. He was on embarkation leave. Greenwood provoked a new thought. 'Look after yourself, mate! Forget anyone else.' If they wanted to smoke - that was their business.

Finally home, everything was forgotten in his mother's embrace and father's gentle bear hug. Rachel held his hand all afternoon. Christopher had grown now, broad-shouldered and tall. Mary Cork never took her eyes off her son.

"Pat, you look great." The afternoon was filled with catching up on all of the family's news. His father asked,

"Any word on a posting or when?" Between mouthfuls of food, he answered,

"No." Christopher and Rachel asked about army life. Pat told them about Greenwood and the army in general. Then Connor spoke.

"There has been a change of plan. The children and your mother intended going to Kerry next week but will now stay here until we can get the house rented." His mother continued, "The Ministry of Housing are looking for flats and houses outside the city and West End for the large numbers of military personnel in London. We've been offered a reasonable rent and have signed a lease which gives us one month's notice to vacate."

Patrick was shocked. Christopher was growing up very quickly. Rachel could be a young woman before he saw her again. Then came the pain of not knowing the next time he would see his mother.

Where would his father stay when the tenants moved in? These thoughts were just about to burst forth in a verbal torrent driven by fear and self-pity.

Then Patrick took a quick glance at the family. His mother's heart was breaking because her beautiful family and the home which they all loved so much were being torn apart. His father was clearly, if silently, distraught at losing his family, for he did not know how long. Patrick decided the last thing needed now was a hysterical rant from him.

"Where will you live, Dad?"

His father explained,

"As you know, Peter has sold the business. Once your Mum has gone to Ireland, I'll be moving to Portsmouth. When you get leave, you can spend it there. Does that suit you Pat?"

He smiled at his father and mother.

"Whatever is best for all of us? It seems you have all been busy making very sensible plans. We will all come through this madness in one piece, if not one place." He knew it was best to have everyone out of harm's way.

Patrick woke on the third morning at home and thought of Barbara and, during breakfast, told his mother he was going to see her. Mary sat down and, holding his hand, said,

"Pat, if there is anything left between you and your girlfriend, please make the best of it. Take happiness when it comes. Maybe it would be better for you and Barbara to stay friends and no more. These are terrible times, where the only certainty is uncertainty, and there is no place for emotional commitment."

He listened to her words with little surprise; she had always been forthright with him at important times in his life, then kissed her on the forehead and left.

Pat's training had made him very fit; as he walked toward Paxton's shop, a few women sent pleasant smiles, which he returned. Maybe monogamy was not for him?

The sign above the shop read, 'Paxton's', 'General Store'. Patrick saw the owner's face fill with a warm glow when he entered the shop, now full with lucnhtime trade. Some of the local people recognised him as one of their own. Mr Paxton came out from behind the counter and shook his hand firmly.

"Welcome home, Corporal. I see you did more than survive basic training. You look very well, and those stripes suit you. I dare say you want to see my daughter. She's out for the moment, but the minute she comes back, I'll let her know. Are you staying at home with your family?"

Patrick nodded as other people began to gather around; one whispered, "You know Patrick, Mrs Cork's son - that nice Irish family."

Mr Paxton watched Pat deal with the small crowd with ease. As a soldier, Lance Corporal Cork would do very well. Paxton was aware of Barbara's pacifist views that all wars were mass murder, and in his opinion, she was, at times, too outspoken. He particularly worried about her attitude to Patrick when he came home, knowing how close this young man and his daughter were, but that was before the war. Now things were completely different. Paxton was reassured by how much Patrick had matured. Corporal Cork would be able to deal with anything his daughter had to say.

At home that afternoon, Mary made dinner, and he and his father talked.

Patrick was desperately sad at the prospect of not seeing his family when on leave. Insecurity was new and scary. He quickly regained control. There was a war to fight for all of the Cork family. His family was being forced to move their lives to a country the children knew nothing of - his father living alone, away from everything he held dear. They had their battles to fight as well. Then there was a voice.

"Are you going to see Barbara Paxton tonight, son? Her father left an address for you. There you are."

Patrick thanked his dad and, as he left, kissed his mother good night. He had decided not to stay in London much longer, returning to barracks within the next two days. The farewell would be quick and, hopefully for him, unemotional.

Barbara opened the door and led him to a large sitting room at the end of the hall where three people were sitting. As she turned to him, Patrick saw she looked fabulous. Then he heard her say,

"This is a friend of mine - Pat."

And having kissed him lightly on the lips added,

"He wants to kill people."

Barbara seemed to be looking to provoke a confrontation, and he was the chosen target.

"Well, don't you have anything to say?"

Pat thought,

'Sod it! I could be dead in three weeks.'

"Well, I thought I'd start with hello and, as Barbara has not seen fit to introduce you, continue by asking your names. My name, as you know, is Pat. I am a Lance Corporal in the Irish Guards, so there is the possibility I may live up to Barbara's introduction by actually killing someone. As for wanting to kill someone - that's another matter."

Barbara retorted,

"Yes, you do want to kill someone; you volunteered for the army."

The other man in the room butted in.

"Barbara, please stop being so rude."

Pat looking directly at the stranger, continued,

"As I said, I have not been told any of your names, so may I ask who you are?"

The man spoke,

"Let me ask you a question first. What do you think of conscientious objectors?"

There was a short silence before he replied.

"Each to his own - I think it takes courage to go against public opinion."

The answer seemed to surprise everybody in the room, especially Barbara. The man stood up, hand outstretched, eyes directly in line with Pat's collar button.

Pat hoped his surprise had been concealed as the much shorter man introduced himself.

"My name is Peter Williamson; I am from Ipswich, although I have lived in London for some time. I am a conscientious objector, or, as we are commonly known, 'fucking conchies'."

Pat shook his hand.

"Good to meet you, Peter."

The girls introduced themselves as Petra and Josie, both attractive. Barbara, who was now a little less belligerent, told how they had met at college. The atmosphere became more relaxed as Peter explained his pacifism. The point of which was that he supported the war but was incapable of taking a human life. Then the girls told Patrick about the courses they were taking and remarked how much life in London had changed. Patrick concentrated on Barbara, cautious not being seen to stare. Her mouth was a little tighter when speaking as if permanently angry. Patrick told about basic training and of the many characters he had met. How the soldiers' varied backgrounds had taught him even in Britain, people's lives were so different.

Peter explained that he was lecturing on Political Science - a course all the girls were taking. Then they discussed the situation in Russia, Stalin and Hitler. As the evening progressed, Barbara became warmer towards Pat, sitting next to him, her thigh touching his, as she explained how the flat belonged to Petra's family, who were Swedish but now lived in America. Petra continued, as she had two bedrooms; she had been looking for a flatmate and had immediately hit it off, with Barbara when they met during the first term. Barbara finished with,

"Dad was worried about me travelling to North London in the evenings, so everything had worked out well." Then snapped at Pat.

"Why do you wear your uniform when you're on leave?"

Pat remained calm.

"It's all I have. Everything is packed up as my family is going to Ireland. Dad will be away on war work, and the house has been rented."

Barbara looked shocked.

"Your Mum and Dad love that house; it's their home. They shouldn't have to leave it."

Pat retorted,

"Tell that to the Luftwaffe. Goering has said he will flatten London."

Barbara's face tightened,

"If it wasn't for people like you, in uniform, there wouldn't be any bombing or war."

At that, Pat ran out of patience.

"It must be great to have all the answers to all the problems so readily at hand. Take everybody out of uniform, and the bombers will go away? Tell that to the people of Poland and the Jews living in Germany."

Barbara sprang up demanding,

"Is that the best you can do? Is that the only answer you have?"

His voice hardened.

"It's the only answer I have because I have had my world torn apart. I am trying to stay sane during a time when I could die at any moment. I'm sorry for my apparent lack of sensitivity to all your points of view. But, at this moment in time, I am concentrating on staying alive, and for your information, there are thousands, if not millions, like me. If you all choose to disagree with war or opt out, that's your business. I will concentrate on keeping me and as many people alive as possible."

Barbara retorted,

"Would you kill anyone?"

Pat almost pleaded,

"How the hell do I know, Barbara?"

Peter cut in,

"Barbara, let Pat alone. That's a very unfair question. Why did you ask it?"

Barbara almost screamed,

"That's none of your business. You may be my lecturer, but you're not my father. Don't tell me how to behave. Do you hear?"

Peter reacted, in Pat's opinion, very well,

"For god's sake, stop being such a drama queen, will you. This man will be facing god knows what in a few days. Leave him alone. In fact, leave us all alone. You have been a real bitch the last few days."

Pat joined the interchange.

"I think I had better go. I wish you all well and hope none of you are killed." Peter and Josie stood up and put their coats on. It was past midnight, and Josie said,

"We are going because it's getting late and because you, Barbara, are being so bloody stupid. Pat, it is lovely to meet you and good luck for the future, whatever it holds for you and your family. Come on, Peter. Let's go before we get told off again."

Barbara looked up, her face livid but said only.

"I'll see you at college."

Peter and Josie mumbled something like goodnight, shaking Pat's hand as they left. Petra, slightly shorter than Barbara and pure blonde, moved over to Barbara and whispered something in her ear and then walked to Pat and kissed him very lightly on the lips and said,

"Good night Pat. I hope to see you again soon."

Pat looked at Barbara and quietly demanded.

"Excuse me for being forthright, but what the fuck is wrong with you?"

Barbara moved closer, resting her hands on his chest.

"I am a committed pacifist, yet the only man I have ever been close to is going to war. I always knew you would be a good soldier. You will apply that considerable intellect and rationalise everything to allow yourself to do what is best for you and your men." Barbara paused; her eyes swept across his face. "And you will kill people."

Barbara seemed to be thinking before adding,

"My father always says of you and your dad that both of you know when to bend with the wind. I had hoped that your time away from me might have made me feel different toward you. Pat, I am very attracted to you, physically and emotionally, but I could never love you, and I'll tell you why. Although you are always open with me and the perfect gentleman, there is a part of you that is your own and nobody else's. Your mother puts it very well when she says you are very deep. I think what is ahead of you, whatever it may be, will be to your advantage. Forgive me, Pat, I have nothing to prove what I am about to say, but I think you will be very good at war."

Pat's face was still, his eyes questioning.

"What do you want me to say? If I am good at war, it will be because I want to stay alive and come home. If we both live through the war, what chance do we have of being the same people we are now? Will your judgement still apply if I come back in five or six years as a brigadier general with one arm and a knighthood?"

Barbara just moved closer and spoke.

"Once I have my degree, I intend to leave England as soon as I can. I believe this war is being fought to keep people under control, not free and what happens in other people's countries is their own business. I know this is, in your opinion, the easy way out, and there are large holes in my arguments, but right now, it's what I am convinced is the truth." Her stare was firm but not cold or angry, and as her hands moved to his shoulders, she whispered,

"I can't see any future for us other than what we have now."

Pat gently pulled her closer as he asked.

"What do we have now, Barbara?" As her arms closed around his neck, she answered,

"Let's go to bed, and we'll see. You can stay here tonight; after all, you're a soldier now. Oh, by the way, don't worry about condoms; I'm a lot cleverer now."

They had talked for a while as Barbara seemed preoccupied. She gave herself to him enthusiastically. He knew even when deep inside her that she did not love him and never would. During the night, they had sex continuously, excited by each other but at ease with the realisation that they were parting, and that would be that.

When morning came, Pat woke first and gently shook Barbara, who sat up, allowing him to see all of her body. She turned to him and they both became fully awake with one final coupling. He decided to go as he only had the rest of the day to say goodbye to his family. They washed and dressed without conversation. Barbara made tea which was drunk in silence. Pat took her in his arms; she willingly rested in his embrace and said quietly,

"Go, Pat, and please be safe. Just stay alive; that's all I ask of you. I don't know if we will ever meet again. Please put me out of your mind and just concentrate with every fibre of your being on staying alive. Pat Cork, do that for me, please."

She kissed him on the lips,

"Now, go and save the world."

He walked out of the flat into a fresh, bright, spring morning and half an hour later was sitting at his mother's table eating breakfast. Mary sat by his side but did not ask where he had been all night, though she wished her son had been at home. Mary Cork did not know when her family would be together again, and it was breaking her heart. Pat finished his breakfast then once again said,

"Nobody makes a cup of tea like you, mum."

He looked so mature in his uniform - she knew he was ready for whatever lay in front of him. Pat prepared to leave the house where he had known only happiness and fulfilment. The family agreed to send letters as soon as things settled down. His father, brother and sister were watching him. Standing up, he hugged each in turn, then went to his mother, who was crying. Putting his arms around her, for the first time in years, he had no words for her. She looked at him and, as usual, came to his aid. With tears running down her face, she whispered,

"God go with you, and always know that there will not be a moment when I am not praying for you."

Pat picked up his kit bag and walked out of the house without looking back. He would have become too emotional if he had begun to say all he wanted. That could not happen. Walking down the street where he had lived all his life, a familiar voice called out,

"Pat, please wait."

He turned to see Peter Wilde. Another man stood a little way behind him. Peter took his hand, saying,

"For God's sake, Pat, be careful. I've always believed that men could and should settle their differences by civilised means but Pat, my dear young friend, you do whatever it takes to stay alive."

His voice hardened,

"Whatever it takes Pat. Goodbye and good luck."

With that, he turned and walked back to his companion, and both walked away from Pat.

Pat reported to the guard house and was informed that the commanding officer would be giving a briefing at zero nine hundred the next day. He went to his billet and waited for the rest of the platoon to return.

Peter Wilde was aware that Mary and Connor were close to despair and invited them to dinner to meet the man he intended to live with in America. The meal was superb, and the Corks took to Peter's partner, who was tall and slim with jet black hair and utterly charming. By inviting them to meet the man, Peter was showing his complete trust and affection for the couple he had known since their marriage. After dinner, as they were having coffee and Brandy, Peter recalled how their friendship had begun.

"Do you remember how we bumped into each other Connor, all those years ago? What was on your mind that morning? You were so angry with the world."

Connor looked at his friend,

"It's time I told you the full story. This is why I left Ireland."

03

Beginning and End

Connor Cork was born in Dunmanway, West Cork, in 1898. The eldest of four children, himself, his brother Thomas and sisters Cora and Josephine were each born a year apart. William Cork, their father, was a confident man of just under six feet with brown curly hair and broad, strong shoulders. He successfully bred cattle and horses on fifty acres of good land, with dairy cows and pigs that gave fresh food and a bog which produced excellent turf. Their mother, Mary, was a tall, elegant woman with blonde hair and deep blue eyes who showered her husband and children with limitless love.

Despite a British colonial education, the family was steeped in Irish nationalist history. The Manchester Martyrs, Wolfe Tone, Emmet and many more who lost their lives in the cause of Irish freedom were as well known to the Corks as Queen Victoria.

William Cork was outspoken as to who was responsible for Ireland's many woes.

"An unholy alliance of the British Government and the Catholic and Protestant churches. They hold the Irish prisoners in their own country".

His sons listened, rapt, as he continued.

"The church is content with the way things are in Ireland as long as they are allowed to maintain their power. There'll be no rebellions coming from the bishops' palaces."

The boys worshipped their father, sharing his passionate nationalism, but even at an early age showed different temperaments. Their father noticed this and warned them.

"Ireland's history is full of hopeless risings by men armed only with pitchforks and passion. To be free, Irish people will need organisation, patience, education and unity. Always remember that."

Dunmanway was a small town with a triangle-shaped square of pubs, shops, the bank and a few houses. The Catholic Church was on the Bandon road, set high on a hill. The Church of Ireland Chapel was located on the Clonakilty road. Both were fine, ostentatious buildings with spires reaching to the heavens and their respective Gods. The local economy was controlled by Protestants, but there was work for all.

As William and Mary Cork's family and farm prospered, the time approached for the boys to choose a living. Connor was very bright, always reading and good with his hands. Thomas loved the land and livestock and spent many happy hours with his father on the farm and at cattle or horse sales.

Their farm was adjacent to the property of a Protestant builder, his wife and two children. Philip Bagot's ancestors had been part of the first plantation of West Cork. He was a well-built man with a straight back and a kind face which hid a sharp mind. His hair was almost white, his skin pale.

The men respected and trusted each other, and both had little time for religion or churchmen. Their eldest sons were the same age and close friends. It became clear that George, Bagot's only son, was 'a bit slow'. His father knew that George would be unable to run the business alone. From friendship and practicality, Bagot offered William Cork a carpenter's apprenticeship for Connor. When told, the boy accepted knowing of his close friend's problem.

Mary Cork woke beside her husband as she had done every day of their marriage. She found him dead. He had passed away as the result of a massive heart attack. The day after their father was buried, Connor Cork, at fourteen, began work for Philip Bagot. Thomas Cork left school to work on the farm - he was thirteen.

For a year after the death, the Cork family existed in a state of shock. Mary Cork had never been so lonely. Alone she watched her children grow up quickly. Connor worked for the Bagots and each evening, with his sisters and mother, helped Tommy, who did the work of a grown man on the family farm. Then the first anniversary mass was being said, and then the second year without him passed. Mary attended mass every Sunday, but not one priest had been near her house since her husband died. His views on the Catholic Church were well known and it seemed the clergy did not forget or forgive.

Philip Bagot had been deeply saddened by the death of his neighbour, making a point of calling to see Mary every week. She found these visits of great comfort. He was a good listener and described Connor as being 'worth two men.' Silently, Mary thanked God for the regular wage coming into the house.

Their father's death affected the brothers differently. Thomas needed to talk. Connor saw questions in his brother's eyes. "Please help me! Tell me! What did daddy do wrong? Why did he die? What did we do wrong?"

Connor, still in agony, could not answer his questions. Connor turned his back on his beloved brother. Thomas was hurt by his brother's behaviour and became bitter about his father's death and toward his brother. As they grew, the younger Cork's emotions and politics became more extreme.

Thomas believed that all Irishmen should be nationalists. Any who were not were not Irishmen and took his father's point to where he turned his bitterness into total distrust of all Irish Protestants. Connor tried to be balanced. During their rare talks, he pointed out that many Irish Nationalists were Protestant. But life went on, and both grew into young men - Connor the builder and Thomas in his father's footsteps.

The Irish Republican Brotherhood -the Cork brothers amongst them- met one of its leaders, Michael Collins, in west Cork. He asked if any man had ideas for gathering information on British government forces. Connor spoke up,

"We have a contract to build an office in the RIC Barracks in Bandon. Maybe we could get something there."

Collins almost whispered.

"Won't the RIC be suspicious of a Catholic working in the barracks?"

Connor assured,

"I run the jobs, so they think I'm a Protestant in the Army and RIC barracks."

Collins continued,

"I'm a bit worried about you going in alone."

Tom spoke.

"I'm taking a horse that an army officer bought to Bandon barracks stables. I'll go in with my brother."

Connor heard caution in Collins' next words.

"So boys, we're in, but listen, don't take any risks. Anything will do, a list of names, troop movements or government people."

Then as he embraced both boys in fierce bear hugs, he exclaimed,

"Jesus, boys! With men like you - and there are hundreds more - the Brits haven't a chance."

They met outside the barracks in Bandon and told the desk sergeant their business. He had known their father and offered his condolences. As Tom was shown to the stable, Philip Bagot unexpectedly arrived at the front desk. Connor wondered what to do next, recalling Collins' words,

'Don't take any risks lads'.

He followed Bagot, who walked toward the District Officer's office door and knocked. Both heard,

"Come"

District Officer Peters stood up, shaking Bagot's hand. Connor saw a man, at least three inches taller than Bagot, with a ramrod straight back and jaw permanently jutted. His jet black hair made him look about forty years of age, an imposing man by any standards with nothing kindly about him.

"Mr Bagot, good to see you - and who is this young man?" Bagot introduced Connor, explaining about the extension. A constable entered with Tom reporting the horse had been stabled. Peters suggested,

"Why don't we go for a cup of tea, have a look at the horse this army chap has bought, and this man can measure up."

Bagot, Peters and the constable left. Tom was ignored and stayed with his brother. Then, in amazement at being left alone in the office of the senior policeman in West Cork, they began to search. The desk drawers and filing cabinets were locked. On top of the cabinet, Connor found a list headed 'Preferred Contractors', comprising the names of Catholic and Protestant builders in the West Cork area. There was nothing remotely like military papers. Tom moaned,

"Jesus Con! We don't even know what we're looking for." Connor tried to remember how much time had passed since Peters and Bagot had left. His brother saw a piece of paper jutting out of the top of one document cabinet.

"Over here, Con; maybe we can get it out."

Tom slowly eased the sheet of paper from the cabinet drawer. There were two lists. On the left-hand side were names the Corks recognised: some Protestant, some Catholic. The right-hand side contained far more Catholic names, amongst them IRB men. The lists of names covered every town in west Cork. Tom swore,

"What the fuck is it? Are they informers, or what? There's all sorts of people on this?"

Connor questioned,

"I haven't a clue. Will we take it? If there's only the one copy - Peters is bound to miss it."

They heard Bagot and Peters returning; Tom stuffed the list in his pocket, and they were measuring the gable wall as the men entered. Both seemed satisfied with Peters saying,

"Right, so you'll start work tomorrow. I have a meeting in Cork all day, so you can begin in the morning by removing all the furniture."

Bagot agreed,

"Yes, my George can do that. Con will tell the labourers what to do."

The Corks left the office and waited outside for Bagot. Con knew that he could estimate the dimensions of the room if pressed, but it was not raised by Philip Bagot again that day. At home, the brothers examined the list.

"Well, Tom, whatever that list is Collins, will have to find out. There must be over two hundred names all told."

Tom exploded, "What the fuck is it then?"

Con pondered as he looked at his brother, who was now close to seventeen and felt a surge of real pride.

"Jesus, Tom, we got away with it. Peters will never know we took anything once we demolish the office tomorrow. You go and give the paper to Michael."

The following morning, the paper in his pocket, Tom drove cattle to the Cork City railway link in Clonakilty. In Bandon, Connor had the office cleared by mid-morning and the wall knocked by Midday. As Tom met Collins and another man, he recalled Connor's words.

"Tell Collins what we did and then get home. We've done all we can do for the cause."

That night the brothers discussed the meeting.

"Collins and a man called Harry Boland were very pleased and said that we were to do nothing until we heard from them."

Tom did not say that Boland had given him a pistol and ammunition, which he hid on the farm.

A week passed; Connor was at work in Bandon when one of the labourers whispered,

"Michael Collins will be at your house tonight at nine o'clock."

Mary Cork was slightly concerned that someone in the IRB was visiting her boys, though her husband had known Collins and described him as a man who did not take unnecessary risks. At precisely nine, there was a knock on the door; three men stood outside. As Collins came in alone, Connor suggested,

"Bring them in – it's cold out tonight."

Collins smiled.

"The boys are on guard - you never know who you can trust. Always remember that. Do ye hear me - both of ye?"

The brothers nodded and led Collins into the front room, where he began.

"Great things will happen soon, just be patient until you receive orders from the IRB, and remember, lads - trust no one but your own. Everybody outside the IRB is a potential informer."

Mary Cork entered the room, followed by her daughters. Michael Collins stood, and the ladies surveyed their guest. A man six feet tall with wavy, dark hair. Broad shoulders, solid torso and powerful arms. As they shook hands, he commiserated on her loss. Mary smiled.

"Mr Collins, my husband is not dead. He is alive, here, through my children."

The visitor took the cue, and for the next hour, they talked of the many challenges to be faced. Con saw his mother smile in a way she had not done since her husband died. A glance at Tom's face showed peace in his eyes. Both sisters were laughing in a way they had not done since that terrible day. Collins somehow managed to relax everyone. Tea and cake were served and eaten with gusto while they discussed female emancipation and the corruption of the churches. What could be learned from other countries - even the British? But above all else, being Irish. The Cork family now understood why the man was becoming a legend. Michael Collins stood and shook hands with the women; then, in the hallway, he bid goodbye the men with words,

"Con, Tom, we will meet again in a free Ireland."

Connor had met a true leader and silently vowed to obey him without question and almost demanded of his brother.

"Tom, did you ever see the likes of that man outside of Daddy?"

Tom replied intensely,

"That's the first time you've called him Daddy since he died, and no, I've never met or seen anyone like Michael Collins." Then added with fervour.

"Remember what he said about the Protestants? They are all enemies!' Remember, Connor."

On Easter Sunday in 1916, IRB volunteers in Dublin staged a rebellion. News was fragmented. Con heard of the rising while in Dunmanway with Philip Bagot. An RIC constable approached and saluted Philip Bagot, speaking of some trouble in the capital. Fighting was still going on around the GPO and the city centre.

Certain there would be more news in a large town, Connor suggested to Bagot that he and George collect materials from Bandon; Bagot agreed. Running home, he met Thomas, who, when told, exploded with excitement.

"It's what Michael said. Remember Con? 'Great things!' Remember? Let's go to Dublin, join the boys and hammer the Brits. Come on Con, let's go."

His brother grabbed him with great force.

"Shut up before you tell every RIC man within ten fucking miles that we are in the brotherhood. Shut up - for God's sake, Tom – just shut up! Remember what Michael said, 'Say nothing, do nothing, wait to hear from someone in command'." Tom glared angrily.

"How the fuck will we find out what's happening, Connor? Tell me that!"

"The same way I found out this morning," Connor retorted.

"The RIC will tell the Bagots, and they will tell us, or me, to be exact. Does that answer your question, Tom boy?"

Tom was straightening his jacket as he demanded,

"Do you think the Bagots are informers for the RIC, Con?"

Con stopped, then almost shouted,

"Now listen, Tom, we have known these people all our lives. Jesus! George, the crater, is too slow to inform on anyone. They are not spies or anything else. What's given you this set on them anyway?"

The reply was twofold.

"Remember what Michael said about all Protestants being informers, and anyway, why do the RIC men keep saluting Bagot?"

Con countered.

"Jesus, Tom. What Michael said was, 'trust no one but ourselves.' We are surrounded by Protestants. The Bagots are Protestants and support the government. As for the saluting, I don't know." They walked home in silence.

Connor was in Bandon soon after dawn and met the man who told him about the Collins' visit, who was equally confused. Both men listened, in growing disbelief, as a man described how in Cork City, twelve hundred volunteers had mustered under Thomas Mc Curtain, only to receive nine sets of conflicting orders. The volunteers finally dispersed under intense pressure from the Catholic bishops.

Connor and George took the supplies home, and Philip Bagot told of countrywide chaos. There were rumours of sporadic fighting in Dublin, then more reports of the rebellion being suppressed and more troops arriving from Britain.

Within days, the military presence in West Cork increased – strangers, not local garrison men. Connor knew that to commit troops, the British must be worried. Then news arrived that Roger Casement had been captured and a ship carrying twenty thousand rifles for the rebels had been scuttled in Dublin bay.

Things began to settle down. While working around the county, Connor listened to Cork people. Some felt the rebellion was reckless; there were Irish men in the British forces all over the world. The British military authorities ensured a large percentage of their pay was sent home, in some cases the only money coming into some households. The loss of these payments would mean economic disaster. Many Irish people could not afford to be rebels. Connor concluded the majority of people were indifferent to the nationalist cause.

Then, once again, the British displayed their customary stupidity and brutality toward the Irish. They interned hundreds of men who had been involved in the fighting. The leaders were convicted under military law and executed without appeal. The executions totalled fourteen men, with Roger Casement being the last in August 1916.

The brutal deaths of the men brought condemnation on the international stage from Britain's allies in the Great War. In Ireland, public opinion began to swing in favour of the nationalists. By Christmas 1916, many of the interned men were allowed home - amongst them Michael Collins - and they began to plan a war against the British.

During all this, the Cork family carried on. Connor qualified as a carpenter, bringing real pride to Philip Bagot. Tom, still young, was gradually filling his father's shoes. At a personal level, they had grown apart – something their mother was understandably unaware of as her mind was occupied elsewhere.

As 1918 began, both Mary Cork's daughters were being courted. Cora's suitor worked in Cork City and, on one visit to the house, made his intentions plain.

"Mrs Cork, I care greatly for your daughter. I have the means to give her a good life. I have told my parents about Cora and me, and they are happy for us."

Mary believed her eldest girl, at eighteen, was too young to marry, though her admirer Dan was clearly in love. Why not? Cora Cork was a very beautiful young woman with golden brown hair and willow-like grace. She listened to her mother caution her on the possibility of becoming an unpaid maid to Dan's ageing parents. Her reply was forthright,

"Mammy, I have known Dan for two years. He loves his parents, and he loves me. We have talked about how things will be. I will be the woman of the house."

Mary bowed her head. Her daughter's mind was made up.

"That could have been your father speaking. You have his way with words and his sensible view of life. Go, my darling and be happy with your fine, young, Leitrim man."

The boys were delighted when told of their sister's coming marriage. Three months later, in March of 1918, Cora Cork became Mrs Dan Flaherty of Leitrim. Con gave her away. The wedding was enjoyed by all. The parish priest officiated and spoke of a bright future. The celebrations went on long into the night. The guests sang; some were very good, some not so melodious. Everybody sang 'The Banks of My Own Lovely Lee.' During the celebration, Cora cried a little, missing her father, and Mary felt a pang of longing for her husband, as occasionally, at Mass, she felt a shiver of envy and anger because her family was not complete.

Josie, the youngest, had received a proposal from a young Tipperary man - a builder working in Bandon. She accepted as he was about to go home. Mary was delighted that her girls would not end up being unpaid servants to their brothers, as so many other Irish women. As for her boys, they were, to the stranger's eye, grown men. Mary feared her sons were involved in more than stock trading and building. It was rumoured the RIC had suspicions about stolen weapons being hidden in West Cork, and Collins' visit to her house involved more than paying respects. Her boys were never questioned. Mary believed it was because of Philip Bagot's influence and his respect for the family.

Their sister's marriages brought social pressure on the brothers. Connor was twenty years of age and foreman carpenter, a responsible position. Tom, now nineteen, was a successful breeder travelling the country, trading high-quality cattle and horses. Both men were now expected to be settling down. Neither man had given any thought to marriage. Tom's mind was elsewhere. He was utterly committed to the nationalist cause and secretly hiding stolen weapons for nationalist groups on the Cork farm. Guns that his brother or Collins knew nothing of. Connor was a very busy man with contracts to run all over Munster.

When the Great War ended, the Colonies of the British Empire began to demand increased independence from London. Throughout the Empire, soldiers returning from the front demanded social change. These demands were loudest from Ireland. A General Election was called in 1918. The Irish united under a political party called Sinn Fein.

All over Ireland, the men released from British Internment were elected as Sinn Fein MPs. In Cork, Michael Collins – who joked that internment had made them respectable- was elected along with Harry Boland and Thomas McCurtain. The party now had seats all over the country, except for Ulster, which, even with a large catholic population, voted for the Protestant Unionist party, which was bitterly opposed to an independent Ireland. Sinn Fein, representing the other provinces, demanded Irish independence.

The Sinn Fein MPs began their campaign by refusing to attend the Westminster Parliament. The British government knew that, should Ireland gain independence, other colonies might soon follow.

In West Cork, Michael Collins and others were organising the Irish Republican Brotherhood (IRB) to fight the British using guerrilla tactics. They were not the only the only nationalist group that would use violence against the authorities. Hostilities began in 1919 with attacks on RIC barracks. The aim of the raids was to steal weapons which were then hidden throughout the country.

There was little coordination amongst the nationalist volunteer groups resulting in the RIC and British Army discovering weapons caches and guns being transported. The volunteers caught were given lengthy jail terms or even executed out of hand. The killing of volunteers provoked equally brutal actions by the nationalists. Atrocities were committed by both sides in an increasingly vicious and growing tragedy. Secrecy was hard to maintain amongst the IRB; weapons continued to be discovered, resulting in many nationalist and IRB men suspecting every Protestant of being an informer. Many innocent Irish Protestants lost their lives at the hands of nationalists who refused to believe that arms discoveries were due to lack of planning, stupidity or just bad luck. The RIC and the British Army had commanders that were stupidly convinced that brutality would break a people already hardened by centuries of cruelty and violence. The IRB and Nationalists blindly and dangerously believed they could defeat the strongest military power on Earth by force.

At the end of March 1919, Connor Cork left for Mallow on Monday morning to return on Wednesday, having priced a job in that town. George Bagot had driven him to the Bandon station and bade him goodbye in Irish, a language he loved.

"Six o'clock Wednesday night."

The same night, Tom Cork was waiting in the Square, Dunmanway, for men from Middleton to deliver stolen rifles. As the darkness grew, so did his anxiety. Then he saw Philip and George Bagot. They waved and moved toward him. Tom caught sight of a pony and cart with turf baskets pull up in the Square as he listened to George joke about how their walk got them out of the washing up. Suddenly four RIC constables appeared from a shop front and grabbed the men in the cart. A search discovered four rifles. Tom looked at George, whose face showed his shock, then noted the calm of his father. Tom spoke, hoping to allay any suspicion of him.

"Jesus! What the hell has happened here?" George was still; his father walked over to the trap and lifted a somewhat rusty firearm. Tom was certain he saw a satisfied look on Philip Bagot's face as he said.

"Bloody Fools! When will they ever learn?" As the Middleton men were taken prisoner, one looked straight at Philip Bagot as he shouted,

"Fucking informers!" Tom remained silent, as did the Bagots. Then he went home, his head reeling.

Connor Cork stepped from the train, and perplexed, began looking for George Bagot. The man was religiously punctual. Suddenly two RIC constables grabbed his arms and, while taking him to Bandon RIC station, informed him he was under arrest. In the District Officer's office, Peters shouted.

"Where is your murdering brother, you IRB bastard?" Then punched Connor repeatedly into the face and stomach. Connor managed to shout,

"What the fuck do you think you're doing? What the fuck did we ever do to you?"

Peters stood still, chest heaving, his face displaying pure hatred.

"What did you ever do to me? There is nothing you could ever do to me, you bastard, you or your fucking brother."

Connor yelled,

"What do you want with me and my brother? What has happened?"

Peters grabbed him by the throat and very slowly said,

"At four o'clock on Tuesday afternoon, on their land, next to yours, Philip and George Bagot's bodies were found. They had been shot dead."

When the RIC sergeant, stationed in Dunmanway arrived, he was visibly shocked and feared for Connor Cork's life. Realising Peters was out of control he calmed him by pointing out in blunt terms that injuring Cork would close all of west Cork to the RIC, and quoting Philip Bagot's opinion of the Cork brothers.

"Those Cork boys grew up young; they don't have the time for politics. They're too busy working."

Peters retorted venomously,

"Don't trust any of them; they regard us all as foreigners. Don't ever forget that. Never turn your back on a Catholic - they're all the same. Do you hear me?"

The sergeant asked Connor about his whereabouts for the previous three days. His answers, along with the sergeant's calming influence, finally convinced Peters to release him. Connor Cork left Bandon RIC Barracks at nine o'clock in terrified disbelief. He wracked his mind. 'Where was Tom?' At a cattle sale, but where? They were busy men and lived separate lives sometimes, not meeting for days. Then he thought of Philip and George Bagot. Why would anyone shoot them? Suddenly he found himself crying for them.

In Dunmanway, Connor saw neighbours paying respects at the Bagot home, his mother amongst them. He waited and followed her home. Mary Cork gasped, seeing his cuts and bruises and began cleaning his face. Connor saw pure agony on her face. Mary would never forget the utter desolation on Emily Bagot's face, or the hatred and suspicion on her daughter's.

His mother demanded

"Where is your brother, Connor? Do you know?"

"I don't know, Mammy, but we have to find him. That RIC District Officer is set on killing someone tonight, and he's not bothered who, as long as they are Catholic."

Her fearful voice trembled,

"Con, do you think Tom was involved in this awful thing?"

Her son's face showed his shock,

"Jesus, Mammy. Tom would never do anything like that. What gave you that idea? Tommy would never kill anyone."

Mary Cork pleaded.

"Then where is Tommy?"

He whispered,

"I don't know, Mammy. I just don't know."

Her voice hardened.

"Get Michael Collins over here, now. Now! Do you hear me?"

Con pleaded.

"I don't know how to get on to him. He always contacts us."

His mother shouted,

"Get Collins here now. Now, Connor! Now!"

Collins was already on the way to the Cork's house, having been told of the murders by an informant in the Cork RIC. Collins and Tom Cork arrived at the same time. Connor greeted his brother with a relieved hug.

"Jesus, thank God you're alright. That bastard, Peters, has you in his mind for the murder of the Bagots."

Tom defiantly stated,

"The last time I saw the Bagots was yesterday, in the fields next to ours."

Connor noted his brother was not shocked at the deaths. Tom went on,

"I watched them searching the fields next to ours."

Connor, becoming concerned, demanded,

"What do you mean, that's their land. Why would they be searching it?"

Tom ignored the questions.

"Then they started looking into our ditches and fields - searching our land. I told you they were helping the RIC. How many times do you have to be told?"

Now deeply worried, Connor asked,

"Why would they do that?"

Tom's raised his voice.

"They were RIC informers. All Protestants are informers. Michael said so. Didn't you, Michael?"

Collins remained silent, his face darkening. Connor, with growing anger, demanded.

"Tell me why those men should be searching our fields. Give me one good reason." His anger began to turn to fear.

"Tommy, do those men searching the land have anything to do with the shootings?" Tom shouted,

"You want a reason for them searching. Well, here's one. I have been hiding guns in our ditches. Philip Bagot found two rifles." He pulled a revolver from his coat pocket, exclaiming,

"That's why I used this on them. I shot them both"

Mary Cork let out a low wail of despair. Michael Collins watched as Connor's face twisted into a picture of confusion and disbelief. He shoved his brother away and exploded with rage.

"You've been hiding guns on this farm, putting everybody here at risk – Mammy, the girls and me - without telling anybody? Jesus Christ! Did you listen to one word Michael said?" He looked at Collins.

"Michael, did you know about this?" Collins' face hardened.

"Not a damn thing, Con boy, not a damn thing." He continued,

"Now, Tom, tell me more about these guns."

Tom, now losing his defiance, was about to answer the question, but Connor spoke first.

"Jesus, Michael, forget the guns! He shot the Bagots; the Brits will hang us if they find out. They'll hang all of us, including Mammy. You stupid man! Jesus! What did the Bagots ever do to you or this family? Answer me, you stupid, murdering bastard!"

Tom stared at his brother threateningly and with renewed defiance.

"Watch out who you're calling a murdering bastard. You work for them; maybe you're an informer too. You're always too close to those Protestants for my liking. All that time you spend in the army and RIC barracks. As far as I am concerned, they were informers and got what was coming. If they weren't, why were they searching the ditches in that field? Tell me that, big brother, tell me that."

Connor's reply was riven with horror.

"What in the name of God has happened to you? All this time spent working with the beasts has made you as stupid. What were they doing in that field? I'll tell you. Philip was thinking of building a house on that field for George. They were looking at the ditches to see where to cut a boreen, you stupid fool."

Tom stood his ground.

"That makes no difference to me; they were looking for guns... I saw Philip Bagot's face when the Middleton boys were caught. He knew about the RIC trap. Now the Middleton and Antrim lads will probably die because of the Bagots and their kind."

Connor was almost derisory,

"Is that how it is with you and your friends in Middleton and Antrim? Anyone who doesn't agree with you gets shot. Is that the kind of Ireland you want?"

Tom challenged,

"Who gave you the right to judge me or anyone else? You do what you do to free Ireland, and I'll do what I do. Do you understand that? If you or anyone else gets in the way, they can have all the trouble they want."

Con realised Tom had shot the Bagots because he believed they were informers, like all Protestants, nothing else. No proof, nothing. He felt he was going to vomit as he looked at his brother and voiced his contempt.

"If that's the kind of Ireland you want, you can have it."

Tom glowered as he hissed through gritted teeth,

"We have no choice but to fight them this way. Every one of the Protestant bastards will have to go. It's us or them, Connor. That's it; us or them."

Michael Collins stood up and moved toward Tom.

"Tell me, young Cork, where will you hide for the next ten years?" He queried in an emotionless voice.

Now unsure, Tom replied,

"What do you mean, Michael?"

"I want to know where you are going to hide until we have driven the British out. You can't stay here; you'll be caught and killed. You can't hide in Ulster; we're outnumbered up there by the Orange men. Nobody else will hide you. You're a loose cannon. You were supposed to be taking orders from me, and now I find out you're doing jobs for every man in the country. As for the Bagots giving up the Middleton men, anyone could have."

He raised his voice,

"Jesus Christ, you're still wet behind the ears, and you're freeing Ireland on your own."

Tom slumped in a chair, all defiance gone. Collins was merciless.

"Jesus Christ almighty! We had Connor in the middle of the RIC and the army, and you, with your cattle business, free to cross Ireland without fear of being stopped or followed. He could get us information, and you could carry it anywhere. Yet, for the sake of a few rifles, you throw it all away by murdering two Protestant Irish men. You stupid, little man."

Tom screamed.

"I did it for a free Ireland!"

Collins laughed in a mirthless, cruel way that made Connor very afraid for his brother.

"What free Ireland? There is no free Ireland. There are twenty thousand British troops here and more coming back from the trenches. Battle hardened men. What about the Protestants? Are you going to murder all of them? Well, are you? What about the Orange men in Ulster? There's nearly half a million of them. Are you going to murder all of them, on your own, with a few rusty rifles, you stupid little boy? The British have just defeated the Kaiser and destroyed his empire. Right now, they're sitting at a conference table with the French and the Yanks, dividing the world between them. He paused. Then said sarcastically.

"So you think you can defeat one of the greatest Empires the world has ever seen with some ancient rifles and the murder of two Irish Protestants."

Tom Cork, now silent, still convinced he was right, had the sense to keep quiet as Collins moved toward him. Connor involuntarily moved to protect his brother. He was now seeing the other side of Collins, a cold, ruthless, calculating man capable of anything.

Collins looked at Mary Cork, stating,

"This is the end for Tom, here or anywhere else in Ireland. We have to get him out, or the Brits will torture and kill him. He knows too much."

Mary Cork sat beside Tom and held his hand. Knowing once he left, she would never see him again.

Connor asked.

"Michael, what will we do?"

Collins explained,

"We will get him to Cobh. He can get a ship there for America; then we'll have to get you out as well."

Connor was about to protest, but Collins cut across him,

"Connor, boyeen, do you really think they're going to leave you alone? If they can't hang Tom, then you will do. Justice doesn't mean anything to those bastards. All they want is an Irishman hanging on the end of a rope - if not now, then in six months' time."

Con shouted.

"I don't understand, Michael."

Mary Cork spoke first.

"What Michael is saying is that both of you have to leave home as soon as you can. Tom will have to go tonight, you soon after him. The Corks will leave this town forever; do you hear me, both of you? Forever!"

Collins tried to help her.

"Mary, things will change when we win independence. There will be a time when the boys can come back. Don't give up hope, ever."

She looked at all of the men and said,

"Come back to what? We can no longer stay in this town. Our neighbours have been murdered by one of my sons. What Tom has done has destroyed us as a family in this town and West Cork. We no longer belong here. We are a family of murderers. We will all have to go and never come back."

Tom spoke, his voice breaking,

"Mammy, I'm sorry for all the trouble."

Connor lunged at his brother, screaming,

"Sorry! That's all you can say, you murdering bastard! Look what you've done to us all. Our family could hold our heads up anywhere. You and me, we were part of a movement that was going to help all Irish people. Where are we now, Tom? Tell me that, you madman. That's it! You're stone mad! Only a madman would do what you did here today. Those men you murdered were our friends and neighbours. Yes, Tom, the Bagots were our friends. When that bastard Peters was beating me, he was told by another RIC man that the Bagots will speak for the Corks; they trust them completely. Why do you think the RIC left us alone? Because of Philip Bagot, that's why. And you kill him and poor George, only the carcass of a man. Freedom fighter, my arse! A stupid, thick cow peddler is all you are and a now murderer. Get out of my sight."

Tom launched himself at Connor, and they were locked in a clinch fuelled by grief and anger. Mary Cork screamed,

"Stop! For the sake of your father's memory and me. Stop before anyone else dies tonight. Please, my beautiful boys, please stop."

Collins separated them, shoving Connor into a chair. Then grabbed Tom by the lapels and spoke slowly,

"You will have to be out of Ireland in the next two days. If you're arrested, you won't get a trial; you'll be shot trying to escape. To stay alive, you must go."

Tom retorted,

"I can look after myself."

Collins pulled him closer and spoke in a cold clear voice,

"Do you ever listen? If you're blamed for the murders, the British will implicate your brother and mother. The farm will be seized; she'll be out on the road, and they'll get Con one way or another. The IRB command will never trust you again; why should they? You shot a man who spoke up for you and have drawn down the army and the RIC on us, looking for you under every bush and outhouse. Volunteers will have to move every gun we have hidden now. You've messed everything up, and still, you won't listen. Well, I'm telling you boyeen, for the next two days, you shut up and do as you are told. If you don't, it may not be the British who kill you. Do you understand that?"

Mary Cork said goodbye to her son Tom in their home in Dunmanway, knowing it was the last time she would hear his voice. Connor never spoke to his brother; he shook his hand, turned his back and walked away.

The situation in West Cork became desperate, as Collins had predicted. The army and the RIC tore the countryside apart to try and find the murderers of the Bagots.

The day of the funerals of Philip and George Bagot was one of the worst of Connor's life. Searing emotion almost overwhelmed him. Grief for Mrs Bagot, now widowed, who wouldn't look at him when he had tried to offer his condolences. A woman that, for the previous ten years, even up to last week, would call him into her kitchen to give him delicious homemade cakes for being so good to her 'Georgie'.

Sorrow for his mother, who had had her world torn apart again. Anger and loathing for the man who had caused all of this, his brother, now gone from Ireland, probably forever. Then a numbness gripped him, close to that when his father died. George was his friend. Philip Bagot had listened to him talk about his father, sometimes for hours. Bagot did listen for no other reason than he was a kind and decent man. Now he was gone, murdered by a Cork.

Connor wanted to settle the family's affairs in Dunmanway quickly and had to be able to travel freely. To achieve this, accompanied by a solicitor, he walked into the RIC barracks in Bandon and asked if he was under suspicion regarding the killing of the Bagots. Connor was informed the case was still open; he was not under investigation and was free to go about his business. No one could murder him now without uproar throughout Cork.

He and his mother sat in the house that had been their home for so many years. "We must sell the farm as soon as we can and get out - the girls have told me to stay with them from now on. Con, I want just enough money not to be a burden to the girls. How do you feel about that Con?"

Connor hugged his mother.

"Mammy, all I care about now is that you have some kind of peace in your life. If it means you going to Cora and Josie, that's fine with me. I'll look after myself. Just as long as you are settled, that's all that counts".

She looked at her son and burst into tears.

"Connor, I'm dying of worry about Tom. Where is he? Do you know?"

Connor steeled himself.

"Mammy, I don't know where he is, but you must stop worrying yourself. He will survive. You know how tough he is, and we both grew up young; remember that when you think of him. Please do that for me, Mammy."

They talked on into the night about the good times they had all had in their home, but there was no laughter. Mary told her son how she had missed her husband when he died. How it was as if half of her had been taken away. She felt the same way about Tom. For a fleeting second, Connor felt anger and jealousy but said nothing knowing there was years for anger. He listened as his mother talked until she fell asleep.

The farm was put on the market, and he took his mother to her daughters.

When he returned to Dunmanway, an offer had been made for the farm, which fulfilled his mother's financial needs. Connor accepted and visited his mother and sisters to tell them he had sold everything the Corks had owned in West Cork. One evening his sisters asked Connor to tell them about what had happened in West Cork. Connor knew he owed them at least that much and much more. He knew both women were angry about his even being involved with the IRB. So he tried to put the horrible mess into words. Cora, who was now very much the married woman of the house, listened for a short time, then butted in forcefully.

"If Daddy had lived, none of this would have happened. He'd have kept you both under control. You can be certain no man in my family will ever be involved." Connor nodded his head in sad agreement. The next morning Cora's husband warned,

"Connor, the RIC and the army have been asking questions about you - you'd better move on soon. These fellows have no respect for anything other than their own law but listen, whatever happens, you are always welcome here. Don't mind herself; she really thinks you're the bravest man in Ireland. But Tom -I'm afraid he's cooked his goose with my Cora. She won't even mention his name without getting into a fit of temper."

Connor left his sister's farm, and after a brief visit to Josie's home in Tipperary, he returned to West Cork, where Collins sent word for him. For one minute, Connor nearly told the messenger to tell the whole IRB to go to hell, but Collins was still his friend. When they met, he was surprised at how quiet Collins was about the rising and the movement. Michael gave him the names of men who would find him work in London. Then with a wry smile suggested,

"Jesus! Connor boyeen, if we'd never asked for a list, maybe none of this bloody business would have happened."

Connor almost managed to laugh.

Connor left West Cork, got the train to Dublin and then the ferry to England. With his tools and a few pounds in his pocket, he had no idea what the future held for him, but he had to get away from the sadness and grief before he went mad.

Connor remained on good terms with his sisters and their families. When they wrote, none of them ever mentioned Tom. He would return to Ireland just once more to bury his mother, who passed away in 1922. His sister told him that her last words were about Tom. Connor replied,

"As far as I am concerned - he killed her."

Cora and Josie never forgot the look of pure hatred in his eyes as he spoke the words.

The Bagots buried their dead husband and brother in the Protestant Church in Dunmanway, sold their house and moved to Londonderry, where they lived with relatives until 1937, when they moved to England. They never returned to West Cork.

Mary Cork was buried in Leitrim, far away from her beloved husband and their own lovely Lee, and in the same year, 1922, Michael Collins was killed in a gunfight in West Cork. When Connor heard, he turned his back on Ireland forever. As for his brother, he still could only feel hatred for the man who had, as far as he was concerned, destroyed a part of Ireland forever.

— 04 —

Taking Control

Having completed winter training and commanded by Brigadier Gareth Davies, the 24th Brigade of Irish Guards sailed for the town of Bodo in Northern Norway. Aboard the Chobry - a Polish crewed troop-carrying vessel – during a briefing by Brigadier Davies, all officers and NCOs were instructed to state their names and units. Lance Corporal Pat Cork listened and was surprised as the brigadier ignored blatant insubordination by an Irish Guards captain and two Royal Norwegian Navy officers who remained silent. Davies concluded his involvement.

"Gentlemen, I will leave the details to Colonel Fitzmaurice. Good luck."

The brigadier, his staff, and the Norwegian naval personnel disembarked. The Irish Guards officer remained to confirm his unusual departure from Sandhurst had not caused other army officers to recognise him. Satisfied about the continued secrecy of his unit he prepared to go ashore.

Neither Captain Lewis nor Lance Corporal Cork heard anything after the first explosion. The second and third hits were completely silent, as both men were in shock. Lewis felt only searing heat and then a cool sea breeze. Below deck, Pat Cork was blown against a bulkhead, his legs and arms immobile. He shouted at the battalion commander, Colonel Fitzmaurice, and the officers seated with him. Their eyes seemed lifeless in expressionless faces, and as a wave took the ship, they fell forward, dead. Pat felt a desperate need to breathe clean, fresh air, forcing him to climb the gangway, which seemed to take an eternity, his eyes concentrating on the daylight at the hatch.

On deck, the sounds of men shouting and the crackle of fires were muffled in his addled brain. The deck underfoot was red hot. He heard the Irish Guards captain shouting orders to the Polish-speaking crew, who, to Pat, surprisingly obeyed. All except one, who was screaming hysterically as the captain held him by the jacket? Now beside the captain, Pat yelled,

"What do you want me to do, sir?"

The reply was concise.

"Corporal, my name is Lewis. This man is the ship's radio operator. I know he speaks passable English. Get him to the radio room. Make him signal the navy escort ships to come alongside to take the men off."

Pat drew his sidearm. The sailor was still screaming in barely coherent 'pidgin' English.

"The fucking ammunition will blow, you stupid bastard. I getting off now. I not to die."

Pat's head had cleared. He pointed his revolver at the man's left temple,

"We are going to the radio room, where you will signal the navy ships, or I will kill you. Now, move, you useless bastard."

Realising his life was in danger, the man stopped shouting. Pat suddenly remembered Barbara's words. In the radio cabin, the operator sat at the set as a man bleeding badly from a head wound in a merchant navy officer's uniform entered. In excellent English, he announced,

"I am the captain of this vessel, corporal."

Then demanded to know why the radio operator had a pistol at his head. Pat explained. The captain nodded and swore in Polish as he punched the operator viciously in the face. Then added in almost apologetic tones.

"Corporal, I will take over. This man will transmit until I tell him otherwise. If he doesn't, I will kill him with my bare hands."

Another of the ship's officers, visibly shaken, came into the cabin. The captain conferred with him, resulting in another blow to the operator's head, followed by a string of guttural curses. Again he addressed Pat.

"Corporal, I am informed by my second officer that this man is half German. We may kill him anyway. I am sure you are needed elsewhere; please go; we are in command now."

Cork was about to offer his pistol, but the radio operator, now transmitting frantically, needed no further encouragement.

On deck, some fires were doused by sea spray caused by the German bombers near misses, but over a short period, Pat felt the ship rock as a number of direct hits wreaked havoc. Then a wind cleared the smoke to reveal bodies everywhere. Despite the atrocious conditions the highly disciplined Guards' men were descending by nets to immensely brave local fishing trawlers who had steamed alongside.

Further off, the outlines of the Royal Navy escorts became sharper as they closed in on the Chobry. Suddenly Lewis's voice rang out.

"Report, Corporal," Pat told him about the radio operator.

"Right, any idea what is happening below decks?"

"No sir. I'll get below and have a recce." He turned to see Brigadier Davies, with a number of army officers and the Norwegian Navy officers from the briefing, climb onto the deck. Lewis signalled him to wait on deck as he began briefing the Brigadier. Then a bomb dropped under the stern detonated, which was lifted out of the water, for what seemed an eternity, then the ship crashed down on to one of the trawlers, sinking it without a trace.

The instant death of so many brave men shocked everyone. Davies was quick to take control. Lewis was ordered to take two officers to the stern cabins.

Corporal Cork, another two to the forward cabins. Everyone was to return in exactly five minutes with situation reports.

Pat arrived at his platoon's billet. Flames had engulfed the cabin bedding; the smell of burning flesh filled the ship as the vapour escaped from the large jagged hole blown through the upper deck, which had been the ceiling of the cabin. His friends of the last few months were lying dead. As the officers counted the bodies, the junior of the two noticed Pat's ever-darkening face and shouted,

"Corporal, have a look further down. See what's in there, please."

He knew the man was trying to be considerate. Greenwood's wisdom came to mind as he stepped into the corridor,

'Never make friends; they could be dead within seconds.'

Well, this was ample proof. Pat checked his watch and shouted.

"Gentlemen. The brigadier will be waiting."

On deck, Davies was talking to the Chobry's captain. As Pat approached, he assessed the senior officer. A big man with an evenly proportioned, powerful body and straight back. His hair was cut short and would have been almost ginger if allowed to grow. His clear voice carried in the wind, commanding and confident, summoning the returning officers.

Cork stood silently and watched the remnants of the battalion disembark. Then the brigadier called him to his side.

"Corporal, I have received reports regarding your conduct during recent events. I am promoting you to sergeant with immediate effect. Do you accept this promotion?"

Pat, without thought, said,

"Yes, Sir. " Then added.

"Permission to speak, sir?"

"Feel free, sergeant."

"If I may, I would like to thank Captain Lewis for the way he assumed command."

The brigadier moved closer until their faces almost touched,

"Sergeant, you will forget that that officer was ever on board this ship. Do you understand, laddie?"

There was little choice.

"Yes, sir."

They saluted, shook hands and left the doomed Chobry.

Sergeant Patrick Cork and Brigadier Davies aboard HMS Dolphin watched Captain Lewis, and the Norwegian sailors embark on a Norwegian warship. The former silently vowed to thank him if they ever met again.

Those aboard the Dolphin watched as the Chobry sank slowly with the dead of a battalion of the finest front-line troops in the British Army. There was a groan which became a roar as the air was forced out of her lower decks. Pat involuntarily blessed himself and suddenly felt very alone. The ships which had rescued the survivors turned away and steamed for the Norwegian Coast and comparative safety.

Over the next two weeks, Sergeant Cork learned how much red tape was involved in the death of one of His Majesty's soldiers. The original platoon officers had been killed, and their replacements insisted on writing to the next of kin. Pat was the only man who had personal knowledge of the men lost. For hours, the young officers sat and wrote letters they knew would break hearts and destroy lives. Pat stayed with them, trying to conjure up a unique memory of the soldier who was the subject of the letter. Finally, the task was over, and he secretly acknowledged that the exercise had probably kept him sane. Convinced no training could have prepared him for the deaths of his comrades. Pat somehow felt he owed them something more than the letters. But what? Maybe the answer would come with time. His confused anger raised questions. Where was the RAF fighter cover? Why had no one seen the bombers? Again, no answers. There was one certainty. During the bombing, he'd felt real helpless terror. A sensation he did not want to experience again. Pat decided somehow, he must take control of his part in the war.

In Bodo, the survivors recuperated and came to terms with the losses. Brigadier Davies had difficulty controlling his emotions when informing the survivors of the fatalities of the First Battalion of the Irish Guards. The Battalion CO and five officers. Then Pat's platoon. The regiment had lost one hundred and eighty-two men. Brigadier Davies finished with,

"Along with our comrades, we have lost all our heavy equipment. Gentlemen, this expedition can only be described as an unmitigated disaster."

He then spoke of the future, citing the reputation of the Irish Guards and the Brigade of Guards as a basis to build from. Davies then voiced his belief that every recently promoted man, regardless of lack of training, would acquit himself admirably in action. Which, he stated, would be very soon, as the enemy were pushing deep into Norway. Davies then wished the assembled company 'Good luck.' As Pat left the room, an officer approached him.

"Sergeant Cork, the brigadier wants to see you immediately. Follow me, please."

"Ah, sergeant, how are you?"

Pat, slightly surprised, replied,

"Very well, thank you, sir." He paused. "Good of you to ask."

Davies nodded acknowledgement and continued,

"I have received more good reports regarding your assistance in the writing of letters to the bereaved families. That couldn't have been easy for you. At a ridiculously young age, you are now one of the senior men in the battalion. This has brought extra responsibilities for you, as it has for others."

Cork felt the senior officer's eyes concentrating on him.

"Now, I want to explain something. You are a soldier - and a good one. I know you appreciate the value of good intelligence. As of now, I have little coming to me on anything. Now tell me, what do you know about something called C squad?"

Pat was frank.

"Never heard of it, sir."

Davies went on,

"The officer you commended on board the Chobry is part of a unit which is unofficially attached to the brigade. The squad is commanded by Commander Bakken of the Norwegian Navy. He has requested a liaison officer from the battalion. I am unaware of the precise nature of their mission; however, I know they specialise in operating behind enemy lines. The liaison officer will be in the field with them. I want you there, sergeant. I need good intelligence on the enemy, and I need it as soon as possible, so I am asking you to take that position. You will not be under the orders of any officer in C squad – or any other unit. You will report to me alone. Do you fully understand what I have explained and what I am asking you to do?"

"Yes, sir."

"Then will you take this posting?" Davies asked.

Pat thought quickly. The battalion had been wiped out. Captain Lewis had been exceptional on the Chobry. What did he have to lose? Then it hit him. This gave him control. Christ! He would be reporting to a bloody brigadier. Nobody could tell him what to do. Once again, in his head rang Greenwood's wisdom. 'Never volunteer.'

He ignored the voice.

"Yes, sir, I will."

Davies stood, and they shook hands.

"Right, let's meet C squad. These men are part of an organisation called the Special Operations Executive - SOE for short. Thank you, sergeant. Oh! - And good luck."

Pat watched as Captain Lewis, two Norwegian naval officers, and a seaman entered. The latter's untidy dress did not make a good impression, as Cork thought ironically.

'Christ! I am beginning to think like a sergeant already'. The senior Norwegian naval officer was over six feet with jet black hair, tanned skin and piercing blue eyes, lithe and very fit, shaking hands as he spoke.

"Commander Bakken - Royal Norwegian Navy." Then he introduced the second officer Fran Larsen and the seaman as just Freddie. Davies explained Pat's role. Captain Lewis was pleasant, "Good to see you." Bakken explained he was part of Norwegian Naval Intelligence, which had under surveillance, the leader of a Fascist political party which, they suspected, intended to assist the Germans to conquer Norway. Their reward being they would become the puppet Nazi government. C squad's mission was to locate the party leader. He added,

"What we require from you, sergeant, is to provide logistic support from the Irish Guards."

Pat asked the brigadier.

"Sir, may I speak freely?"

Davies nodded.

"This is an open-ended operation behind enemy lines. What happens if the team has casualties? Do the others carry on? If so, we all need to know the target's identity."

Bakken looked at Lewis who nodded.

"The man's name is Quisling."

Cork continued,

"Thank you. Just one more question, if I may? Tell me, sir, what happens when we find this man?"

Bakken answered slowly,

"If we find out that this man has conspired in treason, he will die and will do so at the hands of a Norwegian."

Just as feared, the German invasion of Norway was successful, primarily due to the coordinates of defensive minefields being given to the Germans by Norwegian Nazis.

The Guards marched north to a town called Pothus, where the 1st battalion immediately engaged the Germans in fierce fighting. C squad was deployed as a reconnaissance unit, far behind enemy lines, from where Sergeant Cork radioed reports to Brigadier Davies and gradually got to know his comrades. Bakken was a highly intelligent man who commanded with dignity and ease. The leading seaman, Freddie, was raised in England of Norwegian parentage. He taught Pat how to steal everything needed to survive behind enemy lines. His victims could only remember a plain, ordinary man, nothing special. The perfect description of the consummate thief. Pat never questioned his scruffiness again.

The second in command was Fran Larsen, of self-proclaimed Viking blood. A tall, rangy man with blonde hair and fair skin. Who, when told Pat was Irish, delighted in suggesting, because of Viking raids over the centuries, that they might be related? Lars, as he became known, was the communications expert and could operate any radio set invented.

Lewis switched from one language to another with infinite ease – and killed with equal zeal. Pat learned from them all as they blended into the civilian population like Chameleons.

During the squad's recce missions, Pat spent many hours with Lewis. Their conversation ranged from basic training to each other's backgrounds. Pat mentioned Greenwood's wisdom. Lewis expressed his approval.

"Very wise man."

Pat moved on to his Irish background. Lewis had at first been a solitary, remote man, told of having strong Irish connections and his passion for all languages Irish amongst them. He finished with the words,

"I was born in Ireland - though it's been years since I was last there. Things happened." Despite his reticence to talk about the past, as each day passed, Lewis became more relaxed with his comrades. After ten days behind enemy lines, the squad returned to base and listened along with Davies to Bakken's detailed situation report. A signal was then handed to the Brigadier, who, remarkably for a senior officer, overtly vented his frustration with the British Prime Minister.

"That bloody man Chamberlain is useless beyond belief; either withdraw us or reinforce the entire operation. No more fudging!" Then thanked and dismissed C Squad. Later in a Guards rest area outside, Bakken summarised.

"The intelligence gathered is helpful to the brigadier but useless for us. We need to tell SOE HQ what's going on."

For this, a very powerful radio was required, and as luck would have it, the Germans were about to provide one. The squad were in the field and were watching a checkpoint when four German military police -or 'chain dogs' as they were known, turned up for what seemed a snap inspection. The police were equipped for overnight travel and amongst their kit was a high-powered radio. Larsen observed,

"That set is just what we need." Lewis spoke.

"We'll wait 'till the Germans bed down for the night." Then he detailed the assault. Bakken would kill the first policeman. Larsen, the second. Freddie would despatch the third. Bakken reminded everyone the radio must not be damaged, so Larsen must make that his priority. Cork spoke up.

"I'll take his man."

Lewis nodded and advised.

"Pat, just keep him busy until I get to you." He cautioned them.

"Remember, silence and get the radio intact." The Germans were camped in a quiet wooded area some distance away from the checkpoint, all sitting with their backs to the vehicle, watching a field kettle come to the boil. Bakken killed his target with a knife inserted between the collarbone and the spinal cord. Freddie strangled his man with a fine wire garrotte which cut his windpipe in two seconds. Pat forced his man forward, pulled his chin back, and slid his knife along the German's throat. He felt the warm sensation of blood flowing over his hand and remembered Lewis's instructions.

"When you feel the blood spurt, do not squeeze the handle. It will cause your hand to slip. Just relax and continue to slide the blade along the length of the target's throat." Pat did as instructed, and the German died silently, as did the fourth policeman Lewis killed by breaking his neck with his bare hands.

Larsen quickly mastered the radio, and Bakken made his report in English, answering 'yes' and 'no' to prepared cryptic questions. A method of reporting designed by the SOE signals experts to minimise exposure to enemy tracking units.

After three minutes, Bakken summarised the situation.

"Well, there is nothing more on Quisling; except that the order to kill him has not been confirmed by the Norwegian government. He paused to stress his next words. "So we are on our own."

Larsen spoke with a cold voice.

"We should just cut the bastard's throat and let him bleed to death. He is a traitor, and that's the end of it. He makes me ashamed to be Norwegian."

No one spoke; Quisling's actions were deeply hurtful to the Norwegian people. Bakken was about to continue but was interrupted by the sound of heavy artillery. Pat stated.

"That sounds very close to brigade headquarters."

Bakken agreed.

"Let's go and have a look."

The squad approached the headquarters on a road held by the enemy. The stolen German vehicles and uniforms gave them cover as they moved toward the British front lines. In the general mayhem, no one was going to be looking at regimental insignia too closely. Pat mentioned to Bakken that getting into the brigade headquarters in German vehicles and uniforms might prove difficult. Bakken ordered the squad into a small wood five hundred meters from the perimeter of the British position, looked at Pat, and said,

"Well, sergeant, you're the Guardsman man here. Get into the HQ and find out what the fuck is going on, please."

Cork had learned it was relatively easy to pass through advancing troops as they never expect anyone to come from behind. Having crawled to within fifty metres of the first line of defence, he removed the cape revealing his battledress to the perimeter defenders and yelled.

"Incoming patrol, don't shoot."

Then repeated twice before a reply came as a challenge.

"Who are you, and where the fuck have you come from?"

Pat answered both questions and heard,

"Come ahead."

The brigadier asked urgently.

"Have you been in touch with the UK, sergeant?"

"Yes, sir. We stole a radio from an enemy patrol. The information I'm about to give you was transmitted earlier this morning. We have had no contact from the Norwegian Intelligence Service. We do not know where the target is."

The brigadier ordered,

"Sergeant, would you now please go back to C squad and tell them to come into the divisional HQ immediately."

Pat commented,

"There might be a problem there, sir."

Davies prompted, "Go on." Pat explained the squad's current uniforms. The brigadier laughed.

"Sergeant, I need to speak to those men now. Do you understand that? Bring them in. They're supposed to be especially talented - let's see if they can get through the sentries. Bring them in, Cork, and do it now, please."

Once through disorganised German lines, Pat relayed the orders. Bakken shrugged his shoulders.

"We'll go in after dark."

The brigadier swore quietly when C squad appeared in his command room. "Jesus Christ! This goes from bad to worse." Then raised his voice.

"I don't want to know how easily you got past our guards. I trust you did not harm any of my soldiers."

"One or two may have sore heads in the morning, sir, but they'll all recover," Bakken replied.

The brigadier ordered all the men in the command room to leave and asked,

"Commander, I need information on the enemy positions."

Bakken obliged.

"Captain Lewis, please make your report."

Lewis nodded.

"Sir, the enemy is about to flank Brigade HQ on the left and right with infantry units with full armoured support. With respect, sir, the situation is quickly becoming untenable."

The brigadier looked at the command room desk as he said,

"Captain, please show me on the map where the enemy is, and please estimate at what speed they are advancing."

As Lewis finished, the brigadier looked up from the chart.

"Gentlemen, I am assuming command of C squad. I am aware of your mission. If we have to evacuate the Brigade HQ, any decision to continue that mission will be Commander Bakken's. Is that clear?" Bakken answered,

"Perfectly clear, sir."

For the next five days, the squad roamed the Norwegian countryside. Contact with the enemy resulted in the loss of thirteen German lives. Pat watched Lewis kill quickly and silently - he always led the attacks. Bakken did not argue.

As predicted, the military situation soon became untenable. C squad returned to brigade headquarters, aware the HQ was nearly surrounded by German forces. Brigadier Davies signed the order that instructed the brigade to move to the coast to be evacuated by sea. The Norwegian expedition of the Brigade of Guards was an unmitigated defeat. Davies spoke to Bakken.

"Commander, that is your authorisation to go ahead with your mission should you choose to do so. Good luck."

Later that day, the squad were concealed in a wood just inside the British perimeter. Bakken spoke.

"We have our orders, but as you all know, we have no idea where the target is or if we have authorisation to kill him." Larsen nodded, still trying to raise SOE headquarters by radio. Bakken continued.

"Gentlemen, we have a choice. Stay here or head for Oslo and probable capture. We have been very lucky so far, fighting men who are under orders to keep advancing. The Germans will figure out that some of the dead were killed at close quarters and not by regular troops. Then they will start looking for us." His comrades digested the words in silence. The Commander went on.

"If we stay in Norway and attack the enemy, there will be reprisals. The Germans have threatened to shoot ten Norwegians for every soldier killed." Again there was no reply. Bakken approached Pat.

"Sergeant, I need to talk to you immediately."

Cork's astonishment was clear as Bakken gave him the details of the order issued regarding Lewis.

"I have to tell the brigadier; you know that, don't you? If this order is legal - which I doubt - no soldier can be expected to obey it." Bakken replied.

"That's fine by me Pat. Meanwhile, we'll move up to the harbour and see if we can help there."

Pat made his way to battalion HQ, where, outside the building, he shouted at a corporal.

"Where's the brigadier? I need to see him urgently." A lazy voice replied,

"Sarge, everything is fucking urgent. Just how fucking urgent is your urgent, Sarge?"

Pat let rip.

"How about you being known as 'Private' from now on, you cheeky bollocks."

The corporal stood to attention, saluted and pointed toward a large canopied truck.

"The brigadier is in that lorry, sergeant."

Pat yelled,

"You behave as a corporal in the Irish Guards or else. Do you hear me?"

The reply was instant.

"Yes, sergeant."

The brigadier jumped from the lorry in a sprightly fashion for a big man. Seeing Pat, he said,

"Still fairly fit for an old man, hey, young fellow?"

Pat saluted and cut across him, saying,

"Sir, I have to speak to you immediately."

Seeing Cork's face, Davies realised something was very wrong.

"Get to the point, sergeant".

Pat very carefully summarised Bakken's words. The reply was in a voice barely concealing astonishment.

"Sergeant, I have been in the army all my adult life, and in that time, I have been involved in many operations and projects. The majority of them were legal if, in some cases, slightly underhand, but never, in my entire service, have I heard of such an order being issued. Are you absolutely certain of what you have been told by Commander Bakken?"

Pat almost whispered,

"Absolutely certain, sir."

Davies exploded,

"Quite disgraceful! Absolutely disgraceful. I am aware that C squad are special, and they have been using methods that could not, by any stretch of the imagination, be called regular. However, we are fighting for what we regard as common decency - amongst other things. Sergeant, we have to go and find out exactly what is going on here with Captain Lewis and Commander Bakken. If I understand you correctly, and I think I do, should certain circumstances prevail, this order is to be carried out very soon. Is that correct?"

Pat nodded his head.

"Right, laddie, jump in the cab of this lorry and get me out to C squad."

Pat objected,

"Sir, we will be on the front line. There is a chance you could be taken prisoner."

The reply was simple.

"Let me fucking worry about that, son."

They approached the front lines and found the brigade had captured a road giving access to the port and the vessels waiting to evacuate them. The Royal Navy was laying down a barrage of shelling in the harbour. The advance on land and attack by sea had caught the German defenders surrounding the harbour by surprise. The brigade had secured a number of jetties and was preparing to begin embarkation. Davies quickly assessed the situation, and under the circumstances, it was a minor victory. He and Pat abandoned the lorry and crawled to within shouting distance of C squad, which was involved in hand-to-hand fighting with the enemy.

Unknown to the brigadier, his staff officers, brigade HQ troops and body-guards had followed him at a discreet distance. Now, they threw themselves into the fighting. The Germans, finding themselves now fighting on two fronts and overwhelmed by the sheer ferocity of the attack, were suffering heavy casualties and began to retreat. Davies ordered a controlled action to force the enemy away from the port.

German soldiers had set up a general purpose machine gun in a warehouse near the jetty, which was inflicting heavy casualties on the men waiting to embark.

Lewis, wearing a German uniform and Bakken in his naval uniform, sprinted toward the warehouse, firing from the hip. They reached the building, and Lewis kicked in a window, throwing in a phosphorous grenade which exploded imme-diately. Screams from inside could be heard over the sound of battle - both men disappeared into the smoke-filled building. Pat followed, and, to his surprise, so did the brigadier and one of his bodyguards - a redcap.

The machine gun was located on a mezzanine floor in the warehouse, and all five attackers opened fire. There were explosions as the machine gun was silenced. The Redcap had been killed by shrapnel which opened his abdomen - intestines clearly visible. The brigadier had been knocked over but was conscious. Pat, having been blown on top of Davies, regained his feet and watched a dazed German soldier stagger. Lewis cut his throat. The brigadier shouted,

"I will forget I saw that captain. Come on, let's get aboard the ships."

Lewis turned and said,

"Sorry, Brigadier Davies. I am not going back."

With that, he rendered Bakken unconscious with a chop between his neck and shoulder. Turning to Pat, he said,

"Sorry, Sergeant - nothing personal. Please tell Odin that Erebus will be in touch." He fired, and Pat felt a burning feeling in his left lower leg, followed by the sensation that his shin had been hit with a sledgehammer, then unbelieva-ble pain. As he slumped to the ground, he saw Lewis shoot the brigadier in the arm. Davies was a big man, but the force of the bullet spun him around as he fell. Then, as the soldiers of the brigadier's support group began to arrive, Pat watched Lewis stand over the prostrate Bakken and salute. He then disappeared through a window, and everything went quiet.

The next thing Sergeant Pat Cork of the Irish Guards knew was when he woke in the sick bay of a troopship. Standing at the bottom of his cot was a serious-looking doctor reading a file with 'Cork' written on it and a large capital

B in red. Pat knew he was bound for Blighty as 'wounded in action.' He looked around the cabin and saw the other three men from C squad and Brigadier Davies. The doctor looked up from the file and smiled as he said,

"Sergeant, your war is over for the near future until we get the bone in your shin rebuilt."

He placed the file in the bracket at the foot of the cot, and as he opened the cabin door, Pat saw two armed redcaps on guard outside the cabin. He then fell asleep for what seemed an eternity.

Erebus

Charles Peter Lewis was born in the county of Kilkenny, Ireland, in 1919. Since the Norman Conquest, the Lewis family had been soldier-servants of the English Crown and had been rewarded with land in Yorkshire. During the reign of Elizabeth the First, they were suspected of covert allegiance to the Catholic faith and lost their Yorkshire estate. As a loyalty test, the family was exiled to county Kilkenny to assist in the suppression of the recalcitrant Irish. The methods employed by the Lewis men were assimilation and marriage, with all Lewis children born in Ireland. When presented with no alternative, they resorted to eviction and execution so their souls were not entirely unblemished. Despite bringing as little hardship to the local population as possible, they were looked on as relatively civilised landlords, but still English invaders.

For their efforts in Kilkenny, they were granted lands in Leinster and became one of the oldest, if minor, members of the Anglo-Irish aristocracy. The family adroitly survived the mayhem of Cromwell and quietly flourished. As the British Empire expanded, the Lewis family played its part. In 1704, Lieutenant Gregory Lewis was with Admiral Rooke aboard a ship of the Line when Gibraltar was taken. There was a Lewis at the relief of Khartoum and in all of the major campaigns which secured British colonies in Canada and Africa and the 'Jewel in the Crown', India.

Whilst on leave in London, a single man of the Lewis family met and fell in love with a young woman of an old English family from Suffolk. The marriage secured a small estate in that county and an English hereditary title which was passed to the eldest boy of each generation. As the nineteenth century ended, the Lewis family felt comfortable in their small ancient seats. One in Suffolk, where Sir Geoffrey and his wife Felicity lived. His brother, Peter Lewis, resided in the estate in Kilkenny. Throughout their long and quietly illustrious history, the family had invested in banks all over the world. A policy which resulted in the minor aristocratic family having substantial property and considerable cash assets.

The Lewis brothers saw active service in the British Army in the First World War. Sir Geoffrey as a major in the Coldstream Guards, while Peter served as a captain in the First Battalion of the Suffolk Regiment.

Sir Geoffrey's life had been that of an upper-class officer - something he had never questioned until he saw the unshakable bravery shown by other ranks during those four indescribable years. His opinion of the British soldiers was forever cast, not on the playing fields of Eton, but on what he had seen in the mud of Flanders, Ypres and the Somme. He had heard a young Army Colonel, called Macmillan, describe British Infantry as 'Lions lead by Donkeys'. Sir Geoffrey had never heard truer words, as a good soldier had come to profoundly respect and, in his own way, love the men he commanded.

Peter Lewis was a shattered man from combat and mustard gas. In 1919, Sir Geoffrey and his heavily pregnant wife arrived in Kilkenny to maintain the family tradition and their son was duly born in Ireland. Despite fears that he might not be able to deal with the excitement of a baby, Peter was delighted, immediately perked up and became the doting uncle.

Once Charles Peter, as he was christened, was old enough to travel, he would spend every summer with his beloved Uncle Peter. The Dublin-based physician attending Peter Lewis stated that the boy was the best medicine in the world.

Charles Peter Lewis was six years old and again enjoying an idyllic holiday in Kilkenny with Uncle Peter. In England, his father received an urgent call from the local police. The Lewis's immediately went to Kilkenny to be told Peter Lewis's body had been found; he had been shot dead.

Sir Geoffrey and his wife comforted their son and explained that Uncle Peter he had died from his war wounds. The boy was calm and never cried. The local police, such as it was, reported that Peter Lewis had been targeted as an absentee landlord and sympathiser with the RIC and Black and Tans. There was also the possibility that the car was to be used later in a bank robbery. Sir Geoffrey listened but didn't believe one word.

He knew Peter's involvement with any side in the War of Independence was impossible. His brother was a Great War survivor who could barely walk. Peter was buried in his beloved Kilkenny soil while the house was closed up, and two hundred and fifty-odd acres of land were rented out. As Sir Geoffrey was leaving, a man approached and spoke with genuine sorrow about Peter Lewis's death. The men exchanged addresses, and over the years, became correspondents and friends of sorts.

Charles, always a gregarious boy, became a recluse in his father's library. Then at school began to show an exceptional aptitude for languages. After his tenth birthday, he asked to go to boarding school and was duly dispatched to a suitable prep school and then Eton. He spent a number of years as a diligent student, with his ability for languages stretching his teachers to the limit. Physically, he was immensely resilient, winning all of the cross-country races with ease and excelled as a boxer.

On his fifteenth birthday, Charles' life took one of those irreversible changes of direction that occasionally happen. He was being ribbed by three prefects in the common room. The eldest of the three had demanded.

"I take it English is your favourite language?" Charles answered, "No, Irish."

The prefect in question had lost a relative in Ireland during the War of Independence and took exception to this, as he termed it, a 'disrespectful and insolent answer.' The prefects decided that the young Irish pup needed a lesson beginning with a good thrashing. Unfortunately for them, all the years of pent-up anger and frustration came flooding to the surface, and Charles Lewis inflicted grave injury on all three. The prefects suffered broken limbs and damage to their testicles and kidneys - one had his jaw fractured. The instigator of the thrashing would leave hospital with a limp, which would plague him for many months.

After an internal investigation, Lewis's parents were summoned to the college and told their son had been suspended. His father, an Old Etonian, knew that the matter must be very serious for the college to take such punitive action.

Sir Geoffrey asked the parents of the injured prefects to take into account the immediate suspension of the offender and consider the offer that all fees charged by Eton for their sons would be paid by him. The collective decision not to prosecute was quickly forthcoming. This decisive action allowed Charles Peter Lewis to avoid any in depth examination as to why and how this usually quiet, studious boy caused serious injuries to fellow pupils in such a controlled and ruthless manner.

The faculty members at Eton were perplexed at the behaviour of this pupil with a remarkable aptitude for languages. However, the senior masters concluded that, although the prefects were hardly blameless, the expulsion of Lewis was inevitable.

Sir Geoffrey was confused and appalled by his son's behaviour. His wife, Lady Felicity, though devastated, loved him as any mother would.

The headmaster at Brownleigh School was made aware of the boy's very rare terrible fits of temper and agreed to take him as a boarder, under close supervision. Lewis moved through the school system, passing the necessary exams to enter the Royal Military Academy at Sandhurst. His exceptional talent flourished and, by the age of eighteen, he was totally fluent in Italian, French, German and Norwegian. Polish, Hungarian, Spanish, Russian and Swedish were marked by his teacher as excellent. Irish he had quietly taught himself.

The Commandant of The Royal Military Academy was a personal friend of Sir Geoffrey and his wife. Indeed, as young men, they had vied for her hand. He had seen all sorts of men enter the Academy and felt sure it could sort out any problems the young cadet had.

Charles Lewis quickly concluded he must control his temper and violence. His father and the commandant ensured that his progress was incident-free by arranging for an NCO who had served with them in the Great War to join the Academy as an instructor. As his first term came to a close, the cadets were given weekend leave. Nobody was surprised that the less than gregarious Lewis remained in his quarters.

The training period for cadet officers is eighteen months, enough time to turn boys into officers and gentlemen, and Sandhurst is rightly proud of its graduates. Lewis's grades at Sandhurst were above average, and when he requested permission to go to London, the commandant and his NCO instructor agreed.

Three weeks before Cadet Lewis was due to graduate from Sandhurst, he was returned to the Academy under arrest by officers of London's Metropolitan Police Force, having been in a fight in the Limehouse area of the city. The police reported to the commandant that a young man had attempted to blackmail Lewis, alleging he had offered money for sex. The boy had been supported in the coercion attempt by two older men who had threatened Lewis with violence. Lewis had beaten the men unconscious, the receiving hospital describing the individual's conditions as serious. The boy had been slightly injured. The police were accustomed to such violence, a common occurrence in parts of London. What was unusual was the involvement of an officer cadet from Sandhurst. The 'Met' was practiced in dealing with 'Hooray Henrys', as someone from Lewis's background was known. The idiots were returned to whatever 'Toff' colleges they came from, suitable compensation was paid to the aggrieved party, and life went on. Except in this case, how the injuries were inflicted was of grave concern. Witnesses said that the 'Toff' had beaten the men senseless in a controlled way without thought or pause. The police had no choice but to refer the case to the Director of Public Prosecutions.

The commandant discussed the situation with Sir Geoffrey, and they agreed on three areas of concern. The casualties, the reputation of Sandhurst and the name of the Lewis family. Sir Geoffrey had the casualties moved to a private hospital. The sixteen-year-old was to attend a school which would educate him until his eighteenth birthday. Cadet Lewis was under arrest at the Academy and, under military law, would remain so until the commandant said otherwise. Sir Geoffrey negotiated with the DPP and the War Department, persuading both to prosecute Cadet Lewis under military law.

Maintaining confidentiality was relatively easy as the aspirant blackmailers were career criminals and were dealt with simply. The sordid details of their new venture -attempting to extort money with male prostitutes -was leaked to the criminal fraternity in the Limehouse area. When released from hospital they were advised to leave the 'manor'.

Cadet Lewis was examined by numerous psychiatric experts who could not diagnose any specific mental condition which caused the terrifying rages. Physically he was as fit as any other cadet.

The year was 1939. Sir Geoffrey and the Commandant were acutely aware that the future of Charles Lewis would be decided quickly.

In 1939 the British Empire had been forced into a war it did not want. Society in Britain had changed drastically, with working-class people and trade unions demanding a better society for all.

Pacifism was a widely held political view in Britain. Years of spending cuts had left the armed forces ill-prepared for war. Global conflict would put the already stretched colonial administration under further pressure. Britain's colonies all had substantial pro-independence movements, which were monitored by intelligence officers and indigenous police forces, supported by military garrisons. These officers, police and military units were under orders to maintain British rule.

The British Military High command was aware that in the event of a world war, intelligence would be a fundamental weapon in the fight against an enemy and possibly the independence movements in the colonies. There are two elements which make up what is known loosely as British Intelligence. These are the gatherers and the analysts. The gatherers are recruited from every part of the Empire. The Gatherer's recruitment officers maintain a covert watch on the armed forces, universities, schools, performing arts and prisons. The officer stationed at Sandhurst quickly recognised Lewis's potential. The cadet's mastery of languages was outstanding. His penchant for less than pleasant behaviour was a bonus. Both could be harnessed to great effect.

The recruitment officers were not averse to operatives who were not exactly normal. The function of the department was to gather intelligence. Who did it and how was nobody's business but theirs. Once selected and trained, the role of the gatherers is to pass all information on to the second element – the analysts.

The role of the analyst is to find, somewhere amongst the mountain of information supplied by the gatherers, that which is closest to the truth. Once the raw intelligence is analysed and refined, it is hereafter referred to as 'the product'. Both gatherers and analysts guard the source of the product jealously.

The product is then at the disposal of the customers, who comprise of prime ministers, cabinet members, senior military officers and colonial administrators, governor generals and such. All those responsible for decision-making within the British Empire.

It had been decided that Lewis' talents could not be wasted in prison. There was a role for him in the Intelligence world as a gatherer.

The Commandant of Sandhurst sat in his office, recalling his recent telephone conversation with Sir Geoffrey Lewis.

"Please come to the Academy immediately. No. I cannot discuss it over the phone." The refusal was based on a long-held suspicion that his conversations were being listened to by others. He was now convinced they were.

Sir Geoffrey arrived and quickly read the documents handed to him. The former soldier sat back in the chair, astounded and utterly confused. Cadet Lewis entered the office and was ordered to sit. Sir Geoffrey spoke slowly, concealing a mental and emotional maelstrom.

"What do you know of intelligence work, my boy?"

His son replied,

"Nothing sir."

Sir Geoffrey handed the letter to the cadet, saying.

"Please read this letter very carefully. It may have a profound effect upon the rest of your life."

The commandant silently approved as Lewis read the letter twice and then spoke.

"Permission to speak, sir?"

"Granted."

"I would like to accept this posting immediately, sir."

Sir Geoffrey indicated agreement.

"Very well, please sign the paper in your hand. What is contained therein are your orders until further notice. You will leave the Academy in the morning, and good luck."

Cadet Lewis was escorted to his quarters and reread the orders. It was a legal contract binding him to serve with the Special Operations Executive for not less than ten years. His rank would be captain in the Irish Guards regiment, which would be unaware of his existence. Any breach of security, such as revealing the name of the organisation or criminal acts, would result in him being returned to the civilian authorities for trial on the offences committed in Whitechapel. Finally, he was to make his own way to a training camp near Aldershot. Failure to arrive on time would be regarded as desertion in the face of the enemy and punished as such – meaning, upon capture, he would be shot.

In the Commandant's office, the two old friends looked at each other in total amazement. Sir Geoffrey spoke first,

"When was all this decided, and how long have you been aware?"

The Commandant looked up, exclaiming,

"Geoffrey, I profoundly resent the implication that I would do anything less than honourable toward your family. I have stuck my neck out for you and your son and have placed my career at risk, and, unlike you, I am not a man of means. The army is my life; it is all I know and want to know. As Commandant of this academy, I am completely unaware of who, other than us, had knowledge of Charles' problems and his performance here. I have never heard of this organisation he has signed up for.

However, I am fully aware of the authority of signature on the covering letter attached to the orders your son received, and before you ask, no, you cannot see the fucking letter."

He continued,

"We are both fully aware that Charles has profound problems and sooner or later he was going to be killed or kill someone. This chance, if that is what he has been offered, has been given by people who are certain they can make use of his talents. He will be commissioned and will have a role to play in this bloody awful war we have to win. He may die, but then so may we all. I suggest that we do two things tonight. We go and see his mother and tell her as much as we dare, and then we get drunk at your expense."

Sir Geoffrey stood up, tears in his eyes, his voice trembling,

"Come on old friend."

Charles Peter Lewis approached the base at Aldershot with a mixture of trepidation and anticipation. The top secret orders he had signed placed him at the disposal of perfect strangers. Being alone was normal, fear was not. Lewis was nineteen years old, just under six feet tall, weighed thirteen stone ten pounds, with blonde hair and blue eyes. Boxing and cross-country running had developed his broad shoulders and strong legs. His reflexes were exceptionally fast, and, apart from the occasional killing rage, he was a very attractive young man.

As a boy, he had felt little emotion despite his mother's loving, tactile affection. His father had always displayed as much emotion as was deemed acceptable for his class and upbringing.

Uncle Peter had been very different but had been taken away, and no one had explained why. After his uncle's death, Charles felt safer alone. Studying languages was his route to solitude. His classmates were unable to keep up as he learned of different tongues and cultures. Everything would have been fine if he had been left alone. When the prefects attacked him, the memory of Uncle Peter returned, and his fear quickly turned to anger. The insult about being Irish was enough to send him into an uncontrollable rage. The boxing training and high level of fitness had done the rest, converting anger into a controlled state of mind with every blow and kick planned and executed. Lewis was not surprised at being expelled.

At Brownleigh, he had played games and studied hard. His parents tried to talk to him - as had the medical people, both clinical and psychiatric. These people cared for him, but there were no answers. Lewis could not explain to them how once the anger started, he channelled all his strength in a totally controlled manner. The rages had not occurred again until the night in Limehouse. The boy had jumped on his back. One blow had been enough. The attackers were beaten until he felt safe. He never caused the fights. If people were stupid enough to provoke him, he would respond.

Charles Peter Lewis entered the guard house at Aldershot barracks, presented his orders and was ordered to wait in a seven-ton lorry with a tarpaulin canopy and wooden benches that ran the length of the body. He was joined by three men, the lorry departed, and an hour passed before it stopped. They alighted and were called to attention by an NCO.

"Good afternoon, gentlemen. My name is Sergeant Major Tomlinson. I will be your squad leader during training. Please do not ask any questions, as you will not be given any answers. Your training for the next three months will prepare you for whatever the people who run this organisation have in mind for you. While on this base, you will be known collectively as C squad and will remain unaware of each other's identities and backgrounds. This is an essential part of your security when you go on active service."

Lewis surveyed the other men - wondering what their talents were. His were languages and causing injury with great speed and efficiency. During the next three weeks, C squad was literally run into the ground to satisfy the Sergeant Major's required fitness level. Then the squad was addressed by a man they presumed to be the commanding officer of the unit, whose speech was concise and informative.

"You are now part of a unit that has yet to be recognised by the military establishment. The SOE has been set up by people who have experience in fighting insurgent or rebel groups throughout the world. This knowledge will now be used to establish resistance groups in occupied countries. To do this, men and women will enter and live in occupied territory assuming the identities of those countries' nationals." He then made a specific reference to C Squad.

"Your mission will be in a Scandinavian country with which you are all familiar by birth or fluency in language."

The man went on to say,

"You are all from different backgrounds and have different skills to apply to the task at hand. We are here to fight the dirty war that no one wants to talk about. The Nazis are the most dangerous enemy civilisation has ever faced. We have to use all means to destroy them, and if the reports of their actions in Germany are remotely accurate, they will have to be destroyed - not just defeated but destroyed completely. So be aware if you are captured, your death will be agonising and guaranteed."

He paused.

"The SOE uses methods which are regarded as unethical or illegal by the military establishment and is already under intense scrutiny. Any mistake would result in calls for the organisation to be shut down. So this could be your first and only mission. I won't invoke God's help because what we have to do and how we do it has very little to do with God. So good luck. I will not speak to you again."

The next three weeks involved the construction of bombs and booby traps and how to improvise explosives from natural substances such as manure. The three weeks after that were dedicated to silent killing. At the end of this training, their instructors were delighted. Every man in C squad could take human life silently and at close range, but Lewis excelled. The members of C squad knew no more about each other than when they first met. Lewis had seen enough to know that the other men were highly intelligent and motivated by a sense of duty or freedom. He threw himself into all of the training and exercises, physical and intellectual, and understood the nature of the fighting the SOE had in store for him, but still felt nothing other than he was here because he had no choice.

Colonel Simpson-Coyle was very suspicious of the types of people now involved in the war, specifically in intelligence. Some departments had, to his mind, recruited utterly unsuitable people. Sections breaking enemy codes were made up of eccentric geniuses. Academics, Artists, actors, playwrights, now had vital roles to play. Some with idiosyncrasies and unsavoury habits. Simpson-Coyle had to accept all were committed and loyal to their country, but he still did not trust them.

During his training, Lewis was interviewed weekly by a man he presumed to be a psychiatrist. The questions asked were not about his background but about his powerful, violent urges. He had no answers for why he hurt people - he just did.

His guess about the psychiatrist, come interviewer, was correct. The officer in command of C squad finished reading the report and faced a dilemma. Lewis was amoral, asexual, apolitical, and utterly ruthless - in fact the perfect killing machine who would kill because there was no reason not to. Captain Lewis was an ideal operative for the SOE and also a potential serial killer who could desert on active service and murder, at will, across war-torn Europe. The CO decided to make his own contingency plans for Lewis and be circumspect with the medical information when meeting his superior officer.

The next morning, Lewis was called to a meeting.

"I am Colonel Simpson-Coyle of the Norwegian section of SOE and in command of C Squad. I have reviewed your performance and am fully apprised of your past record. Your linguistic gift and the war have kept you out of prison. The other members of your squad are men who have ties with Norway - one is a convicted thief and smuggler who knows the Norwegian coast like the back of his hand. The other two are serving officers in the Norwegian armed forces of impeccable character. See if you can figure out which is which." Lewis remained silent as the man continued.

"You will soon be on active service, where you will be the translator for C squad and will eliminate any threats. I will now tell you your code name. From the moment you land, when you make contact with SOE, this is the only identification which will be acknowledged. From now on Captain Lewis, you are 'Erebus'. Please carry on with your training."

Lewis was dismissed and he saw another member of C squad waiting. The man entered, closed the door and was greeted with the words,

"Commander Bakken, how are you?"

Bakken saluted and replied,

"Very well, thank you, colonel."

The next ten minutes were dedicated to Lewis's psychiatric report. The colonel concluded the discussion.

"Commander, it is, unfortunately, obvious that we cannot wholly rely upon Captain Lewis, even though his expertise in languages and his ability to kill are essential to the operation which you will command. In the event of the pending capture of Lewis by enemy forces, or his desertion, you will kill him. Is that order clearly understood, commander?"

Bakken replied in a clear voice,

"Perfectly, sir."

The Colonel continued,

"Bakken, your call sign is Vali." Vali was given operating procedures and dismissed.

Colonel Simpson-Coyle pondered on the men he had just spoken to. Vali was a decent man, and Erebus was probably unwell, but he could not allow any of that to interfere with his job. He was fighting his kind of war, having been involved in the dirty side of the military service all his life. After leaving Sandhurst in 1918, he was posted to Ireland and cut his teeth fighting the IRB and other rebellious groups. He had gone head-to-head with Michael Collins. He had not flinched in his methods of interrogation. Finally, after numerous protests from army officers and civil servants, Simpson-Coyle was recalled in 1922 after, in his opinion, being betrayed by the politicians in Whitehall. Then posted to the Middle East and Africa, where again there were allegations of overzealous interrogation of suspects - namely torture and cruelty. Numerous investigating officers believed the allegations to be well-founded but could not prove anything. Colonel Rupert Simpson- Coyle was adroit at leaving no evidence.

Simpson-Coyle had hoped for a regimental command, but the allegations of cruelty had convinced the high command that he was best kept out of the limelight. In fact, if it had not been for the declaration of war, he was to be retired early. Now his vast experience in counter-insurgency made him a very valuable asset, ideal for the SOE, even if certain people in the army had their doubts. He was appointed to command the Nordic section of SOE because of his record in nearly all of the other areas of operations. No one had heard of him in Norway, and hopefully, there would be no more complaints.

Simpson-Coyle's life was the army and the Empire, and he was not going to risk his career by being held solely accountable for issuing what was an illegal order. He was about to make a report to the man largely responsible for the SOE being founded and would have to choose his words very carefully.

He stood to attention in front of an admiral of the Royal Navy called Spenser, who looked up and greeted the officer.

"Good evening, colonel. What do you have for me?"

The colonel reported that C squad was ready for action; however, he was a little worried about the operative codenamed Erebus. The admiral requested.

"Please expand upon the word, 'worried'." The soldier's words were chosen with extreme caution.

"Erebus may be a little unpredictable in the context of his ability to carry out orders to the letter. He may be a bit of a loose cannon, sir."

Spenser looked at the colonel and, for the first time in thirty years of military service, realised he was being subjective about a fellow officer. He simply did not like this man, who seemed to radiate mistrust. Simpson-Coyle was a small man, bald with a pencil moustache which, in Spenser's opinion, was quite ridiculous. The man's record was unwholesome. His reputation for avoiding blame was well-known but unconfirmed by evidence. Spenser pressed.

"Colonel, can you control this loose cannon?"

Simpson-Coyle answered,

"Yes, sir. I think I have devised a method which will be effective."

The admiral's suspicions increased geometrically, but he would have to take the Colonel's report at face value.

"Right, carry on. Dismissed."

Admiral Spenser was dining in Bond Street at the residence of the chief of British Intelligence. His name was known to a few of the establishment in Britain, but his function was not. Admiral Sir Kevin Menzies had been in the Royal Navy since he was fourteen and had seen active service all over the world. In 1933 he was ordered to modernise naval intelligence and then military intelligence. He was known throughout the war only as 'C'.

Menzies briefed his guest before dinner on the current situation regarding the war. Now his dining partner learned just how pessimistic his host was regarding the ability of Britain ability to defeat the Germans. His reasons had been presented to the Prime Minister, Neville Chamberlain, and met with disdain.

"Peter, we are going to lose the war unless the people in the cabinet realise the Nazis do not want peace. Hitler is bent on world domination. We will have to break all the accepted rules of war to stop them, The German people have backed Hitler and his gang to the hilt thus far, and it seems they will not be persuaded from supporting him further." Menzies then underlined his pessimism by outlining the plans for a resistance movement should the country be invaded. The SOE was to disappear into British everyday life as civilians and organise an effective resistance movement. Then he became slightly more upbeat.

"Now, Peter, bring me up to date on current operations.

Spencer did as asked.

"Sir, please understand all decisions on Norway must take into account the Norwegian government is far from secure. We have confirmed reports of a very senior member of the Norwegian government having very close links with the Nazis." Menzies remained silent, so Spenser continued.

"We have decided to send our own people in to assess the situation. " C asked.

"What sort of team do you have?" Spenser described C squad. Then spoke slowly,

"If the individual in question is a traitor, the Norwegian military has requested we eliminate him." C broke the ensuing silence.

"Go on."

"The current Norwegian government has forbidden any form of violence on principle. This policy may increase the danger facing our men."

C looked at his fellow flag officer, his face displaying slight anger.

"Admiral Spenser, we will have to take all opportunities and risks in pursuing our objectives, there will be mistakes made, and these we will learn from or just have to live with. The operatives face risks which are unavoidable." He continued.

"Now, speaking of danger, we have to secure your identity. From now on, you will use only the call sign 'Odin'."

Then he finished the briefing by raising a whisky glass.

"A toast to those of us who live in the world of smoke and mirrors and the dark arts - may God help us all."

Spenser decided not to mention his concerns about Simpson-Coyle. He had been given his orders, and that was enough for him. Both men emptied their glasses and began to eat.

Spencer returned to his command and signed the order that authorised C squad to go into action. They would go to Norway with the Guards Brigade.

— 06 —

Tom's Story

Shaking with anger, Tom Cork sat in a tiny cabin aboard a ship in Cobh harbour. Collins' earlier warning had been rammed home in a harbour pub used by other stock dealers. Tom was seen waiting to board the ship and was forced into a snug bar by a number of men. A nervous landlord kept watch as one demanded,

"Cork, what the fuck are you doing here? Why did you shoot those good men? Jesus, Cork, one of them was touched. You've every RIC man and soldier acting like madmen. Why did you do it? They were Irish men like us, or don't you give a fuck as long as you can boast you killed some Protestants?"

Tom retorted,

"We are at war - didn't anyone fucking tell you?"

Another man hissed,

"We're all at war against the British, not innocent Protestants. You can call that war if you want but don't try and involve everybody else. Who said you could declare war for me? The best thing you can do now is clear off. You fight your fucking war somewhere else."

Later, Cork told Michael Collins, who was there to ensure he left, and he was equally abrasive.

"What did you expect; you're no hero to them. The Bagots were well respected all over the County Cork. You had no proof they were informers; I swear if you were caught and tried now, a jury of Cork men would hang you. Now just go. You have no friends here Tom, at least, not now."

Collins shook his hand and wished him well, but Tom wouldn't give in completely, not while he was still in county Cork and tried to convince Collins he could stay. The reply was mercilessly logical,

"You say you can hide here because you know your land and country, but there are men who will not rest until you are dead. You're on the wanted list for years to come. Remember that. This is not your country now and might never be again."

At sea, Tom watched the Fastnet rock light shine bright until it disappeared astern. In Dunmanway, he could almost touch the silence. Now, in his bunk the engine noise and his anguish made sleep impossible. Images running through his mind - the pure hatred in Connor's face - Cora and Josie crying, and the terrible goodbye to his mother who had demanded answers.

"Why did you kill the Bagots, Tom? Tell me why please tell me, why? Look what you have done to me, your sisters and Connor. Do you think your father and I raised you to be a murderer? Well Tom, tell me please, before I go mad?" She had kissed him and, crying, told him to go forever.

He couldn't answer his mother then, and there were no answers now. Thomas Cork slowly realised that all he had done was destroy the Cork and Bagot families. Suddenly, he was sobbing uncontrollably.

The next morning on deck, Tom thought about how an ocean dwarfed everything he had seen before. Then a shape took his eye, a ship, and panic welled up. It was a warship flying the White Ensign, declaring Britain's dominion of the seas. Suddenly, he was no longer alone. A sardonic voice broke into his turbulent thoughts,

"Welcome aboard, Mister Cork. Don't worry about the cruiser. We are in international waters; not even the mighty Royal Navy can stop us. You have escaped from Ireland."

Tom watched the cruiser as the man continued.

"My name is Schultz. I am the captain of this vessel. I hope your cabin is not too uncomfortable."

Schulze explained that it would take three weeks to get to San Francisco, where Tom would go ashore as arranged. He then suggested that as the only English speakers aboard, they eat together. During the meals, Tom learned that his dining companion had 'No love for the British', having spent three years interned in a British African colony.

The master of the Belgian steamer was a small, rotund man in his late thirties with a growth on his face desperately trying to be a beard. His ship had a live cargo of high-value Aberdeen Angus cattle bound for Texas. The balance was antiques from Britain for the auction houses of San Francisco. Tom's interest was sparked by the mention of Aberdeen Angus. The Captain allowed him to spend time with the livestock, which lifted his spirits. The cattle gave him an idea. Galveston was a port in Texas - a state famous for ranching and cattle. Maybe there was work for him on one of those ranches. Suddenly he decided to disembark in Galveston and disappear into the huge state of Texas. When told, Schultz replied a little fearfully,

"I was paid by Michael Collins to take you to your comrades in San Francisco. Men I would not want to upset." Tom replied with wisdom that belied his years,

"Don't worry about them; they'll soon forget about you and me. The lads in San Francisco will send word I'm OK. Half of those lads are on the run like me. Michael needed to get me out of Ireland quickly; there's no danger to you, Captain. You see, we Irish are too busy killing the British and each other to have time to hurt anyone else."

That night, Tom told Schultz why he had left Ireland. The elder man had warmed to the young passenger and advised.

"Get into America and never worry about anyone but yourself. You got out in one piece; your mother knows you're alive, and that means everything to her, don't ever forget that."

The steamer beat through heavy seas, steadily nearing the east coast of America. During that time, Tom relived the Bagot's deaths many times. It always began with Philip Bagot's reaction to the volunteers' arrest and how they had shouted at him about informers. Tom had decided to wait for Connor to come home before he did anything, but then so much happened so fast.

The next day he was walking in his land and saw two figures in the fields opposite. Moving nearer, he recognised the Bagots. They were looking at the ditches which separated the farms. Ditches with concealed Poitín chambers, now hiding weapons. One, a pistol Tom had got from Boland, and with which he'd become a good shot. George Bagot waved to him; as he returned the gesture, he saw Philip Bagot prodding a part of the ditch which hid two rifles. If the guns were found, there would be hell to pay. Suddenly, fear growing, he was tucking Boland's pistol in his jacket. Then relief, as Philip Bagot looked over the ditch into what was left of an old boreen but then returned to prodding. Tom's heart raced as the walking stick suddenly disappeared into the earth. He heard Philip Bagot call his son to help him. There were only a few feet between them as the younger Bagot lifted a rifle. Suddenly he was firing the pistol, and George Bagot was falling, blood pouring from his head. Then seeing Philip Bagot's face calm and the light of life leave his eyes after being shot twice by his neighbour.

The birds had not been disturbed, no one had heard the shots; he had time. The rifles were moved to the next field, it was late afternoon, and he finished the day's work as if in a trance.

Burned in his memory was that there was no surprise on Philip Bagot's face as if he expected to be killed by Tom Cork. If only there had been time to talk to Connor to explain all this. Things could have been so different.

As the ship docked, Captain Schultz asked about Tom's plans for getting ashore.

"I've a good bit of money from home, and I know a fair bit about cattle and horses. I'll find work on a ranch and take it from there." Schulze offered.

"The Americans are using Galveston as a port of entry, so there shouldn't be any problem. If you want, I can give you a letter of reference."

Tom thought, then shook his head,

"Thanks, but I think the least known about my past, the better. What if there's a wanted notice from the British?"

Schultz shrugged,

"It's unlikely that a wanted notice would be here so quickly. America is huge, and so is Texas. You will be asked questions, tell them just enough to keep them happy. No more."

The captain continued,

"Say you have come to settle in Texas, no more".

Tom asked,

"What about my name? Do you think I should change it?"

The captain laughed cynically,

"All I'll say is that I tried it once, forgot at the wrong time, and you know the rest. Use your own name, and you'll be okay."

Tom went ashore just as dawn broke and stated to US customs he was an Irishman wanting to live in America. Having completed the paperwork, he was asked to show the means to support himself and counted out a large amount of money. The customs officer asked a number of questions finishing with,

"Have you ever been convicted of a crime?" Tom's answer was honest.

"No." Then there followed a quick medical check, after which the émigré Irishman was told to take a seat and wait, which he did nervously. After what seemed hours, his name was called. The officer explained how long before he could apply for US citizenship. Thomas Cork was then officially welcomed to the United States of America and walked through customs at Galveston to begin his new life in Texas.

Tom had a very basic plan. To find work with livestock, keep a low profile and start to rebuild his life. Texas was a cattle state, something Thomas Cork knew all about. He got the name of the man who imported the Aberdeen Angus; he'd find him and maybe work.

In 1900 a catastrophic hurricane had nearly destroyed the port and city of Galveston, after which the city elders welcomed immigrants from all over Europe to settle. In 1919, Galveston was flourishing, with work in the cattle, grain and Tallow industries. The population was a mix of Texans, Europeans, Indians and Mexicans. Tom rented a room and avoided any police, also the relatively large Irish and British populations. The cattle importing companies were located in an area known as the 'Wharves'. One must have dealt with the owner of the stock from Schultz's ship. This is where he searched every day for two disappointing weeks. Then on the first morning of week three, he found himself in an office bedecked with images of the Aberdeen Angus breed. Tom asked once again.

"Good Morning. Would you have any information about a rancher who has bought Aberdeen Angus cattle from Britain recently?"

The man at the desk looked up,

"That's a strange accent you got their son, you Scottish or something?"

Tom replied,

"No, I'm not Scottish; I've just been travelling a lot. The war and all that, you know what I mean?"

Tom's spirits fell as he denied being Irish for the first time.

"Your luck's in son. There's a man collecting British cattle from quarantine today."

Spirits lifting, Tom asked,

"Can you tell me his name, please?"

The answer was double-edged.

"No, but I will point him out." Tom thanked him and waited outside. A stock wagon and a pickup truck arrived. A very big man stepped out of the pickup and strode toward the office. On the truck door were the words 'Double B Ranch', 'Bill Buchanan, Cattle and Horse Rancher, Big Bend, Texas.'

The same name as the captain gave him. Tom ran after him shouting,

"Excuse me, sir, can I talk to you?"

The tall man spoke as he walked,

"Son, I am here to collect some valuable cattle. I don't know you, and even if I did, I'm too busy right now."

Tom kept up with him, saying,

"You have Aberdeen Angus cattle, and I know all about that breed of cattle, and I know horses too."

The tall man turned his head.

"Come with me son."

In the office the big man was shown to concrete floored holding pens. The Aberdeen cattle were obviously in distress, and he demanded of the manager,

"What the hell is wrong with those cattle?"

Tom saw his chance,

"These cattle have soft hooves, and they need to be taken out to pasture with soft grass and plenty of give in the ground. They have been standing on concrete for at least two weeks. They're not damaged; they're just sore."

Buchanan looked quizzically at Tom,

"How old are those cattle, and how much do the heifers weigh?"

Tom answered both questions immediately.

"Are you looking for a job?"

Tom said,

"I am, and I can start right away."

Buchanan reached out a very large hand and shook Tom's, then said in a full Texas drawl,

"Son, you're hired. Now, why don't you tell me your name?" Tom looked at his new employer. The man was at least six feet four inches tall with broad shoulders and skin an almost leathery brown and weighed between sixteen and eighteen stones. Everything about this man was solid and hard. Tom was told he was working for the Double B Ranch of Big Bend, Texas, which was just over 700 miles away, and the cattle had to be taken there safely. The big man explained the cattle would be loaded onto an adapted, very large Model T Ford. Without thinking, Tom voiced his concerns about the bulls being so close to the heifers. Mr Buchanan answered,

"It won't be a problem."

Immediately a truck pulled into the yard towing a low flatbed trailer with two pens on the back. Buchanan continued.

"The bulls will be on this trailer and towed by the pickup."

It was the first time Tom had encountered Buchanan's can-do attitude – he felt it would not be the last. He and two Negro men, who said very little and were called 'Boy' by Buchanan, loaded the cattle.

Tom was used to young men being called boy or boyeen in Cork, but the way Buchanan used the word, was not with humour or affection. Maybe Texas was not as far from Ireland as he thought.

Then he was perplexed as Buchanan introduced Simon and his companion Felix. They shook Tom's hand smiling, faces open, welcoming. Buchanan explained the trip would be a long one and cautioned.

"These Aberdeen Angus are the future of the Double B, so we'll do whatever it takes to get them home healthy. If it's too hot, we'll travel early in the morning and late evening, resting midday and overnight."

Tom had an idea to speed things up. But Bill Buchanan seemed like a man who was used to being obeyed. Jesus! What if he was like that bastard Peters in Bandon? He decided there was time enough to get his own ideas across. Buchanan spoke to him directly.

"Tom, you keep an eye on the cattle; if they look too distressed, we'll stop. The trucks are capable of speeds between twenty and twenty-five miles an hour and I want to cover at least fifty miles per day and more if the heat is not too bad. The boys will cook and keep watch; we'll buy gas and food on the road. I've booked some corral space in farms owned by cattlemen I know, but they are at least two, maybe three days apart. He paused as his eyes swept across the small convoy. Then said confidently.

"Right, it's fifty miles to Houston; let's go."

The truck was doing about twenty miles an hour. Buchanan, at the wheel, was silent. Tom, beside him, enjoyed the warm sun while concentrating on the cattle. He would have rather been in the pickup with the bulls, which were more likely to become agitated. He leaned out of the truck, looked back and was satisfied that all the livestock was at ease.

After two hours, Tom thought he could see the outline of a town ahead. Buchanan explained,

"Houston dead ahead. Tell me, are there any cities like this where you come from?"

Tom answered quickly,

"No, Mr Buchanan."

Buchanan continued in a relaxed voice,

"Ok, Son, you can tell me where you're from when you're good and ready."

They had reached the city limits and, once off the highway, pulled into a farm with a large two-storey house and cattle grazing. Buchanan jumped out of the lorry and was greeted with a handshake as he said.

"Tom, this is Mr Berne", and continued,

"Tom will be looking after the Aberdeens while we're here."

The livestock was offloaded to separate paddocks. Tom had a quick look at the grazing for poisonous shrubs, then saw healthy cattle in other fields and relaxed.

The night was quiet, and the food cooked by Felix was welcome and filling. There was little talk as all three were exhausted. Tom dozed and watched as the owner's ranch hands patrolled the grazing fields with rifles at the ready. Sleep came quickly, as did the sunrise, but the Irishman had enjoyed a good night's sleep and was now finishing a breakfast, again cooked by Felix.

Buchanan appeared and asked.

" How are the cattle?" Tom said.

"All fine." Buchanan, clearly agitated, went on.

"Tom, Houston to San Antonio is about two hundred miles. We did well yesterday, but today we'll hit serious heat out in the open scrubland. I'll see how the first four hours go, then decide what to do."

Tom raised his voice,

"Mr Buchanan, is it that you're worried about cattle being harmed by the heat? I have an idea which could help."

Buchanan replied cautiously.

"Alright, Tom, go ahead."

"We need to rig up some sort of canopy that will keep the cattle out of direct sunlight and generate air flow to cool them." Then went into detail.

Buchanan looked at him,

"Young fella, we'll give it a go."

He called Felix and Simon over. Mr Berne supplied some sheets of light plywood. Felix showed how good he was with his hands and tools. The plywood was nailed to the uprights on the pens of the truck. The convoy was soon speeding due west to San Antonio, and Buchanan reckoned they travelled seventy-five miles by noon. The canopy and crude air conditioning were working, and the cattle passive. Buchanan exclaimed,

"At this rate Tom, we could be in San Antonio by night fall or soon after it. Now let's get some gas."

Tom was suddenly feeling good and eagerly helped in refuelling the trucks.

As the small convoy pulled into San Antonio seven hours and 125 miles later, Buchanan was ecstatic. As the sun set, the cattle settled into rich green paddocks. Tom asked about some shrubs, Felix assured him they were safe. He began to roll out his bedding when Buchanan, who was staying in a small hotel near the paddock, called.

"Tom boy, there's a room for you, then come and have dinner with me. Your idea has put us two days ahead of schedule."

During the meal, Buchanan gave a very brief history of his family leaving Scotland after the defeat of Bonnie Prince Charlie at Culloden. It was clear to Tom that his boss was a Texan from the best state in the USA - after that, what else was there? Tiredness caught up with Tom, and he asked,

"Mr Buchanan would you mind if I went to bed? I'm absolutely bollixed." Buchanan laughed.

"Son, you can go to bed when you tell me what bollixed means." Tom's attempt to explain caused more mirth.

"Go away to bed Tom, and we'll do another stretch tomorrow."

Tom was up with the sun and ate a full breakfast while he watched as the boys got up after a night under the truck and felt a twinge of guilt, then remembered advice given by good people.

"Tom, look after yourself and no one else."

Buchanan gave the route for the day.

"It's nearly 180 miles to Sonora, but with the canopy, we can do it today. What do you think?"

Tom replied.

"I can't see any problems there, Mr Buchanan. Let's go for it."

The weather was good, and the road smooth except for the odd bad stretch, which slowed them, but they soon made up any lost time. Buchanan asked sporadically.

"How are the cattle, Tom?"

He answered confidently.

"They're OK, Mr Buchanan; let's keep going."

They arrived in Sonora on time, where the cattle were placed in a large complex of holding corrals patrolled by armed guards. Felix explained this was to prevent attacks by Mountain Lions, Wolves and Coyotes. Tom said nothing, knowing Aberdeen Angus were too large for any animal other than a Tiger or Lion to bring down. For the first time, and to his great surprise, he saw a Texas Long Horn.

Again Buchanan had booked a room for Tom in the hotel. The boys were under the trucks. During dinner, Buchanan began asking questions about Tom's background and, being so young, how he knew so much about cattle. Tom gave a brief history of his father's death and going to work at thirteen with the stock. Then proudly said.

"We had a good farm. My family always worked hard." Buchanan asked straight out.

"Then why did you leave?" Tom replied sharply.

"I left because of British rule", expecting another question. Buchanan surprised him.

"Tom, I need to know if you have broken any laws in America. We'll be in Big Bend in a few days, and you could help me to develop my ranch." Then in a firm voice he continued.

"Tom, I have no quarrel with any British people, and I take a man as I find him." He paused."

"And they do have fine cattle."

Tom felt relaxed enough to ask a question on his mind.

"Mr Buchanan, why did you get me a room and not the boys? They work just as hard as I do?"

Buchanan spoke sadly,

"Tom, I can only live as those around me do. In the Civil War, many Texas men declared for the Confederacy, which caused great wounds; some are still raw. There are towns in the state where the boys wouldn't be allowed inside the town limits, let alone into a hotel. I don't like it, but there's nothing I can do about it, so I just try and forget about it. Anyway, things are much different back on the Double B, believe me, Tom."

Cork went to bed with a lot to think about. Buchanan had not tried to disguise prejudice in Texas and apologised for it. Then only after a few days work had offered him a long-term job on the Double B, a ranch he had never seen. Would part of that job be to enforce the rules of segregation on the ranch? Then Buchanan's words about things being different at the Double B finally brought on an uneasy sleep.

At breakfast, Tom realised he was starting to like Buchanan's optimism. Now he was thinking about the future. The past was gone, if not forgotten. He missed his family desperately, but Texas seemed a great place to get on with life.

During the 143 mile run from Stockton to Sonora, the convoy approached a small roadside store. Buchanan signalled to the following pickup to pull in.

"Tom, keep an eye on the cattle."

Tom nodded and noticed a sign which advertised that the store served food all day. Buchanan, now wearing his gun, called the men from the pickup and led them to the part of the store labelled 'Cantina'. Tom watched as Buchanan went in. The boys hesitated, then followed. Tom whispered.

"Jesus, what's going on here?" Some twenty-five minutes later, they came out of the cantina laughing as Felix and Simon climbed back into the pickup. Buchanan jumped into the Model T.

"I just bought the boys breakfast in that cantina. I thought about the question you asked me the other night and decided the least I could do was to try and change a little."

Tom couldn't resist asking,

"Why carry the gun, Mr Buchanan?"

As he turned the truck onto the road, Buchanan replied,

"First of all, it's my gun, and the owner of the cantina may have had a problem serving us. Tom, this is Texas, where the law still favours the use of guns. Tom, if a man finds his wife in bed with another man in his own home, he can shoot both of them. Now that is the law, do you hear?"

Seeing Tom's face aghast, his mouth wide, Buchanan just roared with laughter.

"Listen, Tom Boy, can you use a gun?"

Tom showed his growing confidence.

"Not to shoot cooks, if that's what you mean."

Buchanan's laughter was infectious as the men in the pickup sounded their horn and the remaining hours and miles flew by. By eight o'clock that evening, the stock was inside a holding area with armed guards for protection. Simon and Felix were bedded down relaxing, and Tom was with Buchanan in the guest house. During dinner, Buchanan explained.

"Tom, we are on the border down in Big Bend, and there are still men who don't want any foreigners, Mexicans or Negroes. So we'll have to be careful a little while longer." Tom was about to answer when the big man went on.

"Now, before you ask, the boys are camping under the trucks tonight, but this should be the last but one night. We have one more night, maybe two on the road."

As the convoy started out, the heat, even at six in the morning, was intense. Tom sitting in the cab of the Model T, began to think that life in this vast country made anything possible. Buchanan asked.

"Tom boy, we have about 180 miles to go. How long is that going to take at top speed?"

The answer came quickly. Buchanan smiled, and Tom found he was relaxing a little more as the hours went by. The silence was broken a little later.

"I have some business to do in Marathon, and we'll head for the Double B tomorrow."

The cattle had been settled, and Tom considered his situation. If the Double B was like what he'd seen of Texas so far, it would be a good place to deal with the shock of losing everything. His cautious side warned him the real test was

Buchanan on his own territory, though after a week, Tom was pleased with the way things had gone.

The afternoon was hot as they lay in the grass, all waiting for Buchanan. Felix and Simon were asking questions about the Aberdeens. He answered and cautiously asked.

"What's Mr Buchanan like on the Double B?" Simon answered.

"We have seen many white men who are a lot worse than Mr Buchanan." Then asked.

"How come you know so much about these cattle for someone so young?"

Tom talked about the cattle but said little of Ireland and then asked a pointed question.

"Why are you both so friendly when I get special treatment?" Felix answered.

"Tom, we can handle any cattle in America. But know nothing about the Aberdeens." Simon continued.

"When you loaded them that first morning, we knew you did, and you've made the trip a whole lot easier." Buchanan then arrived with a group of men who were clearly cattle ranchers. After inspecting the cattle, one fired a question at Tom.

"Some people might think cattle without horns, and different colours might be poor beef quality?" Buchanan nodded to Tom, and he assured all present the meat from the Aberdeens was as good as any in the world. Tom then listened as herds of over one hundred thousand heads were discussed and realised, like Buchanan, to these men, Texas was the centre of the world. As the evening came in, Buchanan approached Tom,

"Tom, I'll be going into town with these men to have a few beers."

Tom replied,

"What about the cattle Mr Buchanan? Who will guard them?"

Buchanan said.

"The boys will look after the Aberdeens tonight. We are close enough to home now for them to carry guns without causing a ruckus. If the sheriff turns up, asking questions, you do the talking. Do ya hear?"

Tom had another question.

"That's fine with me, but why would the law take my word, Mr Buchanan?"

Buchanan laughed quietly,

"Because that's his daddy over there, and you are white."

Tom tried to look calm, his mind racing, seeing arrest warrants and the hope of a new life being torn away.

"Jesus!" he swore as panic nearly overwhelmed him. He had money. He could run and, by morning, could be a hundred miles away. Felix's voice brought calm.

"Mr Buchanan said you're in charge, Tom. You'd better have this. Have you used one before?" Tom found a Colt 45 revolver pistol pressed into his hand

and automatically checked if it was loaded with the safety on. Then again, panic, as he thought.

'Don't look too familiar with guns.'

Simon joined them, and before Tom knew what had happened, he had a gun belt strapped on. The boys were admiring and teasing him. There was no way out, so he asked Felix,

"What do you want me to do tonight while we're on guard?"

They all moved closer to the corrals, as Felix replied.

"There's no big cats down this far. Sure, there are plenty left in the mountains. We'll just sit here while you sleep for four hours, then I'll sleep, and you keep watch with Simon, then we'll watch, and Simon sleeps. OK, Tom?"

Tom went to sleep under the Texas sky and was woken by Simon with the words,

"Tom, the sheriff is here."

Cork stood slowly, hoping he looked casual, the lawman approached, looked at the Aberdeens, then spoke,

"Hi, you must be Tom Cork from Ireland. My name is Deputy Sheriff Rawlings of Marathon County. Bill Buchanan said you're ramrod on this cattle drive, so you're in charge of these men as well."

Tom nodded and put his hand out to shake; the lawman made no attempt to return the gesture. He stared at the boys, who remained silent and still as Rawlings moved past and then walked behind Tom and in front of him.

"You're a long way from home, aren't you?" Then ignoring Tom, he turned to the Negroes and said,

"There are folks around here who don't like to see Negroes carrying guns. They might take offence and come over here shooting."

Tom replied in a calm voice,

"Well sheriff, what do you want us to do to make sure nothing happens?"

Rawlings gave a last look at the cattle as he said.

"Just tend the cattle and keep the guns out of sight."

Then turned and walked away.

Felix informed Tom.

"He's deputy Sheriff because his father bought the job for him. He's a son of a bitch, and everybody round here thinks he's the worst lawman they've had in years."

They told Tom that Buchanan had done business with Rawlings' father, and around Marathon, he was known as a 'spoilt brat'. The County Sheriff kept him on a short leash as he had been known to overstep the mark with all folks. Felix continued,

"Tom, don't let that little bastard worry you. Most of the folks in Big Bend are good people. He is just a useless bastard." Both men sat down by the fire as Felix finished.

"Forget him; the sooner we get home the better."

Tom offered to cover the rest of the watch while the boys slept. Sleep was impossible because of the incredible Texas night and concern that Rawlings might return.

Later, looking at the stars, he realised that there were people like Rawlings all over the world. Tom thought about Connor and how he ignored him and caused so much trouble and pain for so many people. Rawlings was not his business; Buchanan, Felix and Simon could handle anything Rawlings or his like could throw at them. It was then that Tom began to accept that he had no right to appoint himself as everybody's bodyguard. He was free and had a good job with people who seemed to genuinely care about him.

Cork watched the sun come up and was burning at this early hour. The boys had begun making breakfast. He decided to start loading the cattle as the boys put everything away. About seven thirty Buchanan appeared, looking slightly the worse for wear, and went into the small guest house. He reappeared twenty minutes later and, climbing into the truck, said,

"It's about three hours to the ranch. Let's take it nice and easy, Tom boy." Buchanan was driving and asked Tom,

"How was last night? The cattle look in good shape. Were there any other problems?"

Tom answered.

"Everything was fine. The cattle have made the trip really well; they're in great shape after nearly a thousand miles. I met Deputy Sheriff Rawlings as well. Are all the lawmen in Texas like him?"

Buchanan his eyes fixed on Tom, replied forcefully,

"No! That son of a bitch has been holed up there in Marathon since he got the job. Don't worry about that jackass Rawlings. His daddy helped the County Sherriff with his election campaign fund - for that matter, we all did. The jurisdiction covers Fort Stockton to Big Bend. His name is Jim Cosgrave, a fair man and a hell of a lawman."

They drove for an hour, and Tom began to see the beauty of the Big Bend country. The green pasture and the hills grew into mountains with at least a hundred waterfalls which ran into lakes and rivers. Buchanan spoke.

"Tom, we are about an hour from the double B, and I want to tell you I put every last cent into buying them. I was up most of the night trying to get some investment from those guys you saw. They got drunk, I didn't. I didn't get the cash either. There is one thing though. Charlie Rawlings - he's the father of that clown of a deputy sheriff - has a daughter. She's a little wild, and he wants her to come and live with us on the Double B for a while to cool off." He stopped, as if thinking what to say, then continued.

"Listen Tom. I gotta tell you how much it means to everybody getting these cattle here in good condition. I was mighty worried back there about the whole cattle drive, but you made it so easy. You got them here and they look good. We can make a real herd from these beauties. There's a home at the Double B for you as long as you want to stay, Tom."

Cork was fighting back the tears; he looked at the giant of a man and decided he would stay with these good people in this beautiful country.

07

No Choice

The papers announced Winston Churchill was Prime minister. Neville Chamberlain had resigned. The troop ship SS Artemis docking and the transfer of Brigadier Davies, Pat Cork and C squad to SOE headquarters were not reported. The top secret meeting of the commanding officers of SOE and the Guards Brigade began with some feeling. Davies demanded.

"Whoever you are, I have one question. When, in the history of His Majesty's Armed Forces, did ordering one officer to kill another become operating procedure?" The admiral gasped a question.

"Brigadier, what are you talking about?"

Davies gave more details.

The admiral probed,

"May I ask from whom you received this information?"

The Brigadier's words were measured.

"You may ask, but I have no intention of telling you. I must ensure the safety of my men in all operations."

Spenser, in civilian dress, ceased all subterfuge.

"Brigadier, I am Admiral Spenser. This base is the headquarters of the Special Operations Executive." He continued,

"I suspect the order may have been given by an officer in this command." Davies spoke slowly.

"I suggest, admiral, that you choose your words very carefully. That order was illegal, and the consequences could be extremely serious." Spenser looked at the incandescent soldier.

"Brigadier, I want you to see some files." Davies stared hard at the admiral as he handed him a file marked Erebus.

The soldier read quickly, then listened to a question.

"Brigadier, what exactly do you know about the members of C squad?"

Davies replied,

"Other than as fighting soldiers - very little."

Three other files were handed to him as he demanded,

"Is this man, code-named Erebus, Captain Lewis?"

Spenser replied.

"He is."

Now the brigadier probed,

"Tell me, admiral, in the opinion of your medics, just how abnormal is the captain?"

Spenser offered,

"Well, according to the medics, abnormal doesn't apply - he's off the scale."

Davies bristled.

"Then I will say this to you. In Norway, he fought with courage, purpose and loyalty to me and his comrades. According to this report, he will not accept responsibility for anyone other than himself. Then tell me, admiral, if that is the case, why did he assume command of a sinking ship, ensuring that two hundred men were evacuated? He left the ship only after having been ordered to by me. How is it that he placed himself at risk when, according to the man who wrote this report, he should have done exactly the opposite?"

Spenser couldn't answer, so pressed on with another question.

"Can I have your assessment of the fighting capabilities of C squad, please, brigadier?"

The soldier perked up.

"Absolutely first class, within the context of infantry and armoured warfare. Best reconnaissance unit I've ever had, reasonably good discipline too. All of them should be decorated - even though we did get stuffed."

Spenser spoke openly.

"Brigadier, I trust these men implicitly. As I need to trust you, there is a question I must ask."

Davies's eyes hardened as he almost ordered,

"Go on."

"Brigadier, I need to know the soldier who reported the illegal order. I suspect there are men who will silence him at all costs."

Davies spoke.

"Admiral, I think we both need a short break to assess where we stand and how to ensure the safety of my man and the continued existence of your organisation."

Davies needed the break. That Sergeant Cork's life could be in danger astounded him. Spenser returned.

"Brigadier, I think we agree that someone in this command gave the order to kill Erebus. I do not have proof. We must protect that man that might give us that proof."

Davies agreed.

"Then we'd better look out for our young sergeant."

Spenser spoke slowly.

"Brigadier, the ethos under which my command operates makes direct questions and answers abhorrent – but there are times when they are unavoidable. Are you stating the 'kill order' was reported to you by Sergeant Pat Cork?"

Davies answered in an equally direct manner.

"Yes, admiral, I am."

Without any idea why Spenser asked.

"How is your wound?" The reply was succinct.

"I'll survive." Both officers went over Cork's medical file. The fibula in the left leg was smashed but not irrevocably damaged. There were no other injuries. The admiral summarised.

"Cork was extremely lucky, or Erebus is an excellent marksman. He could be back on active service within five months." He paused then. "Brigadier, please give me an opinion on this sergeant of yours." The reply was short.

"The sergeant learns quickly and puts that knowledge to use quickly and ruthlessly. He cut a German's throat without hesitation. There's a lot more to the sergeant than meets the eye, so don't pigeonhole him."

Spenser finished with.

"Brigadier, I think you'll agree secrecy is paramount. So perhaps we can make use of Cork. He's seen too much of us to be allowed to roam around free - we've enough trouble already on that front."

They decided that Cork was to be given three months recovery time. If unfit for service, he could be invalided out of the services and advised to forget everything. If classified fit for duty, he was under military jurisdiction. A decision would be then made as to his role in the war.

Pat Cork spent three weeks in the base hospital where, despite the heavy plaster he was, with crutches, mobile. Now he sat in an office, hoping to be allowed home leave. At twelve hundred hours, the door opened, and an Admiral entered. Pat silently swore,

'Jesus! What's this got to do with the Navy?'

Spenser, his demeanour polite, began.

"Sergeant, I would like to thank you for all your efforts in Norway."

There was a pause, and then the admiral's voice hardened.

"I must warn you, regarding that action, any divulgence of names, ranks or military units will result in the most severe punishment under military law."

He placed a sheet of paper on the desk and demanded.

"Sergeant, before you is the signature sheet of the Official Secrets Act, which you will sign and be bound by until the end of the war. Do you understand?"

Pat silently summarised the flag officer in front of him and the current situation.

'This is the man who commands an officer who, though on our side, shot two men - me being one, the other a brigadier and half-killed another one. Let's see how he handles this?'

"Sir, may I ask a question?"

Spenser replied testily,

"Yes, but please hurry up."

"Sir, who is Odin?"

Spenser sat down and hissed,

"Why do you need to know?"

"I must talk to him, sir."

Spenser's testy demeanour vanished, replaced by menacing authority.

"Why do you need to speak to Odin?"

"I have a message for him."

"Tell me the message now."

Pat persisted.

"I can only give this message to Odin, sir."

Spenser stood up, all semblance of politeness gone.

"Sergeant, I could have you locked up for the rest of the war?"

Pat controlled his voice.

"Admiral, stop threatening me. I am a sergeant in the Irish Guards, promoted under fire when supporting your men. I was shot by a British officer in front of witnesses, one of which is my brigadier, who won't let you lock me up. I volunteered for this war, sir. I resent the suggestion that I would do anything to endanger my comrades or this country. Now, will you please tell me how I get a message to Odin?" Spenser's face was emotionless, his voice now less threatening.

"Listen to me carefully, sergeant. If I tell you who Odin is, your entire life could change. Do you understand that?"

Pat replied,

"Perfectly, sir."

Spenser tore up the signature sheet.

"Sergeant, I am Odin. Now, what is the message please?"

"The message is, 'Erebus will be in touch.'"

The admiral's face showed shock; then his expression turned to one of worry.

"Sergeant, there was, until now, only four men who knew the call sign, 'Odin'. He paused, the man who assigned it, one other senior officer in this organisation, a member of the government and me."

". "That is all. Come along, sergeant, you are an intelligent man. Is the man who gave you the message any of these men? Think about it."

All Pat could say was,

"Jesus Christ!"

Odin affirmed,

"Precisely."

Spenser became almost pleasant as he continued,

"Sergeant Cork, I apologise for the attempted intimidation. It was necessary to see how you are under pressure. Look, you're not stupid so you know that C squad are not regular army. They are part of a unit which I command. I owe you an explanation only because, as you forcefully pointed out, you were not expecting to be shot by an officer from your own side."

Spenser explained the SOE's mission and how a breach of security was potentially disastrous. They had some lunch and talked more. Pat sat and ate, his mind working overtime. He was dealing with a very powerful, utterly ruthless man. Disposing of a troublesome NCO would not trouble him in the least. The best thing to do was to listen. He didn't fancy spending the rest of the war looking over one shoulder - let alone both. Lunch ended, and back in Spencer's office, Pat was told.

"Sergeant, allow me to summarise your position as it stands, or, in your case, doesn't. The medical report states you are not fit for active service. You will be given leave until you are passed fit by a doctor to return to duty. Secrecy is essential, so your posting orders will be in a nonstandard format. Is that clear?" "Perfectly Sir."

Spenser then shook Cork's hands.

"Now, go and get some rest and once again, thank you for all your efforts."

The admiral had closed Cork's file as his office door opened. A naval officer entered.

"We have received an intelligence signal, sir."

Spenser asked,

"Why hasn't it been passed to the analysts?"

"It's been requested you read it, sir. "

Spenser became demanding.

"Why should I read it, Curtis?"

The young man spoke up.

"Well, sir, three reasons. One, it makes reference to a German surface raider. Two, the sender is using a code name on the classified list."

Spenser demanded.

"What is the third reason?"

Lieutenant Curtis's voice was clear.

"It is addressed to someone called 'Odin'."

Spenser reached out.

"Let me see that please."

The admiral went to the large chart on his office wall and checked the coordinates; his index finger came to rest on the Norwegian Atlantic coast. He handed the signal to the lieutenant.

"Read that, would you please."

Curtis began.

"To Odin, priority. Enemy capital ship located. Surface raider identity con-firmed by sight. Scharnhorst. Repeat. Scharnhorst. Enemy will sail approximately 48 hours from time of transmission. Erebus." A smile came across Spenser's face, his eyes glued to the chart. The gatherer had done his job. Now it was up to others.

The admiral broke the silence, asking Curtis,

"Have a look at that chart, check the coordinates and then tell me where the raider is."

The lieutenant concentrated on the signal, then the chart.

"The raider is in a fjord near a village called Hagnor in Norway, sir."

Spenser nodded, saying,

"Good man. Now get that signal over to the relevant people, please."

Despite all of his worries about security, as Curtis left the office, Odin smiled and said in a low satisfied voice,

"So! The great game goes on. Erebus is alive in Norway - and he's located the bloody Scharnhorst."

08

Choices Made

Erebus woke to a gruff voice demanding,

"Hey! Get up!" Then a pause.

"I'm sick and tired of you bastards breaking into people's property. Get up now."

Exhaustion, hot food and a warm fire had finally overwhelmed him. Two men held shotguns. His instinct was to attack. The armed men spoke Norwegian; maybe they were friendly and elderly. Escape would be easy. No need to hurt anyone - and he did not want to. As the sun rose, they walked, his armed escorts close. No one had mentioned the stolen German vehicle, which must have sunk without trace in the sea beneath the cliff edge. Erebus recalled the events of the previous three days.

When told of the order to kill him, he had to run. Then plan what to do. He would be alone in occupied territory. Being alone was not a new feeling. Since Uncle Peter had been murdered, he had been a loner. That was the easy bit of what was ahead. He was isolated. A fugitive from both sides. Wanted by the British Army for desertion and attempted murder. If caught by the Germans, he would be shot instantly as a spy. Erebus smiled. Pat Cork might say. 'Only an Irishman could finish up in the middle of a world war being hunted by both sides.'

He was in the present again, angry at being caught while asleep - how stupid was that? The driving had exhausted him. Two to three days at least - non-stop.

Leaving Bodo in the Mercedes staff car, Erebus saw the personal belongings of the driver on the back seat and again felt anger. All the German had to do was walk away. Well, now he was a hero of the fatherland. On the seat lay a satchel full of stolen identification papers, military and civilian, which would give him multiple identities. Languages to match were not a problem.

The Nazis had invaded Norway through the main ports. He would go to Narvik. The huge increase in displaced people and German military would provide camouflage for the identity changes needed to stay alive. Lewis was now in the recesses of his mind. Erebus was his call sign and mental anchor. 'You are on your own from now on,' he whispered fiercely. A quick glance at the map brought a curse to his lips. 'Jesus! Wake up.'

The map was British Army issue. If caught with it, there would be no second chance. The dockside battle came to mind, and C squad being evacuated. Despite feeling utterly betrayed, Erebus made sure of his comrades' safety. A series of explosions had silenced any enemy fire that threatened them. He had been part of the squad and the brigade and felt a sense of belonging - a new and pleasant sensation. Wounding Sergeant Cork was a necessity. Odin would want to know why he was shot, and Pat would deliver his message. His shin would heal but only after a long rest. Cork deserved a rest; the others were in good shape.

He drove continuously - stealing gasoline, sleeping when needed, living on water and anything he could forage. Towards evening on the third day, he had been asleep in a small wooded copse, and when woken by hunger, saw a rough road leading to a small fishing port with a short pier and a few trawlers tied alongside. Maybe he could find shelter there. The car would raise too many questions. Nearby was a sheer cliff which overlooked a rocky fjord. Erebus watched, gasping for breath, relieved as the car sank into the depths of the fjord. Any trace of a vehicle could result in a police report.

Erebus marched to a small shed. Once inside, the view confirmed the hut was halfway down the track and completely hidden from the road and village. The room was dusty and had drying and smoking ovens which gave him heat to cook and warmth. Next was food. He caught a few small fish and silently thanked the fisherman who laid in the makings of a fire. He would have a relaxed night. The fish tasted superb, and the warmth was welcome. Erebus began to analyse his situation. The choices were simple. Spend the rest of his life on the run or do the job he had been trained to do. He must find a way back into the SOE, and to do that, he needed leverage.

The order to kill him was illegal, and the man who issued it knew that. The British didn't do that sort of thing - Sandhurst convinced him of that.

He knew the code name of the SOE commanding officer, who would be desperate to know how that code name was leaked. Only he could tell him. Inside SOE, there was one man he could trust. The man who told him the code name and of the kill order. First, h had to choose an identity.

Erebus went through the identity cards and decided to become Laudrup, a Danish seaman, just one more of the large number of transient Scandinavians in Norway. Then sleep overcame him.

Now, he was fielding questions in broken Norwegian from an avuncular police officer who was suspicious of his prisoner's identity papers.

"Come on; you can wait in a cell until I decide what to do with you."

Erebus listened as the police officer explained to his friends,

"I'll hold him for a while. There's a new police chief appointed to the district. One of Quisling's men, I suppose."

The words were greeted with oaths and curses. Erebus got the impression that his captors were not supporters of the Nazis or the puppet government. One of the old men talked about a battleship under repair in the fjord.

Erebus knew immediately he had to take the biggest gamble of his life. If it went wrong, it would mean death. He stood up and called the police officer in perfect Norwegian.

"Officer, I must speak to you. It is vitally urgent." The policeman enquired sarcastically,

"That's the best Norwegian I've ever heard from a Danish deckhand. Now, why don't you tell me who you are, young fellow?"

Erebus told of being in Norway with the British Expeditionary Force and being separated from his unit. The scepticism in the policeman's voice lessened.

"If you're British, let's hear some English."

He spoke about the bombing of the Chobry and named the towns where the fighting had been heaviest. The police officer did not speak English but heard enough to open the cell door. His captors shook his hand, asking him to speak Norwegian. Their former prisoner said a silent prayer and asked.

"Gentlemen, can you tell me more about this battleship?"

They sat, and each gave different details, but there was enough to convince him that the information was sound. Erebus ventured almost in desperation,

"Do you know where there is a radio transmitter?"

All three men looked at him in total confusion. The police officer took the lead.

"We do not have such a thing in the village, there may be a small radio on one of the fishing boats, but the Germans have stopped everyone putting to sea while the big ship is in the fjord. Some people are going hungry; those bastards couldn't care less."

Erebus pressed on.

"The British must be told about that ship. Is there somewhere you can hide me? Before you say anything, I must warn you that the Germans are going to be brutal with anyone helping me."

The sergeant asked,

"May I ask you your name, sir?"

Erebus cautioned,

"Perhaps it is better that you do not know, the Germans will have no reason to question you."

The oldest of the men said,

"Sir, we are a conquered country. At my age, to die fighting these bastards would be an honour and a privilege."

The former captive stood and introduced himself as Captain Charles Lewis of the Irish Guards and then saluted the three old men.

The next hour was spent planning his new identity. The old men agreed with his choice of a Danish seaman and padded out his story. He had been aboard a cargo ship- the Freya - which sailed to evade capture, stranding him - like so many others in Norway. It helped he looked haggard which made his story believable. Erebus relaxed and was briefed on his new home. Olaf Strand, a widower for several years, enthusiastically offered Erebus a warm, clean room in his cottage. Which he learned later, was kept spotless by Strand's fiery niece Hilda. The fishing port of Hagnor was some one-hundred and twenty kilometres west of Narvik, off the main road to Oslo. It was located on a narrow and very deep fjord which ran into the Norwegian Sea.

Laudrup was accepted by the villagers as another victim of occupation and the harsh regime of searches and roadblocks, practiced by the regimes police militia. He was questioned twice in one day. The first, they waved him on quickly. The next was more in depth. The larger of two policemen demanded the name of his ship and where it had docked. He was told Freya and Narvik. His interrogator demanded,

"Why weren't you on it when it left port?"

"I was owed six week's pay. The owners wouldn't pay until the ship docked in Denmark. It could be sunk, so I took what I could sell and came ashore," he answered submissively.

There were mutterings about Jewish owners. Laudrup got his papers and was told.

"Get going."

The village food crisis was serious enough to force a confrontation with the Germans. The plan was leaked to ensure there was a controlled response.

A large crowd watched at the shore as the fishing boats were readied for sea. A boat owner, Berg, had agreed to Laudrup as his crew. German infantry appeared on the shoreline, supported by an armoured car armed with a heavy machine gun.

The Wehrmacht major ordered the fishermen to stop, and the German speaking village school teacher approached him. Erebus listened as the teacher talked about the shortage of food.

Berg was called forward and, via the teacher, showed where the boats would fish. The officer agreed for ten boats to go out as long as they remained visible. He signalled to the gunner on the armoured car to demonstrate the consequences of disobedience. Large calibre rounds tore up the water at least eight hundred metres from the shoreline shattering the morning calm.

Erebus whispered as he was preparing to cast off.

"Is there a radio aboard any of the Trawlers?" Berg whispered back.

"You are welcome to use mine. The German idiots are not seamen. That showed that when they searched my boat."

Suddenly, the German major and the teacher were alongside.

"The major wants some fish, so catch him something profoundly poisonous, my friend." Berg nodded just as a sergeant ran to the major, reporting in German,

"Major, the Scharnhorst will be ready to sail in forty-eight hours."

Erebus looked at the armoured car. It was unlikely it had a radio tracking kit. He decided to take the risk.

Once at sea, Berg enthused about his boat.

"She built for the fjords and the Atlantic. She looks small but has a deep draft to carry a very large catch." Erebus was shown a series of bulkheads with hidden compartments and enquired.

"Why so many secret spaces?" Berg smiled.

"My friend, your country has a King. Yes?"

Erebus nodded. Berg continued,

"Well, we as well, but he keeps asking for tax to pay for his services. I pay some, not all. Do you see?"

Erebus laughed out loud.

"Berg, you're a smuggler." The big Norwegian laughed.

"Well, some of the time, maybe."

Standing at the wheel, blonde hair half matted, his body solid and supple, at least six foot two, eyes of Nordic blue. The hands on the wheel were strong and tough from the sea. Erebus mused. 'So that's what a Viking looks like.' The trawler moved out to sea as the sun burned off the surface fog. They looked forward, and as one, their jaws dropped - but neither spoke. About two thousand metres dead ahead, was the huge superstructure of a battleship. Dominated by the outline of the huge fifteen-inch guns in batteries of three mounted on four turrets, the ship was the complete killing machine. Erebus whispered,

"She weighs thirty thousand tons at least."

Berg gasped a reply,

"No, my friend, she is at least forty thousand tons," then added eagerly.

"Now, let's get this radio going."

Erebus decided the aged radio would do the job. He transmitted his call sign, named the raider and estimated the coordinates. Then repeated the signal. That was all. The rest was up to the British. Then quickly stowed the radio as he heard boots and voices on deck. The trawlers were ordered ashore by sailors from the battleship. One had boarded the trawler from a motor-driven whaler. Berg played dumb and gave the German fresh fish. Who, clearly satisfied, disembarked with a friendly wave. Erebus made some decisions as the trawler headed to shore.

For now, he would stay in Hagnor but only as long as he did not endanger the villagers. Using Berg's radio regularly would do just that. So another must be found.

His attention was drawn by Berg as he explained during winter, most of the trawlers tied up in port. A few anchored on the ice edge to fish if the village ran short of food. Now the Germans ordered all boats to tie up until further notice. Berg told his crew member the only way to fish was through the ice. Laudrup and Strand began the next day. One evening, as they returned from another freezing day, he asked his landlord about Hilda. The obliged in sad tones.

"She is a good kind girl but those mood swings! She can be very difficult," then, "after what she has been through. Her mother – my sister - died in childbirth. Her father never forgave the child. She was fourteen when he took a boat out into the fjord one night and disappeared. Hilda is now twenty-two."

Without thinking, Erebus asked,

"Why isn't she married? What are the village men doing?"

Then as Olaf continued, Erebus realised he really cared about these two people and had just broken the fundamental rules of an agent behind enemy lines. 'Do not get too attached to anyone.' Be ready to move on at a minute's notice.' The old man's gentle voice again reached him.

"There are many men who tried to court her. I think she is very angry about her father and takes it out on the village men." That night Erebus lay thinking. Hilda's angry rages. Those he knew about. Other thoughts came. SOE had to be contacted. Was he a deserter or agent? Who could be trusted? Bakken may not even be in the base. Pat Cork was in sick bay long term. Spenser was too senior. Erebus was certain Simpson-Coyle had given the kill order. Brigadier Davies was the best option. But how would he be contacted? The man could be anywhere. Then came the practicalities. Getting a radio was now priority. One must be stolen, from the enemy. Not near hagnor.

The next morning, Erebus told Strand he was going inland. Strand asked a very good question.

"What do we tell that idiot policeman if he asks where you are?"

After a few minutes they agreed on a cover story. He had gone looking for work.

Erebus headed inland, thumbing until picked up by a lorry carrying timber. The driver's suspicion was overt, asking blunt questions. Erebus stuck to his deckhand story. Then his interrogator announced.

"As long as you're not German or Austrian, that's fine with me." The man began to chatter incessantly until Erebus asked about the timber load. The reply was vitriolic.

"This load is the best timber, stolen by the Todt organisation, which is using forced labour to build U-boat pens in the Atlantic ports. Slave driving bastards."

As the lorry approached a road block the driver suggested.

"I'll say you are my driver's mate if the bastards are being awkward. What's your name?"

He handed over his papers and heard,

"Hello, Laudrup."

At the roadblock, Erebus watched the Norwegian, at least six foot three and sixteen stones, glare down at the Germans but remain calm. Again, on the road he was told.

"My name's Moen". He wore steel-rimmed glasses, had deep blue eyes and receding hair line and proposed.

"Why not stay until I deliver in Hammerfest? It will take a few days to get there, and I'll be glad of the company." It was good cover, and he could assess occupied Norway.

"Fine by me, thanks." Erebus knew SOE would want any intelligence on the U-boat pens as viable bombing targets. The need for a radio increased every hour.

Sergeant Pat Cork was officially on three months sick leave, during which he was to report to the regimental medical officer monthly. He could stay anywhere in the UK but must tell the Regimental Sergeant major. The NCO finished with.

"Right, we can contact you at your dad's in Portsmouth. Sergeant Cork, you've had a hard time. You never know; it might be all over by the time you get back."

Connor Cork thought he heard cheering in the yard. He looked out of the site hut and saw his son on crutches, being greeted by his former workmates. Within seconds the Corks were alone in the hut. Emotions pent up from Norway, and seeing his father crying with relief and joy was just too much. Pat burst into tears, as father and son embraced. A few minutes of silence passed, then there was a knock on the door, as Connor opened Peter English spoke.

"Connor, please introduce me to your son, and would you allow me the pleasure of driving you both home."

English rambled and continued to do so in the house. After several attempts, Connor politely persuaded English to leave. Then explained to his son.

"Peter has always wanted to meet you. His only son was killed at Dunkirk. God alone knows what he is going through."

Connor brought Pat up to date on how the family was. Christopher was doing well in school apart from being called a 'Black and Tan'. On the upside, he was excelling at Gaelic football, which in Kerry was much more important than virtually anything else. Rachel was happy and planned to train as a nurse. Mary's family were all well, and the food situation was good, with plenty of fish. Pat interrupted,

"Mum hates the smell of fish. She'll be cleaning the kitchen day and night." His father continued as he handed his son a bundle of letters.

"Read these in your own time."

Pat said goodnight as tiredness forced him to bed. The next day finding himself alone, he decided to explore the local area and decided walking was the most beneficial method.

The village was just under two miles from Portsmouth. The first walks were exhausting, but slowly leg and fitness improved. A telegram arrived from the Guards' divisional office, instructing him to attend Portsmouth Hospital, where a doctor would assess his progress and brief the Guards' Medical officer. A welcome development as journeys to London were not appealing.

Pat tried to assess his feelings about Norway. He had killed Germans; that was war. The deaths of the platoon members still played on his mind. Why he didn't know, he felt no guilt about being alive. His father had been emotional and tactile, and it felt good. He was thankful that all his family was safe and didn't care who knew.

Pat called to his father's yard and was given a tour by Peter English, who explained they were making anti-tank traps and developing concrete which set in near-freezing conditions. At home that evening Connor told his son about Peter English. A highly qualified civil and construction engineer who, like Wilde, treated him as an equal. Pat sensed his father liked the man so he asked a personal question. Why English never mentioned his late son's mother? The answer was unexpected.

"Three days after his son was killed in action, his wife told him she had been having an affair with a man in London and left him. Seemingly, it had been going on for a couple of years." Pat, now shocked, listened as Con added.

"Pat, I believe he is working every hour sent to forget the boy's death and her." Pat gasped.

"Jesus! This bloody war has done some damage."

Then he wished his father "Goodnight."

The doctor finished Pat's first check-up with the words.

"You have made reasonable progress. We'll know much more in a month."

He walked through the crowded hospital canteen wondering how to occupy himself for the coming month, bought a cup of tea and saw a nurse sitting at a table alone.

"Can I sit down?"

"I don't know. Can you?" The reply came with heavy sarcasm, then was followed instantly.

"I'm sorry. That was very rude of me. I've just finished night shift and am very tired. Please join me."

During idle chatter. Pat asked.

"Why are there soldiers here? Isn't this a naval hospital?"

She was silent for a moment.

"Well, as a soldier, I suppose you deserve an explanation."

Pat warmed to her as he heard.

"We take all sorts here. We're not in the least fussy."

He thought quickly.

"Well, you let me in, so that's true."

They both laughed, and then suddenly, the nurse said.

"I need to get some sleep. I'm sorry, but I really must go."

Then she was gone. For the first time since Norway, Pat thought about Barbara. He took a taxi home. His father came in after work.

"How's the leg." Pat tried to be upbeat but walking across the room showed his true condition. He needed to find a way to exercise, which took the weight off his leg. Portsmouth provided a possible answer. While walking, Pat stopped at a local yacht club and asked about sailing lessons. The reply gently pointed out sailing was physically very demanding as kind eyes covertly dropped to his wounded leg. Visits to similar clubs produced similar replies, and he went home more than slightly fed up.

Sergeant Cork waited for his second check-up. The hospital corridor was full of people moving purposefully. Suddenly he saw her – 'his nurse', as he named her. Then she was gone. He was called by another nurse.

After a very painful hour, he waited in the corridor. Then she appeared again, but this time with an x-ray folder and called his name. In the consulting room, the doctor spoke.

"Well, sergeant. Your leg has not healed as well as we had hoped. We'll see how things go in a month's time. But as of now, active service is impossible."

Trying to remain upbeat, Pat asked,

"I had an idea that sailing might help strengthen my leg. What do you think, doctor?"

The doctor was cautiously supportive.

"Go ahead - just be careful. But support the leg well. I'll see you in a month."

The nurse followed him out.

"I've just recognised you, and maybe I can help with the sailing. My uncle owns a small marina down near Southsea, so we could start whenever you want. I'm off next Saturday."

Pat, now showing his delight, continued,

"That's great, thank you. Could you just tell me one thing?" The nurse looked puzzled.

"Yes, of course."

"What's your name, please?" Laughing, they sat down.

"My name is Penny White of Portsmouth and all points of the compass, and I have been sailing since I was old enough to tie a reef knot. Who are you, sergeant?"

Pat introduced himself and told her about coming home from Norway.

"Now, when can we begin, Penny?"

"I had a look at your file; your leg is still very fragile. Any ideas on supporting your leg?"

Pat was at home wondering how to support his leg. Maybe his dad's eccentric friend could come up with something? Pat explained what was needed. Having listened, Connor cautioned.

"I'll speak to him straight away, but be warned, once he gets his teeth into something, there's no stopping him."

English was waiting for Pat at the plant the next day.

"Pat, we need some medical input. Will anyone from the hospital help?"

Pat nodded.

"When"

English replied,

"The sooner the better."

Penny had been told she was going to the pictures but met Peter English and Connor Cork instead. The cast was made of a mixture of cement, and very fine sand, reinforced with a very light metal mesh, with a soft padded inner lining and was virtually waterproof. English named his creation Frankenstein's foot.' After an hour of walking, Penny examined Pat's leg finding little chaffing and pronounced that trial had been a success. All concerned went to the local pub to celebrate.

Pat Cork enjoyed the sailing lesson but ached all over. He persevered, and eventually, his coach Penny conceded that he knew more than just which was Port and Starboard.

The third medical came, and Pat was convinced he had made significant progress. The doctor agreed to a degree.

"Much stronger, but another month at least, sergeant."

Later, at the yard, Peter English asked for an update on 'Operation Frankenstein', then suddenly, he became serious.

"Pat, please do not tell anyone where the cast originated. We made it out of an experimental material which is still classified."

Connor listened and later advised his son.

"Pat, Peter is extremely tense and may have a nervous breakdown at any moment. Just play along with him, please. The material is nowhere near secret. Being so clever, Peter acts differently to the rest of us." Connor paused. Pat saw real concern on his father's face.

"He is working very hard on a number of projects which may one day help us to win this bloody war - but I'm afraid of the price he may have to pay."

Pat did as asked. What else could anyone do but listen to Peter and hope the man managed to stay sane? He often called to the works when bad weather made sailing impossible and endured another tour finishing with the words.

"We are building concrete tank traps, which are shipped to all parts of the country. The beaches will be impossible to sunbathe on when the war is over."

Away from the yard, his time was spent sailing and learning from people ranging from Penny to a friendly old seadog.

"Single-handed is fine in the marina but never put to sea alone." Penny and Pat became part of each other's lives. Pat told her about Barbara, and he knew of the man in her life who was now in the Far East. There had been no word in eight months. One night in the kitchen of Pat's house, Penny asked about Norway.

"I know a little about military life and you are very young to be a sergeant. What did you do to be promoted so quickly? Was it in Norway?"

"Which question do you want answered first, the one about Norway or the reason why I was promoted?"

Penny's face darkened slightly.

"I'm sorry, Pat - I didn't mean to pry."

Pat knew he had hurt her.

"No, please don't apologise. It should be me saying sorry. Penny, I was promoted because I was one of the few men left alive after enemy action. The whole thing in Norway with the Irish guards was a complete disaster, and to this day, I can't figure out why it all went so wrong."

He went into detail about the bombing, the platoon being wiped out, and the ship sinking. Then talked about Greenwood's wisdom. The thought of the Sergeant made him smile as he spoke the words.

"Never make friends. They could be dead within ten seconds."

Pat looked up and saw his sailing partner's eyes were full of tears.

"Christ! Penny, I am sorry. First, I bite your head off, and now I've got you in floods of tears. Ask me anything."

She took up the offer.

"Tell me more about Greenwood's wisdom and the man himself."

The evening flew by as Pat told of basic training, the platoon - even the 'uniform hanger'. They were in fits of laughter. Then Penny sat in silence as he told her about the letters the young officers had written with his help. Suddenly Pat felt ready to talk and explain how he felt about Norway. Then the words just dried up. Penny sensed he was not going to say anymore and asked. "Tell me Greenwood's wisdom again."

He repeated the sergeant's words. Penny stood.

"Pat, please take me home now."

The taxi came quickly. During the silent trip, Pat saw that Penny was deep in thought. Suddenly she asked the driver to stop by a two-masted schooner. Pat followed Penny aboard and into a large deck-level cabin.

"The Lydia is owned by a very wealthy man who went to America when the war started. Not very patriotic, but when you own half of Hampshire, you can do that sort of thing. She is maintained by my uncle. I live here, which allows us privacy."

She paused as if preparing.

"Pat, why don't we use Greenwood's wisdom? Let's be together just being friends. Let's make each other happy without hurting each other when we say goodbye."

She kissed him gently, at first, on his lips, then with more pressure. Then pressed her index finger to his lips, saying.

"You've done enough talking for tonight, Pat Cork."

She opened her coat and then removed her dress, leaving just her bra and panties. Then led him to the double bunk in the main cabin. Sex had not crossed Pat's mind since Norway, but with Penny, he relaxed. There was an understanding that what was happening was right and good for both of them. He looked at the beautiful woman lying next to him and asked,

"May I talk now?"

The reply was in a very low, sexy voice.

"No, not till I tell you."

They made love slowly. Pat slowly began to feel easier about the disaster in Norway. Then sleep came. The best night's sleep since getting home. Reality hit him as he woke and blurted out,

"Jesus, Penny, I never used a condom."

She gently kissed his lips before he could say any more.

"Pat, I'm a nurse. Please don't worry about it - we medics have our ways; just remember Greenwood's wisdom."

They talked as the sun came up. Pat felt at peace as Penny snuggled in his arms. Then questions began to run through his mind. He was safe, but for how long? A medical discharge was unlikely; he knew too much about SOE operations. Then Erebus, was Charles Lewis dead or missing behind enemy lines? They dressed, and Penny went to work. Pat went back to his father's house, where a Royal mail messenger was waiting. The telegram was in Norwegian, which, when translated at a local library reference section, read. 'Dartmouth College - fourteen hundred hours - in mufti' - and a date, two days hence.

It was signed, 'Odin'. His orders had come.

09

Maiden Aunt

Admiral Spenser was escorted into the dining room in Ten Downing Street. Admiral Kevin Menzies shook his hand, and Spenser knew the evening was far from social. As both men sat, their host approached, waving an American newspaper, demanding.

"When will the Americans enter the war, gentlemen? When? It is vital for us that they do." Before either could answer, the door opened, and a steward came in with a tray of brandies.

Churchill continued.

"We need them in the war very soon. We face a long, hard, brutal struggle."

Spenser replied frankly.

"Prime minister, it will take something of biblical proportions to bring them into this war. They are three thousand miles away from us and any threat of attack from our enemies. Their armed forces are nowhere near active service level. I think we should bank on miracles before the cousins."

As they sat to eat, Menzies requested Spenser brief them on events in Norway.

The report was greeted with silence until broken by Menzies.

"The Erebus affair is profoundly disturbing. I trust it is the first time such an order has been issued."

Spenser was ambiguous,

"As far as I am aware, that is correct, sir."

Menzies pressed,

"It must be the one and only time understood."

"Very good Sir."

Menzies continued,

"I have to tell you both that there are elements on the Joint Intelligence Committee who are set against the SOE. So, to partially disarm these elements, we are giving you a second in command. Brigadier Davies - he commanded the Guards in Norway. How do you feel about him, Peter?"

Spenser knew how he felt was irrelevant - the decision had been made. He silently summarised the situation.

The brigadier was now inside SOE and, being army, better equipped to deal with Simpson-Coyle and the safety of Erebus and Sergeant Cork. He answered.

"Davies is a good man, sir. I think we'll work well together."

Menzies looked at Spenser hard and said,

"Make sure you do, Peter. There will be no second chances if the JIC get its way. Is that clear?"

"Perfectly, sir," came the reply.

"Right, that's that sorted. Carry on with all operations as planned, and maybe, just maybe, we can win this war. Peter, I believe you're the junior officer present."

Churchill smiled as the King was toasted. Then lighting a cigar said.

"You chose this man's code name well. In Norse mythology, Erebus is the God who brings darkness and chaos."

Menzies returned to his office and made a note in Spenser's file, which was not fully supportive. Before midnight, Spenser had returned to his London base and drawn up orders that reactivated C squad and removed Erebus from the wanted list and returned him to active service.

Moen and Erebus sat in the truck outside the Hammerfest port office.

"The transport manager is a mate of mine, he's promised me a load to take back, but it'll take a day to clear the docks; it's German office equipment for the bastards inland. I'll wait for that. What about you?"

Erebus had decided to move on, but a question sprung to mind.

"Did the transport manager tell you anything about the furniture?"

"No, maybe it's for the army. We could sabotage it. So it blows up in the bastards' faces or blows their balls off." Seeing Laudrup was serious, he handed over a list.

"That's the delivery addresses." They sat in silence then Laudrup spoke,

"The furniture is for different administration offices all over Norway." Then asked.

"Why would they ship desks from Germany they can commandeer here?"

Thirty-six hours later, Moen and Erebus were in a wooded copse a hundred kilometres from Hammerfest, opening the shipping crates. Erebus' interest was increased by the shipping documents being printed in German and Norwegian.

"Well, Laudrup, is there anything we can booby trap?"

There was no reply as an opened crate revealed heavy packing around a smaller case marked 'fragile.'

Erebus wondered out loud.

"Why would furniture be marked 'fragile'?" The smaller box was opened, and Moen heard the word.

"'Transmitter" Quickly followed by,

"Open all of these cases." Fifteen minutes later, as he looked at six radios, Erebus knew he had to risk trusting the big Norwegian.

"The way I see it is these radios are to be delivered as furniture to officials within the new administration. I think the officials are Abwehr agents who are spying on everyone, German and Norwegian. Hence the civilian transportation." Moen asked,

"How come you know so much about the bastard's spies? Who are you?" Erebus explained about the SOE and why he needed a radio urgently and finished with,

"Understand, if we get caught, we are both dead." Moen's reply swept away any doubts.

"Well, I might as well go along. The bastards are probably going to shoot me for calling them bastards." He laughed, then became serious.

"Now you say you need to keep one of these radios and the rest of the load destroyed." He went on.

."So we'll have to arrange an accident. But not here. Somewhere on the delivery route." Erebus prompted.

"Go on."

Moen told him about a customer who supplied equipment, including radios to the mountain rescue teams in Norway.

"He'll know how to make the accident look convincing."

Erebus was interested but cautious.

"So, how do we meet this man?"

Moen, now more downbeat, answered,

"We have to go cross country, which is dangerous?"

Erebus stated.

"Right, we'll stop in the first big town we find."

Moen looked to the sky as he exclaimed.

"Well, I did say yes."

The town was large and full of German military. Laudrup ordered.

"Park about a hundred metres away from that police station and wait." Moen sat and watched Laudrup bump into one of two Wehrmacht officers on a busy road crossing point near the police building. He made a great act of apologising which seemed to satisfy the Germans. Moen then gasped as Laudrup walked into the Police station.

Erebus was gambling the police would be in disarray as the new puppet government officials took over. He approached the desk officer and showed the German military ID cards along with the official dual-language shipping papers. The pompous man looked at them and him,

"You don't look like an officer." Erebus spoke Norwegian, then German telling the increasingly nervous official he was interfering in matters that did not concern him. The man, now feeling the pressure obeyed obediently as Laudrupdemanded nationwide transport permits for two officers and an open-ended gasoline permit.

The documents were duly produced. Laudrup climbed into the passenger seat of the truck and exclaimed.

"Good job he wasn't a police officer. They always ask questions. It's in their nature. Let's get out of here before that idiot realises what he's done!" Then added,

"Thank God for fanatics."

He need not have worried. The newly appointed official, so eager to curry favour with the Germans, realised he had not taken the names on the ID cards. Now terrified, he ensured that all records of the permits being issued disappeared.

The warehouse was reached after three days of hard driving. Laudrup again voiced concerns about security. Moen guaranteed the people they were meeting.

"Everyone here feels the same. We all hate the bastards." Then instructed.

"When we get there, I'll do the talking." Laudrup just nodded.

Lars Hagen was a married man with two teenage sons. Images of him; tall and slim with light brown hair. The warehouse was busy. A stream of vehicles coming and going. He examined the radios.

"These are very powerful radios, not standard issue."

Moen asked,

"How do we conceal that one or maybe two have been stolen in transit?"

Hagen continued enthusiastically,

"Leave that to me. The Germans confiscated all my good radios and left damaged sets. We'll replace the radio you took with a busted radio. Then steal a truck like yours and crash it down a ravine" he paused.

"In fact, I've got a hairpin bend in mind. You carry on with your truck home without any load."

Moen asked.

"What about the registration plates?" Hagen was cheerful.

"This ravine is deep, and we'll make certain everything burns." He paused. Then warned,

"These radios are never found outside Germany. Anyone caught with one in Norway better have a good reason."

Moan asked.

"Won't the Germans wonder why the truck was so far off the main roads?" Hagen replied.

"Where we are going crash the truck is a well-known but dangerously icy shortcut to the main road. The Germans think all Norwegians are stupid. So will blame the driver."

Hagen and his sons took over the repacking of the crates. Moen watched them until there were two crates left. He turned, looking for Laudrup, and saw him enter one of the warehouses carrying one of the stolen radios.

Erebus decided to contact SOE. He placed the stolen radio on a bench in the warehouse and began transmitting his call sign. Out of the corner of his eye, he saw Moen approaching. Within a minute, the call sign was acknowledged, then he heard.

"Go ahead Erebus, over." Erebus demanded to speak to one man only. The reply was short.

"Please wait, over."

The Brigadier was summoned to the radio room and told.

"Erebus wants to talk to you." Davies took the radio headset and, with his heart pounding, began his first agent-handling operation. Erebus recognised the Brigadier's voice.

"Erebus, your last postcard had some very interesting gossip. Got a lot of fish heads and skimmers talking? It was well received, over."

Davies had used slang terms known only to British Military. Erebus knew they received the Scharnhorst signal.

"Delighted that you got my card and you could read my handwriting." Erebus paused, then asked.

"Do you have anything for me, over?"

Davies thought quickly.

"All is forgiven after the misunderstandings this end. You tell us what you need, and we will supply. Do you concur?"

Erebus felt his heart lift. The shootings and desertion had been expunged. He was back on active service.

"Your offer is too generous to allow me to refuse. Over"

Davies replied,

"Nonsense! Pleasure is all ours. Especially your maiden aunt. Propose you write only to her at this address. She will tend to your needs, over."

Erebus understood fully. Davies was his handler.

"Understood. Will drop postcards as and when. Over and out."

Moen was now by Laudrup and, seeing him smile broadly, said.

"Laudrup, that's the first time I've seen you smile. I get the feeling the bastards could be in for a hard time."

Erebus looked at the big Norwegian.

"You know you could be wanted until the war is over." He replied,

"Laudrup, this is the first time I've felt alive since the bastards conquered us. I even sleep at night. I'll go wherever you tell me to and wait for your next road trip, OK?"

Erebus smiled.

"How do we arrange to meet?"

Moen thought,

"I deliver for a sawmill on the main road near Hagnor. You can leave a message there for me."

Later that day, Erebus briefed Maiden Aunt on his situation except for the radios. Maiden Aunt was to the point.

"Local resistance groups are unknown entities. Stick with known contacts only." Erebus felt safe in telling Moen. Who responded.

"Right, we'll go ahead as planned and burn the rest."

The crash was staged on a hairpin bend, the ravine at least fifty meters deep. A local farmer informed the police, and they reported it to the German authorities. A perfunctory examination confirmed that an accident and the ensuing fire had destroyed the load and truck completely. There was no interest in the welfare or identity of the driver. A copy of the report found its way to an Abwehr agent in the guise of a regional administrator who presumed all the radios were destroyed. The pair returned toHagnor. Erebus hid the radio, and Moen carried on his business.

During a later briefing, Erebus asked for detailed information on the Abwehr and the Organisation Todt. Davies agreed. He then repeated the policy on resistance groups and signed off.

"Good luck and be careful. Over and out."

What Erebus was not told was that Odin was profoundly concerned there was a double agent within UK intelligence services.

"Brigadier, welcome to the world of smoke and mirrors and the dark arts." Now officially second in command of SOE, Davies asked.

"What do we do with Sergeant Cork?"

Cork walked into an office to be greeted by Admiral Spenser and Brigadier Davies. He was told he was unfit for Infantry service and asked to consider a proposition.

Admiral Spenser pulled over a chair and began,

"Sergeant, do you remember when I made clear to you the consequences of any breach in security surrounding this organisation?"

"Perfectly Sir." Spenser went on.

"If you accept this proposal, those conditions still apply."

"Understood sir."

"So be it, sergeant. It is your choice alone – you have made it." He explained that Lewis was alive and behind enemy lines. Then said.

"You are one of the few people who know this, and you also know the man is unpredictable."

Pat thought.

'That's some understatement. He's 'stone mad'.

Admiral Spenser continued.

"The man trusts you, so you are rather valuable to us".

Again he thought, 'you mean I've seen too much of your top secret little section here.'

Pat said.

"Permission to ask a question, Sir?"

"Permission granted."

"Where does the brigadier fit into all this?"

Spenser stood exclaiming,

"Now look here, laddie! All we need to know is whether you are with us or not." Then calming down, he continued.

"To answer your question, Brigadier Davies is officially second in command of the section."

Pat thought to himself, 'What have I got to lose? – and this lot could still have me killed!'

"When and where do we begin, sir?" He was ordered to report back to Britannia in seventy-two hours.

The Cork's were about to say goodbye. Connor explained that Peter English would be moving into the house.

"It's the least I could do. Jesus, Pat, he's just the carcass of a man. This house is too big for me anyway. God bless you, my boy, and stay safe. I'll tell your mother that all is well with you." Since Norway, the Corks took nothing for granted and hugged unashamedly.

Penny's goodbye was more emotional but still short. They went to bed but slept in each other's arms. In the early morning, woke and made love gently and slowly. Within five minutes, they were dressed and had gone their separate ways without a word being said.

Having reported as ordered, Pat was escorted to an office where Spenser and Brigadier Davies were waiting. The admiral spoke.

"Sergeant, as I got you into this, I feel duty-bound to offer you an alternative way to fight. Ships might suit that leg of yours. I am asking you to join the Royal Navy. Are you willing to do that?"

Pat didn't hesitate.

"Yes, sir. Absolutely."

Spenser advised,

"The correct response is, 'aye aye', but we can work on that."

Both Brigadier Davies and Spenser came to attention.

"The rank of admiral, although having great responsibility, occasionally has its pleasurable side. I am allowed to promote or commission men whom I consider to have served their country with distinction and valour. There is no doubt you have done both."

Davies gave a hearty,

"Here, here!"

Spenser continued,

"It is with great pleasure I now commission you into the Royal Navy in the rank of sub-lieutenant. You are required and requested to report immediately to the commanding officer of HMS Britannia, where you will undergo such training as is considered necessary to enable you to carry out the duties assigned to you by their Lordships of the Admiralty. God save the King."

Sub-lieutenant P Cork had finished training in what one admiral called an obscenely short time. He had excelled at gunnery and Sonar. Despite being wounded, he had passed the fitness test, just barely. While training Pat reported fellow cadets for breaches of discipline. Some took exception and told him so. They received a dressing down which would have done any army NCO credit. Pat didn't explain why to anyone. He knew active service was waiting for all of these men. Any slip, any lapse, could be fatal.

Some commented on the campaign colours he wore as a 'sub', but the scuttlebutt said he had permission from a flag officer in the Royal Navy, that was that. The other cadets celebrated 'passing out.' Pat didn't. The war would be the same as it was in Norway. Then his orders came.

Brigadier Davies was in full uniform.

"First of all, please accept my congratulations on a very respectable training performance and pass mark, bearing in mind that leg." Then said

"Admiral, I'll leave the rest to you."

Odin began.

"You're being posted to the Black Swan-class sloop HMS Snow Eagle, rated as gunnery officer, with a watching brief on signals and radio communications. We have someone on board you know - Lieutenant Commander Larsen. He is electronics and signals. HMS Snow Eagle is part of the home fleet, which has two primary tasks. The first is to blockade a number of enemy capital ships. The second is escort duties for convoys in the sea areas around Ireland and the North Sea. Do you have any questions, sub?"

Pat did.

"Sir, does the captain of Snow Eagle know about Lieutenant Commander Larsen and me?"

The admiral replied,

"The captain has been fully briefed."

Davies stood and shook Pat's hand, followed by Spenser, who said.

"Right. Good luck and good hunting."

During the winter of 1940, Erebus requested details on two German organisations which made up part of the Nazi occupying forces.

The Organisation Todt was responsible for all major construction projects in the Reich. Its officials had free run of all German installations in Norway. The Abwehr was the counterintelligence arm of the Nazi state. It silently monitored and struck terror into all people. German or otherwise. Erebus received forged ID papers and uniforms used by Todt and Abwehr officers, which he would use to impersonate and infiltrate their operations, causing as much chaos as possible.

Erebus summoned Moen by the agreed method. The message read. 'Be ready for a job in early March.'

Laudrup settled in with Olaf and Hilda, who stayed nights as the winter became bitter. He listened and laughed with the many visitors who came to Strand's house. One morning he asked Hilda why the house was so popular with the villagers. The young woman had begun to like this quiet, interesting man sat down.

"My uncle is the village historian; he keeps the legends and sagas of the Norsemen alive in word and song."

Erebus thought of the storytellers in Ireland - the 'Seanchai'. Then reminded himself. 'You have no past before Laudrup. Don't get too involved.'

Later that day, Olaf called up to his room.

"I am going to Berg's house for a drink. You are invited as well."

A clearly delighted Berg handed two large glasses of brandy to his guests.

"This brandy was for a German colonel in Narvik but was liberated by a friend of mine who owes me many favours. 'Skol', my friends."

Berg regaled them with tales of exploits as a fisherman and smuggler. Laudrup drank very little, making sure his glass was nearly full when offered a refill. Strand was not so abstemious and had to be helped home. As he put the old man to bed, Hilda came into the room and covered her uncle in a warm blanket and led Laudrup into his room.

She gently kissed him, then stood back and dropped her nightgown. In an instant, he understood what the boys at school had been obsessed with. She moved toward him, unbuckled his belt and reached down into his trousers, searching for his penis. She took him in her hand and then kissed him, pushing her tongue into his mouth. He was aroused, and his penis swelled to full size. He felt a burning desire to have sex with this lovely young woman. For the first time in his life, he was beginning to understand how touching was another form of communication. For the whole night, he was gentle and caring. Morning came, and with it, a new experience for Erebus. Her body heat was incredible and, after a lifetime of living and sleeping alone, he knew he would never forget the night he had spent with Hilda. She awoke and whispered.

"You are a lovely, gentle man - that is why I decided that you should be the first man I would be with. I do not want anything from you other than to come here to you when I want. You do not own me - nobody owns me. Do you understand?"

All he could say was.

"Yes."

She dressed in silence and left as Erebus thought his life was becoming very complicated for a man who was supposed to be a loner.

Erebus could see the Germans regarded all Norwegians, including the fishermen, as stupid and no threat to Nazi strategic plans. During many hours of ice-fishing, Olaf Strand told him of reports by fishermen from all parts of the coastline. Reports which provided accurate intelligence on the building of U-boat pens in the coastal ports of Norway. Erebus passed this information on to SOE. The analysts demanded further proof of the accuracy of the intelligence. Erebus replied.

"These men have vast experience of the coastline. The Germans are so arrogant they don't know they are being watched." The situation inspired Erebus's contribution to Greenwood's wisdom.

'Get your enemy to underestimate you. The man who has been underestimated will always have the advantage'.

In March 1941, Moen arrived, eager to go into the timber business again.

"How are you, Laudrup? If that is your name. Still ahead of the bastards, I see. Well, so am I. Come on, tell me how we can kill a few hundred of these bastards before we all go to hell." His attitude to the Germans was part of the man's constant ebullience, and the SOE officer replied in a similar vein.

"I am well, my friend, and how are you in these difficult times?"

Moen shrugged his broad shoulders. Erebus continued.

"What is the latest on the building of U-boat pens?"

"There are large numbers of forced labour being shipped to Bergen along with requisitioned building material."

"Where did this information come from?"

Moen explained in detail how his network of owner drivers from all over the country had been delivering huge amounts of materials to Bergen. Enough for a very large construction job. Erebus asked

"How do we get in to have a look?"

Moen answered.

"I'm not sure. I could get a contract to deliver timber?"

Erebus remained silent for a while. Then explained,

"There is an organisation, Todt, which does all the Nazi's building work."

Moen countered. "Don't you have to be German?"

Erebus replied.

"No, some Norwegians have joined already." Moen looked shocked. Erebus went on.

"I'll get us uniforms and papers, and we'll go to Bergen." Moen laughed.

"Life is never boring with you, Laudrup, or whatever your name is. Let's go and give the bastards some trouble."

Two Todt officials entered the Bergen construction site. Laudrup, a senior superintendent. Moen, a shift master, both looking every inch loyal Nazi functionaries. Erebus saw bullied and broken men in numerous work gangs labouring while being shouted at by Todt overseers. Erebus watched his companion's eyes harden as he spoke in a low voice.

"I'll get every one of these Norwegian bastards if it kills me."

They approached a uniformed man who was overseeing two labour gangs. One loading a conveyer belt with concrete, the other shovelling it into a huge shutter. Laudrup ignored the man's greeting and demanded directions. Moen stood behind him, eyes hardening at the overt brutality. Erebus signalled his companion to follow him toward the site office as an elderly man collapsed onto the conveyer belt. He instinctively moved to help. Moen, his face now cold, blocked him and hissed,

"Leave him! We have to think and act like the bastards to pull this off. Now leave him." No attempt was made to save the man being swept into the chamber, where he drowned in concrete. Erebus began to walk away, his eyes fixed dead ahead. Moen followed.

The site office door flew open as Moen charged in and ordered everyone to stand. A man who tried to speak was silenced by a heartfelt insult. Erebus entered and, in German, demanded the plans for the upgrade of all U-boat facilities in Norway, beginning with Bergen. Moen cleared a desk with a sweep of his arm, then, as Erebus sat, spread the plans given to him. Erebus glanced up and saw Moen's eyes were glistening with tears of anger and shame. The death of the nameless old labourer had profoundly upset the big man. The drawings revealed that Bergen port was being upgraded to service at least two U-boat flotillas. Similar plans had been drawn up for the ports along the western seaboard of Norway. The Nazis were preparing for a massive U-boat assault on the convoys. Erebus stood and, on leaving the office, saw men in the remnants of British uniforms. A nod to Moen indicated that they walk toward the prisoners. Moen asked.

"What's this?"

Erebus motioned toward the labourers.

"They could be British. Let's find out."

"Leave it to me", that guard's Norwegian. The bastard!"

Erebus saw a small site hut with a table and chairs and the makings of hot drinks. Moen was leading the prisoners toward him; the guard at the rear was dismissed with a cursory,

"This officer is going to question these men."

The guard protested.

"My boss is a fanatic and a right bastard, if he catches us leaving the workers unsupervised. He wants them working every minute."

Erebus, now standing by the hut, showed impatience. Moen raised his voice.

"My officer is senior to yours. Now just fuck off - right."

The man did so.

Erebus ordered Moen to send in the first prisoner. Inside the man was ordered,

"Identify yourself. You know the drill." The prisoner gave name, rank and serial number. Erebus turned around and said,

"Stay calm and quiet. I am part of the resistance, and so is the guard outside. Right, get some of that hot coffee inside you."

The highly suspicious sergeant replied,

"Germans can speak English too. How do I know you're not Gestapo?"

Erebus nodded.

"Good point. I am a captain in the Irish guards on special duties in Norway. Ask me any question you want."

The man did so.

"What's the nickname the British Army has for the Irish Guards?"

Erebus thanked heaven for his time spent with Pat Cork.

"They call us the 'Micks'."

The sergeant stood to attention, saluted and said,

"Sergeant Cormac Reilly. First battalion Oxford and Buckinghamshire Light infantry. Sir."

Erebus shook his hand as he handed over a mug of steaming hot coffee.

"Please sit down. Now, what can you tell me about this place?"

Sergeant Reilly reported that all the men were British expeditionary force and were captured during 1940 and added.

"They're all good men, sir. We've been through a lot together." Erebus said.

"Sergeant, please listen and then tell me what you think." He explained the possibility of the pens being bombed and maybe a mass escape of allied POWs. Reilly's eyes lit up as he sipped hot coffee. Erebus found himself desperately wanting to free the allied prisoners.

"Right, Sergeant Reilly, let's have everyone in."

During the next hour, all six men drank something hot and were told to stay hopeful of escape. Reilly sat in on each 'interview.' The last man was Private Mullen, who listened, nodded and asked.

"There's one bastard I want to settle with, whatever happens. Is that alright with you, sir?"

Erebus answered.

"That's up to you. But the aim is to get everybody out. The bombing could kill anyone left. But Private Mullen, if you get the chance, the German's all yours."

Mullen's smile said everything. Then as he turned to leave.

"Cormac, you know one of us always gets a hiding. The goons might be watching, and not all the fuckers are stupid."

Reilly punched Mullen in the mouth, producing a cut lip. The soldier said.

"That should do it nicely, sarge." Moen watched as the guard took charge of the prisoners and noted a spring in each man's step. One looked at a German guard with almost sadistic pleasure.

Five days later, on board Berg's trawler, miles from landfall, Erebus turned off his radio, having given Maiden Aunt an in-depth briefing.

10

Sea Legs

The shipmates stood outside the captain's cabin as Larsen knocked on the cabin door.

"Enter."

Captain Tom Loftus commanding the escort group of six Black Swan-class sloops, was an officer of senior standing on the captains' list. Pat saw a man of six foot two, slim with grey hair, his voice firm, appearance and demeanour distinguished. The very essence of the Royal Navy.

"Gentlemen, welcome to Snow eagle, a sloop of war. My compliments on your service in Norway. Admiral Spenser has briefed me on SOE. We will assist in every way, but the business of HMS Snow eagle and this escort group is paramount?" The reply was instant.

"Aye aye, Sir." Loftus continued.

"The first officer will assign your duties. Larsen, there will be extra duty for you in the SONAR and radio cabin." Lars replied.

"Excellent, Sir, and thank you for having me aboard; it is great to be at sea". The captain nodded.

"Right, you will share a cabin." Loftus concentrated on Cork.

"Sub, well done at Britannia. It is my policy to have a fit crew; I need to be certain that you can cope with the demands of sea service. I'm a bit concerned your wound may have taken a good deal out of you. So first, run ashore; you are to get a medical report. Do you understand?" Cork replied.

"Perfectly, Sir."

"Right, once again, welcome to Snow Eagle, and good luck to you both."

As Pat stood watch, he recalled his first days at sea.

He joined HMS Snow Eagle in January 1941 and was greeted by Larsen.

"Hello Pat, wrap up well; we're about to cast off. Now, my friend, we'll see if you have your sea legs." He remembered the cramped conditions, then standing watch in the radio room just below the bridge, as Lars said.

"Rough weather ahead, Pat." As if on cue, the ship heeled over at an unbelievable angle, then righted herself. Larsen laughed

"She is tough, our Snow Eagle."

Pat concentrated on the lookouts on deck who - like the men in the radio room - ignored the weather. Then the ship reeking of vomit - salt water everywhere. The relentless rocking motion. At first came nausea, followed by vomiting and empty retching, then exhaustion and delirium. A haze of heat and smoke, fire, explosions, screams, burning flesh. Faces, voices, names. Norway would never leave his memory. Then sleep and finally some sensible food and the magical cocoa. Now back on watch.

The first officer named Campbell, a solid man of six foot with jet black hair and a slight Scottish accent, acquainted Cork with his 'new home.' HMS Snow eagle was a Black Swan-class sloop with 180 officers and men; top speed was twenty knots. Three four-and-a-half inch guns, four anti-aircraft guns, torpedoes, Oerlikon guns and 'hedgehog' depth charges were the ship's weapons. Captain Loftus captained her and commanded five of His Majesty's ships, Snow Leopard, Snow Lynx, Snow Tiger, Snow Wolf and Snow Cougar. Their primary functions were to escort convoys and sink U-boats.

Off duty, in the cabin, they caught up with each other's lives. Cork asked.

"Why aren't you with SOE?"

"In Norway, anyone whose relatives are suspected of being resistance fighters are being arrested, and I have three sisters and my parents there." Lars' face reflected his fear and sorrow. Then he perked up.

"Plus, someone in the admiralty remembered I have a degree in electronics and, so I am aboard to develop Sonar systems and HFDF kit." He added with venom.

"Pat, I intend to send every U-boat to the bottom."

Pat asked.

"Any idea where Erebus is." The reply was succinct.

"God only knows." Lars continued.

"That reminds me." He handed Pat a sheet of paper.

"Came in from Maiden Aunt; anyone spring to mind?" Pat read the signal.

"There is someone who might fit the bill."

The escort group assumed convoy duty, and Cork stood watch with Campbell, who explained convoy escort tactics.

"Pat, the first thing to learn is that a convoy is only as fast as its slowest merchantman." Scanning the fleet with binoculars he continued,

"Captain Loftus and the C in C Western Approaches have some ideas which should kill more U-boats." And explained.

"The enemy is weakest straight after an attack because he's shown his position. If he's on the surface or not, we can and must attack accurately with speed using experienced escort and aircraft crews." Campbell spoke slowly.

"Something which the Admiralty are refusing to accept."

Meanwhile, Captain Loftus sat in his cabin fuming. He received orders for his first officer Lieutenant Commander Campbell to take a command.

Campbell was highly experienced in convoy escort and anti-submarine warfare. If 'Number one' had been given a ship in the escort group, he would have been delighted. No, the Admiralty, in their wisdom, had sent him to minesweepers. Loftus had objected to the C n C convoy escorts many times but was told that Atlantic escort duty was ideal preparation for command of any ship. Basically, Tom Loftus was politely told,

"Captain, please keep up the good work and shut up."

Campbell's duties were reassigned. Larsen took over all RADAR-ASDIC and radio duties. The crew nicknamed him 'Sonar' because it sounded Nordic. He was secretly delighted. Cork though inexperienced, took command of the ship's armament and assumed the nickname 'Guns'. Captain Loftus stood on the bridge, aware the situation was not ideal but was feeling more comfortable, having noted how the crew, new and experienced, supported each other. He ordered the escort group to make steam for Londonderry and another convoy.

The losses of merchant shipping during 1940 and early 1941 were disastrous. But slowly, the escorts began to gain the upper hand with occasional help from coastal command long-range bombers. The U-boat high command then varied their tactics, hunting in 'Wolf packs' or strung-out lines of U-boats across the convoy routes, and the losses began to increase.

The Royal Navy and the Canadian and allied navies waged a brutal, desperate battle with the U-boats. Pat was learning his duties and how to cope with all sea conditions. The ship was in the middle of a ferocious mid-Atlantic storm, with some of the most experienced crew falling to seasickness. Pat stood watch with the lookouts, alert for danger lurking in the boiling black water. Captain Loftus appeared on the bridge. Then looked at Pat and, with a slight nod of his head, indicated total confidence in him. Pat knew he had found his sea legs and belonged aboard Snow eagle.

Larsen was becoming expert on SONAR and the High-Frequency Directional Finding system, HFDF, or "huffduff" and was told to prepare to be the training officer for the escort group. He practised his teaching methods on Pat.

"Right Guns, listen." He explained how when a surfaced U-boat transmitted a signal, allied coastal HFDF listening stations calculated its position by directional cross reference. The target's location dictated if it was attacked by escorts or shore-based aircraft. He finished.

"Pat, if we get this right, Huffduff will become a vital weapon against the U-boats."

As training officer, Larsen was made a Commander. Pat Cork was promoted to second officer, and Lieutenant Commander Jack Crowley joined as first officer. He had experience in carrier-borne aircraft tactics for convoy escort gained aboard HMS Victorious. He was gregarious with a shock of blonde hair, just over six feet and, as he put it, 'elegantly built.' He and Pat hit it off from the word go. Crowley was convinced crew morale was of fundamental importance, and once aware of the nationalities aboard; he started the practice of celebrating national days.

Each group prepared an entertainment on the date in question. The Welsh sang on St David's day, as did the Irish on St Patrick's. The Scots recited Burns and smuggled some bagpipes aboard, and the English had to be reminded when St George's day fell. There soon developed a competitive spirit between the men. In the wardroom on St Patrick's day, Pat surprised everyone with a thundering rendition of 'On The banks of my own lovely Lee.'

Crowley's plan was not wholly altruistic. He had seen morale ripped apart by the 'no stopping' order, and fire at sea brought horrors that were enough to break the strongest of men. The smallest diversion helped everyone.

It was not long before Crowley's excellent seamanship, and genuine concern for his shipmates made him a popular and respected first officer.

In mid-1941, Captain Loftus had gambled on Snow eagle taking station 9000 yards astern of the westbound convoy. The ship's radar picked up an unknown surface contact 3000 yards astern of the fleet. The watch officer reported to Crowley.

"Radar here, Sir, we have a contact 6000 yards dead ahead." Crowley ordered,

"Wake the captain." Loftus and Crowley suspected the contact was a U-boat on the surface looking for a convoy straggler; it would then radio other U-boats to gather in that sea area. Captain Loftus ordered,

"Battle stations, engine room full ahead both". Pat's station was forrardat the 4.5-inch gun where he heard from Campbell.

"Guns. Target five thousand yards dead ahead." Pat confirmed.

"Very good, Sir, well within range." The excitement grew as lookouts vied to make the first sighting. Campbell ordered.

"Flags, give me our position, and copy C in C convoy escorts. Western approaches command." The reply was instant.

"Ships position one hundred miles and twenty due west of Ireland." The forrard lookouts shouted,

"Conning Tower dead ahead". Captain Loftus spoke,

"Guns, we'll close, then you try to knock his tower off. Number one, ready depth charges." As Pat responded with,

"Aye, Aye, Sir", he heard.

"Radar picking up aircraft astern, Sir." Loftus demanded.

"What the hell is it number one?"

"Single aircraft Sir, range 10,000 yards, speed about 200 miles an hour, closing on us fast." Loftus remained calm.

"Battle stations. Cork, you concentrate on that U-boat."

Crowley's cut across him.

"Aircraft is one of ours, and I think he's after our U-boat. Sir." A bomber flew over Snow Eagle and attacked the enemy with bombs that fell either side of the target and at least a hundred yards short. The U-boat submerged as the ship's crew watched in stunned silence as the aircraft peeled away. Struggling to keep control, Loftus ordered.

"Standard search pattern, number one."

Three hours later, the first officer entered the captain's cabin.

"Report, please, Mr Crowley."

"Sir that was a Coastal Command aircraft and attacked as a result of the U-boat being located by HFDF stations on the west coast of Britain." Loftus motioned him to sit and then exploded with rage.

"Number one, we had a U-boat, and due to crass stupidity, it escaped." Still seething, he asked.

"How are the men?" Crowley was frank.

"The crew are very angry. The U-boat escaped, and they all know what it could do. Morale has taken a bit of a pasting". Captain Loftus said.

"I commend you on your understatement. This kind of cock up has got to stop. Thank you, Mr Crowley; please carry, on. Dismissed."

Loftus drew up a signal which he sent to the C in C Western approaches and the commander of Coastal Command. The signal was, in the long term, to have profound effect upon all the men of the escort group.

The men of the ships of the escort group learned to sleep when equally vicious enemies - the Atlantic or the Germans - allowed them. They learned how to, at night, steam to a torpedoed merchantman and lay depth charges which would explode with survivors in the water. They obeyed the no-stopping order, and some cried as they heard the screams of the men in the water covered in oil and on fire. They learned munitions ships were stationed on the perimeter of the convoy, so if torpedoed, the damage to other ships was minimised. They learned how to get drunk in Liverpool and Derry and never say a word to anyone outside the escort group about what they had seen and done. Their jobs were perfectly simple, get the convoys through and kill U-boats at every opportunity. Pat Cork learned all this alongside his shipmates and never a word from Erebus.

In Liverpool, Pat was in the operations command office collecting charts and was given a tour by an officer who said in a complimentary tone.

"We have a name for your escort group. The Snow ships." Pat smiled as he noticed a ledger entitled 'Civilian seaborne losses.'

"Why civilian losses?" The officer looked up.

"This is the list of civilians who were killed when the merchantmen they had passage on were torpedoed." Pat didn't know why he asked.

"Would you mind if I looked?" The reply was pleasant.

"No, I don't mind; please help yourself". Pat knew the name and the date of every ship lost from the 'Snow Ships' convoys. He read the manifest of all the other ships until he found two names. Pat controlled his reaction, closed the log, thanked the officer in charge and went back to war.

At SOE HQ, Odin, Maiden Aunt, and Vali were planning the Bergen raid. Odin spoke.

"The RAF have yet to prioritise this target as they are desperately short of crews and long-range bombers." The mood was quickly downcast. Odin lifted his voice, realising that perhaps he'd been too frank.

"Still – that's for me to sort out." He continued.

"Vali, let's have your thoughts and please speak freely. We are planning to bomb your home."

The young Norwegian did as asked.

"Bergen will be rebuilt when the Germans are defeated, but to do that, we have to stop the U-boats. That is the price we pay for being conquered."

There was silence, so he continued,

"As for the other proposal, it would be extremely risky for Erebus and his comrade. They are providing first-class intelligence. We can't afford to lose two excellent gatherers."

Maiden Aunt commented,

"Your objectivity is admirable." As he thought.

'Jesus! I thought the English were cold fish,' then went on,

"It would be a great fillip for morale; plus, these men know how the Organisation Todt works."

Then he showed why he was a brigadier.

"There is more; these men are all army regulars who have the priceless experience of active service. The more of these men we can get back to train other troops, the better prepared we are when we go back and get amongst the Germans." Odin ordered Vali to produce an operational plan for the prisoners' escape. Erebus was signalled to put his men on standby. Then out of the blue, orders came from Downing Street. The raid and rescue was to go ahead. Churchill wanted a message sent to the occupied countries that they were not forgotten. The air raid and the prisoners' escape would do just that.

In early August, Erebus was at sea on Berg's trawler listening to a cryptic message from Maiden Aunt.

"Certain items are to be moved overland, then transferred to seaborne elements for export by local contractors. A head office consultant will be on-site to confirm details. Dense fog will provide cover."

Ashore Erebus translated for Moen and Berg.

"A man is coming from Britain to command the operation."

Moen replied bluntly,

"Do you know him, and do you trust him?"

Erebus answered,

"Yes, to both questions, but you have to make up your own minds. In the meantime, listen up." Erebus outlined the details.

"The escape will take place as the bombers flatten the pens." He looked at Moen.

"You and your mates will take the POWs to the sea." The big man smiled as Erebus met Berg's expectant gaze.

"Your fishing boats will then take the men to Royal navy warships waiting out to sea." Both men left already planning the fine details. Erebus re-read his personal orders. He was strictly forbidden to endanger himself by re-entering the port of Bergen or by taking part in the escape.

Maiden Aunt did not know that three weeks later, Erebus completely ignored his orders. As far as the German guard knew, the British prisoner was under questioning by an Abwehr officer. The Irish man was delighted to see Erebus, who hid his concern at the sergeant's weight loss. Reilly sat down as the plan was explained, and despite obvious weakness, he enthusiastically answered Erebus's question.

"Tell me a little about the men?"

"There are one hundred and twenty-six allied servicemen here. We have thirteen NCOs, six English, four Scottish and three Welsh, who will supervise the other hundred men." He rested as Erebus handed him a mug of coffee. Then said.

"They're all good soldiers. They won't let us down." His voice lifted.

"All regulars, except me and Tomas Mullen."

Erebus felt the man just wanted to talk.

"Tell me about yourself."

"I am a Leitrim man and always wanted to be a soldier, so I joined the Irish Army. By 1938 I could see war was coming, and De Valera was keeping Ireland neutral. I deserted, crossed the border and joined up." Erebus had heard enough to know Reilly's experience and intelligence ensured rapid promotion. The sergeant continued.

"Tomas did pretty much the same, except he enlisted in a different regiment." Erebus asked about the sick. Reilly answered,

"There four who are too sick to walk," He vowed.

"We'll carry them. We're not leaving anyone."

The matter of non-British prisoners was raised. Reilly told how the Dutch and the French would get home on their own. He added,

"There is one more thing, sir."

Erebus nodded.

"There are about twenty Jewish prisoners here. Rumour is that all the Jewish people are secretly shipped out to Germany." Erebus could only say.

"Of course, we'll take them."

Laudrup was collected by Moen on the outskirts of Bergen, and on the way to Hagnor, every detail of the escape was dissected. Despite having huge doubts, Reilly's attitude, coupled with Moen and Berg's enthusiasm and determination, made Erebus believe they just might get away with it. His mood improved as the idea of how the Jewish prisoners could help the escape came to him.

At SOE HQ Bakken's return to Norway threw up personal issues. The Germans knew he was in England, so his family in Norway would be under surveillance. He desperately wanted to see them, even from a distance. His wife had left him before the war stating that he cared more for the Norwegian navy than her. At least he had done her some good. The Nazis would leave her alone.

Sitting on the plane, Vali considered his briefing just before he left. Odin had informed him that with immediate effect, all operations involving Erebus and C squad were now commanded by Maiden Aunt. He was unconcerned. Davies knew little of Norway but was a good commanding officer. He'd proved that on active service.

Vali's new CO was wondering why Odin had given him sole command of Erebus and C squad. The Admiral did not explain, and orders were to be obeyed. Simpson-Coyle remained in charge of all other SOE operations. So, in theory, their paths should not cross.

Odin did not explain the command changes had taken place because King Olaf of Norway had informed Churchill that Norwegian resistance leaders refused to obey Simpson-Coyle's orders, which were to inflict maximum casualties on occupying troops. Such attacks provoked terrifying reprisals against civilians.

Churchill instructed Odin.

"The Norwegians have every right to decide how they fight in their own country. SOE is to provide advice and material support. Not issue direct orders."

A protracted and difficult interview followed, during which Simpson-Coyle dismissed the ultimatum of the resistance leaders as blatant insubordination. Odin stated the command changes. Then went on bluntly.

"Your demands for absolute obedience and refusal to accept that the war must be fought by professional soldiers working alongside courageous, dedicated and talented volunteers." Odin paused,

"Has resulted in a complete breakdown of relations between the Norwegians and the SOE." The Colonel remained silent as he was dismissed.

Simpson-Coyle's intransigence was of deep concern to Odin, who already disliked the man. This was now coupled with mistrust.

Maiden Aunt's total knowledge of Norway was based upon a disastrous campaign. Expert advisors were needed quickly. A signal was sent to all SOE personnel requesting they forward to HQ immediately the name of any acquaintance who had knowledge of the social and political history of the occupied countries. Larsen gave Pat Cork that signal, and he forwarded a name.

Professor Peter Williamson was approached outside UCL by two large men and asked to accompany them to a meeting in a civil service office in Whitehall. There he met Maiden Aunt and was asked to assist in the production of reports and analysis of political factions in the occupied countries before and during the war. Williamson stated his position as a conscientious objector. Davies was in no mood for negotiation.

"Listen, I can have you charged, convicted and digging the roads within a week. Do you understand?" Williamson replied.

"If that is the price I must pay, so be it". As an afterthought, he added.

"Where did you get my name and subject expertise from?" Davies, now a little calmer, answered.

"You were recommended by a man who is fighting, the son of an Irishman, in fact". Williamson's interest was aroused.

"Can you tell me his name?" Davies felt the man was worth that if he was willing to go to jail.

"The man's name is Pat Cork." Williamson remembered the objective young man from that night in London.

"Will he benefit from my assistance?" Davies answered, his voice now expectant.

"Yes. He and many like him."

"Very well, Brigadier; where do I sign?" Williamson returned to UCL and cleared his desk, satisfied he had not compromised his principles. Within a week, the former 'conchie's security vetting had been completed, and the Official Secrets Act signed. Davies repeated his request for political overviews and would the Professor please begin with Norway. Privately, Davies was hugely relieved at not having to make good his threat. He would have to handle this man carefully.

The SOE pilot touched down twenty kilometres north of Hellebakken, a coastal village eight kilometres north of Bergen. Vali's papers identified him as a schoolteacher returned from Denmark. He was met by a member of Norwegian Naval Intelligence.

Erebus, accompanied by Moen and Berg, neared Hellebakken, having agreed to meet Vali only because of Laudrup. Moen spoke first.

"I am here because my friend Laudrup here says you are to be trusted and because I want to help those poor devils in Bergen. I can get you ten Lorries driven by men who think the same as me. There is just one thing, Laudrup comes with us, or it is no deal. I'll tell you why. I've seen the way he works. I've got to know him; so, I trust him. I don't know you, so I don't trust you. Nothing personal, but that's the way it is".

Berg spoke.

"I can bring eight ocean-going fishing boats. The skippers know every inlet on the coast. They are not local men, so the Germans will not be able to take reprisals against the local people. Again I feel as this gentleman does, Laudrup is with us, or we'll free the boys without you."

As a career naval officer, Vali had become accustomed to absolute obedience. He looked at the civilians and saw as much determination and courage as any serviceman. Then glanced at Erebus, who nodded. The Commander smiled.

"Gentlemen, whatever you say, I agree with. Let's be honest the professional soldiers did not do much of a job in keeping the Germans out, did we? Now please tell me what you have in mind."

First, Berg explained how the eight boats could be put to sea immediately after the 'go' order was given. The only information needed was the embarkation harbour to calculate the time it would take to muster the fleet. Berg was totally confident as he finished with,

"Each vessel would be crewed by the owner/captain, who are all highly accomplished seamen. No crew means better security, and we can carry more men."

Moen got straight to the point. He needed the same information as Berg, Nothing more. Erebus had remained silent, then looked at Vali as he said in English.

"These Norwegians are tough aren't they? I'm beginning to become dangerously fond of them, especially Moen." The civilians demanded Norwegian be spoken. Erebus nodded his head.

"Gentlemen, I apologise." He continued.

"I must speak to our colleague alone." Both nodded and left the house.

"I've been told to make sure you don't take any risks. Especially the escape of the POWs." Bakken paused, then posed a question.

"How are you going to play this one, Erebus?"

"You heard those men. It doesn't leave either of us with much room for manoeuvre. Anyway, those orders were issued at HQ; things are different here."

Bakken spoke forcefully,

"Those orders were issued with your best interests at heart. We can't afford to lose you. We nearly caught the Scharnhorst, thanks to you."

Erebus changed the subject.

"I can look after myself. But you'd better keep a low profile. Is there anyone this far south who is likely to know you?" Bakken shrugged.

"It's unlikely my family is from Oslo." Bakken had accepted Erebus would be on the raid and moved on to other matters.

"Is there anything you need? We have much more compact radios. One might make life a bit easier." Erebus shook his head.

"No, I'm doing fine. Tell me, how are things in Britain?" Vali sighed.

"Things are tough. Shipping losses are very bad, and most cities are taking a pasting from the Luftwaffe" Then his face hardened.

"But everybody is willing to see it to the end." Erebus was forthright.

"We have to beat these bastards if the last thing we ever do, they really believe all this stuff about the master race and Hitler is stone mad." And then demanded.

"Have you any idea when the RAF will bomb the Bergen pens?" Vali explained.

"It will be early October. The weather controls everything. The RAF confirm a raid forty-eight hours ahead of take-off." Erebus commented.

"October! Well, that's something." He wondered out loud.

"How long can the men in that labour camp hold out under those conditions?" Vali was positive.

"They have more hope than six weeks ago. Now listen, you and I are to go to Oslo" Erebus looked up.

"Quisling?"

"Yes, Quisling".

Erebus suggested.

"Moen can take us. What else do we need?" Bakken answered.

"Nothing, just keep a low profile. My contacts will find and brief us." Bakken finished with.

"Oh, by the way, I am very impressed by the men you have found to work." Erebus nodded his appreciation.

Then both agents briefed Berg and Moen on the possible date for the raid and why nothing could be confirmed because of the weather.

"Right, I'll start planning." Erebus warned him and Moen.

"Security will always be a problem. Just one slip! That's all the Germans will need; they're not all stupid. So, tell no one yet."

Moen dropped Vali and Erebus on the outskirts of Oslo with the words.

"I'm staying with a mate about ten kilometres away. When do you want me to pick you up?" Before Vali could answer, Erebus said.

"Twenty-four hours from now." Vali's contact reported that Quisling was embedded heavily guarded by his own version of the Nazi Brownshirts. Assassination was impossible. Later, Vali asked.

"What do you want to do, stay here or go back North?" Erebus replied.
"There's nothing we can do here." Then surprised his comrade with,
"Why don't we find your family? At least you can see them."

Vali watched his mother and father. They looked older and careworn. His heart was breaking as he walked away. He consoled himself with the thought that to say hello may cost them their lives. Erebus was at his side and saw the pain in his eyes but remained silent. He suddenly thought of his parents. Then as if by fate, within eight hours, the signal came that the air raid had been confirmed. They left Oslo with excitement, all thoughts of Quisling forgotten. They were now concentrating on helping brave men, not killing a traitor.

— 11 —

Settling Down

Tom saw a set of long horns suspended at the centre of a crossbar, just as in the cowboy stories from his childhood. The trucks came to a halt. Buchanan stretched up an arm, and in a sweeping gesture, tore the horns down.

"No more Texas Long Horns. From now on, we breed Aberdeen Angus pure and cross cattle, and here's to all of us for making this great journey."

He jumped out of the truck, walked over to the pickup, and shook hands with Felix and Simon. Then turned and said.

"Welcome to the Double B, Tom Cork. This is your home for as long as you want it to be."

Felix and Simon were cheering, grins across their faces as wide as Tom had seen since he had met them a week and nearly a thousand miles ago. The trucks rolled through lush flat soft grazing land with a backdrop of magnificent hills and mountains. The sky was as blue as Tom had ever seen. They were heading for a canyon made up of hills which ringed a lake on three sides and a river that flowed past a large house with several smaller houses nearby. Vegetable patches and, what Tom took to be, orchards were on both sides of the big house. They continued past the houses to a large corral where there was a small herd of grazing dairy cows.

Tom jumped out of the truck as some children ran to Felix and Simon and leapt into their arms. They were followed by two women who embraced their husbands. The reunion lasted until both men shooed their families away and started to unload the precious cargo.

Buchanan opened the gates of two corrals as Tom cast a very careful eye over the cattle, and then they all watched as the cattle ran free, tasting and then rolling in the rich grass. Buchanan asked enthusiastically,

"They look in great shape - what you think of them?"

The Cork man answered calmly.

"Let's wait for a week and then see if they have settled."

Both men walked toward the Big House, as Buchanan said.

"Right, Tom, you can sleep in the house for the time being."

Consuela, the housekeeper greeted him with a lovely smile and a meal, during which Buchanan explained at the Double B when the sun rose, so did the ranch; at sundown, it slept. Tom learned the history of the ranch. Buchanan's father and grandfather were buried on the Double B with their wives; both marriages had produced only one son. He was the third generation of Buchanans on the land. The Double B was a five hundred thousand acre ranch which, in Texas, was not very big. Three hundred thousand acres of that land was rich and lush. The ranch had run a profit until Buchanan's father had turned some of the ranch to tillage to supply the demand for grain during the First World War. The crop failed due to a rare drought. Most of the existing herd was sold to pay the seed grain suppliers and bank. Soon after Buchanan's mother died of a burst appendix; within two weeks his father suffered a fatal heart attack. Some said brought on by grief and the debt hanging over him. Buchanan buried them without time to mourn and borrowed heavily to restock the ranch. It was at a cattle sale he'd met Felix and Simon. Both were experienced cattle hands, so Buchanan asked their former boss why he'd sacked them. Without shame, the dealer explained both men had mixed-race marriages, and he didn't like 'breed' kids. Buchanan went to the railway siding where the families were camped. Where he was told in no uncertain terms by the men they loved their families above anything. Buchanan was angry at the prejudice they had faced and offered them jobs and homes if they were willing to move their families to the Double B. That had been three years back, and he had never regretted the move for one minute. Buchanan suddenly became very serious.

"Tom, the reason I am telling you all this is because, as beautiful as this ranch is, it can get very lonely here. The winters are severe - maybe more than you've ever seen. At round up, we hire in men but they only stay long enough to earn their pay and then move on."

At this point, the housekeeper wished them both 'goodnight'. Buchanan continued,

"Tom, my wife walked out two years ago. I found her later in Houston, teaching at an elementary school. Don't get me wrong, Tom, she is a good woman, but when the children didn't come from our marriage, she realised that she needed more than just me and this ranch. Hell! - there is nothing for a woman to do here for four months of the year."

Then looking very tired, the big man said.

"It's time we hit the hay. I have a lot of catching up to do. Good night, Tom and once again, welcome to the Double B." Tom lay in bed, his mind racing, despite being exhausted.

Buchanan's frankness; had taken him unawares. The man was lonely here in his beautiful home. Suddenly, thoughts of his family, the farm and all he had left behind and lost brought pain like a punch in the stomach. Then quickly, the optimist in him came to the surface; things could be a lot worse. There was so much here to help him forget his heartbreak and move on with his life.

Suddenly he was being shaken; someone was yelling.

"Sun up, Tommy boy, there's work to be done."

Tom heard his father's voice, 'Come on Tommy boy, sleep is nothing but a rehearsal for being dead'. He went into the large kitchen, where Buchanan handed him a cup of coffee and the day began.

Milking the dairy cattle was the first job, then the Aberdeens checked. In no time came breakfast, a huge plate of steak and eggs with fried potatoes, all washed down with lashings of coffee. Having picked a horse, Felix gave him a basic lesson in riding. Soon he was at ease in the big American range saddle, astride his horse secretly named, 'Corkman'. He was offered a handgun and told it was never to be worn near the houses or children. Felix repeated the word, never. Ammunition was freely available. When out on the range Tom practised, soon becoming accurate with the Colt 45. He picked up the routine of the ranch and quickly concluded the round-up would need a lot more men.

At breakfast on Sunday morning, Buchanan said.

"Tom, do you remember I told you how I raised some investment from a man called Rawlings."

Tom asked.

"Would this man's son be the Marathon lawman?"

Buchanan replied, between gulps of coffee,

"Yep, that's the guy. Well, he'll be here in the next few days with his daughter." Cork recalled,

"Isn't she coming to stay at the ranch to cool off a bit?"

Buchanan confirmed.

"That's dead right, Tom. That's the only way I could get the money from Rawlings; she'll be here for the winter. Seemingly, she is a little wild."

With a mischievous smile, the young man enquired,

"Mr Buchanan, in Texas, what exactly does, 'a little wild' mean?"

His boss laughed out loud.

"Well, Tom boy, I guess we are about to find out."

The next question was slightly hesitant.

"We are not holding this girl here against her will, are we, Mr Buchanan?"

"Hell no, Tom. It's just that her daddy is a bit worried she might get herself into deeper trouble in Fort Stockton and embarrass the family even more."

Tom couldn't resist pointing out,

"The Rawlings family couldn't be any more embarrassed than by that bollix of a lawman, could they?"

The big man agreed loudly.

"Well, Tom, you're not wrong there. No, it seems this girl had a stand-up row with some bigwig in Fort Stockton. Everything happened in front of a reporter from a state-wide newspaper. The man she attacked represents an even bigger bigwig who doesn't appreciate publicity of any kind. Now there's all sorts of legal stuff being threatened. Charlie Rawlings loves his daughter; problem is, she is young and, to use his word, 'impulsive'. Anyway, we'll have to make her welcome. Is that OK with you Tom boy?"

The answer was immediate.

"No problem, Mr Buchanan."

Sunday was always a lighter day, workwise. Tom thought about this woman who was coming to the ranch - headstrong, impulsive – well, that was something he had in common with her. The rest of the day was spent on a long ride, just thinking about being enveloped by the beauty and silence of the Big Bend country. Tom considered how Buchanan had talked to him more in six weeks than Connor had in two years. 'But it takes two to talk Tommy boy', as Daddy would always say. Jesus! If they had talked more, things could have been so different. What was Connor doing now, and where? He was working. Tom was certain of that. The Irish always found work. And the Catholic Church always found them. A wry smile broke across Tom's face. Not here in Texas. Not once had he been asked his religion. Maybe he was lucky it was the British who were looking for him. If it was the Catholic Church, there would be no escape.

Thoughts of home set Tom thinking. Two days later, in Fort Stockton, Buchanan posted the ranches mail. Amongst it was a letter written by Tom addressed to Harry Boland asking for news of his family. On Monday afternoon, Buchanan announced.

"Tom, the Rawlings will be here for a night. Jessica Rawlings will stay in the Big House until deciding where to live on the ranch." Tom looked at him, and half laughing, said,

"Mr Buchanan, do you think she'll really settle here?"

Buchanan poked fun.

"Tom, you sound like you know about women?"

"I have a mother and grew up with two sisters; I think that gives me enough experience to make a call - don't you?" Tom fired back.

Then they heard a distant motor engine.

'Well, now we'll know what this lady is like', The Cork man whispered.

The vehicle stopped, and a tall large man got out, followed by a young woman. Buchanan shook hands with both. Felix took the bags, and as Tom went to help, he was introduced to Charlie Rawlings. While carrying the bags, the woman introduced herself.

"Hi, my name is Jessica Rawlings, and I'm here for the winter. Who are you?" At her room, he answered.

"My name is Tom Cork, and I work here, so I'll be here longer than just the winter, all being well. Now, I have work to do, so I'll see you later on."

Dinner was eaten in silence, apart from Buchanan asking Tom about the Aberdeens. It was obvious that father and daughter were not getting on. He answered as many times before, sensing that Buchanan just wanted to make conversation. The minute the meal was finished Tom said,

"Mr Buchanan, if you don't need me anymore, I'll go to my room. I have an early start in the morning."

Buchanan said,

"OK, Tom, I'll see you tomorrow."

Jessica Rawlings looked at Tom and demanded,

"Get lots of sleep. You'll need it as my prison guard. It's your job to make sure I don't escape."

Charlie Rawlings cut in.

"Jessie, you behave. I'm getting tired of you taking your anger out on everyone but the person who deserves it."

"And who is that?" she shouted. Rawlings looked at Buchanan and said,

"Bill, I'm sorry about this. I was hoping Jessica might show some respect for you, at least." Then turned to Tom, who spoke first.

"If you'll excuse me, I'll say good night to you all."

Jessica was about to shout at her father again as Tom left the room. He'd seen enough family rows to last him a lifetime. The girl's raised voice was clear until he walked out of earshot. Jessica demanded

"Tell me, who is to blame, daddy?"

Rawlings exploded.

"You are! This is entirely your fault, you silly little girl. You think you can break all the rules and daddy will get you out of trouble? Well, not this time."

Jessica shouted,

"All I did was to tell the truth about that land grabber. What's wrong with that, daddy?"

Buchanan stood up and moved toward the fireplace as Rawlings spoke.

"Bill, I'm sorry. This was never going to work. We'll go home in the morning. This is not your problem - it's mine. I'll apologise to Tom Cork in the morning." The big man replied with a question.

"Charlie, what is so terrible that you need Jessica out here? From what you told me, all she did was shout at this guy in public." Rawlings looked at his daughter.

"Tell him please, Jessie." Buchanan stood still and listened.

"Daddy, I am sorry, but I felt threatened when I went to confront him. He was surrounded by his cronies, so I took a gun and threatened to use it if he took the land off those people. Worse, I threatened him in front of witnesses - his witnesses." Buchanan spoke up.

"Hell, Jessica, this is Texas. Everybody has been threatened with a gun in this state at one time or another, with the exception of no one. Why are you so worried Charlie? We'll take care of this thing. Who is this guy anyway? If he's from Texas, I'm sure he'll listen to reason. Hell, it was only a few words."

Rawlings was silent for a minute then, as he sat down, said,

"It's more complicated than that, Bill. This man represents a very influential silent partner from Houston, and what Jessie did not only scared him, it made him lose face - in front of some of his backers." Jessica cut in.

"But he is stealing the Indians' land, isn't he, daddy? Yes or no?"

Charlie Rawlings looked at his daughter and spoke in plaintive terms.

"Let's be honest, honey; he's only doing what has been done repeatedly over the last hundred years. There's not one rancher who hasn't taken land from someone one way or another." Jessica exclaimed,

"So, you're a land grabber as well. Tell me, daddy, what do we do with the Indians when we have all finished grabbing all their land?"

Rawlings looked imploringly at Buchanan for help, who reluctantly obliged.

"I am not going to get caught up in family matters. Having said that, Jessica, you're welcome to stay here as long as you want. But I want you to consider this." The big man moved closer to Jessica, his voice now gentle.

"Jessica, ten thousand cultivated acres can feed a million people. It takes a million wild acres to sustain ten thousand nomads." Her face was now confused as he continued.

"This country was made by people who wanted or needed to change their way of life; the Indians were never asked about their lives. Everyone else just took it for granted the days of the nomadic hunter were long gone." Buchanan looked

at Charlie Rawlings, who nodded encouragement and continued.

"So are the days of pulling guns on people whether, in your opinion, they deserve it or not. Your daddy needs time to sort this out. He's on your side – as am I - but these people from the East have to be handled differently these days. Give him time. Now, how many Indians are we talking about Jessica, and how have they been wronged by this guy?"

Jessica explained how there were four families. In all, about twenty-five people. Buchanan asked,

"How many of them are men, Jessica?"

She answered enthusiastically.

"Five adults and some teenagers, but they have never been in trouble, and all are good with horses. The children are bright - I used to teach them until that greedy little man closed the school."

Rawlings joined in, his voice now kind.

"Jessie, it was an unofficial school. It would have been closed sooner or later."

She looked at her father, her voice plaintive.

"Yes, daddy, I know, but he did it so quickly and without care for what happened to the children."

Buchanan, having sat down, raised his hand as if to ask for silence.

"OK. How does this sound to you both? Charlie, you get the best price you can for the land. Jessica, the Indians can come and live here at the Double B. I need men who are good with stock, and we have plenty of houses for them to live in. We have some children here already, and you could teach school here if you wanted to. What do you think?"

Rawlings looked at his daughter, who glared at both of them for a while before saying,

"I'll believe it when I see it, but OK, I will go along with it."

Tom carried on as usual the next morning, unaware of what had been agreed the night before. That evening as he was stabling 'Corkman', he saw Jessica Rawlings and Felix's wife, Maria, tidying the empty houses.

The next morning Felix, Simon and Tom headed out to work. As they rode, Simon estimated there were between ten and fifteen thousand Texas Long Horns loose on the Double B. Felix confirmed Tom's earlier thoughts as they rode back to the ranch.

"It doesn't matter how many cattle there are out there. We need more men to bring them in. That's all there is to it." They went to bed facing another long, backbreaking day come sun up.

Jessica Rawlings was clearing the last house as Tom watched Buchanan and Charlie Rawlings driving their cars out of the ranch, followed by Simon in the pickup. Tom recalled yesterday's talk with Buchanan.

"Tom, I'll be away for a couple of days. Jessica will need a hand tomorrow. You and Felix stay here and help her with those houses. And before you ask, I have thought about the round-up. I think I've got it covered, so just look after the place till I get back."

Now Tom thought about Jessica. Their paths had crossed only enough for him to know she had moved into one of the unused houses. Occasionally eating with either Simon or Felix's family and was clearly adored by the families from the other houses. He knocked on the door, hoping she would be in a better mood than the last time they spoke.

"Good morning Tom; how are you? Come and have some coffee."

Cork was dumbstruck. This wasn't the woman he remembered. The sun had turned her hair almost blonde. It fell around her beautifully tanned face. She was about five foot four with a slim, shapely figure. Before him was a very beautiful young woman with a glorious smile called Jessica Rawlings?

Arranged inside the cottage were ornaments and flowers; Tom thought, 'only a woman can do this to a house. This is more than somewhere to live - this is a home'. Memories of his mother's always-welcoming house overwhelmed him. Suddenly, he was face to face with Jessica. She asked, handing him a mug of coffee,

"Tom, are you OK? You seemed miles away."

He didn't answer, just took his coffee and drank quickly, which was scalding hot, causing him to spit some back into the mug. They both laughed. Tom was grateful for the diversion as he was close to tears. They talked all day, but he could not remember one word afterwards. Tom didn't feel any sexual desire for her – he just felt good to be near someone gentle and warm. He had made friends since arriving on the Double B. But this was different. The last eight hours reminded him a woman brings out completely different feelings in a man. As evening came, she realised she had forgotten to prepare a meal for herself. Tom said.

"Come up to the house. Consuela always has more than enough to go round, and I think you've earned a little bit of being waited upon."

The meal passed quickly, and Tom felt confident enough to ask.

"How long are you going to be here on the ranch?"

She smiled,

"Tom, it will be much longer than I thought." His heart sped up as she explained Buchanan's idea for the Indians and how her father would help them. The Indians were now going to live at the Double B.

"So that explains the convoy," Tom said, then asked.

"How many people are we talking about, Jessica?"

When told, he let out a yell.

"So that's what he meant." Then fearing she might misunderstand Buchanan's motives, specifically the round-up, he continued.

"Mr Buchanan was talking about how the Double B needed new blood. I thought he was talking about bringing new stock, not people."

She laughed and said.

"Well, Thomas Cork, there is new blood coming in and soon. Now, where do you think we should build the school?

Tom relaxed as she took him by the hand onto the veranda and explained where the building should be. He didn't get a word in edgeways for the next half hour and couldn't have cared less. She was a person who cared about herself less than about other people. As the sun went down, Tom walked Jessica to her cottage, said goodnight and attempted to get some sleep as faces appeared. His mother's, then Connor's. Daddy's, his sisters' then, out of nowhere, Jessica's. The sun woke him, and he walked over to Jessica's cottage.

"Good morning, and what do we have to do today?"

She turned, gave him another winning smile and answered,

"Well, to be honest Tom, everything was finished yesterday." Tom feigned disappointment but was relieved. He needed time alone to think. He teased.

"Good, I can get on with some real work."

She laughed a reply.

"We still have to plan for the schoolhouse - don't forget Tom, will you?"

He lifted his hat. Then as he saddled his horse, Felix stood at the stable door.

"There's nothing more to do with the cottages. So what should we do today? Both laughed.

"I don't know about you, but I'm heading for the East Pasture - there are a few long horns to bring in. OK with you?" Felix's voice hid concern.

"That's a long ride for one man. I'll stay here and wait for the boss to get back; you never know. Yes, go ahead."

Tom nodded. Both men silently observed another ranch rule. The families always had a man on guard.

Tom headed out of the ranch and up toward the mountains looking forward to the solitude. He was inexperienced in handling the Texas Longhorn. So during the following few days, he rounded up eight to drive onto the ranch. Alone on the trail Jessica came to mind. Why he didn't know; they hardly knew each other. He felt nervously excited that such a lovely woman was part of his life and maybe, just maybe, he was part of hers.

Tom guessed it must be Friday as he shut the gate on the corral. The long horns had proved challenging, but he had learned a lot, using familiar landmarks to find the ranch. He was making for the Big House and supper when he heard a call and turned to see Buchanan and Jessica walking toward him,

"Tom, Jessica's been telling me about the schoolhouse she wants built. Well, we've just had a look in the old barn, and that will do fine for now, so don't worry about it. Ok?"

Jessica nodded toward Tom and then said,

"Goodnight gentlemen," and headed for her cottage. Buchanan asked,

"How are you, Tom? Felix said you had nothing to do, so you went out after cattle. Listen, Tom, I appreciate the effort you made, but the range can be a very dangerous place, and you don't know it yet. So don't go out on your own again until I say so. Do you hear me Tom?"

Tom nodded as Buchanan put his arm around him.

"Come on. Consuela kept some dinner for you, and it's good."

Tom wasn't sure whether he had been told off or whether Buchanan was genuinely worried about him. Along with Jessica's, this was the second show of affection he had been shown on the Double B in the last twenty-four hours. He went to bed that night twice as confused as the night before. The next morning Tom saw all five cottages were full. The Indian families had been settling in while he had been out on the range. After breakfast, Buchanan called him into the Big House.

"Tom, I need to talk to you. Sit down, will you?"

Buchanan explained why he brought the Indian families to the ranch. Once he'd met the men, it was clear they were experienced cattlemen and would solve the problems of the round-up. They had accepted the terms offered to them, which meant security and safety for their families. Jessica Rawlings would continue her school. Charlie Rawlings had got a good deal for the land. They would have money in the bank.

Buchanan went quiet for a minute and then said,

"Tom, the other thing I needed was a first-class foreman for this ranch and you come out of the blue all the way from Ireland - a man who knows cattle and horses. I didn't mean to bawl you out last night Tom. I wouldn't find another man like you if I waited till hell freezes over; that's why I want you to be careful. These Indians are good men. They know the ways of the range, the land and the mountains. Their ways are different from ours, and they are good ways. They have beliefs that go back before time as we know it. Listen and learn from them Tom, and with you in charge here, we can do really well now. It's all up to us, Tom - all up to us."

At that instant, Tom made his mind up to stay on at the Double B and make a new start with Bill Buchanan, the boys, the Indians and the Aberdeens. Jessica Rawlings was someone he could only dream about, and anyway, there was too much work to be done to pay any heed to his personal life. He shook Buchanan's hand and said,

"Mr Buchanan, I'll be here as long as you'll have me, and I'll do my best to take your advice and that of those who know better than me."

Buchanan looked at him and said,

"Tom, from now on, you call me Bill. Do you hear me?"

With that, a million memories flashed through his mind as his eyes filled with tears. He walked away from Buchanan, and the big man knew it was better to let him go.

Fighting Back

"**J**esus! It really is going to happen."

Moen's words were whispered with the reverence of a vow. Berg remained silent, but his eyes showed the excitement coursing through his veins.

"At last, we're going to really hurt the bastards," Moen, his voice louder, demanded, "Tell me again Laudrup. How many Lancaster bombers? Tell me again?"

"Two squadrons - a total of twenty-eight bombers will attack the Port of Bergen to destroy the U-boat pens."

Vali advised caution.

"Please remember gentlemen, the weather is the controlling factor in this operation but, as of now, the raid will take place on the Friday evening of the second week in October."

Erebus maintained the cautious vein.

"Right, from now on, everyone is told just what they need to know." Moen and Berg vigorously nodded in agreement. He continued,

"Moen, your lorries must gather no more than six hours driving time from Bergen." Berg's face was a study in concentration, as he heard.

"The trawlers are the same, six hours steaming from Hellebakken." Moen spoke for both men.

"Why six hours?"

"Six hours is the Lancaster's flight time from base to target, you will be signalled the minute the bombers take off." The entire night was spent checking every detail.

In England, Odin knew the operation must succeed to rebuild the trust of the occupied countries in the capability of the British armed forces and for morale in general.

Odin and the C in C Home Fleet were old shipmates, and he knew not to ask why when requested to provide two warships for unspecified duties by the spymaster. He confirmed one Norwegian Royal Navy warship and a ship from convoy escort duty would be deployed. Odin felt personal responsibility for the seaborne element of the rescue mission and unofficially requested permission to put to sea with the warships. The reply came in official terms. "Remain ashore!"

As Vali considered six hours steaming time from Hellebakken to the warships at sea, visions of conditions aboard overloaded trawlers in heavy seas became terrifyingly stark. He took refuge in silence and details of the raid. Security was an uncontrollable factor, he and Erebus constantly reminded themselves that they were working with civilians, and the least innocent remark could be fatal for all involved.

There was one more dangerous task. Sergeant Reilly, captive in Bergen port, had to be briefed. Erebus insisted he was the best equipped. Moen countered that materials were being delivered constantly and a lorry load of timber and his Todt uniform was good cover. Erebus raised an objection.

"My friend, you don't speak English." Vali spoke,

"I'll go in with him." It was agreed there was no other way. On the Thursday before the raid, Vali and Moen would brief Reilly. Moen finalised the decision exultantly.

"I'll get a load organised. Now there's no going back."

Erebus relaxed as Vali commented, then questioned.

"Over the last few weeks things have been getting worse for the people of this country. The Nazis are arresting Jews, Gypsies and even those who are reported as being, 'less than loyal.' I wonder just how much the people can take before they give up completely."

Erebus spoke defiantly.

"Don't worry about the people in this country - they fight in their own way." Bakken pressed,

"How do you know that? You're not Norwegian."

The defiance continued.

"You're not British, but you're certain they won't give in. What makes you more of an expert on them than I am on the Norwegians?" His comrade smiled.

"Touché!"

Moen and Vali drove into the pens spotted Reilly and pulled up beside him and his men. Moen yelled at the guard supervising the prisoners.

"Unload this lot, now." Then listened to the guard shout in broken English.

"Get bloody move on, lazy bastards! We teach you British bastards lesson when we go to London."

Moen added the man to his list as he called him over.

"Leave this lot to us. Go and have a coffee."

The guard, seeing he was outranked, walked away, saying,

"OK. You're in charge."

Reilly did not recognise Vali, then his face changed slightly as Moen approached and shouted in broken English.

"Round other side of lorry, now." Moen stood guard as Vali spoke.

"Next weekend, my friend. The raid is planned for the weekend, but we won't know for certain until the bombers take off. Have everybody ready to go from Friday onwards. Can you do that, Sergeant Reilly?"

Reilly, untying ropes, looked at Moen and then Vali with a glow in his eyes. "We'll be ready. Have no doubt about that. We'll be ready."

Moen started shouting as a German officer appeared and demanded.

"Where is the paperwork for this timber?" There was no paperwork; then inspiration came to Moen.

"I gave it to the other guard when I got here. Jesus, how much paperwork do you fucking lot want?"

The German looked at him with contempt, ignored Vali, and strutted away, saying something about Norwegian imbeciles. The lorry left. Moen smiled as he spoke to Vali.

"Next time I leave this place my lorry will not be empty."

The first week of October came to a close. The escort group was hove to at the Liverpool Buoy, waiting for a convoy to form. The days were becoming short - as were some of Loftus' sailors' tempers. The Captain was trying to find a way to lift morale. He was becoming increasingly convinced some senior officers in the Royal Navy had no experience of the pressures of modern warfare and certainly not those exerted by almost constant convoy escort duty. Then Loftus received a signal from the operations office in Liverpool requesting the release of a ship for special duties. The ship was to, with another warship, take station off the Norwegian Coast. Then on a given signal, make a dash into a fjord inside enemy waters. The order detailed that the ships would make contact with an inshore fishing fleet and transfer approximately one hundred and twenty escaping prisoners of war and return them to the UK. The captain thought the whole thing, though risky, was the chance he'd been looking for to lift morale.

Loftus decided that, as Larsen and Cork were experienced with Norwegian waters and covert operations, Snow Eagle was the best equipped for the job. He asked for the senior captain in the escort group to come aboard. All escort captains were ordered to ready their rowing crews to come aboard Snow Eagle at an hour's notice.

The captain of Snow Tiger was an Australian who, when war broke out, had been working in the London office of the family maritime insurance broking company in Sydney. His name was Warne, and he held the rank of Commander in the Royal Navy Volunteer Reserve. RNVR. He was also the senior officer in the escort group after the men he now faced.

"Captain Warne, as of now, you are in command of the escort group and the merchantmen which will remain on station until I return, or should Snow Eagle be lost, a senior officer is appointed to the command. For your information, there will be a total of fifty-one merchantmen in the convoy. Is there anything else you need to know from me?"

Warne looked up from his written orders, confirming what Loftus had said, and replied,

"Jesus Christ! Skipper. Where the bloody hell are you going?"

Loftus laughed inwardly at the way Australians always said what was on their minds.

"I, Captain Warne, am going to kick Gerry in the balls, and you will be just fine. Now let's get on with it."

"Aye, aye, sir."

Reilly briefed the group leaders as soon as darkness fell. The men would move to the perimeter wire during the nights of the weekend. If the raid did not happen on the first night, they would spend up to eight hours in freezing conditions but would have to put up with that. They would be back in the barracks before sun up. The guards were indolent, lazy bastards, for which Reilly was grateful as it allowed the prisoners to move around the camp at night with ease.

The lorries and the trawlers were in position at sundown on the Friday evening of the second weekend in October 1941. At eighteen hundred hours, twenty-eight Lancaster Bombers lifted off from two RAF bases. They set a course due east then turned north toward the North Sea and then the Norwegian Coast. The take-off was confirmed by SOE in a signal to Vali. The lorry fleet began to drive toward the town of Bergen. Erebus was in the lead lorry with Moen. The convoy was timed to arrive at the perimeter fence as the bombers attacked. Moen's mind was full of just how much could go wrong; then he cheered up as he pictured the German guards and their Norwegian allies getting a lethal surprise from the RAF. Moen also forgot the blind anger in him, knowing Laudrup - or whatever his name was - had given him a deeply satisfying way of working off that rage. The big man was feeling really good about what he was doing.

Erebus was worried about the prisoners who had suffered so much. If the RAF overshot the target, the bombs could kill them. The warships could meet foul weather; there may be U-boats and Germans E-boats patrolling the coast. He, too, worried in silence.

Berg and his smugglers were hove to just offshore of the village of Hellebakken, having made good speed from their home ports. Every captain knew the allied warships' coordinates. Now all they needed were some passengers.

Reilly and his men were ready to move to the fence once the air raid sirens sounded. Except for one group of escapees. It had been agreed for security reasons the Jewish prisoners knew nothing of the escape plan. As for the Germans, there had been a number of practice drills held in the past, but these were just for the guards - nobody cared about what happened to slave labour during an air raid.

The night was moonless as the men moved toward a fence at the northern end of the camp. The lightly reinforced timber fence had been ignored by the

Germans along with the track outside, which had been hardened by construction traffic just enough to support Moen's lorries. The air raid sirens sounded just after midnight, and the bombers delivered their lethal load. Reilly watched the camp descend into chaos and whispered.

"So far, so good."

Then he swore slightly louder.

"Jesus." As he watched the Jewish prisoners forced from their hut and rounded up by the guards and herded toward a lorry by the main gate. This unexpected development made rescue very difficult. His attention was drawn from the growing problem by lights approaching. Within minutes sections of the fence were torn away, and Erebus and Moen greeted him with handshakes. Reilly savoured the gesture of both men and, for the first time in months, felt like a free human being. He handed a large canvas sack to Erebus, who asked,

"What's all this, sergeant?"

Reilly replied,

"We took as many documents from the planning office as would go into that sack, sir. There may be something in them of interest to the boffins. Once the RAF has finished, the Germans will never know we've got them."

Erebus threw the sack into the cab of Moen's truck, thinking,

'This man has got to join us; he's a born gatherer'.

Reilly reported that all allied prisoners were present and then pointed toward the Jewish prisoners, now on a truck with a Todt driver and two guards. Then both watched as Moen, in his Todt uniform, demanded to know from the driver where the truck was going. The driver pointed to his ears to show he couldn't hear Moen as the second wave of Lancasters came in. Moen jumped in the cab and drove the truck to the fence. The Norwegian guards stepped down from the back of the lorry and were instantly attacked by the allied prisoners, who took swift and brutal revenge. Moen dealt with the driver in an equally robust fashion. The Jewish prisoners were overwhelmed as friendly faces appeared at the back of the lorry and offered words of encouragement.

Erebus had an idea the Jewish prisoners amongst the convoy might help rather than hinder the escape - he would soon find out. The POWs climbed into the trucks quickly as the fence had been levelled along a hundred-metre stretch. Reilly and the group leaders made sure all were loaded. Erebus and Moen climbed into the cab and moved to the head of the column. Private Mullen approached, with a German at bayonet point. He yelled,

"Do you remember my request, Sir?"

Erebus recognised the German sergeant who had made the POWs' lives miserable and made a decision.

"Carry on, Private Mullen."

Mullen nodded.

"Thank you, sir."

The German was on his knees, pleading for his life as Mullen drove the bayonet into his chest. The blood spurted from the man's mouth as the blade was twisted and withdrawn. Mullen removed the bayonet from the rifle and slit the German's throat. He turned to Erebus and said,

"I've waited a long time to do that, sir. I will never do it again, but he was a savage of the worst kind."

Before he could speak, Reilly's voice rang out.

"Jesus Tommy! Will ya come on! Let's get the fuck out of here."

With that, he saluted and disappeared into one of the trucks. Reilly's organisation had been first class; the escapees had taken less than five minutes to board the trucks. The pens were ablaze, and the sound of the Lancaster Bombers Rolls Royce Merlin engines began to fade as they headed for the open sea and safety.

The convoy, led by Moen, with the truck carrying the Jewish prisoners second, began the journey to Hellebakken. The escaping men watched total chaos as the fuel and ammunition exploded. Erebus had counted on the Germans taking some time to organise any sort of headcounts. They would certainly, as standard procedure after an air raid, set up checkpoints around Bergen. The convoy was stopped at one under the command of a Wehrmacht officer with Norwegian militiamen. Moen whispered to Laudrup.

"We're about four kilometres from Hellebakken". Erebus -dressed as a Wehrmacht officer - climbed down from the lead lorry and counted twenty heavily armed men; that many could be a problem. The POWs were weak and certainly unable for hard hand-to-hand fighting. He spoke first to the German officer telling about the Jewish prisoners. The officer, now animated, demanded to see them, completely forgetting to ask details about the source and destination of the convoy. When shown the men in the back of the second lead lorry, the Wehrmacht officer swore under his breath.

"Fucking Nazis, there's no need for this carry-on." Before he could express any more dissent, Erebus cut his throat. Then turned to see that Reilly, Mullen, and the stronger POWs, along with the lorry drivers, were out of the trucks, and attacking the Norwegian militia men with surprising forceful vigour. Erebus saw Moen personally account for three of his countrymen with a tree-felling axe. There was hatred and tears in his eyes as he hacked them to death, shouting,

"Filthy scum! You filthy murdering traitorous scum!"

The slaughter was over in less than two minutes with Private Mullen to the fore. Captured weapons were distributed as the convoy began to move. A light was spotted approaching from the direction of Hellebakken. The column and the oncoming vehicle came to a halt. Vali stepped out. He saw Erebus and climbed into the cab beside him.

"Everything in Hellebakken is ready."

As the sea village came into view, a sense of belief was growing amongst the prisoners that they might make it. For the regular soldiers who had been captive for so long, the defeat of the enemy guards and militiamen had been almost therapeutic. The natural leaders began to assert themselves and encouraged and cajoled the weaker men into believing they were on their way home.

As the convoy stopped in Hellebakken, the villagers came out with hot food and drinks and any warm clothes that could be spared from their sparse supplies for the bedraggled men. Vali felt an overwhelming surge of pride. Moen found himself fighting back the tears of admiration and pride.

Out of the darkness, the small flotilla closed to the water line, and the POWs eagerly climbed aboard. Some of the Jewish escapees were pleading to be allowed to go home to see their families. One man wailed,

"But without my family, why should I want to live?"

Erebus looked at them and felt utterly helpless; going home was out of the question. One name given in error to the enemy could mean death for so many. Vali took hold of a man's arm and, as gently as possible, began forcing him toward the water's edge. Moen followed, then Erebus and Reilly, Mullen and some of the stronger POWs were involved in a number of scuffles, but within minutes the small fleet was heading out to sea. Erebus was aboard Berg's boat, which took the lead in the perilous journey to the waiting allied warships eight hours away. He recalled some of the former prisoners on the seashore had shaken the truck driver's hands saying,

"Thanks for everything lads. Don't worry - we'll be back, we promise you, we'll be back."

The drivers shook hands all round and dispersed with feelings of pride in a job well done. Moen, in his lorry, wondered if he would ever see Laudrup again. Before boarding the trawler, Erebus had repeated the warning he had given him many times since the escape had been planned.

"Do not trust anyone in the resistance, and wait until I get back before you try anything against the Germans - sorry, the bastards."

Moen decided for once to do as he was told. This guy, Laudrup, had brought meaning into his life again, and he knew there was much more to do before the bastards were driven out of Norway.

The lead fishing boat cut into the icy water. The stars were soon lost in the cloud cover as light rain began to fall. The escapees were packed on and below the decks of the boats, which were in two 'single line ahead', formations, with Berg's boat in the lead. All of the skippers had agreed to follow Berg as it was agreed he was the most skilful and successful smuggler on the Norwegian Coast. He was, though not many would admit it, the best seaman as well. Navigating with a boat's compass Vali estimated the small fleet had about another two hours of darkness before they were visible from the sky. Erebus was standing next to Berg in the small wheelhouse when the fisherman spoke.

"Tell me, my friend, have you ever prayed for anything?"

Erebus shrugged.

"It's a long time since I prayed, let alone for anything specific. Why do you ask?"

Berg answered,

"Pray for cloud cover now, my friend, because if the Germans catch us out here, we are really for it, believe me."

Erebus looked around and saw cold, wet, hungry men; he motioned for Reilly to come to the wheelhouse. Having made his way through the crowded deck, the sergeant stood in front of Erebus.

"Jesus! Sir. You have no idea how good this feels. Whatever happens now, it was worth it all. If we die, we'll die free men, not under the lash from those bastards."

Berg picked up the curse and asked Erebus,

"Is he related to Moen?"

Erebus laughed and then explained the joke to Reilly.

Reilly said,

"Tell him please, sir; it would be an honour to be related to any of the men who helped us."

Erebus translated, and Berg, almost emotionally overwhelmed, mumbled.

"I need to look at the engine."

He was about to go below but not before taking Reilly's hands placing them on the wheel, and pointing dead ahead.

As the morning wore on, the weather worsened, which would keep the German air patrols grounded. It also caused the most appalling seasickness amongst some of the men already weak from captivity. The small fleet was struggling against heavy seas, and Vali, like all the ships' captains, was worried about the fuel levels.

The boats were loaded to danger level, and the engines were under real strain, shown by the heavy smoke from their exhaust pipes. Vali estimated they were running at least two to three hours late. Despite the danger of the signal being detected by enemy listening stations, he decided to signal the naval vessels with his position course and speed. Now all they could do was hope the warships got the signal and that the trawlers would survive the weather.

Snow Eagle departed the escort group and, four days later, rendezvoused with the Royal Norwegian Navy ship Norskall. Under the command of Loftus, the ships waited off the mouth of the, Buy Fjordnight giving cover and low cloud after sun up. Loftus was on station but sensed there was something wrong. He decided to brief Cork and Larsen,

"Gentlemen, this operation is being run by two officers, one codenamed Erebus, the other Vali. I need to know if either of these officers have experience in the transfer of men from ship to ship in heavy seas?"

Larsen replied,

"Vali is a Norwegian naval officer, but Erebus has no experience of sea warfare at all, sir."

Loftus remained silent and, seeing the weather worsen, could only imagine conditions aboard the trawlers. His voice forceful

"Right, we may need to go in and get them out.".

A signal was sent to the Norwegian captain. As the ships were steaming into the fjord, Snow Eagle's radio officer reported Vali's signal, which confirmed the trawlers were way behind schedule. The warships captains ordered 'full ahead both' and sped to rescue the struggling fleet.

As the sea became heavier and the cloud thicker, the temperature began to drop. Reilly, who was still at the wheel of Berg's boat, suddenly gave a shout.

"Sir, there's something ahead of us; I think it's coming in our direction. No – wait - there are two ships, and they're coming straight for us. What do we do if they are German, sir?"

Vali looked into the gloom and mist and saw the outline of two warships. Since they were nowhere near the designated pickup position, he had no idea which side the ships were on.

All lookouts on board the warships were at high alert as a shout went up from the starboard, forrard lookout.

"Vessel ahead, green ten. Just off the starboard bow."

Loftus ordered,

"Slow ahead, both."

The small ships began to appear through the cloud and rain. On the bridge of Snow Eagle, Cork said to Larsen,

"Can you hear cheering?"

Larsen had no time to answer as the order came from Loftus,

"Number One! All ship's boats to sea, and I want an officer in each boat." The reply was instant.

"Aye, aye, sir."

Pat and Larsen were aboard whalers, and soon the escapees were aboard and pulling hard for Snow Eagle and the Norskall. Pat now knew why Loftus had brought the extra sailors. The whalers were, with expert crews handling them, highly manoeuvrable, but the rowing was back-breaking work. After each pickup, the crews were relieved. Each fresh crew cut through the rough seas and kept the boats steady as the escapees were disembarking using the webbing laid along the sides of both warships. The Norwegian warship took aboard half of the men, and the entire operation took less than an hour. Then as the weather worsened, reducing the risk of being spotted by German air patrols, the fishing boats were refuelled. Captain Loftus invited all captains aboard Snow Eagle. In the wardroom, the gathering quickly became a party, as Berg caused uproar by offering to supply Snow Eagle with brandy if a regular pickup point and a reasonable price could be agreed. The ship's sick bay staff, with the help of countless volunteers not on watch, were checking the former prisoners of war for any serious illnesses or injuries. Loftus looked at the faces in the wardroom and acknowledged how he had changed since he had met these men under his command. Pat and Larsen joined the group, and there was a moment of silence as a tall man entered the wardroom. Then one of the fishing boat captains began to applaud and as the other captains recognised the man they joined in. Sergeant Reilly stood in the wardroom, somewhat embarrassed by the reaction of these brave men. As Erebus placed a drink in his hand, he saw how Reilly, even though he was in a make-shift uniform, stood straight-backed, maintaining his military bearing. Then a commanding voice was heard.

"Gentlemen, as much as we have enjoyed your company, we must get under-way. So, please board your vessels."

Erebus and Vali went to the radio cabin, where Larsen briefed them.

"Maiden Aunt says you can come home if you wish." He paused.

"If you want my opinion, you should - God knows you've earned some leave." Erebus thought for a moment,

"No, not yet. I can do more damage where I am. There is one thing you can do for me at home, please."

Having heard the request, he mused.

"Maiden Aunt will have to approve it. If he does, I'll do it."

Erebus handed over a soaked bag which Vali took with the words,

"What's this? Laundry?"

Erebus laughed as he explained the contents and where the bag had come from. Vali gave a low whistle and said,

"The analysts will have a ball. Sergeant Reilly is a bit special; I'll brief Maiden Aunt on him."

Erebus agreed,

"Perhaps you should."

Erebus reached the ships side to disembark and found Reilly waiting. As they shook hands the ex-prisoner simply said.

"Thank you, sir."

Then watched the man who had brought him freedom go over the side and, with Berg and the other fishermen, head into the stormy North Sea. On board Snow Eagle, Pat watched the man who had shot him leave. He and Larsen had greeted Erebus formally for security reasons. Captain Loftus noted the ship's crew were delighted with the escape and every minute of the action would be retold over and over again.

In the radio room of the SOE, Colonel Simpson-Coyle had ordered the radio operator to signal Vali to arrest Erebus and bring him to Britain, in chains if necessary. The radio officer looked astounded as Maiden Aunt cut in.

"Ignore that order and carry on, please."

He moved in front of Simpson-Coyle, saying,

"I am ordering you to leave this room now. Do you understand, Colonel?" Simpson-Coyle's eyes bulged as he almost shouted,

"There is a serious security breach, and Erebus is the key. I am ordering you to arrest him immediately."

The sight of two senior officers behaving in such a fashion was unusual even for the SOE. Davies was fully aware of the disturbing effect this could have upon the entire section but knew he was right.

"Colonel, you have no authority in operations or personnel here. Please leave the room and do it now. If you refuse, I will have you placed under arrest. Do you understand?"

Davies' demeanour left very little doubt in the mind of anyone that he meant exactly what he had said. Simpson-Coyle stormed out, and Davies said,

"I would ask all here present to forget what has just occurred. Ladies and Gentlemen, I am relying upon your utter confidentiality. Is that clearly understood?"

All answered,

"Yes, sir."

The operation had been successful, and all of the men were free. Vali had reported on Sergeant Reilly, and Davies had requested that the man see him before returning to his unit. Then Brigadier Davies went to his office and arranged a meeting with Odin. The agenda being the excellent Reilly and Simpson-Coyle.

Snow Eagle and Norskall headed at full speed for the open sea. Five days later, the escapees had been transferred to a Liverpool-bound merchantman, part of an inbound convoy. Although the operation had been classified as secret by the SOE, Loftus knew naval tradition would take over once the boat crews returned to their ships. He was correct; all first officers reported a marked improvement in morale when the story spread throughout the crews.

The weather that had nearly brought disaster now became an ally as the trawlers all made their home ports evading air and sea patrols. On board Berg's boat, Erebus was feeling very satisfied. The prisoners were on their way home, and he had made many trustworthy, reliable and brave contacts during the planning and execution of the escape. Berg was silent as the ship beat its way through heavy seas and felt deep contentment at the success of the mission and his growing bond with Laudrup. All of a sudden, he said.

"Why don't we catch something? The weather is easing; it should be much softer as we head inshore." Erebus just laughed as the boat slowed and, with his friend, threw a net over the side and did a day's fishing.

The debriefing of the Bergen raid ended with Maiden Aunt passing on the Prime Minister's congratulations to all involved. The team was stood down, and as the brigadier returned to his office, Vali approached him. Davies listened as the request from Erebus was outlined, then posed a question.

"Tell me, Commander, has Erebus changed much since he first came to us?" Bakken replied,

"Enormously, sir; he is a thoroughly brave and balanced man. He's even developed a sense of humour."

Davies gave a short laugh.

"I'll have to think about this one. Oh! The papers you boys got out of Bergen are providing some very interesting reading. Right, if there's nothing else, dismissed."

Davies sat and pondered on Erebus's request. God knows he had earned some reward for his extraordinary efforts in Norway. He would see to the matter personally - no need to bother Odin.

On a warm spring afternoon, The Lewis' were judging a village fete in aid of the war effort. Sir Geoffrey found the whole thing hugely frustrating. Despite, as his wife put it, some Herculean string-pulling, he had not secured an active service role.

Lady Lewis had just completed judging the rose competition when a young man approached her. He introduced himself; then suggested a cup of tea might be nice. Lady Felicity scanned the array of tents to locate her husband and saw him waving to her to go to him. She looked at the young man with perfect though slightly accented English and noted the immense tiredness behind his deep blue eyes. She had seen this same tiredness in so many people, and her thoughts went to her son Charles.

"Please lead the way."

She joined her husband, who was sitting with a man considerably older than her escort, but with the same weariness and a hint of sadness in his eyes. The men stood as Lady Lewis took a seat then her husband sat next to her. The visitors were opposite. Sir Geoffrey took his wife's hand.

"My Dear, these gentlemen have news of Charles."

Lady Felicity looked into the stranger's eyes, trying to discern if the news was good or bad. The elder man spoke.

"Good afternoon, Lady Lewis. May I apologise for this unusual introduction. However, once I have explained why we are here, I hope you will understand. I am Brigadier Davies, Brigade of Guards, and this is Commander Bakken of the Royal Norwegian Navy." Bakken bowed imperceptibly as Davies continued.

"Please forgive us if we forgo the usual courtesies, but our work is top secret and being here is highly irregular, so please remain as calm as possible."

Sir Geoffrey replied,

"My dear brigadier, I can assure you that my wife and I are masters of calmness under any circumstances. Now, what is it you have to tell us?" Then Lady Lewis spoke.

"Brigadier, will you please tell me of my son."

Sir Geoffrey leaned forward and whispered fiercely,

"Right man, out with it; what do have to say about our boy?"

Davies knew he had done the right thing.

"Well, first things first - he is in perfect health. As you are aware, he is part of an organisation which is secret in its existence and operations. Your son has been overseas for some time, where he is making an immense contribution to the war effort. I am his commanding officer, and Commander Bakken has been working with him in the theatre of operations. He asked that we come and see you, pass on his best wishes and tell you both that he is well. This request was granted because of his exceptional service."

He watched as Lady Lewis began to cry very quietly into a handkerchief provided by her husband. Sir Geoffrey, although attempting to comfort his wife, looked straight at both men, his face aglow with pride.

"I know you cannot tell us more. I appreciate the risk you have taken coming here, and for that, I thank you from the bottom of my heart. If you can, would you send him our love and tell him his home is waiting for him."

Lady Lewis looked up,

"I really do not know how to thank you; will you both please join us for dinner this evening?"

Bakken spoke.

"I am afraid that is impossible as we must return immediately, and I must stress that, as far as anyone is concerned, our having a cup of tea was a coincidence. Secrecy is everything in our operations. I will make contact with you if necessary, so please assume that no news is good news. I assure you, your son is a very brave and able soldier."

With that, both men stood up and walked away. Sir Geoffrey looked at his wife,

"Exceptional service, my dear! Did you hear those men? Exceptional service!" Felicity Lewis was shaking, and then she heard a voice call,

"Lady Lewis! It's time for the cake competition."

She looked at her husband.

"Come along, dear. We have to carry out some exceptional service."

That night in his study, Sir Geoffrey was about to open a bottle of Vintage Hennessey Cognac in celebration of the earlier news, then stopped as he almost prayed,

"I will open this when my boy comes home, and we will drink to his exceptional service together."

— 13 —

Lone Star State

Any suspicions amongst the newcomers to the Double B soon disappeared. The men were quickly involved in the first round-up of the year. The women mixed as the work to be done around the ranch house was shared out. Jessica set up her school, where the children mixed freely.

Out on the range, the Indians' experience with cattle soon became obvious. Mutual respect grew as, at night, the men shared stories of their people. Tom spoke of Ireland. Carlito and Chato told of the Apache. Felix and Simon of the Southern States. Tom learned from and appreciated the men's deep respect, understanding and knowledge of the Range, river, and mountains.

Tom was shown Cacti that held water, the shrubs and plants which were poisonous. How to survive on little water, and where to find that water. How to track mountain lions. Over the next two months, eighteen thousand head of beef was rounded up and divided. The cattle in season were covered by the bulls, and with the younger cattle, released into summer pasture. The rest was sent to meat processing plants.

As the round-up concluded, Tom sat with his boss on the veranda of the Big House. Buchanan had satisfaction in his voice.

"With the families here, we've handled the workload. We're getting a good name with meat plants, and the 'Bank' is a good bit happier. Tom, we gambled on the British cattle, and I think we are slowly winning." Tom remained silent as Jessica joined them and spoke of her students.

"I can only teach them so much; some will need more." Buchanan said,

"Jessie, we are a cattle ranch, not a college or charity. They can learn about cattle and horses, but that's about it. But we only have so many jobs for those who want to work here."

Tom joined in, trying to lighten her mood.

"Jessica, they all get a pretty good start, better than many in America or Europe."

She replied passionately,

"Tom, do you know how much prejudice these young people with Negro and Mexican parents will face when they leave here?"

Buchanan answered for him, his voice gentle but firm.

"Now, just one minute Jessie, Tom's right. We can only do so much. I'm sorry, but that's the way it is."

Jessica's mood seemed to bow to the facts, as stated and lighten.

"I know, Bill. Anyway, to be honest, all the boys want to do is be like Tommy and you; big-time cowboys." All three laughed then Buchanan spoke,

his voice and face suddenly serious.

"Jessica, how long do you mean to stay here? If my memory serves me right, you were only to be here for a winter, and that ended over a year ago."

Tom's heart raced; he desperately wanted her to stay. The woman's face was as open as her voice was clear.

"Bill, I can't think of anywhere else I'd rather be for the next few years. Do you mind if I stay?"

Buchanan's smile said everything.

"The place is yours, young lady, as long as you want."

Tom calmed down as his heart slowed. Now there was time to look to the future and see if Jessica might be a huge part of his future.

The next year was all work for the Double B Ranch hands, and as foreman, Tom learned Spanish surprisingly easily. The herd grew beyond anyone's wildest guess on the lush grass of the Big Bend country. Each day of the long, beautiful summer was spent surrounded by creation at its most bountiful. Tom decided he must find out if Jessica Rawlings was anything more than a dream. One evening he walked over to her cottage. A horse ride was suggested and eagerly accepted. The rides took up each weekend. Then began earlier and lasted longer until one night, they decided to camp out under the moonlight. Tom told Jessica all about Ireland and West Cork, about how his father had taught him about cattle. He never mentioned Connor or the Bagots.

Jessica told of the Rawlings family history. She knew her grandparents had come from England. Her father had confirmed this but said nothing else. There was just her and her brother, whom her mother had died giving birth to. Tom was silent as Jessica told him about how before she left for college, she asked her dad if he was lonely and why he never married again. Her eyes filled with tears as she repeated his answer.

"Jessica, where would I find someone like your mother and honey, there is only so much pain a man can bear."

He put his arm around her, and they gently kissed. She said,

"Tom, how long are you going to stay here?"

He had been dreading the question but said what was in his heart.

"Jessie, if you want me to, I'll stay here forever, but only if you will marry me."

She threw her arms around his neck.

"Yes, Tom, I will marry you. This is the place for us Tom, here on the Double B."

At that precise moment, a rattlesnake slid from under a stone, startling one of the horses. Tom drew his Colt 45 and killed the snake instantly. Jessica was exultant.

"Well, that's one way to celebrate becoming engaged, and, I guess, in Texas, it's as good as any."

They laughed and huddled together against the increasing cold. There was another rustle in the bushes near the river bank, and out of the darkness rode Buchanan. The big man dismounted and smiled.

"So this is where you young'uns have been coming. Can't say I blame you. It is surely beautiful. I heard a gunshot. Everybody OK?"

Jessica replied,

"Tommy did two wonderful things tonight. He shot a rattlesnake as if he was born in Texas, and he asked me to marry him."

Buchanan sat down beside them and remained silent for some time. He then put his arm around Jessica and then Tom.

"Hell, that's just great - killing the rattler and you both getting engaged. Just one thing, how do you both think your father is going to take the news? Tom, in Texas, it's customary for a young man to ask his intended's father for her hand in marriage."

The couple looked at a loss for words. All Buchanan could see was that the couple were deeply in love and carried on.

"As it happens, your father sent word that he's coming out to the ranch tomorrow night to talk some business. Couldn't have worked out better, could it, Tom?"

That night, all three slept under the Texan sky, and, despite what having to face Mr Rawlings might bring, Tom slept soundly. They were back at the Double B before Charlie Rawlings arrived.

Buchanan was delighted about the engagement. But decided not to tell Jessica or Tom that of an earlier conversation with Charlie Rawlings, who had asked him if there was any chance of his daughter marrying Tom. A man he respected and liked and viewed as having helped the Double B grow into one of the most successful ranches in Texas.

Rawlings was met in the Big House by his daughter, and then Tom and Buchanan joined them. The big man made an excuse to take Jessica out to the veranda. Less than five minutes later, Charlie Rawlings and Tom came out. Rawlings embraced his daughter and exultantly turned to Buchanan,

"Bill, we've done many things together in our lives, most of them well, a few might have been better. But bringing these two young people together is, without doubt, the best of all. Will you do me the honour of allowing my daughter to marry her young man on the Double B?"

Buchanan stood up to his full height, put his arms around Jessica and Tom, and demanded.

"Now, where else would they get married but here?"

Harry Boland, the member for West Cork, received Tom's letter, which asked one question. 'Can you please tell me of my family and my home?' He sat down and began to write to the young man burned in his memory from the night in Clonakilty with Michael Collins in 1916 and the disastrous events after that. Every word was written with caution and genuine concern. Boland had long since stopped believing in God, but he prayed that this young man would not be alone when he read the letter. Boland would not risk anyone knowing the whereabouts of young Tom Cork. The murder of the Bagots was still raw in many people's memories, as were many other acts of madness that had taken place in the name of the Crown and Irish freedom. Cork was better out of it. The letter would be posted from a town in England.

The planning for the wedding was in full swing. Tom was glad to be riding out for a day's work. Buchanan called him.

"There's a letter for you, Tom." Then paused,

"Is it from home?" Tom replied,

"Bill, this is my home." Buchanan smiling said.

"Take your time and read your letter."

Tom did so, and Buchanan watched as the colour drained from his young friend's face. Tom gave a low guttural groan and shouted.

"No!"

He threw the letter away, scrambled onto his horse and raced out of the ranch. Buchanan picked up the crumpled paper and read of the death of Tom's mother, now buried in Leitrim. Of his brother now in England, returning only to bury their mother. The family farm had been sold. Then, a family called Bagot had left Dunmanway forever. There was some news about Tom's married sisters' families; he had three nephews, and two nieces, one of the boys was named for him, the second for his father, the third boy was called Connor. The writer went on to describe how Ireland was in the grip of a seemingly endless terrible civil war. Finally, there was no way of knowing when, if at all, he could come home.

Buchanan called the Indians and explained some of the letter, then asked them to trail Tom. Then found Jessica; as he handed her the letter, the concern on his face convinced her that she must read it.

Carlito and Chato had come to detest all white men, but when Tom told them of Ireland and the British, they felt something in common with him but sensed right now he must be alone. The Indians watched from a distance, as for two days, the men rode. Tom did not eat or sleep and stopped only to rest his horse. Finally, in the middle pasture, he dismounted and collapsed. The Indians lit a fire, wrapped him in a blanket and then they slept. Tom woke some hours later and saw them watching. Chato said,

"There is much that causes you pain. When the Apache has pain, he rides to the high country to be near his ancestors, the wise ones."

Carlito announced.

"Now the healing begins." Then they started riding again.

The men rode on for two more days up into the mountains. They camped in the mouth of a cave. Tom had never been as high before; the air seemed thinner. His laboured breath was mist as he gathered firewood. The Indians watched him sit down, and the tears came. At first, slowly, then uncontrollably. He cried for his mother and father. His tears flowed for Connor and his sisters, for the Bagots. He cried for Ireland, the lost years. All the anger and sorrow inside, the frustration, the, the self-loathing came out, and he wailed to the moon that shone above him. Then exhaustion brought sleep. For how long, Tom did not know. When he woke, the Indians once again were watching over him. He stood up saying.

"Thank you, my dear friends; now let's go home."

As they rode down the mountain, Tommy realised how badly he stank and, at one of the mountain streams, stripped off and washed himself from head to toe. Chato said as he handed Tom a change of clothes.

"Thank the elders for that, Tom; you stank worse than the cattle in heat,"

Carlito's face broke into a wide grin, and Tom began to smile. The ride down the mountain seemed shorter, and it was not long before the Big House appeared in the distance. Tom made the decision to tell Jessica and the people in his life what had happened in Ireland; otherwise, he would never have peace. What Jessica and his friends did after that was out of his hands. As they neared the ranch, Chato rode ahead and spoke to Buchanan. Tom got off his horse and said to the big man,

"Bill, I need to talk to you."

Buchanan answered bluntly.

"Son, you need to talk to your woman first."

As Tom told Jessica of Ireland, his eyes began filling with tears. Seated and calm, she listened, then as he described the shooting of the Bagots, her face filled with horror as she stood up.

"Tom, are you telling me you killed two human beings?"

His voice trembled with fear.

"Yes, I believed I was fighting for freedom. I was young and stupid."

Jessica demanded.

"Why didn't you tell me before I fell in love with you?"

Almost pleading, Tom answered.

"Jessica, I was escaping from the British. I never thought in my wildest dreams I would find a home and the people who have become my family. If you don't marry me, you stay here – I'll move on." Jessica sat down next to him and, in a quiet but firm voice, announced,

"This is where we belong, my wild Irishman until we decide otherwise. Just us, Tom, nobody else. Of course, I'll marry you. But listen up; if you ever keep secrets from me again I'll shoot you myself."

She kissed him long and hard, forcing her tongue into his mouth. He responded, his hand gently cupping her breast. She opened her blouse and guided his eager lips to her nipple, which he kissed with a tenderness that surprised her. She took his other hand and placed it between her legs and then found his erect penis with her hand and said,

"Tom, we have so much to live for, so let's get married and have lots of children."

There was silence; then Tom asked.

"About the killings? I know now it was wrong."

She replied,

"Thomas Cork, I am a teacher, and when I began to feel something for you, I did some research on Ireland. Now I know what you did, I think I understand why. As for your brother, well, that's between you and him. We'll tell my father the whole story together."

Tom told Buchanan and Jessica's father the story of his life from 1916. British rule, supported by Irish Protestants. about Connor and the IRB, the hidden guns and the Bagots' deaths. He ended with,

"Bill, when I met you, I had just escaped from Ireland." Buchanan replied.

"Tom, a man has to fight for what he believes in, and if someone wants to pay a price for hurting loved ones, so be it. Son, I think you have just about paid that price and more. Your momma's in heaven, and your brother's gone from your life - maybe forever. Whatever happened in the past, this is your home and will be until you tell me otherwise."

Charlie Rawlings stood and asked his daughter,

"Jessica, is your mind made up?"

She responded forcefully.

"Yes, daddy, completely."

Rawlings turned to his future son-in-law.

"Tommy, less than eighty years ago in Texas, men had to fight for freedom at a place called the Alamo. What you did was become part of the fight for freedom in Ireland. People have been fighting for freedom since history began." He paused and put his arm around Jessica.

"Now listen, you can't go on blaming yourself forever. What you can do is marry my beautiful daughter. Do you hear me?" Tommy said,

"Yes, I hear, but there is something else." Charlie Rawlings nodded.

"Go ahead." Tom explained,

"There might be an arrest warrant out for me from the authorities in Ireland."

Rawlings was silent for a minute,

"Tom, you leave that to me. I'll see if Jim Cosgrave can help us."

Tom recalled the Sherriff, who was Jessica's brother's boss and then suddenly felt exhausted. Jessica saw this and ordered.

"Tom, my cabin and sleep for you." Which he did for twenty-four hours and the next day went to work as usual.

Before the wedding planning was finished, Jessica asked her fiancé.

"Tom, maybe we should wait a little before getting married. In mourning for your mother." His reply was instant.

"Jessie, my mother would have said, 'you go ahead and marry the woman you love.'" Then within a week, Charlie Rawlings told Tom discreet enquiries had confirmed there was no warrant with his name.

Tom and Jessie were married on the ranch they had made their home. The guests were the people on the Double B and all of Charlie Rawlings' and Buchanan's friends from Marathon and Fort Stockton. The celebrations lasted long after the happy couple retired to Jessica's cottage. Their lovemaking was easy and immensely fulfilling. Jessica held her husband tightly, and the night seemed to fly as the couple were brought closer together by the act of love. The sun shone in Tom's eyes as if in a dream when he woke to feel his wife beside him the next morning. The bed was warm and their bodies were entwined as Jessica slowly began to wake up. He looked into her eyes.

"Jesus! I love you, Jessica Cork."

There was a round of applause as the couple approached the veranda of the Big House, where breakfast was being served to at least twenty people. Jessica was sure she knew most of them and then saw the man she had threatened. He stood up, smiled and laughed, putting his hands up as if being held at gunpoint. Jessica was uncertain, but her father came to the rescue.

"Jessica Cork, meet Mr Elmer Riddle of Fort Stockton and Marathon."

Jessica introduced her husband, who shook hands with the man who was, in a way, responsible for bringing them together. He spoke.

"Mrs Cork, your father and I have become friends over the last year, and I am delighted to be at your wedding. I am from the East, but the gentleman I represent is from Houston, and he would like to meet you both."

With that, a man stood up and introduced himself.

"My name is Holman Hundes, and I am also delighted to be here for this celebration. When Elmer came back to Houston and said that you had come at him with a gun, all I could do was laugh. I told him, 'Welcome to Texas.' Mr and Mrs Cork, your father and Bill Buchanan, along with the people I bought the property from, have shares in the Hundes Tool Company. I intend to expand my company by building an engineering works on that site. Please accept some shares of the company as a wedding present with my best wishes."

The celebrations carried on as the guests gradually left the ranch. The newlyweds couldn't wait to be alone, and they nearly tore each other's clothes off as the feelings of love and excitement overwhelmed them. Their sex was passionate but more controlled as they began enjoying the freedom of being naked in each other's arms.

Within eight weeks of being married, Jessica felt a change in her body, and after confirmation from a doctor told her husband she was pregnant. The couple waited a further week before telling Charlie Rawlings and Buchanan.

Both men immediately decided to build a house for the young couple without asking the parents-to-be their opinion. The house would have five bedrooms on the edge of the lake that Jessica and Tom loved so much.

When informed of the plan, Tom refused point blank. Buchanan told him straight. This was their first child, and they should take all the help they could get. He then gently reminded Tom how Jessica's mother died, and maybe his wife and father-in-law were terrified of what might happen. The big man finished with.

"You have family now and are going to be very busy working to keep them."

Tom never left his wife's side for more than eight hours for the next eight months as Jessica experienced morning sickness and mood changes that baffled her husband completely.

The boy came into the world in the new hospital in Fort Stockton, and then mother, father and son moved into the Lake House, as it became known. Buchanan and Charlie Rawlings celebrated with the whole of the 'Family', as the people who settled on ranch called themselves. The boy weighed seven pounds eight ounces which, according to the hospital, was above average. Grandfather Rawlings, utterly delighted, quietly purchased a thousand shares of the Hundes tool Company, which would be given to the boy on his eighteenth birthday.

Once Jessica had regained her strength she asked her husband to make the first decision of the boy's life.

"Tom, what are we going to call our son?"

His father, who still couldn't take his eyes off his son, replied with a plea.

"Honey, could we name him after my father? His name was William."

"OK, that's settled. We'll name him for your father and mine."

She picked up her son and said,

"Good morning to you, William Charles Cork." Jessica and Tom soon became accustomed to the child being the centre of their lives

They told the boy's grandfather and then Buchanan, who was asked to be godfather, a role he clearly intended to take very seriously, picking out the finest pony on the ranch for his godson. Charlie Rawlings took great delight in asking Buchanan.

"Bill, how is a six-week-old lad supposed to know how to ride a pony?" Buchanan laughed at himself and with Rawlings as he answered,

"How? - because he's from Texas, that's how."

William's christening was held in a relaxed atmosphere at the Lake House. Afterwards, Buchanan - the boy's godfather - and his Grandfather, Charlie Rawlings were sitting on the veranda of the big house with large bourbons in their hands. Charlie looked around him with a guilty glance and said,

"Bill, I watched this morning as Jessica was changing my grandson's diaper. I tell you Bill, my grandson and your godson is hung like an Aberdeen Angus." Having checked again to make sure that no one could hear them, Buchanan raised his glass and said,

"Hell, Charlie, what do you expect? He's from Texas."

Both men began to giggle and then roared with joyous laughter until they very nearly cried. In the Lake House, the baby was asleep, and Jessica and Tom had gone to bed. They heard the men laughing, hugged each other and went to sleep.

The passing years saw the Double B grow in prosperity. The cattle industry experienced sustained expansion helped by a worldwide fragile peace which allowed trade to grow. Tom and Jessica had another boy, Patrick, five years after Bill and then a daughter, Mary, three years later.

Jessica was teaching at the ranch school, where the number of children increased yearly. Charlie Rawlings spent every weekend on the ranch and was, by his own estimation, the luckiest and happiest man in Texas and, therefore, the whole world.

One Sunday afternoon, after lunch with the Cork family, as they sat on the veranda of the Big House, Charlie looked at Buchanan and said,

"Bill, I was in Houston recently and called in to see your wife. She looked well Bill."

Buchanan looked at his old friend,

"She looks well, you say? She has that fine auburn hair?"

Rawlings nodded and continued.

"She was asking me all about you and the ranch. I told her about the way things are, how much life there is here now. She kept asking me about you; every second question was about you."

Buchanan said,

"What is she doing now? Is she still teaching?"

Rawlings nodded his head,

"Bill, go to Houston. Say hello, talk to her. At least do that."

The next day Buchanan took his car and headed out of the ranch without a word. Two days later, he returned with a beautiful woman he introduced to Tom and Jessica as his wife, Catherine. She began to teach in the school, and within two weeks, she came to his bedroom and took her husband in her arms and deep inside her body. The next morning, Catherine Buchanan moved back into her Big House, and they became man and wife once more. Buchanan's world changed that day, and his beautiful, intelligent wife fell in love with the Double B all over again. She had always been as deeply in love with Buchanan as he was with her.

William, his brother Patrick and sister Mary grew to be healthy and happy. The 'Great Depression' came almost overnight following the Wall Street crash. The ranch, thanks to astute negotiation of contracts with the US Government and the US Army by Buchanan and Tom Cork, continued to flourish.

Unknown to the people of the Double B, one of the wedding guests, Holman Hundes, had died in 1924. His son had taken over the business at twenty-one years of age. Hundes Junior, a solitary man, lived in New York and had complete control of the companies he was building. He intended to gain a similar position in those inherited from his late father. When told that a number of shares were held by the Corks, Hundes instructed Riddle to bring the shareholders to New York immediately, all expenses paid.

On the tenth anniversary of their wedding, Jessica and Tom Cork visited the great city. From the hotel, Tom looked out over the vast metropolis and reflected on his life. The Cork family was relatively wealthy and enjoyed a very comfortable standard of living compared to many people in America, let alone Ireland. Out of the blue, he wondered what kind of life Connor had. Jessica brought him out of his thoughts, reminding him,

"We have to see Mr Hundes in half an hour. Come on, Tom."

Once in Mr Hundes office, the meeting did not last long. He was willing to pay a very high price to get the shares. Jessica and Tom Cork left New York wealthy people. Charlie Rawlings was also approached, and he sold both his and his grandson's shares. A substantial amount of money was deposited in Rawlings Bank in Marathon, Texas, to the account of William Charles Cork.

Buchanan and Catherine were very happily settled. He was running the ranch he dreamed of all his life, and she was the full-time teacher of fifty pupils from the families on the Double B. Amongst the children Catherine was teaching were the Corks. She came to see Jessica one day after school, and as they sat and talked, she said,

"Jessica, we may have a problem with William."

Jessica looked startled.

"What do you mean by 'a problem', Catherine?"

Catherine raised her hand.

"Forgive me. I put that very badly. When I said, 'a problem', I meant that he is far too clever for our school. I think you and Tom should consider moving him to a grammar school in Marathon."

Jessica told Tom of Catherine's suggestion, and he agreed. That evening there was a conference between the Corks and their eldest son. His father began.

"Bill, you'll need a good education if you want to run the Ranch." His mother pointed out.

"The school is in Marathon, and you can stay with your grandpa from Sunday to Thursday and come home on Friday afternoon after school. How does that sound?" Bill was silent as he considered that Marathon was only two hours away and life at grandpas.

"Ok, Mum, Dad, I'll give it a go."

The most disappointed man on the ranch was Buchanan, who was teaching the children to ride after school, and Bill was his best horseman.

William Charles Cork entered the Marathon Grammar School for Boys in the winter term of 1930. Having grown up around cattle, Bill was able for the horseplay of his classmates. Rumours soon spread that his family were part owners of a large ranch in Texas, and the invites from classmates' parents to tea or supper came quickly.

Working on the ranch made Bill strong and fit, which helped in his selection for the school football team. As a solidly built young man with a good turn of speed, he excelled as a running back. Those on the field who poked fun at the country cowboy were the recipients of a bone-shaking tackle. Off the pitch, any derisory comments were answered with comments such as.

"Next time you want some real steak, see me," Bill Cork was growing up a Texan and an American.

Travelling state-wide with the football team, Bill saw Mexicans, Indians Negroes, all living in near poverty. Which provoked him to question Charlie Rawlings, why? His grandpa explained as best he could but frankly felt he was not qualified to answer.

When at home, similar questions were put to his parents. Who were pleased their son felt strongly enough to ask. His father remembered some of Buchanan's words.

"I don't like it, but there's nothing I can do about it for now."

Then on a range ride, Bill asked Buchanan. He expanded upon what he'd said to Bill's father years before.

"Son, Texas won its freedom from a Mexican dictator, Santa Anna, by fighting. The men who fought were not perfect, but they did get a hell of a lot right and good. No matter wherever you go never forget, you are a Texan first and foremost." The big man was silent for a while, then continued.

"Billy, your father came here a man alone. I don't know what made us meet up, but we have done our best to see that all around us have been treated fairly. At the moment, there are people in power who don't want change. They are in the majority for now, but that will change with your generation and those that come after you. That's democracy."

As they rode on, Buchanan looked around him and said,

"Billy, this is one of the most beautiful places on God's earth. The whole world should be able to come and see and enjoy it, just as we can."

Jessica and Tom Cork were content with their lives. Their second boy, Charles, was like his elder brother in temperament but clearly loved ranching. Mary Cork was growing into a fine young woman. Tom and Jessica silently dreaded the day when they would go away to school. Then they looked at Bill's academic report. He averaged 'A' and loved all sports, and was growing up as an outgoing rounded young man. Both accepted their children going away to school was a price to be paid for living on the Double B.

Life on the ranch moved on. Buchanan was not getting 'any younger' to use his own term, and he and Catherine were quietly preparing for their elder years together. They had spent too long separated. Tom and Jessica had decided they would not leave the Double B. There was a problem, it was home, but the only part they owned was where the Lake House stood. They decided to approach the Buchanans. The couple listened in growing amazement as Tom explained his and Jessica's intention. Then the big man demanded.

"Do you really know me that little after all these years?"

Jessica was about to point out the exact number of years; Tom shot her a look, signalling that silence was the best policy. Buchanan went to his desk in what had always been called the office and unlocked a drawer. He returned with a large envelope, and as he handed it to Tom. Catherine said,

"Please read that, both of you."

It took the Corks about five minutes to read and digest what was the last will and testament of William Campbell Buchanan, otherwise known as, 'Buchanan'. Tom stood up and said.

"I don't know what to say, Bill."

Buchanan said,

"Well, I'll say it for me and my wife. We've talked it over, Catherine and me, and there is no way we would have anyone else on this land except you and your family. Hell, Tom, Jessica, your children were born here - on the land by the lake. You're the only family I've ever known. When I met you, I was just another cattleman trying to survive, but now we're more than comfortable, Cathy and me, and that is, in a big way, due to the both of you. To you, Tom, for years of backbreaking work with me to build this place up, and to you, Jessie, for bringing life to this place. Not alone your own children, but the other families who've settled here. Tom, I've never seen anything as beautiful as the land around here, and it needs to be looked after by people who love it. There it is in black and white; the Double B is left to both of you when we're gone."

With that, he and Catherine stood up and went to bed.

When Jessica and Tom got back to the Lake House, they sat in silence for some time until Jessica said,

"Well, that solves that problem."

"What problem is that, Jessie?" Tom asked with disbelief in his voice.

"Where we're going to live in our old age," she answered.

"Right," said Tom, and they went to bed. For some reason, that night, they felt completely at ease and, turning to each other without any words, began to undress. They made love through the night as if they were twenty-one again and enjoyed every second. Finally, after some blissful hours, they slept soundly.

– 14 –
The Aggies

In 1939, The British Petroleum Company BP was one of the largest companies in the world, with massive interests in the strategically vital oil exploration and production industry. Petrochemical Engineering was an integral part of the industry, and the company was offering degree scholarships places at Oxford to exceptional students worldwide who, when qualified, would join BP. Bill Cork's graduation marks at Marathon Grammar school placed him in this category, and he received a formal offer from the British company. He was also offered a place at Texas Agricultural and Mechanical College, or A&M. Bill faced a dilemma; both colleges were excellent as he explained to his immensely proud parents. The news put Tom Cork in a difficult situation. He viewed British Petroleum as a bastion of the British Empire which had inflicted so much pain on his country. If he tried to influence Bill too much, he could face uncomfortable questions. He decided to stay silent as his son made his decision.

Bill chose Texas A&M because of the worsening political situation in Europe, and he would miss the Double B too much.

Bill threw himself into college life, joining numerous student groups. One, in particular, took his interest. The Reserve Army Officer Corp-ROTC, Engineer Platoon. His parents and the Buchanan listened eagerly as he told them about being an 'Aggie', the nickname for all A&M students. Catherine Buchanan noticed Bill talked more about the ROTC than other groups. How the 'Aggies' were immensely proud of the contribution made by the ROTC to the US armed forces. Catherine felt that perhaps Jessie and Tom were underestimating Bill's commitment to the ROTC.

Texas A&M had found oil on its land, and the money earned enabled the college to grant scholarships to students from less affluent backgrounds. Meeting these people reinforced Bill's views on two things. Life was not perfect in Texas, and how lucky he was to be raised on the Double B. 'Aggie' Bill Cork was becoming a man who believed in equal opportunities.

In his second year, Bill met a young woman studying Journalism and European history at Lubbock College. As they became friends. Mandy Bruce and Bill talked about their families. Mandy was intrigued by Thomas Cork's Irish background and asked.

"Bill, would you mind asking your dad some questions about Ireland for me?"

Bill wanted his family to meet her and suggested.

"Come to the ranch for a few days and ask him yourself," then added quickly,
"I think he'll talk to you, and I want to show you the beautiful land where I live." Mandy, a little hesitant, replied.

"I'd have to ask my parents" Her parents were delighted.

Catherine Buchanan was always up to date on current affairs. The main topic was the war in Europe. One evening on the Big House veranda she spoke.

"Bill, I think America is going to be in the war very soon, maybe around Christmas. Something fearsome is going to happen."

Buchanan's voice conveyed his concern.

"Honey, I hope to God you're wrong." His wife agreed.

"God! So do I, Bill. Some of our beautiful family will have to go to war and won't come back."

Mandy was introduced to the Cork family. She soon felt welcomed, not judged. After lunch, Bill saddled horses and explained the ride on the range would be short as sundown brought bitter cold. She quickly understood why Bill came home so often; the range was stunning. Dinner was at the Big House. She then asked Tom if he would discuss the Irish War of Independence. Tom smiled.

"Mandy, it was a long time ago. I'll tell you as much as I can remember." For a student of contemporary history, meeting someone who had lived through a war was worth a semester of lectures. This man was living Irish history. As he talked, Mandy listened to a man profoundly committed to his family and ranch. Mandy began to understand how important land, ranching and farming were to people born on and made a living from the land in Texas, Ireland or anywhere in the world. There was something else. He seemed to answer her questions in a guarded way as if he had been keeping a secret for a long time.

Sunday came, and as lunch ended, Mandy and Tom were in the study when Jessica came and turned on the radio. The announcement they heard ensured that Americans would never forget the first week in December 1941. The United States Navy Pacific fleet at Pearl Harbour had been virtually destroyed by a surprise attack from Fighter bombers and Torpedo planes of the Imperial Japanese Navy. The United States' declaration of war against Japan and Germany followed within twenty-four hours. All US armed forces, including the ROTC. were put on war footing. Tom Cork took his horse and rode out into the range and cried. In London, Winston Churchill rejoiced.

General Omar Bradley saw the Reserve Training Officer Corps as a significant part of the US military and, as part of war planning, determined that the ROTC officers would serve in units where their educational qualifications were maximised. To ensure this, he recruited a number of professional men into the ROTC at senior command level. Travers was one.

Colonel A. Travers had been in the Army reservist for two years and full-time for three months. As an oil production engineer, he had worked in London for six years during the late twenties and became a self-proclaimed Anglophile. General Bradley knew that to station American troops in Britain successfully would take an enormous diplomatic initiative alongside the military operation. Travers' myriad of contacts in business and friends in London society would help to advance Bradley's plans.

Bill returned to college a day after war was declared and was immediately summoned to the campus ROTC office. He met Colonel A Travers, who, seated at his desk, began,

"As of now, I am the commanding officer of the ROTC engineers at A&M." Looking at a file, he continued.

"Now, Cadet Cork, your grades tell me you will be a first-class petrochemical engineer. This is going to be a war fought by men with machines; gasoline and diesel-powered machines that will float, crawl, dig and fly. That fuel must be supplied by engineers, who have invented processes that extract, refine and deliver the fuel anywhere in the world."

Now standing, Travers paused, giving Bill time to view a tall, wiry man with thick grey hair and slightly weather-beaten skin. His blue eyes reflected the increasing fervour in his voice.

"What I want you to do is you complete the basic officer training at Texas A&M and as much of your degree course as possible before you are posted." Travers again paused as he looked Bill in the face.

"Cadet Cork, I have no idea when you will be posted. What I can guarantee is that you will be." His tone hardened as if to underline every word.

"These Nazis and Japanese are evil sons of bitches, with long histories of aggressive wars. It is going to take an almost incalculable effort by all good people to defeat them. Don't imagine this war will be over soon. The enemy wants world domination and are prepared to do anything to achieve that. So don't rush anything, young man. There is plenty of time for dying. Well, what do you think?"

Immensely impressed by Travers' forthright manner, Bill agreed.

"I'll go along with you, sir, and thank you."

The colonel reached out his hand, saying,

"Good. Goodbye for now, and good luck." Bill divided the days between college and riding the beautiful Double B range with his family and Mandy. He sensed, despite the tranquillity of the range, an urgency in them all. One evening just father and son rode.

"Dad, at college, we have a song for just about everything. Teach me a song about where you come from."

Tom Cork was silent for a minute and then began to sing. Any Irishmen within earshot would have recognised the 'On the Banks of My Own Lovely Lee.' Before long, Bill Cork could nearly sing it in his sleep.

The war increased the workload on the ranch, and Tom and Buchanan only caught up on personal matters as they rounded up cattle. Tom remarked how the evenings could be lonely now that the kids were away at school. Buchanan mentioned this in passing to Catherine. From then on, every Friday night, the Buchanan's entertained at the Big House. Food, drink and conversation were on the menu. The practise soon became a tradition and then an institution. One such evening, Bill saw Catherine sitting alone on the veranda. He asked.

"Auntie Catherine, where do you think they will send me?"

She spoke in a knowledgeable concerned voice.

"Bill, there are only two nations in the world capable of invading Europe. The US and Britain with its allies. Don't ask me when, but I am convinced that Hitler is quite mad and will make a mistake which will change the course of the war." She smiled.

"Then I might be able to tell you. Bill, I think you will be sent to Britain within the next year and may God go with you, my beautiful young Texan."

Back at college, he listened as the radio news announced that Hitler had invaded Russia. From that moment on, Cadet Bill Cork swore he would ask Catherine Buchanan for her advice on everything.

Bill concentrated on becoming a good officer and engineer as the college hummed with rumours of oversea posting. In the Atlantic, the allied navies were slowly subduing the U-boats, and the once invincible Wehrmacht was falling victim to Russians armies and the terrible winters of that vast land.

Bill's parent's nightmare became a reality just as he completed his degree. Colonel Travers told Bill he was appointed to Second Lieutenant in the US army engineers.

"You are now officially on active service and will take a vacation which will be regarded as embarkation leave. In the near future, you will be posted to Britain and begin combat engineering training with the allied forces. This information is confidential. You may tell your immediate family only." Bill was driving to Mandy's, after which he planned to go home. Suddenly the words 'embarkation leave' hit him, followed by panic.

Jesus, he was going to war. Why? He could with his engineering qualifications arrange for a posting in the US. Bill began to calm down as General Patton's words came to mind. The American Army was the best equipped and fed in history. As a Texan and an Aggie, he believed that defeat for the US Armed Forces was unthinkable. Now more composed, Bill thought of his family.

His mother, though scared, would deal with him going overseas. His father was different. Bill knew his father disliked the British intensely. Then he laughed.

This enmity never stopped Tom Cork from buying their cattle and boasting of the quality meat. Logic now took control. The motives of the Nazis waging war in Europe and the attack by the Japanese on Pearl Harbour left him in no doubt; he was right in going to fight not only for America, but civilisation as a whole. Britain was a war-weary country that stood up to them and now needed help from the young and vibrant USA. As for his father's views, once in Britain, he'd make up his own mind. Things were far from just right and wrong; leave it at that.

As Austin rose from the horizon, Bill thought about Mandy, who was as well informed on European current affairs as Auntie Catherine. He laughed. How much information do you need to stay alive?

The Bruce home was in a suburb of Austin, with wide tree-lined streets. Mandy met him at the gate, her family at the front door. The Bruce boys were some years younger than their sister and unlikely to see service. Bill sensed sadness in the family.

Mrs Bruce, a petite Texan lady with a mother's smile, had made a full lunch. Her husband, tall and well-built, was almost overwhelming in his efforts to make Bill welcome.

The Bruce family's eyes showed their concern and affection for this Texan of Irish descent from the Big Bend country, who was about to go to war to defend them all. After lunch, they sat in the living room, and Mr Bruce voiced his conviction the continent would have to be invaded. Finally, Bill said he must go. Mrs Bruce put her arms around him and hugged him for some time; her husband took his hand,

"Good luck to you, Bill Cork. I'm sorry that my generation should have seen this coming. There are too many people in this country who want to forget that the rest of the world is out there and who think that we can exist without it. God bless you, soldier and godspeed."

Mandy walked him to his car, then suddenly suggested.

"Bill, why don't I come back to the Double B for just one more ride on the range with you before you go? Please, Bill?"

He saw real yearning in her eyes.

"That's fine with me. What about your folks? What will they say?"

She turned, and her parents walked down the path with her bag. All Mr Bruce said was,

"It's such a beautiful night. Drive carefully."

Bill had always assumed they were just friends. She was far too intelligent to fool herself about love. From the start, both had made it clear they had definite plans for the next few years. Mandy's didn't include getting married and waiting for the hero's return. On the contrary, her plan was to go to Europe as a war correspondent. Bill had intended to qualify and travel. Now they were different people and much closer. The war had changed everything and not just for them.

The vast American production machine was getting into its incredible stride and beginning to arm the free world. The highways were full of trucks supplying the production plants and factories that had made, as only Winston Churchill could have described, America 'The Arsenal of Freedom'.

Jessica Cork, as any mother, knew immediately that her son was home as his car pulled up and that his young lady was in a separate room. Well, that would go the way it would. Now, all Jessica cared about was her beloved Bill being back on the Double B and that he would soon have to leave, maybe forever. Ice-cold tremors ran down her spine. To drive the horror away, she rose and got ready for another day in what she held to be the most beautiful place on earth.

Bill and Mandy rose in the late morning to a large meal. Bill saddled the horse he had ridden since he was a teenager and a quiet, mature mare for Mandy. His mother suggested,

"Bill, there is a full moon tonight. It might be the last one you see over the Double B for some time. Why not take Mandy and let her see our beautiful ranch under the moon? If it gets too late, stay at the cabin on the middle range. Your father and I would be much happier knowing you are there and safe and warm instead of trying to get back here in darkness. We'll talk in the morning."

She kissed him and then gave Mandy a hug. At this point, Buchanan came across the yard and was about to invite everyone to dinner when Catherine arrived, hugged Bill and Mandy and told her husband for once in his life to be quiet. Buchanan looked hurt, then said,

"I'm gonna find Tom and have a beer. Is that OK, Mam?"

Catherine kissed him and gently said,

"Good man Bill. Jessica and I will join you soon."

Buchanan strode away smiling. Catherine took Jessica's hand as she said,

"I can only imagine what you, as a mother, must be going through."

As they walked toward the Big House, Jessica spoke.

"Catherine, you were always as much a mother to me as I was to my children. I always knew that if anything happened to me, the children had nothing to fear as long as there was breath in your body. They know it as well."

Tears welled in Catherine's eyes, as Jessica continued,

"Do you remember all those years ago when you said to me that Bill was very bright?"

Catherine had linked Jessica's arm and, brushing away a tear, smiled as she nodded her head.

"I knew I raised a boy to become a man who would go his own way. I just didn't imagine for one minute it might be to a war halfway across the world. Catherine, let's join our husbands and have a drink. I need one."

Tom and Buchanan appeared with a small table and some bottles and glasses. All four sat and watched the moon rise in all its glory. Buchanan's deep voice broke the silence.

"That moon is glowing all over the world. I wonder where Bill will be looking at it a year from now."

Jessica began to cry, and Catherine put her arm around her and answered her husband's question.

"You were right to bring it up. Bill and many more young men will be going overseas, and some will not be coming back."

Tom Cork spoke before anyone else.

"I know I may be wrong here, but I have to say this. We have a bit of pull in this state, and maybe we should apply a little of it to get Bill a posting at home. Damn it, he's our boy, and I'm scared for him and us. I know it's selfish, but I think it had to be said."

He finished as he looked at his wife.

"Jessie, what do you think?"

She said,

"Tom, I think both of us know our boy. He is a Texan first and an American. He believes in this country and everything it stands for. If he wants to fight, there is nothing you can do about it."

Tom looked at his wife and said,

"I can take him fighting for America, Jess. But not fighting, let alone dying, for Britain. That would be too much for me; please try to understand."

Her reply was instant, her face flushed with anger.

"Tom Cork, for two years, the only thing that has stood against this evil which is now loose in the world has been Britain. There is a much larger world out there than you and your hatred of the Brits, as you call them. We are at war; they are our allies and it's all or nothing now, Tom. You can't have your own private war and decide who you will or will not back. Forget what happened and get behind our boy and all the other boys who will leave these shores in the months to come." She seemed to be finished, then continued fervently.

"I've got news for you, Tom Cork; as things stand now, nobody could care less what the Irish think about anything. Catherine tells me this guy De Valera is keeping Ireland neutral. Well, that's his business, but it won't be forgotten when the war's over. Many people won't be too fond of this Ireland you keep fantasizing about. Our Texan, our boy, is going to fight the Nazis; do you hear me, Tom Cork? What you are going to do is make certain he is well fed and well-armed and that the young Australian, New Zealander, British and yes, probably Irish, soldier fighting by his side is equally well fed and well-armed."

Bill and Mandy rode in silence through the middle range arriving at the cabin as the sun went down. Mandy could not think of words to describe the sky. The fire was soon roaring, and Mandy cooked beans and tinned corn beef, which, at that moment, was the best food she had ever tasted. As they ate, she spoke of her attempts to get to a position as a journalist. He decided to offer help,

"Mandy, my grandpa has a few contacts in the press in Texas and the State Department. I'll ask him if he can help."

Mandy replied desperately.

"Bill, if he could help. I've been banging my head against a brick wall for the last month and can't get as much as an interview with any Texas newspaper."

Bill said,

"Ok, I'll speak to him before I go."

Now Mandy was cautious.

"When are you going? Do you know exactly?"

"I know when I will be at base but not when or where we are going. My Auntie Catherine thinks I'll go to the UK, and believe me, that lady is never wrong."

Mandy asked about the Buchanans. Bill told her about Catherine coming back to the ranch. She continued,

"They are very happy, aren't they, Bill?"

"Yes," he paused,

"Everybody on the Double B seems to find peace in the end; it just takes some people longer than others. Dad was very unsettled when he came to Texas. He has never told me why he had to leave Ireland so quickly and so young."

Mandy put her head against his shoulder and said,

"The civil war in Ireland came after the war of Independence and was very bitter and divisive; many families were split irrevocably. Your dad was just begin-ning to tell me about what happened in West Cork when the news about Pearl Harbour was broadcast."

Bill laughed,

"I hope he doesn't have that effect every time he starts to talk about his home and history."

They laughed and then Mandy kissed him, slipping her tongue into his mouth, hesitant at first, then more sensually. Suddenly she stood and, while turning down the lamps, said.

"We'd better get some sleep. Do you think I'll be safe if we share a bed, Bill?"

He turned his eyes to heaven,

"Definitely, Miss Bruce." Adding.

"I just need to check the horses. Ok?"

She replied,

"Ok, Bill. I'll be in bed; it's getting cold."

Having locked the door, Bill checked the fire and slid into bed wearing just his shorts. He expected to feel Mandy's clothes against his skin, but to his surprised delight, she was naked. Her voice was low and husky.

"Bill, I want us to be lovers." They began kissing, and just before he entered her body, Mandy reached up to a bag and handed him a packet of condoms. No words were necessary. They made love for most of the night, and after waking from a deep sleep in the morning, Mandy spoke.

"Bill, I've never been so close to anyone as now. So intimate, physically and emotionally, it's new and wonderful."

All Bill could say was,

"You're going to be a great journalist. You've just put into words exactly what I'm feeling."

Once back at the ranch, Mandy called her father to take her home, despite Bill wanting to. She explained.

"Bill, you must spend as much time as possible with your family." Bill had to accept her logic was unimpeachable, but neither had had bargained on another man on the Double B called Bill.

Mr Bruce arrived with his wife and the boys. Buchanan invited them to stay for dinner and, before anybody knew what was happening, had convinced them to stay the night. Then Charlie Rawlings arrived, and the ensuing impromptu party was a great success if tinged with sadness. Everybody knew that within a few days, Lieutenant William Charles Cork of Big Bend, Texas, would be going to war.

The next morning, before they said goodbye, Bill told Mandy his grandpa said he would try to help; just give him time. The Bruce family said goodbye to the young man they held in great affection and respect.

Bill had left the ranch hundreds of times before but this time was different. The previous evening, he told his parents of being told his posting was in the Northern Hemisphere, in other words, Britain. The Cork family stood by him as all of the men who had seen him grow up said goodbye. Felix and Simon, and then Chato and Carlito, who were all now as much part of the ranch as the high ranges. Carlito quietly gave him a razor-sharp hand-made knife. Buchanan and Catherine hugged him and then just got on their horses and rode off into the range. Jessica watched Buchanan, certain he was crying. That giant of a man was always in complete control of all situations, but when it came to his godson, he adored the ground the boy walked on and now could not hide his sadness.

Charlie Rawlings stood with his daughter, then said goodbye to his beloved grandson, who was to him everything that was good about Texas and America. He had secretly explored getting Bill a home posting, then realised it was completely wrong. Families all over the free world were going through what they were. Grandpa Rawlings decided to channel his energies into Bill's brother and sister. Both were desperately upset and old enough to know that the situation was very serious. Charlie tried to be casually jovial, but the Irishman in him came out, and he hugged his brother fiercely. His sister Mary was already with their grandfather finding comfort, having kissed her brother goodbye for at least five minutes.

Tom and Jessica took Bill back to the A&M. His car would remain on the Double B for his use when he returned. The drive was made in silence, and then, at the door to his dorm, he hugged his mother, who was sobbing as she kissed him.

"Bill, you are my life. Your birth bonded your father and me, and whatever happens to you, I will know if you are alive. I gave you life, you are me and your father, and there will not be a second when you are not in our thoughts. Whatever happens you are never alone; we'll be with you; never forget that my blessed Bill, my handsome William, my beautiful Texan."

His father stood in front of him,

"Bill, I left Ireland many years ago because of a war that I declared without telling anybody else and hurt many people. You are now going to fight another war. These Nazis and Japanese are the worst thing to come to God's earth in many years, and it is the responsibility of your generation to stop them and everything they represent. Bill, this is a just war, so my dear, sweet son, you do whatever it takes to send those murdering sons of bitches to hell and come home safe and sound. You'll be in Britain, the home of the empire that I have always hated, but listen to me. There are good men in that country, and they know how to fight wars; listen and learn from them. You're an American with new ideas, so make sure they listen to you. God bless you. my boy, and, as your mother said, you will never be alone as long as there is breath in our bodies."

He kissed his son and walked back to the car. Jessica looked at her son and then once more kissed him on the lips and the forehead as she had done since the day he was born, and then she walked away.

Inside the building, Colonel Travers watched the Cork family say farewell. As Bill entered the hallway, he was told to pack his overseas kit. The Aggies would be shipping out straight away. After roll call, they boarded a bus. Travers called them to attention.

"Gentlemen, we are going to Austin, then aboard an armed merchantman which will join a convoy under escort by the Canadian Navy to the mid-point of our passage. He paused, trying to assess the reactions of the young men.

"The Royal Navy will then be our escort until we reach Britain and World War Two." As the bus pulled away from the A& M, hundreds of Aggies appeared and began to cheer and wave the flag of Texas and the Stars and Stripes. In all the noise and emotion, nobody noticed that Colonel Travers was sitting at the front of the bus and that he was in combat uniform too.

‒ 15 ‒

Over There

Bill Cork stood on deck trying to break the boredom with another attempt to count the merchant ships in the convoy. His eye caught one of the Royal Navy escorts and again lost count. Suddenly, the warship rose out of the water as the sound of an explosion rolled across the ocean. Bill heard alarm klaxons as the troopship's decks filled with men in life jackets and then a yell.

"The bastards got one of the escorts." All eyes watched two warships converge to a point west of the convoy, then depth charges exploded. The escorts re-joined the convoy as it steamed on. There was another more controlled shout.

"'No stopping', order received, captain."

The captain of the SS Bailey was on the bridge, binoculars trained on the stricken vessel. His agonised voice was loud.

"Jesus Christ! I have been at sea twenty-five years and never left a man in the water; this is worse than torture!" Then he was on deck, binoculars locked on the chaotic scene.

Colonel Travers heatedly demanded.

"Captain Fleming, what the hell do they mean 'no stopping'?"

A big passionate man, Fleming spat out the words.

"Colonel, we cannot stop and pick up survivors - we must keep going. We can't break formation; that's what the U-boats want. We have to leave the men in the water; there's nothing we can do. Jesus Christ! Jesus Christ, forgive me." Travers pleaded in desperation,

"There must be something we can do."

Then came a yell from the bridge.

"I think it's Snow Cougar that's been hit."

The captain, now calmer, explained.

"The escorts will try and organise one of the merchantmen at the rear of the convoy to slow down and pick up any survivors in lifeboats."

Exploding ammunition rocked Snow Cougar, and she began to show her keel. The speechless US Army Engineers watched a merchantman slow to pick up survivors, the sea around them dotted with corpses. The silence was broken as Captain Fleming announced to his passengers.

"Gentlemen, welcome to the Second World War."

Ten days later, Bill Cork scanned Liverpool port with binoculars. After the loss of Snow Cougar, the 'Aggies' quickly became familiar with the escorts. Bill recognised Snow Eagle and saw activity forward of the bridge. Lieutenant Pat Cork was on watch as the ship steamed for the Liverpool buoy. He checked ahead for clear water, swung his binoculars around for a final sweep of the port and came eye to eye with a US army officer. Bill saw the Royal naval officer and, wishing him good luck stood to attention and saluted. Automatically Pat returned the salute and wished the same to the unknown American who had come so far to fight.

The US Army Engineers were billeted near Swansea harbour and began studying the theory of landings on defended beaches. In July, practical training put the theory to the test in tidal seawater with diesel vehicles of all designs. In a few days, it was obvious the theory was just that, as salt water quickly blocked all filters in every engine. Travers pointed out as the engineers waded ashore from abandoned half-tracks and tanks,

"Thank Christ, we're not under fire!" The next day he summarised the previous exercises.

"Gentlemen, it is plain we know nothing about amphibious operations, or the equipment needed. We will divide into two groups. One to work with engineering companies' design staff to produce waterproof filters, gaskets and snorkels for all engines currently in military use. The other group will go to the shipbuilders to design landing craft. This is an open-ended operation, so get it right because it will be Americans using this equipment one day soon."

He raised his voice.

"Now listen, do not be overawed by the British; speak your minds, and if you have an idea, shout it out!"

Bill went to the shipbuilders, and after a short time, Travers summoned him and two other engineers. The CO began,

"Gentlemen, a top-secret operation will soon take place. Canadian and British units will land on the continent of Europe to test the amphibious landing capabilities of the Allies. We have been ordered by the US high command to observe. I am asking for volunteers to go on this test of equipment."

The officers stepped forward, knowing the 'test of equipment' was a full-blown commando raid and would provide priceless experience of a beach landing under enemy fire. Travers smiled.

"OK, there are four of us going in. Cork, you and I will assess the landing craft and fuel and ammunition delivery procedures to the troops in combat."

The other officers were to observe the planning and logistics operation at the embarkation ports. Then come cross channel aboard the supply vessels to see supplies being landed for the attacking units. Travers then vigorously stressed.

"Now listen. Our presence is secret and must stay that way. Make sure you stay alive; we are not going to be the first Americans killed in Europe. You'll get twenty-four hours embarkation notice. Please carry on."

Peter English ran his life and company in a way which ignored his wife and monopolised their only son. This caused his wife to suffer great loneliness and finally drove her to seek affection elsewhere. Oblivious English carried on and, in doing so, met Peter Wilde at an architectural exhibition in London in 1936. They became business acquaintances, and English made an offer for Wilde's business. He was given first refusal. In 1939 Wilde kept his word with the stipulation that all employees be kept on; English agreed. When war came, his son, an army reservist, was sent to France with his regiment. Peter English's world collapsed when his boy was killed at Dunkirk. An equally devastated Mrs English finally left him, citing his complete inability to share their grief. Wilde had told Connor a little of Peter English's past when he sold the company. Cork accepted the job anyway and, in time, found English a fair if eccentric man. Now, in August 1942, Peter English was coming to terms with the loss of his son and marriage. Connor, also living alone, suggested they share a house. English accepted and assured Cork,

"Connor, I was consumed with grief when my boy died and very callous toward my wife. The time has come to move on. Seeing Pat here has done me the world of good."

English did more than move on personally. He was exceedingly impressed with the quality of the work by the tradesmen who had come with the buyout. He called Connor to the site office.

"Connor, I have something to say. Thanks to you and the other Irishmen here, we now have a highly-skilled, experienced and virtually perfectionist workforce. I want to show my appreciation by offering you a partnership."

Connor Cork was pleased knowing the business was profitable and would give his family long-term financial security. He agreed if allowed to invest some of his own capital. English accepted. The finalised agreement was dependent upon Connor passing scrutiny by the security services. Unknown to either in 1935, because a number of Peter Wilde's clients were establishment figures, Connor Cork had already undergone vetting. His clearance came through within a week, and the partnership was formalised.

Then without explanation, orders came from the Ministry of works to cancel all projects and prepare to start building large unnamed floating structures. Material specifications and outline drawings began to arrive within days. Neither partner knew the project was a direct result of a secret raid on the French port of Dieppe.

On the 17th of August, Colonel A Travers and First Lieutenant Bill Cork sailed on the morning tide aboard a troop-carrying landing craft, which was part of a small flotilla heading for Dieppe. As ordered, they assessed the vessel and reported it was totally unsuitable for sea passage, even in fair seas. The Colonel knew the main attack force of 75 landing craft carrying nearly five thousand men had gone ashore in Dieppe at 05:40hrs - it was now 09:30, and the landing beach was visible. The engineers were horror struck by the sight of overturned, sunken landing craft and bodies strewn all over the attack area. Bill pointed to a bombed, burning Royal Navy destroyer. Any vessel that had got to the water line had been cut to pieces by mercilessly deadly accurate enemy fire. The waterline was filled with wounded men. On the beach were at least twenty stranded tanks, tracks ripped apart by shingle. The German defenders had shown no mercy.

The commander of the LRC yelled he had been ordered to transfer the troops aboard to a warship and head inshore to pick up the wounded. Travers stated.

"We'll stay aboard; you'll need first aiders and maybe mechanical help."

The transfer took just under an hour. Eventually, the landing craft edged to the water line and came under surprisingly light fire. Bill quickly saw why. The Canadians ashore had managed to destroy some enemy gun emplacements. Bill was halfway down the ramp to help a badly wounded Canadian trooper when he completely lost his footing on a wickedly slippery substance and fell into the freezing water. As he righted himself and grabbed the wounded man, a mixture of blood mixed with salt water and diesel oil covered his hands and uniform. Travers grabbed Bill's webbing and pulled both men onto the ramp and then into the landing craft hold alongside more wounded. Then the Aggies heard.

"Colonel, we've been ordered to withdraw; the operation has been abandoned. We have to get off the beach now." Bill had been desperately trying to stem the flow of blood from a gaping wound in the casualty's back, but the young Canadian died in his arms. Travers watched as Bill stared at his blood-covered hands, utter despair on his face.

Dangerously overloaded, the LRC began to turn and head out to sea. Then a spray of bullets hit the steering wheel mounting at the stern. Travers saw the crewman wave his hand to show he was OK. The Petty officer lifted a shattered radio dial. His shipmate began using a semaphore to contact the ships off the beach. Travers shouted to Bill.

"The radios shot through!" Bill almost laughed.

'What's one more disaster?' Then sardonically whispered to himself as he tended to another young man fighting for his life.

"Well, Cork, you wanted active service."

The landing craft hove to alongside a destroyer, and the transfer of the wounded began. The American engineers were amongst the last to leave the LRC and looked astern as the warship gathered speed. The abandoned craft hit by German artillery was sinking. Their eyes moved to the receding beach and surveyed the tragic evidence of a total disaster.

As the destroyer docked in Southampton, Travers, aware that certain senior officers would be looking for scapegoats, issued an order.

"Lieutenant, contact our officers where ever they are and instruct them not to speak to anyone but me." Bill soon saw why.

A senior British officer asked Colonel Travers to make a statement before he disembarked. He refused, stating he did not know the objectives of the operation and could not draw an objective conclusion. Bill quietly confirmed the other US officers had received Travers' order.

After the 'Battle of Dieppe', allegations were made, questions asked, and answers demanded. The US army engineers remained silent. Travers and his commanding officer were convinced a witch hunt by opponents of Admiral Louis Mountbatten in the British Joint Chiefs of Staff was underway. The US Army Engineers and others submitted their reports to Mountbatten's staff and waited. Five weeks after the raid, Travers and Cork were ordered to London for a meeting with Mountbatten. All present were thanked for their efforts. Then Mountbatten went into detail about what had been learned at Dieppe. He assured them that nothing would be ignored from their reports which would greatly assist in the invasion of Europe. Travers and Cork were leaving when an Admiral's aide approached.

"Compliments of the admiral, sir. Would you and the lieutenant be kind enough to spare him a minute."

Louis Mountbatten rose from his chair and shook hands, asking them to sit.

"I had my honeymoon in America and have always had a deep love for the country and the people. I would not wish any nation to be at war, but I am very glad that you are here. Feel free to contact me at any time if you feel that bureaucracy or reactionary elements are at play. Now is there anything you want to do before you return to your base?"

Bill sat in astonishment as Colonel Travers and a member of the British Royal family chatted as old friends. What would his father say if he knew his Irish, Texan, American son was taking a drink with a senior British royal, not a stone's throw from Buckingham Palace? He was brought back to the present when the colonel stood and thanked Mountbatten. Both men saluted, and when outside, Bill enquired,

"Which train should I book, sir?"

Travers replied,

"Tonight, lieutenant, we stay in London as the guest of the admiral, and we have tickets for a West End show. Now my young Texan, I am going to take you to the Cafe Royale, where we are going to drink the best pink gin in the world." That night, Bill Cork saw a side of Britain and the colonel that he never knew existed. He began to realise why so many people had come from all over the world to fight on Britain's side. He met many of Travers' British friends and discussed the arts, theatre, literature and music. Travers beamed,

"Here it is, Bill boy. All here, in one big, beautiful city, and long may it remain so."

That evening they painted the town red.

He watched the troops on the train to Wales laugh and joke and silently made a vow. At Dieppe, Bill Cork grew up and swore he would never allow another young soldier to die as that young Canadian had. Next to him, Colonel Travers was satisfied that he now had a conduit to the top, which gave him real leverage. Back at base, they began to rewrite the manual on American Combined Operations Amphibious Landings based on knowledge that had been learned the hard way.

16

Advances on All Fronts

Allied High Command could not countenance a similar disaster to Dieppe on D Day. The success of the assault depended utterly upon invading troops being supported with heavy equipment and supplies immediately after landing. After much brainstorming, a plan was adopted, which was described in a few words by a senior officer.

"If we can't capture a harbour on the European coastline, we'll have to take one with us. In essence: We will build a harbour in sections similar in size to Dover and tow it across the English Channel. The assembled harbour will be a safe landing for men and supplies until a port is liberated."

English and Cork had renamed the company E&C Fabrications. The senior partner returned from a meeting with detailed plans of the top-secret project. The British construction industry was tasked with a formidable challenge, the development and manufacture of components for the floating harbour. Connor took responsibility for the shuttering, which would mould the concrete and steel structure. Peter English would guarantee every calculation and measurement was perfect. When not on site, he was at planning and review meetings in London, causing him to work twenty-hour days.

Connor worried about Peter's long days until it occurred to him that the project was probably keeping him sane. With Peter away so much, Connor became the public face of the company, hosting the occasional dignitary who called to raise morale. Those who came to ensure that public money wasn't being wasted. Then the unannounced security checks made by slightly less pleasant gentlemen.

As a partner, he was now called Mr Cork and comfortably changed from employee to owner.

Connor wrote to his wife every week and received a reply by return of post. Mary wrote that everyone was fine and life was good. There were shortages, which were balanced by plenty of fresh food. Christopher was becoming a very good Gaelic footballer, but for Kerry - not Cork. Something Connor managed to laugh at. He missed his family terribly, but they were safe. Portsmouth was bombed almost nightly. The Ministry of Information was saying the RAF was getting the upper hand - whatever that meant. In early September, great news came. Pat had a week's leave. Connor counted the days. It was with disbelief he watched his son shown into the office by a clearly smitten secretary. When alone, father and son embraced fiercely. Connor sat wondering about the change in service and rank and then said.

"From your uniform, I'd guess you have a lot to tell me, but first things first. Everyone in Ireland is fine, all well and not feeling too isolated. Now let's have a drink; from the look of you, you've earned it - I know I have."

Pat sat down, looking around the plush office and, as his father handed him a brandy, asked.

"Dad, since when have you worked out of an office?"

Connor explained about the partnership and the company taking on very important war work. Pat's next question was about Peter English.

"As far as I can tell, he is ok, but to be honest, I hardly see him outside work. He works a twenty-hour day."

Pat continued,

"How are the living arrangements going?"

"Really well; we have a housekeeper who lives in and does everything for us. She is a widow who wants to mother us all the time; I'm spoiled rotten," Connor replied. Then he changed the subject.

"Tell me, have you given any thought to what you will do when the war is over? If you want to join the business, there is a place here for you. However, if you want to do something else, maybe go to university. We are fairly comfortable." Pat mused.

"I haven't given much thought as to what I'll do, to be honest dad, but if you press me...."

His father gently interrupted.

"I'm not pressing at all, but you are a vastly different man to the one who joined the Irish Guards. Don't feel you are bound to anything; that's all I'm saying."

Sitting back, Pat replied,

"I'm not the only one who has changed but, as you bring it up, Maybe something in the legal profession – possibly a barrister. How does that sound?"

Connor smiled.

"Just fine with me, my boy. Now, more brandy?"

As the evening closed in, Pat explained about his commission in the Royal Navy. Connor spoke about Ireland and Mary pressing to return with the children. There was silence for a moment as both men considered the possibility and simultaneously said.

"No."

Pat carried on,

"Dad, the bombing is still too heavy, and they are perfectly safe in Kerry."

Connor nodded his head vigorously, saying,

"Your brother has become a very good Gaelic footballer, although for Kerry - not Cork."

Pat laughed out loud.

"How does that make you feel, dad?"

Connor's voice contained all the joy he felt talking of the family with his eldest son.

"How do you think any Cork man feels when one of his boys plays for Kerry?"

Pat told his father about singing 'The Banks' on board Snow Eagle on St Patrick's Day. As the men went off shift, they heard the sound of singing coming from one of the partners' offices. The Irishmen among them recognised the song as 'The banks of my own Lovely Lee.' The Corks went home after midnight. The housekeeper had left a cold meal which they ate with the hunger of men who had drunk too much. Both were asleep and did not hear Peter English pull up in his car later that night.

Mrs Stokes served breakfast and told him his father and Mr English had left for work much earlier. Pat arrived at the plant and became increasingly impressed by how good a director his father was. Lunch was a sandwich in the plant, and then English showed him around, describing the work. In the evening, they had dinner at home and listened to Peter English talk incessantly for two hours without actually saying anything. He finally said goodnight. Their faces showed pity for the man as Pat asked,

"How long has he been like this, dad?"

"Since we got the new contract. As I said, twenty-hours a day."

Pat asked,

"How long do you think he will last?" Connor speculated.

"I have no idea, but he says there will be stopping; what we are doing is too important."

Pat suggested,

"It could kill him, dad."

The reply shocked him.

"Pat, my boy, I've lived with that man for the last year, and believe me, from what I have seen, he is already as good as dead."

Pat relaxed; then, in no time, he was making ready to leave. Father and son said goodbye in the evening, privately and with a good deal of emotion. The condition of Peter English made them very grateful for each other and their family. Pat had one more thing to do and called to see his father in the office the next morning.

"Dad, as you know, I have been on Atlantic convoys for some time. I was in C in C Western Approaches and came across some information which involves you and possibly Peter. Would you ask him to come in, please?"

English sat in the chair next to Connor.

"In the operations room is a list of civilian casualties comprising people who took passage to America and were lost when their ships were sunk. Dad, Peter, Peter Wilde is on the list. I'm sorry, but he and his companion are dead."

He waited for a moment,

"Gentlemen, I have to go. I'm sorry to tell you in such a brutal fashion, but there really is no other way."

After Pat left. Looking at Peter, Connor asked,

"Should we have some kind of service? Do you know what religion he was? What should we do?"

English almost scoffed,

"We get on with our part of this awful bloody war, my friend; that's what we do."

That evening, Connor did something out of the ordinary. He arranged for a Catholic Mass to be said for the repose of the souls of Peter Wilde and his friend. Then wrote to his wife with the dreadful news.

At SOE headquarters Brigadier Davies, now unexpectedly in command of the Norwegian section, knew he needed trustworthy people with knowledge of that country. Colonel Simpson – Coyle's behaviour was extremely worrying, as highlighted by the radio room incident. Odin, unusually for SOE, again granted Davies' request to recruit his own people. Professor Williamson had proved him to be a good judge.

Sergeant Cormac Reilly was sitting in his outer office after four months sick leave. Davies reminded himself not to expect too much; the man had been to hell and back. However, Cormac Reilly was a career soldier and ideal for the job in hand. The Irishman heard his name, and after a handshake, was asked to sit.

"Now, sergeant, please tell me, how have you been in the last few months?"

Reilly spoke, his accent rounded but unmistakably Irish.

"Good of you to ask, sir. My time in German hands weakened my system to the extent that I developed dysentery, which, at one time, threatened my life. The medics also tell me that I suffered a bit of depression - not something I want to experience again, but I've had great medical care and am feeling much better now; thank you, sir."

Davies noted the sergeant had put on weight and guessed he was a few pounds light of sixteen stones which, with his height of six foot three inches, made an imposing man. The colour had returned to his cheeks, and his hair had regained its thick, wavy texture; his blue eyes smiled again. On the desk was the psychological profile, which summed up the sergeant in one sentence, 'This man possesses tremendous willpower'.

Davies decided to get to the point.

"Sergeant Reilly, I can offer you an honourable discharge on medical grounds. You could return to Ireland."

Reilly smiled at this and explained.

"Brigadier, I deserted the Irish State Defence Forces to join the British Army and am now a wanted man in Ireland. There is an unpublicised civil war going on at home as De Valera's people are in power and are trying to destroy some of their former allies in the War of Independence." He paused.

"There is more; in 1936, I was lied to by the Government and went to Spain believing I was fighting communism. I soon realised we were on the same side as Franco's Nationalist murderers. I've seen the Nazis in action." Davies saw deep anger in the big man's eyes as he heard.

"I'll stay here and help to finish off the Nazis. Whatever the nationality."

Reilly noticed the brigadier's face become taught as he asked,

"How do you feel about running my personal security team, sergeant?"

"How many men are in the team, sir?" he asked.

"Just you." Reilly probed,

"Why would you need a bodyguard, sir?"

"I need a man I can trust implicitly, but before we go on, I must have your decision, sergeant."

Reilly looked at the man who was responsible for his escape from living hell in Bergen,

"When do I start, sir?"

Davies stood and shook Reilly's hand,

"Immediately. Oh, and by the way, from now on, it's Sergeant Major Reilly. Now, in answer to your earlier question, we are the new boys in this bloody awful game. I am putting together a group of people who will operate in Norway, a country of which you have invaluable experience. Security is everything in what we do. You will lead the recruitment and vetting team, which will ensure that the Norwegian Section is airtight. The threat of a leak is always present and not alone from the enemy. That is the part of the job that is not so pleasant."

He looked Reilly in the eye, saying,

"Congratulations on regaining your health - it's good to see you looking so well."

Then continued,

"Now, I've put together a training programme, code and cipher writing and breaking, sabotage and demolition, the use of signals equipment and a bit of field tradecraft. Which involves undergoing surveillance training and how to lose someone should you be the one being followed. Plus, you are to assist Professor Williamson in a project he is beginning, which is a study of the current political situation in Norway and then in Southern Ireland. We may need a comprehensive understanding of the situation over there soon. One never knows in this line of work."

Reilly laughed.

"I'll be happy to offer any help I can to the professor, sir. But as for a comprehensive understanding of the Irish by the British! That, sir, is asking for the impossible. We've been looking for that for the last eight hundred years."

Davies knew enough about Anglo-Irish history to stay silent, but his Celtic humour came through, and he joined in the laughter. Reilly spoke again.

"There are a number of things I need to mention."

Davies encouraged,

"Go ahead."

"Firstly, I need to retrain on weapons and my marksmanship needs sharpening," he continued as Davies nodded.

"The second relates to the team. There was a soldier in the camp, Private Mullen; he's a very useful man in a tight corner."

Davies agreed.

"Give me his details, and we'll track him down. You explain the job. He will report to you only."

Reilly smiled as he continued,

"Third, sir, there is something which may be of importance. In Bergen, we were labouring on a submarine bay different from the others in that it was sound-proof. One of the French prisoners spoke German and kept hearing the words 'acoustic' and 'torpedo'. The whole thing was run by a German scientist who was reportedly a doctor, as well. If he was, we didn't see it." He paused.

"Sir, it may be nothing, as the bay was probably destroyed by the RAF and hopefully the scientist as well. But you never know."

Davies looked at his new recruit with growing satisfaction.

"Get me the Admiralty Scientific Research Unit, please, Mr Reilly and then signal Erebus. We need to talk to him. Please ask Commander Bakken to see me at his earliest convenience?"

With that, Sergeant Major Cormac Reilly entered the world of smoke and mirrors and the dark arts with both eyes wide open.

Professor Williamson asked Reilly endless questions about conditions in the camps and how the civilian population were dealing with the occupation. Then about the Norwegian monarchy in exile. Were the people still royalists? Sergeant Major Reilly reminded Williamson that he was held in various closed labour camps. Then summarised.

"Professor, my opinion is that the majority of Norwegians still support the monarchy and will after the war. As for the occupation, they know it will be over one day."

Private Seamus Tomas Mullen was walking down Aldershot High Street when a car stopped on the kerbside. The rear door opened, and a familiar voice called,

"Jump in, you bloody Blue Shirt."

Within twenty minutes, he was on his way to the SOE headquarters. He was introduced to Maiden Aunt, promoted to sergeant and became a member of the Special Operations Executive. His former commanding officer received notification that Mullen had left the battalion permanently.

Brigadier Davies heard from Naval Intelligence. Sergeant Major Reilly's report, added to those from convoy escorts of ships torpedoed from previously impossible firing positions, pointed to one conclusion. A form of an acoustic torpedo which 'homed in' on engine and propeller vibrations was in use by the enemy. Davies was ordered to discover if such a weapon was being developed in Norway. If so, the development was to be stopped, at all costs, permanently. As 1941 drew to an end, Davies briefed Erebus. All resources were to be concentrated on locating and identifying the acoustic torpedo development team. Erebus put Moen and Berg on standby.

Vali was parachuted into Norway and was met by officers from Norwegian Naval Intelligence. They were asked to check if any lecturers in Hydrodynamics or Marine engineering were absent from their university posts. Then he briefed Erebus, Moen and Berg.

"Once we find the torpedo test site and research team, we have two courses of action. One, we steal a prototype torpedo and get it to Britain. Then get the RAF to bomb the works.

Two, we kill the men involved in the research regardless of their nationalities or motivation." He paused.

"Is there anything I've missed?"

There was silence. The 'courses of action' were extremely perilous, if not fatal, for all concerned. The meeting broke into an open discussion. Erebus advised. "The Germans are upgrading the U-boat pens in Bergen, Narvik, Trondheim, Hammerfest and Kirkenes. Which one is being used to develop the torpedoes?" Vali added more information.

"UK research scientists believe prototype torpedoes can only be tested and recovered in shallow waters." Berg pronounced,

"That narrows down the number of harbours."

There was silence until Erebus suggested.

"The trawlers could fish off those ports and keep an eye out for anything strange." Moen posed a question.

"The only problem is how to get the extra fuel needed without the local militia getting nosey." Then suggested an answer.

"I'll get the lorry drivers to buy fuel in different parts of the country, then take it to isolated harbours where the trawlers can refuel." Vali added,

"I'll get the cash from the SOE."

Just before he left, Berg was approached by Erebus and Vali, who said.

"I have been asked to tell you by the commander of the Norwegian section of SOE he has complete confidence in you and your fellow sea captains."

The Norwegian fisherman left with a broad smile on his face.

In his office, that commander was aware that, on his order men, would die whether they worked for the Germans willingly or not. Maiden Aunt remembered how and why he had joined SOE and felt more than a little uneasy.

In early 1942, one of Berg's smugglers confirmed a sea area just outside the Narvik U-boat pens had been restricted to German vessels only. The four men met, and Vali began.

"How do we find out if this torpedo is being tested there?" Erebus spoke.

"It would help if we knew what equipment is being used to develop this thing."

Vali agreed.

"SOE will have to tell us what to look for; we're not scientists."

Berg spoke for the first time.

"Don't forget we still have to figure a way in and out safely, maybe more than once." Erebus proposed,

"I'll go in as a Todt supervisor." Vali would not hear of it.

"No, you're our last resort as an Abwehr officer."

Moen was as ebullient as ever.

"Why don't Vali and I go as Todt men?" His idea was, after some discussion, accepted. The next day, after Vali contacted SOE, he briefed his comrades with the expert information supplied.

"We're to look for cylindrical objects with a rudder and tail fins and floating crane rigs, all housed in soundproof bays" His comrades looked on in stunned silence, which deepened when he added.

"Maiden Aunt has ordered this operation be carried out only those who were involved in the Bergen escape. No one else."

As two Todt officers, they moved freely around the outer part of the port of Narvik. When they tried to talk their way into a restricted area, German Military police guards told them to 'fuck off.'

Erebus approached the restricted area guard post with Maiden Aunt's words fresh in his memory. 'We need to know what's inside that restricted area and soon.' Moen had voiced his concern.

"It was fine you going in alone with those idiots in Bergen, but the bastards have guards here of a completely different calibre." He then questioned.

"What if there are real Abwehr agents in there poking around?"

Erebus tried to reassure the others and possibly himself.

"Good question. But we know the Abwehr is obsessed with secrecy. Their agents do not know who else is working for Canaris."

Moen demanded.

"Who the hell is Canaris?"

Vali explained,

"Admiral Wilhelm Canaris is the head of the Abwehr, a counterintelligence organisation similar to SOE in that both use a cell system. All operations are stand-alone." As he neared the guards, Erebus felt more confident as he at least knew what equipment to look for.

His papers were accepted by the Military Police Guards, who were not overawed by a senior Abwehr officer. Erebus realised there was no chance of intimidating these hardened 'Chain dogs.'

He moved on to the inner part of the site, where a gang of emaciated men were dismantling a timber shutter, revealing a very high, long concrete structure with one door space cut into the wall. Immediately past the door was another single unmanned guard post. Looking into the newly constructed pen revealed a number of smaller jetties running down to the sea and the inner harbour. A cursory inspection of the thirty feet concrete pen roof slab confirmed bombing was pointless. Then with slightly more optimism, Erebus watched a group of men at the water's edge standing over an object nearly identical to that described by SOE. Just behind them stood an SS trooper, all noted for their devotion to Hitler rather than intelligence. Erebus sensed an opportunity as the guard turned and challenged him.

"Who are you, and what are you doing here?" The reply came in a cold voice.

"Had you been at your post, you would know the answers to both questions."

The arrogant SS man immediately reached for his sidearm but stopped when Erebus produced papers and hissed.

"Now you know who and what I am. If I say so, you will face a charge of deserting your post while on duty." The SS man, now visibly unsure, surprisingly offered an excuse, almost pleading.

"I am not to blame." His tormentor retorted.

"So, who is?" Erebus's mind was racing. The SS idiot was ready for burning, but how? He gambled on the man's sycophancy.

"Report everything you know." The guard burst into a self-preserving torrent about incompetent commanding officers and arrogant scientists. He finished,

"If only the Fuehrer knew." Erebus ordered.

"Follow me."

They moved within earshot of the group circling the torpedo and heard a man who appeared to be in charge angrily say.

"The guidance system is functioning, but the level of interference from the seawater must be reduced." Erebus asked.

"Can you guarantee all of these men have security clearance to see that object?"

In an obsequious attempt to answer the question, he opened the door for Erebus.

"Yes Sir. They are the prototype torpedo development team."

Erebus went for the kill, his voice low but ice cold.

"You have just committed treason. You have told me what the object is and what those men do." Then remained silent until he saw the fear in his prey's eyes.

"It is obvious you have not been trained properly in security. I must establish how much information is at risk." He walked away from the waterline, the guard following. Then in a conspiratorial tone, he spoke to the shaking man.

"You have stated your senior officers are at fault. I need proof." He saw a relieved look on the SS man's face as the firing squad, and the Russian front began to fade.

"You will now escort me to the gate."

Once through the security gate, Erebus instructed.

"As of now, you are working for the Abwehr. Tonight, at twenty hundred hours, you will meet me in the town." He named a cafe by the river. The guard vigorously agreed. Outside the plant, Moen was waiting.

"Well, Laudrup, how did we get on?" Erebus smiled.

"I think we did very well. Now, shut up. We have to see Vali straight away." Moen replied,

"Jump in. I know exactly where he is."

That night the German was introduced to Vali and Moen and told they were field security agents. Vali instructed him on how to provide the Abwehr with proof of the incompetence in security. He would bring out the personal files of the scientists. One every evening. His reward was a promotion and posting to Germany. The files were delivered as planned. Vali stayed with the guard as Moen took the files to his truck and quickly microfilmed them. He said later to Erebus.

"We've got a problem. Most of these files don't have any photographs."

By the eighth night, both men concluded the German was becoming suspicious and very nervous. When told, Erebus met and informed the guard there was enough evidence, and his promotion and transfer would be confirmed the following night. Four men enjoyed a drink at a riverside café in Narvik. Just after midnight, one had a knockout drug poured into his beer. On the way back to base, he slipped, fell into the river and drowned.

In the morning, his absence at roll call instigated a standard search by military police. The body was discovered, and after a perfunctory investigation, accidental death was confirmed. Suicides and desertions amongst German troops were rising as the war turned against the Thousand Year Reich. A fact kept top secret.

His mother received a telegram expressing the Fuehrer's gratitude. Moen gave the SS man a slightly different epitaph.

"One less bastard to kill tomorrow". Adding,

"Do you know Laudrup. I can't remember the idiot's name?"

The analysts in SOE produced a report which was summarised by Maiden Aunt to Vali and Erebus via radio.

"Right, gentlemen. This is the current position. The research on the weapon is being carried out in the shallow water off Narvik, making it impossible to retrieve an abandoned prototype as the risks involved are unacceptable even for your men". He paused, not mentioning his concern for Berg, Moen and their countrymen, whose bravery and dedication were now almost legendary amongst the SOE. Erebus reported.

"The pens are made of concrete too thick to be penetrated by any bomb we currently have; over." Maiden Aunt concluded the briefing.

"Right, go ahead with planning for option two and good luck. Over and out." The Oslo University contact had provided two names which matched the Narvik files. The project leader was named Karl Hartmann, a medical doctor and a professor of acoustics and hydrodynamics. A fanatical Nazi who experimented without conscience. Hartmann was unassailable for two reasons. One, there was no photograph and two, he never left the Narvik base.

The other man was a different matter. Jurgen Mueller was a professor of Hydrodynamics who had spent many years in the USA, returning to Germany at the outbreak of war. The SOE men were relieved in many ways and had no qualms about killing both men. They were German.

Erebus and Vali could not trust the resistance, so Moen and his truck drivers became watchers, quickly confirming Mueller resided in a small, expensive hotel near Narvik city centre. As he did not go out without armed bodyguards, an assassination attempt was ruled out because of the inevitable gun battle and civilian casualties. Erebus remembered being told 'watchers' earn good luck. Olaf Pedersen, one of Moen's men, managed to get a contract delivering fresh vegetable produce every morning to Mueller's hotel. He soon learned from the goods inward porters that the hotel guests were mostly self-important high-ranking German officials. One, in particular, constantly complained about life in Narvik and made it clear he would only be content in Germany. Gentle probing confirmed Mueller or the 'bigmouthed American' as the unhappy man. The porter, now in full flow, complained that because 'the American' liked to shoot most weekends, hotel staff were forced to act as beaters and to serve lunch to his guests.

On a Saturday morning, while listening to a porter moaning about his holiday being cancelled, Olaf Pedersen struck gold. Mueller was hosting a large number of German and Norwegian ruling hierarchy officials in the woods outside Narvik. The complaining man supplied the date. Two weeks away. Erebus and Vali knew it was a chance too good to miss. The attack must be convincingly camouflaged. The Germans exacted brutal revenge on anyone remotely suspected of resistance activity.

This information was relayed to Maiden Aunt, who gave the go-ahead for the attack.

Pedersen, now a 'Watcher' and 'Gatherer', learned from hotel staff that during a shoot, Mueller's bodyguards were spread out as the shoot covered a large area. He also discovered the guests usually drank heavily, as did the guards, though covertly. Erebus had counted on some of the hunters being drunk, which would help convince investigators that Mueller's death was a shooting accident. The night before the hunt, Erebus was cleaning the rifle and round when Moen asked.

"What's so special about this rifle and bullet?"

Erebus explained slowly,

"It is a soft-nosed round that will explode once it enters the target and tear his chest to bits as if he had swallowed a grenade. What's left of him will look like a close-range shotgun accident."

Moen's reply was an aghast,

"Jesus!"

The Saturday of the hunt was warm and clear. Erebus, Moen and Pedersen followed the party, which was spread out in a line nearly a kilometre in length. The beaters were another kilometre ahead of that line. Mueller was located in the middle of the hunters, using shotguns, all more interested in killing than target shooting. Pedersen's information was accurate; some of the party officials were still half-drunk. Just behind all the drunken laughter, Erebus waited for the right moment.

The hunting party took lunch which was, for some, mainly liquid. Erebus, Moen and Olaf followed with relative ease, the guards being more interested in food and drink than guarding anyone. In the afternoon, the hunters raucously began shouting at the beaters and readied to shoot guinea fowl and grouse. Erebus positioned himself, then, in an instant, a large flock of birds flew up from the scrubland, and all the hunters fired.

Erebus took aim, then gently squeezed the trigger and, through the telescopic sight, watched Mueller's torso explode. The hunters were all blasting away at anything that flew, and only those in the immediate vicinity of Mueller saw him fall. Erebus and his comrades were already heading to Olaf's concealed truck.

Moen's lorry had been left a further five kilometres back, on the road near the hunt, to enable an escape if the shot had been taken earlier. As the men climbed into the cab of Olaf Pedersen's lorry, Moen said,

"One bastard less to kill tomorrow."

At Moen's truck, Olaf said.

"I've got another week of the job. Better not just disappear; the police might get suspicious."

The investigating police officers were profoundly sceptical about the scientist's death, but with high-ranking Norwegians and Nazis and the level of drunkenness in the hunting party, the officers took the politically safe option. Mueller's death was classified a tragic accident, and he was given a hero's burial.

Olaf Pedersen's bravery paid dividends later that week as he made his final hotel delivery. A very expensive leather holdall had been thrown down by the rubbish skip on the loading bay. Olaf asked,

"This is good quality. Why is it being dumped?"

"It belonged to the German scientist, but we were told to throw everything away – personal belongings – everything. Do you want the bag? There's a bloody swastika on it, or one of us would keep it," the porter replied as he threw the bag to Olaf. The Norwegian stopped the truck outside Narvik and examined the contents. There were photographs and papers, some personal, some official.

Within a week, Vali had sent the contents to the analysts at SOE. The photographs were very helpful; one was of a group of twenty men who were standing over what looked like a torpedo. The men were known to naval intelligence, and by process of elimination, identified. A high-ranking naval officer, some U-boat captains and a number of scientists. The group was important as, in the middle, was Grand Admiral Doenitz, commander in chief of U-boat fleet. Only two remained unidentified. One tall and blond, the other of similar height but with slightly dark hair. The analysts agreed both fitted a vague description of Hartmann, but which one was he?

Back in Norway, Erebus briefed his team that SOE had confirmed, through other sources, that Karl Hartmann had gone to sea in a merchant ship which was, they presumed, being used to test the acoustic torpedoes and supply them to U-boats at sea. Everyone went home and waited for the next time Erebus called them.

Colonel Travers and Lieutenant Cork, as ordered, submitted reports with recommendations on the equipment used on the Dieppe raid. The reports were forwarded to Admiral Mountbatten, who had resisted all attempts to remove him, and was now compiling the report which would be the blueprint for the invasion of Europe.

Keeping a very close eye on the whole affair was Prime Minister Churchill; who made unannounced visits to the plants working on the invasion equipment. Peter was again in London, and Connor was informed by telephone, a very important visitor would be calling to the plant. Work was to be as normal. At two o'clock, a police-escorted Rolls Royce pulled up at the gates. An astounded Connor Cork accompanied Winston Churchill around the plant. He took time to speak to most of the men, asking some cogent questions. Finally, he turned,

"Mr Cork, may we go to your office, please?"

Churchill sat down, and all Connor could think to do was to offer him a brandy. The Prime minister commented how the bottle was nearly empty. Connor explained how he and his son had drunk most of the bottle during his leave. Churchill looked through his glass and asked.

"Mr Cork, you are an Irishman. May I ask which part you are from?"

Connor replied,

"I am from County Cork, Prime minister."

His guest smiled,

"I knew a man from Cork, Michael Collins. I had hopes of a long relationship with General Collins and, in turn, Ireland, whatever place the country may have taken amongst the nations of the world. Tragically, he was killed as a very young man."

Before he could control himself, Connor spoke.

"I knew Michael Collins well, Prime minister. He was born and lived close to where I was raised. He was a few years older than me." He paused and confidently stated.

"I feel his death was tragic for Ireland and Anglo-Irish relations."

Churchill nodded his head slowly, stood up, shook Connors' hand, saying,

"Thank you for your hospitality and your excellent work here."

As the prime minister left the plant, he again spoke to many men. Connor heard him say to one Irish man,

"Thank you for staying to help us."

About to get into the car, he turned to Connor,

"I am staying in Portsmouth tonight, Mr Cork. Would you join me for dinner?" In a daze, Connor accepted. At half past seven, he was collected by two detectives and taken to a large secluded country house. In the dining room brandy was served. His host said,

"Thank you for coming tonight at short notice. I hope I did not inconvenience you too much."

Despite all he had heard about this Englishman who was despised in Ireland, Connor could not help warming to him. They sat, and as they were served the starter, Churchill said,

"Now, Mr Cork, tell me all about your countryman Michael Collins."

Connor told how he knew Collins years before in West Cork. Churchill invited him to talk about his life in Ireland and how he had come to be in Britain. Connor was completely relaxed and spoke with great pride of the family, his wife and children in Ireland and Pat being in the Royal Navy. The Prime minister listened with great attention, and occasionally Connor would be interrupted by the steward entering the room to ensure that their glasses were charged. Connor was surprised at how easily he talked and how much he remembered. Churchill voiced his approval of Connor, having sent his family to Kerry for safety. It was, he said,

"The honourable thing to do – to place non-combatants out of harm's way." Connor then heard himself apologising for talking nonstop. Churchill laughed,

"My dear Mr Cork, I spend half of my life listening to men who redefine the word loquacious. To listen to you is a pleasure; I believe the English language is spoken magnificently by the Irish. Just think of Oscar Wilde, James Joyce, Shaw, and so many others."

The evening ended, and Connor hoped he could remember just some of it. Churchill had spoken of many things, and before the dessert was served, he said to Connor,

"We will win the war, Mr Cork, now that the Americans are with us. The British Empire and her colonies have all rallied to the fight, but this war means the end of the old order. There will be no more empires; they are a thing of the past, Mr Cork."

Connor sat entranced as Churchill continued.

"The people who will bring about the end of the British Empire are men like your son. A man who was starting his working life as a carpenter but who, through circumstance and his own ability, is now an officer in the Royal Navy. The very essence of the British Empire. Tell me, Mr Cork, will your son be content to return to a carpenter's life when he has helped to defeat the Nazis? Will he be content to doff his cap to the so-called, 'upper classes? I doubt it very much, and I ask you, Mr Cork, why should he? And there are millions like him; why should they? He has earned his place in a free world, and in that free world, he can go where ever his ability allows him to, and rightly so."

Connor sat in stunned silence as the great man stood up and came round to his end of the table.

"Mr Cork, I spoke to one of your countrymen this morning and thanked him for staying in this country and helping us in our hour of need. I now extend that thanks to you, sir."

He raised his glass, and both men finished their drinks. Churchill continued,

"Mr Cork, I saw your plant this morning and how the work is going. Is there anything else you need to assist you in the completion of your vital work?"

Connor came back to earth and realised that Churchill was always prime minister and was always at war. He answered,

"Prime minister, I know we have everything we need, but I believe there should be more input from the men who have to transport the structures we are building. It concerns me that we may produce something which we may be unable to move to where it is needed."

Churchill nodded his head and said,

"I believe we need more input from the Royal Navy. The Royal Engineers have vast experience in building military installations all over the world. However, they have no experience in moving structures by sea. Thank you for your cogent input."

Connor stood and began to prepare to leave. Before he did, Churchill said,

"Mr Cork, I have enjoyed tonight immensely. Thank you very much. I note that you said earlier that when your son has leave you both like a glass of brandy. Perhaps I can help you there. Good night to you, Mr Cork." Connor could not help himself as he said,

"God bless you, Mr Churchill."

The prime minister smiled,

"I thank you for your kind thought, but I feel I should explain that we English devised a mechanism which relieved God of all responsibility for our actions and spiritual welfare some three hundred and fifty years ago. We called it 'The Reformation.'"

With that, Connor Cork left the presence of a man he would never forget and was driven home. That night he found sleep impossible. Lying in bed, he heard Peter English come in, and a thought occurred to him. During the dinner, Churchill had never once mentioned Eamon de Valera. As the sun came up, Connor Cork rose and prepared for a long day, made longer by lack of sleep, but after the previous evening, he couldn't have cared less.

17

Scatter

Captain Loftus sat, signal in hand. Commander Crowley stood waiting for the reaction of an angry and frustrated man.

"Please sit down, number one." Crowley did. Wearily Loftus continued.

"We are ordered to dock at Liverpool, provision and escort a convoy to the Russian port of Murmansk. Mr Crowley, please remind me, how long have we been at sea?"

"This commission - nearly twelve weeks, sir."

Loftus demanded.

"How are we to maintain an efficient fighting unit if our men are exhausted and demoralised? I wish somebody in the Admiralty would tell me." His voice exasperated; the captain continued.

"We steam to Iceland with ten merchantmen, where we collect another twenty-nine ships and on to Russian waters. Correct me if I'm wrong number one. By my reckoning, at seven knots, it will take seven days to make Iceland and a further fourteen to dock at Murmansk - a total of twenty-one days."

The captain's navigation skills were excellent, so Crowley didn't reply and continued in a similar vein.

"So if we double the time for the return passage and allow for bad weather, we're looking at another forty to fifty days at sea."

Loftus concluded the brief but heartfelt exchange.

"Add that to the three months we've just spent on Atlantic crossings, and our men will have run up nearly six months on active service without a single run ashore."

After a further minute's silence, Loftus sat up in his chair.

"Well, Mr Crowley, that's the self-pity over. Ask Mr Cork and Mr Larsen to see me straight away and brief all escort captains we will dock in Liverpool in forty-eight hours. They have seventy-two hours to fully provision. After which, we head for Russia, and God alone knows what."

Cork and Larsen stared at the charts as the captain briefed them.

"Now you have both seen our passage; we need to know just what aircraft are based in Norway and, as far as possible, how they will attack us. Also, the weather conditions for this time of year - not alone the long-range weather forecast, the summer conditions, hours of daylight, fog and such. Is that clear, gentlemen?"

Lars had been to the Meteorological Office; Pat, the naval operations centre. They stood in front of a now ebullient Loftus.

"Well Larsen, what can we expect?"

The Norwegian's voice was clear.

"The weather is completely unpredictable, sir. Though the daylight is not, we will have continuous daylight for the next three months. Perfect weather for all air operations - a bomber's paradise."

The captain looked at Pat.

"Tell me, Mr Cork, what good news do you have?"

Pat cleared his throat.

"Sir, we can expect attacks from Messerschmitt's, Stukas, Dornier and Hienkels, also, Condor long-range bombers. All based in airfields in occupied Norway."Loftus thanked and dismissed both officers. His mood was now one of determination. The provisioning had gone very well. The men were in relatively good spirits despite being treated, in his opinion, appallingly. Loftus made his views known to the C in C, 'Western approaches', who sympathised, but that was all. Well - not quite. The admiral had promised extra firepower to combat the air attacks but had not been specific. The elegant Englishman and his escort ships would have to wait and see; Loftus looked at the signals on his desk. One requesting all ships' captains to prepare a list of sailors taking leave was silently thrown into the wastepaper bin. There were reports from some escort captains that ships' companies were beginning to show fatigue. These were filed but not forgotten. There was a note from the first officer, a new radio, radar and ASDIC operator joining the ship. Loftus ordered the man to report.

Petty Officer Selby Constantine was from the West Indies and had trained as a radio operator aboard a merchantman. When war broke out, he had worked his passage to the UK and joined the Royal Navy. The man was just over six foot, very fit and was obviously highly intelligent. Loftus shook his hand and welcomed another addition to the growing multinational crew aboard Snow Eagle.

The ten merchantmen convoy made up of thirty-nine merchant ships steamed north to Scapa Flow and then into the Arctic Circle. Pat Cork was on watch and saw a squadron of British warships approach the convoy from the southeast. He informed the captain and was almost struck dumb by the sight of the battleship HMS Renown, thirty-two thousand tons of pure firepower. He was estimating the size of her main armament as the captain came onto the bridge.

"Fifteen and eight inch guns backed up by substantial anti-aircraft batteries. She's ideal for escort duty," Loftus informed the bridge watch and went on, "The cruisers Belfast and Sheffield have ten and eight inch guns and equally effective anti-aircraft batteries. They can take care of the Luftwaffe, and we will deal with the U-boats. Mr Cork, signal Renown that the convoy is making seven knots."

"Aye, aye, captain."

The Luftwaffe attacks began after the convoy cleared Iceland and were incessant for the next ninety-six hours. The smoke of explosions from the guns of the battleship, cruisers and escorts seemed to dim the daylight and caused mayhem amongst the attacking Germans aircraft. Pat finished his watch and, on the way to the wardroom, overheard some of his shipmates.

"That's good enough for the bastards. We should have had those battleships from the word go. There goes Renown again. Jesus! Its aft and forrard fifteen-inch guns. Christ! I swear the ocean shook with that broadside."

Another voice joined in.

"Bloody hell! That lot knocked out four Dornier. That'll teach 'em to fly in formation. Go on, you big bastard, give it to 'em."

Pat stood in the wardroom as Crowley handed him a mug of cocoa.

"How are your lads, Pat?"

"Well, from what I've just heard, Renown is lifting everybody, including me. Christ! I have never seen anything so big that floats," The convoy steamed on as attack after attack was driven off. Then a vicious storm blew up, making flying impossible. The escort crews relaxed, knowing not even the 'Master race's' Luftwaffe could better nature. Pat repeatedly checked the charts, and each time the convoy was a little closer to a safe port. At his last reckoning, the convoy was five days from Murmansk.

Everybody began to look forward to Murmansk; some of the crew were already practising how to order beer in Russian. The captain was on the bridge when Larsen handed him a signal from Renown.

Loftus read the signal out loud.

"Renown, the cruisers and her escorts have been ordered to a westerly position to intercept a German surface threat. We should be able to take care of the U-boats, and with this weather, the Luftwaffe won't be flying."

The first officer approached the captain with a second signal, his face white with astonishment.

"Well, what else, number one?"

Crowley controlled his voice with difficulty.

"We have been ordered to steam with Renown, sir."

Loftus took the signal, then, in a calm voice, ordered.

"Number one, please ready the escorts to depart the convoy. I will be in my cabin."

Loftus had spent his adult life in the Royal Navy and had always followed orders without question. Had he voiced his concerns on the bridge, it could be seen as a serious undermining of discipline. In the privacy of his cabin was a different matter where he spoke without knowing it.

"This will leave the convoy without any escort at all; do they know this, do they?"

There was a knock on the cabin door. The captain steeled himself.

"Enter."

Pat Cork came in with another signal.

"Read it, please, Mr Cork."

Pat spoke very slowly, trying to hide the disbelief in his voice.

"Sir, the signal is from Convoy Operations. It instructs PQ19 merchantmen to scatter and to proceed to Murmansk individually."

There was silence as Pat watched the blood drain from his captain's face. Loftus forced himself to be optimistic.

"Well, if the storm continues, they should have a good chance to make port. How many days are we from Murmansk, Lieutenant?"

Cork's voice was increasingly emotional.

"Five days at the most, sir, but the Luftwaffe, sir. The bloody U-boats?"

Loftus spoke with force.

"Lieutenant Cork, we have to obey orders." Then voiced the terrifying truth.

"And every man aboard this ship knows how vulnerable merchantmen are without escorts." His voice softened.

"Pat, please keep me informed of the mood of the crew. Tell Commander Crowley I will be on the bridge directly. That's all, thank you. Please carry on."

As the Royal Navy steamed to meet the enemy, thirty-nine small ships scattered to all points of the compass and continued on their lonely way to the port of Murmansk.

Captain Loftus briefed the ship's company on the possible battle ahead.

"The size and makeup of the enemy is unknown. Until further notice, we are attached to the battle squadron commanded by HMS Renown."

Despite the pending action, the convoy was still on most sailors' minds, and Pat sensed anger and frustration never experienced on Snow Eagle before.

The days went on without any enemy engagement. Loftus tried long and hard for permission to return to Arctic waters and escort the convoy. From the Admiralty, there was just silence. Finally, HMS Renown and her squadron were redeployed. Loftus contacted the Admiralty requesting information on the Murmansk convoy. C in C Western Approaches confirmed the almost total destruction of convoy PQ19. The feeling of desolation and guilt was overwhelming. Then another signal confirming leave for the escorts in Liverpool or Londonderry. Loftus chose the Northern Irish port, because there his men could vent their anger. In the pubs of Londonderry, the boys could sound off without being identified by security officers or naval police. In Liverpool, near Western Approaches Command, that might not be the case.

The escorts tied up in Londonderry, and before long, the terrible fate of PQ19 became common knowledge. Any attempts to contain details of the convoy losses failed as the German propaganda machine went into overdrive. Lord Haw-Haw was broadcasting to the whole world, telling the number of ships sunk and how the Royal Navy had fled from the Luftwaffe and the U-boats in the Arctic Circle. Of the thirty-nine ships, thirty-two had been destroyed. The Luftwaffe and U-boats hunted them down at their leisure.

Once ashore, the crews read Royal navy 'Daily Orders'; all Russian convoys were to be suspended until further notice. This order was greeted with derision by the men who regarded it as a trick by the Admiralty to save a senior officer's career. Or as one sailor put it.

"Just another fucking whitewash!"

Lieutenant Pat Cork and Lieutenant Commander Larsen sat in silence in their cabin, emotions out of control. Pat, seething, needed time to calm down and Larsen, straight-faced, hid his agony as he thought of how many of the ships lost were Norwegian. The silence was as complete as words were useless. The desolation was broken when a midshipman knocked and put his head around the door.

"Wardroom in ten minutes, please, gentlemen." They arrived to find the captain, Commander Crowley, and the officers of the escort ships. The doors were closed, and in an overcrowded wardroom, Loftus spoke.

"Gentlemen, I have asked you all here to convey my appreciation of the service of you and your men over the last six months. By now, you know of the losses suffered by convoy PQ19. I am aware of the discontent amongst our shipmates. I am now speaking as a man who also feels the same."

There was silence for a moment, and then Crowley spoke.

"Right, let's get it all out in the open. No holds barred." Commander Warne, captain of Sea Tiger, spoke first.

"Jesus, skipper! What the hell is going on? We left all of those men to die – and for nothing. Where were these bloody German battleships? What I'm saying, sir, is if we'd sunk some German bastard, it just might be easier to take."

Loftus looked around the room,

"Who's next? Come on, I said, 'clear the air." More officers spoke up during the hour finally; Pat spoke

"Sir, I am a conscript; the war is why I am here today. I believe that what we are doing is the only way to beat these Nazis. Why is it, sir, that we are still under the command of men who are, to put it politely, dinosaurs? All we did last month was chase shadows and allow good men to die for nothing in hell's own waters."

Then there was just silence. Captain Loftus spoke.

"Gentlemen, I joined the Royal Navy many years ago and saw action in the First World War where, if I am being honest, the course of that terrible struggle was decided in the trenches of Europe. The navy had a secondary role, but in this modern era, we face a different challenge. The orders to sail with Renown were issued by men who see enemy battleships as the most serious threat to the allied war effort. I disagree; I see a far more effective and ruthless enemy in the U-boats. The last few weeks have tested us all to the limit. I am certain that you all care passionately about the convoys we are tasked with protecting. This meeting is, I feel safe in saying, the first and probably the last of its kind in Royal Naval history. I cannot stress enough the need for you all to keep secret what we have discussed here. There are elements within the Admiralty who would look upon this gathering as mutiny. They do have influence in the service. What you have said has made me certain of two things. The first is that we can win the war with all of you part-time sailors. The second is that we must have air support - and soon."

Loftus paused to regain his composure.

"Commander Crowley and I have been ordered to the Admiralty; we leave tomorrow at four bells in the noon watch. The ship's companies have all been given three weeks leave. Please make the best use of it; it may be sometime before the next. Now please vacate the wardroom as a buffet lunch to which you are guests of Commander Crowley and me will be served in thirty minutes."

The sun being way over the yardarm; there was plenty to drink and eat as the officers of the Snow Ship Escort Group relaxed and began to come to terms with one of the worst disasters in Royal Naval history. When concerns about their crews were raised, they were told similar functions had been arranged in a number of pubs in Londonderry.

The next morning, Pat and Larsen waited for Loftus outside his cabin. They came to attention when Loftus appeared accompanied by Crowley and a four-ring captain. Loftus introduced Captain Bradbury, who was in charge of the installation of new radar and sonar equipment. Bradbury explained the work would involve the rebuilding of certain cabins, one being Pat and Lars'. Loftus took over.

"We've booked you into a small hotel near the yard but nicely in the centre of town. So you'll have some time ashore, so enjoy it, gentlemen. Now Captain Bradbury and I will have a look round the ship. Number one, please carry on with the briefing." As the senior officers left, Crowley spoke.

"All of the ship's living quarters are being refurbished, so there will be builders everywhere. Security is being provided by the Military Police and the shore patrol. Sorry about this Pat but we need someone here for at least one hour a day. Apart from that, your time is pretty much your own. The majority of the crews have gone home, and the remainder of the men have been billeted ashore."

He continued,

"Lars, later on during the work, Captain Bradbury will need you on hand as the new kit is commissioned. You will be responsible for training the crew on the new system. Now both of you go and have some fun."

Like schoolboys allowed home early, Pat and Larsen excitedly collected their personal kit and left the ship. As briefed, the hotel was near the city centre. Having checked in, Pat's first priority was to find a doctor to examine his leg. As the receptionist gave him the address of a local GP, Pat asked,

"Should I call and make an appointment?"

The girl just smiled and said,

"You're in Londonderry now; nothing's too much trouble for the Royal Navy. I'll call now, just a wee minute."

Lars was enthralled by the girl and enquired,

"Pat, what is a wee minute?"

As if on cue, the receptionist spoke.

"Doctor McBurney will see you straight away!

Five minutes later, Pat was being examined, and the doctor asked how he had been wounded; Pat hesitated and was assured.

"Lieutenant, all I need to know is the cause of your wound, not where or when it was inflicted."

Pat replied,

"Sorry, Doctor. It's just that you get into a habit of not revealing anything."

The reply was unexpected.

"Don't worry about anyone here, young man; there are no Taigs around here. We are all loyal to the Crown and the British empire."

Pat concealed his surprise at the declaration and then explained how he had been wounded. Dr McBurney, a slim, slightly balding man, spoke in a relaxed, professional manner,

"I was a young medic during the First World War and saw many wounds, so I do have a deal of experience in this field. I consult at the Royal Victoria in Belfast. Your leg is not too bad but far from ideal."

He put his head down as if speaking to himself.

"Perhaps a second opinion."

Then looked up and continued,

"Be careful not to allow too much exposure to extreme conditions; otherwise, you are fit for active service." Then Pat was introduced to the doctor's wife.

"Please make the lieutenant an appointment for next week, my dear."

Turning to Pat, he said,

"There is a colleague of mine; I would like his opinion before you return to sea."

His wife took up the conversation.

"I'll arrange a time and drop the appointment card around to your hotel. Is that OK with you?"

Pat nodded and left, a little overawed by the kindness.

The officers stood outside a small pub. A quick look found it quiet. Pat ordered two pints, and Larsen drank his first pint of Irish stout – it wouldn't be his last. Pat left him in the bar, talking to some of the locals. Later, he was called to reception, where a visitor waited for him.

Mrs McBurney was considerably younger than her husband. Very attractive, about thirty-five years of age, with dark green eyes and waves of jet-black hair. Pat tried not to stare as he guessed her to be about five foot six inches tall with a full and well-proportioned figure. They were having drinks Pat had bought to thank her. Her voice was soft.

"A consultant will see you in a week's time in my husband's surgery." He nodded and was about to order another drink when the door to the small hotel burst open, and in came a very drunk Norwegian. Lars had obviously been made very welcome by the regular clientele at the pub. He saw Pat and ambled over,

"Hello, Pat."

Then, peering at the woman, he added,

"Hello, Mrs Doctor." He continued with what Pat would later describe as an unbelievably stupid grin on his face.

"I have been drinking Jinness."

Pat corrected.

"Lars, Guinness - that's how it's pronounced."

The Norwegian made an attempt at the word, failing miserably, but continued,

"Jinness is really good. Why didn't you tell me about it before Pat? I have never tasted anything like Jinness."

"How many pints did you have, Lars?"

Larsen looked around him, saw the receptionist, smiled,

"Hello."

He quickly turned to Pat.

"I had about twelve pints, I think, with some friends in the pub. Mrs Doctor, everybody here is so friendly."

Mrs McBurney smiled.

"Nothing is too good for the Royal Navy, Commander Larsen. Welcome to Londonderry."

Lars leaned forward, nearly in tears.

"I shouldn't be drunk, but my home is occupied by Germans, and I can't forget the convoy or Snow Cougar."

He straightened himself and said,

"Goodnight, Mrs Doctor and goodnight, my friend, Pat," then staggered out of reception, climbed the stairs and disappeared. Pat began to apologise.

"Please forgive him, Mrs McBurney, he is.........."

She interrupted.

"Please don't apologise for anything, and my name is Victoria. Now let me buy you a drink."

Pat accepted, and after another round of drinks, the lady went home.

The following morning, Pat found Larsen at the breakfast table very much the worse for wear. Later aboard Snow Eagle, Bradbury briefed both officers. "Gentlemen, we have reports of some of the crews getting out of hand in some local pubs. Nothing serious, no one hurt or anything, just damage to fixtures and fittings." Pat spoke.

"Right Sir, we'll do the rounds and settle any outstanding matters." The first stop was RUC headquarters, where they were advised the pub landlords would be happy just having any damages paid for. The rest of the day, Pat watched with sadistic pleasure as Lars drank the best pint of Guinness in Ireland with each of the publicans as a final settlement of all dues. There were no more complaints as the initial flurry of drunkenness waned; the men relaxed and enjoyed their leave.

The specialist from the 'Royal' advised Pat his leg would do, on the condition that he undergo surgery, to improve circulation to the lower leg when the war ended. Pat expressed his thanks as Dr Trimble advised him a report with recommendations for further treatment would be sent. When Pat tried to pay for the examination, the consultant quickly explained as a lifelong friend of 'Mac' he would not accept any fee and also because nothing was too good for the Royal Navy. As he was leaving, Victoria began chatting.

"Where is Lars today, and has he had any more 'jinness?"

They laughed.

"He's on-board ship. Why don't you come and see the ship; she's beginning to take shape now that the work is near completion. I'll arrange a tour for you. Please come; every ship needs a woman's blessing."

Before she could reply, Pat heard,

"Yes, you must go, Vicky."

It was her husband, and he added,

"Nothing is too good for the Royal Navy, and you are the best."

Victoria agreed to visit Snow Eagle. Pat cleared the lunch with Captain Bradbury, who had his head buried in a box of some sort and just grunted his assent.

The following day, just before noon, Lars and Pat were on the bridge, bored stiff with nothing to do other than scan the dockyard with binoculars. The yard was a hive of activity with at least thirty ships tied to numerous jetties. Finally, Pat broke the silence.

"Everyone is very busy apart from us." For a second, he felt a flash of anger that he could have seen his dad, instead of doing nothing on board all day every day. Lars replied.

"We'll soon be busy, Pat; they're not installing this kit for us to go fishing."

Captain Bradbury appeared on the bridge saying,

"Sorry, it's so bloody awful boring for you boys. I did try to persuade the powers we could handle everything but to no avail. They ordered a ships' officer be on call during the refit. Now, I have a surprise for you both. With that, Victoria McBurney appeared on the bridge.

"Sorry, am I early?"

Bradbury answered,

"From what I've just heard, your timing is perfect. Lieutenant Cork, when are you going to introduce me to our guest?"

Pat did so, and Captain Bradbury was charm itself as he entertained all of them for the afternoon. The wardroom had been cleared of builders' rubbish, and a cold collation was served with a delicious wine – wherever he got it from. The foursome toured the ship and then returned to the wardroom, where the conversation went into the evening. Bradbury said,

"Look, I'm sorry, but I've got to go. This was my way of saying thank you for being so professional about the last ten days. The refit is almost complete, and you both have made a substantial contribution."

Larsen spoke.

"That's very kind of you, sir, but we didn't do anything."

"Precisely, Commander, that's why the refit has gone so well. There are certain officers on board ships who cannot leave well alone. We are dealing with highly complicated kit, and some still think they know it all - well, they don't. You acknowledged that, and you two are a good deal brighter than some I've met recently. Well done."

He stood up, kissed Victoria's hand, then looked at Lars and said,

"We begin training the day after tomorrow. Understood?"

He nodded at Pat.

Pat walked Victoria home after a day, she excitedly told him she would never forget. Her voice softened.

"Pat, I am married to a man who is nearly twenty years older than me. He is my second husband. My first died, aged thirty, from alcohol poisoning. When I married him, I had no idea he had problem, and for the first year, he was the ideal man. We have very good Guinness in Northern Ireland, but we have very good whiskey as well, believe me. What I didn't know was that the poor man was addicted to Bushmills. God, I am rambling. How's your leg? Are you tired, Pat?"

Pat encouraged his companion,

"Go on if you want to. I have all night and only the hotel to go back to."

She smiled and linked him as they slowed their pace.

"What I found incredible about my first husband was that he could drink anything and yet function perfectly. His business was going well and I never suspected anything until there was no children coming. We tried, but, as I was told after his death, the alcohol made him sterile. He died at work of a massive stroke, and the irony is he left me very well off."

Pat asked,

"Why did you marry again, then?"

Immediately as he said the words, he regretted the question and wanted to say so, but Victoria put her finger on his lips and smiled to show she understood.

"Pat, I was in shock for a while and then I met Dr McBurney, who had lost his wife about a year earlier. We are not in love, we never were, but he is a kind man and when we decided to get married it was for company and, would you believe, to go to America. My husband is a very accomplished doctor, and as a married man, he would have settled in America far easier. There was nothing for me here, so I agreed to become his wife, but then the war came and, as you know better than any of us, Trans-Atlantic travel is not recommended. Neither of us holds the other responsible for the war, and now we are just the best of friends."

By now, they had reached the house where Pat wished Victoria goodnight and walked back to his hotel. The next day, the commissioning of the new equipment began. Pat had a little more to do, but it was Larsen, Captain Bradbury and shore-based technicians who were heavily involved all day. He finally had a chance to speak to Captain Bradbury and ask him when the cabin would be restored to them.

Bradbury explained,

"The problem is that there are essential cables running behind that bulkhead, so we won't be securing that wall of your cabin until everything is tested to full capacity. I'd say at least another week at the earliest."

Pat nodded.

"Thank you, sir."

Another week in the hotel. He wasn't going to complain about that, and neither was Lars, who was working very long hours indeed. In fact, he had seen him aboard the ship but not in the hotel. Pat was in reception. The weather was nearly perfect. August was in full bloom, but he had been told there was the chance of a shower now and by no less an authority than a Londonderry taxi driver. Victoria came through the hotel door looking distressed, saw him and motioned to come outside. There, in the back seat of a taxi, was an almost unconscious Larsen. Pat put his arm under Lars' body, and he and Victoria got him to his room. Once on the bed, Pat asked,

"Where did you find him, Victoria?"

She turned.

"I was about to drop your medical report when I saw Lars asleep in the taxi. The driver was about to call the shore patrol. Pat, what's wrong with him? Why is he drinking so much?"

Pat sighed.

"Victoria, I have to tell you what has been eating away at Lars and maybe me. But first of all, thank you for looking after him - and me."

She looked searchingly.

"Pat, what do you mean?"

He told her all the details and fate of PQ19. Then finally said.

"All I wanted to do was to get drunk and maybe do something really stupid."

Victoria queried.

"What do you mean by stupid?"

"I thought about jumping the border and spending the rest of the war with my family in Kerry. You know, I haven't seen my mother in two years. I don't even know why I'm boring you with all this. I suppose it's just so good to have someone listening to me who I think actually cares."

He paused and then regained control.

"Victoria, what time do you want to go home?"

She answered as she looked in the bar mirror.

"It's still early, Pat, and I don't mind listening some more." Then asked.

"Can I go to your room to straighten my clothes?"

He gave her the key. About five minutes later, having checked Lars was asleep, he went to his room. The curtains were drawn, and Victoria was standing facing the window with her raincoat on. The moonlight made her outline stark, Pat said,

"Thank you for your help again this evening."

She turned and opened her raincoat, which fell from her body. She was naked except for her high heels and stood with her hands on her hips,

"As I said, nothing is too good for the Royal Navy."

Pat stood and looked at her, his heart racing, mouth dry. Amazingly, a question crossed his mind.

'Did I say all that just to get her here?' There was no answer. He took Victoria's hand and led her to the bed, never taking his eyes from her as he undressed. She ran her hand through her hair, and then he was beside her. She kissed him and, within seconds, whispered,

"Now, Pat, now."

They moved down the bed until both were lying flat, and then he slid over her; she parted her legs and moved her body very quickly as he moved into her. He gasped as she impaled herself on him. Pat began to move in and out of her, their eyes locked. Her hands were all over his body, touching, caressing, directing him where to kiss her, where to touch her, and all the time as he moved into her, she made him sink a little deeper into her body. She drew her legs up and locked them around his back. Amidst all the passion, he marvelled at her control; this beautiful woman was in complete control of their sex, then she kissed his neck and ear in such a way that he came inside her. They lay in each other's arms for some time in silence, and then she sat up, inviting Pat to enjoy her nakedness.

"Well Pat, I think we both surprised each other there."

He sat up, reached out, cupped her left breast and said,

"I'll never be able to look at a raincoat again without getting an erection."

His mouth closed on her nipple as she laughed.

"Come on Pat, surprise me again."

They made love for the next two hours, both of them becoming aroused within minutes of reaching orgasm. She was an experienced lover and took the lead. Pat willingly followed. Just after midnight, she dressed and said,

"Pat, I have no idea why this happened, but I don't regret it for one minute. I want to be with you until you go to sea – if possible, every day, and if there are consequences, I'll worry about them later. I'll call again tomorrow night about six. Is that ok?"

Pat got out of the bed.

"Let me get dressed and take you home."

Victoria kissed him and said,

"No, I'll be fine. I'll get a taxi. Goodnight, lieutenant."

She kissed him again and left.

Pat was on deck early as the first of the crew were returning from leave. Snow Eagle's crew got to know the changes. There was increased railing on the weather deck, and lashing rings had been fitted to bulkheads leading to the open deck area. As with all sailors, everybody knew why so much new equipment had been installed and told anyone who would listen. Pat was busy as the ship came alive, then he saw Larsen and tore into him.

"Jesus, Lars, what the hell were you up to last night. Christ, you were as drunk as a skunk. If you need that much liquid, why don't you just throw yourself overboard and have done with it. Christ Lars, what is wrong with you?"

Larsen looked at him and said,

"Pat, I am very busy, so this will be quick. First, thanks for last night. Believe me; it won't happen again. You know why; because you are not talking to me, you are, in fact, talking to my ghost. When I woke up this morning, I felt dead. The night porter in the hotel gave me something called a hot toddy. Which did one of two things, it either cured my hangover or it killed me. I don't know which, but as I can now feel nothing, I presume I am dead."

All Pat could do was laugh as Captain Bradbury came on deck.

"Ah! Just the man I've been looking for. Lieutenant Cork, I have just spoken to Captain Loftus; he will be aboard in three days. He's been briefed on your cabin condition and agrees that you stay in the hotel until further notice. Commander, let's go; we have a lot to do today."

A number of the junior officers were aboard, and Pat set a duty roster to cover the running of the ship, which inadvertently left him with more time on his hands. At six o'clock, Victoria stopped outside the hotel in a car and ordered.

"Jump in." After about twenty minutes, they were at what looked like an army customs post. The traffic through the checkpoint was light, and everybody seemed to be on first-name terms. The soldiers chatted to the people crossing the border by foot, bicycle, horse and cart and occasionally car. Having watched for a short time the couple drove further into the countryside. Pat was about to ask Victoria a question when she kissed him passionately. He responded willingly; their tongues engaged in a delightful wrestling match. When the kiss ended, Victoria gave him the most beautiful smile and said,

"Hello Pat, how are you?"

He replied,

"Very well, thank you. Now what was all that about?"

"That, my darling man, is the border between the North of Ireland and the Free State. So, if you still wish to jump the border, as you so melodramatically put it last night, you won't have to jump very high."

Pat countered,

"I didn't say what I did last night just to get you into bed, or at least I don't think I did."

She leaned over and said,

"That little bit of honesty is going to be well rewarded later on, Pat, my handsome sailor."

She then explained the reality of the border. How allied servicemen were simply allowed to walk across the border and rejoin the fighting. The Germans were different, as they stuck out like a sore thumb on either side of the border. Those happy to sit out the war did so. Those who didn't were arrested because of the risk of sabotage to the allied installations in the North. Pat began to understand how impossible the situation in Ireland was. As they walked through the beautiful land, Victoria told him how the war had been the best thing that had happened to Londonderry. There were over one hundred and twenty warships based in the docks in Londonderry. The crews had brought money and trade to the town. Pat cut in,

"Hence, nothing is too good for the Royal Navy."

She turned, smiled and said,

"I always knew I was in the presence of a genius."

He pulled her close and kissed her; she pressed her body against his, and he asked,

"Vicky, what is a Taig?"

She sat down in the long grass and pulled him with her.

"A Taig is a catholic with nationalist leanings; some people in the North regard all Catholics are Taigs."

Pat asked,

"What do you mean by 'nationalist'?"

"Well, in a nutshell, there is an element in the Free State or 'The South', which claims all of the six counties as their own. Some northern Catholics share that view. Many people - mostly Protestants – in the North of Ireland totally disagree. As a result, all Catholics are now identified as nationalists or, as Taigs," she answered.

"Vicky, why haven't you asked me what religion I am?"

She whispered in his ear.

"Well, you are definitely not Jewish." She scoffed.

"Pat, who cares about religion, there are far more important things in life." She gently bit his ear lobe and lightly caressed his growing erection.

"And you, my beautiful man, are full of life. Now come on, let's get back to town."

After a quick dinner in his room, he undressed her and explored her with his fingertips and tongue. She whispered fiercely.

"Pat inside me now, now! He obeyed. Victoria played him with her tongue and fingers as if he were an instrument. He came deep inside her, almost at her will. They lay in each other's arms, and as midnight approached, she got up and dressed. She kissed him on the lips and said,

"Goodnight, my Royal Navy."

Pat was on deck, determined that the captain would not find any faults upon his return. Eight o'clock struck on the dockyard clock, and the next forty-eight hours were spent checking and double-checking every operation on the ship. When Captain Loftus was piped aboard, the crew stood to attention on deck. Pat noticed immediately that Loftus had the rank of Commodore. A commander boarded with him, but the first officer was not in attendance. Loftus accepted Pat's salute as the senior officer present,

"Lieutenant Cork, stand the crew down and follow me. Would you please join us, Commander Larsen?"

In the captain's cabin, Pat and Larsen were stood easy by Loftus.

"Gentlemen. This is Commander Buchan of the Royal Canadian Navy. He has been transferred to the Royal Navy until further notice or until we win the war, whichever comes first. He is, as of this moment, captain of HMS Snow Eagle. Lieutenant Cork, you have been given a half stripe and are now the first officer of this ship. Commander Larsen, your considerable aptitude for operating the new radio shack equipment has been reported to me by Captain Bradbury. You are now the fleet radio officer with responsibility for working out the maximum benefit to be gained from this kit to kill U-boats in single ship and fleet attack. The other escorts of the group are making steam from Liverpool, and we will rendezvous with them and resume convoy escort duty. You sail in thirty-six hours. Captain Buchan, I'll leave you to introduce yourself to your officers, and I'll see you in three days off Scapa Flow."

Buchan replied,

"Aye, aye, sir," and with that, he was gone. Buchan shook hands with Pat.

"Number one, congratulations on your half stripe. I'll meet the other officers as we make our way to Scapa Flow. Please arrange times for each officer to speak to me on a one-to-one basis, and I'd like you to be present. I understand you have been sleeping ashore because of the refit. Make tonight the last, would you. I spoke to Captain Bradbury, and he tells me all should be in order in your cabin by midday tomorrow."

Pat stayed as the captain spoke to Larsen. He saw a tall man with a strong, honest face, solidly built, with dark hair tinged with grey and skin tanned brown as all men who had been at sea. Pat estimated the captain to be about six foot one inch tall. His demeanour was confident and efficient.

"Commander, I have been informed that you are the man who is leading on the equipment installed in all of the ships in the fleet. Hopefully, you can bring me up to speed before we get into too much trouble."

He added,

"Number one, there is another addition to the ship's company, a senior chief petty officer who was with me on my last ship. His name is Adams; please make yourself known to him as soon as you can. Right, that's all for now. I want to be at sea within thirty-six hours. All understood, number one?"

"Very good, sir."

Pat's head was spinning; ninety minutes ago, he'd been a second Lieutenant. Now he was Lieutenant Commander Cork, first officer of His Majesty's ship Snow Eagle. Coming on deck, he saw a chief petty officer directing the crew provisioning ship. Pat presumed this must be the CPO the captain had spoken of.

"May I have a word, please, chief?" The chief petty officer immediately came to attention and saluted. Pat returned the salute as the man answered,

"Yes, sir."

Both men moved to the rail. Pat introduced himself and explained why he would be ashore that night. Chief Adams shook his hand.

"I understand completely, sir. These are strange times; leave it all to me. Might I suggest that we load the ambient supplies whilst you're away and then the ammo when you get back?"

He lowered his voice and continued,

"I've been with the captain in two commissions, sir, and I think he'd prefer it if you were aboard tonight." Pat got the message loud and clear and made a promise to thank the chief when he had time.

"Right, I'll get my kit and be aboard in an hour; please carry on chief."

Then he called the second officer and told him to stick close to the chief until he returned. Having cleared his room and when back aboard Snow Eagle, Victoria came to mind. Pat assuaged a sense of guilt with logic. There was far too much to do to call her, even if he could. He didn't allow himself to give her a second thought. As for somewhere to sleep, the question didn't arise as the ship was provisioning throughout the night and, as first officer, it was his responsibility to guarantee that all was in order. He found CPO Adams to be of immense assistance. His years of experience in the navy showed as every problem was dealt with quickly and without fuss. Finally the ship's company were ordered to load the ammunition which would enable HMS Snow Eagle to destroy kill U-boats and enemy aircraft.

Pat noticed that the crew were in better spirits and worked with eagerness. The leave had done them all the world of good. These were the same men who had been close to mutiny three weeks earlier. Now they were a ship's company again. The dawn came up over Londonderry as the captain began his round, and after four hours, pronounced himself reasonably happy. He then turned to the assembled ship's company and said,

"I gave you thirty-six hours to ready the ship for sea. You did it in twenty-four. Well done. Men of Snow Eagle, I'm very happy to be here, and I think we are going to get along. Now we put to sea."

In a completely spontaneous response, one hundred and eighty men saluted and shouted.

"Aye, aye, sir."

18

Mulberries and Nephews

Connor Cork lived for his family's letters. His wife's last letter read everybody was well and wanted to come home. Pat's mail was erratic because of sea duty. The last told of a new captain and his promotion. That was all. Connor had started to give serious thought to bringing the family home. There were still sporadic air raids, and the sea crossing from Ireland to Britain still terrified him. Pat said a U-boat could attack anywhere - including the Irish Sea. Connor mentioned his dilemma to Peter English, who voiced another view.

"I would love to meet your family, but Connor, it's the risk of travelling. That's the problem, my friend. God, if anything happened to them, you would never forgive yourself – never."

Those words settled Connor's mind, and he wrote a letter to his wife explaining his fears. Replying immediately, Mary again displayed riveting common sense, writing she fully understood, adding that the time for her and the children to come back was when they could all go into their home together. Connor again thought how lucky he was to have met her, and it only made him miss her more. In a dark moment, he remembered how different things could have been.

As 1942 came to a close, English decided to brief the entire E & C workforce on the aims of the work in which they were engaged.

"Gentlemen, we have been tasked with the following. To build what are called 'pontoons'. Concrete structures which will float. When built, these pontoons will be joined together and form a roadway with enough flexibility to allow for sea wave motion. The pontoons will be attached to caissons that will be anchored to the sea bed. Laid on top of the Pontoons will be a steel road. A number of jetties will be attached at right angles to the main structure at which cargo ships will unload supplies for the invasion forces. Now, are there any questions?"

The men, all highly experienced and skilled, were stunned into silence. One did manage to ask,

"How long does this structure have to last, Mr English?"

Connor spoke,

"It will need to last until the allies liberate a port in Europe."

Peter English finished with a flourish.

"Gentlemen, the civil engineering industry has received its orders from the men and women fighting for freedom. To construct a floating harbour in component parts." He paused as if for effect.

"Then tow it across the English Channel! Once we get to our destination, we put the parts together."

The work was incessant as design revisions arrived on an almost weekly basis, and a growing sense of belief spread through E & C Fabrications as slowly the pontoons began to take shape.

In September, the pontoons were moved to Dungeness on the South coast of England for sea trials. The components now attached were anchored on the seabed. When the tests were completed, the Royal Engineers were to remove and store the structures under secure conditions. Having attended the trials, the partners of E & C fabrications were quietly pleased with their work.

Many other civil engineering companies involved in the project were in hotels and boarding houses around Dungeness. There was general satisfaction, enhanced by a sense that the civil engineering industry was making a real contribution to the war effort.

As a result of this rare opportunity to meet in uncommonly pleasant circumstances, an almost party atmosphere prevailed as old friends had a few drinks. The geniality was somewhat dampened when rumours began to circulate that the commanding officer of the Royal Engineers, a Colonel Morley, had allowed the pontoons to sink. Confirmation came via a civil engineer, who had been informed by a Royal Engineer junior officer that Morley had stated the structures would remain in the sea.

At a heated meeting during the next week, Morley was told by the builders the pontoons were, to an extent, evolving and must be brought ashore for examination. Colonel Morley seemed to take exception to being told anything by anyone - least of all civilians and became increasingly defensive. Finally, the owner of a very successful civil engineering company wondered out loud whether the Colonel, 'wanted to save the pontoons at all. Indeed, he seemed to be concentrating on giving spurious reasons for not doing so.'

Eight days had passed since the structures were immersed, and no information was coming from the Colonel or his men. Peter had returned to Portsmouth. Connor and RS Kennedy, the man who openly challenged Morley, stayed on to try to find an answer. Attempts to see the colonel were politely ignored. Both stood on the beach where at low tide, the heads of the pontoons were visible. One of the younger officers commanded by Colonel Morley was on the beach and introduced himself.

"Lieutenant Rodber, Royal Engineers, or Sappers. Gentlemen, sorry about the situation." The civilians introduced themselves. Connor then asked,

"There are no guards here. Why is that do you know?"

The lieutenant replied,

"Off the record, sir, Colonel Morley is adamant that since Royal Engineers weren't in charge of the project, they shouldn't be guarding someone else's mess."

RS Kennedy, in a broad Scottish accent spoke.

"Tell me something young man, does this colonel of yours have any notion of trying to raise these structures before we lose the war?" The sapper's voice was slightly plaintive.

"I can't answer that question, sir. The problem here is that we don't have any experience of working in water. That's because we are rather good at building structures to cross it. This is more of a salvage job, gentlemen."

"My son is in the navy - perhaps he could do it on his next leave," Connor said sarcastically. The lieutenant replied,

"If the colonel has his way, your son might have to, sir. Good day to you both."

Upon his return to the Royal Engineers' camp, Lieutenant Rodber was called to the colonel's office. Morley, five feet ten, with light brown hair and the body of a fit professional soldier, was looking out of the window in the general direction of Dungeness. His open face was troubled. He had guaranteed the Sappers could deliver the harbour. Now, it looked as if the whole project was going to collapse. He heard a knock on the door.

"Enter."

Morley turned,

"Well, Rodber, anything new on the beach?"

"Yes, sir. There were two civil contractors on the beach this morning asking some questions." Morley almost shouted at him,

"Asking questions! What questions? Who were they? You'd have better got their names." The junior officer answered in a slightly defiant tone.

"They were Mr Cork of E & C Fabrications and Mr RS Kennedy of a company of the same name. Mr Cork asked why there were no guards on the beach and Mr Kennedy asked if you were going to raise the structures before we lose the war." Morley's self-control was stretched to the limit, but he did manage to ask one more question of the young man, who he believed was secretly laughing at him.

"Was there anything unusual about these men, Rodber?" The lieutenant spoke with almost tangible sarcasm,

"Mr Cork is Irish and has a son in the Royal Navy, and Mr Kenned– is Scottish - if that's unusual sir."

"Dismissed Rodber." Morley finished the testy exchange.

The office door had hardly closed when Morley was on the phone to an old friend in the security section of the Royal Engineers and demanded that both civilians be scrutinised. He was asked,

"Scrutinised for what reason?"

Morley replied,

"Threat to the security of the project due to the nature of questions asked of my men." When asked for the questions Morley placed them out of context, specifically the query about sentries, adding that one of the men was Irish. The security officer was doubtful, but Morley was a full colonel and old India hand, so he put the wheels in motion.

Connor returned to Portsmouth, where he and Peter English discussed the best course of action to take. To them, inter-service rivalry was irrelevant. Their sole concern was to raise the structures. English said.

"I'll make some phone calls to the Ministry of works. See if they can do anything." At about eleven o'clock, Connor's secretary knocked and came in to his office, grim-faced.

"There is a policeman here to see you, Mr Cork."

A sensation of pure terror ran down Connor's back as he thought of Pat. The policeman entered the office, and the worried woman closed the door.

"Good morning, I am superintendent Spence of Portsmouth CID. I have a number of questions for you, sir."

Connor's voice concealed his relief.

"So you're not here about my son?" The officer looked perplexed, then realised what the man in front of him had been thinking.

"Good Lord Sir, no, I don't have any information on your son, although I am aware he is in the navy." Connor stood up, his relief now clear and shook hands with the policeman.

"Please sit down. Now, what can I do for you, superintendent?"

"May I ask you what you were doing on the beach at Dungeness yesterday morning Mr Cork?"

"I was looking at the result of over nine months of work done by this and other civil engineering companies being left to rot by the Royal Engineers. Well, one, in particular, to be precise," Spence prompted as doubts began to grow, even at this early stage.

"Please carry on, sir."

At this point, Peter English rushed into the office and exclaimed,

"I was told there's a policeman here, Connor. Pat is ok, isn't he?"

Connor replied,

"Pat is fine, and the police officer is here regarding a completely separate matter."

"Right, well as long as Pat's well. That's the main thing. Now, what's the separate matter? If it concerns you, it concerns me." Spence explained he needed to talk to Connor alone.

English stated.

"This man is my business partner, and I know he hasn't done anything illegal.

He's incapable of it. Therefore, it must be related to our business. Now, you can talk to us both or our solicitor unless Connor wants to talk to you alone. Do you Connor?" Connor nodded.

"Peter, the superintendent wants to know what I was doing on Dungeness Beach yesterday."

English sat down.

"Right Connor, you can tell him, but first things first. May I see your security clearance?" Spence almost spluttered the reply,

"Mr English, I am a superintendent of police."

English acknowledged this fact and then said,

"Alright, you may speak to my business partner, but I will be next door. Remember that, please. Great news about Pat, isn't it, Connor?"

Spence and Connor looked at each other and then at English with complete bewilderment.

"The superintendent hasn't said a word about Pat. What great news, Peter?" English nearly yelled,

"That Pat's well."

With that, he left the office. Connor looked at Spence and said,

"Now, what is this all about?"

Spence asked him,

"Why were you asking the officers of the Royal Engineers about the absence of any guards or sentries?" Connor began,

"Superintendent, we and other civil engineering companies have been involved in a project to build components of a floating harbour. What is submerged in the sea off Dungeness is a vital part of that floating harbour. The Royal Engineers have been tasked with securing them until they are needed. Now I am not military man, but I think it is safe to assume that the enemy has an idea of what we are up to. The components are now on the sea bed and are, at low tide, clearly visible from the air. They should be floating and camouflaged. There are no guards to stop people wandering onto the beach at low tide and having a closer inspection. Anyone with even a basic knowledge of civil engineering could figure out what stage we are at in our preparation for the invasion of Europe. It's only one small piece of information, but it might be helpful to them. Does that answer your question?"

Spence thought for a moment and then said,

"Why do you think a complaint was made, sir?"

Connor replied,

"Superintendent, I have no idea, but whatever the outcome of your investigation, those components have to be raised and soon. Still, that's our problem, not yours. Now is there anything else I can do for you?"

"There is one more thing, sir. I couldn't help noticing a full bottle of brandy on your secretary's desk. Brandy is very rare these days; would you mind telling me where you got it."

Connor looked at Spence,

"I'm afraid I cannot tell you that, superintendent."

Spence stood up as he said,

"Then I will have to find out, sir."

"Please do, and good day to you, superintendent. Please feel free to call any time," Connor said.

"I will, sir. We will be speaking again."

As Spence left, he took the consignment number on the bottle of brandy. All alcohol distribution was now strictly controlled. Back at the station, Spence asked his sergeant to trace the consignment number while he did a bit of research on Connor Cork. The company name rang a bell. Spence looked up the local newspapers and found a report on the visit of the Prime Minister to Portsmouth. Reading the names of the yards and factories that had been visited by Churchill, his blood began to run a little colder. The superintendent asked the inspector in charge of the close protection unit to spare a minute and would he be kind enough to bring his file on the Prime minister. Inspector Morgan sat down and Spence asked,

"Can you give me the names of the people who dined with the prime minister when he stayed in Portsmouth recently, please, Inspector?"

Morgan, a Welshmen with years of experience in human behaviour, could see Spence was suffering. He heard him groan,

"Oh my God! This gentleman had dinner with 'Winnie'." Just at that moment, his sergeant put his head in the door,

"Call–for you, sir - from Scotland Yard." Morgan motioned to go, but Spence shook his head. He picked up the phone.

"Spence."

He didn't speak for the next minute and a half as the Assistant Commissioner, Special protection unit asked him, in no uncertain terms, what he was doing enquiring about the Prime Minister's personal provisions, then finished by telling him to find bloody better things to do with his time.

It was coming up to half past six when Connor looked up from his desk to see Superintendent Spence entering his office. Spence quietly began,

"May I come in, Mr Cork?"

Connor nodded his head, stood up and pulled a chair up to his desk. He looked at Spence who was stern-faced.

"Mr Cork, I owe you an apology. You have no reason to worry about my enquiries; they are over, and the matter is closed. Why didn't you tell me who the brandy came from, sir?"

Connor's reply was simple.

"Superintendent, would you have believed me?"

Spence just laughed.

"I'll say goodnight to you now sir."

As he stood to leave Connor asked him,

"Superintendent, would you like to stay and have a brandy or two with me?"

Both men laughed as Connor opened the bottle.

Colonel Travers liaised with all allied engineering units involved in the construction of the Mulberry Harbours with a watching brief over the building of the components. He and Lieutenant Cork checked civilian yards and had occasionally passed by the E & C fabrications plant but were never requested to inspect it. They had two more functions. The first to cross and re-cross the UK surveying sites where bases could be built to house troops gathering in Britain for the greatest invasion in history. The second was to oversee the training of the amphibious units involved in that invasion. As Mountbatten put it.

"Lessons learned at Dieppe must not be forgotten."

Bill Cork began to gain a reputation as a hard taskmaster when training the officers and NCOs who would lead the landings. He was merciless in his demands and criticism of all concerned, irrespective of rank. After one particularly tough training programme, a formal complaint was made to the divisional commander of an infantry unit on exercise with Travers and his engineers. The brigadier general in command of the unit ordered Travers and Cork to his quarters and demanded to know what was going on. Why were the US Army Engineers trying to cripple or drown his men? Travers spoke.

"Brigadier, I'd like to let Lieutenant Cork answer that question if I may?"

The general nodded his head angrily,

"Speak up son, and this had better be good. You put two of my best top sergeants in hospital this morning."

Bill told the senior officer what he had seen at Dieppe; about the tanks losing tracks on the shingle beach, of the ships being blown out of the water because the landing craft were virtually unseaworthy. The radios and weapons becoming water-logged and useless. Finally, he talked about the young Canadian dying in his arms because of the total lack of experienced leadership and support. Bill informed the brigadier that, according to verifiable research, when the American troops hit the beaches, only fifteen in every hundred men will have seen active service. The enemy waiting for them would average around eighty out of every hundred with combat experience. Lieutenant Cork finished with the words,

"Sir, I made a vow that I would never allow another allied soldier to die on a beach because he had not been fully trained and properly equipped."

The brigadier was silent for a moment.

"Please wait outside, Lieutenant Cork; I wish to speak to Colonel Travers."

Five minutes later, Bill was called back into the brigadier's room. Travers was sitting down, and the brigadier, standing, spoke.

"Mr Cork, you just carry on being a son of a bitch. You have my full and complete support. One more thing, from now on, it's Captain. Kick ass, Captain Cork. Kick American ass, kick any goddamn ass you want but get these boys ready for that long, wet, murderous march up those beaches. Well done both of you, well done."

When the engineers had left, the brigadier put his head in his hands and repeated Cork's figures, first in a whisper, then louder.

"Only fifteen in every hundred men with combat experience! We are going to be slaughtered."

Travers was fully aware of the Royal Engineers being unable to raise pontoons. Years in engineering had taught him many things, among them that the sea was a unique environment in which to work. He decided to see the colonel in charge. An appointment was made. Travers arrived early, and Colonel Morley could not have been more welcoming or open about the problem, arranging for Rodber to drive them to the beach at high tide. Travers remained silent but could see nothing. Morley began,

"You see, that's our problem. Too much bloody water. Why won't anybody listen to me on this? It's simply a matter of too much bloody water. Now, if you can find a way to raise those things from the water, please tell me; otherwise, I'll say to you what I said to all the others, 'It can't be done and that's all there is to it.' Now go back and tell whoever sent you what I have just told you. Rodber will now take you wherever you want to go. Good day to you, colonel." He walked down the beach, where another car was waiting.

Travers stood seething. As he opened the door for the colonel, Lieutenant Rodber's face reflected his shock at the way Morley had disgraced the 'Sappers.' Travers saw this and said.

"I'll sit in the front, son, if that's ok with you."

Rodber replied,

"Perfectly, sir."

On the drive back to the station, the officers made small talk. Finally, Travers suggested.

"Tell me, lieutenant, off the record, exactly what is the colonel's problem?" Rodber asked,

"Forgive me, sir, but this is completely off the record?"

Travers nodded his head.

Rodber continued.

"The colonel's problem is that he has not got the remotest idea how to do the job and will not admit it to anyone, least of all himself. The Royal Engineers know very little about water, sir. That's why we build bridges to cross it, sir." Travers said,

"Thank you for your honesty, Lieutenant, and you are to be commended for your loyalty to Colonel Morley."

Rodber answered,

"Sir, I have a degree in construction engineering from Jesus College, Oxford. My loyalty is to the Royal Engineers, not Colonel Morley. The man is utterly loyal to the Royal Engineers and will defend the regiment even at cost to him." He paused, then exclaimed.

"Sir. I volunteered to fight the Nazis, not to be a driver to a man who refuses to acknowledge he and the Royal Engineers are out of their depth and need help!"

Travers returned to Swansea and made a phone call to an acquaintance. An hour later, Admiral Mountbatten asked his aide to put him through to the PM's office. The phone rang, and his aide said,

"Prime Minister for you, sir."

Mountbatten began,

"Good morning, sir. I think we may have a problem with the Mulberry Harbours."

An hour later, the Royal Navy were placed in command of the entire Operation to raise the caissons.

Travers and Cork were in Cardiff Bay a week later, observing US amphibious troops training. Having lunch in the unit's mess hall, Travers noticed that all of the cookhouse staff and kitchen orderlies were coloured. The officer in charge of the canteen saw his colonel's eagles, approached him and asked obsequiously,

"Is everything to your liking, colonel? We provide only the best for our boys." Travers, in turn, questioned him.

"Tell me, captain, why are all the kitchen and mess hall staff coloured."

The reply was immediate.

"Well, colonel, the black boys were no good as soldiers; they just didn't have it in them, so we give them something to do more appropriate to their abilities." Travers and Cork looked at each other and nearly wept. Travers remained silent, then dismissed the captain with a curt,

"Thank you."

He made a mental note to ensure that a similar policy was not being followed in the units he and Cork were training. The British were not the only army that had problems with a small number of officers and their attitudes toward conscripted men or, unbelievably, in this case, the colour of their skin.

The problem with the pontoons had been handed over to the Royal Navy under the direct command of Commodore Stephens, who had twenty years' service building naval installations throughout the British Empire. He sat in his office at Plymouth Naval Base, pondering what to do. Stevens concluded as the problem was primarily salvage, an expert in raising sunken ships was required. His investigations found a US Navy captain Clinton, currently working somewhere in the Pacific Ocean, was the man best suited to the job. This information was relayed to Admiral Mountbatten, who immediately requested the American High Command to have the captain posted to the European theatre of Operations.

Clinton arrived in Britain on a Lancaster Bomber sent to collect him from Pearl Harbour. Rumour had it that the aircraft had been personally ordered by Bomber Harris, C in C of RAF Bomber Command. Clinton had spent two years in the Pacific, and the British climate was somewhat of a shock to his system.

Commodore Stephens chaired the meeting and began by introducing Captain Clinton and gave a brief resume of his experience. The other attendees were introduced. Colonel Morley of the Royal Engineers and Colonel Travers of the US Army Engineers. The civilian contractors were introduced by company name only. As E & C Engineering was named, Peter English stood. Connor remained silent, as did his nephew, Captain Bill Cork, who was seated behind his colonel. The commodore concluded his opening by requesting all questions and comments be addressed to Captain Clinton. Surprisingly, to Connor's justifiably cynical mind, the next two hours were remarkably constructive. A timetable was drawn up and a date fixed for the first, and hopefully only, attempt to raise the pontoons. Colonel Travers was quietly delighted at the cooperation of all the principals. The meeting finished with the directors of contractors being asked to be on the beach in Dungeness for the raising. Peter English confirmed that he and his partner be delighted to attend whenever and wherever they were told to.

As the meeting broke up, Colonel Morley approached Colonel Travers and said,

"This chap Clinton seems to know his business. If there is anything you need, please let me or my officers know immediately. The resources of my regiment are at your disposal, and may I apologise for my behaviour recently? May I say we are glad of all the help we can get?"

Travers extended his hand to Morley.

"Thank you, colonel. Now, let's just get on with this Operation. Tell me, do you have any suggestions as to how we get the water out of the pontoons and some air in?"

With that, both men began to walk away, and Bill and the officer he remembered as Rodber fell in behind them. Bill said in a low voice,

"What's happened to him?"

Rodber answered in a whisper,

"He had a meeting with the general in command of the Royal Engineers. In the British Army, we call that kind of meeting 'an interview without coffee.'"

Bill replied, almost inaudibly,

"In the US Army, we call it, 'getting your ass kicked.'"

Rodber nodded his head.

"Quite."

Connor and Peter English booked into a pub-come-hotel near the 'sappers' camp. The morning came bringing benign weather – a calm sea, little wind. The plan, as explained by Captain Clinton, was to get air into a chamber of a pontoon and raise it to the surface before tipping it and draining the water. The pontoon was to be secured with flotation balloons and brought ashore to be inspected. If successful, the process would be repeated until all were secured. A variety of craft were at the site, and the beach was relatively crowded. Travers and Bill were aboard a launch about two hundred yards from the pontoons. Their role being to ensure no unnecessary risks were being taken and cooperation was maximised. Clinton and Morley were aboard the lead boat with a crew of naval and Royal Engineers.

Connor and Peter English were in the group with Rodber, under orders from Morley to get them close enough to the pontoons to allow inspection. Connor was concerned that too much air pressure might be loaded on the pontoon too quickly and cause it to rupture. E & C had built a total of forty-eight of the structures, and he was sure that if the initial lift damaged one, then the rest would also crack when moved. As the morning went on, the tension mounted. One dire possibility in the minds of all involved was if the pontoons could not be raised, the invasion may have to be delayed.

Slowly the air pressure in the pontoon was increased and it began to move, then float toward the surface. The Royal Engineers secured a fixed line and tipped it slowly until the water was immersing only half of the casing. The flotation balloons were attached, and Rodber signalled Connor and English to board a small fishing boat which took them alongside. Connor inspected as much of the casing as he could see and was delighted, even at this early stage, there were no cracks anywhere above the waterline. The water was very cold, but Peter English insisted on feeling as far as he could below the water level and then said,

"Mr Rodber, we'll go back to the dock with this one; please send the others after it. It looks in good order to me. What do you think, Connor?"

Connor wanted to see the pontoon out of the water, so he gave a qualified agreement. Immediately the salvaged pontoon was towed to the storage bays and lifted clear of the water. Connor and English declared everything was in order. Rodber radioed Colonel Morley, who ordered the raising crew to begin bringing all the pontoons to the surface. The process was repeated with Connor and Peter passing the pontoons as undamaged. The exercise took two weeks to complete.

Colonel Morley and Captain Clinton had become experts in the raising process. When Dungeness was finished, Clinton asked Morley if he would accompany him to the two other sites where pontoons had been submerged. Travers was aware of how Colonel Morley had thrown himself into the raising project. His report later read that this particular Anglo-American Operation had been a great success and was proof that the job could be done if you had the right people.

As the Dungeness salvage came to a close, the engineers involved were either sent to the next site with Colonel Morley or returned to their units. Travers and Bill had brought a squad of engineers based in Cardiff, and as the last structure was secured, word went out that there would be beers in the local pubs that evening. Connor heard and, as he had not had a chance to meet Clinton or any of the American engineers, he felt bad. The effort had been huge by all involved, and he had even begun to like Colonel Morley.

In the pub that night, it wasn't long before the singing started as many of the engineers were Welsh. One called to Bill,

"Come on, captain, give us a song that you boys sing on the range in Texas when you're entertaining all those cows." Bill laughed as he shouted a reply,

"How many times do I have to tell you hill farmers, they are not cows – they are cattle?" Rodber sat with Bill, and both watched in amazement as Morley laughed out loud, thoroughly enjoying himself. Clinton at his side.

Bill's voice was heard above the noise.

"Okay, I'll sing a song that we sing on the range, but everybody had better remember you're all cattle - not cows."

The crowd laughed and then quietened as Bill began to sing. In reception, Connor and Peter were about to leave. As they paid their bills, Connor heard, from the bar, a lone voice singing, 'On the Banks of My Own Lovely Lee.' He was torn between Peter cajoling him to hurry up and finding out who was singing this song that held so many memories for him. Bill Cork had, by this stage, reduced the bar to absolute silence. Some of the men, either due to alcohol or heritage, were close to tears. Outside, his uncle moved toward the bar door then he heard,

"Connor, let's go. We've work to do." He picked up his coat and left.

19

Hurricanes and String Bags

HMS Snow Eagle steamed for Scapa Flow; sea conditions were good. As ordered, all of the ship's officers met the captain before Pat and Commander Buchan finally sat down.

"Number one, I will be frank, I am very surprised that a man of your comparative youth holds such a senior position in a Royal Navy ship. I have two questions for you. One, why were you transferred from the army to the Navy? Two, why are you really on this ship?"

Pat knew it was only a matter of time before such questions would arise, generated by his unusual service record. Because complete trust was essential, Pat wanted to be as frank as possible but did not know how much Commodore Loftus had told Buchan of the SOE and Erebus. The first officer chose his words carefully.

"Sir, I saw active service with the Irish Guards in the Baltic theatre of Operations and was attached to a covert Operations unit. I was wounded and returned to the UK; a medical board classified me as unfit for service in the infantry. However, certain circumstances gave me the opportunity to continue to fight. I was offered and accepted a transfer to, and a commission in, the Royal Navy. My role in this ship is the same as any other officer, and my commitment to the crew and the war total. However, I do have certain extra duties which the commodore is aware of."

Buchan relaxed.

"Ok, that clears that up I think. Number one, we'll get to know each other slowly but surely. Now, do you have any questions for me?"

Pat thought, 'well he wanted honesty, so here goes.'

"Tell me about your previous service, sir." The captain began.

"I was in the Canadian Naval Reserve and at sea for the odd weekend. I could never be regarded as regular navy."

Pat listened as Buchan explained that in 1939, the Royal Canadian Navy had a total of thirteen ships. When war came, as a member of the Canadian Naval Reserve, he was posted as first officer on an old corvette which was part of the lend-lease programme. The ship was thrown into convoy escort duties in the North Atlantic until torpedoed off the East Coast of Canada in 1941. The survivors were in an open boat for five days before rescue came. Buchan relaxed as he told of his return to active service to find the Canadian Navy had grown to nearly two hundred ships and sixty thousand men. Buchan was given command of a Flower Class corvette on convoy escort duties with an auxiliary aircraft carrier. His ship then took part in what became known as the 'Battle of the Atlantic'. Buchan's ship had been bombed later the following year off the West Coast of Ireland. The crew were rescued by a Norwegian merchantman. A short spell in hospital followed by a training course in tactics on convoy escort with an air support group brought the captain's story to the present day. He finished by saying,

"I have had two ships sunk under me and was amazed when given this command, especially with such a competent escort group."

Pat Cork spoke with respect.

"Well, if I may say so, sir, it looks like we have an extremely experienced captain. May I welcome you to the ship and tell you that you have a very seasoned crew who may lack a little in naval etiquette but make up for it in fighting spirit and realism."

Buchan prompted,

"Go on, number one."

"If I might suggest you consider this, sir. We're a pretty mixed lot aboard Snow Eagle - English, Scottish, Welsh, Aussies, Irish and Norwegians and a West Indian- all nationalities really. The majority of us have one thing in common – we are the same as you, sir. None of us are–regular navy - we are drawn from all walks of life. Captain, I have no idea why you were selected to command Snow Eagle, but when Commodore Loftus picked you, he must have had a good reason."

Buchan asked,

"Tell me, number one, in a few words, what is the overriding ambition of the crew of Snow Eagle?"

The answer came quickly,

"We all just want to get the war won and go home, sir."

The captain smiled.

"That, number one, will do for me. Let's get to the bridge."

As she closed on the fleet through the fading light, all eyes aboard Snow Eagle were greeted by an unfamiliar sight. In the middle of the escort group was a large vessel with a flat deck. Buchan spoke to the bridge watch,

"Well, gentlemen, now we have air power. What you see is an auxiliary air–raft carrier - she is also the flagship." Number one, please do the honours."

Snow Eagle took station as a pennant was unfurled at the masthead of the flagship. The naval salute for the rank of commodore is eleven guns. Pat called the gun crew to stand and deliver that salute. The other ships of the group followed suit as a volley of eleven rounds from each ship rang out through the cold North Atlantic air. The flagship acknowledged the salute. Buchan stood beside his first officer and said quietly.

"Perhaps somebody was listening to the 'clearing the air,' session in Londonderry."

Cork relaxed as he thought, 'If he knows about that, Loftus trusts him totally.'

The fleet made steam for the Northern Atlantic and escorted convoys to the Russian ports of Archangel and Murmansk - but this time with air cover. Under Commodore Loftus, the Snow Ships took six convoys into Arctic waters whilst enduring appalling sea conditions with temperatures below minus twenty degrees centigrade. Commander Buchan and his first officer, Lieutenant Commander Cork, were becoming firm friends as their ship and shipmates proved equal to anything the weather or the U-boats and the Luftwaffe could throw at them. The enemy was increasingly desperate as the Nazi High Command demanded the flow of supplies to the Red Army, which was slowly draining the lifeblood out of the Germans on Russian soil, be stopped.

As well as the merchantmen, the sloops had responsibility for HMS Polar Star, an auxiliary aircraft carrier; it had the silhouette of a cigar box, and displaced fourteen thousand tons. She had twelve hurricanes and twelve swordfish - all lashed to the deck when not in action. The crew's quarters were below decks alongside the supplies, ammunition and fuel. Her top speed was around fourteen knots – considerably slower than her escorts. The name was a complete mystery to all of the escort crews, but they all got on with ensuring her safety.

On what had started out as an otherwise normal day on convoy escort, the flagship received an unusual signal. The eagle-eyed crew of an RAF long-range meteorological plane, returning from north of the Arctic Circle, reported objects on the surface which they assessed to be two or three conning towers. The contacts were about one hundred miles astern and south of the convoy. Loftus could only surmise that they were U-boats waiting for a surface supply vessel. The opportunity to attack three U-boats was too good to miss. Loftus ordered Captain Crowley to plan for an air attack. Soon afterwards, Crowley began the briefing.

"Sir, please bear in mind that the targets, whatever they are, are at the maximum range of our aircraft." Loftus acknowledged the fact.

"Very good captain." Crowley began.

"We launch all of our aircraft simultaneously. Half will attack the U-boats while the remaining aeroplanes give cover to the convoy. Once all aircraft are airborne, the flagship steams south toward the enemy position. This will shorten the distance for the attacking aircraft, which we recover first. Polar Star then steams north at fourteen knots. The recovered planes, now refuelled, take off and fly at full speed to cover the convoy. Those aircraft which have been flying convoy cover will head south at full speed for recovery and refuelling. If it all works out, we should never be out of range for recovering all of our aircrews." Loftus was silent. The plan was daring and dangerous, but the prize was worth it. He signalled

'Ready Aircraft.' Snow Eagle was ordered to escort the flagship when she steamed south. Captain Warne of HMS Snow Tiger was given command of the convoy with orders to continue on course no matter what. All aircraft were launched, and six hurricanes and eight swordfish flew due south to attack the enemy.

Captain Buchan had experience of escorting vessels similar to Polar Star. The flagship was slow and cumbersome and to provide a submarine screen with a single escort was- as one of Snow Eagle's Yorkshire born officers put it – 'all nigh impossible.'

The ships steamed south in pursuit of the aircraft, which, by Crowley's calculations, would be on the enemy very soon. The hurricanes carried heavy calibre wing guns capable of piercing a U-boat hull. The swordfish were much slower but were armed with depth-charges and contact bombs. The sailors on all the escorts marvelled at the bravery of the Swordfish crews who risked their lives when taking off from a heaving deck in aircraft known as 'String bags'.

The hurricane pilots were in radio contact with the flagship, and thanks to the electronic wizardry of Larsen and Constantine, the radio traffic was relayed to all parts of Snow Eagle. Absolute radio silence was kept as the fighters closed on the reported U-boat position. Then the airwaves were filled by calm voices reporting two U-boats on the surface and one supply vessel. The attack was twofold. One flight of hurricanes strafed the enemy submarines, describing them as helpless, tied to the supply ship by refuelling lines. The pilots confirmed that both targets had been holed above and below the waterline. The other hurricanes reported strafing the tanker with tracer rounds. Suddenly, the ops room was deafened by the sound of a massive explosion. There was silence, and then an emotional voice spoke.

"The supply tanker has exploded and destroyed both U-boats. The ship is in two…no, three sections, all sinking."

For a few moments there was silence, then,

"Squadron leader here. I have to report two hurricanes were lost in the blast. Jesus! It was as if they were flies being swatted."

Then there was silence which was broken by another radio message.

"Requesting a rescue vessel; there are a number of survivors in the water. I regret to confirm the death of two pilots. I can see their bodies."

Aboard Snow Eagle, Buchan and Pat remained silent, both desperately worried about the whereabouts of the third U-boat.

The order came from the flagship, 'recover survivors.' Every man aboard both ships knew instantly that this left the carrier without an escort. Captain Buchan ordered 'full ahead both', and Snow Eagle quickly reached twenty knots leaving the cumbersome carrier astern. Within an hour, the lookouts saw smoke indicating the wreck of the sinking tanker. Their eyes quickly switched to the seas surrounding the rescue zone for a periscope.

The hurricane pilots' bodies were recovered with the survivors of all three enemy vessels. Some were horribly burned as they lay on the deck of Snow Eagle; the medical orderlies knew there was little that could be done for them. Pat counted a total of twenty-two men out of an estimated two hundred who had made up the crews of the U-boats and supply vessel. One of the survivors stepped forward requesting permission to speak to the captain. Captain Buchan interrogated him, and, in good English, the man explained that he was a Swedish national and a doctor who had been captive aboard the supply vessel. Temporarily satisfied, Buchan ordered the doctor to the ship's small sick bay. The medical orderlies of Snow Eagle offered a silent prayer of thanks. A doctor could do far more for men badly burned and immersed in salt water than they could.

Snow Eagle then set a course for the carrier and the convoy. Uppermost in the mind of both Pat and Buchan was the third U-boat. If it sank the carrier, it would be free to signal for the support of other U-boats in the area and attack the convoy at will.

Aboard Polar Star, Captain Crowley had twenty-two aircraft in the air running out of fuel whilst his ship was under the threat of torpedo attack. There were two choices. He could operate standard anti-submarine tactics, which meant adopting a zigzag pattern and varying speed while on a fixed course. This, though effective defence, would make the landing of aircraft impossible. The second choice was to maintain a single heading to enable the aircraft to land but also presenting any U-boat captain with a sitting target. Snow Eagle signalled that she was still a good two hours away, and the convoy was at least three hours north of Polar Star. There would be no escorts from that quarter. As captain of the carrier, the decision was his to make. The commodore could only advise, even though he was the senior officer. This tradition had worked well for over two hundred years in the Royal Navy, and Crowley accepted the irony of the situation in good humour. The commodore had made the strategic decision; now he had to make the Operational one. Just then, a radio message was received from the returning fighters.

The hurricane pilots flying north toward the carrier saw, in the clear waters, a shadow which they were certain was a U-boat cruising at periscope depth - the captain obviously unaware of the fate of the supply ship. The position of the U-boat was reported, and Crowley did some very quick calculations. The target was between the returning fully armed swordfish and the carrier. The 'Stringbags' were much slower than the hurricane's, which allowed greater durability in flight – one of the few saving graces of the bi-plane.

Crowley made radio contact with the pilots of the swordfish flying north. Their fuel levels were not critical, and when they heard of the possible U-boat target, the crews needed no prompting. All volunteered to attack.

The immediate threat was removed, and during what seemed an eternity, the hurricanes, which had attacked the tanker and the U-boats, landed, refuelled and took off to provide air cover for the convoy. The aircraft that had been flying cover on the convoy were now dangerously short of fuel and were heading south toward the carrier at maximum speed to refuel.

The swordfish found their target. The German submarine captain was utterly perplexed, then terrified, as depth charges rained down on his boat. The swordfish were very stable in the air and were able to pick a spot in the water to deliver their lethal loads. Six aircraft attacked, and, despite the efforts of the target to go deep, the pilots dropped their depth charges with unerring accuracy and, for the Germans, potentially fatal consequences. The U-boat captain became convinced that such a concentrated attack must be coming from an allied task force and very quickly came to the conclusion that the better part of valour was surrender. His boat was irreparably damaged, and the order to surface was given. The scuttling charges were armed, and the German commander left the vessel expecting to see allied warships. There was consternation amongst the crew as they realised they had surrendered to a group of ancient biplanes now circling overhead. The captain sat desolately in a rubber dinghy and watched his boat blow up. The 'stringbags' disappeared, to be replaced by much more threatening refuelled hurricanes as they flew fast and low over the life rafts. Eventually, a large shape appeared on the horizon and closed on the survivors. Capitan Wilhelm Prost of the Kriegs marine and former commander of U131 got his first and only sea-level view of an escort carrier. She was soon joined by another warship which he later learned was called HMS Snow Eagle. Once aboard, he was informed that he and his crew were prisoners of war.

Later that day, HM ships Polar Star and Sea Eagle gained the convoy. Captain Campbell entered the commodore's day cabin. As captain of the Polar Star, Crowley had entered in the ship's log that three U-boats and one enemy supply vessel had been destroyed for the loss of two hurricane fighter pilots and their aircraft. Crowley had drawn up a list of men he was recommending for decoration. Loftus approved all of them; he enquired of the captain if there was anything else before expressing his gratitude and asking him to carry on. Loftus was disappointed about the tanker blowing up. She had been carrying equipment that the boffins at the Admiralty were desperate to examine. Once he had reported the sighting of the U-boats and the possibility of a tanker or supply ship, the Admiralty had requested the capture of that vessel if at all possible. The ship was believed to be carrying secret acoustic torpedoes. In this respect, the action had been unsuccessful.

20

Murmansk and the Dark Arts

The convoy made Murmansk without further enemy contact, and despite the deprivations of Arctic waters, all first officers reported morale was good. The crews' spirits were high, everyone looking forward to a run ashore.

The men expected to meet some of the people of the ancient port. Instead, they were quickly made aware of life in Communist Russia. Being placed under military police observation from the minute they stepped ashore. While the first officers were provisioning the fleet, Commodore Loftus and Captain Crowley were engaged in a diplomatic tussle. The Russian authorities demanded that the German sailors be handed over to them. Captain Crowley faced a dilemma. The situation was crystal clear. Under the Geneva Convention the U-boat crew were British prisoners of war. Privately, Crowley had no doubts that there were dedicated Nazis amongst the eighty-one survivors of U131. Handing them to the Russians would solve any security problem. But he knew the fate awaiting the German prisoners if he did so.

The diplomatic impasse was resolved by Rear Admiral Benbow, officer in command of the allied naval units based in Murmansk. His responsibility was to keep all of the meagre facilities available to allied shipping open. The U-boat crew was handed over. The existence of the Swedish/German national was not disclosed. Fullman was a valuable part of the escort group's medical team, and doctors were a rare commodity at sea. He was transferred to Snow Eagle because, once at sea, the carrier was inaccessible. The escorts could transfer him with relative ease when a medical emergency arose. As the convoy departed Murmansk, a conference concerning the 'Doctor' took place.

The man had never explained to Buchan or Cork's satisfaction why he had been on board the supply vessel. As for speaking Swedish, Pat reminded the Captain how Erebus switched languages. Buchan ordered a background check on the Swede from SOE and the setting up of a cover watch on him. Buchan underlined his concern.

"Number one, keep a very close eye on that man. There is no doubt he is a medical doctor, but the question is - what else is he?"

The CPO who came aboard in Londonderry had become a valuable ally of the first officer in naval disciplinary procedures. Chief Adams was a wise head at the 'Captain's table', where all minor disciplinary infringements were dealt with by the first officer. Pat had no idea of apt punishments for men who had broken what seemed to them and him, one of hundreds of King's Regulations. Chief Adams advised minor reprimands. Careers were not an issue - once the war was won most of the men would return to civilian life. The Commodore supported the somewhat lenient attitude to King's Regulations which generated highly motivated fighting crews on board the ships of the escort group.

It also produced a rather lax attitude to naval etiquette, which allowed a form of release from the constant pressure of the Atlantic convoy runs. These men willingly risked their lives every minute of every day. Commodore Loftus made it clear that he had little time for landlocked officers who demanded punitive measures when sailors who had seen men die in freezing water failed to salute them correctly.

This attitude was disapproved of by factions in the Admiralty who still believed in discipline above all else and those who were just jealous of Loftus and lobbied he should be replaced by a disciplinarian. The escort group did seem to attract 'individuals'. Aboard Snow Tiger was an officer who had been a West End Theatre set designer. The man was an aesthete who had proposed, to an enlightened admiral, a way of effectively camouflaging ships at sea. This innovation had made the silhouettes of certain vessels almost invisible to U-boat periscopes. He was a complete extrovert who captain Warne pleaded with when senior officers were present; please address the first officer as 'Sir', not 'Dear.' His contribution to morale was immense, and his courage unquestioned by the ship's company. Loftus and Warne had to fight to keep him aboard as a certain senior officer regarded him as unfit for sea service. What this officer chose to overlook was that this mildly effeminate man was as capable as any officer aboard, and comfortable in command of ship's stations, from navigation to guns and torpedoes.

There had been no reply to his enquiries at the SOE. CPO Adams and Cork were certain that, if Fullman/Hartmann was an enemy agent, he would be able to improvise a means of contacting the organisation he worked for. They set up a watch on the Swede. The men were selected by Adams and were all volunteers. The first benefit of the watchers came when Chief Adams reported that the Swede kept asking crew members if they knew the destination of the convoy.

The southbound voyage saw the convoy attacked as, in desperation, the Nazi High Command demanded that despite losing aircrews, convoys with or without cargos be attacked. The winter days began to shorten, and the attacks from the Luftwaffe lessened, but the U-boats continued their relentless campaign. Of the convoy that left Murmansk, with a total of fifty-seven merchantmen, two were sunk within eight days of leaving port. This was disheartening as the navy was confident it could defend convoys from all torpedo attacks. Despite the setbacks, the fleet made good speed. Orders were given for the escort group –hips to dock - some at Liverpool and others at Londonderry.

The Swedish doctor was moved to Snow Lynx to tend to a leading seaman's broken leg under orders to be returned to Snow Eagle immediately once sea conditions allowed. The carrier and three escorts, joined by vessels from the home fleet, would escort the merchantmen to Liverpool and Plymouth. Snow Eagle, Snow Lynx and Snow Tiger were to take leave and undergo an equipment upgrade in Londonderry. Pat was upset that there would not be time to see his father. As for his mother, occasionally, he allowed how much he missed her to come to the fore and prayed she would not be too upset. What else could any of them do? Then he cheered up with the thought of a chance to apologise to Victoria McBurney for leaving without as much as a word. A quick calculation confirmed that with seven convoys to Murmansk and the attack on the U-boat supply vessel, it had been fourteen months since the ship was in Londonderry.

As ever, the war called for his attention. The watchers reported that when Dr Fullman heard that the ship was bound for Londonderry, he repeatedly asked about the South of Ireland.

When alongside in Londonderry, the ship's boilers went cold for cleaning. Direct electricity, hot water and fresh drinking water were made available from ashore, as was a direct telephone line.

Commander Buchan contacted the Royal Ulster Constabulary, Special Branch, to be told someone would be in touch. During the next twenty-four hours, the situation became critical. Fullmann had made a phone call to the Swedish lega-tion in Belfast, who immediately asked for their citizen, a neutral national, to be released. Pat was called to the captain's cabin.

"Sit down please, number one. I take it you have nothing to report from the intelligence people on this Swede?"

"Nothing as of now, sir."

Buchan stood, declaring,

"Number one, we have no legal right to hold this man, and if he gets ashore, we cannot stop him crossing the border and disappearing into the South of Ireland. Do you agree?"

"I do, sir."

Buchan looked at his first officer.

"Then what do we do to keep this man under tabs?"

Pat spoke up,

"There are always Chief Adam's watchers."

Buchan mused,

"The RUC have not contacted me, and we have nothing from SOE. Let's see what Chief Adams can do for us."

Adams explained how his watchers could keep the Swede under observation.

"Sir, I have run shore patrols all over the world. This Operation is similar, and we have some really bright lads. Some are from Ireland, and they'll mix easily with the local people around Belfast and Derry. We can track this man using our watchers. They know him well by now."

Buchan gave the go-ahead and signalled Commodore Loftus of his intentions. Loftus replied that taking into consideration the failure of the RUC to act, there was no alternative. Maiden Aunt was contacted and ordered daily reports. Pat was sent to find the RUC officer in charge of the Special Branch in Northern Ireland. He walked into the RUC station in Derry and asked to speak to a senior officer. Now he sat in a detective's office as tea was poured.

"Now, what can we do for you?"

"We need someone watched twenty-four hours a day while he is in Northern Ireland. Can you help?"

The CID officer placed two mugs of tea on the desk and explained.

"Commander, I would love to help, we have a senior officer here who is in charge of all such Operations, and he has his methods. God help anyone who interferes with them. Please believe me; this man believes he is well in with God. Maybe I can ease your mind a little. What are your concerns about this man?"

Pat explained about the possibility of him crossing the border and then disappearing. The RUC detective, now sitting at his desk, replied.

"Commander, publicly, we have little to do with the Gardaí in the South. The neutrality is observed, but they are very supportive of the war effort, unofficially of course. There is no internment of allied servicemen. Every day, a bus comes to the border, and anyone who wishes to do so simply gets off and walks across. Should any German servicemen arrive, we arrest them until they can be shipped to the mainland. Going the other way is much more hazardous. Outside of German diplomatic personnel, the only people who are likely to help this man are the IRA – members of an organisation that is illegal in that jurisdiction, as well as this one and are treated accordingly by the Irish Authorities and the Gardaí." He sipped his tea and continued.

"If the target jumps the border, he had better have contacts there because if he puts to sea anywhere on the coast between here and Mizzen Head, he will drown. The seas are deadly." The sergeant paused before confessing.

"I wish I could help more, but the man in charge of the special branch here would have my guts for garters."

Pat asked,

"When is this man back in the office?"

The Sergeant laughed.

"That, my dear man, is 'hush hush'. We do not know where he is, and frankly, we don't care. Between you and me, that man has a different agenda to the rest of us. He is on some kind of crusade or vendetta, depending on your point of view and religion." Pat looked at the officer's nameplate, which read Detective Sgt. G. Bagot, CID. Then as he left the office, having thanked the detective for his time and the tea, one more question sprang to mind.

"This man - what is his name?"

Bagot stood to attention and mockingly saluted.

"Chief Superintendent Peters of the RUC and formerly of the RIC, may God help us all. Best of luck to you, commander."

Dr Hartmann left Snow Eagle, followed by two leading seamen named Sean Canavan and Fergus McNally. When CPO Adams asked for volunteers, they jumped at the chance - the reason, 'boredom'. The men were ideal for this assignment, coming from an Ulster county in the Free State and knowing the six counties intimately. As very young men, both had been involved in the Irish War of Independence, then the Civil War, which had left them with little regard for politics or politicians. The men were farmers and fishermen, who when De Valera declared economic war on the British Empire, struggled desperately to keep their small farms and fishing boats viable as the guaranteed markets in Britain disappeared. When war was declared, they walked across the border and joined the Royal Navy. The men were Donegal to the core with jet-black curly hair and swarthy skin. They explained their looks and love of the sea as coming from the survivors of the Spanish Armada. The women whose hearts they had broken thought differently.

They followed the Swede to the RUC barracks, then separated outside. At the desk, Hartmann asked if papers were required to travel to Belfast. The answer was, 'no, but the bus has already left.' The next one was at eight in the morning. Canavan waited a few minutes after Hartmann left and then approached the desk. The duty sergeant looked up.

"How's it goin'? Listen! Me and my mate, we're off one of the escorts in the harbour. Never been to Belfast; how would two thirsty sailors get there?"

The mention of the escort group brought a smile to the sergeant's face.

"Fair play to ye boys. There's a bus tomorrow morning at eight o'clock. There was a fellow in here earlier. Maybe you could team up with him for the company."

Canavan played the game perfectly.

"Was there? What'd he look like? If we see him, we'll say hello."

"A tall blonde man, you can't miss him."

The sergeant had told Canavan all he needed to know. Outside, McNally, who had watched the Swede, said,

"He's heading back to the ship. What did the RUC say?"

Canavan said cheerfully,

"The Swede is headed for Belfast tomorrow, and so shipmate, are we."

Fergus laughed.

"I tell you what, boy, this spying game's good old craic."

CPO Adams relayed his watchers' report to the captain.

At the bus, four watchers accidentally bumped into the Swede and joked about a few pints in Belfast. The doctor joined in the banter. When the bus arrived in Belfast, the watchers headed for the nearest pub and started casual conversations with regulars. Pints were ordered and drank as, one by one, they slipped out of a side door to follow the target. CPO Adams had opted for the 'hide in plain sight,' method of concealing his men. Their overt behaviour on the bus trip to Belfast would reassure the doctor that nothing untoward was happening. Adams had made it clear to all of his team that their job was to watch the target, not get involved in espionage. He cautioned,

"Do not attempt to intercept anyone. These people could be dangerous killers."

Hartmann called into the Swedish legation and left after thirty minutes, spent some hours in Belfast city centre, then caught the last bus back to Derry. The watchers, to maintain credibility, had to take a few drinks before getting aboard the bus with him - something which quietly impressed CPO Adams. The next day, Hartmann stayed in Derry city centre, acting as if he was waiting for a contact or signal. The watchers were by now completely at home in their roles and almost invisible. Adams and Cork went into the centre of town and could not spot any of them. As the Swede returned to the ship, the watchers, having followed him aboard, made their report. Canavan and McNally recounted to CPO Adams how he and the first officer had spent the day in Derry - something Adams found hugely amusing and satisfying. He was becoming very proud of his watchers. The following day was a repeat of–the previous - there was no contact. The doctor had seemed very irritated later in the day, and the watchers sensed he was waiting for someone. CPO Adams' report was concise, and Pat watched the captain make notes. It was at this point that the phone on the captain's desk rang. The conversation lasted about five minutes, and then, Buchan said,

"That gentleman was the senior special branch officer. He has informed me that, as of now, the RUC will be taking over surveillance of the good doctor." The cabin door opened, and the captain's steward entered with a signal in which Commodore Loftus confirmed the earlier phone call.

In a way, Buchan was relieved; he had little time for all this cloak-and-dagger stuff, but it was necessary until the target's identity was confirmed. Buchan moved on quickly.

"We are no longer responsible for the Swede, so let's get the crew ashore for some leave and then get the ship ready for sea. Thank you, chief, and please thank your watchers and congratulate them on a good job."

The CPO left the cabin then Buchan turned to Pat.

"Number one, you are entitled to a bit of leave as well. Any plans?"

Pat explained about the injury to his leg and how, during the ship's last docking in Derry, he had seen a specialist in Belfast. Buchan suggested,

"Why don't you take a navy car, get to Belfast, see the specialist and have a couple of days in the city?"

Pat couldn't refuse the offer as his mind strayed to Victoria McBurney.

"That's very kind of you, sir. Perhaps Commander Larsen would benefit from a break in Belfast?"

Buchan enthused,

"Excellent idea! Better call in ever eight hours - after all, we are still at war. Right off, you go and have a good leave."

Pat and Larsen began to relax on the way to Belfast, unaware that in London, some forty-eight hours earlier, Colonel Simpson-Coyle had demanded the observation of the Swede be handed over to him and his contacts in Londonderry. Dr Hartmann was now in the hands of the man in charge of the special branch in Northern Ireland and Simpson-Coyle. They were, according to the Colonel, the experts. The people involved in the Fullman/Hartmann affair did not know the history of the former RIC district officer and the former colonial soldier. Both had fought in the War of Independence and believed they had been betrayed in 1922 by the British government. Both men mistrusted any form of nationalist, but the Colonel did not harbour Peter's fanatical distrust of all Catholics regardless of where they were born.

Brigadier Davies h–d not argued - there seemed little point. His analysts were convinced Dr Hartman was Fullman but had no concrete proof. The SOE had not found any clear image of the man, just faded photographs, so Simpson-Coyle got his way.

From his hotel, Pat phoned the Royal Victoria Hospital and asked to speak to Dr Trimble's secretary - to his surprise it was the doctor who answered the phone. When Pat introduced himself, an appointment was arranged for four o'clock the following day. They sat waiting in the outer office of the consulting rooms, and Pat's thoughts roamed as he wondered how many hospitals he had been in since enlisting. Lars interrupted his reverie.

"Pat, if we get away fairly quickly, we can have a few pints of 'Jinness'. Just then a nurse walked by, and Lars gasped.

"My God, every woman in this city is better looking than the previous one. I think I may be in love again."

Pat was half listening to his friend as Victoria kept coming into his mind, which distracted him from what was essentially small talk with Lars.

The nurse who called Pat into Dr Trimble's office was turning away when Lars whispered in Pat's ear,

"See if you can get her to come out tonight and ask her if she has a friend. Full ahead both Pat." When Dr Trimble entered the room, Pat stood, and they shook hands.

"Right, lieutenant commander, would you please walk up the length of the office and then remove your shoes and repeat the exercise." Pat did as he was asked, and Doctor Trimble continued pleasantly.

"Please remove your sock, and we'll have a look at the injured leg."

After about fifteen minutes of examination and questions, Trimble concluded.

"That's the examination finished. Your leg is in relatively good condition. Well done."

As he wrote in the medical file, he said.

"Congratulations on your promotion. Right, you can get dressed, and I'll let you go."

Pat said.

"Thank you very much, doctor, but there is something else."

Trimble allowed the nurse to leave and sat down at his desk. Pat was about to speak when Trimble cut across him in a gentle voice.

"I take it you know about the McBurneys and their little boy. God rest them and bless him." Pat sensed there was something wrong by the doctor's use of the blessing given to the dead by all Irish people.

"I'm sorry, doctor, I was just about to ask after them. I have not seen them since we docked in Londonderry."

Trimble stiffened as he said,

"May I ask how well you knew them?" Pat sensed the question was more of a concern than an enquiry and answered openly,

"I knew Victoria slightly better than Dr McBurney."

Then instinctively asked,

"Is there something wrong, doctor?"

Trimble's face was sad.

"There has been a terrible tragedy. I'm afraid Dr McBurney and his wife were killed during an air raid. The Germans have been suffering heavy losses recently, and it appears that some of the master race are losing their stomach for the fight. One dropped his bombs short of the dockyard. One destroyed Mac's surgery, by some miracle, the baby survived."

Pat was lost for words as the kindly man in front of him continued,

"Yes, it was very sad. Their son brought a completely new meaning to their lives and marriage. Mac seemed twenty years younger when he saw his son and never looked better. As for Victoria, I didn't think she could look more beautiful than when she was pregnant, but when he was born, she seemed to blossom more with every day as the boy grew."

Pat asked,

"Where is the baby now, doctor?"

Trimble didn't seem at all fazed by the question.

"He is with Doctor McBurney's sister's family - they intend to adopt him as soon as the law allows. They have a substantial farm in the West of the province and have a family where he will grow up believing he is one of them. They'll adore him - he's going to have a good life. He's a fighter, that wee man. We had to give him a blood transfusion after he was rescued from the bombed building; thankfully, he is the same blood group as his late father, so we had no problems with matching. It's a very common group - same as yours, actually."

Pat said without thinking,

"Is there anything I can do for him, doctor?"

Trimble looked at Pat.

"The best thing that you can do for this boy is to win the war and let him li–e in freedom - that's what you can do for him and all of us."

Pat stood up and shook the doctor's hand. His mind was racing. Time to think things through; that's what's needed. Then Lars called him as he left the consulting room.

"Pat, over here, please."

Lars stood by a public phone. Once again, the war called Pat Cork.

"What's all the hurry about?"

Lars answered,

"I've just checked in with Snow Eagle. The RUC, or whatever it is called, has lost the Swede, and we're to start searching here in Belfast. If we don't find him before morning, we are to return to the ship and try to cover the border."

Pat asked,

"Where do we go from here?"

Now very much the SOE officer, Larsen told him,

"We sit outside the Swedish diplomatic representative's house until he turns up or the morning comes – whichever is first."

Pat again asked,

"What do we do if he turns up?"

Lars' face was impassive.

"Pat, we are SOE. If he turns up and refuses to surrender, we kill him."

The next few hours were, in a strange way, just what was needed by the first officer of Snow Eagle. Sitting in the car outside the Georgian building, the numbers stacked up. He could be the baby's father. Victoria told him about the relationship with her husband. They had not been lovers. The little boy must be his. Dr Trimble had remarked that the baby's blood and his were the same but had added that it was a very common group. His mind whirled at the situation. He had no claim to the boy. No proof of paternity. What could he offer the boy until the war was over? He could not even be sure of surviving the next convoy, let alone the war.

Dr Trimble's advice came to him,

'Win the war. Give him a new world. Give him peace.'

Pat began to assess the baby's current situation. The little boy was in the best of homes - where he would be loved all his life. Lars nudged him.

"Sun up, Pat, and no sign of the Swede. Orders are to head for the ship. Do you want to drive?"

Pat turned the ignition key and put the boy out of his mind. The Swede must take priority. Victoria was a beautiful, glorious memory, but that was all. Now it was time to go back to war.

Back in SOE HQ, the staff had agreed that if Simpson-Coyle wanted to take over the surveillance, so be it, but there had been secret doubts in everyone's mind. Simpson-Coyle had moved in too quickly. In a situation where one team of watchers takes over from another, there must be a reasonable handover period. Granted, the RUC knew the ground where the Swede would be at large, but they didn't know him as a person. The watchers on Snow Eagle had been in close proximity to him for at least a month, and even the most accomplished deceiver couldn't hide everything. He would, in time, reveal a unique trait. His favourite food or a saying repeatedly used in conversation. It was a proven fact that nobody could change their gait viewed from behind. A number of SOE operatives had been captured or shot at after they had been through checkpoints - their walk had been recognised and given them away, nothing else. All of this knowledge which the gatherers, analysts and watchers knew as the gospel, had been ignored by Simpson-Coyle and Superintendent Peters.

The analysts were told that the RUC and the men who had been sent to Northern Ireland to watch the Swede had lost him. There was initially shock; then some felt a small sense of satisfaction and inevitability.

Maiden Aunt had the situation under control. Simpson-Coyle had lost the biggest fish the SOE had reeled in so far in the war. If he escaped, there would be hell to pay. As the Operation was handed back to Maiden Aunt's people, Simpson-Coyle was nowhere to be seen; now, the amateurs, led by a new boy in the game, would have to retrieve the situation. The report on how the RUC had lost the Swede made unbelievable reading to anyone who had been raised outside Northern Ireland. Maiden Aunt gave a brief and alarming summary of what had happened.

"It would appear that unknown to us, there is, in the RUC, an appalling sectarian bias. This prejudice is aimed at any and all Catholics, and, as a result, there are certain areas of the cities and towns of Northern Ireland where RUC officers will not go for fear of their safety. Now, either by luck or planning, once the Swede arrived in Belfast, he entered one of these areas and lost the RUC men. We must forget this and find him. He cannot be allowed to escape to Germany; he must be captured or destroyed, is that clear?"

The teams signalled their understanding by trying to find a place where he might head in the North or South of the island of Ireland. The first thing that the analysts did was to revisit the papers brought out of Bergen. Every document was analysed for anything that might give a clue as to where the Swede might go. Then, found amongst the documents was a list of names of villages located on the coast of the British Isles and Northern Ireland. Closer examination revealed just one village situated close to the border between Northern Ireland and the Free State. Immediately, Sergeant Major Reilly and Sergeant Mullen were despatched to Londonderry with a grainy photograph and the village name - Donaghmore.

The officers of Snow Eagle were called to the captain's cabin along with CPO Adams and introduced to Sergeant Major Reilly and Sergeant Mullen. A photograph was shown to them. Captain Buchan asked the question,

"Well, gentlemen, is he our man, Yes or no?"

Pat answered immediately,

"Yes, sir, I am convinced he is."

Larsen then spoke,

"I agree with number one, sir. I am convinced he is the man we are looking for." Buchan remained silent as the other officers expressed opinions ranging from 'not sure' to just, 'don't know.' The captain thanked them all and dismissed them, with the exception of Pat and Lars, who remained with CPO Adams, Sergeant Major Reilly and Sergeant Mullen. Buchan briefed.

"I am convinced that this man is Hartmann/Fullman and that he is one of the men responsible for the acoustic torpedoes. I will read to you a signal received from Commodore Loftus this morning. Reference the matter of Dr Hartmann/ Fullman. I have been fully briefed by Brigadier Davies, and we have decided the following. The suspect is now the responsibility of the SOE and the Royal Navy. In the event of the suspect attempting to escape to the South of Ireland, he is to be apprehended or destroyed."

Buchan put the paper down.

"In the event of this man attempting to escape, are you all willing to shoot him dead, even if he is unarmed and possibly on neutral territory? I will ask each of you individually for your answer. Commander Larsen?"

Lars replied.

"Yes, sir."

Buchan continued,

"Lieutenant Commander Cork?"

"Yes, sir."

"Chief Petty Officer Adams?"

"Yes, sir."

"Sergeant Major Reilly?"

"Without hesitation, sir."

"Sergeant Mullen?"

"Yes, sir."

Buchan continued the briefing.

"You all know what's happened; now we have to find him. The analysts have an inkling that the Swede may make for a small village called Donaghmore. Why, they don't know, other than this place was mentioned in a document recovered from enemy territory. There is one more thing; we do not have definite identification. Remember that we are not one hundred percent certain this man is Hartmann/ Fullman. Either way, if he looks as if he is escaping, we take the shot."

CPO Adams had deployed his watchers in the centre of Londonderry, just in case the Swede doubled back. He had suggested this to the captain, who readily agreed. Both men did not want them on the border. The sailors were watchers, not marksmen.

One hour later, five men were arranged in a semi-circle on a gently rising hill overlooking the village of Donaghmore. Pat needed time to think and always did his best thinking when on active service.

Earlier on, during the drive from Belfast, his mind had been a maelstrom caused by Dr Trimble's news. Now in the green countryside, he rationalised thoughts and emotions. The boy was safe with a good family. So the short term was covered. A thought came to mind; if the boy was his son, he could not allow him to be raised in a society with so many contradictions and blatant bigotry. Then reason came with the conclusion that whoever the child's father was and where he was to be raised would have to be left until the end of the war. Everything was, until then, academic. Pat cleared his mind and concentrated on the five-man team deployed just on the British side of the border in wait for the suspect to arrive - if he arrived at all. There had been no sighting of him anywhere in the North of Ireland. The RUC Chief constable had ordered Peters to withdraw from the Operation. Simpson-Coyle received a similar message from Odin. It was made clear that the mess they had created would be sorted out by Maiden Aunt's men and the Royal Navy.

The team members stiffened as a coach approached the border post from the British side and stopped. People got out and began walking toward the road that was regarded as the border by the locals. Just as it seemed that the Swede was not on the bus, a figure slipped out of the coach door and moved toward the border with a determined stride. His head and face were covered with a large fedora-styled hat. He wore a coat, almost full length, draped from his shoulders. There was no way that Pat could be certain that this was the Swede. At the border post, the man looked around, but his face was not visible. He then turned and walked onto neutral territory, at which point a car appeared from behind a copse of trees. As it came to a stop, a man got out and approached the individual in the raincoat and hat, who began to walk faster the nearer the two men came. Pat later recalled that they were about twenty yards apart when the shot rang out. The man in the Fedora dropped vertically on the spot, clearly stone dead.

Pat turned to see who had fired the shot and saw Sergeant Mullen discharge a cartridge casing from his rifle. Pat said,

"Sergeant, was it him, and if so, how the hell did you know?"

Mullen replied calmly,

"The walk from the back, sir. I'd seen it before - in the camp at Bergen. I was getting a beating from two of the guards, and they were told to stop as some top brass were nearby. I remember having my head pushed into the mud as this man walked by. Then, as he walked away, I heard one of the guards saying, 'There is Herr Professor Doctor Hartmann'. I never saw his face, but I saw him walk away from me as he told the guards to keep beating me. I never forgot that walk."

All five men headed for the cars and then on to Londonderry, where Sergeant Mullen and Sergeant Major Reilly were secreted aboard Snow Eagle until arrangements could be made to fly them out of the province. During the next twenty-four hours, Snow Eagle made ready for sea, and Captain Buchan had a visit from an RUC Chief Superintendent. Buchan had asked his number one and Larsen to be present when the policeman arrived in his cabin. Both stood in silence. The police officer, who didn't deem it fit to identify himself, enquired as to whether any of the Snow Eagle's crew knew anything about a body which had been found lying just on the British side of the border, near a village called Donaghmore. Captain Buchan replied to the question with barely concealed contempt.

"Chief Superintendent, my ship's company know their jobs and do them to the utmost of their ability, irrespective of the cultures and faiths of the people they come into contact with. The answer to your question is, none of my men have anything to do with the body your men discovered, or should I say, tripped over."

The RUC officer was obviously unaccustomed to being spoken to in this fashion and immediately reacted.

"The body has been dumped back across the border by the Gardaí. It's obviously a message they're sending us, 'Tidy up your own bloody mess.'" There was a short pause.

"This man was of interest to the department which I run in Northern Ireland."

Buchan fired back.

"Your interest being based solely upon his religion."

The RUC officer stood in silence for a minute and then said,

"We do things our own way in Northern Ireland, and it is our business alone." Buchan said,

"Well, if it is your business, how did you lose this man?"

The RUC officer hissed,

"That information is classified by special branch."

Buchan looked at Peters, then Pat Cork.

"This is my first officer Lieutenant Commander Cork. Number One, please escort this person off my ship."

The policeman remained silent as they approached the gangway, then, about to leave the ship, he spoke.

"Your boss called you Cork. Would you have any family from the South commander?"

Pat couldn't resist.

"That information is classified by the Royal Navy."

Behind him, as if from nowhere, the watchers' Sean Canavan and Fergus McNally materialised.

Pat greeted them,

"How are you both?"

"I'd watch him if I were you, sir," Fergus advised, looking at Peters as he walked away from the ship. Sean joined the conversation.

"Aye, sir. We did some digging about your man in Derry and Belfast. That one's a nasty piece of work."

Pat looked at his shipmates.

"Thank you, now please carry on gentlemen."

In broad Donegal accents came the timeless reply,

"Aye, aye, sir."

Captain Buchan spoke to his senior officers when Pat returned.

"Gentlemen, I can only imagine how much trouble this whole affair is going to cause for someone. However, it will not be anybody from this ship or the escort group. I have received an order from Commodore Loftus. If any of you are contacted by this so-called policeman or any other unknown officer or persons, you are to report it to me immediately. Is that clear, gentlemen?"

The officers replied,

"Perfectly, sir."

Buchan nodded his head.

"Good, now please carry on. We put to sea with the next tide."

Back in his office, Peters ordered one of his men to find all he could on the first officer of HMS Snow Eagle. Detective Sergeant Bagot heard the order being given and made a mental note to keep an eye out for the young naval officer.

Maiden Aunt was just entering his office when he was informed by Sergeant Major Reilly that a meeting had been called by Odin for that afternoon.

Davies replied,

"Sergeant Major, please ask Sergeant Mullen to drive us."

Davies had, since joining the SOE maintained a low profile, such as using the passenger seat in official cars. On this run Sergeant Major Reilly took the back seat. There was silence during the time it took Mullen to arrive at a closed car park under an office block near Whitehall.

Spenser was not alone when Brigadier Davies was announced, his face revealing nothing. There was another man in the room, 'incognito'. Odin spoke in a way that gave Davies the impression every word was carefully considered.

"Tell me, Brigadier; you have been with us for some time now. Are there areas in the organisation where there might be room for improvement and a re-think on Operational procedures and responsibilities?"

Davies sat silent, now aware that he had just been accepted into the inner circle of the Intelligence community. The question Odin had put to him was twofold. Firstly, he had been asked to consider proposing changes to the Operational procedures which had been designed by Simpson-Coyle. Secondly, did he have confidence in Simpson-Coyle to do his job? He was about to speak when Odin continued,

"Before you answer, I have some more questions. I want to know what happened regarding the shooting in Northern Ireland."

Davies recounted the incident from HMS Snow Eagle docking to when the suspect was shot. Odin asked,

"When did Colonel Simpson-Coyle insist upon taking over Operational surveillance?"

Davies replied,

"When he learned that we may have the man responsible for the acoustic torpedoes in our hands."

"When was he told of the situation regarding this man, and why?"

Davis again told of the standard Operational briefing.

"Why do you think he took over the Operation, brigadier?"

Davies was precise in his answer.

"I cannot tell you what motivated him, but he was within his rights as the incident was in the Operational area assigned to his command."

It was then the other man spoke.

"What are your views on the attempt to have an operative arrested and returned to base in chains?"

Davies's mind raced as he tried to fathom how either man knew of that incident. 'Jesus!' he swore to himself. 'These people know everything we do.'

"Sir, there are areas in which the colonel and I disagree. He is primarily concerned about security and has a perception of operative's suitability based upon background and nationality rather than ability."

The man spoke again in a manner which made it clear to Davies Odin deferred to him.

"You mean he is obsessed with his security, he is a snob, and this has left him somewhat preoccupied. However, we still have a war to fight. There are a number of projects which are in the advanced planning stage, all in Norway. Do you have any knowledge of these?"

Again Davies answered precisely.

"Sir, I'm aware only of my projects."

Odin spoke.

"Right, well now I am going to tell you, so listen up, Maiden Aunt."

Within twenty minutes, Davies had been briefed on plans involving units of the resistance, active in the Trondheim region, which were under the Operational control of Simpson -Coyle. The senior man spoke again.

"Under no circumstances whatsoever are any of your people to get involved. You will continue with your Operations on a stand-alone basis. Is that understood?"

Davies replied,

"Yes sir, perfectly."

"Good; now, regarding our initial questions. I am aware of the colonel's perception of the people we have and the kind of war we are fighting; I will deal with those issues. Are you happy with that?"

Davies replied in the affirmative.

"The second is the code name of the agent in Norway. I assure you it will only be passed on to an equally brave and dedicated man."

Davies looked at Odin.

"Please supply the name, brigadier."

"The code name is 'Erebus'."

The man smiled, saying,

"The bringer of chaos - how apt."

Odin wrapped up the meeting.

"Right, that's that. Just to say that everything seems to be going well at your end of the house. Let's try and keep it that way. Thank you, brigadier and good day to you, and good luck."

Davies sat in the front of the car as Mullen enquired,

"Where to, sir?"

Maiden Aunt replied,

"That, sergeant, is a very good question, but in the immediate future, I think we've earned a good meal, so stop somewhere on the way back to base. Anywhere you like - and it's on me!"

21

A Hunting We Will Go

After the raising of the Pontoons, Cork's thoughts turned to gaining more combat experience to enhance his training skills. Bill approached Colonel Travers, who played the devil's advocate, saying his knowledge of the Mulberry Harbours was of equal value to the US Army Engineers as his active service experience. Cork persisted, and reluctantly Travers agreed that he contact Admiral Mountbatten's Combined Operation command.

After the Mulberry harbours success, Mountbatten issued a directive to his command, demanding that when the invasion of Europe took place, the level of cooperation between the Allied forces be seamless. Captain Cork of the US Army Engineers was summoned to Poole in Dorset to undergo basic commando training. The Royal Marine NCOs, impressed by his attitude and fitness, recommended him for close combat training. This completed, Captain Cork was considered by his assessors to be a very capable officer able to think clearly under pressure and was listed as 'available for covert Operations.'

His Colonel noted that on his return to Wales, Captain William Cork was a changed man and a hugely different individual to the one who left Texas. Bill was much quieter, as if deep in thought, but about what - Travers didn't know.

In September 1943, Cork was ordered to report to a base in the Scottish Highlands, where he joined a squad of Royal Marines training for action behind enemy lines. None knew yet, what they were to do once they landed.

Erebus summarised for Moen and Berg the details of a series of briefings from Maiden Aunt, Vali and Professor Williamson.

"Now listen. Despite the best will in the world, the Norwegian Resistance is dangerously compromised, so, my friends, we involve them in nothing and tell them even less. We take orders from Maiden Aunt only; we are a completely stand-alone unit." His listeners stayed silent.

"Now, we've been asked to find targets on the East Coast suitable for attack. Newly built pens or warships, anything which will, if destroyed, damage the Nazis' war effort. There is one more thing – we are to keep an eye and an ear out for any reference at all to something called 'Heavy Water.' Ok, what do you think?"

Moen had been thinking while listening and replied straight away.

"I'll ask my drivers to report anything unusual in any of their drops." Berg didn't speak, just nodded to signify he fully understood, and his men would do the same for all ports.

As the spring began to thaw the Norwegian countryside, Hilda spent more nights with Erebus. They made love, and while giving herself to him completely, he felt she was still distant from him, hiding something.

One morning, as he and Olaf were having a hot drink in the kitchen, Hilda came into the house, having chosen not to sleep with him after sex. Her uncle spoke.

"Hilda, why didn't you stay last night? I may be an old man but do not think I am stupid. It is good that you young people are happy together. God knows we need some happiness in this country. Have you thought about maybe getting married?"

Hilda exploded.

"Nobody owns me. I do what I want to do, and I will not marry anyone until I want to. Do you hear that, both of you?"

She stormed out of the kitchen. Erebus looked at the bewildered old man.

"I am sorry if I have done something to offend you. I am very close to Hilda, and if things were different........"

The old man raised his hand.

"Hilda has far more of her father in her than she cares to admit - he too was a 'free spirit', as he put it. If you ask me, he was just a selfish, conceited thug with a restless streak which she has inherited. The girl has never forgiven him for walking out on her and her mother. Erebus asked,

"Has she ever heard from father?"

"Not a single word in years," Then added.

"I am worried about her."

Much later, as Olaf dozed, Erebus sat in front of the fire, thinking about the future, knowing Hilda could not be part of his. She was his only lover, so he could hardly call himself an expert on love or women. However, being alone was another matter and isolating oneself from people when surrounded by them he was an expert. He did not know how to help Hilda, and as he was moving on very soon, maybe he had no right to try.

That night, after making love, he asked how she felt about her father. Her reply was instant.

"He left my mother destitute and didn't care whether she lived or died, so, if you must know, I hate him – but not for myself. I hate him for her because she was never strong enough to hate him. No matter how much I may love some-one, if I ever will love, I will always be strong enough to walk away from them if they hurt me."

Erebus prompted,

"Do you really hate your father, Hilda?"

She replied as she moved her naked body against his arousing him instantly.

"I suppose that I do not really hate him, Laudrup. You cannot hate someone who does not exist."

With that, she kissed him, pushing her tongue deep inside his mouth. Then she lifted her body and positioned herself above him. He held her still.

"What would you do if you met him, Hilda?"

She looked at him and said,

"I would do nothing."

Then she lowered herself onto him, and he watched as her eyes closed with pleasure. Even during the act of sex, during the passion, pleasure and affection, maybe even love, he knew she wasn't being completely honest with him, then he forgot everything and allowed himself to be taken over by this beautiful young woman. The morning came, and as Hilda left, she said.

"Don't worry about my father. He will never come back, not if he knows what's good for him. He is despised in Hagnor; hated by everyone. There would be a crowd of people to tell him so. He hurt many good people in many ways when he was here."

Laudrup took her hand and said,

"Hilda, I am going away for some time. I will try and get back as often as possible, but I can't promise anything. Do you understand?"

Her reply surprised and reassured him.

"Laudrup, I do not know who you are or what you do when you go away. What I do know is that the people in this village hold you in great respect. I don't know if I love you but what we do together gives me great pleasure and, for a little time, peace of mind. I will miss you, but I will live without you. So don't worry about me; just be safe and be careful."

She kissed him on the lips and left. He put Hilda out of his mind and started to think about the campaign when the thaw set in. Then packed his kit-bag and walked out of Hagnor to the main road where Moen was waiting with the lorry. Both men remained silent for some time until Moen spoke.

"Well, Laudrup, where are we headed?"

Erebus replied,

"Since we have heard nothing from your men, we are going to check out all of the coastal ports and see if we can find a target important enough for commandos to destroy." Moen gave a low whistle,

"Jesus, things are really going to get serious for the bastards now."

Driving along the Atlantic coast of Norway allowed Erebus to see the country. The Germans were taking everything, and people were suffering from food shortages, with conditions being far worse inland than on the coast, where the sea provided food. The Norwegian people were engaged in a campaign of non-fraternisation. An instance being not to sit next any German military personnel on public transport. Moen's comments were heartfelt.

"The bastards have made it illegal to stand up on a bus or such if there is a seat available. The bastards must be feeling lonely. Poor sensitive bastards; my heart bleeds for them. May they all rot in hell?"

Erebus didn't reply, now concerned about the security of his comrades. Hunger and fear were powerful motivators in the most loyal, brave people.

As agreed, when Erebus and Moen neared a port, the local contact would meet them. So far, there was no enemy activity strategically important enough to risk commandos or bomber crews - and no mention whatsoever of heavy water.

They were near the home of Hagen, the man who helped to steal the Abwehr radio. Erebus asked Moen,

"When were you last in touch with Hagen?"

Moen replied,

"Not since the radio thing. We could call in and say hello. He may have something."

Erebus agreed.

"I'm tired of sleeping in this truck; we'll check their place out. If they have room for us and it looks ok, we'll stay overnight."

Moen increased speed. They parked out of sight on the edge of Hagen's property and watched the warehouse for most of the day. All seemed normal; Hagen and his sons went in and out of the buildings. Moen led as they entered the loading bay, where Hagen recognised and approached them smiling. Shaking hands warmly, he enquired,

"How are both of you?"

One of his sons joined them and whispered something in his father's ear. Hagen motioned he understood. Erebus replied to his question,

"We're fine. Do you mind if we go in?" Moen did most of the talking, asking Hagen for his estimate of the German strength in the region and if he had noticed anything out of the ordinary. Hagen spoke as both of his sons joined them.

"We have been busy with our own resistance cell here; the British have given us weapons. The local resistance are saying we should wait until we get proper targets - machinery and such - but our man in the UK says to go ahead with attacks on the Germans." Erebus and Moen remained silent, aware of the agreement between the resistance and the British. Moen asked,

"Do you have anything planned at the moment?"

Hagen answered, his face grim,

"There are a number of German camps set up in the forest around here. There is a lot of heavy equipment going into the forest; forced labour too, but the surrounding area is restricted. We are trying to find out what is going on in them, but that kind of snooping can be very dangerous. The Germans shot two men who got too close."

Moen went on to ask,

"You have no idea what the bastards are up to? There's no way you could guess from the loads going into these camps?"

Hagen just shook his head; then invited both men to stay for the night.

"You must stay here under wraps; the sight of two strangers sleeping in a truck might arouse suspicion. Because of those camps, we are swamped with German troops, not ordinary infantry but those Waffen SS bastards, Fanatics to a man and far from stupid."

Erebus lay in a camp bed in the warehouse, thinking over what he had been told earlier. Maiden Aunt would want far more information before ordering a raid. Security could be a problem. Hagen's group had grown with people not known to him or Moen. At breakfast, Hagen apologised to his guests for the 'bloody awful coffee.'

"Next time you have breakfast with us, maybe after the war, we will have some real coffee for you. Times are hard now - the Germans are stealing everything they can get their filthy hands on."

When they had finished eating, Hagen spoke directly to both of his visitors.

"Just to add to what we talked about last night, we intend to have a closer look at those cam—s in the forest - maybe give the British something of use. We also have some new recruits who would like to meet you. Would you mind? The escape Operation from Bergen has become an inspiration to a lot of people." Before Erebus could speak, Moen answered,

"We need to move on, so we won't meet anyone this time. Good luck and be careful." As they drove away, Erebus, in mock sarcasm, asked.

"Since when have you been so cautious and giving the orders - I thought I was in charge?"

Moen looked at him worriedly.

"I've learned a lot since I met you. There is something wrong back there, and as for meeting new recruits - we are not bloody folk heroes. Hagen is good, but he's too lax on security. We're better off well away from them. Where are we going now? See, you are still in charge."

Erebus instructed,

"We'll continue to head up the coast and see what comes up."

For the next two weeks, they got as close to the ports as possible, but Moen was almost paranoid about talking to strangers, so they kept very much to themselves.

The Nazis had set up networks of spies and informers - some Norwegian. A report about two strangers could cause real trouble.

At the end of July, outside Trondheim, one of Berg's men came up with just what they had been looking for. A German destroyer was anchored in a fjord about three kilometres from the open sea. The first thing to be done was to make a camp that was secure enough to satisfy Moen's strict requirements. They found a cabin which was located five kilometres from where the ship was anchored. After a week of watching, Moen decided it was unused and secure. Having moved in, provisions were bought locally but never from the same shop or farm on consecutive days. The men remained apart, meeting only in the hut. Each day they walked to the point which overlooked the vessel and set up a small observation post and began slowly building a picture of the work being carried out on the vessel and how the guards and crew operated.

The guards were Wehrmacht conscripts, not Waffen SS elite. The repair crews were sailors, not engineers. As a result, work seemed - to the watchers' untrained eyes – be progressing very slowly. 'Richard Beitzen' was visible on the hull from the observation post. The name of the vessel and a description of the work were radioed to Maiden Aunt. Davies forwarded this to Royal Naval intelligence and Combined Operations planners. He later received a request that the men watching the ship get a photograph. Intelligence folklore has it that Davies' reply to the planners was along the lines of,

"I have *men* in the field - not fucking magicians!"

During the second week of observation, Vali was flown to a makeshift airfield nearby and met by Moen. Erebus stayed on at the OP and, when joined by his long-time comrade, thanked him for meeting his request in England. Vali briefed his companions.

"The name, as you know, is the Richard Beitzen. A destroyer damaged by heavy weather in the Norwegian Sea and the North Atlantic. The hull has been bent out of shape and the propeller has been slightly warped; the ship is barely seaworthy. The Germans, in their wisdom, have decided to carry out essential repairs in the fjord. The guards are a Wehrmacht company - about a hundred soldiers. Her crew totals three hundred and sixty men. Once repairs are complete, the destroyer will join a battle group and attack the Russian convoys." He paused and looked at his comrades; both were staring at the ship.

"There is one more thing. Hitler is losing patience with the German Navy and demanding they deliver on the promise to stop the convoys to Russia. Things are going seriously wrong at the top in the Third Reich, my friends."

There was silence from the men he had just briefed; they continued to look at the destroyer. Vali asked,

"Why the silence? was it something I said?" Moen spoke for both of them.

"The bloody thing gets bigger every day."

They concluded the anchorage was well chosen; the fjord cliffs gave little cover from the land side for attack and escape after the assault. The sentries were well-trained in efficiently appointed gun emplacements. Aware of the risks involved, Vali - who had operational command - listened as Erebus explained that as Moen was the leader of the Norwegian drivers and Berg was responsible for all seaborne resources, they needed to be included in planning the raid. There was no objection.

The planning began with a highly detailed report on the target. No work done after dark. The sentries were alert during the day but, after dark relaxed. Only one officer stayed aboard overnight. Interestingly it was the same man who was not Kriegsmarine or regular army. The men worked a two, eight-hour watch rota system, and the guards had standard armament. Vali radioed the report to Maiden Aunt, who forwarded it to Operations planners with the comment, 'This, I believe, will do, instead of a photograph.'

In the first week of August, it was confirmed the raid would be in early September. Vali said to Erebus.

"We need to talk to Berg and his men as soon as possible." The meeting took place just outside Trondheim, where the plan was explained in general terms.

"The ship displaces six thousand tons and would, in normal circumstances, would have been attacked by bombers." The men laughed at the phrase, 'normal circumstances.' Vali continued,

"When this was raised by Maiden Aunt at a senior level planning meeting, he was told that RAF Bomber Command had a list of over three hundred priority targets they had been requested to bomb." Erebus spoke.

"Before we go any further, there are some things you must understand."

Vali began.

"Berg, what we are doing is very dangerous for all concerned. I want you to know that you do not have to do this." Erebus continued.

"There are problems in the Third Reich. Hitler has ordered that all commandos, or 'pirates', are to be executed after a trial of sorts. He is so incensed that these men can get to his glorious Reich; he intends to kill everyone taken prisoner and anyone helping them. So we have to make sure that all involved bear that in mind. Everyone on this job must be a volunteer, understood, gentlemen?" Vali was silent but heard the passion and concern in Erebus' voice and thought.

'Jesus! You've changed from the cold-hearted bastard I trained with.'

The three men nodded, and Berg asked,

"What do you want us to do?" Vali answered.

"We have a plan to get the commandos to the target, which is totally dependent upon you and your fellow smugglers." Berg demanded.

"Tell me more." Vali did.

"The commandos will transfer from a sea-going vessel to the trawlers. After dark, they will steam the three kilometres up the fjord, destroy the ship and return to safety the same way." Berg remained silent.

Moen's only comment was,

"Jesus, Laudrup, are all you Brits completely, bloody mad?"

Erebus couldn't resist,

–I'm not British - I'm Irish, and yes, we and most of the Brits are mad."

Berg's comrade spoke.

"Gentlemen, my name is Nielsen which is a Norwegian name, and my blood goes back to Norsemen and beyond. I was on the sea run when we took the POWs to freedom. I have never felt more alive than I did on that night. I am a single man; this is my country, which you are here to help us free. We will get the boys up to the ship, and then, when they have blown it to hell, we will get them all out. Let me give you some local knowledge. The fjord cannot be mined. It is too deep. The Germans would need anchor cables at least three kilometres in length to secure the mines to the bottom at any point on the channel out to the sea. The only problem is the boom that the Germans have laid across the fjord about one kilometre from the destroyer."

Erebus took up the conversation.

"We are aware of it – it is anchored either side of the fjord. The marines will eliminate the troops in the guard houses and then allow the boom to sink. Then go onto the target."

Nielsen nodded, then added,

"If we attack in September, the days are long, but the night, when it comes in, is pitch black. The Germans won't be able to see their hands in front of their faces. We'll muffle the exhausts for the last kilometre. We know every current, every eddy and every backwash in the channel. I repeat, we'll get the commandos into the channel and, if necessary, alongside the destroyer. How many men are we talking about, how do they intend to attack, and what arms will they have?"

Berg remained silent, but his silence was thunderous in its complete support of everything Nielsen had said. Vali was the first to speak.

"Right, let's get down to details. We will need transportation for fifty heavily armed Royal Marine Commandos."

The planning went on long into the night, and, as Erebus, Vali and Moen listened, the raid on the Richard Beitzen began to seem more possible. It was agreed that the commandos would attack in the second week of September; this date being proposed by Nielsen as the tides would be most suitable for three heavily laden trawlers to navigate the fjord undetected. The suggestion was made that the local resistance be involved to attack the land-based troops; Erebus explained the security issues. The others did not argue.

In London, Maiden Aunt met the liaison officer for 62 Commanddo Royal Marines - the unit from which the raiding party would be drawn. When told that there would be a number of non-marine personnel on the trip, he demanded the names of these people. Davies ignored the protests and was given the information. He went straight to SOE headquarters and instructed a team to begin vetting. Maiden Aunt's earlier meeting with Odin had sharpened his determination to maintain security. The vetting cleared all the personnel, including Captain William Cork, U.S.

Moen and Vali stayed at the OP as the planning reached the final stages. Erebus and Berg had six offers to join the raid. Berg had the final choice and selected his men carefully, opting for Nielsen and a man called Gustafson. They were given more details of the attack plan; after the boom had been lowered and boarding the target. Then the rest of his comrades were told of their role. They would keep watch from just over the horizon just in case the Germans fortified the entrance to the fjord. Any German air patrol would report a small inshore fishing fleet and hopefully nothing else. The transfer of the commandos to the three attacking boats would take place in the midst of this small fleet.

Moen, Vali and Erebus were driving the last fifty kilometres to the embarkation point on a forest road which avoided the heavily policed main roads. Suddenly, they saw a man by the side of the road frantically waving his arms with a bike beside him. Moen pulled the truck to a halt.

"What's wrong with you? Have you had an accident?"

The man replied,

"No, I'm fine. I just wanted to warn you. The Germans have a roadblock two kilometres ahead. They're searching everyone and everything. Look after yourselves. The German bastards are stirred up about something."

Moen spoke.

"Thanks very much. Can we be of any help?"

"No, I live down the road. Be careful," the cyclist replied.

Moen instructed his passengers.

"Listen, there is a path that runs through the forest parallel to the road about five hundred metres from the tree line. You take it. I'll be fine getting through the roadblock. Wait for me five hundred metres past the checkpoint."

Erebus and Vali found the path, and the undergrowth was light enough to allow them to approach the roadblock without being seen. Two vehicles were waiting to be checked, but, to the consternation of the SOE men, neither was Moen's. They watched as a staff car pulled up, and an officer joined the soldiers who were searching people. Erebus whispered,

"It's been nearly an hour - where is he?"

In answer to his question, Moen's lorry approached the checkpoint. The men in the forest looked at each other in amazement. It was laden with logs. If the Germans wanted to search the lorry, they would have to move at least two tons of timber to do so. He was questioned for roughly five minutes; Erebus prayed that the big Norwegian would not lose his temper. But Moen seemed very calm and was looking at the staff car intently until finally he was flagged on. After he had left the roadblock, Vali and Erebus cleared the forest and climbed into the waiting lorry. Moen was almost hysterical.

"Jesus Christ, the Hagens, they're dead."

Erebus demanded,

"What are you talking about?"

The reply was spluttered.

"The man I saw in the back of the bastard's car was at Hagen's the other night. He didn't see any of us, thank God. He is one of Hagen's new recruits who wanted to meet us, remember?"

Vali wondered out loud,

"How long would it take us to get there? What do you think is happening at the Hagens?"

Moen retorted,

"At the most two hours, but it could be crawling with Germans, and they could be waiting for people like us to turn up and then we're dead as well. The Hagen's do not know that the man I saw is a traitor and are probably up against a wall waiting for a bullet or being tortured by the Gestapo. Take your pick. How the hell do I know what's going on there?"

Erebus spoke quietly but firmly.

"Why do you think they put the roadblock up all of a sudden? Is there any way they could know about the commando raid? We have told no one. I'm certain the smugglers are all secure. None of them knows Hagen."

"As far as we know!" Moen snorted.

Vali spoke.

"We have to find out what is happening at the Hagen's. When we know that, then we can decide about the raid. Agreed?"

Vali nodded silently. Moen qualified his agreement with,

"I'll get us good and close, but this is my territory, so I will call it if we are in danger. Is that understood?"

Within an hour and a half, they were lying behind an overgrown, heavy hedge which provided excellent cover and an unimpeded view into the warehouse yard. The Hagen's were being held at gunpoint along with two other men. Even at a distance, Erebus could see that all the men had been brutally beaten. The Germans were tearing the warehouse to pieces. Suddenly there was a shout from one of the men who was searching the Hagens' house. The officer who was in charge went into the house and emerged with a radio.

"Jesus Christ!"

Erebus and Moen swore at the same time.

"Jesus Christ! The bloody fools! The stupid, bloody fools!" Moen added to his earlier curse and gasped.

"Laudrup, it's one of the radios we stole from the Abwehr. They told us they'd destroyed the lot."

All three watched in silence as flames began to rise from the warehouse and then the family home. The Hagen's were about to be thrown into a lorry when, out of the flames of the warehouse, rushed two men. One with his clothes on fire. Both began firing machine guns and killed some of the guards. The watchers looked on helplessly as the Hagen's wrestled with the soldiers nearest to them. One of the Hagen boys managed to rip a gun from his guard and opened fire. In less than a minute, all three Hagens were dead, and so were at least five more Germans, along with the other prisoners. The staff car from the roadblock sped into the warehouse yard and the officer, and a man got out. Moen swore viciously.

"That's the same man who was in the car at the roadblock; he's working for the bastards."

Feeling helpless, the three men headed for Trondheim. It was now clear that the German had been told about the radio by the traitor. The Hagen's must have been using it to contact the SOE. Erebus thought, 'Jesus! Simpson-Coyle again.' Moen slowed the vehicle as they neared the OP.

Erebus spoke quickly.

"Moen, pull up here. We'll have a look at the OP from a distance, just in case there is a problem. Vali, you approach from the West. I'll do the East flank. Moen come in slowly with the lorry. If anything nasty is in there, you'll have to get us out." The driver nodded his head.

Exercising extreme caution, the approach took an hour before all three were in the OP and satisfied that there had been no leak. Vali repeated his earlier thought.

"Listen, we know that Hagen doesn't know Berg or his men. In fact, he's only met you and Laudrup." Moen bowed his head, saying,

"Well, he won't be meeting anyone else, poor sod."

Vali continued,

"To be brutal, the capture of the radio and the destruction of the Hagens' resistance cell might get the Germans to relax for a time. They'll never expect a major military attack within such a short time of a major blow to the resistance." His comrades remained silent.

Maiden Aunt sat in his office. The report received from Vali was deeply worrying. The men killed were under the command of Simpson-Coyle, another disaster and possibly another leak.

He tried to reassure himself. A very small number of men knew of the impending raid. The phone rang. Ten minutes later, Davies sat in a room with Odin and the man he had met in London earlier in the year. The meeting began with the man introducing himself as Admiral Sir Colin Menzies, head of British Intelligence Services and known simply as 'C'. Maiden Aunt was asked to make his report on the Hagens' deaths. Odin remained silent throughout. Once Maiden Aunt had finished, 'C' summarised.

"Gentlemen, it is clear that there are problems with all aspects of Colonel Simpson-Coyle's operating procedures and security. The decision to ring-fence all of Maiden Aunt's projects has paid dividends, and as a result, the order to go ahead with the raid will be given. 62 Commando go in as planned."

As he radioed the 'Go, order to Vali, Davies said a silent prayer for his men.

22

Pirates and Crown Jewels

Bill Cork reported to the secret HQ of 62 Commando Royal Marines. One of the bases from where attacks on Hitler's fortress in Europe were mounted. The raids had a single objective. To convince the German High Command that Norway was the target of one arm of a pending two-pronged invasion of Europe. The objective had been achieved as over six thousand battle-hardened Waffen SS troops were stationed in Norway rather than mainland Europe.

Bill Cork sat on his bunk, glad to be seeing action again. Images of Dieppe vivid in his memory. Suddenly the order to board came, and Bill was sitting aboard a seagoing trawler affectionately known as the 'Shetland Express.' He had come here for active service experience but learned more. During training and now aboard ship were men of all nationalities. All with one aim, to destroy the Nazis. And in contradiction to his father's words, many of these men were Irish. Not alone on this raid, but in the Commandos, the British army, the RAF and the Royal navy. All Irish, all fighting for freedom. His eyes swept around the deck and saw Royal Marines; some were laughing and telling jokes. Some were trying to sleep, others silent, pensive. One was deep in a book, another smoking an unlit cigarette. The trawler hit the open sea and began to heave rhythmically. Bill laughed as one of the marines joked,

"I always get seasick, and it makes me turn green. I want to look my best for the Germans; anybody got any make-up?" Several marines replied in the crudest of terms, but one wisecrack appealed.

"I'll explain your problem to them; maybe they'll give you a dressing room."

The laughter that followed was full and part of the commandos readying for action. At ten knots, the trawler would take about twenty hours to reach the transfer point, plenty of time for everyone to think about Hitler's order which left no doubt to their fate if captured. The Texan amongst them had other thoughts. Captain Cork of the US Army Engineers had impressed his superiors to such a degree he had been appointed second in command in conjunction with a Scottish/Canadian officer who had also been at Dieppe. The men discovered this during a twenty-mile route march and became good friends. The senior officers planning the raid had noted this and decided to take an unusual step. The raid required two executive officers, so Captain Cork would lead the attack on the Northern guard post, and Captain Frazier would lead men to neutralise the other. The inherent perils of a split command had been raised, but the demands of the mission and the friendship of the men had ameliorated concern. Both were leading men who volunteered for the dangerous work of commandos for many reasons. The most common being boredom, others for reasons which were better left unsaid. Now all were aboard the Shetland Express heading for active service.

The big trawler hove to and was quickly surrounded by a number of smaller vessels. The commandos boarded three trawlers and, along with the rest of the 'fishing fleet', watched for the Shetland Express to head out to sea and wait to return and pick up the raiding party.

The trawlers which would make the attack were drawn up on either side of Berg's boat for a briefing by the officer in command. On deck was Major Ken 'Spike' Campion of the Royal Marines - a tough, outspoken Englishman who did not suffer fools gladly. Campion had been given the nickname 'Spike' at school due to his thick bushy 'spikey' hair, and it had stuck. The Royal Marines and Rugby Union football were his passions and at fifteen stones and six foot two inches, most sensible people played and stayed on his good side. Major Spike Campion began in a clear, strong voice,

"We are going to attack a warship which displaces six thousand tons and is guarded by three hundred and sixty enemy personnel, so let's get in and out with a minimum of fuss. All contact with the enemy must result in the permanent silencing of that contact. If we get into a firefight, we will do badly because we are outnumbered. This is about stealth and speed. Now gentlemen from the onshore party will brief you on the terrain and the final approach to the target. Before that, are there any questions?"

One of the platoon lieutenants said,

"What about prisoners, sir? Should we try to take any?"

Campion answered,

"Good question. If we get our hands on a senior officer, we'll bring him along,–but other ranks - no. They will have to be eliminated." Then another officer, in a very rounded Scottish accent, asked,

"Do you think they'll offer to surrender the ship to us, and if so, what do we do with it, sir?"

Campion smiled,

"Bring the bloody thing back, I suppose. Anyone know how to drive one?" There was laughter all round. Bill's view of the British was changing by the minute. They prepared for battle and possibly death in a unique way, being facetious and yet profound; Bill suddenly felt proud to be with these men. Campion finished his briefing by saying,

"As I said, these gentlemen have seen the target at close quarters."

Erebus began,

"You do not know me or the organisation I work for. All I will say is that I have spent some time behind enemy lines, and it is this gentleman to my left and myself who recommended the target. You are here because of us, and thank you all for coming."

He then went into detail of the attack and escape. The Operation was to begin with Berg, Nielsen and Gustafson taking the commandos to the guard posts, which teams from two trawlers would eliminate, then lower the boom. The third would stand in reserve. All three trawlers would then proceed to within sight of the destroyer. The decision would then be made either to swim the last short distance or lay alongside the ship. A number of commandos would board and eliminate the sentries on deck, and then the main force would follow with the charges and destroy the ship.

Vali then spoke.

He paused.

"It would appear that the destroyer's hull is badly warped, the repairs have closed the living quarters aboard, and the crew and guards disembark every night. They are in a camp three kilometres from the anchorage. The cliffs surrounding the ship are too steep to allow any tents or even a guardhouse to be set up within sight of the ship. We estimate with confidence, at night there are never more than thirty guards on board."

He finished with the words,

"Gentlemen, the Norwegians have had a hard time from the Germans, so this action will hopefully do something to lift their morale and also reduce the enemy's capabilities in the Norwegian Sea. Finally, as I am sure you have all been told, Hitler has developed a dislike for chaps like you. In fact, he calls you 'pirates', so let's all get in and get out. The Nazis respect no one, and there is not a shred of decency in any of them. Right! Good luck."

The raiding party comprised three squads of fifteen marines in each trawler, with Berg's boat carrying Vali, Moen and Major Campion. Captain Weir was aboard Nielsen's boat. Captain Cork was in Gustafson's boat with his men and Erebus. The trawlers entered the fjord, single line ahead as the light faded. Just as Nielsen said, the sun disappeared behind the cliffs of the fjord, and darkness fell as if a light had been switched off. The craft separated, and Cork's boat headed for its target; the other trawlers disappeared into the blackness. Bill watched Gustafson, a calm, bearded man who, for some reason, reminded him of his Uncle Bill Buchanan – utterly dependable no matter what. The skipper's eyes were almost on fire as the trawler closed on the guard house. There was a sliver of light coming from the lookout hut by the boom cable anchor. Otherwise, pitch darkness. Bill facetiously promised to send a note of thanks to the allied bomber forces who made the enemy darken everything after sundown.

Everything depended on the enemy guards not seeing them from either the boom anchor guard house or, later, the deck of the ship. As the trawler touched the shoreline silently, Gustafson gave a small laugh of satisfaction. His seamanship had been superb. The commandos, led by a large Norwegian, closely followed by Erebus and Bill Cork, moved soundlessly toward the hut. Six men immediately began to disengage the boom anchor rigging as Cork, and the others entered the guardhouse.

The big marine killed the first enemy soldier with a chop to the Adam's apple, followed by a knife blade through the spinal cord. Bill Cork found himself calmly issuing orders to his men as he drove his service knife into the heart of a German who had been lying on a makeshift bunk. Within two minutes, the post had been neutralised. The marines at the boom anchorage had finished releasing the cable, which was at least three feet thick, and watched it slide into the fjord. Bill checked his watch - eight minutes from start to finish. Gustafson watched as all of the commandos boarded, and then he eased the trawler back into the fjord. Erebus stood beside Bill Cork and said,

"Well done, Captain. You commanded very well back there."

Bill simply replied,

"Thank you, sir."

There was a question on his lips, but Gustafson signalled to all aboard to be silent. Nielsen's boat came alongside, and then Berg's trawler came out of the darkness and took the lead, edging toward where the boom should have been. The sea was clear - the boom had sunk. The water was as coal black as the night as Bill Cork crouched next to Erebus and whispered,

"When will we know if we swim or go alongside?" The answer was instant,

"In about thirty seconds."

With that, Erebus signalled to two commandos to climb over the side. Cork said,

"I'll go with you, just in case something goes wrong."

Erebus was not concerned; he knew that any man on the mission could swim the fifty metres to the ship in full combat gear. Anyway, the young American had proved himself to be an able and ruthless killer. Erebus slipped into the bitterly cold water, followed by the man from Texas.

Bill Cork felt the air being forced out of him by the icy water and thought of the lake at home in Big Bend and suddenly missed it enormously. The hull of the ship rose before them as eight commandos swam toward the gangplank. The two guards at the bottom of the gangplank were in a relaxed pose as the daggers thrown by two commandos found their targets just below the carotid arteries. The men died instantly but, far more importantly, silently. The commandos who had swum ahead of the knife throwers were at the bottom of the gangplank to stop the bodies falling into the sea. Both dead men fell, one almost vertically, unfortunately, the other did look as if he was going to tumble into the sea. The commando who took the force of his falling corpse was knocked almost unconscious.

The landing stage was now crowded with two dead bodies and the commandos. Erebus signalled to Cork to follow, and both began to climb the gangplank. Once on deck, Bill felt he was the only man on earth as he followed Erebus to the first available cover. The other commandos, now on deck, went in search of the guards. The first German to die did so at the hands of Erebus; his spinal cord snapped by a sharp jerk of his head to the left. Almost simultaneously, Bill Cork crept up behind the second guard and, as he recalled later, with consummate ease, took his life with the knife given to him by the Indians. The blade was razor sharp and cut the man's throat without a trace until the blood began to flow. At the landing stage, the dazed commando had regained his senses and was signalling to the trawlers to come alongside. Once the initial assault team of eight commandos, with Cork and Erebus, had cleared the weather deck of lookouts, the full commando force occupied the ship. There was absolute silence, and the report of the raid would read that only one enemy prisoner had been taken - all other opposition had been eliminated. Bill Cork remembered hearing a German pleading,

"Bitte, bitte," then there was just silence. The big commando came out of a cabin where the sound had come from, looked at Bill and said,

"Captain, I am Norwegian. My sister killed herself after being raped by a German."

Cork said nothing; how could he judge anyone? In the last few hours, he had killed two men. He looked at the blonde giant and shrugged his shoulders. One of the many thoughts that went through his mind at that point was that it could have been *his* sister if things were different. If anybody asked, the German tried to raise the alarm. Vali was now assisting in the setting of the charges with Major Campion. A marine sergeant reported to the major that an officer had been captured. Campion ordered.

"Bring him; we'll interrogate him later."

The raid had, so far, been almost perfect, and there was a sense of disbelief as the raiders boarded the trawlers and made for the open sea and safety. The small convoy cleared the fjord as the first explosion rang out to be followed by others in quick succession. Major Campion counted the sound of each explosion as the charges went off. He looked at Vali with a gleam in his eye,

"Four on the port side, four on the starboard and one in the engine room— totalling nine - she'll never see daylight again. Right! Let's go home."

He then added,

"Captain Frazier, let's have a roll call - and bring that German prisoner."

A lilting Scottish accent replied,

"Yes, sir."

The trawlers headed out to sea as the fires on the destroyer grew in ferocity, as did the explosions when the ammunition on board exploded. The plan was simple thereafter. The trawlers were on course to a position where they would be met by the Shetland Express, which would refuel them, take the commandos on board and head for home. Major Campion sat in the cabin of Berg's boat with a frown on his face. The Shetland Express was not answering any hailing signals. Even Campion, with his minuscule knowledge of the sea, knew that the fuel situation on board all three trawlers would soon be critical. Erebus said to the major,

"How long before the rendezvous, Major Campion?"

He looked at Erebus and said,

"I have been briefed on your organisation and your role in the resistance in Norway, so I feel quite proper in telling you that we are in serious danger of being left out here. I cannot contact the trawler which was to have picked us up and refuel our friends from Norway. Erebus, we are at a crisis in the mission."

Erebus replied,

"If you know my code name, I can only presume you were briefed at the highest level. So tell me, major, just how much trouble are we in?"

Campion said,

"I don't think I have to go into too much detail other than to say that when the day breaks, if the Germans spot us, we will be sitting ducks when the fuel runs out, which, in my opinion, will be in about fourteen hours. We do not have enough fuel to make Shetland, and we certainly can't go back. Even with your remarkable record of achievements in Norway, I doubt you could hide fifty of us until the end of the war. There is also the death sentence handed down to all commandos by Hitler to consider. Having blown up one of his ships in his backyard, so to speak, I imagine the deaths of my men would not be quick." Erebus asked,

"All right major, as we are being frank, what was so important on that ship that it couldn't be destroyed from the air? I saw the RAF, in the early stages of the war, flatten U-boat pens from ten thousand feet. Now, if they wanted to, they could have hit the bridge without scraping the paintwork anywhere else."

Campion smiled and replied,

"Your reputation is well earned. The Scottish officer with the facetious questions was tasked with getting what we came for, and the bonus is that we got one of the men who designed it as well. The box, which he has not been out of his hands since we put to sea, is an Ultra Machine, the most recent update. We had received confirmation that a machine had been allocated to the destroyer. When the proposal to destroy the 'Richard Bietzer' was made, we got to hear about it and decided it was a calculated risk but worth it. The ship has now been destroyed, and, with luck, the Germans will believe the machine went with it. As you know, the fjord is very deep, and there is no way they can know what went down. The only problem, Erebus, is that we seem to be all at sea. I have no idea what happened to the trawler that was detailed to collect us."

Erebus went to the wheelhouse,

"I need to use the radio and quickly."

Berg's face reflected his comment.

"I thought things were going too well."

Snow Eagle was escorting a 'fast' convoy of fuel tankers as it steamed south down the Norwegian Sea. The first officer was summoned to the radio cabin as a signal designated for his eyes only had been received. The signal, just one word, 'Erebus,' brought an order from Cork to the radio operator,

"Please contact Commander Larsen and ask him to come and stand by in the radio cabin."

Captain Buchan was silent as his first officer explained the utmost importance of the signal, as it indicated a member of the SOE needed assistance as quickly as possible. He also requested the captain's permission to signal Commodore Loftus. Buchan knew in covert Operations this signal was a last resort. Before going to signal the flagship, Cork was asked one question by his captain.

"Number One, in your opinion, as a result of this signal, is it likely that we may have to leave the fleet at short notice?"

Cork replied,

"It's only an educated guess, but I would say that is a realistic assumption, sir." Buchan replied,

"Right then, we had better get ready."

Buchan's steward was told to find Chief Adams. In the radio cabin, Larsen was in contact with the flagship and minutes later with the Commodore. The exchange of signals was short. Loftus ordered Cork and Larsen to make contact with Erebus; he would contact Maiden Aunt.

At the SOE base in England, the signal from the Polar Star raised the temperature in the communications room. Within minutes, Maiden Aunt was in contact with the officer in charge of Special Forces transport and demanded an update on the location of the trawler assigned to pick up the raiding party. The reply was simple - no one knew. All he could offer by way of explanation was the weather off Shetland had deteriorated rapidly. Heavy seas, some strengthening force ten, had been reported by patrol aircraft which had struggled to land in the weather conditions and finished with,

"Her call signs were on schedule, then silence, and we've not heard from the Shetland Express for sixteen hours; believe me the North Sea is treacherous." In the meantime, 'C's office was informed of the developing crisis in the Norwegian

Sea. Menzies took personal command of the situation and, breaking every rule in his and everybody else's book, phoned Maiden Aunt. He began to speak, and Davies recognised the slow controlled voice.

"Please listen carefully; the items in the location which we have discussed must be extracted at all costs. They have amongst them the crown jewels; therefore, they must, I repeat, must be retrieved. Pass the reference crown jewels to the officer in charge," then the phone went dead.

Davies sent a signal to Loftus, who immediately dispatched a signal to Captain Buchan, which was read to him by Larsen in his cabin seconds later.

"All efforts must be made to retrieve elements at issue. Detach you and one other unit and retrieve elements and crown jewels."

The signals officer on the Polar Star expressed a view later that it seemed an awful lot of fuss to get the Norwegian Crown Jewels out of enemy hands. This was exactly the perception 'C' had planned. He had agents spreading rumours around enemy intelligence agencies that the Americans were demanding security for the huge loans they were making to all the allies to fund the war. The Norwegians had put up the Royal Crown Jewels, which had been given to the British Commandos by the Norwegian resistance. The destroyer had been sunk as a diversion. Under normal conditions, Commodore Loftus would never have allowed the amount of radio traffic transmitted in the last hour. The Commodore sensed whatever had happened in the last twenty-four hours off the coast of Norway was far from normal, even by North Atlantic convoy and SOE standards. The flag officer still had to get the convoy home but was confident he could release two ships. Snow Eagle and Snow Tiger were ordered to make ready to detach the convoy.

As hoped, the Germans were also listening. The high command in Berlin had been shaken by Hitler's anger when told of a warship being blown up inside what he regarded as German territory. The Fuehrer ordered that the ships carrying the raiders be found and bombed. However, when the signal about the Crown Jewels was intercepted, he demanded that the 'pirates' be captured, brought to Germany to stand trial and executed. It was this stupidity that gave the Royal Marines a chance of escape. The Krieg marine was somewhat loathe to carry out Hitler's orders - to do so would involve sending their rapidly diminishing surface fleet to the open seas where the Allied Navies were waiting to sink them.

On board Berg's trawler, Erebus was at the radio as the signal from Cork came through. 'What do you require?' Erebus looked at Major Campion.

"This is a signal from a ship of the Royal Navy; some of the officers aboard have knowledge and experience of SOE Operations. What do I tell them that will bring them here without the enemy realising what we have with us?" Campion looked out to sea from the small wheelhouse of the trawler and replied,

"Erebus - tell them we have the Crown Jewels with us."

The signal was sent, and Erebus enquired.

"Is it possible for you to tell me what is so important that you were willing to risk the lives of fifty good men and also these very brave Norwegians?"

Campion looked at him.

"Erebus, in the increasingly unlikely event of us getting out of this mess alive, I feel that your request is justified. As I have already told you, on board that destroyer was the latest Ultra Cipher Machine, which was being fitted by the German we have taken prisoner. If the Germans believe that the cipher box was destroyed by the explosion we are ahead of the game, at least for a while. That is why we started spreading rumours about the Norwegian Crown Jewels. Apparently, Hitler and his cronies feel the need to acquire State jewels to add to the hoard of stolen masterpieces. If the Germans knew we had the Ultra-Machine on board, we would have been bombed by now. We have not, so it would seem the idiots in Berlin actually believe that we have the Norwegian Crown Jewels."

Erebus smiled.

"I don't suppose, by any chance, you know where the Norwegian Crown Jewels actually are?"

Campion's reply was,

"Not the faintest idea, old boy. Why do you ask?"

"Just that the men who own these trawlers all do a nice side-line in smuggling, that's all."

Both men laughed, and then Erebus called to Berg,

"Set a course due west."

Aboard Snow Eagle, the signal was received and relayed to the flagship, which issued the order within thirty seconds. 'Recover crown jewels and other elements.'

Captain Buchan ordered 'full ahead both', and the ship surged forward; aft of her, Snow Tiger got up to full speed. The signal from Erebus had been tracked by Snow Eagle and gave a bearing. The exact location of the trawlers on that bearing could not be calculated unless a second location, or 'fix signal', was received. Captain Warne, on Snow Tiger, took station three thousand yards abeam of Snow Eagle, then resumed the original course to get that target bearing cross triangulation. Aboard Berg's trawler, Erebus sent a second signal giving the second fix required. If the trawlers stayed on the same course, the sloops would intercept in six hours.

In the port of Trondheim, the orders from Berlin were being put into Operation. The 'pirates' were to be taken alive. They were not to be bombed under any circumstances. If necessary, a U-boat was to be ordered to surface and escort the vessels back to Norwegian waters. The Norwegian Crown Jewels were to be taken to Berlin. The officers of the Krieg marine read the details with astonishment, but no one dared question the orders. Rumours were rife, amongst the German military, of men being shot for questioning the Fuehrer's infallibility.

Aboard Berg's trawler, Erebus received the signal that the allied ships were closing. Every effort was to be made to shorten the distance between the converging ships. Snow Eagle and Snow Tiger both pushed their engines to the limit as the sea began to lighten. At times, much to the consternation of the engineering officer and his men, both ships were exceeding maximum safe engine revolutions. This concern was voiced to his fellow engineer when he exclaimed,

"Jesus! She's only designed to do twenty knots. If the skipper wants any more, we'll need paddles!"

Aboard Berg's trawler, Erebus knew he could do no more than wait for the navy, so he sat beside the young American captain and began to talk.

"Tell me captain, do you have any relatives in the Irish guards?"

Startled, Bill's tone was incredulous.

"Not as far as I know, sir. Why do you ask?"

Erebus explained.

"It's just you carried out your duties at the guard post and on board the target with great alacrity. You reminded me of another man I have been in combat with. His name is Cork, and he has an Irish background; don't suppose there's any Irish blood in you, is there?"

Bill, now on firmer ground, informed his comrade.

"Well sir, as it happens, my father is an Irishman from County Cork. My mother is a Texan. Do you know Ireland well, sir?"

The captain's voice was wistful.

"I used to know it very well, but I left as a very young boy. I haven't been back in years." Cork recognised a similarity.

"Then we have something in common, sir. I could say the same of my father. He left his home in Cork at a very early age and settled in Texas. He has never told us why and none of us have ever pressed the point with him." Erebus suggested.

"Rather coincidental, don't you think, that two men of the same name should be involved with this part of the world."

Bill asked,

"Do you mean Norway, sir?"

"Yes, I do mean Norway. Still, perhaps one day you and your namesake will meet, and we can chat about the whole thing."

Bill's mind went to the raid and his actions.

"Sir, may I ask a question?"

"Yes, of course."

"When does a man know when to stop killing?"

Erebus paused, then answered,

"When you start to enjoy it!"

At that point, an aircraft with German markings flew over the ships. Within a minute, it had returned.

"It's a long-range Condor Bomber," one of the Marines shouted, then continued, "Now we're for it."

But to the astonishment of the men on the small flotilla, the aircraft just circled. Erebus calculated that it must be at least five hours since he had received confirmation that help was on the way. With little else to do other than wait, he began to think about maybe going home and seeing his parents. The pleasant daydream was shattered by a huge hissing sound, which became a roar. Off the port side of Berg's trawler, a U-boat surfaced. The conning tower hatch opened as a gun crew appeared from the forrard hatch. The U-boat captain used a speaking trumpet to order the trawlers to heave to. Just to give emphasis to his command, the deck gun on the U-boat sprayed the water just ahead of Berg's boat with large calibre shells. Erebus and Berg were in the wheelhouse as the U-boat captain issued further orders.

"You will all follow me until further notice. Any attempt to escape will result in the destruction of your vessel. I assure you, gentlemen, we will shoot to kill."

Berg said to Erebus,

"I estimate that there is about two hundred metres between us and the U-boat. Gustafson's boat is a small ice breaker with a powerful engine and solid steel prow and could punch a hole in the hull of that U-boat easily. It's got to be worth a try."

Erebus signalled to Major Campion and Captain Cork to come to the wheelhouse and told them Berg's idea. Campion listened, then called a marine over,

"See if you can get a message to Captain Frazier; try not to let the box-heads see what you are doing."

Campion then turned to Bill and said,

"Now, captain, would you be kind enough to put together a plan for storming that enemy vessel."

"Yes, sir."

The German captain had now handed over the marshalling of the trawlers to his first officer, who was shouting at Nielsen and Berg, who, in turn, were shouting back something about 'not understanding German – they were just poor fishermen.' Meanwhile, as the officer came close to losing his temper, his captain was getting into a rubber dinghy with three other men to board one of the trawlers. Campion almost whispered to Erebus,

"Jesus! They must have believed that Crown Jewels rubbish; otherwise he would have sunk us immediately. Either that or they want their Ultra Machine back. Listen, all of my marines are armed with machine guns and hand grenades - we can fight our way out of this."

At that precise moment, Bill Cork approached him and said,

"Major, if we can get one trawler onto the other side of the U-boat, we will divide their fire sufficiently to allow us to get aboard the casing. Then it's sailors, or whatever their crew is, against marines. That shouldn't take too long, sir."

Campion smiled and said to Erebus,

"There you have it - American ingenuity, and if that idiot captain boards any of the trawlers, we have a ready made hostage."

Aboard Snow Eagle, Lieutenant Commander Cork was in the radio room. The surface radar was registering three contacts single line head about a hundred yards apart and underway at about ten knots at a distance of seven thousand yards. Their course was converging with the sloops. Petty Officer Constantine said,

"Fourth contact, sir. Just ahead of the trawlers." There was a pause, and as Cork was about to turn away, the radio operator spoke again.

"All contacts now at a stop."

Cork looked at the radar screen. He had spent many hours on the radar and regarded himself as good as anyone, but Constantine was the acknowledged master aboard.

"What do you think it is, PO?"

"Constantine's voice was confident,

"It's U-boat conning tower, sir."

Cork asked,

"How do you know?"

"It must have surfaced, sir. Until a minute ago, there were only three images. That is a U-boat - definitely."

"Right! Don't take your eyes off it. Hear me?"

"Aye, aye, sir."

Cork lifted the speaking tube and said,

"Radio room here. First officer for the captain."

"Bridge, aye, the captain here. Go ahead number one."

"We've found the trawlers, sir, but it would appear that the enemy have as well. There is U-boat alongside them as we speak."

"What's the range?"

"Seven thousand yards, sir."

"Come to the bridge straight away, number one."

As Cork left the radio cabin, Larsen entered and said,

"Tell the Captain that the Condor has gone. I think we can presume because of low fuel."

Pat Cork entered the bridge of the Snow Eagle, where Captain Buchan was estimating how close he could get before being spotted. On seeing Cork, he said to the signals officer,

"Flags, ask Commander Larsen to establish an open line with Captain Warne on Snow Tiger- we don't want any misunderstandings."

Buchan spoke.

"Number one, we need to knock out that U-boat without endangering the trawlers. Do you agree?"

"Yes, I do, sir."

"Right, who is the best man we have on the four-inch forrard mount?"

Pat answered,

"I am, sir."

The captain continued,

"Right! We agree again. I will get you as close as possible then you take the shot. Make it count number one; you will only get one chance."

Pat moved to the for'ard mounting, where his service on Snow Eagle began. The gun commander was stood down then Pat briefed the gun crew on the situation and imminent action. Then, knowing each man well explained the possibility of hitting friendly ships and their own marines, finishing with,

"Whatever happens, I take full responsibility. Is that understood, gentlemen?" The men nodded, and the leading seaman, who was the gunner, asked.

"Sir, do you want the conning tower hit below or above the fleet number."

The men focused on the gun. The shell loader was searching through the magazine as if looking for the perfect round – one which was true in every way, to ensure there would not be any deviation from the trajectory that would take the shell to its target. All of the crew knew a four-inch shell hitting a small, crowded vessel would kill everyone on board. They also knew that the shot had to be taken and there were no more qualified men aboard to do that. Cork felt the ship surge as the engineers squeezed more speed out of the engines. The speaking tube whistled. Cork picked it up.

"Captain here, number one. At two thousand yards from the enemy, I will signal the trawlers to disperse. I will close to fifteen hundred yards and reduce speed to give you a stable deck to fire from. You take your shot when you want. Any questions?"

Pat replied.

"No, sir."

"Right! Let's get on with it, and good luck Pat."

Cork lined up the gun, the shell was loaded, and he checked his calculations twice mentally, his mind racing through the basic mathematics of elevation of barrel, velocity and distance. He then allowed for the unknown factor of wind - but this he had done many times; he felt he knew this gun intimately. Then thought, 'who am I kidding, it's just a naval gun; they're all the same.'

Then a shout from the radio cabin announced,

"Trawlers ordered to disperse, sir."

As the dinghy carrying the German captain neared Berg's boat, the radio came to life. Erebus listened and swore.

"Jesus! Berg, get the trawlers under way. Don't argue - just do it. Major, give the order to your men to open fire on the U-boat - now."

Campion and Cork ran from the wheelhouse as the German captain began to climb onto the deck. Cork went to the stern of the trawler as Campion went to the bow; both shouted,

"Commence firing."

The marines sprayed a hail of lethal fire across the casing of the U-boat. Berg was on the radio and shouted to Nielsen and Gustafson,

"Get away from the U-boat, now, and don't ask questions."

On board Snow Eagle, the ship slowed as Pat heard the leading gunner call out.

"Range, Fifteen hundred yards, sir."

Pat calmly ordered.

"Shoot!"

The lanyard was pulled, the report of the gun was instant. Pat Cork watched, convinced the shell was visible all the way. Then there was wild cheering from the bridge. Looking around, he saw every vantage point had been taken by the crew. The gun crew was silent; one man looked as if he was praying. Then Pat heard a shout from 'flags' on the bridge.

"Christ, number one! Bloody middle stump."

With that, the for'ard mount of Snow Tiger opened fire. The distance between the escorts and the enemy was reducing rapidly as Snow Eagle closed on the target, the trawlers, the Royal Marines, the crown jewels and Pat Cork's first cousin.

All three trawlers got underway as the heavy calibre machine gun on the U-boat opened fire, aiming at Gustafson's boat. Within seconds, the crew of the machine gun were dead, killed by the direct hit of a four-inch shell from Snow Eagle. The trawlers strained their engines to get away from what was now a target for the Royal Navy warships closing at maximum speed. The shells continued to fall, and the U-boat sustained another three hits, but the trawlers were still in mortal danger.

Erebus, seeing that the U-boat was now no longer a threat, signalled to the Snow Eagle, 'cease fire immediately - enemy destroyed'.

Then, there was just silence as the enemy vessel slid beneath the waves, and the German captain and his men were taken prisoner by Captain Cork and the Royal Marines. The action had taken no longer than five minutes.

The marines began to cheer as the escorts closed on the small trawler fleet. Aboard the warships, it had been decided that the commandos and their prisoners would be taken to the Shetland Islands by Snow Tiger. Snow Eagle would refuel the trawlers and then return to the convoy. Each trawler disembarked its complement of commandos; the men climbed the netting rigged along the port side of HMS Snow Tiger. One of those men was Captain Bill Cork of the US Army Engineers, who, once aboard, went below for food and debrief. Roughly two hundred yards away, his cousin First Lieutenant Pat Cork was supervising the trawlers refuelling. Aboard Snow Eagle, Erebus reported the action by radio to an SOE analyst. Vali joined him as he finished. Captain Buchan greeted both men with a handshake and a message for Erebus,

"I believe my first officer has an update for you from Maiden Aunt, who has also asked me to say, 'Come home if you want to.'"

Buchan continued,

"Will you be coming back with us? I am afraid I'll have to press you for an answer. I think if we hang about here too much longer, we may get stuck in rush hour traffic."

Erebus laughed.

"Say goodbye to the Royal Marines for me and thank them and the American officer - they're a first-class bunch of men. In answer to your question – I will go back. I have a little unfinished business to attend to."

Buchan nodded,

"Very well, it's your decision. Good luck to you and your comrades in arms."

Once provisioned, two trawlers had steamed for their home ports. The smugglers were extremely cautious; nothing aboard could be linked to the Royal Navy, knowing the Germans would be brutal with anyone thought to be involved in the raid and the sinking of the U-boat. Erebus approached Pat Cork as Berg's boat finished refuelling.

"How is your leg these days?"

Pat looked up from the diesel tank control panel,

"We'll get to that in a minute. How the hell are you? Well, I trust?"

Erebus asked with overt respect.

"That shot with the four-inch gun saved a lot of lives; was it you, Pat?"

They moved out of earshot of the crew.

"Yes, I wouldn't let anyone else take the responsibility, Charles."

Erebus smiled and spoke.

"To answer your question, I am fine. In fact, I couldn't be better - all things considered. It's been a long time since anyone called me Charles. Anything for me?"

Cork looked around to ensure their privacy.

"I have some general information for you. Maiden Aunt sends his best, as do your parents. They are very well. Getting back to my leg, in many ways, I would not be here today if we had not met what seems like a lifetime ago. I am an officer in the Royal Navy now, up to my eyes in secrets and seawater. You, however, have changed. When I first met you, I thought you were stark, raving mad."

Erebus butted in,

"Don't you mean stark staring mad?"

"No, you never stared at any time, which made you harder to figure out and even scarier. I think you've mellowed a good bit!" He paused, then exclaimed.

"Good god! You've not gone and fallen in love, have you, Captain Lewis? Oh, I beg your pardon. I should say, Major Lewis. Congratulations. That's official from Maiden Aunt." Lewis nodded silently, then prompted,

"You haven't finished have you, Pat?"

Cork again glanced around.

"Charles, please listen very carefully. Maiden Aunt is extremely concerned about Simpson-Coyle. There has been a serious security leak in his theatre of Operations, and men have lost their lives. Maiden Aunt has told me to tell you to trust no one. Do you hear me, Charles? No one at all – ever! And on a personal note, which I agree with, he believes you are pushing your luck to the limit by staying in Norway any longer. That's everything he asked me to say. Now your trawler is nearly ready, so you'd better board her. Goodbye Charles, and good luck." Erebus shook Pat's hand.

"Thanks, Pat. Oh! By the way. You wouldn't by chance have any relatives in the US Army Engineers or living in America, would you?" Pat, surprised, asked.

"What made you think of a question like that?"

Erebus shrugged.

"Oh, nothing really. Forget it. Good luck to you, Pat."

— 23 —

London and Love

The hot chocolate drink and corned beef sandwiches tasted as good as any steak from the Double B. Memories and images driven by hunger and adrenalin raced around his head, then slowed and merged into a question. How could he go back to his old life after Dieppe and Norway? What could top the last two years? Then came a voice at first indistinct, then clear. It was Captain Frazier,

"Just wanted to say how you impressed us. You have an invite any time we get ourselves into trouble. Well done Bill, you're one of us now." Bill replied.

"My pleasure. Anytime I can help." Frazier took the offer up.

"Well, now you mention it. We might need a little help with the Crown jewels."

Now fully attentive, Bill said.

"Lead on", and followed the Scotsman. Warne was leaving his cabin, and they heard him say to Major Campion.

"Take as long as you want. My ship is at your disposal. We have what's left of the U-boat crew under lock and key until you say otherwise."

Bill and Frazier saw a small case with a barrel lock complete with four numbered tumblers on a small table and heard Major Campion speaking German to the dishevelled prisoner. On seeing them he switched his attention.

"Ah! Captain Cork. I take it Frazier voiced our appreciation. It seems our German guest does not speak English and is unable to help with the combination lock on the case. We may need to impress on him the importance of offering assistance. How do you feel about that?"

Bill smiled. It was the second very British compliment he'd received that day.

"I have no problem at all, sir. What do we need to know?"

He saw the surprise on the German's face on hearing his accent and recalled Buchanan's words,

'Bill boy, bullies can't take what they dish out."

Campion redirected Bill's question,

"Your witness, Captain Frazier."

Frazier explained that if an incorrect combination was used, it might trigger a destruction device in the Ultra machine case. He finished with.

"It would not take a lot to render the crown jewels valueless."

Bill asked.

"Major Campion, may I have the assistance of one of your men?"

The officer nodded. Bill found the Marines and spoke to a particular commando, explaining what was required. They returned to the captain's cabin, and Bill spoke to the German in Texan-accented English.

"Maybe you should listen up good and clear. I'm going to explain the situation. I am an American and on this ship unofficially." He took out his. 357 magnum side arm and held it at shoulder level.

"So it follows that anything I do never happened." Bill paused for a few seconds.

"Your position is slightly similar. Everyone thinks you were killed when the ship was sunk. Aboard this ship I do not exist." He paused, then finished the sentence in a cold voice.

" Neither do you?"

The prisoner's face betrayed he understood every word. Bill continued.

"If you do not tell us what we need to know in ten seconds, my comrade and I will take you on deck, where I will blow your left hand off at the wrist. Sixty seconds later, I will do same to your left kneecap."

The German's face drained of all blood as the Norwegian marine grabbed him by the collar and dragged him toward the door. The panicking prisoner shouted at Major Campion in German,

"You must help me; these men are insane. I am a prisoner of war."

Campion spoke to Captain Frazier.

"Don't know about you, old boy, but I'm rather thirsty. Fancy a cup of tea?" Captain Warne, who had been listening outside the cabin, walked in. The German shouted in English,

"I am a prisoner of the Royal Navy. You are the captain of this ship."

The Australian answered with venom,

"Don't invoke the Geneva convention here, you Nazi bastard. Hitler has given orders that all commandos are to be executed. I don't care if the Yank and the Norwegian gut you. Give us the combination."

The German screamed,

"Your crew will know what happened."

The Australian vented all his feelings.

"My boys have seen too many good men die because of you and your sort. Theywon't say a word - not now or twenty years from now."

The German, his head bowed, moved toward the case as Bill Cork aimed the Magnum at his left temple.

"If I get one hint that you are trying something on, I will kill you instantly. If you think I won't - I was at Dieppe."

The German slowly moved the tumblers, and the lock snapped open. Captain Frazier confirmed they had an Ultra Machine. Captain Warne signalled the flagship. 'Crown jewels confirmed'. Loftus signalled 'C.' His reply was instant.

'Secure crown jewels immediately. Proceed Shetland'

Snow Tiger steamed for the Shetlands, where the Royal Marines disembarked along with a US Army Engineer.

Bill Cork was thinking about the last week and towelling himself after a very welcome shower. He was satisfied about his part in the raid and becoming part of an elite band of men. As for the enemy killed, there were no regrets. Their deaths were an unavoidable part of the job.

Bill headed for the officers' mess and the real malt whiskey promised by Captain Frazier. Surprisingly the room was full of all ranks. Frazier approached

"Sorry, Captain, the whisky will have to wait. The colonel would like a word." They entered an office where Major Campion and another officer waited.

"Sir. May I introduce Captain William Cork of the US Army Engineers and a true commando if ever I saw one."

The colonel of 62 Royal Marine commando saluted and shook Bill's hand,

"My name is Weir – welcome to the Royal Marines captain."

Bill looked at all three men quizzically. Weir continued,

"Captain Cork, as you may have gathered, we in the Royal Marines regard ourselves as being an exclusive bunch, and we guard our traditions and insignia jealously. We do, occasionally, make exceptions. It is with great pleasure I now present you with the badge and insignia of the 62 Commando Royal Marines, Combined Operations."

Bill was given a small box along with a scroll of what he took to be parchment, which read Captain William Cork had earned the right to wear the insignia and badge of His Majesty's Royal Marine Commandos. A second scrip commended him for outstanding service during Operations with the Corps. It was signed, 'Mountbatten'. Bill saluted and said,

"Colonel, I am lost for words other than, 'the drinks are on me'."

In unison, all three marines said,

"Oh no, they are bloody well not."

The colonel continued,

"Tonight, our American Irish friend, the drinks are on 62 Commando."

During the night's festivities, Bill was most struck by the Marines' camaraderie - the mutual respect and loyalty to each other and the corps. Just before it all got rather hazy, Cork remembered thinking,

'Jesus! These bootnecks can drink.'

Next morning, Captain Frazier, who was remarkably fresh despite the night before, was driving Bill to take a flight to Swansea under orders to report to Travers immediately. Within hours they sat in the colonel's office, his tone congratulatory.

"Welcome back, and well done." He waited for comments on the raid. Cork remained silent. Travers moved on.

"We have to push ahead with the training for the invasion – we are going to be flat out from here on in. Are you ok with that, Captain Cork?"

Bill asked.

"When do we start, sir?" Travers voiced his approval.

"Good; we'll assess each unit's readiness for the invasion. Now tell me, what did you learn from your recent experiences?"

Bill answered, at first slowly.

"The British military is steeped in tradition; they pride themselves on the history of the units in which they serve. The US Armed Forces do not have that kind of history. What we do have are some of the fittest and best-equipped men in the world. What we must build upon is the tribal element like the British have." Travers butted in,

"What do you mean - 'tribal'?" Cork's voice was more emotional.

"Sir, in the British Armed Forces, it doesn't matter what nationality the men are; their overriding loyalty is to the regiment, warship or squadron. The Royal Marines I served with were loyal to the corps and each other, almost as brothers. We have to get our men to think the same. The unit is what they fight for, above all else. On the beaches, their only friends will be the men from their unit, and the fastest way off that beach is to fight as one man."

Bill realised he was almost shouting, and he looked at a smiling Travers.

"Captain Cork, you had better take care. You're becoming almost British, but you have learned what I did. The men must be convinced loyalty to each other is the most important thing - after that, anything is possible."

Travers then surprised Bill by telling him he had two weeks leave. Bill thanked the colonels.

"It's good of you, Sir. Being honest, I need some time to think things through." Bill left and Travers sat down and pondered, 'Well, I took a boy from Big Bend, Texas and turned him into a cool, professional soldier.' Travers was concerned - as any commanding officer - could a man kill? Colonel Weir's report made it clear Captain Bill Cork of the US Army Engineers 'did so without hesitation.' Travers was aware what an honour the Royal Marines had accorded Bill, but he hadn't mentioned it- maybe he just didn't want to brag.

At the officers' quarters was a large bundle of mail for Bill, which he sorted through, and stopped only when a soldier delivered an envelope. Having thanked the Private, Bill looked at the contents. A note from Colonel Travers and a train ticket for London in the morning, plus details of a double room in the Cumberland Hotel booked for two weeks. Then a sealed envelope. Inside a folded sheet of headed paper. Bill read that the undersigned authorised him to wear the insignia of the Royal Marines as part of his US uniform. The signatory was Omar Bradley, General, US Army. He settled down for the night and was on that first train in the morning.

London was incredibly busy; Bill spent the first day just walking around the city. Everywhere there were uniforms, accents and languages - all different but all with one aim - to get the war over and get home. After one drink in the Café Royale, he was approached by a British Army Officer with a large pink gin who without introduction, quietly acknowledged the unusual insignia and campaign colours on Bill's uniform.

"Looks like you have been rather busy old boy; this one's on me." He was invited to join them. Bill watched servicemen who were boisterous and determined to have a good time. He could tell those who had seen active service; they became quiet and introspective as the alcohol hit them. Glancing in the back bar mirror, Bill saw his reflection and suddenly realised that he felt much older than he looked. As another drink came, he decided enough was enough and slipped quietly into the late summer night.

The next morning, during breakfast, Bill started to work his way through the bundle of post. There were letters from his mother, father, brother and sister -also one from his grandfather. He silently vowed to reply to all of them that day. A Houston local newspaper, sent by his Auntie Catherine, came to the top of the pile. It was about twelve weeks old, and Catherine had ringed an article which was about the different types of food available in Britain despite rationing. Bill scanned the article but found little of interest until he saw the credit, which read, 'From our London correspondent, Amanda Bruce'.

Breakfast and vow forgotten; he contacted the US press bureau in London where all American press personnel were registered. The voice on the phone spoke with an accent which sounded definitely East Coast. The man flatly refused to give any information over the phone; private details of press personnel were given only on a personal basis. Within an hour, Captain Bill Cork was at the bureau desk asking about Miss Amanda Bruce. Standing off to one side was a senior officer of the Royal Navy who asked to see Bill's ID, then suggested they step into a small office for a moment where the captain spoke his face emotionless and hard.

"Captain Cork, may I ask why, immediately after being involved in a top-secret Operation, you wish to see an American journalist?"

Bill's jaw dropped but he answered,

"We were at college together; we have been more than friends - if you see what I mean."

Bill watched the captain's face soften almost imperceptibly as he spoke.

"Well, that solves that little riddle. Allow me to explain. My interest is solely in what the lady might ask you. I cannot impress upon you enough the need for absolute secrecy regarding your activities. The crown jewels are delivering product which is priceless."

Cork was defiant.

"You can trust Mandy - and me, for that matter."

The Royal Navy captain relaxed.

"Captain Cork, please understand our concerns - concerns which have now been addressed. You see, in Britain, we have always prided ourselves on having a free press; however, in these difficult times, we like to ensure it is not too free."

The atmosphere was convivial as the captain accompanied Bill into reception and nodded to the people seated.

"Captain, you will find all of the information with the officers at the desk. May I wish you and your young lady a very enjoyable leave and good luck?"

The information officer was an American woman of senior years who made it perfectly clear that she was very protective of her lady reporters. She looked at Bill, so young and already battle-hardened. She thought of her husband on active service somewhere in the Pacific. His eyes had the same fatigue about them - and he had been in the army all his life. Her voice was soft but firm.

"Captain Cork, you will find Miss Bruce at a press briefing at the Ministry of Food. She will be there until two o'clock but then has the afternoon off. I think she is owed some vacation."

Bill thanked the lady and left, wondering what he was going to say to Mandy. Behind him, in the press bureau, the senior lady said to her male counterpart,

"So that's what he looks like. Mandy was wondering if she would be able to find her Texan. Well, all I can say is that he's different to the man she saw leave the States. I hope she's able to deal with the change."

Her colleague replied,

"See those battle colours? He's been in the thick of it - and recently."

The Royal Navy officer had disappeared.

Mandy stood at the back of the hall, thinking, 'how the hell am I going to make this interesting,' while a stuffy civil servant droned on about nutritional units per head of population. Suddenly, she felt a presence a little too close behind her and was about to turn around and berate the person when she heard the words,

"We're a long way from the middle pasture, Mandy, but I know a nice park where we can go for a walk."

She turned and saw Bill Cork. Her immediate reaction was to hug him, but she stopped and looked him up and down and saw a tough, lithe, almost tensile man. Very fit - there was not a ripple of loose flesh on his face or neck, and skin almost weather-beaten. His eyes were glowing with delight, and yet she sensed he was very tired. Mandy compared him to the other civilian men in the room; he looked bullet hard and with an aura of quiet ruthlessness. All this took an instant; then, with her arms around his neck, she kissed him long and hard. The civil servant giving the briefing coughed awkwardly, and one wag asked,

"Do the rest of us get similar rations?"

The audience laughed, but for all Mandy and Bill cared, they could have done so all day. The early October sun greeted them - bright but without summer warmth. For the first hour, they just walked and talked about each other. The afternoon became the evening, and both realised they had been walking for hours, yet neither could remember where. A small restaurant seemed to appear from nowhere, Mandy said,

"Bill, I am starving; let's eat here."

They enjoyed the best that the war-weary menu could provide. There was no question they would be lovers again that night. The hotel concierge had become accustomed to seeing young couples come and go. Some happy, some sad, some desperate. The captain and his lovely companion were definitely in the happy grouping. He had seen so many young people leave his hotel never to return and silently and fervently wished these young Americans all the best they could have. As the hotel room door closed, they kissed, and both realised how lucky they were to find each other in the middle of the madness that had gripped the world. They lay on the bed, naked, kissing, then both, as if by telepathy, stopped. Without speaking, he reached for a rubber. There were no words necessary, and if there were, that would be for later. After what seemed hours of lovemaking, they lay in each other's arms, sated and blissfully happy. Bill asked,

"Ok, so please tell me how you got to London one more time because I still don't believe it."

Mandy sat up facing him, naked, with the confidence of a beautiful woman.

"As I've told you, I was in Washington for a conference of women journalists. Mrs Roosevelt decided, at the last minute, to attend. By chance, I sat next to her and told her how so many papers had turned me down for overseas postings because I was a woman."

She kissed him.

"She asked me about my education and background and if I had anyone close on active service. I told her you'd been posted overseas at short notice."

Bill returned her kiss, saying,

"Go on."

"Well, she agreed that it was tough, but such was war; then said she would see what she could do. Within two weeks, I was offered the job of London Correspondent with my paper in Houston and was on the next ship sailing for Britain. Jesus, Bill! The Atlantic's a big ocean when you know there are U-boats out there."

They lay back in each other's arms, and Bill whispered,

"I swear, only you could have got here against all the odds. God! I am so glad you did."

"Really! I can see you were planning ahead! Where did all these rubbers come from?"

He burst out laughing and then went into a story about how, as an officer, it was his responsibility to ensure that his men... but before he could say any more, Mandy reached for him, saying,

"That's enough of that nonsense - you're dealing with a friend of the First lady. Now make love to me again."

They explored London as lovers and people with an insatiable thirst for knowledge and history. The city did not let them down. Bill considered his father's view of the empire as he walked the streets of its capital. He questioned so much of what he had been told. He was particularly struck by the close proximity of the seat of the Church of England - Westminster Abbey and Westminster Cathedral - the home of the Catholic Church in England and posed a question.

"If Catholics were so oppressed in the British Empire, why are these churches so close together - and in the heart of the capital of that empire?"

They visited St. Paul's – standing defiant to all who would attempt to conquer Britain. The museums were open, many had wisely, in the opinion of the young visitors, moved their valuable and, in some cases, irreplaceable exhibits to safety. At night they discussed everything and anything that came into their heads then they made love until they fell asleep in each other's arms. As the fortnight came to an end, they realised that, never once had they discussed each other or where their relationship would go.

On the penultimate morning, Bill said,

"Mandy, I am going back in twenty-four hours. What do you want to do? Where do we go after these two weeks?"

She took his hand.

"Bill, I'd say that at home, we would never have felt as free as we have in the last two weeks. As a journalist, it is my job to ask questions, but I sensed that you did not want to speak of what has happened to you since leaving home." She moved closer.

"I have my career, and, at this moment in my life, it means as much to me as you do. The reality is that you go back to war tomorrow. I want to believe that you will survive the war – then maybe there will be a future for us. I think I love you, Bill - I just don't know how much. To do my job properly is very important to me, but I also want you in my life. All I can say, Bill, is that I will think of you every day and will not see anyone else until you safe are finished or......" She stopped speaking. Bill picked up her words,

"......or until I am reported KIA! I so desperately wanted to hear those words from you. Mandy, you're a journalist and a good one. I know there are so many questions you have since we met again, and I can only thank you for not asking any of them - but I will say this. I have seen some terrible things, and yet I have met some magnificent human beings who are fighting this evil called the Nazis. With them, I feel I am part of something much more important than me. I have killed, and I did so without hesitation or guilt. I want you to know this, Mandy, if anything happens to me, I do not want you to waste your life. There are men who will never know what I have known with you, and for that, if I die, I will be happy."

He paused - then laughed—

"Listen to the hero - all I've talked about is me. You're here in London, facing air raids every day. I don't know how you feel, but I believe you would not want me to be alone if anything were to happen to you."

Mandy smiled as tears ran down her face.

"God, Bill! How we have grown up. That's just how I feel too. You must find happiness - promise me that. We both must. we've earned happiness - hopefully, with each other, but if that is not possible, then with someone else. They were silent for a moment then Mandy asked,

"Bill, what do you think about before you go into action?"

"Now that's a question I *can* answer," he laughed, then became very serious.

"I put everything, other than my comrades and the mission, out of my mind. There is a mantra I repeat before action. It is, 'Stay together, stay alive.' So we'll do the same and do our best to come through this in one piece."

With that, Mandy stood up and said,

"We don't have too much time left, so let's make the best of it. I think we should have one more look at London in all its beauty and then spend our last night together in here, just being us."

Bill agreed. As they ran out of the hotel, the concierge smiled and said to his hall porter,

"Tommy, maybe with young people like that, we can win this war."

Travers knew what Cork had been through in the previous months. He decided to keep him out of active service for now. The man would need to be fit and rested for what was coming. Captain Cork was dispatched on a roving commission to inspect the American Forces arriving in Britain from campaigns in Sicily and North Africa under Generals George Patton and Omar Bradley. Bill was impressed. His report to Colonel Travers summarised the US troops as battle-hardened, serious men who knew what to expect when they 'hit the beaches.' Travers was also aware questions were raised by the security section of the team preparing for the invasion of Europe about Cork's involvement with a journalist. He decided to make enquiries in a very British way. Travers was a conduit between the American and British High Command. His links with Lord Mountbatten had opened doors on the British side, and he believed that all Americans were secretly covert royalists at heart. He raised his concerns for Bill with Mountbatten's staff and was assured the matter had been investigated to everyone's satisfaction.

The planning for the invasion of Europe was in the final stages. Travers was called to attend a planning meeting in Whitehall, where he met General Omar Bradley, the man with Operational command of all US troops going into Europe. Bradley was acutely aware of the potential for misunderstandings between allied forces – having spent the previous two years watching Patton and Montgomery behave like Prima Donnas and vowed such behaviour would not be repeated. He placed experienced men in strategic positions to monitor cooperation between American and British Forces. Bradley asked one such man to update him.

"Well, sir, we had problems in the early stages of the war, but we think we have ironed out most of the issues. If I may give you an example, the construction of the Mulberry Harbours was proving particularly difficult, mainly because of the intransigence of a senior officer of the Royal Engineers. I thought the man was just being difficult out of arrogance, but I learned that he had been given a project for which he had little training or experience. However, rather than have his regiment look bad, he took all the blame on himself by appearing to be completely against the project. Once he received the proper support and training, he became and is now a leader in Anglo-American cooperation. His name is Colonel Morley of the Royal Engineers or 'sappers', as they like to be called." Bradley said,

"Colonel Travers, what you have told me encourages me greatly. So, where do you go from here?"

"Well, sir, we will be on the Mulberry Harbour project and the ensuing laying of a pipeline until the invasion is over and we have captured a port on mainland Europe."

Bradley asked,

"We?"

"I have a captain assigned to me who has been with me since we left Texas." Bradley said as he opened one of the files on his desk,

"Yes, that would be Captain Cork - I have your file here as well. You have both been doing excellent work - well done. Please carry on, and if there are any problems, please let me know immediately."

Travers left the general's headquarters and headed for his base in Swansea. From now on, he and Bill Cork would be concentrating on the Mulberry Harbours and the provision of a pipeline which would bring fuel to the fighting men and machines in Europe once the invasion was successful.

— 24 —

Home Comings

In Portsmouth, Connor Cork's pulse raced. Mary had written saying it was time to come home. Finally, after a sleepless night, he wrote, telling her he couldn't wait to see them. The next letter told him they would be landing at Fishguard on the second of November - in four days' time!

He hadn't slept since the letter arrived, terrified for them during the crossing. Now he sat alone in the sitting room of his house, his family upstairs, safe in their beds. The morning they landed in Fishguard was calm but cold. Not that he felt anything. Emotions ranging from petrified terror to sheer delight left little room for physical senses. Mary had never looked calmer or lovelier as she hugged him, and then Rachel, now a young woman kissed him as only a daughter can kiss her father. He had looked for the luggage only to see a fine young man organise a taxi, then come to hug and greet him with a definite Kerry lilt in his voice. Mary, as ever alert, asked how he'd got past the security gate. When he replied that working on government contracts had its advantages, she teased him about the boy from West Cork and the IRB, now with British government security clearance.

He'd booked into a typical wartime hotel doing its best to be warm and welcoming, and discovered his first mistake. The double room booked for his children would not do for two young adults.

He laughed, remembering how embarrassed he'd been and how everyone else had been amused and understanding as the problem was solved. The first meal together flew by. His letters kept everyone informed of the 'day to day,' of his life. Pat's promotion was news, and his heart fell when seeing their disappointment as he told them there was no mention of leave. The family talked about where to live. He'd suggested they stay near his work in Portsmouth and added London was still not safe. Then Mary had asked about Peter English's plans. Connor replied he planned to move out. Rachel commented he might be lonely all on his own, and Mary began to support her daughter as she asked,

"Con, how big is your current house?"

He went into detail.

"There are six bedrooms, but only three are occupied. Why? What are you trying to say?"

"Well, Dad, it seems the house is big enough for all of us."

Christopher had answered his question with nods of approval from his sister and mother. Con smiled as he remembered the joy of reaching family decisions.

"Well, if that's what you want and if Peter is happy with it, that's what we'll do."

Now they were at home, and Peter English was beside himself with excitement at the thought of sharing the house. Mary had asked the housekeeper to stay on. The lady explained she preferred to live with her elderly mother but would work three days a week if 'the gentlemen' were agreeable. Mary soon had Con and Peter coming home to a house of warmth and fresh home cooking. She saw in Peter English a desperately sad, lonely man and encouraged her children to make him feel part of the family. Christopher went to the local grammar school and quickly lost his Kerry accent and made the first fifteen rugby team. Saturdays were never the same again for the side as Peter English galloped up and down the side-line, roaring encouragement for the school and especially Chris Cork.

At school, Rachel quickly settled. Most of her time was spent at home with her beloved father. Mary Cork found the Portsmouth people to be friendly and her husband a relatively well-known and respected man. He had changed from the efficient, confident foreman to the successful executive and business partner with ease. His partner was another matter; Mary hoped that her family could give Peter some peace and happiness. Deep down, she was convinced it would take very little to drive him over a precipice.

As Christmas approached, Mary and Con talked, catching up on time lost. Pat was the main topic as she explained how not seeing him made her more understanding of Peter English. When alone, Mary had repeatedly read Pat's letters, her way of knowing, as any mother does, that he was well, though nearly four years without seeing him had torn her heart apart. Pat being on active service, called to mind her fisherman father's words, 'The Sea will have her own.' On many a stormy night on the Atlantic Coast of Kerry, she had thought of her son in mid-ocean and had prayed from dusk till dawn. It was all she could do for him and to keep her sanity.

Con tried to ease her pain but knew if she saw Pat once, it would mean everything to her - and him too. All they could do was wait and pray for the Admiralty to give his ship leave.

As with the Mulberry Harbours, private industry was tasked to provide another crucial requirement for D-Day. Plans were made to develop a pipeline to cross one of the most inclement stretches of water known, the English Channel. The project was to be carried out by British and US military Engineers and Navies in conjunction with UK and US oil companies. Captain Bill Cork found himself part of the development team testing equipment off the South Coast of England. The proposed procedure was to weld pipes aboard ship and lay a continuous pipeline. Cork and his team, along with civilian engineers, were testing pipe joints immersed in sea conditions for fourteen consecutive days.

As if to taunt the men aboard the pipe-testing vessels in clear weather, they could see the coastline and imagine the warmth of the hotels and houses ashore. As the weeks passed, the pipeline test team became certain the joints were leak-proof in all sea conditions. A certainty Bill reported to Travers when ashore. He also wrote and received letters from all of his family. Every letter Bill wrote was under the shadow of the censor. As a result, Bill did not reveal his feelings, not even to his mother. Occasionally, Mandy came to mind. Then, at the beginning of March, all leave was cancelled, and Captain Bill Cork of the US Army Engineers prepared for his part in the invasion of Europe.

In Portsmouth, Peter English and Connor Cork had finalised the production of the pontoons, which were part of what would be forever known as the Mulberry harbours.

The head of British Intelligence 'C' chaired a meeting with Odin, Brigadier Davies, Commander Bakken, and Professor Williamson. The 'Prof' was presenting a report on certain factors that may have affected the Operations of a number of Special Operations units under the command of Simpson-Coyle. It had not made comfortable listening.

"Sir, I have carried out an analysis of the people involved in Operations mounted by Simpson-Coyle's sections in the occupied countries, and there is one common thread. All of the resistance groups which fell into enemy hands were drawn from what were established political parties before the war. These groups were not fascist by any means, but they would have been opposed to any form of socialism similar to that which is currently being practised by some of our allies. There is a definite pattern here, sir. It is safe to assume that these groups would have a significant input into the re-establishment of democratic governments in the occupied countries when the war is over."

'C' sat at his desk and said,

"What you are saying is that these resistance groups, which are primarily anti-communist, are being wiped out as part of a campaign which will allow the communists a head start in free elections when the war is over. Is that correct?" Williamson replied,

"Yes, sir, and we know that some of the communist resistance groups are receiving support from the Russians now that the Germans are retreating on the Eastern Front."

'C' spoke very slowly.

"Gentlemen, the only conclusion to be drawn is that we have a communist agent or sympathiser within British Intelligence, and we should begin looking in the section commanded by Simpson-Coyle." He looked straight at Davies.

"I want a reason why should we not suspect your sections brigadier?" Unfazed, Davies replied.

"If you have no objection, Sir, the professor will answer your question."

Williamson took his cue readily.

"Well, sir, we got started a little later than the other sections, and none of us have official intelligence backgrounds."

Menzies raised his hand,

"What you mean, professor is that we have a spy in the camp who is from the upper class or from Oxbridge and is a professional career civil servant."

Williamson confirmed.

"Yes, sir."

The meeting then concluded that the situation for Erebus was now critical. Menzies said,

"Order Erebus home, then keep him under wraps and away from Simpson-Coyle. Under no circumstances are you to brief anyone outside your own section on any Operations from this moment on. Thank you, gentlemen and goodnight to you all."

'C' returned to his office, knowing he had to find who was causing the loss of so many lives. Some agents were captured within twenty-four hours of landing in the occupied territories. He had no doubt of Simpson-Coyle's loyalty, but the war had taken its toll on all of them, and some men felt every death personally, perhaps too much so. He had considered replacing him at one stage, but his vast experience and knowledge was, at this moment, irreplaceable. However, the leak had to be plugged, and soon, as the invasion date was getting closer. C's problem was that he did not have the remotest idea of how to catch the person who was responsible. There was, though, one course of action open to him - he could transfer people from their current duties using the invasion as an excuse. This may help to disrupt the flow of information, but it would also make the traitor far harder to catch and only push the problem away in the short term. The security of the invasion was of paramount importance, so perhaps that was the best way forward. As he walked through the front door of his home in Bywater Street, his wife asked, as she had done every day for the last fifteen years since he had come ashore for good,

"How was your day, dear?"

He replied, as he always did,

Smoke and mirrors, my dear. Smoke and mirrors.

Connor Cork and Peter English were ordered to a meeting in London which was chaired by Captain Clinton of the US Navy, with Colonel Morley of the Royal Engineers. The Royal Navy was represented by a number of senior officers who were responsible for shipping the components across the channel. Along with the directors of E & C construction, all other civilian contractors involved in the construction of the harbours were present. A realistic time scale for the harbour to be sailed across the channel was agreed upon, and then volunteers were called for to accompany the sections at sea. Before Connor could do anything, Peter English had put his hand in the air and was immediately accepted. The officers present, led by Captain Clinton and Colonel Morley, all volunteered. The meeting then went into detail and stretched into the evening. Connor was struck how security was extremely tight, and there were no apologies for this. All papers used at the meeting were placed in sealed cases before any one left. Then, just before ten o'clock, Connor heard the words spoken by Captain Clinton that he would remember for the rest of his life.

"Gentlemen, we are now as prepared as we will ever be for our contribution to the invasion of Europe. Good luck to you all, my friends."

As the meeting broke up, Connor could not wait until the room had cleared to voice his anger and astonishment.

"Peter, what the hell are you doing? Why did you do volunteer?"

English spoke in a low, calm voice.

"Connor, I have spent the last three years of my life mourning my son and my marriage. Now I have finally come to terms with my problems and am ready to start a new life. I intend to see the harbours up and running, and then I will decide what I will do after the war. In the meantime, I have rented a house on the far side of Southsea where I will live until the war is over. I will be moving out over the next few weeks."

Connor calmed down as he replied.

"Ok, it's good that you are looking forward, but don't you think that men of our age would be better employed making kit for younger men to use against the Germans, rather than risking our lives in the front line?"

"Connor, we have been friends for some years now, and I value that friendship and all of the help and love your family had given me too, but it's time for me to stop using the Corks as a crutch."

Connor listened with a growing belief that Peter had turned the corner and felt pleased as well as admiring him for dealing with the problems that had plagued him for so long.

He said as much to his wife Mary later that evening as he told her Peter's news and when he would be moving out. Mary queried,

"Con, are you sure that that is what is making him do all of this? He knows he is welcome here for as long as he wants; there is no pressure on him to move out - he knows that."

Connor sensed his wife had her doubts and asked what was troubling her. She replied,

"Con, I don't know Peter English the way you do. All I am saying is that I think there may be more to this change in him than new found self-confidence. It seems such a drastic change in attitude, and it has happened so quickly. That's all I am saying."

"Well, all we can do is wish him well and let him do what he wants to do, Mary," her husband replied.

Mary said nothing, and within a week, Peter had moved out of the Cork household and had set up home in a small but very comfortable house. He hardly called after that, and, as the month of May came to a close, he was asked to join the other commissioning team in a secret base in the invasion assembly area. Connor did not know where he was and what he was doing, so there was little else to do but wish him well.

Connor's involvement with the Mulberry Harbours finished when security personnel visited him at the yard and gave him a week to collate and hand over all of the working drawings and paperwork relating to the Harbours. There was no mention of the invasion or Peter English, who Connor presumed was still with the Mulberry Harbours - wherever they were.

25

In Harm's Way

Pat was about to begin a letter to his mother when the captain's steward appeared.

"Captain's compliments, sir, and he would like to see you immediately."

To be summoned in this manner was odd – tradition being that the captain's steward was not involved in the daily routine of the ship. When he arrived, the door was ajar, and the steward was just leaving.

"Please go straight in, sir. The captain's waiting for you."

Buchan looked up from his desk and motioned him to sit.

"Number one, there are a couple of things I'd like to discuss with you. The shot you took today could have gone disastrously wrong for all of us, so well done from me on a personal level and from the crew as well. How are you feeling? " Pat answered,

"I am fine, thank you, sir. I have given some thought to what might have happened. A shipmate told me that if the marines had been captured by the Nazis, they would all have died. If the shot I took went wrong, only some of them might die, but the others would be free and the enemy vessel destroyed. I took the shot with a clear conscience."

Buchan smiled, saying,

"I presume you're not going to tell me this man's name?"

Pat explained,

"He asked me not to, sir."

Buchan said,

"Good, but if I need to know, I will ask, and you will tell me. He sounds like a very wise man. Agreed, number one?"

"Yes, sir."

Buchan continued,

"Right, let's move on. I have just received a signal from C in C, Western approaches requesting the names of any officers I consider fit for command. If you agree, I intend to forward your name."

Pat paused.

"May I have some time to think about that, sir?"

Buchan spoke firmly.

"We will have to be careful with this, Pat. I respect your reticence. But there are people in authority who know you are capable of command and might take your reluctance as something more than prudence on your part and draw less than pleasant conclusions. Bear that in mind, please."

Pat Cork chose his words.

"Sir, I have a number of issues which need resolving. I would rather stay aboard Snow Eagle for now."

"Pat, I'll mark this as 'waiting confirmation', which will give you a couple of weeks. Are you happy with that?"

Relief was clear in the answer.

"Perfectly, sir."

Buchan closed the file with the words,

"Right number one, set a course to close on the convoy, then we can get these tankers home in one piece."

Snow Eagle's first officer replied,

"Aye, aye, sir."

Snow Eagle was on station with the fast convoy made up of fuel tankers which were capable of maintaining up to fourteen knots. The relatively high speed of these vessels gave greater security as U-boats could not catch them in a protracted stern chase. The Admiralty prioritised the fast convoys as the supply of fuel was critical. Only certain classes of escorts could steam at between twelve and fourteen knots. An unspoken reality amongst the escort crews was the cumbersome auxiliary carriers, such as Polar Star, which could not keep up, were, in the final analysis, relatively expendable. On the bridge of Snow Eagle at sundown Captain Buchan said,

"Number one, you have the ship."

Pat confirmed,

"I have the ship, sir."

He had considered commanding a warship, but there were other factors to be considered - some had nothing to do with the Royal Navy - and then there was Erebus and the SOE. It was a wonderful clear night, the stars almost guiding the fleet home. Lars joined Pat on the bridge.

One of the junior officers said to himself.

"Two more days - we turn left at Ireland, then sharp right, and we're home."

Pat said in a low voice,

"It could be so much easier if we had the 'Treaty Ports'."

Lars heard him and asked,

"Pat, what are the Treaty Ports?"

He motioned the Norwegian to move to the rear of the bridge.

"Ok - a quick lesson in what is laughingly called 'Anglo-Irish relations.' Please feel free to ask questions a part of your tutorial - just don't expect any straight answers."

He went on to explain how, in 1938, the Irish State took possession of three harbours which had been when Britain ruled Ireland - Royal Navy bases, known as 'The Irish Station. Lars' interest increased,

"Where are these ports, Pat?"

"Now, that is one question I can answer directly."

They moved to the chart table.

"Spike Island on the South Coast, Berehaven on the West Coast and finally Lough Swilly on the Northern Coast. The use of these ports would make our lives a lot easier. It might also allow me to see my mother, so maybe I'm not the most objective person to talk to."

Larsen demanded,

"So why aren't we using them? Jesus! Pat - we could be in a safe harbour now."

Pat laughed.

"Now, I ask you to cast your mind back to my earlier comment about straight answers. Right here goes."

Lars listened, his facial expression changing from curious to bewildered as his shipmate tried to explain how, despite intense and detailed negotiations, no one on either side, British or Irish, had confirmed that, in time of war, the Treaty ports, as they are known, would be available to the British Armed Forces. Lars replied,

"But they know we are at war. The whole free world is at war - not just Britain. Everybody needs those ports."

Pat, to his surprise, found he was defending the Irish position.

"Agreed, but Ireland is officially neutral and, since the fall of France, well within the range of German bombers. It's another case of a complete cock-up between the British and Irish governments. Eamonn de Valera the Irish Prime Minister - and Churchill do not get on, so I gather. So, Lars, don't hold your breath while waiting to be alongside in any of the ports - or me seeing my mum!"

Just then, he noticed the radar officer looking concerned and enquired,

"Is there a problem, Flags?"

The officer answered,

"There is a large vessel losing the fleet, sir. I think it's the flagship."

Pat scanned the screen and confirmed that the vessel off-station was HMS Polar Star. For the previous twenty-four hours, the convoy had been steaming at thirteen knots. Snow Tiger, having made Shetland, was ordered to take the 'crown jewels' to Portsmouth. Lack of speed and shortage of one escort multiplied the risks to the slower flagship. After the commodore and the captain of Polar Star, Captain Crowley, Captain Buchan was the senior officer in the fleet. Pat ordered,

"Flags, wake the captain and ask him to come to the bridge."

Once on the bridge, Buchan was briefed by his first officer.

"Would you look at the radar, please, sir? I think we may have a problem with the flagship."

Buchan studied the screen.

"Are we still on radio silence, Flags?"

'Flags', otherwise known as Lieutenant Nigel Bellay, replied,

"Yes, sir - until we come under attack or hear from the flag to the contrary." Buchan moved next to Pat and almost whispered,

"The old man knows what's what. We cannot leave station without a very good reason."

Cork replied,

"We could do an extra sweep, sir, just to show we are aware of his problem."

"Good idea, number one, but the old man would see through it and probably beach both of us. His orders are explicit; the tankers are priority."

The night passed peacefully, and as the sun came up, the flagship was clearly visible astern of the convoy. Her aircraft took off, on course for Britain. Commodore Loftus had given the order in case of attack, the valuable aircraft would be safe and the convoy would now have air cover from land-based aircraft. The day passed without incident, and darkness descended. Spirits lifted on the bridge of Snow Eagle when Snow Tiger signalled she would make the convoy in three hours. Then an explosion was heard. The flagship, just visible astern, had lost another three thousand yards and run out of luck. A torpedo struck her amidships, and even as a second explosion was heard, a signal came from the flagship. Bellamy read it.

'All escorts maintain station. 'No stopping' order confirmed.' There was nothing anyone could do but hope that the stricken ship would sink in a way that would allow the lifeboats to be deployed. Another unspoken fear of all aircraft carrier crews was the height of the deck from sea level. If a ship listed more than five degrees, lifeboats were unusable.

Captain Buchan continuously signalled Polar Star, but without reply, then Snow Tiger signalled she was taking station with the convoy. Buchan acknowledged, and Snow Eagle made for the last known position of HMS Polar Star.

Aboard Snow Eagle, the first officer was angrily frustrated for two reasons. Firstly, the time it would take to make the flagship's position and secondly, the Treaty Ports. As a man of Irish descent, he felt angry but not ashamed. There were thousands of Irishmen from the 'South' fighting the Nazis, but still, the nagging question. How many lives could have been saved if the Allies had safe harbours in Ireland? He calmed down and concentrated on the flagship.

Snow Eagle steamed for Polar Star; Captain Buchan received signals from US Navy escorts from another fast convoy offering assistance. Buchan acknowledged and advised the US ships to exercise caution when closing on Polar Star because of the possibility of her aviation fuel tanks exploding. Another US destroyer reported contact with a U-boat and was attacking. The escorts closed on the carrier's coordinates, and for what seemed an eternity, there was nothing on the horizon. Suddenly the lookouts shouted almost as one,

"Smoke, dead ahead!"

The rescue ships steered for the pall of smoke and slowed as the situation became clearer. The carrier was listing to port but still deploying lifeboats. The ship was lost, fires were raging on her deck as the list was increasing. On the bridge, Buchan spoke.

"Number One, ready the ship's boats. Contact the American ships and suggest they do the same."

"Aye, aye, sir."

Now in the radio room, Pat watched as Lars attempted to make contact with the US Navy frigates and the stricken carrier. Chief Adams reported.

"Ships boats ready." Pat acknowledged and observed.

"Everything seems to be orderly - judging from the way the crew is evacuating the ship. Any idea how we can find out if the commodore and Captain Crowley are still in command?"

Lars, who was speaking into a radio mouthpiece, suddenly raised his hand for silence. A voice was heard over the cabin speaker.

"Commodore to Snow Eagle - do you read, over?"

Pat dashed to the bridge.

"Commodore on the radio, sir."

"Number one, you have the ship."

Buchan left the bridge, as Pat confirmed,

"I have the ship." Buchan soon returned,

"The carrier is sinking - Commodore Loftus has given the order to abandon ship. Captain Crowley was killed by the explosion from the torpedo strike; casualties are heavy. Most of the lifeboats are badly damaged. We will close on the flagship and launch the sea boats. Off you go, number one."

Pat was underway towards Polar Star. As the smoke cleared, he saw that nearly all of the internal decks were ablaze, the steel bulkheads beginning to glow red as the fire spread through the now exposed compartments. The fabric of the hull had been blown away by the torpedo strikes. Then they began to take survivors aboard. Soon the sea boat, now full with wounded men, made for Snow Eagle. Pat recalled the Chobry and Norway. The US Navy boats were motorised - rescuing survivors quickly. For nearly two hours, the sea boats continued to pluck survivors from the water. Then, as Pat's boat again came alongside Snow Eagle, Captain Buchan called him to the bridge.

"The commodore has decided to transfer his flag to us. Chief Petty Officer Adams will take command of the sea boat - I need you on board. I am going to be tied up with the Americans to find the best way to deal with the wounded and maintain a convoy escort. Number one, I need to know how many survivors have been rescued."

"Aye, aye, sir," Pat replied as he was handed a mug of steaming cocoa. As the ship's boat cast off, Polar Star was beginning to settle in the water. The fires that enveloped the hull were extinguished by sea water as she began to sink. Pat watched the sea boat make its way to the carrier, and Adams' signalled to the remaining men on the flight deck to abandon ship. The Commodore was clearly visible as the carrier began to slide into the ocean bow first- very slowly at first, then faster, accompanied by a rumbling which grew to be a huge rending sound of tearing metal and hissing water. Suddenly the stern came out of the water, the ship's back broke, and, in an instant, she was in two sections, both of which rose vertically, then sank into the ocean. Aboard Snow Eagle, all hands rushed to the side with binoculars and lifebelts. Pat steered towards the place where the carrier had been. The American sea boats, to their eternal credit, sped to the spot without care or concern for themselves but all to no avail. Polar Star was gone - and so was the Snow Eagle's sea boat along with Chief Adams and eight shipmates. Commodore Loftus, the man who had pioneered the principle of seaborne air escort for convoys, was lost too. Buchan came onto the bridge, his face white with shock.

"Good God, number one."

Pat couldn't reply. He tried to close his mind to the loss of shipmates who were now just more names to be added to the casualty list.

"I'll start the roll call, sir - we need to know who has survived." Buchan regained his composure,

"Very good, number one."

After several sweeps of the area, three ships made for Liverpool - the seriously wounded needed proper care. Pat reported to Captain Buchan that over two hundred men had been rescued from Polar Star, and above them, the skies filled with fighter escorts from the RAF and the US Air Force.

Liverpool was dark as the ambulances took the wounded to hospitals and the dead to the morgues. Buchan had given the order for the deceased to be brought home rather than buried at sea because of the nearness to land. The American destroyers had acted courageously throughout the action, and gratitude was expressed at all levels. Pat had spent some time on board both vessels, the USS Rockhampton and USS Riverfalls, identifying the dead and accounting for the living. Again, his mind went back to Norway.

Despite the deaths of many friends, he refused to be depressed, his responsibility was to see that the wounded were cared for and the dead buried. The next two weeks were taken up with funerals and writing letters to the families of the men of the ship's boat who perished. The affairs and personal belongings of Chief Adams were taken care of by Captain Buchan. The Admiralty convened a board of enquiry to examine the loss of the Polar Star, and the officers of Snow Eagle were ordered to give evidence. The enquiry was not a Court Martial, so the atmosphere was one of enquiry rather than apportionment of blame. The evidence given by Captain Buchan and Pat was straightforward, and the board recorded its findings quickly. Officially, HMS Polar Star was lost to enemy action.

"No recriminations or witch hunts – the old man would have been pleased with that. He would have said, 'At last, the Admiralty is thinking in this century not the last,'" Captain Buchan said as he and Pat sat in a hotel bar near the centre of Liverpool. Pat asked,

"Another one, sir?"

Buchan nodded his head, adding,

"Today, Pat, we get drunk for all of the men who never came home from the last voyage of HMS Polar Star."

As Pat approached the bar, he thought about those men. A total of three hundred and six had been lost from the crews of the carrier and Snow Eagle. Many more would have drowned if the American ships and Snow Eagle had not gone to the rescue. He had feared the board of enquiry might prosecute Captain Buchan for leaving the fast convoy without permission from the C in C, Western Approaches, but nothing had been mentioned. Maybe someone had thought it best, as Commodore Loftus would undoubtedly have done, to let the matter rest along with the bodies of over three hundred good men. As the day went on, the officers of Snow Eagle joined the officers from the US warships who had given evidence to the board of enquiry. They were also trying to dilute their memories with large amounts of alcohol. The atmosphere was quiet; Pat wondered where Captain Buchan had gone when one of the American officers approached him.

"Maybe you should go and see your skipper - he's not very well. He's in the heads."

Pat thanked the man and went into the toilets. Captain Buchan was hunched on a stool in the rest area of the large room, crying quietly. Pat went to his captain and, for the first time, other than when he shook his hand when they first met, touched him, putting his arm around his shoulder. Buchan whispered as he continued to cry,

"All those good men – the finest of men, the finest of men!"

Pat spoke very quietly.

"Do you remember when I shelled the U-boat? You asked who gave me the advice on the rights and wrongs of the shot."

Buchan nodded his head. Pat continued,

"It was Chief Adams."

"Number one, would you get me a taxi. I think I'll go back to the ship. What about you, my friend?"

Pat declined, and having seen his captain away; he continued to drink through the night. Even though he had the Americans with him, he felt completely alone. A feeling he was comfortable with.

Captain Buchan with Snow Eagle was assigned to command a flotilla of mine sweepers and landing craft. His orders were to train the crews in close-quarter manoeuvres when transporting troops from larger ships to landing beaches.

After the German destroyer attack, Erebus, Berg and Moen spent a week fishing in secluded inlets to let things quieten down. Moen was collected by a fellow driver at a small jetty in a fjord north of Hagnor.

Moen shook the hand of the man who was now an important person in his life and smiled as he watched the trawler put to sea. The drive to collect his lorry allowed him time to think. The big man had Laudrup's warning ringing in his ears,

"Trust no no-one! Do you hear me? No one at all - in fact, do not even speak to anyone unless you know their grandparents." He secretly hoped that come the New Year, maybe an invasion would come as well. His wife had never asked him about his absences, saying he always returned in a relaxed and almost contented mood. Through his many contacts in the transport industry, she and the children were well looked after. When the country had fallen, in her husband's opinion, so easily, it had broken his spirit. Now, all that had changed – she sensed that he had regained pride in himself and Norway.

They steered the trawler into the small harbour in Hagnor already beginning to freeze over and when Berg saw the ice said,

"Are we going to need the radio? I want to anchor the trawler on the ice edge, nearly mid-channel."

Laudrup replied,

"The radio's fine in the boat - so it's up to you. Mooring out here means we can put to sea whenever."

Berg nodded, and both began to unload the fish. They strolled through the village as often before. This time they were stopped by a police patrol made up of men they had not seen before. The usual questions were asked, and, as usual, Laudrup's language skills proved faultless. After the customary show of authority, both were told to move on. Later, Olaf told them a new police chief had been appointed who had not been seen in public. When he was consternation reigned, the man was Hilda's father. He was a senior member of the most despised organisation in Norway.

Laudrup sat at the breakfast table as Olaf, riven with fury and shame, told him about the man. Hilda came into the kitchen with tears in her eyes. He stayed silent, knowing she would talk to him when she was ready.

They sat in shocked silence until shouting came from the road outside the house. The men moved to the window, and with growing concern, saw the Police chief and his men set up a roadblock. They searched men and women, irrespective of age. Nearly every villager was stopped then, a group of teenagers were being searched, and one of the girls refused to submit. The boys joined in her protest, and a tense standoff developed – the policemen reaching for their pistols.

Suddenly Hilda approached her father and spoke to him. The man quickly recognised her, they hugged, and he ordered the teenagers be allowed to pass. Then both walked to the police station. Her actions had averted what could have been a massacre, and the whole village knew it. Later that day, she returned to the cottage and told them her father had asked her to move in as housekeeper. Olaf asked,

"What will you do?"

"I asked for a little time to think," Hilda replied. Laudrup remained silent. The girl was under enormous pressure. Could she be trusted? Despite being lovers, he had told her nothing about Moen - in fact, she had never seen him. Berg was another matter. How much did she know? This was a small village with few secrets amongst the fishermen. Somebody may have heard or seen something and mentioned it to Hilda.

As deep winter closed in, the disruption to village life became worse as the police chief ordered houses to be searched during the night. Christmas came, cold and cheerless, and the New Year seemed without hope. Hilda had stopped sleeping with Laudrup since her father had arrived, and he saw very little of her at all during January.

One night in early February, the village was woken by a general search. Olaf and Laudrup were made to stand with all the villagers in sub-zero weather. The fourth cottage away from Olaf's was the home of two brothers and their elderly mother. The boys were fishermen. Laudrup had an idea they were involved in the resistance, as one of them had tried to recruit him about a year earlier. The militia marched both men out of the house as the police chief went in and emerged with a number of firearms, after which the boy's mother was dragged out. Standing in the middle of the square, the chief of police ordered all of the villagers to be in the schoolyard at exactly eleven o'clock that morning.

Laudrup and Olaf returned to their cottage kitchen. Within minutes they were joined by Hilda, who had clearly been crying. Olaf spoke.

"Why are you so upset, my dear?"

"Those brothers are going to die because of me."

The men were silent, so she continued,

"I moved in with him because I had been helping the Sigmund brothers. I thought that if I was around him for any length of time, I might pick up some useful information for them. He was half drunk the other night, boasting to his buddies how he'd got the job of police chief by catching a family north of here called Hagen, who had a stolen German radio. He joined their group, and they trusted him enough to reveal all of the other people they knew involved in the resistance. He has the names of everyone in the resistance around here. Being made chief of police is his reward for betraying his countrymen." Her face was agonised as she pleaded.

"What are we going to do, Uncle Olaf?"

Her uncle stood up and took his niece in his arms in a gentle, protective way. He looked at Laudrup, and his eyes spoke volumes – pleading for help for his niece and his village. Olaf said to his niece,

"Try and stay calm and tell me, do you think that man knows about you and the Sigmund brothers?"

Hilda quickly regained her composure.

"I don't think so. He is stupid. He seems to think I admire him for what he has achieved. I just want to kill him."

Olaf continued.

"If you feel safe, go back and wait until the morning comes. I will know what to do by then."

Hilda left, and Olaf demanded.

"Now, whoever you are. What the hell do we do? Please help us. Please!"

Laudrup stood up and, as he left the kitchen, said,

"I need some time to think. Goodnight."

The truth was terrifyingly clear. The Sigmund brothers were dead, no matter what. In the room where he had slept safely for so long, Laudrup considered the options– Erebus, Laudrup, Lewis - he was all three. As Erebus, the men in the resistance cell and the officers in SOE were the limit of any responsibility on his part. Moen was not from the village and was safe. Berg had been made aware of the possibility of leaving until the end of the war, but this village was home to the Viking, and the choice must be his.

Killing the police chief would serve no purpose other than to provoke the most appalling reprisals by the Germans and militia. SOE agents were not in the business of making futile gestures or carrying out revenge attacks. He suspected that there were people in the village who mistakenly believed the Sigmund brothers could be rescued. Even the most passionate resistance fighters must know that any attempt could only end in disaster. On a personal level, Hilda was someone who was real in his life, and as such, she would not be forgotten easily. As for the local resistance - it was totally compromised. The conclusion was inevitable. He must leave Hagnor immediately. Erebus stood up in the small room and began to pack his kit bag. All that was left to do was to tell Berg and Hilda, if he could get to her, of his decision. Laudrup would no longer exist.

At eleven o'clock, the villagers gathered in the schoolyard, where the Sigmund brothers were denounced as traitors to the new Norway by the police chief. The people of Hagnor were told that the brothers would be executed the next day in the town square. Everybody was to be there. As the police chief made the proclamation, Laudrup approached Berg and said in a whisper,

"I need to talk."

Berg nodded his head.

"How about a quick fishing trip? I need some fresh air after this lot."

Aboard the trawler, Berg asked.

"Well, my friend. What do you have planned for us now? Are we going to blow up Berlin with Hitler in it?"

Erebus saw the gleam of battle in the big man's eyes.

I need to use the radio - now."

Erebus made contact with Maiden Aunt, advised him of the situation and asked for advice, which was forthcoming almost immediately. He had a choice; either come home straight away or relocate with Moen. The second option carried the proviso that Erebus would have to establish a new identity which, under current circumstances, was extremely dangerous. The situation was summarised with the words,

"Erebus, you have twenty-four hours. If you have any doubts as to your absolute safety - get out. That is an order. Over and out."

Shutting down the radio, Erebus turned.

"Berg, things are getting too dangerous here. The resistance is riddled with informers, which puts everyone at risk. So, my friend, it's time for me to move on. Maybe you should think about doing the same."

Berg was silent and eased back the throttle. The boat settled in the water.

"What are you saying that I should leave Hagnor - forever?"

Erebus shook his head as he spoke.

"No, my friend - just until the war is over. We have talked about this. Remember?"

"We talked about a lot of things, but I never thought it would happen. I hoped you were going to tell me how we were going to stick it to the Germans again. Or maybe kill this bastard of a police chief."

Erebus saw the hurt in his eyes.

"We've been over this, Berg; my superiors have sent me word to leave should the situation here become too dangerous. They have work for me elsewhere. Work you could be involved with. Come with me - the Germans have to be fought everywhere, not just in Hagnor"

"How long do I have to make up my mind?" Berg asked.

"Twenty-four hours at the most."

Berg was silent as he put the trawler about and headed for the mooring. Ashore, the men went to the square where the villagers had gathered in silent protest. The police chief had responded in force. Erebus found himself wishing that it was German troops that were in town as they, at least, were disciplined. These so-called policemen were little more than uniformed thugs and dangerously stupid. Berg spoke quietly,

"All of the villagers are using the silent protest. We do not speak to the police, and as for the police chief, he has been told that his family name will never be spoken in Hagnor again. He no longer exists as far as the people are concerned. When people address him, they call him by his official title - not even his first name will be used."

Erebus asked,

"How will that affect Hilda? She is his daughter."

"She's the one who came up with the whole thing. We all know he is her father in name only - Hilda is one of us."

The man paused, then added,

"I thought you were too, Laudrup."

Erebus felt Berg had a right to demand his help as they had been through so much together. Except, everybody from Maiden Aunt to Pat Cork kept telling him, sooner or later, his luck would run out, and his duty lay elsewhere. In reply, he asked,

"Have you decided what you are going to do? Are you going to come with me?" The Norwegian smiled.

"This is my home – I was born here, and I will die here, my friend."

Erebus went back to the cottage and collected the prepared kit bag. Walking out of the village, Berg's words came back to him, 'I was born here, and I will die here.'

Erebus had a growing suspicion that something was going to happen at the execution of the Sigmund brothers, which would involve the resistance and the villagers. He went to the hut where he had first found safety in Norway and waited until the morning came.

Lieutenant Commander Pat Cork stood on the bridge of Snow Eagle and watched the ships ahead of him make steady progress toward the beach dead ahead. The exercises in fleet coordination in open water off the South Coast of England were beginning to bear fruit. The minesweepers stationed at the flanks and ahead of the flotilla were keeping station well. The landing craft were maintaining reasonably straight lines with speed constant and direction good - but this was fair weather. When bad, the result had been chaotic. Constant speed and course had to be maintained in all conditions. The men in command of the landing craft must be able to turn them in their own length and take them alongside vessels of all shapes and sizes in all seas.

The captain was in his cabin, having been on duty all night. The ship had been escorting a large convoy of merchantmen carrying troops to another top-secret camp for final training for the invasion. Pat watched the men who were on duty with him. Since the ship had been commissioned, they had all been very lucky, taking into consideration the amount of action the ship had seen. The death of so many shipmates had taken some getting over, but the crew was young and soon began to recover. Whilst below decks, earlier in the week, Pat had heard one old hand advising a young sailor who had just joined the ship,

"Look after Snow Eagle, and she'll look after you." The old hand was a Cockney, all of twenty-one years of age.

On the personal front, Pat had refused a command position. He had discussed the decision with Buchan. The reasoning was simple - he was not a career navy man, taking a command would mean a new ship and an inexperienced crew which would need training from scratch. He'd been at sea and at war too long, and his patience was not what it used to be. The crew of Snow eagle knew him, and he knew them. Then Pat spoke off the record to his captain. There was another factor. His mother and family had returned from Ireland and were quite close by, at home, in Portsmouth. A command could mean a posting anywhere. Snow Eagle was to be involved in the invasion of Europe in some capacity, which could mean they might be getting leave. He finished by saying.

"Captain, I have not seen my mother in four years." Buchan accepted and endorsed the young man's decision.

The exercise was coming to an end. The minesweepers, all commanded by experienced sea-going officers, had performed well and were ordered to return to home port. Tomorrow, the fleet would practice again. Snow Eagle was back on escort duty that night as more supplies were brought ashore. Pat concluded, silently, that it might actually be some time before he got leave.

Pat and Lars stood on the bridge of Snow Eagle and watched the evening close in - Captain Buchan had been called to a briefing in London. The ship was at sea but moored about six hundred yards from shore. The crew could see the lights of Portsmouth as the sun went down until the blackout regulations came into force and the town became cloaked in darkness.

From the outskirts of Hagnor, Erebus watched the centre of the town that had been his home for the previous three winters with concern. The police had forced all of the villagers into the square to watch the execution. Standing next to her father, the police chief, was Hilda.

Scanning the crowd for Berg, Erebus noticed some strangers- which increased his concern as the brothers were dragged out of the police barracks. The crowd became restless, seeing both were bruised and bleeding. Erebus's concern became fear of a disaster as the police, who were ignorant louts, acted as if the villagers would obey without question, a very dangerous assumption.

As the two men were tied to posts, the crowd moved forward, and then Erebus saw Hilda take a pistol from under her coat and hold it to her father's head. The strangers he had seen earlier produced weapons and overpowered the policemen in the crowd - there were reinforcements in police trucks which had machine guns mounted in the rear of each. Erebus then saw a column of lorries, carrying German troops, approaching the village. Within a minute, there developed a standoff with the chief of police shouting garbled orders to his men and the crowd becoming increasingly agitated and loud.

Suddenly without any warning, Hilda shot her father in the head. He dropped dead instantly. The police who were being held prisoner by the strangers were also shot. The militia men in the lorries opened fire with machine guns killing men, women and children. The strangers in the crowd opened fire on the machine gunners, and as the German reinforcements arrived, the shooting died away.

The German troops entered the centre of the village and stood in silence as they surveyed the scene of carnage. Erebus saw Hilda lying prone next to her father's body. It was clear that she was dead, as were so many others. Erebus could see Berg's body - a machine pistol in his hand and the bodies of three policemen around him. The German troops were trying to help the wounded as best they could but were ordered to return to their trucks and quickly drove out of the area. Erebus took one final look at the body-strewn village square, then headed for the harbour, walked out onto the ice and boarded Berg's boat. With the engine running, he set a course for the mouth of the fjord and the Norwegian Sea. The radio was on the line, there was a full fuel tank and adequate provisions. Berg always kept the vessel ready for sea. Of course, he could also catch some fish, another skill taught him by Berg, along with sailing the trawler. Once in the open sea he began transmitting a single word. Erebus.

As another exercise finished, the officers aboard Snow Eagle were quietly pleased. The formations had stayed on station. The minesweepers and landing craft had maintained accurate courses and consistent speed. As the vessels anchored, Captain Buchan came onto the bridge and said,

"Well done everybody. Please signal the other ships of the flotilla to that effect, Flags."

Pat approached Buchan's side from the radio cabin and said,

"May I have a word, sir?"

Buchan signalled his assent.

"Erebus has been in touch. We have to go and get him, and I also have orders from Maiden Aunt. Under no circumstances are we to let Simpson-Coyle know that he is on board."

Buchan again nodded his head as he said to the crew on the bridge,

"Gentlemen, we are heading for our old hunting grounds up around the Jutland peninsula." Then ordered.

"Engine room, full ahead both."

Erebus headed out to sea, remembering all the brave and proud people he had met during his time in Norway and Hagnor in particular. Berg was dead– and Hilda was gone too - very much by their own hands. Norway had changed him in so many ways. There were many memories, but above all else was Hilda's vow that she would never love anyone so much that she could not leave them. Those words made a huge impression on him. So much so that he decided that's how he would live his life - however long it lasted. Never love anyone so much that you cannot walk away from them. Then, he thought of Moen and smiled; maybe even now he was somewhere making a deal or waiting for the call from Laudrup or 'whatever your name is,' to wreak havoc on 'the bastards'. The night was cold as the fishing boat began to rock with the swell of the open sea. Erebus set a south westerly course to take him to the Lower North Sea and tied off the wheel. He then sat in the wheelhouse and tried to remember the song he had heard Pat and Bill Cork sing. It wasn't long before his remarkable memory allowed him to fill the wheelhouse with the sounds of "On the Banks of My Own Lovely Lee." He thought of his mother and father, Uncle Peter and Ireland.

HMS Snow Eagle was making good speed to the rendezvous point but had at least thirty-six hours steaming on dangerous waters ahead of her. Buchan spoke to his first officer in the privacy of his cabin.

"Number one, we are going to have to hide our friend from all eyes when we get him ashore in Portsmouth; any ideas?"

Pat immediately thought of his time in Pompey and remembered the 'two master', which he and Penny had shared. He answered,

"I think I have a possible solution to our problem, sir."

Captain Buchan smiled,

"Number one, I think you have developed a liking for all this clandestine stuff - must be the Irishman in you."

With that, Pat left the captain's cabin and sent a signalled Penny's details to Bakken ashore, certain she would help. Erebus sent a homing signal every eight hours and eventually saw the shape of the warship close; a crew was assigned to sail the trawler astern of the warship. Within forty-eight hours, Erebus saw landfall and prepared for his debrief. Then a signal was received from Maiden Aunt - there was a change of plan. Immediately upon landing, Commander Bakken would take Erebus to a location known only to Odin, Maiden Aunt and Vali.

26

The Wild Geese

Maiden Aunt closed the file marked Erebus. A call to Odin followed, during which he proposed a plan which was greeted with silence and then agreement. Erebus would be debriefed in a location where no one, least of all Simpson-Coyle would expect him to be - a classic case of 'hide in plain sight.' Vali was briefed to inform Erebus when he collected him from Portsmouth Naval Base. Later, as they drove through the English countryside, Vali began,

"Listen, Charles; we are not staying in Portsmouth." Erebus answered with a question,

"What about security - aren't we top secret?"

"Yes, we are, Charles, but there are greater minds than ours looking out for us."

Bakken then explained the plan in full to his SOE comrade, finishing with,

"I can think of no better place to spend a few days in complete solitude and safety if your father is agreeable, and it will allow you to spend some time with your mother." Erebus didn't hesitate.

"Why not? I'll put it to my father. I can't see any objections. To be honest, I want to spend some time with them— It's been far too long - in more ways than one."

Vali remained silent, surprised by the emotion in his companion's voice.

Sir Geoffrey Lewis and his wife were sitting in their drawing room when the doorbell rang. Normally the butler would open the door, but Lady Felicity went instead as he was not as quick as he used to be. She chuckled to herself. The man should have retired years before, but he loved the house and the family- and they loved him in equal measure. Sir Geoffrey entered the hall as his wife opened the heavy door to see her son, Charles, with Commander Bakken by his side. As her tears flowed, all she could say was,

"Oh, Charlie! Welcome home, darling."

The Lewis family and their guest sat in the drawing room as dinner was served by the cook who, at short notice, had managed to produce a hot meal. Sir Geoffrey sat in silence and watched both young men eat and then, remembering his promise, went to the library and returned with the bottle of Hennessey Cognac. The men had finished eating as he poured a glass for all present. Even his wife, who was not a drinker by any standards, joined them in a toast to the delightful and seemingly brief visit of their son and his comrade-in-arms. Sir Geoffrey asked,

"Where are you staying tonight, boys?"

"Father, I need to talk to you about that. We haven't booked anywhere," Charles replied as Sir Geoffrey's face lit up with pleasure at the term his son had used.

"You will both stay here tonight," Lady Felicity almost shouted with excitement. She continued in an unstoppable voice,

"It will only take minutes to make up your rooms. There now, that's decided." As both men nodded their agreement, Bakken sensed that Erebus was beginning to relax in a way he had not seen before. As the evening went on, the conversation turned to the family history. Then Sir Charles spoke to his son about what had happened at Eton and events after he joined the army.

"My boy, I remember when you were a small child. You were as mischievous and naughty as any little boy should be, and we delighted in you, but after your Uncle Peter died, you changed - almost overnight. You became introverted, a virtual recluse from the world and particularly from your mother and me. Now, I see before me an officer whose service behind enemy lines has been described as 'exemplary' by his superiors. Of such a standard that you have been awarded the DSO. One can only come to the conclusion that you have undergone a form of 'Pauline' conversion, which has returned to us, not only our beloved son but a gallant officer and brave soldier of whom we are immensely proud. Charlie, please tell us what happened to take you away from us all those years ago and what has brought you back to us now?"

Bakken stood.

"Perhaps it would be better if I left you alone as a family." Charles answered him first.

"We have been through a lot together. I think you should know - you are part of the reason why I am now able to talk about it. Father, I am glad you asked. It is only recently I have been able to come to terms with many things in my life." Lady Felicity motioned Bakken to sit.

"Please stay, commander. I believe my son wants you to."

Sir Geoffrey prompted his son,

"Please speak in your own time, my boy."

Charles Lewis began,

"Do you remember all those wonderful summers I spent in Kilkenny with Uncle Peter?" His parents nodded, and Lady Felicity explained to Bakken about her late brother-in-law. Charles continued,

"I did not tell you all that happened when Uncle Peter was murdered. We used to play games during the summer holidays. Sometimes, Uncle Peter would drive his car down the drive, and I would hide in the trees and then run alongside as if racing the car. He would slow down so I could run faster than the car. It was a game– and I was just a child - he was so kind to me. The afternoon he was killed, I was hiding in the woods, waiting for him to make another drive. I saw his car and was just about to leave the trees when the car stopped, and four men walked toward Uncle Peter. They were not strangers; Uncle Peter seemed familiar with them. Then they pulled him out of the car. They were shouting at him and at each other. Then one screamed,

"You land-grabbing, English, Protestant bastard."

Another taller man yelled,

"Leave him alone. Jesus, the poor man is as weak as water."

Uncle Peter stood upright and said,

"I am as Irish as any of you."

Then there was a gunshot, and he fell to the ground. The men seemed to panic, yelling at each other and almost coming to blows. One of them - the smallest -shouted,

"He's a Black and Tan bastard and RIC informer," and shot Uncle Peter for a second time. The tallest man yelled,

"We'll have to finish him now, or we'll all hang." He shot Uncle Peter as he lay on the ground. They all got into the car and drove away. I ran to Uncle Peter, who whispered to me,

"Run to the house and hide until your daddy comes for you."

"He was in great pain, but there was nothing I could do. I was so scared I just went into a shell and stayed there because it was safer to do so. I never told anyone."

Lady Lewis moved to the sofa and sat beside her boy, taking his hand in hers. Charles continued,

"Father, you asked me about Eton and the prefects. When I went to school, I realised there were subjects that I could do well at, ones which would allow me to work alone. The teachers were nearly always struggling to keep me busy, particularly in languages, and studying is a solitary pastime - as are boxing and running. Both require skill and discipline, but you have no teammates. Boxing is just you against your opponent, and running is all about willpower – keeping going no matter how tired. I didn't trust anyone after Uncle Peter's death. When the prefects tried to punish me, the memories of how helpless Uncle Peter had been when he was killed came back to me. The way those men showed him no mercy. I was under threat but was not as helpless as Uncle Peter. The boxing trainer always said. 'Channel your emotions. Make every punch count. Never miss.' It was as if there was another part of me that just took over. Every punch was planned, and all landed on target. I was outnumbered, so I attacked their weakest points. They were not trained, and the odds were evened up quickly. I left two of them temporarily disabled and the other badly hurt. If they had left me alone nothing would have happened. Whitechapel was the same – those people attacked me, and I defended myself. Afterwards, it was much easier to go along with the psychiatrists and be left alone. Those people never asked questions about Uncle Peter - only about uncontrollable anger and fits of temper. Never about the fear of a little boy who had seen his uncle's brutal and pointless murder. Those men shot Uncle Peter because they wanted to, and there was nothing I could do about it."

Bakken thought he could see the smallest tear in Charles's eye as he continued.

"In Norway, the people needed help to stand up against the mindless brutality of the Germans - except this time they were not helpless because there was help at hand, from us."

He motioned towards Bakken and carried on.

"I could do something about it. Whilst in Norway, I made many good friends and helped them. Yes, men died in the course of what we did, but that is war, and we have to win this war. For the first time in years, I feel that I am part of something much larger and far more important than me and even Uncle Peter." Sir Geoffrey Lewis stood up,

"Major Charles Peter Lewis, DSO, Irish Guards." He paused, and his voice softened,

"Charlie. Give your mother a hug, then do the same for your dad."

Some minutes later Lady Lewis left the dining room to ready the bedrooms.

Charles stated.

"Father, I believe you met my commanding officer."

Sir Geoffrey replied,

"He did swear me to secrecy, my boy, but your belief is well founded in fact." His son continued,

"He has asked me to propose something to you. Commander Bakken will be leaving in the morning - I will not. Would it be convenient for you to see Brigadier Davies early tomorrow morning?"

The gatekeeper's house had been unoccupied since the outbreak of war except when the Home Guard were on night exercises. 'The Lodge' was a small cottage with four clean, dry rooms, located by a large gate which was permanently closed and surrounded by mature trees making it virtually invisible from the road. As agreed, Sir Geoffrey met with Brigadier Davies, who was accompanied by Professor Williamson and two SOE analysts. Davies got to the point.

"Sir Geoffrey, I need somewhere secure to debrief Major Lewis. We will provide all the necessary security, which will be invisible and silent, and we will only occupy this cottage."

Sir Geoffrey replied with quiet authority,

"Brigadier, the lodge is at your disposal. The major will be staying in his room at home. The other gentlemen are welcome to rooms as well. If I might suggest, we make this as informal as possible. Just a group of servicemen on leave seems the most sensible way forward. Don't you agree?"

Davies spoke.

"That is a very practical suggestion, if I may say so."

Sir Geoffrey smiled,

"I take it no one else in your command knows of this arrangement."

Davies lightened the mood further.

"Sir Geoffrey, my department is accustomed to bending regulations. What we are doing here has thrown the rule book out of the window."

The debrief process had been extensive, but very little repetition had been required - his memory being what it was. The debriefing officers were delighted with the information supplied. Professor Williamson had sat in on most of the sessions, learning an enormous amount from this quite extraordinary young man whom he found utterly charming.

'C' returned to the office, and his signals officer handed him a recently decoded signal marked, 'Action immediately'. The top-secret communiqué bore the coded reference of the office of the Chairman of the Joint Chiefs of Staff of the Armed Forces of the United States of America.

Menzies sat and read. General George Marshal raised a number of issues. Top of the list was Southern Ireland. 'C' was aware that Winston Churchill and President Roosevelt had discussed the ongoing anomaly described as the 'benevolent neutrality' of the Irish Free State and the potentially disastrous security situation. Marshall wanted to know if the enemy embassies located in Dublin were in radio contact with their respective intelligence organisations. Menzies presumed that the prospect of thousands of Americans dying on D-Day on a beach in France was uppermost in everyone's minds. The raid on Dieppe and the casualty forecasts for D-Day had terrified a number of senior US generals and an even larger number of American politicians on Capitol Hill.

Marshall ordered, at the request of Generals Eisenhower, Bradley and Montgomery, that an accurate assessment of the security situation in the Irish State be made. If it was found to be unfavourable to the allies, corrective action was to be taken immediately. Menzies sent for Odin, who, having read the signal, summoned Maiden Aunt. Davies read the communique and indicated he understood the request and waited, his heart pounding. Finally, 'C' spoke.

"You will put together a team immediately to resolve this problem. The operatives will need to be highly specialised and possess intimate knowledge of the theatre of Operations."

Odin took up the dialogue.

"It is obvious, for past and potential security leaks, Simpson-Coyle cannot be involved. As for Chief Superintendent Peters, that man's attitude to the Irish, and Catholics in particular, precludes him totally."

Davies spoke to the spymasters.

"I have just finished reading the Erebus debriefs, and the Lewis family may be the answer; they have local knowledge which is the key. I need a little time, maybe forty-eight hours at the most."

Menzies nodded, saying,

"Forty-eight hours is all you can have. Sorry, but that's the way it is."

Maiden Aunt began to see possibilities. The team would need to blend into the landscape and be experienced in covert Operations. If none of the target's theatre of Operations, local civil and military forces, were hurt, they just might get away with it. Certain rules would have to be ignored, but this was the SOE.

A standing order to all commanders was that members of the same family could not see active service in one theatre of Operations. Maiden Aunt decided to go to the top and explained to Odin who was involved and why they were the best equipped to carry out the mission. Odin listened, then demanded.

"Prove it?" Davies did as ordered.

"Sir Geoffrey Lewis has an impressive service record. Major Lewis's is beyond reproach – with the exception of the occasional shooting of British Army personnel. These men are Irish and know the territory intimately." Odin replied.

"You have my totally deniable 'permission granted.'" Both men knew in their world, the best policy regarding disobeying orders and breaking laws was to worry about the consequences if and when you were caught. Before he could leave Odin's office, an officer appeared and said.

"C would like to see you, gentlemen." The briefing was short.

"Give the Lewis's whatever is needed to get this done. I'll deal with any political problems."

Colonel Sir Geoffrey Lewis was told by his butler that Brigadier Davies was waiting in the drawing room. Twenty minutes later, Sir Geoffrey was in the Lodge House with his son, Commander Bakken and two men he did not know. Davies suggested,

"If I may, I'll make the introductions, sir."

He worked his way around the room.

"Colonel Lewis, Major Lewis, Commander Bakken of the Royal Norwegian Navy and Professor Williamson, gentlemen, Admiral Spenser."

Odin had been briefed by Maiden Aunt in the car, who was adamant that if the right men were given this mission, they would find a way to complete it. Now those men were read an abridged version of General Marshall's signal. Odin continued.

"Gentlemen, the signal you have just heard explains why we are here. It is imperative that you come up with a plan which will give us the information we require - and quickly. I would now like to address Colonel and Major Lewis directly."

He turned to face both men who came to attention.

"At ease, please, gentlemen. I am speaking to you as Irishmen to highlight the following. The Operation for which you have volunteered is technically not behind enemy lines but could, under certain circumstances for you both, be regarded as hostile, neutral territory."

Colonel Lewis spoke.

"Sir, with regard to the location of the mission, as you correctly said, my son and I are not going behind enemy lines. With due respect, neither are we going to be operating in a theatre of hostile neutrality."

Spenser looked perplexed.

Please explain, colonel - where are you going?"

The Irish aristocrat replied,

"Admiral, we are going home."

Odin allowed himself the slightest smile and then spoke.

"Gentlemen, I believe we have the Operation up and running. Colonel, I will have your commission reactivated. You will retain your substantive rank and seniority. The members of your team, I will leave to Brigadier Davies to select. You will report to the Brigadier codename Maiden Aunt. Gentlemen, I leave the planning to you. The use of lethal force is authorised. Colonel, may I ask you to suggest a code name for the Operation."

Sir Geoffrey replied with a twinkle in his eye.

"I believe Operation Prodigal would be appropriate."

Colonel Sir Geoffrey Lewis was placed in command of 'Operation Prodigal 'and was immediately given the Operation's terms of reference by Professor Williamson.

"You are ordered to provide an accurate appraisal of the intelligence communication capabilities of the enemy in the South of Ireland. Then, to produce a plan to insert a number of men into Dublin and stop that communication. If necessary, by destroying the German and Japanese embassies in the Irish capital city."

27

Nothing Personal

Colonel Lewis decided the only way to ascertain the communication ability of the enemy embassies and agents working for them was to carry out an appraisal in his home country. The Lewis family had owned a large farm in Kilkenny for three hundred years, which, after Peter Lewis' murder, was rented by a local farmer. After the funeral, a sympathetic Kilkenny police force candidly told Geoffrey they had no clues as to who had killed his brother. Then Pearse Brogan introduced himself and, having expressed his sincere sympathies, asked after the health of the boy, 'Charles'. Even now, years later, Lewis remembered the great sadness in his face - something he could identify with. Though strangers, the men began a correspondence which, as the years passed, covered many topics. Brogan began by writing about the mysterious death of his younger brother during the War of Independence. Lewis had lost his brother, so they had great tragedy in common. Lewis asked if there was any progress in the investigation as to the identity of his brother's murderers. Brogan replied there was no political will to investigate the crime or prosecute anyone. Over the years, every letter from Brogan asked after the little boy. The men would never be friends, but there was mutual respect and, perhaps, a little affection from one Irishman to another.

Brogan was not a native of Kilkenny and had lived in Dublin since the end of the Civil War. His most recent letter explained how he was now active in the defence forces in the Irish State. Lewis felt he could ask Brogan for an up-to-date briefing on the security and political situation in the country, which both men called home.

Lewis spoke to Maiden Aunt with authority.

"Sir, I believe we must establish the Irish Government's knowledge of enemy agents and the respective embassies' ability to transmit intelligence."

Maiden Aunt had expected a full Operational plan, but now he listened with growing interest at this new view of the problem.

"Please continue, colonel."

"Sir, my research leads me to believe that the Irish Defence Forces are under orders from the government to maintain neutrality by suppressing any faction that endangers it. I believe we can use this to our advantage. The IRA has made its position clear since the founding of the Free State; it does not recognise any government in Ireland, North or South. Should we insert a team of commandos, the Irish security forces will be taken up by any threat to the status quo rather than with our men?"

Maiden Aunt cut across Lewis.

"What type of men will you want, colonel? We must assemble a team as soon as possible."

Lewis replied,

"Well, sir, the only stipulation is they are Irish. As for their qualifications and training - I think I can leave that to you. Then there is the appraisal."

Maiden Aunt nodded his approval, then spoke.

"Tell me, colonel, I sense you have a different way of dealing with this part of the problem."

Lewis intended to convince Maiden Aunt that the appraisal could be completed by a person with local knowledge and part of the Irish Government. He would return to his family home and meet a long-term acquaintance. A trusted member of the defence forces in the South – who would provide an accurate assessment of the intelligence capability of the enemy embassies. Sir Geoffrey then pointed out,

"Sir, I believe the contact will want some intelligence beneficial to him."

Maiden Aunt made an assumption.

"I take it you have someone and something in mind?" Lewis answered,

"I have, sir. The man is a long-term contact and, I believe, totally trustworthy." Maiden Aunt asked,

"What, in your opinion, will this contact want?"

The Irishman spoke slowly.

"Before I answer, please bear in mind that this person's sole concern is the neutrality of the Irish State. This is what he will want."

Lewis handed Maiden Aunt a sheet of paper. The reply was positive.

"This will have to come from the top, but, as of now, proceed with your trip to Ireland - sorry - home. I will have an answer for you within twenty-four hours. Remember, colonel, we have only three weeks".

Pearse Brogan, as officer commanding the Munster Brigade of the Irish Defence Forces, was inspecting a platoon of men. He had been appointed by de Valera as an old and trusted comrade from the War of Independence and the terrible Civil War. The Brogan family had paid a high price for their involvement in both. Patrick Brogan had died in an ambush of British Auxiliaries under circumstances which were still unclear to his grieving elder brother. After the Treaty in 1922, Brogan had sided with the anti-treaty faction and led the war in Munster until the death of Michael Collins. That was, for him, the breaking point. He surrendered to the Free State Forces and was, for some time, under sentence of death. Then, during a period of huge upheaval, he was released. He moved to Dublin, where he began to rebuild his life.

Living on the outskirts of Dublin through the twenties and thirties, Brogan was not involved in politics. He was asked to take up an apolitical position as chairman of a regional committee that assessed claims for pensions of survivors of the War of Independence and the Civil War. There were many acts of undoubted heroism carried out by men who were granted their due. Other claims, when closely investigated, revealed many sordid actions by men claiming to be patriots. Brogan saw avarice, hatred or just plain prejudice as the real motivation. As chairman, he was ruthless in his examination, dissection and refusal of these scurrilous claims.

In 1939 he was summoned by the Taoiseach - the Prime Minister of Southern Ireland - and asked to take command of the newly formed Irish Defence Forces in Munster. Although a reluctant warrior, he accepted the command and trained a large number of men to defend the country. Brogan had compiled a substantial intelligence file on all those who used the troubled times in the world to advance their own agendas in Southern Ireland. Pearse Brogan's orders were to maintain the neutrality of the country no matter what. To enable him to carry out the orders, he was appointed to the rank of General of the Irish Defence Forces.

Sir Geoffrey Lewis explained to his wife that he had been ordered to organise a number of top-secret Operations which would be classified as covert, at best, and illegal at worst. Lady Lewis, even after years of training in self-control, felt herself shaking. Her only son would soon return to active service, and God alone knew where. Now her husband was to be pitched into the battle for freedom. She could not contain herself as she exclaimed,

"Geoffrey, please tell me as much as you dare. I could not bear to lose both of you. It would kill me."

Her husband reached for her as he suddenly realised how unfeeling he had been - how insensitive.

"Darling, I will not be in any real danger unless things go disastrously wrong. So please do not worry. Now, how would you like a trip to see the house in Kilkenny and visit Peter's grave?"

Having locked away the very brief notes on the Operation, the brigadier picked up a phone. Sergeant Major Reilly and Sergeant Mullen were asked to report to his office. Discipline was slightly more relaxed in the SOE than in the regular forces, as life expectancy was considerably shorter. The men sat as their CO moved from behind the desk and pulled up an armchair next to them.

"Gentlemen, I have received an order from the highest authority to carry out a mission in neutral territory. This mission is necessary to guarantee the security of an Operation which will, if successful, begin the end of the war. I have asked you here to explain as much as I am allowed before requesting you both to consider taking part in this mission."

There was a pause as Reilly and Mullen shifted in their chairs. Maiden Aunt continued,

"There are, in a certain neutral country, a number of installations which are at the disposal of enemy forces. These installations house equipment which is potentially lethal and so must be rendered unusable."

Mullen broke his silence.

"May I speak, sir?"

Maiden Aunt, although surprised, nodded.

"Sir, are you talking about the radios in the German and Japanese embassies in Dublin?"

Had the situation not been so serious, Maiden Aunt would have laughed. He had chosen well. Immediately both men volunteered. Brigadier Davies named their comrades on the Operation. Mullen turned to look at Maiden Aunt as he reached the office door.

"Yes, sergeant. You have a question?"

The soldier closed the door.

"Yes, sir. If I may, what is the code name of this all-Irish Operation?"

Davies smiled.

"What else could it be called but 'Operation Prodigal?'"

Pearse Brogan leafed through the post as he sat in his house, which seemed to reflect his life. He and his wife, a good woman, were both born in West Cork. They had two daughters, and, as his business was successful, his family lived a reasonably comfortable life in a Dublin suburb. Then a letter caught his eye. The handwriting he recognised - but the stamp was Irish.

Brogan approached the agreed meeting point with a little trepidation and anticipation. He saw Sir Geoffrey Lewis and his wife as they left the small graveyard where Peter Lewis was buried. Brogan's mind went back to the murder of Peter Lewis and how he had arrived at the scene as a former soldier. The Free State Police were still trying to organise themselves into an effective body; their information was unreliable. He had taken it upon himself to speak to Geoffrey Lewis to convey the sense of outrage and shock in the local community at the death of Peter Lewis. Brogan was reasonably sure of the names of the murderers but had no conclusive proof and was certain there was no justification for the despicable murder.

Now, some years later, he approached this Knight of the Realm whom he had come to like and respect. The men shook hands then Lady Lewis greeted Brogan, a big man with a fine, strong head of hair and a face that, she would remark to her husband later, had the history of Ireland carved on it. Rugged and careworn, and yet would occasionally light up with a glorious smile – a smile which came from the eyes which otherwise revealed nothing of what was in the heart of this tough Cork man.

She made a ridiculous excuse about needing something in Kilkenny City and left. They had much to discuss, and deep in her heart, she did not want to know anything. Her husband would meet her at the hotel later. The two men walked in the countryside they both called home.

Brogan began,

"Well, Geoffrey, what can I do for you?"

Lewis had given much thought as to the answer to this question and was still not quite certain how to begin.

"Pearse, I need to know if certain embassies in this country are a threat to the allied forces in the European theatre of Operations."

Brogan was silent, caused by a mixture of shock and disbelief. He hoped that Lewis had no interest in unsettling the fragile peace in Ireland. His contacts within the allied armed forces told him that there was a huge Operation in the final stages of preparation. He decided to put firm ground beneath his position.

"Colonel Sir Geoffrey Lewis, do the allies plan to invade this country and take control of the Treaty Ports by force?"

Lewis's face could not conceal his surprise at the frankness but sensed there was a good reason for the question.

"General Brogan, under no circumstances whatsoever do the allies intend to invade the Free State. I have that on the highest authority. You have my word." He then handed Brogan a letter which confirmed in detail what he had just said. It was signed, 'Eisenhower'. General Brogan visibly relaxed as he returned the sheet of paper.

"Well, Geoffrey, what exactly do you want to know?"

The conversation went into detail about the possibility of certain establishments being used to transmit information which, if accurate, could alter the course of the war. Brogan and Lewis fenced with each other, neither willing to state the names of the establishments or the Operation, a closely guarded secret. Finally, Lewis decided to go for broke.

"Pearse, I need a guarantee from you that I can take back to my command that no information will leave the German or Japanese embassies in Dublin." Brogan didn't feel at all victorious in winning the joust, in fact, he was actually scared at how explicit Lewis had been.

"Now look, I cannot control the transmissions from those diplomatic establishments. What I can do is tell you that no person from this country will attempt to pass on any information or assist any foreign nationals' attempts to do so."

Geoffrey Lewis relaxed a little but sensed that his companion had something else to say. He prompted,

"I don't think you have quite finished, Pearse".

Brogan remained silent for a time, then chose every word carefully.

"Sir Geoffrey, I live in a troubled land where no one who fought in the struggle for Independence and then the Civil War is fully certain that those wars are over. There are people in this government who will stop at nothing to vent their anger at the British and Churchill in particular and will use any means to wage their personal wars. We have a security cordon around the embassies, but I cannot control access by members of the public under the protection of influential people in the Irish Government." He inhaled, then continued.

"Let me explain, in 1943, due to pressure from the US Ambassador, Dev ordered us to remove the radio from the German Legation - but that was just one. There may well be others. We have a number of German nationals who work in different departments of the Civil Service. Dev brought them here after the British left. Some of these people are card-carrying members of the Nazi party. I cannot guarantee to control these people. There are also a number of agents based in the North who may still be active within the Abwehr. We have tabs on most of them, but there is still the odd one or two undercover. Of course, let us not forget the IRA - it still causes far more problems than it offers solutions."

Lewis stood for a moment and then began to clarify the situation.

"Please stop me if I am wrong, Pearse. What you are saying is that there is a possibility that a number of individuals may give the enemy assistance, and there is nothing you can do about it due to elements within the government?"

Brogan replied,

"Geoffrey, my orders are to maintain neutrality at all costs. Should I become aware that certain individuals or groups are trying to disturb the status quo, I will take action - if I have the necessary evidence, of course. Where that evidence comes from does not concern me as long as I have it to present to my government."

Lewis was taken up in the momentum.

"May I make the following supposition? What if an organisation had the resources in place to intercept individuals as they attempted to pass on information which would compromise the neutrality of the State? Then if the same individuals, with the relevant evidence, fell into the hands of the appropriate Irish state authority - the problem facing us both could be resolved?"

Brogan continued the theme.

"Well, as we are using suppositions. If someone was aware there was a resource for the interception and collection of evidence to enable the arrest of the miscreants by the proper authorities; it may be possible to provide their travel plans."

Lewis then asked the question, which would have a huge bearing on the entire issue.

"What if the resource was external to the Irish State and had to employ lethal force to gather the evidence and deliver the suspects to the proper authorities." Brogan stood in silence for a while, then spoke very slowly and clearly.

"The suggestion of the use of lethal force in the Irish State puts the entire matter on a different footing. Any persons employing such force would face the full rigours of the law once apprehended. There could be no exceptions. For all those concerned, it would be better if the miscreants were presented to the proper authorities alive."

The men parted, having confirmed communication systems and that the meeting had never taken place.

Colonel Lewis returned to the UK with his wife, who had enjoyed her few days in Kilkenny, knowing her husband was now again a man with a purpose.

Maiden Aunt and Professor Williamson listened as Lewis gave his appraisal. "Southern Ireland is in a state of flux with two large political parties vying for government. At the present time, the party led by Eamon de Valera is in power and is trying to bring order to the country. The IRA is causing problems and consistently resorts to violence both on the island of Ireland and in the UK. Realistically, if there was a threat to the security of the D-Day landings, it would come from people assisted by the IRA. The authorities in Ireland have made the maintenance of neutrality their priority and will act against any group attempting to disrupt that position."

Lewis then named his contact in Ireland with a synopsis of his connection with him. He finished this part of the briefing by confirming his confidence in General Pearse Brogan. Williamson remained silent as Maiden Aunt put a question to Lewis.

"How many men will you need to secure the embassies if there is an attempt to pass information to both at once?"

Williamson cut in.

"Excuse me, Sir Geoffrey, I think I can help to answer that one. The sole interest of the Japanese is war in the Pacific. They have a minimal intelligence presence in Europe. The German embassy will, in my opinion, be the place where contact will be attempted. We have the names of a number of Irishmen who have visited Germany since 1937, and I believe these are the potential contacts with the enemy that we should concentrate on. I see the situation as follows. One, General Brogan has given us the go-ahead to apprehend any elements which are likely to disturb the neutrality of Ireland. Two, we are not, under any circumstances, to use lethal force. Three, we may be being used to clean up a rather untidy and very politically sensitive problem that the authorities in Ireland have."

Colonel Lewis replied.

"Professor, my sole concern is to ensure that no information gets to anyone in the German embassy. Outside this, I see no involvement for the Operation Prodigal team. Once the Irish authorities have the miscreants apprehended and the evidence secured, we will get the hell out of there. Whoever they are and what happens to them is not our concern."

Williamson persisted.

"Colonel, I am concerned that we may be used to settle a personal matter."

Lewis replied with a little sadness in his voice.

"Professor, everything in Irish politics is personal."

Maiden Aunt confirmed that Operation Prodigal would be carried out by Colonel Lewis in command, Sergeant Major Reilly, Sergeant Mullen and Erebus, who was to shadow the Operation at a distance and assist only in a covert manner when needed. Now all they needed was the signal from General Pearse Brogan to go.

Pearse Brogan was driving to Bandon in West Cork, where he received the message that a certain former comrade was looking for transport to Dublin during the last week of May 1944. This man had fought gallantly in the War of Independence. Since then, he had become a dangerous loose cannon who saw the British as the sole enemy and was prepared to do anything to damage their war effort. The man had support in certain parts of the country and was relatively easy to follow, as he insisted on everyone knowing where he was in Ireland. Brogan had established a system of watchers who made weekly reports to the regional offices of the Irish Defence Forces. If a suspect was regarded as very active, then the surveillance was increased as resources would allow. Nearly all of the national bus company drivers were working for the IDF, as were the train drivers and ticket collectors on the national railway system, ensuring an efficient watch on suspects who were travelling. The problems arose when private transport was used by persons who were regarded by Brogan's intelligence section as 'dangerous to the stability of the Irish State.' Such people were motivated by many things, but in the case of the man now under observation, General Brogan knew exactly what drove him.

His name was Patrick George Joyce - a native of County Kerry and a fanatical Anglophobe. At the age of eighteen, Joyce had travelled to England and joined the British Army where, as an intelligent, literate man who revelled in the training and the disciplined life, flourished. He served in various parts of the Empire, gaining promotion to the rank of sergeant with specialist training in explosives and demolition. In 1918, at the end of the Great War, Joyce was demobbed and returned to Ireland with a gratuity and the thanks of the Imperial General Staff. He quickly joined the Irish Republican Brotherhood. He fought in the Munster region, reached the rank of Commandant and lived the life of an outlaw hunted by the British. Joyce organised an ambush of British Auxiliaries which resulted in the death of a substantial number and was regarded, by some, as the turning point in the Irish War of Independence. There were other voices amongst republican commanders who regarded the Operation as less of a success. The Republican volunteers lost a number of men - one being Pearse –Brogan's younger brother - in unexplained circumstances. The same commanders were highly suspicions as to how Joyce always escaped injury or capture. Upon Independence, he was given a government job, and certain suspicions were left to rest. Despite his sinecure, Joyce declared he would never recognise an Irish State made up of twenty-six counties and continued to campaign against the government and stood for election to Dail Eireann - unsuccessfully. In 1937, Joyce had gone to Germany and made contact with the Nazi Party. The authorities in the UK and Ireland were aware of this but had no idea as to the reception he received from the Intelligence Services of the Third Reich. The British regarded him as a potential bomber on the UK mainland. The Irish authorities took him more seriously, being concerned he would inflict maximum damage to the British war effort regardless of the problems caused for the neutral status of the Irish Free State.

There were sympathisers that would offer help to a man like Joyce without asking too many questions. One such man met him at Kent train station in Cork City, recently renamed after the only man executed outside Dublin after the Easter Rising.

Joyce had travelled from Killarney to Cork by train. The ticket inspector at Kent station reported the type of vehicle in which he was travelling and a description of his driver to the IDF platoon commander in Cork city centre. When General Brogan was briefed on the movement of Joyce, he made an educated guess and sent a message to Sir Geoffrey Lewis that an attempt to pass information to the Germans was about to take place.

Colonel Sir Geoffrey Lewis had been patiently enduring his mail being held up as a result the war effort affected Royal Mail services. Since being recruited to the SOE, Lewis' name had been added to a list of people whose mail was to be fast-tracked. Because of this facility, Lewis requested Brogan send all letters to his home address. They were delivered unopened as the censors had been briefed that the addressee was cleared by a higher authority.

Within three hours of reading the letter, the team was assembled and on their way to Dublin. Erebus travelled separately to Northern Ireland where, if he was asked any questions, he was to claim to be a teacher of the Irish language. The 'prodigals' had been briefed by Professor Williamson as to the laws in the Irish State - specifically, those applying to offences covering possession of firearms and the attempted murder of members of the civil authorities, political and uniformed. All the operatives' received one explicit order - under no circumstances was any member of the Irish Defence Forces or the Gardaí (the Irish police force) to be killed. Sergeant Major Reilly and Sergeant Mullen were a little nervous as they walked down the gangplank at Dublin port. They were technically wanted men. Both had been very active in their respective communities, especially the GAA, and might be noticed in Dublin. If all went well they should be in and out of the city before anyone knew of their presence. If not, that was another matter.

Erebus had disembarked from a ferry in Belfast and was now on a bus taking him to Dublin.

Joyce's time in Germany was a complete *waste* of time. The Nazis were far more arrogant than the British and placed little value on any assistance offered to them by the IRA. The Abwehr regarded them as a bunch of loose cannons striking at the British in a random fashion with almost suicidal stupidity. Joyce believed he was only being humoured until the Germans could decide what use to make of him. When finally interviewed, it was proposed that his best role would be to assist agents operating on the island of Ireland. Joyce returned before the war started and, until 1944, was involved in IRA activities. Then he was contacted by the Abwehr and offered a substantial amount of money to escort a German agent from the Northern Irish border to Dublin. Joyce recruited another IRA member from Kilkenny to provide transport. Both men set out from Kent station, unaware of being monitored.

Erebus showed his papers to the RUC border officer. The Gardaí were next, then he boarded the bus, sat down and watched two men waiting on the far side of the border post. So much time spent behind enemy lines had heightened his awareness of human behaviour. They were waiting for someone. Erebus mused, 'Christ! These guys are that amateurs.' The situation played out as predicted when a man crossed the border and seemed lost until the larger of the two men approached and shook his hand. The third man led them to a car parked nearby. Erebus looked at this man and felt a surge of excitement. His phenomenal memory instantly recalled the day his beloved Uncle Peter had been killed. The face was much older, and the walk was more stooped, but there was no doubt; this man was one of the four who had murdered his Uncle. Erebus watched as the car drove away. His orders were explicit. There was nothing that could be done now, the man had escaped, but one of the killers of his Uncle had been found - and the war was not over yet. For the first time in many years, Charles Peter Lewis - not Erebus - felt personal anger and a deep yearning for revenge.

The guest house in Dublin was small and the owner did not ask too many questions once paid in cash. Dublin is not a big city, and Erebus quickly located the German Legation, now under observation by Sergeant Major Reilly with Sergeant Mullen. The men randomly changed locations to avoid becoming a permanent fixture in the street. Off to the left, about a hundred yards from the Legation, Sir Geoffrey sat in a car supplied by an old friend who ran a large garage in Dublin. The vehicle was nondescript, and it would get the team out of the vicinity unnoticed. As Erebus watched from a discreet distance, his mind turned to the job at hand and the man who had called Uncle Peter a 'Black and Tan bastard' as he shot him. As the sun went down, Erebus made contact with his father, telling him about the Kilkenny man. Sir Geoffrey replied.

"Brogan said there was no evidence against him. We'll see about that."

As the second day of the stakeout began, Joyce, his comrade and the German agent approached Dublin. Sitting in his car, Geoffrey Lewis was conscious of a man gradually moving toward him until he leaned on the roof.

"Excuse me, colonel. Do you see the black car about a hundred yards ahead of us?" Geoffrey Lewis nodded.

"Would you be so kind as to walk up to it in about five minutes?"

Lewis was greeted by General Brogan.

"Well, Geoffrey, I have a little information for you. The man you are waiting for is called Joyce. He is accompanied by two other men. One is from Kilkenny, is a small-time farmer, and, in his eyes, a big-time patriot. The third is slightly more troublesome. He is a German citizen who is an advisor to the Irish Civil Service and was collected by the other two at the border. I have unconfirmed information that they will attempt to get into the Legation tonight after dark. I would appreciate it if I could have Joyce and his comrade gift wrapped. As for the German - I do not know what to suggest. He is virtually untouchable."

Sir Geoffrey asked,

"This man - has he been into the embassy before? Would his face be known to the staff inside, do you think, Pearse?"

Brogan answered,

"This man is new to us. As far as I am aware, he has never been involved in any form of espionage. We have him listed as a career diplomat, but he is a fanatical Nazi who goes by the name of Herman Brecht. Now, with regard to the evidence........."

Sir Geoffrey cut across him,–

"I'm glad you raised that - I've had a few ideas. Tell me what you think?"

Ten minutes later, they parted with Brogan's words,

"We will leave certain items in your car later today. Good luck to you, Sir Geoffrey."

Colonel Lewis returned to his car and gave the pre-arranged signal for the team to meet, where he repeated to them, word for word, what Brogan had briefed him.

Mullen was the first to speak.

"Colonel, if this man is unknown to the Embassy staff, then we could lift him. The other two we can take out - but what about evidence for General Brogan?"

Lewis looked at his comrades.

"This is what we are going to do. If you have any questions, please ask."

Ten minutes later, Sergeant Major Reilly spoke.

"Colonel, I think we should go ahead as you and the general have planned. In the meantime, I will keep watch on the embassy until dark. Sergeant Mullen will recce the escape route; by then, you will have the package. We'll meet at 19:00hrs here to confirm there are no changes."

Colonel Lewis quietly replied.

"Please carry on, Mr Reilly."

Erebus approached his old comrade as the clock moved toward 18:00hrs. Reilly turned to meet his gaze. There were no handshakes, but the respect and pleasure were evident. Reilly's eyes hardened when told the targets were on their way. Mullen joined the duo and the greeting was as covert and sincere. General Brogan watched the entire gathering and then returned to his car. These men were fighting for freedom - he would ensure that the Operation would be successful. Irish Military Intelligence had access to both British and U.S. reports on what the Nazis were doing - in his mind there was no doubt what was right and what was wrong. As for the Irish men assisting the German, Brogan's conscience was clear. His sole responsibility was to maintain the neutrality of the Irish State, and that end justified the means.

Joyce had guaranteed to Brecht that getting into the embassy would not be difficult. When asked why it had to be done after dark, his answer was, 'security reasons.' Brecht was based in London until 1937, then when Ireland left the British Commonwealth, he was posted to Dublin. He had been recruited by the Abwehr in 1938; his handler soon discovered that Brecht was suffering from delusions of grandeur. He openly expressed a wish to be posted to Rome or Paris, regarding himself as a sophisticated aesthete. Once briefed on Operation Green - the German plan to invade Ireland when Britain had fallen – his delusions grew, picturing himself as the Reich Protector of the German colony of Ireland. Brecht was a fanatical Nazi, and in the New Germany, that counted for a great deal. Since the rise of the Nazis, the German Diplomatic Service was simply another branch of the numerous German intelligence services staffed by Nazis. All of the career diplomats who were not 'loyal' were retired or disappeared. Brecht was based in Dublin, monitoring the number of allied servicemen heading to Northern Ireland to re-join the fighting. Because of glaring weaknesses, his Abwehr handler was loath to use Brecht, describing him as a 'perfect idiot', never allowing him near the Intelligence section of the German Legation. When the war began to turn against the Nazis, out of desperation, Brecht was put on active service and ordered to Belfast to collect and then deliver an envelope to the Legation building in Dublin. Fearing he would get lost on the journey, Joyce was activated as escort and bodyguard. As the sun went down on a beautiful Dublin evening, Reilly, Mullen, and Erebus took up positions close to the Legation building with a precise plan. The German and his escorts were to be intercepted before getting to the gate. Sir Geoffrey looked on from a distance.

The 'prodigals' watched a car park at a corner of the square, and three men get out. The light was slowly fading as the trio made their way to the side entrance of the Legation. Erebus could not quite believe how amateurish they were. There was no attempt to conceal their intention to enter the embassy. Unknown to the prodigals, Brogan had arranged for the regular Gardaí patrol officers to be relocated under the pretext of a demonstration in O'Connell Street. Brecht and the other two men neared the gate to be confronted by the prodigals. Brecht was knocked unconscious with one blow by Mullen. Joyce was tough, but Reilly was far fitter and highly trained, and after a brief exchange of blows, the Kerry man was lying senseless. The third man, the driver, saw satisfaction in the eyes of his attacker before losing consciousness. Mullen searched Brecht, found and handed an envelope to Erebus, who quickly read then divided the enclosed papers. Some for General Brogan as evidence of Contravention of Neutrality by the German diplomat. Some were added to forged papers from the SOE and would be given to the German Legation intelligence officer. The remainder were of interest to the SOE.

Erebus entered the Legation carrying Abwehr Identification papers and the false documents. The intelligence section was in an enclosed room which contained radio equipment, where he was approached by a small man who remained silent as he examined the papers handed to him. His only comment being,

"The Third Reich thanks you."

Erebus made a mental note of the radio kit specifications. As he was leaving his only thought was, 'Thank the lord for fanatics'.

Outside the Legation, Erebus peered into the gathering twilight and assisted Reilly in carrying the German to the waiting car, where his father handed him a package. Father and son's eyes glowed with satisfaction, as Erebus said.

"This won't take long."

As he moved away, out of the corner of his eye, Erebus saw that Reilly and Mullen had propped the unconscious Joyce and driver against the embassy wall.

He was soon back with his fellow prodigals and removed two pistols from his trench coat, handing one to Mullen, the other to Reilly. Then deactivated the safety lock of a third pistol. All three men waited. In O'Connell Street, the patrol officers were ordered to return to the German legation, and as they entered the square, came under pistol fire. Both officers were experienced and dropped calmly to the floor. One reached the nearest phone box and rang for assistance. His colleague counted no more than twelve shots - all were close to him but not too close. In fact, he'd say later,

"The gunmen seemed to be aiming in my direction but not at me."

Reinforcements took ten minutes to arrive, and in the meantime, there was no further shooting. Joyce and his driver came round panicked, and made a dash for the escape car. A dash seen by the police officers now flooding the square. As the Kilkenny man turned the ignition key, the car was surrounded by armed police officers. Both men were searched, and pistols were discovered in their overcoat pockets. Both had been fired very recently. A thorough search of the car revealed a number of weapons concealed under the back seat, along with a quantity of explosives. Brogan said nothing as both men were arrested and read their rights. The prodigals had disappeared.

A ferry sailed from Dublin port. On board were Sir Geoffrey Lewis, Cormac Reilly, Tomas Mullen and one terrified German who had been promised his life if he came quietly. Sitting on a bus heading toward the border, Erebus was unconcerned about Joyce - that was none of his business. The Kilkenny man, however, was different. The weapons and explosives found in his car were of Irish origin - of that, there was no doubt. The Kilkenny man would never know how the devastatingly incriminating evidence got into his car. Charles Lewis smiled; he could not take the credit as his father had planned the whole thing. Later, in the cells of a Dublin police station, the superintendent in charge of custody asked Brogan,

"What are the charges, General?"

Pearse Brogan looked at Joyce and thought of his brother, then answered,

"They fired on Gardaí. We'll start with 'Attempted Murder', then 'Possession of arms and explosives' to follow."

The Kilkenny man remained silent, as did Joyce. Both knew they were now facing the death penalty.

General Brogan had arrested two IRA men with firearms in their possession – all the evidence he needed – but the death sentence was in the hands of the courts or a military tribunal. The issue of the German diplomat was never raised once Brogan produced some of the documents Brecht was carrying, proving his involvement in espionage and therefore contravening neutrality conditions. Colonel Lewis delivered the remainder of the papers to Odin and Maiden Aunt.

These revealed the names of resistance group leaders in Holland and France, and all had one thing in common - the men were all anti-communist. The information planted by SOE was sent to Germany and accepted as genuine.

In the study of their house in Suffolk, father and son held a private meeting. Had anyone been listening and understood Irish, they would have heard Sir Geoffrey say to his son,

"Word has come through that both Joyce and the Kilkenny man had been convicted. The sentence open to the court is a long prison term or death by hanging."

His boy replied,

"One down, Father. Three to go. As for this man Joyce he just got caught in the crossfire. Nothing personal."

Geoffrey Lewis thought of Pearse Brogan and replied,

"We are Irish, and everything is personal."

Sir Geoffrey and Lady Lewis sat with Charles, who was just about to leave. Felicity Lewis was aware that the death of Peter Lewis now hung less heavily on her husband and son. It was as if they were now one again, engaged in two wars. One against the Germans, the other a profoundly personal campaign. She knew that her men were two things above all else - soldiers and Irish, and may God help anyone who crossed them. The farewell was emotional and heartfelt. She embraced her boy and kissed him goodbye. For some reason, she had no doubt that he would be coming home in good health one way or the other. The colonel hugged his son.

"Good luck to you, my boy."

Brecht was held until the war ended when he returned to Germany and became a civil servant. Pearse Brogan kept in touch with the Lewis. The 'Emergency' was to present him with more challenges.

— 28 —

A Day on the Beach

At precisely nine-thirty, a car pulled up alongside a two-masted schooner named Lydia in a quiet Portsmouth dockyard. An Irish Guards officer wearing regimental campaign colours disembarked and got into the vehicle. Any prying eyes would be misled – the soldier had never been within a thousand miles of North Africa.

The car proceeded to a small army camp on the outskirts of Southsea, where the driver- a corporal - led the officer into a room furnished with leather arm-chairs and a medium-sized coffee table, on which were pots of tea and coffee. When offered both, the officer declined with thanks, the corporal saluted and left. The man sat alone for a few minutes, and then the office door opened. Brigadier Davies came in first, followed by a man unknown to the officer now standing to attention. Davies said,

"Please stand easy, Major Lewis." Then shook his hand warmly as he continued.

"May I introduce Admiral Menzies. He has been keeping an eye on your activities in Norway and elsewhere and has something he wants to discuss with you."

Menzies exchanged handshakes as he enquired of the younger man.

"How are you, major? Before we get to specifics, may I express my admiration of your service so far in the war, and my congratulations on the Operations in which you have been involved?"

Erebus nodded his head in appreciation.

Davies opened a large chart holder and showed Lewis a map which showed the location of the SS Panzer divisions being kept in reserve around the Pas de Calais. He was ordered to observe until the invasion. Plus, any other informa-tion that could be gathered regarding the resistance in that part of France. The plan was for him to be parachuted into France within a week. Menzies stood up again, shook his hand and said,

"On a personal note, I am delighted you spent time with your parents. All three of you have earned that much. You've been away since this blasted war broke out. Good luck to you, Erebus."

In the second week of May 1944, Captain Buchan and his first officer were amongst escort officers ordered to attend a briefing aboard HMS Renown. Admiral Hilliard began by informing them the battleship was, until further notice, the Flagship for minesweeping and escort Operations. Stephen Hilliard was as much an Englishman as a sailor - distinguished, tall and slim with silver grey hair and deep blue eyes. He was very much a man of, and very proud of, the Senior Service he had given his life to.

Each captain received his ship's orders. HMS Snow Eagle was to escort the minesweepers across the channel, then return and make another crossing with the landing craft. A civilian then, clearly ignorant of the fact that every man present had spent at least three years fighting U-boats, tactlessly lectured them on absolute secrecy, reinforced with a thinly veiled threat. The Royal Navy officers listened in polite silence, then got down to the practicalities. The question was raised regarding leave for the ships' crews by Captain Buchan, who, staring straight at the civilian, stated some of his crews had been at sea for nearly six months without a run ashore. The civilian was about to answer when Admiral Hilliard spoke.

"Gentlemen, please use your discretion. I suggest that should you grant leave, do so immediately, but no longer than 96 hours. Right! If there's nothing else, I think we have time for a quick pink gin."

Looking at the civilian, he added with great composure,

"You are welcome to join us in this treasured naval tradition, should you choose to."

Buchan and Pat had one round of drinks with Admiral Hilliard, who spoke of Commodore Loftus with great respect and affection, telling how they had been at Dartmouth at the turn of the century. He revealed how proud Loftus had been of his Snow Ship escort group and the innovative thinking all of them had brought to the arduous task of convoy escort.

Buchan requested permission to disembark the ship, and as he and Pat were leaving the day cabin, Admiral Hilliard's executive officer said to them,

"All paperwork for this Operation will be kept under lock and key until twenty-four hours before getting underway. There are very detailed charts of the French Coastline, which may be worth your while studying as you will be operating inshore. I had intended to bring them today, but our security watchdog wouldn't hear of it – seemingly, he doesn't trust us naval types. Perhaps one of you could pop ashore and collect them from the 'Op's' room in Portsmouth." The very pleasant man finished with.

"Well, good luck to you both."

Once aboard Snow Eagle, Captain Buchan said,

"Number one, please draw up a list of the ship's company who, if given leave, have a realistic chance of getting home and back in ninety-six hours."

Pat returned within an hour with the list which Buchan read.

"Number one, you've done well here. Most of the boys will get home to see their families. I'm afraid the Irish and Scottish boys are out of luck; it's just too far to travel. I notice you haven't placed yourself on the list. Your mother and family are now in Portsmouth, aren't they?"

Pat replied,

"Yes, sir, they returned from Ireland just before Christmas."

Buchan looked up.

"Pat, go home and see your mum and give her a hug for me, will you. I'd say four days should be long enough. You can pick those charts up on your way back."

Cork just managed to say.

"Aye, aye, sir."

Pat walked into his father's office, and within twenty minutes, he was in the house where his mother was totally unaware that her son was coming home. Mary Cork was in the kitchen when she heard the words,

"Hello, mum."

She turned to see her eldest boy and her husband. She walked toward her firstborn, unable to speak. Mary hugged her child for at least five minutes, refusing to allow him out of her embrace and then only for a moment as she said to her husband.

"Con, go and get Chris and Rachel from school - they'll want to see their brother."

Connor did not wait, he left the house, and Pat heard the car start.

All he could think to say was,

"I finally got dad to drive, Mum."

Mary Cork sat her son down, and within minutes, she had a sandwich in front of him and was pouring a cup of tea as she had done since he was old enough to feed himself. She sat beside him and watched him eat, too dazed to speak. She looked at him as only a mother can and knew he was a different person from the man who had left home in London. Then felt a blinding anger at those responsible for taking so much time together from them, but then reached out and touched his hand, and, as she watched, a tear ran down his face.

"No one makes a cup of tea like you, mum."

Then the tears flowed from both of them. Mary had asked her husband to go because she wanted her son all to herself for a brief time. She stood him up and looked at his uniform and the campaign colours on his chest – he had obviously been through a lot.

"How's your leg? Your father told me about the wound."

Knowing he would tell her in his own time, she didn't expect an answer. Rachel and Chris came home, and there were tears of joy at seeing their big brother. Mary Cork had her family around her again, and despite her happiness, she thought of Peter English and could only imagine his loneliness. Then she sat next to her eldest boy and, holding his hand, asked him about his life in the Royal navy.

Captain Bill Cork of the US Army Engineers was called to his commanding officer's quarters on a cold, wet day in late May. When inside, he was asked to sit. The blinds were drawn with guards at the door and windows. As with the rest of the base, the levels of security were almost surreal. Travers passed a chart holder and motioned Bill to open it. On doing so, Captain Cork suppressed a gasp of surprise as he read. 'Operation Overlord'. Immediately beneath, in bold type, were the words 'US Army Deployment, Omaha Beach, Normandy, June 1944'. Travers again checked the windows and the door to ensure that all were secure. Then spoke.

"Well, Captain, now you are aware of what only fifteen other people on this island know - where the invasion will take place. I am showing you this because we have been in Britain longer than most of the US forces, and I think I owe you that much."

Bill, still reeling from what he had seen, started to reply,

"Colonel you don't owe me anything......," Travers cut across him.

"Yes, I do Bill, because I am now asking you to go ashore with the first wave of assault troops. You are to be the eyes and ears of the engineers. We need a battle-hardened man on that beach. You know what happened at Dieppe, and I guess I don't need to tell you what the odds are of walking away from your third Operation unhurt."

Now slightly calmer, Bill asked,

"When do we go, colonel?"

"The first week of June - either fourth, fifth or sixth day - the weather is playing hell with all the plans. We can only hope that it improves - and soon. Bill, I'm ending a small team with you - a radio operator and two more officer engineers. Your job is to decide the best time to start moving armour ashore and when we can start to build the Mulberry Harbours. Bill, you are going to be on that beach for at least forty-eight hours. Even if we push inland, you will have to stay by the water line until the beachhead is secure." Bill enquired,

"How are you coming over, sir?" Travers exclaimed.

"Hell! Bill boy. I'm hitching a ride on the Mulberry harbour!

Aboard his 'two-master', Erebus considered his orders. 'To observe the Panzer divisions.' He laughed.

"Could be a bit lonely after Hagnor and Prodigal." But as the French resistance was, to say the least unpredictable, so be it. Suddenly there was a noise on deck, and he opened the cabin door to be greeted by Vali. They greeted each other warmly. His comrade explained.

"Change of plan, Charles - it seems the RAF can't spare an aircraft for us.

Erebus enquired.

"What do you mean 'us'?"

"Well, precisely that. Maiden Aunt took some persuading but finally agreed that two men could observe more than one and possibly do more damage to the Panzer's communications. So I'm going as well. Hope you don't mind."

Erebus moved on.

"So how do we get to France then? - And no, I don't mind. In fact, I'm glad of the company. How are your French and German?"

Vali laughed as he replied,

"German's ok but my 'francais' may leave a little to be desired. Anyway, you can do the talking for both of us."

"So, my silent friend, how *do* we get there?" He asked, picking up his kit.

"The navy will drop us off. Possibly aboard Snow Eagle. It'll be nice to see Pat Cork and Larsen again. Come on; I've got a car outside."

For the Cork family, the two days seemed to pass in an instant. Pat Cork was packing his bag, ready to return to the war. For a moment, he felt a surge of fury mixed with panic. Once again, he would be in harm's way. Then questions formed in his mind. Why was it always Snow Eagle that got the dangerous orders? Why was it always his ship that had to go where others wouldn't? Pat had desperately missed his mother and his family, and he wanted to stay with them – not stick his neck out again so some Nazi could try to blow his head off. There was so much that hadn't been said in the last two days. Another question leapt into his addled mind. Should he tell his parents that they might be grandparents? His mother called him for breakfast. Instantly, the real Pat Cork regained control and made the decision – which news could wait until the war was over. Making decisions alone felt comfortable – it gave him control. After breakfast, their goodbye was short and silent. Pat's brother and sister hugged him. For the first time in their adult lives, his father kissed him. His mother whispered the words she had said to him the last time they had parted. Then he left and went back to war.

Pat boarded Snow Eagle and found his spirits lifted as the crew were returning. As first officer, he cast an eye over the ship and was pleased to see all was according to plan. Finally, under his supervision, the entire crew took on ammunition. Pat returned to his cabin to find Lars packing his gear.

"Was it something I said?"

Lars finished continued stuffing a shirt into his kit bag,

"It's all over between us; you have played the hussy for the last time. How could you go on leave without me?"

"Don't be so stupid. You know I am thoroughly ashamed of you when you've been drinking 'Jinness.' Need I say more?"

Larsen laughed,

"Pat, my old shipmate, I have been transferred to the Renown as the communications officer. Since Polar Star was lost, there has not been a position for me within the escort group, so Admiral Hilliard decided I am needed on the battle wagon."

Pat asked with real sorrow,

"When do you go, Lars?"

"In about ten minutes," came the reply.

"What! They didn't ask *me* if you could go. I don't know what this war is coming to!"

They went to the weather deck where Captain Buchan was waiting along with some of the ship's company. Buchan spoke.

"Well, commander. I have to say I am sorry to see you go - but needs must. Please accept this small token of your shipmates' appreciation of the contribution you have made to Snow Eagle and the escort group in which we serve."

Petty Officer Constantine came forward and handed him a small box. Lars opened it and found a brass statuette of a Snow Eagle. Everybody present, even the captain, was taken slightly aback by its beauty. The Norwegian managed to speak.

"There is not much I can say about Snow Eagle and all of you that has not already been said. All of you know how much this ship and my shipmates mean to me, and I speak as a man whose homeland is occupied. You have all made me welcome and have allowed me, through this ship, to fight back against those who now rule my home. You have all fought by my side on many occasions, some good; some bad. Now I have been ordered to move on, but my heart will always be with you and this magnificent ship, in which we all sailed with such pride, honour and distinction. Goodbye and good luck to all of you, my friends."

He turned to Captain Buchan.

"Permission to leave the ship, sir?"

"Permission granted, commander - and good luck."

Pat sat in his cabin with the charts collected from 'Operations.' He considered Snow Eagle's orders. The ship would be operating close to the water line, within range of fixed heavy artillery sited on the cliffs. He pored over the charts for possible dangers inshore, his mind oblivious to the noises of the busy ship. Then the cabin door opened, and two officers entered. First Erebus, followed by Vali. Pat knew why the ship had been issued with such detailed and, probably, secret charts.

HMS Snow Eagle departed Portsmouth under heavy cloud and strong seas. The ship was rife with gossip about the identity and destination of the unknown officers on board. Pat discovered the favourite of the sweeps was the Jutland Peninsula. The men in question were in the captain's cabin discussing where on the French Coastline to land unseen. The first officer gave his opinion.

"We are to drop you undetected on a coastline occupied by troops that have been preparing for an invasion for the last two years. I think we have more chance if we move further down the French Coast, somewhere between here and Normandy. There are some secluded inlets where we could get you ashore by rubber dinghy, under cover of darkness, and inland almost immediately. Captain Buchan agreed.

"You know, number one that just might work. What do you think, gentlemen?" Erebus countered.

"Sir, our orders are to maintain a watch on the armoured divisions around the Pas de Calais. It might take us days to get there."

During the discussion, Captain Buchan sensed the weather was worsening. He returned to the bridge to have this confirmed by the forecast. Pat joined his captain as they silently agreed; it was impossible to get men into the ship's boat safely, let alone ashore. The weather was in command in the English Channel, and no orders or prayer would change that. The invasion was four days hence, and Buchan knew he could not get the agents ashore. At least not within the next ninety-six hours.

"Number one set a course for Southampton Water. We have some ships to escort back here in forty-eight hours."

Below decks, Erebus and Vali sat back in Pat Cork's cabin and waited for further orders.

Bill Cork joined the 29th Infantry division and, with his engineers, boarded the ships that were to attack Hitler's 'Fortress Europe'. There followed forty-eight hours of sea sickness and frustration - all spent below decks. Finally, as the ship put to sea, Bill dismissed all his fears and thought of Big Bend and the Double B. His last letter home had been optimistic, maybe overly. He had rewritten it many times, not wanting to give the impression of levity. His mother would see through any attempts to fool her about the gravity of the situation in Europe. Auntie Catherine, of course, would be fully up to speed and read through the propaganda and find the truth if there was such a thing.

Cattle round-ups had taught him to sleep when the chance came. Experience he put to good use during the arduous voyage from the British Isles to the beaches of Normandy. When on deck, Bill stood alone - as much as anyone could on a ship packed with seasick troops. The wind howled, and if anyone aboard could hear, they would have heard the strains of 'My Own Lovely Lee,' being sung by a young Irish American soldier a long way from home. In a few hours, the same young man, prone on a beach, would feel that he was the loneliest man on earth.

The Mulberry Harbour sections were in tow of powerful tugs, which were in turn escorted by corvettes and motor torpedo boats. Some wondered what the MTBs could do as escorts, but everything had been pressed into service for the attack on the French coast. Captain Clinton and Colonel Morley were aboard one of the tugs, astern of Peter English and Colonel Travers, in the vessel leading the convoy of Mulberry sections across the channel. The plan was to make Normandy on D-day plus three. The invasion had begun, and Travers saw his companion was deep in thought and completely calm. Peter English saw the rough seas and foul weather as the convoy set out and did not think twice. He was in the right place and, for the first time since his boy had died and his wife had walked out, he felt at peace with himself. All the necessary arrangements had been made in the event of not returning home. The die was cast, and, come what may, he was ready to accept his fate.

Snow Eagle was part of the first wave of ships that approached the Normandy Coast. The minesweepers ploughed through the heavy seas of the English Channel to arrive on station and start work some twenty-four hours before the invasion fleet. The sea lanes were to be made safe for the troop and the big battleships. Pat Cork watched from the bridge as the mine-sweeping crews went about their task with extraordinary bravery and self-control. The safe speed for sweeping mines was five knots; any faster and the weapons would explode, killing everyone on board. Bad weather had reduced visibility for the enemy shore batteries to near zero, so, for at least twenty-four hours, the minesweepers would be safe. After that, the big guns of the invasion fleet would be on station to protect them. The foul conditions also kept what was left of the Luftwaffe on the ground. Snow Eagle reported to HMS Renown that she was returning to the staging areas to collect the troop-carrying ships. The vast armada, carrying three hundred and fifty thousand men, moved toward the Normandy beaches; amongst them were two first cousins.

Aboard Snow Eagle were two SOE officers awaiting orders from Maiden Aunt or 'C'. Erebus and Vali were remarkably relaxed about the whole situation. Privately they said as much to Pat, who got the impression that both men were much happier - if that was the word - working as a small team. In the current situation, they had little control over anything on or off the beaches - or maybe both had just had enough of the war - a sentiment Pat could identify with completely. Then the beaches were in sight from the bridge of Snow Eagle as a signal was received. Pat Cork was asked to read it over the ship's speakers. He began,

"Ahoy ship's company! Please pay attention. This is a message from Admiral Hilliard."

He continued,

"As you are now aware, we are engaged in the invasion of the continent of Europe. Our aim is to establish a number of beachheads and then push inland to drive the enemy back to his own country, and there defeat him and end this war. I am confident that all of you know that the enemy facing us is in the thrall of a very dangerous and cruel dictator who has shown himself capable of any act of savagery in order to maintain his stranglehold on free peoples. I know, having met some of you, that you are all rational, civilised, educated men who would, in normal times, never contemplate being drawn into a struggle to the death. But we *are* fighting in a struggle to the death, a struggle which is not of our making but a struggle that we must win if we are to preserve the civilisation that we know and love. There is, I know, not a man amongst you who has not seen active service. Rightly, you are all concerned about living through the war. This is your right, and you all deserve a long and fulfilling life when we have defeated the enemy. I can only thank you for your efforts so far. It is an honour to serve with you. I wish God's grace and care for each of you in what we have to do this day."

Pat looked at his shipmates and knew the admiral's words had touched everybody. He knew his shipmates, and they, too, had felt the anger brought on by the belief that it was always the same ships that faced danger. This had been replaced by the feeling that we are the best men for the job, with an air of calm resolution and even confidence. So let's get on with it and then go home.

The barrage of shelling began, and for two hours, it seemed as if the coast of Normandy would disappear under the weight and ferocity of the explosives being poured onto it by the fleet. Every available gun was being used to pound the beach defences. The noise of the fifteen-inch shells passing overhead was similar to that of a steam locomotive at full speed. Snow Eagle was now escorting the minesweepers as they made a final sweep of the water inshore before the landing craft began to advance on the beaches. The dust and smoke from the beach areas gave everybody on board hope that nothing ashore could survive the barrage. Then, the order came to head toward the loading areas. Snow Eagle took station as the British troops boarded the landing craft and headed toward the beach codenamed 'Juno'. The sailors reported that the assault troops were suffering from seasickness, and some were soaked through. There was nothing they could do other than to will them ashore. After three hours of daylight, Pat Cork was on the bridge with the captain as the situation on Juno became clearer. British and Canadian troops were pushing inland. Snow Eagle received a signal from the flagship to take a westerly heading along the shoreline and report anything unusual. Buchan laughed with heavy irony when he read the signal.

"Report anything unusual? How about half a million young men who have just written their last wills and testaments going swimming." He paused, then ordered.

"Number one, tell the lookouts to keep their eyes peeled for anything to report - and I mean anything!"

The smoke along the landing areas was almost impenetrable even to the hawk-eyed lookouts as the ship continued steaming west. Snow Eagle began to close on the American beach codenamed 'Omaha'. On the bridge, the captain pointed to a spot on the chart marked, 'Arromanches-les-Bains'.

"That's where the Mulberry Harbour is going." Pat thought of his dad and Peter.

"My father's company was involved in building those harbours." The captain attempted a joke,

"Well, maybe we'll pop back and give them a hand to put them together number one, but at the moment, we're rather busy," The reaction was total silence on the bridge, so Buchan moved on.

"Anything to report?"

"No sir - nothing from the lookouts or the minesweepers."

The ship continued on a westerly heading, coming upon the debris of three landing craft rising into view on the shoreline along with many floating bodies. The crew watched the corpses in silence as the ship steamed on. Some men said a quiet prayer; others just got on with their jobs - what else was there to do?

Pat made marked the chart with red ink, 'debris.' They might be back this way soon.

As the first wave of landing craft approached Omaha beach, Bill Cork sensed optimism amongst the closely packed soldiers that the intense bombing and shelling had destroyed the German shoreline defences. The landing craft bucked and reared in the choppy sea; Cork's men at the stern were checking their waterproofed radios. Dieppe not forgotten. Then the LRC hit the sand, and the Engineers watched helplessly as the heads of the first two ranks of soldiers disintegrated in a hail of deadly machine gun fire before the ramp had fully opened. The men behind tried to jump off the now-lowered ramp but were shot to pieces. The four engineers crawled the length of the craft and half-swam, half-crawled to the shore as Bill yelled.

"Follow me. Head for the sea wall."

He looked at his men. None were wounded, but even at this early stage of the landing, the radio operator was already in deep shock. Bill grabbed him by his webbing and dragged him toward the seawall, which formed the first line of the German defence. Their fellow engineers followed. They watched every agonising second as the men of the twenty-ninth infantry division were being massacred. At the sea wall, Bill tried to assess the situation. Words failed him. The radio operator was hailing the flagship in command of the Omaha landings. After a short period, when Bill demanded a report, he could only stutter.

"There is no response, sir."

A number of the landing craft had become stranded high out of the water on a sand bar, about two hundred yards from the beach. Perfect targets for the German guns. The troops aboard had to jump into five feet of water. Those that weren't hit by enemy fire drowned under the weight of their kit. It seemed he had been on the beach for hours; his horror grew as the incoming tide increased the distance between the sand bar and the water line. Still no reply radio signals. Bill realised most of the officers and NCOs in command of the first wave of troops had been wiped out. Their counterparts with the second wave were trying to bring some order to a situation which was rapidly becoming a complete disaster. Men were shouting their unit numbers in an attempt to gather in strength, but as numbers of men formed up together, they were being cut to pieces by German fire. The killing went on and on as wave after wave of American soldiers landed on Omaha beach, which was almost concave, a perfect killing field for the defenders. Suddenly Bill heard his radio operator yell,

"I've got a reply, sir, but it's a British ship - HMS Renown."

Bill grabbed the radio, trying to remain calm.

"This is Captain Bill Cork of the US Army Engineers attached to the twenty-ninth infantry division on Omaha beach. Can you patch me through to the US Navy warship in command of this section? She is the USS Ancon. Over."

On board HMS Renown, Commander Larsen of the Royal Norwegian Navy replied, as another sailor wrote down every word.

"We will try to get a message to her. In the meantime, we have ships near you. Can they help? Over."

As Larsen was waiting for a reply, the handwritten transcript of Bill Cork's message was taken to Admiral Hilliard, who immediately ordered the signals officer to transmit a signal to the fleet under his command.

"All frigates, destroyers and sloops near Juno beach, not directly involved in supporting British and Canadian troops, are to make for Omaha beach and assist the Americans by all means."

Captain Buchan did not hesitate.

"Number one, Omaha beach is seven thousand yards west of us. Let's go and see if we can offer some assistance to the cousins -and quickly." Erebus and Vali suddenly appeared on the bridge and suggested.

"Captain, this might be a good time for us to get ashore so that we can get on with our own job."

Buchan replied in a forced, calm voice.

"Bloody good idea! Let's go and do it, shall we?"

As Snow Eagle closed on Omaha, the assistant divisional commander of the Twenty-Ninth Infantry Division was performing miracles pulling his men together. Bill Cork sent word with one of his team that he made contact with one of the ships offshore.

Brigadier Stuart F. Mallem risked his life to get to the radio under the sea wall. He took the handset, identified himself as the senior US officer ashore, then, once Larsen had replied with his name and rank, demanded,

"Is there any contact with any US ships as of yet? Over."

Larsen's reply was twofold.

"Negative brigadier. However, we have been ordered to send you ships to assist in any way they can. Over."

Mallem replied,

"Well, that's something. Keep trying to contact the command ship for this section of the landings, please, commander. Over."

"Certainly, sir. Please do not change your radio frequency. Is that understood, sir? Over."

"Understood. I am going to hand you back to Captain Cork now; he will be the liaison officer until further notice. Do you read commander? Over."

"Yes, sir. Over and out."

As the brigadier turned away, a second voice came on the radio.

"This is a warship of the Royal Navy. Do you read Omaha Beach? Over."

The brigadier took the radio, repeated the identification drill and waited. The reply was in a crisp voice.

"Lieutenant Commander Cork, first officer HMS Snow Eagle. Over"

"Well, Mr Cork. Exactly where is your ship? Over."

"If you look out to sea, sir, you should see us just about now. Over."

The American officers did and saw the outline of a ship taking shape through the smoke and dust. The radio sounded again as Pat Cork continued,

"Is there anything we can do to assist you, sir? Over?"

"Can your forward gun take out some of the enemy gun positions? They're cutting us to pieces. Over."

"We'll start right away, sir. Over."

Pat spoke to an officer.

"Guns, can you knock out any of those firing positions sited beyond the sea wall and the sand dunes?"

"We'll have a go, sir."

"Commence firing immediately."

"Aye, aye, Sir."

The smoke was thickening, and Snow Eagle was being taken dangerously close to the sandbank by the incoming tide. Then the smoke lifted, and the American casualties could be seen. There were bodies all over the beach and many more in the water and on the water line. Adding infuriating insult to injury, Snow Eagle's gun crew was struggling to find clear targets because of the smoke inland. The bridge of Snow Eagle was silent - then the radio crackled into life.

"This is Brigadier Mallem. Can I speak to the captain? Over."

Buchan took the radio as he said.

"Number one, go down and take over the gun, will you. Jesus! The poor bastards are being massacred."

He continued,

"Captain here, brigadier, go ahead, please. Over."

"Captain, we need to get more out of that gun. One of my officers has been on this beach since first thing. I'd like to send him aboard to direct fire. Is that OK?"

Buchan came straight back.

"Yes, of course, brigadier. Tell him to take cover behind the beached landing craft – my ship's boat will pick him up there. We'll cast off straight away. Over."

Mallem looked at Bill Cork,

"Captain, you heard what he said. Get aboard that ship and take out some of those guns."

Bill nodded and started toward the water line. Aboard Snow Eagle, Buchan was about to contact Cork when Erebus spoke.

"Sir, Number one will be needed at the gun. We can take the boat in and bring the American officer aboard." Vali joined in.

"I can handle the sea boat, sir. One of us can stay on the beach and see if we can identify any more targets."

"The Americans do sound a little shaken up at the moment - a little help wouldn't go amiss," Buchan said.

"Carry on please, gentlemen."

Just then, the radio came alive.

"Mallem to Snow Eagle. Captain Cork is on his way to the pickup point. Our 'comms' are shot to pieces. Do you have any spare radios? Over"

Buchan answered,

"Received and understood. We will send men and radios, brigadier. Over."

He turned to the SOE officers.

"I take it you have your radios with you." The reply was instant,

"Yes, sir." As the ship's boat shoved off, Buchan asked the signals officer,

"Flags, what is the name of the American officer coming aboard?"

"Captain Cork, sir."

The captain of HMS Snow Eagle announced,

"Now there's a coincidence,"

Bill had waded to where the sunken LRC was between him and the enemy batteries. He watched a ship's boat clear the prow of the British warship and immediately come under heavy fire with shells ripping the water as the crew rowed against the swell. Bill knew he must shorten the distance and began swimming toward the boat. Another line of bullets ripped the water. Suddenly, the firing stopped. Aboard Snow Eagle, the gun crew had sited the gun targeting Snow Eagle's boat and put a four-inch shell in the middle of the emplacement. Meanwhile, Snow Eagle's Gunnery officer was directing the 'Oerlikon' guns. The ship's engineers had increased the firing arc of the anti-aircraft guns to allow them to drop shells on enemy positions further up the beach. All off-duty crew were firing rifles and machine guns. Every single gun and firearm aboard Snow Eagle was firing at the German positions. In the water, Bill reached the ship's boat and was promptly pulled aboard by Erebus who greeted him with genuine surprise and warmth.

"Good morning Captain Cork. Fancy meeting you here. Now, if you don't mind, we'll get the fuck out of here because some of your chaps appear to have upset the Germans."

Vali slipped over the side with his waterproofed radio and firearms and headed toward the beach. The forrard gun on board Snow Eagle was firing rhythmically as more targets were identified and destroyed. The ship's boat hove to alongside Snow Eagle, and Bill Cork climbed the webbing to the deck at the same time as Erebus. Pat Cork was waiting for them, but before he could speak, Erebus said, with a chuckle in his voice,

"Captain Bill Cork, US Army Engineers, may I introduce Lieutenant Commander Pat Cork, first officer, HMS Snow Eagle."

Then added with a laugh.

"If you two aren't related, then you should be because you could be brothers."

Pat looked at Erebus, asking sarcastically,

"Would you mind if we got on with the war now?"

Erebus, still chuckling, answered,

"Be my guest, old boy."

Pat then spoke to Bill Cork.

"Come this way please, captain. You can site more targets for us, and maybe we can take a little pressure off your men, then we'll get you dried out and fed. Is that ok?"

Bill nodded, trying not to show how delighted he was to be off that bloody beach. During the next four hours, the situation on Omaha eased as more ships came inshore and shelled the German positions. Two American destroyers displayed exceptional bravery as they went abeam to the water line to fire broadsides. Pat and Bill Cork stood side by side as the American branch of the Cork family pinpointed enemy targets, and the British side of the same family blew them to hell.

On the beach, teams of US Army Engineers, assisted by two anonymous allied officers, finally placed explosives which blew holes in the German defences. Aboard the ships offshore, the crews cheered as they watched the Americans pour through the breaches in the walls. A few short hours later, the armour was landing, and the American beachhead at Omaha was established. Nobody said it would be easy, but no one could have guessed that the price would be so tragically high.

Brigadier Mallem, in his command post a good two miles inland, requested the two Special Forces officers who had done so much to help the Twenty-Ninth division report to him to be thanked personally. Despite extensive enquiries and searches, neither man could be found alive or dead.

HMS Snow Eagle was ordered to remain on station to provide anti-aircraft cover for the ships bringing supplies to all the beachheads and the Mulberry Harbour construction teams. Captain Buchan received a request from Brigadier Mallem that Captain Bill Cork remain on the ship until the Mulberry Harbours arrived. Buchan readily agreed. He and 'Number one' could share a cabin. When the first officer came off watch and passed the shower bay, he was surprised to hear the strains of 'My Own Lovely Lee.'

Erebus and Vali headed toward the Pas de Calais using every dirty trick in the book. Acquiring German uniforms, vehicles and identification papers from the living and the dead. The enemy forces were in chaos. Some willingly surrendered. But there were still millions of German troops loyal to the Nazi cause. The fighting was ferocious across a broad front for days after the invasion - perfect cover for the SOE agents to roam free and cause chaos as they headed north.

The weather worsened to a degree that the assembly of the Mulberry Harbours was postponed; Bill spent his time relaxing in the wardroom. Pat Cork came off watch and listened as the signals officer asked.

"Where are you from, Bill?"

Bill told him of the Big Bend country, his family ranch and went on to explain that his parents were Irish and American. Pat Cork listened with interest as he heard the American officer tell how his father had left Ireland around 1919 and settled in Texas. His surprise increased as, during the perfectly innocent conversation, the eloquent American told Flags that his mother was a Texan and his father came from Cork. Flags then talked about his family before Pat joined in, giving a brief history of his family, saying that both his parents were

Irish. When he named the counties, a surprised look came to Bill Cork's face. The conversation continued as these young men tried to find some normality in the brutal madness they were part of. Flags mentioned that the ship had been alongside in Londonderry and asked Bill if his father came from anywhere near there. Bill replied,

"No, my father is from a small town in West Cork called Dunmanway."

Pat just stared at the American in growing astonishment.

"Are you alright, number one?" Flags enquired with the informality of the wardroom.

"Yes, I'm fine; thank you, Nigel. I think I'm going to get some sleep – don't leave the lights on, will you?"

His parting joke got a laugh from the other officers then Bill Cork said,

"I think I'll follow number one's example and get some sleep. Goodnight gentlemen."

Pat sat on his bunk as the American entered the cabin.

"Bill, we need to talk."

"Okay, go ahead, Pat."

Pat explained how his father was from Dunmanway and had left Ireland at about the same time as Bill's father. Bill's reply was a question.

"Let me ask you something, Pat. Does your father ever talk about why he left his home and why he has never returned?"

"The answer to both questions is, 'no', and my father is a pretty cool man - he only gets emotional about Ireland."

He continued the thread,

"Would I be right in thinking that *your* father never talks about why *he* left and that he has no intention of ever going back?" Bill's answer reflected his growing affinity with the Englishman.

"I swear, Pat, if Ireland was the next state to Texas, he wouldn't go near the place. As for why he left - not a word, although I think my mother and grandfather know something."

Pat, now equally relaxed, asked,

"Bill, is your grandfather your mother's dad?"

"Yes, he is. My paternal grandfather died years ago in Ireland."

"Same here, Bill, same here."

Bill enquired for both of them,

"What are we saying here, Pat?"

"I don't know for sure, but I think that we are related in some way. Then, of course, there is always the possibility that your father and mine are brothers and that, my American friend, would make us first cousins."

He continued,

"The problem is, how, in the middle of a world war, do we find out?"

Bill thought of Mandy in London and her interest in Irish history. Maybe she could find out - but how would he get word to her?

"Is there any way I would be allowed to send a message to a woman in London? She's a friend and journalist."

The answer was instant.

"Bill, the words 'snowball' and 'hell' spring to mind."

Both young men lay back on their bunks and quickly fell asleep.

29

The More Things Change and So On

The weather eased. Now aboard Snow Eagle, Colonel Travers met Captain Buchan and 'Number One.' Bill Cork came on deck. Seeing the Corks together, Travers exclaimed.

"Hell, you two boys could be peas in a pod!"

The business of building the Mulberry Harbour at Omaha beach began. Wrecked ships were sunk as breakwaters, and the Mulberry harbour components were slowly assembled. Peter English was in his element - as was Captain Clinton. Colonel Morley was tireless in his efforts to ensure inter service cooperation, and soon the Mulberry Harbour at Arromanches was near completion. Peter English even found time to ask if anyone had seen Pat Cork. He was greeted by a sea of confused and bewildered faces. Someone did try to explain that over three-quarters of a million men had landed in Normandy, which didn't deter English in the least. His quest was finally frustrated as he, along with all other civilians and a satisfied Captain Clinton, were consigned to a merchantman bound for Southampton. Captain Bill Cork, along with Colonel Travers, were to stay aboard Snow Eagle until the Mulberry Harbours were on stream.

The subject of his questions was deeply concerned about the rapidly deteriorating weather as he checked the ship's log and counted nine days since D-day. Despite foul conditions, the invasion had been a success. Looking up from the bridge chart table, Pat watched the elements once again dominate. Then the captain stood beside him.

"Number one, we've been ordered to remain here to provide cover for the Mulberry Harbours. Then we are to provide escort, for what, I haven't been told." He ordered.

"Take her out to sea number one - we don't want to be caught between the weather and the shore."

In a very short time, the wind was gale force. The merchant ships waiting to unload were ordered out to sea to ride out the storm. Experienced sailors watched in disbelief as landing craft were thrown onto the beaches as if made of balsa wood. At Omaha Beach, huge waves tore the Mulberry Harbour apart. On the sea bed, the storm disturbed all sorts of military debris. Sunken mines, hand grenades, mortars and ammunition of all types washed ashore, littering the waterline and beaches with lethal flotsam and jetsam. Eventually, the weather eased and the mine sweepers were recalled to clear channels to the beaches, after which Snow Eagle approached the landing sector. At a meeting on Omaha beach attended by Colonel Travers, Captain Bill Cork and representatives of the US Armed Forces it was quickly decided to abandon what was left of the harbour. The US forces got supplies ashore by simply beaching ships at low tide, unloading the cargo, then re-floating the much lighter ships with the incoming tide. Pat Cork, looking on from the bridge, never failed to be impressed by the American gift for improvisation.

At Arromanches, the weather had been slightly kinder, and the harbour was declared Operational after an inspection by Colonels Morley and Travers and Captain Cork. Snow Eagle, now on station, was ordered to provide bunks for the Colonels.

Security surrounding the invasion relaxed as the whole world knew it was successful. Bill Cork was given permission to send an envelope to a friend in London. When Mandy Bruce opened the item, she found a letter to be forwarded to the Double B. Nothing odd in that, but then a note asking her to see if there was a way to research local Irish history.

The British Mulberry Harbour was on stream. Bill Cork and the first officer were called to the Captain's cabin. Travers smiled as both entered. Pat stood to one side. Buchan spoke.

"Gentlemen, please stand at ease. Captain Cork, we have some news for you." Travers began to read.

"This signal informs and confirms that Captain William Cork is promoted to the rank of Major in the Army of the United States of America. Signed George S Patton General US Army." There was little time for celebration as Colonel Travers shipped out for Portsmouth and Major Cork was reassigned to the vessel laying the Normandy pipeline named 'Ramilles'. Snow Eagle was ordered to escort her. The ship was designed with an open stern section which allowed welded sections of pipeline to be fed onto the seabed. Major Bill Cork was aboard the pipe layer as the technical representative of the US Armed Forces. Lieutenant Commander Pat Cork as naval liaison. After one week of trouble-free pipe laying, an unexpectedly vicious Channel squall blew up, causing a large wave to lift the stern of the pipe layer out of the water. A number of steel pipes broke loose and rolled into the sea. Captain Buchan stood on Snow Eagle's bridge, watching events, his ship two hundred yards to starboard of the pipe layer.

Buchan gave Pat a thumbs up; Pat returned the gesture, all was under control. Then he heard the alert alarm on Snow Eagle and watched in growing horror as at least six magnetic mines disturbed by the squall or the lost pipes surfaced and were swept toward the warship. Suddenly, there was an explosion on Snow Eagle's port side, just forrard of the bridge and radio room. Pat ordered the pipe layer alongside the starboard side of the warship. He jumped to the deck closely, followed by Bill Cork and was met by 'Flags'.

"Where's the captain?"

Lieutenant Nigel Bellamy, though clearly shaken, calmly reported.

"Captain Buchan is dead, along with eleven crew members. The bridge has been virtually destroyed. There is a large hole above the water line, portside, Sir."

The ship's engineering officer and his CPO engineer were waiting for orders. Pat asked for an initial damage assessment, which came within minutes and was Snow Eagle was secure below the waterline and her engines were sound.

The squall moved on, and the sun began to shine on the sloop, now taking water. The engineering officer was adamant the ship could be saved.

"Number One, if Snow Eagle could be taken in tow, we might be able to beach her on the Normandy Coast. The wind and the currents are against us, but it's possible. We've secured all bulkhead doors to isolate the leak, and the ship is reasonably stable." Pat thanked the man, then stood alone for a minute. He was now temporarily in command of Snow Eagle. Ramilles was standing by to take the crew off if she began to sink. As for a tow to the beach, Pat knew that that was not his decision to make. He must contact a superior officer and await orders. A working radio had been salvaged from the badly damaged signals cabin by P.O. Constantine.

Lieutenant Commander Cork made his report to the captain of HMS Belfast - the flagship for the landings at Sword Beach and now for escorts in the Channel. He was told help was coming. Within a short time, the lookouts reported HMS Renown and HMS Belfast closing. Both battleships stood off at a hundred yards of Snow Eagle as a captain with a number of senior engineering officers came aboard and surveyed the ship.

Admiral Hilliard boarded and took command. Pat Cork, with Snow Eagle's engineering officer and engine room division, reported that the ship could be saved if repairs were made to the deck and hull. Citing the availability of the heavy-duty welding gear aboard the pipe layer. A tow to a Normandy beach was also suggested.

Admiral Hilliard had just read the report from Renown's engineers and explained, in an almost gentle voice, Snow Eagle was to be abandoned. Pat was about to protest as a rending sound was heard as the sea tore an even larger hole in the hull. Snow eagle was sinking very quickly. The bodies of the dead would have to be left where they fell.

HMS Belfast came alongside, and the survivors were taken aboard. The admiral called for a service of remembrance, and prayers were said as they have been over British sailors since the time of the 'Wooden Wall.' Then, from the deck of the cruiser, the crew watched as their beloved Snow Eagle sank to the bottom of the English Channel, along with their captain and eleven of the men who had served with them. Belfast steamed for Portsmouth with the men of the lost warship and one American officer. The pipe layer continued with its work and was soon joined by another escort. Another US Army Engineer was assigned to the pipe laying technical duty. Snow Eagle was lost, and, as far as the Royal Navy was concerned, that was that. Major Bill Cork of the US Army Engineers took passage to Portsmouth aboard HMS Belfast and awaited further orders. In the relatively spacious wardroom of Belfast, the officers of the ship commiserated with the men of Snow Eagle and carried on. Pat was silent, his thoughts racing. No one was to blame - least of all him. Everything had been done correctly, but now his ship was gone, and he didn't want another one. He'd been at war since September 1939, and it was now June 1944. That was enough for anyone. All he wanted to do was go home and try to figure out what he was going to do with the rest of his life. Then, as the intriguing presence of a certain American officer called Bill Cork came to mind, his spirits lifted.

In Portsmouth, the crew of Snow Eagle were released by the medical teams and given leave until other ships were found for them. Admiral Hilliard convened a board of enquiry. Lieutenant Commander Pat Cork and the officers of HMS Snow Eagle were restricted to the base at Portsmouth until the enquiry was completed.

Major Bill Cork, US Army Engineers, having made a statement to the investigating Royal Naval officers, was granted leave by Colonel Travers and went to see his friend Mandy Bruce. He was curious to see if she had found a way to research the history of the Cork family in West Cork around the turn of the nineteenth century. Bill waited for Mandy outside the entrance to the British Library. When he saw her, his heart leapt. She was a beautiful, mature woman who dressed as a serious person, wearing clothes that made her subtly very attractive. He found himself lost for words as, when she saw him, she ran and kissed him on the lips.

"Jesus, Bill! You look as if you have been cast from steel. Is there a soft spot anywhere on your body?"

He replied,

"Only my brain – and now my heart."

She kissed him again.

"I thought I'd heard all the smart answers since working in the press bureau, but trust a Texan to still come out on top."

She laughed as she spoke.

"How long do you have Bill, and when are you going to get me a pass to go to France?"

Bill kissed her and continued to talk as he wrapped his arms around her.

"How long I have for leave is up to Colonel Travers. As for France, it is still full of Germans who want to keep it all for themselves and their bloody Fuehrer. It is too dangerous, but I may be able to get you a story which could be of immense interest to people in America and Britain."

"You know, the way you spoke then, you avoided that question like a true Brit. They are masters of ambivalent and ambiguous answers."

During the next two days, they trawled the pages of Irish newspapers in the records section of the British Library. Specifically, copies of national dailies and regional papers covering County Cork for the year 1919. Most were reporting everyday events, although there were reports of incidents involving the authorities and 'Rebels'. Nowhere was the surname Cork mentioned. Then, in a section of one of the papers which covered local Irish news was a story entitled, 'Murder most Foul'. Mandy, separate from Bill, took the folder over to him and whispered,

"Bill, this is a report of a double murder in Dunmanway in 1919 - maybe it is relevant. It's weak, but it is the only reference I could find to Dunmanway in this paper for the year." The article told of two members of a highly respected family in West Cork, Philip and his son George Bagot who had been shot to death on their property. The report continued that no arrests had been made and that the case remains unsolved. The article finished with the funeral arrangements and that the widow had stated she intended to sell the family property and move away.

Mandy had been taught that, as a journalist, if you have any lead follow it until it dries up, so she continued to work her way through the paper's property and farming sections, where she found a report on the sale of the Bagot's two-hundred-acre farm. Then, her eye caught another section of the paper that dealt with the sale of livestock. The details read,

'High-quality Aberdeen Angus make good price'. The story was of cattle from the farm of Mrs Mary Cork, which had recently made a good price at the Bandon Stock sale. Mandy again looked through the farm and land sales section on a hunch which proved to be worthwhile.

She read of the sale of fifty acres of prime farmland and house with farm buildings, in the townland of Dunmanway, by Mrs Mary Cork, the widow of William Cork. The widow planned to move to Leitrim with her daughter. A flash of inspiration came to Mandy as she looked back over previous sales and finally saw the name of Thomas Cork of Dunmanway, a cattle and horse dealer. By this time, her investigative instincts had taken over, leading to the death notices pages, but there was no mention of any Corks. Once again, inspiration steered her to the wedding announcements. After many pages, there was the report of the wedding of Miss Cora Cork to Mr Dan Flaherty of Leitrim. The bride was given away by her brother Mr Connor Cork, the wedding party being the bride's mother, sister and brother, Mr Thomas Cork. The parish priest was also in attendance at the reception. Mandy caught her boyfriend's eye.

Bill sat outside the British Library and tried to come to terms with what Mandy had discovered. He knew he had to tell Pat - and as quickly as possible. He felt at ease. They would decide what to do together. Then he heard Mandy's voice.

"What are we going to do now, Bill?"

"Well, you are going to meet my first cousin, and then we will decide."

"Your first cousin, what are you talking about?"

She was holding his hand, a stunned look on her face.

"Mandy, you asked me about the war. Well, let me tell you about a man I met aboard a warship off a beach in Normandy."

They found a pub which served food, and Bill Cork told his girlfriend about Lieutenant Commander Patrick Cork. Although Mandy ate, she didn't taste a morsel of her meal - her eyes became wider and wider as Bill's story unfolded.

After D-Day, the allies attacked on all fronts to maximise the advance while the Germans were still disorganised. Erebus and Vali reached the Pas de Calais and assumed the identities of civilian engineers brought to work on the Atlantic Wall. They found rooms in a small farmhouse and soon learned that the French had very different views on the German occupation. There were many groups involved in the 'Resistance', most of whom distrusted each other more than the occupying forces. The SOE officers decided that operating alone was the best way to stay alive.

The men frequently crossed into allied lines to brief General Staff Intelligence Officers attached to the headquarters' sections of infantry regiments. The quality of the intelligence coming from Erebus and Vali resulted in Odin ordering Maiden Aunt to set up a dedicated support team immediately.

The team was led by Sergeant Major Cormac Reilly with Sergeant Mullen and a Royal Signals corporal, who, with a number of motorcycle messengers, were attached to the Suffolk Regiment. Which was involved in some of the hardest fighting at the point of the advance. Reilly and Mullen stayed as close to the front as possible to provide Erebus and Vali close support and an escape route. The Gestapo, aided by the SS, had become fanatical about any sign of dissent amongst the military or civilian population. Many innocent people were betrayed out of necessity for survival by the informants, and large numbers of people were arrested without reason.

Parts of the German Army in France were crumbling, and every effort was made by Erebus and Vali to speed up the collapse. All along the front, supply trains were blown up, as were fuel tankers and communication centres. The Gestapo were unable to find the saboteurs because Erebus and Vali were supplied by the highly mobile support unit at many different locations.

All the while, they tapped into the communications of the Panzer divisions, which, for five crucial weeks after D-Day, were ordered to remain in reserve. One reason for this was discovered when German monitored signals revealed that fake allied radio traffic had convinced the Nazi high command another invasion fleet was to land at the Pas de Calais. Something else was heard. An astronomer had convinced the Fuehrer the stars indicated that Normandy was just an elaborate decoy. With the importance of the Panzer divisions waning, the allied high command requested Maiden Aunt to move Erebus and Vali into Paris, where they quickly prepared to recruit gatherers by fair means or foul in the City of Light.

In Portsmouth, the enquiry into the loss of HMS Snow Eagle began. The board comprised of a flag officer as chairman and four senior captains. The board would not be adversarial, hearing evidence in report format. As the officers of Snow Eagle were assured by an avuncular senior captain,

"This is a board of enquiry, not a Court Martial, so don't worry."

Pat Cork, as the senior officer to survive the sinking, was called first. He entered the enquiry room, stood to attention and gave his name, rank and ship. The purpose of the board was explained, and he was reminded that his responsibility was to report the facts - not protect the reputations of the living or dead. The chairman of the board, an Admiral Beatty, asked Pat where he was when HMS Snow Eagle struck the mine. Pat explained.

"I had been ordered by Commander Buchan to board the pipe laying vessel, Ramilles, to ensure full understanding of orders given by naval personnel to civilians during the pipeline laying Operation or in the event of an attack by enemy forces."

"Who else was with you from Snow Eagle?" the admiral asked.

"Major Bill Cork of the US Army Engineers."

"What was his function?"

Pat replied,

"He had responsibility, along with the civilian engineers, for testing the pipe joints."

The admiral continued,

"You had no responsibility for HMS Snow Eagle whilst aboard Ramilles. Is that correct?"

"Yes, sir. Captain Buchan was in command of Snow Eagle throughout."

"Now, Lieutenant Commander, what did you do when the mine exploded?" asked one of the captains.

"I ordered the captain of Ramilles alongside Snow Eagle on her starboard side and boarded her. I was informed by Lieutenant Bellamy that the captain was dead. I then assumed command and radioed for orders from HMS Belfast."

"Please carry on, Lieutenant Commander," the admiral prompted. Pat explained how the engineering officer aboard Snow Eagle had reported he believed that the ship could be repaired and towed to Portsmouth. Then HMS Renown arrived, and Admiral Hilliard assumed command. Finally, Pat recounted how the order to abandon ship was given to the crew and HMS Belfast came alongside, and took them aboard, where a service of remembrance was held. He finished with.

"Then we watched Snow Eagle sink." The room was quiet for a moment. The chairman asked the other members of the board if there were any more questions. There were none. Then he spoke.

"Thank you, Lieutenant Commander Cork. Please remain on base and await further orders."

Pat saluted and left the room. The board of enquiry lasted two days. Lieutenant Bellamy and the engineering officer were called to give evidence, along with the captain of HMS Belfast and Admiral Hilliard. The statement of Major Cork of the US Army Engineers was read into the enquiry record. Then all those involved in the matter of the loss of HMS Snow Eagle were ordered to attend the reading of the Board of Enquiry's findings.

Admiral Hilliard and all the officers present were at attention. Pat witnessed the full gravity of the traditions of the Royal Navy and imagined how ruthless that same tradition could be if it went against you. Admiral Beatty read the summary of the report.

"It is the finding of this board of enquiry that all those involved in the action which resulted in the loss of HMS Snow Eagle acted in a manner which was proper and consistent with that behaviour expected of members of the Royal Navy in time of war. HMS Snow Eagle was lost to enemy action, and every reasonable effort was made to save her. The board notes its deep regret at the loss of twelve members of her crew. This board of enquiry is now closed. God save the King."

Pat left the room and was approached by a captain who said,

"Please follow me, Lieutenant Commander."

Both men entered an office where Admiral Hilliard stood to greet them. Pat came to attention. Hilliard came from behind his desk saying,

"Please stand easy, Lieutenant Commander," and shook his hand. Then returned to his desk and opened a file.

"Lieutenant Commander Cork, I have had you placed under my command until we find something suitable for you in the near future. I have seen your military record, which is, to say the least, unusual. Also to be considered is how your wounded leg affects your ability to serve at sea. Commander Buchan and I discussed your decision to decline command, and I respect your reasons for having done so."

Hilliard scanned the file again, then looked at Pat and continued.

"However, I want you to consider something. You are a highly experienced officer, specifically in escort duties, anti-submarine warfare and covert Operations. The crew of Snow Eagle is similarly experienced and is largely intact. The land forces on the continent of Europe require vast amounts of supplies, and there are still U-boats based in the Bay of Biscay and around Norway that have the capability to attack the supply convoys. I need experienced officers and crews to ensure the supplies are delivered. Commodore Loftus spoke highly of you, as did Commander Buchan. Do you fully understand and appreciate what I have said to you?"

Pat replied.

"Perfectly, sir, and thank you."

Hilliard looked pleased as he announced.

"You have two weeks leave - go and enjoy it. I believe your family is resident in Portsmouth."

Pat had given up being surprised by high-ranking officers knowing more about him than he did and saluted and left. He packed his kit bag and made plans to see his family. Before that, there was another issue to resolve. He telephoned the number Bill had given him and asked to speak to Miss Amanda Bruce.

Pat met Bill Cork and Amanda Bruce in the Cafe Royale, and after a drink, they sat in a pre-booked British Library study room. The newspaper clippings were shown to Pat and Mandy summarised,

"What we have, gentlemen, is proof, undeniable proof, that in the townland of Dunmanway, at the turn of the century and afterwards, there was a successful, highly respected Catholic family. The mother was a widow called Mary Cork, and she had two sons and two daughters. One of the daughters was named Cora - we know this from the report of her wedding. One of the sons, by the name of Connor, was a builder and the other, Thomas, a cattle and horse breeder, who worked on the family farm of about fifty acres, which, at the time, made the Cork family relatively comfortable."

Pat asked Mandy to stop, then said.

"Please go on Mandy and thanks for the breather."

Mandy smiled, her eyes switching between the men in front of her. Even though she had chosen to play the devil's advocate, there was no doubt in her mind. She was looking at two men of the same family and definitely first cousins.

"Well, it seems that the brothers were successful men until something happened which caused them to literally disappear from West Cork. Now whether their emigration was caused by involvement in the War of Independence or financial ruin, we do not know. There is no clue as to why the men left West Cork and Ireland. We know the farm was sold, and the family left – never to return."

Pat and Bill looked at each other.

"We should go for a pint and think about this. Mandy, are you coming?" Pat asked as both men stood. She replied,

"I don't want to intrude, but I think you should consider that if the men described in the press cuttings are your fathers, something dreadful must have happened to drive them apart. Just bear that in mind before you go any further."

The cousins sat in the pub and went over every possible set of circumstances which would allow them to conclude that their fathers were not brothers. There were too many coincidences by half. The names, the townland, the cattle ranching in Texas, the building industry in London and, above all else, their own names. Finally, Pat said,

"Bill, how would you like to meet your uncle Connor?"

Bill just nodded his head as he said,

"Meeting you and finding him might just make this whole war worthwhile, but how do we go about it, Pat? That's the question."

Pat sat for a moment and said,

"I know someone who will have the answer."

That night, all three returned to Mandy's flat which she shared with an American forces doctor, where she and Bill became lovers again. Pat spent an uncomfortable night in the armchair. Mandy's flat mate had been on night duty and when she returned and saw Pat, she said to Mandy,

"Listen, Mandy, next time Bill stays over, if his brother's with him and I'm on nights, tell him he can lie on my bed."

Mandy did not even bother trying to explain.

30

Blood and Breeding

Mary Cork was in the garden as the gate opened. She rushed to her son, hugged him and within minutes was savouring the news that he had two weeks leave. Pat spoke.

"Mum, please sit down. I need to talk to you about dad."

Mary listened as her son simply said,

"Mum, does dad have a brother alive?"

Mary Cork showed her surprise at the question, then looked at her son and saw an officer and battle-hardened man who had been through God only knows what. In an instant, her mind was made up. He could deal with the truth; how much was up to his father to decide. She answered his question.

"Yes, Pat. Your father has a brother named Tomas - but we don't know where he is."

"Mum, this is very important. The split, whatever caused it, didn't involve you, did it?"

"No darling. In fact, I've never met Thomas Cork. Your father told me what happened, but I think he should tell you about that himself. Is that, ok?"

Pat nodded.

"Mum, there is someone I think you should meet. He's outside - I'll bring him in."

Pat walked out of the house and down to the bus stop where Bill was waiting.

"Come on, Bill Cork. Come and meet your auntie."

Mary Cork looked up from the kitchen table and saw a man wearing an American uniform. Pat was about to introduce him when Mary said,

"I know who this man is. God! You are as handsome as your cousin."

She put her arms around him and hugged him as she had hugged her son. Then looked at him and saw her husband's family in every feature of his face, in his body and mannerisms, his shoulders, his walk. She saw Irish breeding that went back hundreds of years. Mary touched his face and then looked at Pat and stood both of them together and hugged both. They told her the story of how they met and had researched the Cork family in West Cork and had realised that they were first cousins. Then, while making them lunch, Bill called her Mrs Cork. She looked at him,

"Please, from now on, my darling Bill, call me Auntie Mary."

When lunch was finished, Bill said to his aunt,

"I will come as a great shock to your husband, won't I?" Mary sat down and squeezed his hand.

"Then he will have to deal with the shock. Don't worry about your uncle, Bill. I'll see that he is well prepared to meet you. Now, what are you two going to do for the rest of the day?"

Pat said,

"Well, since I spend most of my time at sea. I'd like to re-acquaint myself with the feel of walking on a surface that isn't moving."

Mary approved.

"Fine, now both of you put your bags away. Bill, you take the room next to your cousin; it's made up."

As the men left the kitchen, Mary sat down, knowing she hadn't the remotest idea how to tell her husband - but her mind was made up. Even if Con and his brother never spoke again, she was not going to be denied her beautiful nephew. Mary had noticed how at ease Pat was with Bill, in fact, how they seemed to be more than cousins, they were very close friends too, and that was something to be treasured in the times in which they lived.

Mary Cork sat in her living room in the house, which she had come to feel comfortable in. At first, she had wanted to go to London - to their home - but Connor and Pat had persuaded her that it was best to wait until the war was over. Her son cautioned,

"Mum, don't believe for one minute that the Germans are beaten. They still have a few very nasty tricks up their sleeves."

Almost as if he had known all along, within a few days, she was reading of the V1 and V2 rockets falling on the capital.

Mary had reluctantly become accustomed to being the owner/ director's wife; her husband had fitted into the role with far more ease than she. How would he deal with the news that a whole new side of the family had been discovered, and the father of this family was his brother, Tomas? Mary rang her husband's office and spoke to his secretary, asked after her health and then said,

"Will you please tell my husband that I am on my way over to see him - it's nothing to worry about, but I do need to talk to him."

The reply came,

"Yes, Mrs Cork."

That was the part she wasn't quite used to yet - the deference of the employees because she was the owner's wife, but as Con said,

"Mary, it goes with the territory and anyway, we've both earned it - and so have the children."

She couldn't really argue with that, but still, it was something she was uneasy with.

The taxi arrived at the plant, and she walked into the office to be greeted by Peter English, who told her, for the umpteenth time, that he hadn't seen Pat in Normandy but was certain he was fine. Peter worried Mary every time they met and sometimes when they didn't. Her husband came out of his office, every inch the company director, something which she found very attractive, even after so many years of marriage. He really had made the most of the opportunities life had offered. Mary followed him into his office, shut the door and said,

"Con, please sit down and, if possible, can you hold all calls?"

Con picked up his phone and asked for this to be done, then, with a worried look on his face, put the handset back. Mary began,

"Con, Pat is home and has two weeks leave."

She watched her husband's face light up, but as he started to get his coat, she continued,

"Con, he has someone with him – an officer in the US Army Engineers. They met in Normandy during the landings. Con, he is Major William Cork and is your brother, Tomas' eldest boy."

Connor Cork slumped back in the chair, staring at his wife. He had managed to block out the memory of his brother and all that had happened in Dunmanway. He condensed the lost years. So, Tom had a family and a life in America, and, just like him, his son was risking his life for the British. A slight smile came to his face, which made Mary ask.

"What's so amusing, Con?"

He didn't answer as his wife continued,

"Con, let's go to meet your nephew - he's with Pat."

Connor Cork put on his coat and said to his secretary.

"I'll be out for the rest of the day."

As Con drove he voiced the first of many questions in his racing mind.

"Mary, do you think Tom's told him about the shooting of the Bagots? Does he know anything about why the family left Dunmanway?"

His wife answered with great care.

"Con, from what I can gather, until meeting Pat, he knew nothing of us." Then paused.

"There is something else. Whatever Bill wants to know, Pat will as well." Her husband exclaimed.

"Good God! I hadn't thought of that."

Stopping the car, he turned to his wife.

"Mary, I have no intention of telling this young man that his father has killed two men. If anyone tells him, it has to be Tom."

Mary spoke firmly.

"Con, whatever happens today, this boy is our blood, and if he asks the questions we have to answer them."

Connor countered.

"That's fine Mary, but if I tell him what happened all those years ago, it could do damage to Tom's family. When all is said and done, he is a father first and my brother second."

Mary saw the determination in her husband's face as he continued,

"I've done a lot of thinking since Pat went to war, which has made me realise that life is too short for feuds and hatred. I was going to try and find Tom and write to him, if only to find out how he is. Now I don't have to. Shortly we will find out. I will answer any questions our nephew has about the family, Mammy and Daddy and his aunts living in Ireland. But that is all I will do. Anything more will have to be done by Tom. I have nothing to hide from Pat or our nephew. Tom has to decide if he wants to meet us and tell his son why the family left Dunmanway. Remember Mary; he caused the split, not our sisters or me."

Mary sensed how angry her husband was even after all the years and how much he had been hurt by his brother.

Having left the house, the cousins walked a little way, and then Bill said,

"Pat, what was all that nonsense about walking? You navy guys hate walking; that's why you're always laughing at the army."

"I can assure you, Major; there are many more reasons to laugh at the army than that you walk everywhere - but well spotted. Bill, I need to talk to you about something, but first, I have something to say to you. Any real problems I've had in my life have always been solved by speaking to my parents. When I volunteered, I decided any problems caused by the war were up to me to sort out, not them. Understood, Major?" Bill looked at Pat, his voice and face non-committal.

"I think so, but carry on."

"Bill, I need to talk to someone about something. I'm not asking you for a solution, but some advice wouldn't go amiss."

Bill sat down on the grass verge in the country lane, his voice now more confident.

"Pat, we have been to hell and back more than once, and I will fight anyone who says otherwise, so please go ahead. Somebody has to look after you navy clowns."

Pat told about the affair in Londonderry, which had produced a child which may be his. Then how the little boy had been orphaned and was now being raised in a very good home in Northern Ireland. He finished with his decision to wait until the end of the war before trying to confirm if the boy was his. Bill sat in absolute silence and asked,

"You are certain the boy is being well looked after?" The reply was forthright.

"Yes, the doctor's family are well to do, and he is in a very good home. That's all I can be certain of." His cousin continued with a comment which became a question.

"Jesus, Pat, you have been busy. This woman - was it a one-night stand or something long term?"

Pat answered Bill explaining how Snow Eagle had been in for a re-fit, how he met the lady, and they became friends when billeted ashore. The sex was instigated by her and how if Snow Eagle had not returned to Londonderry, he would never have known about the child. As far as he could gather from other sources, the couple had been ecstatic when the baby was born and were planning a great future for the boy. Bill suggested.

"Let me run something by you. Is there the possibility that she always intended to fall pregnant by you? You said the couple were very happy with the child. The plan went disastrously wrong when both were killed."

"I had thought about that," Pat answered and continued.

"The fact that they were both so happy when she gave birth adds weight to the argument. As you say, Bill, they had no intention of ever telling me. Now the situation is what it is but what, Cousin William, do I do about it?"

"Well, I agree with your plan to do nothing until after the war, my fertile friend," Bill said with a smile on his face. Pat raised his hand as if to object.

"There is one more thing, and it is probably the most difficult question to answer. Do I tell my parents, and if so, when do I tell them?"

Bill looked at Pat, his face serious in the extreme.

"Pat, all I can say is, if it were my parents, I know they would want to know and would be desperately upset if they found out from anyone but me. However, that really doesn't answer your question. Pat, what I would advise is, don't say anything until you have definite proof that the boy is yours."

Pat concluded the conversation.

"Ok, that sounds sensible, and thanks for listening. Now I might just be persuaded to buy you a beer - real beer, mark you, none of that Yankee gnat's piss."

After one pint, the cousins walked back to the Cork home.

Connor walked into his house as Mary saw Pat and Bill at the front gate. She was filled with pride but also angry that two such perfect young men, and thousands like them, were risking their lives every day to stop Hitler. Both hugged her, and she said,

"Lads, come on in. There's someone here to see you both."

Connor sat in the living room, his hands shaking, heart racing. He had no idea what to do about anything anymore. He laughed as he said to himself, 'Owner, director? Ha!', then the door opened, and Pat walked into the living room. His father stood and they embraced.

"How are you, Pat? I am so sorry about Snow Eagle and your shipmates. Mum tells me you have two weeks leave - make sure you have a good rest. Get lots of sleep. Have you had lunch? Are you hungry?"

Pat butted in,

"Dad, you're rambling!"

"Yes! I am - like an idiot."

"Dad, there's someone here."

He didn't get any further as Mary Cork walked into the living room - her arm linked in her nephew's. She said,

"Bill, meet your Uncle Con."

Con stood and looked at the young man in front of him, and all he could see was his brother as a young man. The tears rolled down his face as the words came,

"Oh my God. Tom!"

He moved toward his nephew as Bill said,

"Hello, Uncle Connor."

Connor Cork hugged his nephew and dried his eyes, trying to control his emotions and stared into the young man's face and saw his brother, his father and his mother. They sat and began to talk. Mary Cork had three of the men in her family under one roof, and at that moment in time, she could not have been happier. Her second boy Christopher arrived, and then her daughter Rachel. The conversation went on late into the night; they talked about Tom and Connor's mother, then about the Double B, the Big Bend country and Texas. Finally, Mary went to bed - closely followed by the rest. Later in the night she woke and saw her husband was not in bed. She went downstairs to see him sitting in an armchair, crying silently. She approached him and sat beside him on the arm of the chair.

"What's wrong, Con?"

"I saw Tom in Bill's face, and when he spoke, it could have been my father. It all came back; it wasn't all bad at home. We had great times and many happy years. When Cora was married, we danced and sang all night. Mammy was beginning to get her strength back after daddy's death, and Tom and I were thinking about settling down. Mary, there is so much we missed out on and for what? Twenty-odd years later, our son and Tom's boy are at war again." Mary stroked her husband's hair and said,

"There's something else troubling you. What is it Con?"

"I don't know what to tell the man when he asks, as he will ask, about the row between his father and me. Good god! He's as bright as our Pat and, from the look of both of them, just as tough when he needs to be. Did you see the Royal Marines crest on his uniform? That young American has been in the thick of it, just as our Pat has. They both have a right to know, but tell me, Mary, how much I tell them?"

He paused his face a picture of bewilderment. Mary held his hand. She had no words for her husband but sensed he had more to say.

"Mary, I haven't killed anyone, but Tom has. How do you think Pat will react to that - let alone Tom's son? Mary, I don't know what to do. I need time to think. There is one thing certain Bill is part of our family now, God; he is the image of his father at that age." He paused, looking deep into his wife's eyes. "Mary, if he asks me, I cannot tell him what happened. If I do, his next question is obvious. I didn't know the answer twenty-five years ago, and I don't know it now. I won't be able to tell Bill Cork why his father murdered two innocent, unarmed Irishmen."

31

Wars Within Wars

Con had not slept since Bill arrived; now exhausted he sat with Christopher and Rachel, who were given the day off school and, with their mother, sat around the kitchen table. As Bill and Pat joined them, Mary poured tea and prompted.

"Bill, tell us more about your family and your home. Big Bend sounds so beautiful. Where did the name come from?"

Bill was at first reticent, then more relaxed as he spoke of his family, home, the people and the country. Suddenly, an hour had passed, and everybody felt they could almost see Big Bend and the Lake House. Rachel enthusiastically asked.

"When can we go to Big Bend, Daddy?"

Bill joined in the conversation.

"Yes, Uncle Con, when the war is over, you must all come out to Texas and spend time with the rest of the Cork family."

For the first time in years, Con felt absolutely helpless; there was nothing he could deny his daughter. Bill was his nephew and a soldier, a man wise before his time, who Con knew would understand as he said,

"Bill, my boy, there are so many things to talk about. It will take time to tell you everything, and you will understand that there are things that your father should speak to you about. Now, I have to go to work, so all of you have a good day, and you two fighting men take it easy and relax."

Having helped him with his overcoat, Mary pointed out,

"Con, he has a right to know what happened."

The front door was open as he spoke.

"I know he does but do I have the right to tell him? Come outside for a minute, please?"

Con tried to explain his confusion.

"Mary, in spite of the madness around us, having all of the young people around the table was wonderful. But to me, there was one person missing. My mother had a right to be there to see her grandchildren and you. I adore Bill, but I can't forgive his father. He killed Mammy as sure as if he'd shot her. I need time to think - to try and come to terms with everything that has happened. I think the best thing to do is to speak to Pat and Bill and try to explain some of what happened. I won't burden them with the whole truth - that would be unfair - God knows they have enough to do just to stay sane and alive."

Mary kissed her husband as she now understood his torment. His last words burned into her soul. Now all she wanted was for the war to be over and for her darling son and nephew to have the chance to live out their lives in peace. She would let her husband make the decision whether to meet his brother or not and walked back to the house to be greeted by Rachel with a huge hug.

Connor got to work and closed the office door behind him. Now he had time to think. Memories of many years before flooded his mind. When Pat was born he tried to forgive his brother, but his mother's tears, her pain, and, he believed, early death had all been caused by his brother, Tom. Even now, years later, looking at his nephew, Con knew he could not forgive his brother. He had loved Bill since the minute he had seen him. His wife's face, Mary- the pillar in his life, the person he would do anything for lit up every time Bill called her Auntie Mary. Even for her, he could not find a way to forgive.

That night, Connor Cork, his son and nephew, accompanied by his wife and children, went to the local pub to meet Peter English, who, when they arrived, was chatting to the landlord. The Cork party was quickly introduced to the publican, and through the course of the evening, Peter made sure that everyone knew the contribution being made by the Irish, and the Corks in particular, to the war effort. Connor watched his son and nephew charm everyone in the bar. Bill was a mature, balanced man from a stable, loving home, who adored his parents. Con wanted to know this young man - his flesh and blood - and would not risk alienating him even with the truth. There was Pat and the growing bond between the cousins, Con listened to the landlord chat and noticed how the pub had filled up with people of all nationalities. Someone called for a song, and Pat stood up.

In no time, the pub was ringing to the sounds of 'On the Banks of My Own Lovely Lee,' led by two first cousins - one in British uniform, the other, American - singing a song about a river in County Cork - a song they had been taught on different continents by Cork men who were brothers, but who had vowed to forget each other forever.

32

Coming to Terms

June 6th 1944 - a day and date which will live forever. It marked the beginning of the end for the marauders, the fanatics, Hitler's hordes, who had saturated the world with hatred and violence. Now, maybe, the end was in sight. A long way off, but, nevertheless, somewhere in the distance, a conclusion, an ending to the struggle, could be seen.

'It will all be over soon,' the papers and the barrack room prophets predicted. The Allies were ashore in Europe and pushing inland. The Germans were in retreat and could not possibly last much longer. Everyone said it. Everybody dreamed it. The allies were now beginning to hope. Peace was only months away. Now there was so much to look forward to. D-Day had changed everything.

In Britain, the people had endured the terror of air raids, the privations of rationing, the sight of so many funerals and the empty streets devoid of children. Then came the new killer. The 'V' weapons. Once again, people asked the question. When would it all end?

In America, the Pacific War was as brutal as anything ever experienced. As American forces drove toward the Japanese homeland, a new phenomenon was unleashed - the Kamikaze - 'The Divine Wind'. Again the same question. When will it end?

All families on both continents could do was pray for the return of their loved ones. Others prayed for different reasons. The telegrams were delivered, destroying lives, families, homes and dreams. For them, the war, wherever it was being fought, was already lost. What was victory without your son or father or husband or daughter or brother?

In the households of the Corks in London and Texas, both were in terror of their sons not coming home. There was another fear, a secret which could do as much damage to the families as one of the terrible telegrams. The families of brothers who had quarrelled during another terrible war. Their sons had met in the middle of a different war, fought on a scale never seen before. An impersonal, cold, savage and ruthless war. In meeting, the cousins had opened a piece of history that their fathers wanted closed forever.

July 1944 European theatre of Operations.

"Looks like we'll have to turn someone, and quickly. Any ideas on where we find him?" Erebus asked with a touch of cynicism.

Vali was relaxed.

"There was always someone open to blackmail and the Wehrmacht, being the rigid machine it is, allows pressure to be applied to any number of people for many reasons. But the most reliable and productive are love or sex or greed."

The SOE officers were looking for an enemy serviceman to blackmail into working for them. They set a watch on German headquarters, and each evening, followed an officer based there. Most, having been in Paris for some time, were resident in apartments and finishing for the day, had a few drinks and then visited girlfriends or mistresses. None proved suitable. Once again, as a major in the Artillery left the building, Vali signalled to Erebus he was the target. The man entered an apartment and then, some twenty minutes later, reappeared in civilian dress. A tall, slim, elegant man with slightly brown, flat hair, he walked to the Latin Quarter of the city and went into a small building. They waited. Half an hour later, the major came out with a man slightly shorter than him. Slim, with jet-black curly hair. In the falling darkness, the couple walked into a dead-end alley. They watched as the major knocked on a door. Music could be heard as the doorman spoke some words of recognition as they entered. During the next thirty minutes, more couples, all men, entered the club, which was clearly for homosexuals and made the major perfect for turning. He was followed for the next three nights. On two of these, he remained at the apartment in the Latin Quarter all night. The third night, the couple stayed overnight at the officer's apartment. Later, Erebus surprised Vali by expressing an opinion on homosexuality.

"I went to public school; you become almost blasé about the whole thing. I say it's a man's own business."

Vali felt he had to reply.

"In Norway, it's far too cold for that sort of thing. It's hard enough to get a woman to take her clothes off."

The following evening, as the couple left the apartment, they were confronted by two armed men. In German, one suggested they all return to the apartment. Erebus searched the flat, finding photographs of the pair in which the poses, in no way lewd, left no doubt as to their relationship. Vali began,

"Gentlemen, you do not need to know who we are. Suffice to say that we have an interest in seeing the city rid of Germans. Now, to this end, you can help us. Major, your friendship is illegal in the eyes of the German Army on two counts. First, you are a security risk and secondly, the nature of your relationship. Should you be exposed on either count, under the prevailing conditions, punishment would be slow and fatal. As for your friend, the resistance would make short work of him due to the level of collaboration in which he has engaged."

There was silence - Vali continued.

"Further, if there is a battle for Paris, the resistance will make every German soldier a target. Cooperate with us, and we will ensure that you and your friend get out of the city alive and to safety."

The Latin looking man screamed,

"But we are in love. Don't you have any emotions? We are going to live together after the war."

Vali spoke, a slight optimistic air in his voice.

"Ah! Now there, we may be able to assist you both......"

He looked straight at the German officer, his voice now hard.

"....if you help us."

The major spoke.

"What do you want from me?"

Erebus and Vali exchanged a look that said it all – 'Turning' complete. This man would do exactly as he was told and, of equal importance, would remain in position while supplying intelligence. The civilian was asked to leave the room.

Vali went on to explain what information was required. Ammunition levels, fuel reserves and troop strengths around Paris. All in small light files. He then outlined the drop box procedure. The major, whose name was Brumner, was given the address of a dilapidated building ten minutes' walk on his route home from German headquarters. Documents were to be placed in the letterbox of this building every evening. The other man was then invited to join them, and both warned they were quite safe while the information kept coming. Before they left the apartment, the German major asked.

"What will happen if I refuse to cooperate?"

Erebus, who had remained silent throughout the encounter, answered.

"You would both be dead before you hit the floor."

The information began to flow on a daily basis. Erebus ensuring the German had not been followed before collecting the documents and passing them onto SOE contacts in the approaching allied units.

Then, after two weeks of successful Operation, Brumner, ignoring all operating procedures, waited at the drop box. Erebus, watching, sensed this was not a trap and allowed the major to spot him, then walked slowly away. Brumner followed at an equal pace, then sped up as his contact seemed to have disappeared. Erebus appeared behind him. The German spoke quickly and quietly.

"I don't know who you are, and I want you to know that I have always been a loyal German officer, but there is something I must tell you, not as an enemy but as a fellow civilised man."

He was encouraged.

"Go on please, major."

"A new general has been appointed as second in command in Paris. He is from the Eastern Front and is noted for ruthlessness. His orders are directly from Hitler." Erebus prompted.

"Those orders are?" The major spoke slowly.

"He is to destroy Paris before the allies take it."

Instructions came quickly from his listener.

"I need all the information you can get on this man, and fast."

The next day, the drop box contained a small file on General Wolfgang Breitner, which was passed on to Sergeant Major Reilly and delivered to Maiden Aunt within twenty-four hours.

Meanwhile, Erebus raised with Vali, his growing concern about the major's friend. The man was becoming unstable. Perhaps a closer watch on him was needed to give him a little reassurance. Major Brumner and his friend went to a club in the Latin Quarter. When returning to the apartment, they were accosted by three very drunk, large Wehrmacht infantry men who made it abundantly clear what they thought of 'queers'. Brumner could do nothing as the soldiers began to hustle and push both men. Erebus appeared and, in perfect guttural German, told the aggressors to 'Fuck off.' The ensuing fight was over in less than two minutes, with all three soldiers clutching their groins and bleeding badly from broken noses. Erebus turned to Brumner.

"We'll keep our part of the bargain; Please keep yours."

At a secret location in London, a meeting was attended by Maiden Aunt, Professor Williamson and C. The agenda was possible developments in Paris based on Vali's report and supported by the Breitner file. Professor Williamson was briefing his synopsis of the document.

"General Wolfgang Breitner joined the Nazi party for personal advancement. Hitler has posted him to Paris from the Eastern Front, where his reputation for ruthlessness comes from carrying out numerous atrocities in Poland, Hungary and Russia. He is driven solely by personal ambition. This, I believe, we can use against him. If he is convinced that destroying Paris will be of no benefit to him, we can persuade him to surrender the city."

Cnodded, then spoke.

"How do you propose to do that, brigadier?"

Maiden Aunt replied,

"We have put together a plan which will cause the general to think very carefully about his future."

"Proceed," 'C' ordered.

"Erebus and Vali will gain access to his headquarters' office and kidnap him. He will be held prisoner, and a number of points will be forcefully put to him. The first being that should he obey Hitler's orders, he will be a wanted man on every continent for the rest of his life. Two, he can surrender the city to the resistance and the advancing allied forces and be given safe passage to Allied lines, where he will be treated as a prisoner of war."

C continued his questioning.

"And what if he refuses the initial approach from our men? What happens to them and the general?"

Williamson thought, 'this man is human after all.'

Maiden Aunt answered,

"Our men have an escape route planned, and the general will be freed. To kill him would provoke the most vicious reprisals."

"How do we put the general in contact with elements of the resistance?" C enquired. Williamson spoke.

"We use Odin's contacts to liaise with the general to arrange the unconditional surrender of all German forces under his command."

C was now almost interrogating the SOE men.

"What about the Gestapo and those elements within the German forces in Paris which remain loyal to Hitler? How are they to be neutralised?"

"That would be arranged by the general, the resistance and the Free French forces."

C continued,

"And Breitner? How do we manage his escape if we need to get him out?"

"Our men will be on hand to take him out of the city, but only after Paris has been liberated," Maiden aunt replied.

C looked over the file and said,

"Gentlemen, I have briefed the Prime Minister on this matter, and he is adamant that Paris must be saved from Hitler's insane plan. Please go ahead with the proposed action. Good day, thank you both and please extend my thanks to those remarkable young men, Erebus and Vali."

The Cork cousins began to discover how much they had in common despite being born on opposite sides of the Atlantic, with a similar sense of humour and temperaments. Their leave was spent at home with Connor and Mary, and of course, they had to visit the concrete plant. Mary and her daughter spoiled both men as if trying to make up for all the years that had been denied them. The whole family visited the local pub on warm summer evenings, where Christopher was never too far away from his brother and cousin. One morning, Mary heard her youngest son telling two of his school friends.

"Listen, we have got to join up and become officers. My brother and my cousin were awash with women last night in the local." All she could do was laugh. He was only just sixteen, and she prayed it would all be over long before he came of age.

Pat and Bill found some time alone and slowly went into detail about the action they had seen and how much it had affected them. Pat recounted how he had joined the Irish Guards and his commission in the Royal Navy. Bill spoke of the raid on Dieppe and his time with the Royal Marines. Then, as only men who have taken a human life can, tried to talk about it.

"Did it affect you, Pat?"

"To be honest, Bill, it didn't – or at least, it hasn't yet. I just got on with it. In Norway, I was involved in hand-to-hand fighting and killed up close. In the Navy, we sank U-boats so I didn't see the crews die. Neither affected me too much. What did get to me was experiencing something in the convoys called the 'no stopping' order." Bill butted in.

"Don't say any more, Pat; I know all about it. I was aboard a troop ship when one of our navy escorts was torpedoed. The captain of my ship was completely devastated because he was leaving good men in the water."

After a pause, he continued,

"When we blew up the German destroyer, I killed two men, as you say, up close. I asked a man when it was time to stop killing. He told me, 'When you start to enjoy it.' I always settled any doubts I had with that statement. I never enjoyed it, but being honest, it never troubled me too much." Then Bill surprisingly changed the subject.

"Pat, do you know what happened to cause the rift between our fathers?"

Pat shook his head.

"I don't know what caused the falling out. All I know is that dad doesn't have any time for Ireland. He has lived in England since he was nineteen and, at times, seems more English than Irish. Dad usually avoids talking about the past with some sayings. 'Ireland is a lost cause,' and 'There are no winners in Ireland.' He always tells me that I should be my own man and never get drawn into lost causes."

Both men were then silent until Bill suggested.

"Come on, cousin, let's go and tell Uncle Con to stop worrying about what happened with my dad. He can tell me in his own good time."

As they approached the house, they saw a police car pull up, and a tall man get out and knock at the door. All Pat could think to say was,

"God! Not Churchill's brandy again."

Bill had to ask.

"Churchill's brandy? What are you on about now?"

"I'll tell you later, but, believe me, you won't believe me," The tall man was about to speak to Connor as the servicemen reached the front door. Seeing them, he turned.

"Good morning, gentlemen."

Bill and Pat shook hands and were introduced to Superintendent Spence of the Hampshire Police.

"Perhaps I could speak to all of you together inside. Under the circumstances, it might be better."

Connor led the way into the living room. Superintendent Spence began,

"Mr Cork, I am sorry to have to inform you of the death of Peter English. He was found hanged this morning in his rented house. As of now, we are not treating his death as suspicious."

Connor Cork's face drained of all colour. He sat down and remained silent. Pat and Bill stood and watched. Experience had taught both that there was nothing they could do to ease his pain. Pat asked,

"Bill, will you find Mum. She's in the village, shopping. I'll go to the schools and get Chris and Rachel." Bill nodded as he said,

"Should I tell her, Pat?"

Connor answered the question.

"Yes, Bill, please tell your aunt. You're part of our family now."

Paris was alive with rumours as the allied forces advanced, and the resistance became bolder. Brumner was about to leave the headquarters building when his desk phone rang. The voice he knew instantly terrified him. Erebus spoke.

"Major, you will go to the drop box apartment building at five o'clock tomorrow evening. Wait in the doorway, and please be in uniform."

Erebus and Vali, in German uniforms, greeted the punctual Brumner with the words.

"Now we go back to German HQ." All three were silent until arriving. Erebus demanded as he motioned toward a first-floor window.

"Can you confirm that is the general's office?"

Brumner nodded. Erebus opened the door of a Wehrmacht jeep parked directly beneath the window in question and signalled the keys were in the ignition. Then unseen, he secured an object under the driver's seat and carefully closed the door, all in less than sixty seconds.

Brumner asked,

"What are you going to do?"

Vali's look to Erebus was questioning, 'Do I tell him?' The answer was an indifferent shoulder shrug. Vali spoke.

"We are going to create a diversion, and then we are going to kidnap the general." Brumner asked,

"How."

Vali briefed Brumner, who responded with,

"I can help."

Vali said,

"Go on."

"You will need someone to drive the staff car and set off the decoy. With my rank, I can supply both." Vali looked at Erebus, who, this time, nodded his head.

In his office, General Breitner was confronted by two Waffen SS officers. One spoke.

"Good evening, general. We are here to offer you a way to stay alive as a civilized man or die be executed as a barbarian."

Ignoring and alarming the general at the same time, Vali went to the window where Brumner, at ground level, saw him close the blind - the signal to detonate the booby trap. He saw a particularly obnoxious homophobic Wehrmacht corporal and ordered.

"Corporal, move that car now."

The man opened the driver's door, which was attached by wire to the firing pin of a hand grenade Erebus had secured under the seat, which, four seconds later, exploded, killing him where he sat. Despite being dazed as the window was blown in, Breitner tried to call for help, forcing Erebus to knock him out. The headquarters sentries were sufficiently confused by the explosion not to challenge the two senior Waffen SS officers who helped the new commanding general to a car driven by Major Brumner. The four men drove away from the building toward the outskirts of Paris and the Allied lines.

Breitner woke with a thundering headache to find two colonels of the Free French forces and a Polish General along, with three men in civilian clothes, all pointing weapons at him. He was sitting on a chair in a barn of some sort and quickly realised he was in extreme danger. One of the colonels explained in English the general's current situation.

"You are a prisoner of the Free French Army and units of the resistance, so I suggest you listen exceedingly carefully."

The general was told the allies knew of Hitler's order, and they had an alternative plan for the surrender of Paris to Free French forces. Breitner was photographed and told his image would be circulated to all intelligence sections of advancing allied units. If Paris was destroyed, he would be known to every soldier in France and shot on sight or, if captured, tried for atrocities. Then it was explained if he agreed to assist in the surrender of the city, the allies would ensure he stayed alive. Breitner snapped nervously.

"Who is in command here?"

One of the men in uniform spoke in perfect German.

"That, general, is none of your business. We have explained your situation." Breitner was silent for at least two minutes, and then he spoke very slowly.

"What do you mean, 'assist in surrendering Paris'? There are many SS and Waffen SS units loyal to Hitler. How will you deal with them?"

The reply was instant.

"That, general, is why you are here. Now listen, any units likely to resist are to be ordered to defensive positions where they are exposed to air attack. If they refuse to surrender, the allied air forces will annihilate them. Any other units undecided about surrender will be persuaded by the resistance and former comrades under your orders." The man paused, then declared.

"If I put it another way, those troops which would prefer to stay alive and eventually return to Germany."

Out of sight, Erebus and Vali listened. Breitner was not stupid and clearly had survival uppermost in mind, reminding all of the reprisals if he was killed. A Polish general retorted,

"Should you remain loyal to Hitler, we will have to free you. But how long can you remain at liberty with the whole world hunting you? Once captured, you will hang, be in no doubt of that. This is your way out of the noose." The concealed listeners smiled at the pressure being applied so expertly.

Brumner drove the general back to the headquarters building and was officially appointed to Breitner's personal staff. He made the necessary arrangements and issued the orders as given by the general, which ensured that on the 18th of August 1944, the German forces occupying Paris surrendered virtually without violence. General Breitner was taken by Erebus and Vali to a safe house for onward transportation to British Military Intelligence for debriefing. As Brumner surrendered to the Free French forces, he was given parole to help with the many German troops and their dependants in the city. As he went to his friend's apartment a week after the surrender, he saw two men waiting outside the building. Vali and Erebus followed him in. As they sat and sipped wine, Brumner asked Erebus,

"You never seem to say much to me. Is it because you are homophobic, whoever you are?"

Erebus replied.

"Major, I went to an English public school where I was taught many things, amongst them, to play rugby, to sing in the choir and never to spend too long in the showers. Does that answer your question?"

Superintendent Spence gave evidence at the inquest of Peter English. His investigation into the deceased's affairs concluded that English had not been in debt and had recently filed a new will with his solicitor. The inquest returned a verdict of accidental death, and the Cork family attended his funeral and ensuing cremation, which was also attended by Mrs English, who did not introduce herself and, in fact, arrived late. After the service, the Cork family were approached by the executor of the English estate and informed that they were all beneficiaries of the 'Will' and would they please attend the reading.

As requested, they were present in the solicitor's office in Portsmouth when the 'Will' of Peter English was read. Also there was Mrs Margaret English, who arrived on time, but left the offices of Shawcross and Partners in a state of high agitation. She learned, through a process of elimination, that the Cork family had been left her late husband's entire estate with the exception of an amount of money, which was hers.

Connor had been willed the controlling interest in company shares. Rachel and Christopher had been left one thousand pounds each for, as the late Peter English wrote, bringing laughter and light into his life. Mary Cork was willed the contents of a furniture storage unit which she later discovered contained many beautiful and precious objet d'art, which were the result of Peter's many trips to antique and bomb damage sales in London. The remaining shares in E & C fabrications, along with a substantial amount of money, went to Lieutenant Commander Patrick Cork RN.

The Cork family desperately missed Peter English. The way he died caused Connor and Mary great concern about how the children would react. The younger Corks were told that they were in no way responsible. Suicide was a word that they all understood. Loneliness was what had driven the poor man to take his life. Peter had been a profoundly lonely man since his son had died. There was nothing anyone could have done for him.

The only person Mary couldn't console was her husband, who felt totally responsible for the suicide. He sat and stared into space, a pained, puzzled, sorrowful expression on his face searching for the missed signals which might have allowed him to help Peter. Added to this was his brother and how much to tell his nephew, who, she could see, he adored. Mary was desperately upset about the death herself, but she had a family to look after, and that family had now grown. For as long as Bill Cork was stationed in Europe, her house was his home.

Major Bill Cork returned to duty. Colonel Travers confirmed his reappointment as liaison officer to the British team responsible for the cross-channel fuel pipeline. The Channel was a literal minefield, and the pipe laying vessel would have a Royal Navy escort and minesweeper on station. Bill was quietly relieved at the posting. He would have time to further his engineering skills, especially in deep, intemperate water, and it meant he was based on the South Coast of England, so he would have the opportunity to get to see his new family as much as possible. But mostly, it meant he would not have to kill again, and all of a sudden, that had become of vital importance to him. Why - he didn't know - but it had.

Lieutenant Commander Pat Cork reported to Admiral Hilliard's office and was shown in by a sub lieutenant who was trying hard to conceal his admiration of Pat's battle honours. The admiral stood, shook his hand, motioned for him to sit and began.

"Well, lieutenant commander, how was your leave?"

Pat felt at ease with this man, for him, a good sign. Maybe a ship under Hilliard's overall command might not be so bad.

"Very good, thank you, sir."

Hilliard stood and closed the office door and, in an earnest voice, spoke.

"Well, Pat Cork, are you going to help me and the others under my command finish off these bloody Nazis?"

Amazed by the man's informality, Pat asked.

"What do you have in mind for me, sir?"

Hilliard's face broke into a broad smile as he exclaimed,

"Good man, Pat Cork. Good man." And continued.

"Admiral Spenser has expressed an interest in where you are going to serve." As he paused, memories of Norway and Simpson-Coyle surfaced.

"Now, there are a number of issues I would like to discuss. I don't like or trust these people involved in the so-called 'secret service.' There are far too many hidden agendas. I say this because Spenser has briefed me on a certain colonel and his methods. I think that you have had your bellyful of cloak and dagger stuff and maybe of this war as a whole. You have been through a lot - but so have many others."

The admiral sat in his chair.

"What I want you to consider is the command of a Castle Class Corvette, which was badly damaged by bombers in the Bay of Biscay. She's just completed repairs and refit. Then be assigned to the escort of the cargo vessels supplying the armies in Europe. The sea area is the English Channel and the North Sea. All she needs is a captain. I am desperate for experienced officers who know those waters. There are over a thousand ships bringing supplies to the armies on the European front on a daily basis. Will you become part of the escorts?"

Pat made an instinctive decision.

"When do I take command, sir?"

Hilliard was elated.

"Excellent! You take command immediately. Well done, and good luck Captain Cork."

Pat boarded HMS Longbow as commanding officer and was afforded all the rites and honours on the captain of one of His Majesty's ships. Command of any kind was one thing Pat had never wanted. Now, by force of extraordinary circumstances, it was what he had, and it gave him independence. The defeat of Germany was in sight, and all Pat Cork wanted was to see out the war and get on with his life. On escort duty in the English Channel, that just might be possible.

The new captain sat in his cabin and read the ship's list, which contained many familiar names. Nearly all of the highly experienced survivors of Snow Eagle had volunteered, so commissioning HMS Longbow would be relatively easy. Snow Eagle's officers had all been snapped up quickly by other ships crying out for battle-hardened men, except for Nigel Bellamy. Pat allowed himself to take the presence of 'flags' as a good omen for the ship.

Captain Cork had a total of one hundred and twenty men aboard HMS Longbow. A Corvette, much smaller than Snow Eagle, but a highly effective fighting ship in the right hands. He had yet to meet the new officers. The senior chief petty officer aboard, named Baker, was from Snow Eagle. A cockney who Captain Buchan had spotted as being a capable man and had promoted through the ranks. Now he was the captain's representative to the crew. Pat heard a knock on the cabin door, and it was Baker who entered and announced,

"A steward has been posted aboard, Sir."

Pat looked up, a little flustered. He was to have a steward! Well - so be it. It was naval tradition.

"Very good, chief."

A small, dapper rating entered the cabin. Pat was struck by the smartness. Chief Baker stood him to attention and then began to speak. Pat cut across him; he wanted to see if he was as smart as he dressed.

"Thank you, chief, but I'd like to hear this man speak for himself."

"Very good, Sir."

The rating began.

"Steward Fredo Grimaldi, sir."

"What were you doing before this, Grimaldi?" Pat asked, trying to sound like a mixture of Buchan and Loftus.

"This is my first ship. I recently enlisted, sir. I was steward aboard a merchant-man running meat from South America to the East Coast of North America. I then worked my passage on a tanker bound for Britain."

"You have an unusual name. Tell me about it, please?"

Grimaldi drew himself up to his full height.

"Sir, my family is originally from Monaco, and we moved to Uruguay when I was a boy. My father opened a hotel on the waterfront in Montevideo. He is still there, sir."

Just at that moment, there was a knock on the cabin door.

"Enter!" Pat said as he signalled to Baker to sit down. He would run the ship as the Snow Eagle had been commanded with disciplined informality. Respect and loyalty he would have to earn. A leading seaman put his head around the cabin door.

"Two officers reporting for duty, sir."

"Show them in, Tomkins."

"Aye, aye, sir."

A face he had not expected to see appeared in the door as he heard,

"Commander Larsen of the Royal Norwegian Navy reporting for duty, captain." Behind him was a much smaller man who looked as if he could have been of Italian or Spanish extraction.

"Lieutenant Forrestal, sir, reporting for duty on HMS Longbow."

By now the cabin was crowded. Pat ordered Baker and Grimaldi to carry on with their duties. As the captain's steward was leaving, he said,

"What time would you like your tea, sir?"

Pat looked at Baker, who, as usual, had the answer.

"I'll brief you on the captain's routine, now carry on."

Then in relative comfort, Captain Cork and Commander Larsen listened as the new officer explained that he had been in the navy since 1943. Before Longbow, he had been at the Admiralty in administration and planning, which could mean anything. Baker, as if by telepathy, knocked on the cabin door. He informed the captain that the officers' cabins were ready for them. Forrestal was dismissed and then, as they shook hands, Pat laughed.

"Lars, what are you doing here?"

Larsen, clearly delighted, replied,

"I am your First Officer, captain sir and Pat, may God help us all."

"Lars, how can you be my number one? You outrank me, and there must be far more important things for you to do. This ship is on escort duty back and forth across the channel."

"Captain, I have no idea other than I was requested by an admiral in the Norwegian Navy to take up this posting. Once I heard you were to be in command of the ship, I agreed immediately."

"Alright, I dare say someone will tell us what is going on, but this all begins to look like the workings of our former lords and masters in the SOE," Pat was surprised to hear himself almost whispering the words.

During the next two weeks, the ship was provisioned and underwent sea trials. She was quick and very responsive, with a top speed of fourteen knots which was fast enough to catch any U-boat. Longbow was well armed with anti-aircraft guns, hedgehog depth charges, torpedoes and three of the latest four-and-a-half-inch guns.

As he and Larsen got to know the ship and the crew, Pat began to settle into his role as captain and took stock of the ship. There was a curious extra cabin built into the wardroom that had two berths; it was more comfortable than the officers' quarters and halved their rest area.

Due to the experienced crew and hard work, by mid-September, HMS Longbow was declared ready for sea duty. A signal was received to make steam to the furthest point of the Portsmouth Naval Base and await orders.

In the middle of a long, late summer's afternoon, Longbow was hove to off a rarely used landing site. Visible from the bridge, a number of cars escorted by military police motorcycle riders and heavily armed Royal Marines were parked. A launch closed on the corvette as Captain Pat Cork received a signal which ordered him to restrict all access to the wardroom and not to disrupt the routine of the ship when certain individuals came aboard.

The first man up the side steps was Admiral Hilliard, closely followed by Brigadier Davies, then a colonel unknown to Pat. All three were polite but went immediately to the wardroom, where the colonel checked every porthole, bulkhead, floor, ceiling and piece of furniture. Finally, the soldier returned to the gangway with Pat then another man boarded the ship and astounded everybody by addressing the captain of HMS Longbow.

"Permission to come aboard, captain?"

Pat looked at the face of Admiral Menzies or, C, to those who knew he existed.

"Permission granted; come aboard."

The wardroom was sealed, and Maiden Aunt began.

"Lieutenant Commander Cork, you are probably somewhat surprised to see me here."

Pat thought, 'damn it - this is my ship'.

"Not in the least, sir."

Davies smiled and continued,

"You see, my boy, your experience and training have made you rather unique in two areas. You are an experienced and capable naval officer, and you have first-hand experience of covert Operations."

Pat saw Hilliard was watching him intensely as Davies continued to speak.

"Commander, I have a number of agents behind enemy lines; some of them you know from previous Operations. You know the welfare of these people is top of our list of priorities. The availability of a warship to effect escapes from enemy coastlines has been invaluable to us in the past. I have the utmost confidence in you to continue to provide this facility."

Pat knew he had been ambushed by the men in front of him and said,

"What, specifically, do you have planned for us, admiral?"

Hilliard nodded his head and looked a little guilty as he replied,

"The admiral will explain."

C began,

"Captain Cork, your ship has been equipped to carry rather unusual passengers. The cabin here is designed to accommodate two men. The walls and fittings conceal the latest listening devices. I believe the 'Cousins' refer to them as 'Bugs'. These devices are connected to tape recorders which will record every word said by your passengers whilst they are aboard your ship." The head of British Intelligence paused his eyes on Cork, then continued.

"This ship, alongside convoy escort, has a specific function which is to transport, in absolute secrecy, captured high-ranking German officers to the UK. The men who have joined your crew, Steward Grimaldi and Lieutenant Forrestal, are multi-lingual. Their role is to listen to every word these people say while aboard your ship. Forestall will also have responsibility for security. It is vitally important that utmost secrecy is maintained about this Operation. Larsen is the communications expert and will ensure that the recording equipment is on line. Your responsibility is to take this ship wherever a pick up is required, disappear into a convoy escort, cross the channel then detach when you are close enough to Portsmouth not to be noticed. Colonel, please carry on."

The Colonel explained how the German officers were to be taken to a secret location where they would be housed in relative comfort, where every word they said to each other would be recorded. C spoke again.

"Gentlemen, the enemy still has six million men under arms; we need to know the mood and morale of the high command in Germany and elsewhere. That is why we must analyse every word these men say."

Pat thought about how the wheel continued to turn. Now he was a gatherer along with his entire crew. As the briefing ended, Admiral Menzies said,

"Captain, please escort me to the launch."

As Pat and C walked the deck toward the ship's gangplank, Menzies stopped and looked around, then began to speak.

"Captain Cork, it is imperative that you maintain the appearance to all other ships in this theatre of Operations as just another escort. However, there is another pressing matter which is the identification of the person or persons who have been feeding the enemy information on resistance groups in the occupied territories. The war is drawing to a close, and already the new secret battle lines are being drawn up. What I cannot permit is the presence of a traitor deep within British Intelligence as we go into the peace."

Pat saluted the admiral as he left the ship with Brigadier Davies and the colonel, whose name still had not been disclosed. As the launch shoved off, Larsen came to him and said,

"Captain, we have our orders."

Pat read the orders and said to his number one,

"Right, let's set a course for the English Channel and the convoys."

He then asked to see Forrestal, who, when he entered the captain's cabin, was asked,

"Are there any members of the crew that you have suspicions about in your role as security officer aboard my ship?"

Pat was surprised at how angry he was that anyone could imply that the crew could be anything but trustworthy. He had sailed with these men since nineteen forty-one. Forrestal had no sea duty and had no idea of the authority of a Royal

Navy ship's captain when he replied,

"I really don't think that's any of your business, captain."

Captain Patrick Cork exploded.

"Oh, you don't, do you? Well, let me tell you something, Forrestal; I was playing cloak and dagger games for real in Norway while you were still doing your homework. On this ship, everything is my business because I have the responsibility of keeping the ship's company and this vessel safe. Now the men on this war canoe had a ship sunk not long ago. Prior to that dark day, every one of them had crossed the Atlantic more times than we would all want to remember."

Forrestal was beginning to lose colour in his face, and Pat found himself speaking with great confidence as he continued,

"The role of this ship is to protect convoys and sink enemy submarines or anything else with a swastika on it. You will do well to bear that in mind. Now I ask you again, are there any members of the crew you consider to be security risks?"

Forrestal, by now, had lost any arrogance and said,

"No one in particular, sir, but I have noticed from the ship's lists that there are a number of Irish men on board." Pat relaxed a little as the answer given showed Forrestal had no answer.

"I see, and how do you equate being Irish with potential treason?"

The security officer's answer was unexpected.

"I can't, sir."

"Then, lieutenant, why did you say it?" Pat snapped, his anger rising again.

"Sir, I have an Italian background on my mother's side. My father, being English, had me reading English and Italian history to allow me to have, as he put it, a balanced view of my parents' countries' history. If you'll forgive me, sir, the way the English behaved in Ireland, you could hardly blame the Irish. Pat relaxed completely and said,

"Good point. Sit down, please. What is your first name?"

For the next half hour, Franco Giacomo Forrestal received a potted history of the Snow Eagle and his captain's family tree. He left the captain's cabin far more aware of the importance of having a crew on your side rather than against you. He recalled the captain's words as his meeting came to an end.

"Every Irish man on this ship has had opportunities to breach security, none have, and that goes for the Welsh, Scottish and all other nationalities aboard. Lieutenant, let me tell you about the Irish since I am one. Tell an Irish man to do something; he'll ignore you. Ask him, and he will die for you. Remember that."

Bill Cork was becoming increasingly bored as the weeks went on. The weather in the English Channel was foul. The pipeline was working perfectly, and he was getting leave on an almost fortnightly basis, which allowed him time with his new family in Portsmouth.

Auntie Mary had also suggested he bring a friend if he chose to, so he asked Mandy to meet his uncle and aunt. She had initially refused, but when Bill said.

"Well, you're partly responsible for me finding them in the first place and I would love you to meet them. Pat and I mentioned you once or twice in passing."

Mandy answered,

"After that masterpiece of diplomacy, I really don't have any choice, do I?"

The routine of the pipeline posting allowed him to write on a regular basis. He could not reveal his whereabouts but could put more into his letters, much more. Soon after D-Day, Jessica began to receive letters on a regular basis, almost weekly, which delighted her. Each letter contained more day-to-day content - how Bill was living on a ship and every second weekend was able to get ashore.

Jessica Cork read her son's letters many times and often fell asleep with them in her hands. She tried to fathom from the letters how he was feeling. The words were crisp, and his handwriting was steady, which indicated he was well. She remained glued to the television and cinema newsreels for information on the conditions and the dangers her son was living in and facing.

Jessica was in contact with the Bruce family, who received letters from their daughter, from which she learned Mandy and Bill were meeting regularly in London. Charlie Rawlings had done his utmost to get information on his grandson's unit, but, again, the US Army was very tight-lipped about certain units and their activities. Then a letter arrived which was longer than usual, and the first page explained how she must keep the contents to herself until they could both decide what to do. Jessica read on and learned of the extraordinary events of D-day and Pat Cork. The ensuing introduction to Connor Cork and his family, 'our family' as Bill put it. How they had made him so welcome and the love they had showered on him, and how he was spending all his leave at their home. He wrote of Auntie Mary and Uncle Connor and his cousins Christopher and Rachel. Jessica was reading the letter on the porch of the Lake House, and without being aware, the tears were rolling down her cheeks. Bill then went on to talk about his cousin Pat Cork in detail, how they had met on a warship in Normandy and since then had become close friends. He wrote of the bravery and courage shown by all the men on the Normandy beaches and how nationalities and religion meant nothing in the middle of a battle. Jessica read of the question in Bill's mind as to how his father would react to the news that he had found his uncle, who was a kind, loving man who worried about Bill as much as he did his own son. How Auntie Mary made certain there was always a bed for him when ashore and that the war was now far less lonely. Finally, he needed her advice as to what to tell his father. Jessica put down the letter and cried for her son for many reasons. He was at war, and that terrified her. He was alone in a strange world, but, from his letter, his discovery of the Corks in England had made his life much better. She sensed that he was at peace when with Connor and Mary Cork and could only imagine what he had experienced. Just then, Catherine Buchanan approached her, saw she had been crying and asked.

"Jess, honey, what's wrong?"

"I don't know if wrong is the correct word Catherine," she replied and handed her the letter. Catherine read the letter and then looked at her dear friend, saying,

"Bill has gone to war and found some kind of peace in England. He sounds far more mature and seems to be at ease with himself. It's good that he has met Mandy. Oh, Jess, I'm just talking nonsense. How are you going to tell him that his father killed two men, and that's why his uncle hates his father? What are you going to do, Jessie?"

Jessica Cork cried as she answered,

"Catherine, this could bring the family together or tear it apart forever. I don't know what I am going to do. All I know is my son is alive and well and has found some peace and happiness. I want to meet my sister-in-law and my niece and nephews. I want to meet my brother-in-law. I feel so helpless. I wish I could cross the Atlantic now and thank them all for being so kind to my boy."

Catherine Buchanan waited for a minute and then said,

"Jessie, honey, they're not being kind; they're just being family."

33

Real Politik

Commander Larsen and Lieutenant Forrestal were testing the bugs. The regular one-two, one-two mantra had become boring, so Shakespeare, with an interesting Norwegian lilt, was heard in the wardroom. As the convoy neared the Normandy coast, Captain Cork was informed by Lieutenant Bellamy the ship would pass over the wreck of HMS Snow Eagle. Permission was requested from the C in C Channel escorts to hold a brief memorial service, which was quickly granted. HMS Longbow's crew made their tribute to fallen shipmates, twenty fathoms below. Then silently thanked heaven for the respite from the battle of the Atlantic and gladly returned to a relatively monotonous routine. Then the war caught up with them as Captain Cork received a radio signal, 'Detach escort group and steam for the North French Coast – coordinates to be confirmed later.' The signal was verified by the code word Maiden Aunt. The onshore contact was Erebus.

"Gentlemen, we have been ordered to deliver certain assets to British custody without the knowledge of our allies. Under no circumstances whatsoever are any of these assets to fall into Russian hands. If that seems probable, they are to be destroyed."

In silence, Odin and Maiden Aunt contained their distaste for the campaign about to begin. C thought of his early years at sea- before joining Naval Intelligence- in command of a fine ship and good crew and a fresh, clean ocean. Since then, he has lived in the world of smoke and mirrors. Where in a very short time, one could witness the dark side of humanity, lose God forever, and struggle to retain one's sanity. All the officers knew that they had to obey the given order, which was to provide the means for senior Nazis to escape justice.

"Do we tell our men why they are being ordered to risk their lives to save murderers and war criminals?", Davies asked, making no attempt to conceal his disgust. Spenser shrugged his shoulders.

"Our men are all highly intelligent - it won't take them long to figure out what is going on. Now let's get on with the details. Maiden Aunt, may we have an update on the current Operation, please?"

Davies began his report.

In Paris, the first man to benefit from the secret policy was acting in a less than grateful fashion. General Breitner was arrogantly demanding that the British meet their obligations.

"You have Paris undamaged. Now get me out of here. If the French catch me, they'll tear me apart."

One of the SOE officers, fast losing patience with their 'guest', radioed HQ that the 'package' was ready for collection. As ordered, Breitner was to be extracted under the noses of Britain's allies. Sergeant Major Reilly and Sergeant Mullen, codenamed the 'collectors', were already en route. Having watched a US Army driver refuel and park his battered, five-ton army truck and go for his coffee break, they stole the vehicle and began their journey to Paris. Mullen, sitting in the passenger seat as Reilly drove, remarked,

"I've always wanted to see Paris. What do you think its like, Cormac?"

"A bit like Dublin but with more people and wine instead of Guinness,"

Reilly responded emptily as he read on a stone road-side marker, 'Paris 10 Km'.

"Not far now," he mumbled. There was silence until the city began to appear on the horizon. Mullen enquired.

"What about our civvies? How do the French dress? What do you think, Cormac? How do we look in Mufti – like locals?"

Reilly replied,

"As long as they don't take us for soldiers! We are looking for the Avenue Victor Hugo here, you read the map."

The Parisians were boisterous. Sporadic gunfire could be heard. Reilly whistled at the Arc de Triomphe.

"That is beautiful. Maybe I'll come back here after the war."

Mullen's voice was urgent.

"Fine. Come back whenever you want, but right now, we make the collection and get out in one piece. Take the third exit off this roundabout, and then we're looking for the fifth building on the left. There it is, Cormac; stop here. You want the second floor, room 202."

As the truck came to a halt, Mullen stated.

"I'll wait here."

Reilly nodded and, climbing from the truck, went through the door of an elegant building, quickly finding room 202. Inside he was greeted casually; they had all shared too much to bother about rank when away from the top brass. Erebus started to update Reilly, then they were interrupted by Sergeant Mullen.

"I found a parking area at the back of this building, away from prying eyes and trigger-happy Frenchie's. We can leave using the back stairwell." The briefing resumed.

"The package is wanted by everyone, starting with the French and ending with the Russians. The Parisians Resistance has set up armed checkpoints and are demanding that all Germans surrender to them." Mullen silently assessed the package, Breitner. A tall, well-built man with pure blonde hair and, as Vali described it, 'an infuriating arrogance', personified by a refusal to wear civilian clothes. His pale eastern front pallor made him stand out from the SOE men tanned from active service under the French sun. He demanded.

"Who are these men?" Erebus answered.

"Allied servicemen." The German's arrogant stupidity continued.

"You will salute me. I am a general in the German Army."

Reilly spoke for everyone.

"You are a prisoner of war, you bollocks." Mullen scoffed as he sat down,

"Master race, my arse."

Erebus continued,

"Any ideas how we get him out?"

A quick conference concluded that the package –if it kept acting so stupidly – would be concealed in the lorry toolbox. Breitner loudly refused.

"I am a general in the German Army!"

Erebus spoke in a firm voice.

"You are no longer a general in anything. Listen, if you are captured, you will stand trial for war crimes in either Washington, Moscow or Paris and will hang. We, general, are your only way out."

Vali picked up where his comrade finished.

"Breitner, there are civilian clothes in the wardrobe which are roughly your size. Put them now. We need to be well away from Paris by nightfall. You will wear a hat and scarf to hide your face. We will not protect you unless we have your full cooperation."

Now visibly shaken, the 'package did as ordered. In his absence, Erebus asked,

"Why the Yank truck, gentlemen?"

Mullen explained,

"The countryside is in chaos; the French resistance is stealing anything they can get and fighting between themselves for anything that's left. The Yanks are giving them transport to stop them shooting at each other. They were using captured Gerry kit, but the flyboys in the RAF and US air forces are strafing anything German that moves. It's not ideal, but it's the best option. Believe me, out there in the countryside, it's like the Wild West."

Breitner appeared minutes later dressed like, as Sergeant Mullen later described, a 'pox doctor's clerk'. His lower face was concealed by a scarf and a hat sitting down across his forehead. The men left the apartment.

The 'yank truck' was standard design - a solid cab which opened into a rear section with benches that ran parallel to the front seats and covered with a tarpaulin hung on a tubular frame. Reilly and Mullen were in the front. Erebus and Vali sat on either side of the German on the next bench. Just as Mullen was about to pull into the main street, Erebus warned the German.

"Breitner, should you make any attempt to escape between here and our destination, I will kill you."

Breitner was silent as he seemed to shrivel. The lorry crawled west through streets packed with celebrating Parisians. From his driving seat, Reilly could see German troops herded together in make-shift corrals. The crowd were shouting abuse as they pelted them with rotting food. After Norway, the Irish man could feel little sympathy and concentrated on driving. A glance in the rearview mirror showed Reilly that Erebus and Vali were relaxed, as if taking a breather. Suddenly, a very drunken aggressive man jumped in front of the truck waving a machine pistol, demanding identity papers. Erebus shouted a reply in French from the rear seat; the man stood his ground. Mullen, side-arm at the ready, accompanied Erebus as he climbed down from the cab. Reilly assessed the crowd as merry and ignored the developing stand-off. On the road, the drunk started to shout louder, waving his weapon dangerously. When disarmed by Erebus, he reacted by wildly lunging at him. Mullen rendered the man unconscious with a short chop behind the ear and gently slid him to the pavement. The firearm disappeared into the lorry cab. Some of the revellers approached the prone man looking aggressively at the SOE men. Then laughter ensued as Mullen held an imaginary glass to his lips implying the man had too much wine. As the truck moved away, Erebus spoke.

"Sergeant, you must show me that concealed chop. Never saw you take him out." Mullen acknowledged the compliment. Vali finished examining the machine pistol, then showed it to the prisoner.

"Is this one of yours?" Breitner displayed his worth even at this early stage, replying tersely,

"This weapon is used by the NKVD, Soviet Red Army political police."

Vali nodded; already, the questions were beginning. What was a Russian made weapon doing in Paris while the Eastern Front was still active?

The journey to the North West Coast of France began revealing. The French authorities were trying to re-establish law and order. Reports of some people arrested at unofficial roadblocks, facing kangaroo courts, which meted out cruel punishments for fraternisation or collaboration, were common. Any challenges to the SOE men were cleared up quickly by Erebus, who could speak French with a regional accent if need be. About twenty kilometres from the coast, Reilly radioed confirmation that the package was ready for despatch.

Odin acknowledged the signal and replied with a grid reference for the pickup point on the French Atlantic coast and orders for Erebus, Vali and the 'collectors' to return to SOE HQ.

Spenser assuaged his disgust at helping Nazis to escape justice by acknowledging that Breitner and his kind possessed invaluable information about Russian counterintelligence. The 'KGB'. Its operatives were in the allied area of Operations, gathering information and recruiting agents for the new, peace-time intelligence war. The Russians were kidnapping scientists and engineers from the defeated German units in the East. The allies did the same in the west. The list of German specialists was long, and everybody wanted them. The Cold War, as it would be called, was just beginning.

Captain Cork checked the coordinates supplied by Odin and set a southwesterly course which would take HMS Longbow away from the English Channel to the island of Ushant.

Breitner remained silent during the forty-eight-hour journey, his arrogance gradually wilting as his isolation became real. The truck stopped by a small jetty where a Royal Navy sea boat waited. The men boarded, and as the crew rowed away from the shore, a kilometre inland, a lorry burned. All traces of the collection were erased. The US Army driver never did find out where the truck went to, and his CO put it down to the fact that the American troops were not used to the habits of 'foreign folks'.

About two hundred and fifty yards offshore, the outline of HMS Longbow became clear. The captain, Lieutenant Commander Patrick Cork, stood on the deck. Breitner came aboard and was escorted by Cork and Chief Petty Officer Baker to a cabin. Neither man spoke until inside. The door was closed, and the captain began.

"General, this will be your accommodation until we reach our destination. Under no circumstances will you leave this area of the ship. Your meals will be served in the wardroom next door, where you will eat alone. Should you feel seasick, you will call for the wardroom steward, who will escort you to the heads. At no time are you to speak to any crew members other than your guards. Please cooperate during the passage. Are there any questions?"

Breitner, trying to maintain his arrogant demeanour, announced.

"I have two questions."

Cork nodded.

"One, what is your name, captain?"

The reply was monotone,

"You have just answered your question. My name is 'captain'. Next."

"Captain, what are the heads?"

"The steward will explain. Now, if there is nothing else. Goodnight to you," Cork said as he turned away.

The ship set a course out into the Bay of Biscay, where it joined a convoy coming up from South Africa and resumed escort duties. The officers' quarters were somewhat crowded, as Erebus and Vali shared with Larsen and the captain. Reilly and Mullen used the chief petty officer's mess deck. HMS Longbow again detached from the convoy escort group just off the South East Coast of England and made for Portsmouth Naval Base at full speed. During the voyage, Breitner's contacts were the multi-lingual steward, Grimaldi, and Lieutenant Forrestal. His guards were the recently promoted Petty Officers, Sean Canavan and Fergus McNally. Lars ensured the recorders were online. There was some alcohol available; surprisingly, Breitner found Rum pleasant. A reasonable amount quickly loosened the German's tongue, revealing some of his personality. Breitner's every word was recorded, and the tapes went with him as he was driven to the stately home, which was to be his comfortable prison.

The weapon taken from the drunken resistance fighter was sent to Intelligence and substantiated Williamson's theory that the Russians were arming communist resistance cells in Western Europe, further confirming the Soviets were active in allied countries. Longbow's crew were given leave as Pat Cork had a few drinks aboard with some old friends who would if asked, declare, in the highest court in the land, that none of them had ever met before.

Admirals Menzies and Spenser were pleased with the first collection - the intelligence coming from Breitner was initially good. The General's willingness to cooperate increased greatly when told the British had received a demand from the Russians that he be arrested on sight and handed over to them to stand trial for war crimes.

C attended a meeting with the Prime Minister, where it was explained that Roosevelt had proposed increased cooperation between the newly formed Office of Strategic Services, or OSS, and British Intelligence. Both old Trans-Atlantic Hands they knew what the Americans 'Cousins' really wanted and why? The OSS believed the British Intelligence community was - as usual - withholding product. Specifically, technical data and identities of captured scientists. C's reaction to this inference was standard for any intelligence service - deny everything. Churchill was supportive, but the war was not over, and needs must. Paris had fallen, and the push into Europe and Germany was gathering momentum. The meeting ended with C being asked to arrange for a number of American officers to work with the 'collectors'. An hour later, Maiden Aunt was summoned to C's office.

Mr Paxton waited. The Doodlebug engine was loud and close, then a terrifying silence followed by an explosion. This time Dollis Hill had been lucky. Paxton had seen his family and business through the Blitz and air raids. Mrs Paxton refused to leave her home, and Barbara, his daughter, despite her ambitions and politics, would not leave her Mum. Everyone had hoped after D-Day, the bombing would stop. Now, in 1944, the strain caused by the terrifying 'flying bombs' was wearing everybody down. Paxton thought, 'How much longer? How much more do we have to take?'

He whispered,

"When are we going to find peace? When will it be over?"

At that point, the door of his shop was opened by two young people. Paxton greeted them.

"Good morning, and how can I help you?"

The answer came in the form of a glorious smile from the young lady as her companion spoke in a broad American accent.

"Good morning to you, sir. Could you tell us where the Cork family house is?"

Major Bill Cork had been given seven days leave and spent it with Mandy in London, from where she was hoping to get to Europe and report from the warzone first-hand. Their reunion had been as passionate as ever, but now there was something more. Both sensed it. The war was coming to an end. When; no one knew. Mandy felt that Bill was looking for something more than a deep friendship and a need to be near someone from home. As a couple, they had stayed with the Corks many times. Mary Cork had given Mandy an open invite to stay anytime when Bill was away, an invitation she willingly accepted and often left London for a long weekend in the country.

During the week, Bill talked of how the discovery of his family in England had changed his perspective, and how he wanted a family. How important family was to all people. Then, on a whim, he announced they were going to see where his cousins had grown up.

"Pat is always talking about this part of London and how happy they were there." The young Texans headed for Dollis Hill, where Bill spotted, as he put it, a 'landmark'.

"Paxton's - the local store. Pat met his first girlfriend there. Her father owns it." Mandy grabbed his hand.

"Bill, will you please wait for a minute? Let's have a look around the area. It's really pleasant here. The English love their trees. Look, every house has one planted outside - and by the way, the word is 'shop,' not 'store'."

Bill responded by squeezing her hand,

"The word is, 'lovely'. The English always say, 'lovely'. Nobody says 'pleasant' except maybe Noel Coward."

Mandy laughed out loud.

"Major Bill Cork, I believe you're becoming an Anglophile. Noel Coward – wow - I didn't expect that!" he fired back.

"You reporters are far too cynical. Let's go and say hello to Pat's friend, Mr Paxton."

Once Bill had introduced himself and Mandy, Paxton could not help but say,

"Major, if I may say so, you and your cousin Pat are so alike. You could easily be taken for brothers." He was delightedly surprised as Mandy reacted with delicious laughter.

"Now the Cork's house is just up the road. Take the first left, and it's the third house on the left, opposite the park. There are some military people staying there, so it might be best not to knock. Now, when you've finished, come back, and I'll make a sandwich for you to eat in the park, which is lovely right now."

The day went quickly, and Paxton kept to his word, dispatching the couple with a sandwich each, but not before asking after the Cork family and especially Pat.

"He's an officer in the Royal Navy now - a Lieutenant Commander, no less. Well, wish them all my best."

As the young couple walked out of the shop, Paxton smiled at the thought of his daughter's reaction when he told her about her former boyfriend. As for him, he was immensely proud of the Corks for the way they had become part of the war effort. He told his wife and Barbara later over dinner,

"They could have all gone to Ireland. They didn't; they stayed and helped us. Pat has risked his life many times - so have many other young Irish people. Look at his cousin Bill Cork, all the way from Texas, a major in the US Army and his lovely girl, Mandy, a journalist. There's the Australians, the New Zealanders, the Canadians, the Indians and West Indians, people from all over the world. Hitler never thought the good people of the world would stand up to him. Well, we have, all together, and we're going to beat him and soon."

His wife and daughter sat in silence. They had never seen him so animated; his voice filled with excitement and pride. Paxton continued,

"The war will be over soon, and we will be there to see it. Thanks to people like the Corks and millions of others like them. That young lady, the journalist Mandy, wants to write a story on the shop and how people coped during the bombing. I said yes. She's going to call back soon and interview me."

Barbara sat in silence, and later, she remembered her words to Pat,

'I think you'll be very good at war'. Now he was a Lieutenant Commander - he had proved her right. She had always sensed that her former boyfriend could be anything he wanted to be, but she had also always harboured the silent fear that he was capable of doing anything if it was necessary and justified. As he once remarked,

"It doesn't matter what the job is if it's necessary - get it done."

Mandy woke first and sat up in a half daze, then saw Bill and laid her head on his chest. She let him sleep as the story about people like Mr Paxton and all

Londoners formed in her mind. She would write about the humour, the resilience and the struggle to survive the Blitz and the rations. This might just interest Americans who had never known food shortages or nightly bombing raids. She would not write about the grief of loved ones when the dreaded telegrams arrived. The press office was already fully aware of the US losses after D-Day. American families need not be told about grief. That was now universal. Her lover stirred and whispered,

"Good morning."

Mandy replied with a kiss. As she settled again on his chest, Bill spoke.

"Mandy, I go back today, and there's something I want to say. I don't know what I want to do when the war is over, but this I do know - this I am as certain of as much as anything in my life - I do not want to do anything without you beside me."

Her head still, she picked her words slowly.

"Bill, what are you saying? Are you asking me to marry you? Because if you are, you've changed in a huge way. Bill Cork does not do things spontaneously. What's happened? I need to know now."

"Mandy, since I've met my family here in England, I've come to realise how important family is. I kidded myself I was a loner. I'm not. You ask me what's changed. I have. I need you with me – but not as a part-time thing. Life is empty without love, and I love you. You are everything to me now. So, yes, I am asking you to marry me when we get home. Properly - with all the trimmings, in front of our families on the Double B. Mandy, will you marry me?" Mandy sat up and brushed her hair from her face.

Yes, Bill, I will marry you. But you must ask me again when we get home, and I will say yes again."

Looking delighted and confused, Bill asked,

"Why again?"

"Because lover, when my friends ask me when did Bill propose? I can hardly tell them after we'd spent the night making love, and I was naked in his arms."

Major Bill Cork of the US Army Engineers returned his posting and was on station when he received a signal to report to Colonel Travers ashore immediately.

Travers was profoundly suspicious of the men in his office. Four had arrived without notice. The man who appeared to be in charge carried a letter of authority signed by General Omar Bradley, now a four-star US general. The letter ordered Travers to compile a list of officers with experience in covert Operations. Then, draw up procedures to assist the Office of Strategic Services (OSS) in establishing teams to work in the European theatre of Operations.

"Office of Strategic Services? What exactly does that mean, may I ask?"

The answer was extremely slow in coming.

"Colonel, we are the intelligence arm of the US Armed Forces. That is all you need to know. Is that clear?"

Travers just about controlled his reply.

"Ok. Now that you have explained what you people do, would anyone care to identify himself? I'm not looking for your ancestry, just a name, perhaps? This is a custom in the real world. People tell other people their names. It's a long-established tradition and works rather well."

Travers waited in silence, hoping he had caused enough offence to provoke a reaction from the man with the letter, who was at least six feet two. Thin with hair crew-cut nearly to the scalp, skin pale and long spindly fingers attached to bony hands and looked so physically weak that Travers was certain he had never done any military service. His eyes, on the other hand, were clear, signalling a very alert mind. The other men varied in shape and size. One who stood just behind the long one -Travers had already nicknamed him - was the exact opposite. Just over five feet and rotund - his raincoat must be boys extra-large - Travers thought spitefully. Skin colour was a similar hue to the others - deathly pale. Again, the hair was crew-cut to the scalp. His glasses were small and almost embedded in the skin of his nose. Surprisingly, he began to speak.

"Colonel, we do not have to tell you anything. You have seen our letter of authority. That is all you need."

Travers remained calm.

"As you do not see fit to give me a name, I will speak to all of you. Now listen well. The officers you are requesting to establish teams are men who have seen active service. They are accustomed to working with men who are physically fit and who can deal with extreme conditions. Gentlemen – and I use the word guardedly – you do not look like men who would meet those basic criteria." Travers looked at the remaining men, who were both a standard height with brown and black hair, respectively. The raincoats seemed to be almost a uniform, although none seemed to fit particularly well. The 'long one' spoke.

"Colonel, we appreciate your concern for our welfare."

"Your welfare!" Travers exclaimed.

"Whatever your name is, I don't give a damn what happens to any of you. I worry only about my men. They have been in this war from the get-go, and I am going to make sure they get home alive. You will be a liability to them, and that I will not allow. As for your veiled threat, Omar Bradley and I have known each other for years. Why don't we go and see him and see what he says about the whole shebang? As for the intelligence arm of the US Forces, you may be spooks but only in the context of being ghosts. God! Don't you people ever get any fresh air or exercise?"

The 'long one' looked shaken by the outburst and began to speak, hoping he was being more respectful and certainly more open about who they were.

"Colonel, please forgive me. If I may, I will tell you as much as I can. We, sir, are all physicists. We are alumni of various Ivy League Colleges. We know very little of Intelligence, and we have received orders to make contact with you and your officers to gather information on the V1 and V2 weapons."

Travers sat down and invited the men to do likewise. They were definitely not trained intelligence officers. If they were, their interest would be not in the rockets but in the man who designed them. These men had been assigned the task of gathering as much information as possible about the German rockets. What they hadn't been told was that they would have to work with Travers' officers in tracking down and capturing the man who invented the bloody things. He asked the men to return later the following day. He would need time to draw up a list of suitable officers. The 'long one' readily agreed.

The next morning, another member of the OSS arrived in Travers' office. A medium-sized man with short, black hair and a disarming smile, which, he thought, put people at ease. In the case of the colonel standing in front of him, he could not have been more wrong. Travers had always prided himself on his ability to weigh men up quickly. The man named Oppenheim worried him - this guy he could not figure out. He gave no signals which would allow Travers to begin to like, dislike or be indifferent to him. One thing he was certain of, from the second he laid eyes on him, his senses were silently screaming, 'This man is not to be trusted.' The object of Travers' profound mistrust spoke.

"Colonel, I will tell you terms of reference for the mission we are about to begin. The US Government has taken a considered calculation on the position which will be taken by the Russian dictator, Stalin. The Red Army has been ordered to capture as many specialist scientists and technicians as possible, regardless of the human cost. We in the OSS, Colonel, have to adopt a similar policy. Secrecy is everything in this type of work. Therefore, I think I should tell you that any of your officers who are assigned to this mission will be subject to secrecy regulations which are themselves secret."

"Now, just a minute," Travers butted in.

"Are you telling me that my officers will be under your sole command?"

The dark-haired man simply nodded his head. Travers was grateful for his silence - the man's southern drawl was hugely irritating. He continued trying to extract information from Oppenheim.

"What about leave and communication with the soldier's families? Are they allowed to write home?"

"Only with my express permission, colonel."

He then produced an identification card which revealed his authority. Travers doubted even General Bradley would go head-to-head with this guy. For the first time in a long time, Travers had to admit he was completely outgunned and out-flanked.

Bill Cork was introduced to the scientists, or the OSS operatives, as they were officially known. The men introduced themselves, 'the long one' as usual doing most of the talking. The meeting took the form of an interview with Bill asking the questions. What Cork needed to know soon became apparent. Each scientist was eminently qualified in his academic discipline but, as a field operative, failed every requirement for active service. Travers listened as Bill summarised the interviews.

"Sir, irrespective of the gentlemen's scientific eminence, there is no way they can operate in the field. To put it bluntly, they're about as suitable for active service as a wheelchair is in a minefield."

The Colonel did not attempt to contain his laughter. Bill looked at him with concern on his face.

"Sir, what are we going to do with these men? Our orders come from General Bradley. We have to think of something - sending them into the field is a death sentence."

Travers recovered his composure,

"Bill, we are going to propose the following to Bradley. The scientists will be placed with a unit near the front. Each man will be accompanied by an experienced officer acting as bodyguard and field operative. We will find the German scientists or engineers the OSS is looking for. The scientists will be given full access to them once they have been secured behind the front. What do you think, major?"

Bill relaxed - which Travers took as approval.

"What name do we give this Operation, sir?" Bill asked. Travers answered with a hint of irony,

"Why! Operation Javelin, Bill. What else would we call it?"

Before he could reply, Bill Cork was asked to select three officers to join the Operation.

"Excuse me, sir, may I comment?"

Odin nodded.

"Please do, brigadier."

"Thank you. If I am reading this properly, there is now a distinct change in our strategy regarding the man who is responsible for the 'V' weapons. Is that correct sir?"

Spenser sat down.

"Yes, brigadier. Our orders are to keep this man under surveillance and then, at the first opportunity, get him out of German hands into ours."

Davies went on regardless.

"Sir, are you saying, if necessary, we keep this man alive whilst he is still working for the Nazis?"

"Yes, Maiden Aunt. That is precisely what I am saying."

Having been debriefed on the extraction of Breitner, Erebus and Vali were ordered to a meeting with Odin and Maiden Aunt. Admiral Spenser began with a brief statement.

"Gentlemen, The V1 and V2 or 'flying bombs', are causing heavy losses amongst the civilian population of British cities. We have been ordered to insert agents into occupied territory to find the man leading the design team responsible for the V weapons. His name is Werner Von Braun."

Erebus spoke first.

Do we know where he is, sir?" Spenser shook his head as he answered.

"We can assume he will close to the launch sites." Vali contributed.

"I take it the sites are in the Baltic region." The Admiral confirmed.

"That, commander, is exactly where they are."

Vali continued.

"Sir, we know that region well. It wouldn't be too hard for us to hide there until we find the package." Maiden Aunt spoke.

"Gentlemen, I appreciate your enthusiasm but understand, unlike other packages, this man must be brought out alive at all costs. Is that clear?" Both replied.

"Yes, sir."

"Right, as of now, you are both on standby for this Operation. You will return to active service with the front-line units until the order is given to activate the mission."

Erebus beat Vali to the question.

"Why the delay sir?"

Maiden Aunt replied in almost conspiratorial tones,

"The V1 and V2 rockets are produced at a research centre near Peenemunde in northeast Germany. Four nights ago, 617 squadron of Bomber Command attacked the facility killing many of Von Braun's team. We received our orders after the raid." He paused, then looked into the SOE agents' faces.

"Gentlemen, we do not know if Von Braun was killed or gone to ground. Your job is to make your way to Peenemunde and wait until he or his team appear again. If the V1 and V2 rockets start flying again, it will be safe to assume Von Braun is alive, and your mission will go ahead. Right, that's all I have to say other than good luck to both of you" Odin left the room as Professor Williamson came in. Davies said,

"The Prof, here, will give you some personal information on Von Braun."

"Thank you, sir," Williamson began,

"Werner von Braun is a man steeped in Nazi ideology who believes fervently in the final victory of the 'Master race'. The Nazis have allowed him to carry out experimentation supported by unlimited labour and resources to develop technology which is, as we know to our cost, highly advanced. Because of his success, Von Braun has the full support of Hitler and is accordingly heavily guarded. If he has a weakness, it just might be his brother, who is nowhere as academically gifted and never leaves his elder brother's side." Maiden Aunt concluded the briefing.

"Trailing him will not be easy, but we must know where he is at all times."

As German units were overrun, the number of prisoners taken to the debriefing centre increased. The Wehrmacht command structure was falling apart, and regular soldiers were being replaced by fanatics or raving madmen with one thing in common - adoration of Hitler. During this period, HMS Longbow was to the unknowing quietly on convoy duty between England and the Channel ports. Some senior officers from other escort groups, aware of her vastly experienced crew, requested the ship join their commands. The reply from the Admiralty was that Longbow was needed where she was, and please do not ask again.

Captain Cork and his crew ferried men from various points on the coast of France and became experts in ignoring the high-ranking prisoners in the wardroom. They did not discuss the matter when ashore. The security officer, Lieutenant Forestall, was pleasantly surprised at this attitude. He learned why the ship's company was so security conscious from Chief Petty Officer Baker.

"Sir, the crew of this ship, have one aim in life, and that is to get through the war in one piece. We have all been Mid-Atlantic in a force ten with U-boats all around us and merchantmen burning. We know full well that the current deployment of the ship is as cushy as it gets. None of us are going to spoil that. If Adolph Hitler himself was aboard, it's none of our business; does that make it clear, sir?"

Forrestal, though stunned, managed to say,

"Perfectly clear, chief - thank you."

When he reported the conversation to the captain, he was told,

"These men have been at sea for nearly five years. Sailors, as you will know by now, are ferociously superstitious. What is on everybody's mind is how much further we can push our luck. We are a taxi service to some very nasty people. That is, however, none of our concern; we just do as we are told. Now relax and let me know if you have any problems with your report to whomever it is for."

The news from the front was good, and the fighting men of all services openly talked of being home for Christmas 1944. On a lovely afternoon in September 1944, Mandy Bruce and Mr Paxton were sitting in the park near his shop where she and Bill had eaten sandwiches. The article, in her opinion, was very good. A draft sent to her editor had been warmly received, and Mandy was asked to write a series of articles to describe the social history of London during the war years. Paxton had opened up to this lovely young American about the English feelings about the conflict; his insights were cogent and passionate. Paxton's compassion for all people involved in the war shone through, including the German and Japanese peoples. The park was full of people enjoying the sunshine - a few servicemen home on leave and some older couples, but there were no children. The atmosphere was relaxed as if everybody was beginning to dream that the end might be in sight. No one in the park that afternoon heard the V2 rocket as it exploded, killing everyone instantly. The houses all around the park were destroyed, bringing more death. The silence after the explosion was all-enveloping. The bodies of some of the victims were never found, such was the force of the explosion. There was some relief that the remains of Mandy Bruce and Mr Paxton were not amongst the bodies obliterated. News of the tragedy spread amongst the people of North London quickly. The final death count was 121. Paxton's store, which had been in business for nearly thirty years, was destroyed. Barbara Paxton had been at college when her parents were killed. Mrs Paxton was in the shop, covering for her husband. The news from the military authorities that the Cork family home had been destroyed reached Connor first. He automatically asked after the tenants and was told they were all alive and well. The person on the phone had no idea of civilian casualties and, when Connor asked, refused to comment on the cause of the explosion. Mary Cork was at home when the phone rang. Her husband told her as much as he knew and then left the office, having agreed with his wife that they would go home to Dollis Hill early the next morning.

HMS Longbow was tied up in Portsmouth Naval Base - her crew on leave. The ship had been at sea for four months and was due an overhaul and boiler clean. It was early in the morning, and Lieutenant Commander Cork was just about to leave the ship when his landline cabin phone rang. Baker picked up the handset.

"HMS Longbow, good morning."

A woman asked,

"May I speak to the captain, please? It's a personal matter."

Baker didn't doubt the caller.

"Captain, a call for you, sir."

"Thank you, chief. Oh, by the way - I'll be leaving soon. I'll be at my parents' if you need me." Pat took the handset.

"Hello! Lieutenant Commander Cork speaking."

He knew the voice instantly.

"Pat, its Barbara. Pat, they've killed mum and dad. There was some sort of rocket. They're both dead, Pat; they've gone forever. Help me, please, Pat, help me."

His mind was calm.

"Barbara, where are you now?"

"I'm at college in London. The house has been destroyed. Everything is gone, Pat, everything."

He tried to reassure her as his mind went over the train timetables.

"Barbara, I will be in London by one o'clock. Stay where you are - I will come to you. We'll work out what to do after that. Is that alright with you?"

Her voice was verging on hysterical.

"Yes Pat, I'll wait in college. Please come, Pat, please come."

The Cork family met at Portsmouth station. The coincidence was kind and cruel. Pat sat his parents down and told them of Barbara's phone call.

"Mum, Dad, Mr Paxton and his wife have been killed by a flying bomb of some description. I'm going to London to meet Barbara." Connor felt sick as his wife explained to her son why they were on the train then she broke down. The other passengers sympathetically looked away. Public displays of grief had become common. This family was as entitled as anyone to grieve. The train journey seemed to take forever. Then the capital made its presence felt as the train pulled into Waterloo Station - noise and smoke - even on a summer's day. They decided that Pat would go to UCL, collect Barbara and then bring her to Dollis Hill. If she had nowhere to stay, she could come back to Portsmouth with them. Dollis Hill seemed as welcoming as it always had. Memories flooded back for Mary and Connor as the taxi drove away. The street where they had lived was devastated, and the houses on one side of the park literally flattened. The area was cordoned off, with ARP wardens and police everywhere. Ambulances were coming and going. Connor approached the chief warden, a man he had known before the war who, when he saw him, gave a smile of recognition.

"Hello, Connor. It's not good, I'm afraid. Over one hundred dead - we are still trying to identify some. God rest them. The park was full of people - it was such a lovely day. It's been confirmed that the Paxtons have been killed, him in the park, his wife in the shop. How is your family, Connor - all well, I hope?" The man seemed to be rambling. He looked at Connor with tears in his eyes.

"We'd hoped and prayed that this sort of thing was over. Jesus, we lost fifty people from the road on the park alone. Your house is gone, Connor."

He waved to Mary, who was speaking to a policeman. Connor turned to see her put her head in her hands, and he rushed to his wife's side. The police officer spoke with a soft clear voice,

"Mr Cork, we are having the devil's own job identifying the casualties even though most of them are local people. I am sorry if I upset your wife, but we are asking everybody for help. Would you confirm what your wife has told us? Do you know an American journalist by the name of Miss Amanda Bruce who was based in London?"

Mary Cork answered the question.

"Con, they want us to identify a body - a young woman - to confirm that it's Bill's girlfriend, Mandy. She's dead Con."

34

Greenwood's Wisdom

Pat sat next to his mother as the hospital orderly approached. His father had attempted to contact Colonel Travers in the hope of reaching Bill. The hospital switchboard had been very helpful, unlike the US Army, which flatly refused to give any information on Colonel Travers or Major William Cork. Connor tried to explain about Mandy and Bill but was told politely,

"Sir, if the couple aren't married, there is nothing we can do. Perhaps the next of kin could help?" He returned to his son and wife as they stood to follow the orderly - an elderly man with soft eyes who ushered them into a chapel where Mandy Bruce was laid out. Her hair had been combed. Her face was peaceful. A policeman – again elderly – introduced himself as the coroner's officer.

"All that is required is confirmation that the deceased is Amanda Bruce."

At that point, the door to the chapel opened, and the American Press Bureau lady came in with her male colleague. Both broke down in tears at the sight of, as the lady sobbed, 'Our beautiful Mandy'. The Bureau man had official identification papers, which solved the policeman's problem. The body could not be released to anyone other than next of kin. Thankfully, the US press bureau personnel were de facto next of kin under US wartime legislation. The tearful man advised Pat that, as the deceased was a US citizen, the US Press Bureau would inform Miss Bruce's family of her death and would make all the arrangements for her body to be taken home. Pat Cork breathed a huge, silent sigh of relief. Now Bill had to be told of Mandy's death with no obvious way of contacting him or his CO. Then Pat thought of the Royal Marines. Wherever Travers was, the CO of 62 Commando should be able to contact him. After an hour of phone calls, Pat found himself speaking to Colonel Weir. The conversation was to the point. Both men had become accustomed to receiving and imparting tragic news. Pat asked if he could tell Major Cork of the tragedy. Weir was kind but adamant that Colonel Travers would be informed of the circumstances. He finished saying.

"The men are US Army personnel; the chain of command will be used as in all cases." Pat thanked him.

Now another bereaved person called for his attention. Barbara was staying at her flat near college while the arrangements for the burial of her parents were finalised. Pat was by her side constantly throughout the terrible week which followed their deaths. Each night he stayed in the flat. They slept in the same bed, but there was no sex. Barbara just held him as she cried herself to sleep. During the day, she talked incessantly about her parents as if trying to bring them back to life. Pat only spoke when asked a question. Experience taught him nothing could ease her grief - which she would have to deal with alone. Then came the funerals, held simultaneously. Local dignitaries, the Mayor, local councillors and the MP for the area were all polite and suitably respectful. Mary and Connor Cork were in a state of shock, saying very little. Barbara managed to speak to everyone and, on the surface, appeared calm. When asked to stay just for a few more days, Pat reluctantly agreed. Refusal was impossible. He saw his parents off at Waterloo but desperately wanted to be with them as in a few short days left before going to sea. HMS Longbow and the war were calling. So far, Barbara had mourned her parents and had mentioned her plans for the near future – something vague about going to America. Lieutenant Commander Cork had seen many people grieve. There was a reasonably predictable pattern of behaviour – first the numbness, then blind anger. Pat never left Barbara alone and waited for the inevitable explosion of rage that comes with unexpected, unexplained death.

Travers listened carefully to his Royal Marine counterpart. The Scotsman had made as good an impression on him as his officers and men had made upon Bill Cork. Weir tried to give Travers an idea of how Bill would react. The conversation lasted some time as both men showed their respect and affection, not alone for Major Cork but for so many young men like him. They knew they could not lessen his grief. If they could just give some little relief from the pain, then both believed they had fulfilled their primary responsibility as commanding officers - the welfare of their men. Travers put down the handset and thought about the dead young woman. He had never met Amanda Bruce, but Cork was not a promiscuous man, this woman meant a lot, and her death would affect him profoundly. Travers wanted to recommend Major Cork for compassionate leave but knew the army would take the view that, as the couple were not married. There was no more to be done than inform the officer of her death, especially an officer who was currently engaged in top-secret Operations. But first, he had to find him. Travers knew that Cork had been working on the selection of officers as 'Minders' to the scientists from the OSS. He made some enquiries through regular channels as to the whereabouts of the major but received no information on his location or current posting. Apparently, the OSS did not exist. Travers contacted the office of General Bradley requesting information on Major Cork. Finally, he was given Bill Cork's current location.

Pat told Barbara that he wanted to spend time with his parents and would have to return to his ship within 72 hours. She agreed, then asked him to accompany her to the reading of the will. Her parents had proved to be astute business people and, as the sole beneficiary of the estate, Barbara was now a fairly wealthy young woman. She bought dinner for them, and now they were in her flat. Sitting next to him, she posed a question.

"Pat, how often do you come into contact with the Germans when you are at sea?"

He answered with a little trepidation,

"There is no straight answer to that question. In fact, the number of contacts has dropped away since our recent deployment."

He continued hesitantly,

"When we were on the arctic convoys, we were fighting them on an hourly basis. Those were very long days, Barbara."

Looking straight into his eyes, she probed,

"How many do you think you and the other ships killed?"

Pat asked,

"What do you mean? How many ships or aircraft, U-boats or men? I don't understand your question. I'm sorry."

Suddenly Barbara blazed with anger,

"I want to know how many Germans you killed. How many died in the water? How many were burned to death in their bloody bombers? How many drowned in their rotten U-boats? I want to know how many of them died and how much they suffered. Do you understand now, Lieutenant Commander?"

Pat was almost glad that, at last, the release of the pent-up anger was beginning.

"I don't know in detail, but at least four hundred."

This figure was off the top of his head, but she needed an answer. Barbara screamed,

"Four hundred? Is that all my parents are worth to the Royal Navy? Four hundred fucking Nazis? Is that the best you could do? - You and all the other warriors who marched off to war. Is that all?"

Now standing, her voice almost breaking.

"Pass out a message for me - a message from me to you and all the other highly trained killers. Tell them I've got money. I'm offering a bonus. For every German sent to hell, I'll pay. Just kill Germans for me and never stop. Do you hear me, Pat? You and all the other heroes? Just kill as many as you can and never stop killing them."

She broke down and fell into his arms, sobbing uncontrollably and within minutes, was asleep. He put her on the bed and sat in an armchair at a loss to know what to do for her. Then there came a knock on the door; when it opened, Pat saw a tall, well-built man who looked at him through horn-rimmed glasses and said,

"Hello, my name is Lyle Tucker. I'm Barbara's fiancé. You must be Pat Cork. Barbara has told me a lot about you. How are you?"

Pat picked up an American accent and watched as the man entered the flat. He turned and shook hands with Pat saying,

"Where is Barbara?"

Pat replied,

"May I ask you where you have been for the last two weeks? There has been a terrible tragedy."

The American's face showed his concern and surprise.

"I'm a war correspondent. I have been in Europe. What's happened? Is Barbara alright?"

Pat suggested,

"Lyle, perhaps you should sit down."

An hour later, Barbara came out of the bedroom. Seeing Lyle, she rushed to him and began crying. Pat, put on his uniform jacket and got ready to leave. Barbara had calmed down and spoke to him.

"Pat, I am so sorry for those things I said."

Raising his hand, Pat spoke.

"Please don't apologise or explain. Lyle has been telling me how you met and your plans for the future. I hope you settle in America. Forget about what was said. Just look after yourself. Maybe drop a letter when you get settled in the US. I think I might be visiting the country soon - after the war and all that." Barbara hugged him and kissed him as a friend.

"I always knew you would be good at war, but Jesus, Pat! Captain of a Royal Navy warship?"

She paused.

"I will write - I promise. Your mum gave me her address. Pat, there is so much I want to say. Please wait, just for a few more minutes. Please."

He shook his head.

"No. It's best I go now. Lyle has promised he will look after you, and I have to get back to my family and then my ship. Goodbye and good luck to both of you."

Pat needed to return to Portsmouth to spend time with his parents, and he knew there was nothing more he could do for Barbara. She had mentioned her intention to go to America. Now he knew how and hoped the decision to go was not driven by attempts to escape her grief. Pat found himself genuinely wishing them the best. Maybe there was a degree of selfishness because now Barbara's anger would be dealt with by someone else. It seemed all she wanted to do was to blame everybody for the death of her family. Her anger was justified but taking it out on other people was not. He had done all he could. Sitting on the train, Pat thought how ironic it was that Barbara, the great pacifist, had demanded that he exact revenge upon the entire German nation on her behalf. It would seem that pacifism is fine when violent death is at a great distance and exogenous to the pacifist. Although he felt sympathy for Barbara, his mind was concentrating on his parents and his cousin. They, too, had grief to deal with and, for that matter, so did he - those men he had fought with side by side - as Captain Buchan had put it, 'The finest of men'. Now he had joined them.

Loftus, Crowley. Chief Adams - then Peter Wilde and Peter English. The loss of so many good men - all gone. The list was endless. Just he and Lars were left, along with Erebus, Vali and Bill Cork - Reilly, Mullen, Constantine and Warne. His head sunk to his chest as he realised that all that was in front of the men who were still alive was more killing. Pat fought back the tears and willed for the train to arrive in Portsmouth. He longed to be with his family as he had never longed before.

Major Bill Cork was sitting in a tent some five miles behind the front line in Northern France, scanning a list. He had been seconded to the OSS section run by Oppenheim. Bill was concerned about taking orders from a civilian, especially a man as secretive as this one. Briefings were non-existent. When asked a question, Oppenheim's mantra was, 'need to know.' Oppenheim's obsession with secrecy added to Bill's suspicions. The OSS section chief had been applying pressure on him to sign the 'secrecy papers', as he called them. So far, he had stalled. Bill could see only one advantage to signing the papers, which would give Oppenheim and the OSS control over him until the end of the war. This posting might just allow him to see out the war and get home safely. Bill recalled Colonel Travers' advice 'not to do anything until they had spoken.' Returning to the list, he saw it contained the names of German individuals who were to be offered residency in the US as soon as they had been collected from the combat zones. Each name had, alongside it, an occupation or speciality, most being scientists or engineers. He suspected that amongst the forty people on the list were intelligence officers - but that was none of his business. All he had to do was to spirit them away once they had surrendered to advancing American troops. The section had been attached to General Patton's Third Army and was moving through Europe at speed. Again, Bill reassured himself with the thought, 'I'll talk it through with the colonel'.

While he waited for Travers, his scientist' came to mind, John Eldridge of Harvard University and Ohio. Bill had got to know this eccentric genius who had been dragged from the hallowed halls of Harvard to a tent a few miles behind a war. At first, he was not too sure what to say to the man. As time passed, he found that Eldridge was an academic par excellence but not very worldly-wise. John had explained that he had been virtually press-ganged, threatened with Internal Revenue Service tax audits and the withdrawal of research grants by

Oppenheim if he did not sign up. Bill and John lived in each other's pockets and were soon good friends. When speaking to the other 'minders', US Army Engineers, Bill was told similar stories of the other scientists. The soldiers would meet and discuss the best way to guarantee the welfare of these men who were utterly unsuitable for the environment Oppenheim had forced them into. The suggestion was made that the scientists be given basic weapons training. This had lasted about fifteen minutes as all three had little or no hand-to-eye coordination and, when given side arms, were potentially lethal to all around them. Unarmed combat was even worse, with Bill and his colleagues deciding that the best way forward was to stay close to these men. They were all brilliant, but life outside a laboratory or lecture hall really did not suit them. On a personal front, the scientists were affable, charming, very entertaining men. The minders became very fond and protective of all three academics.

When Eldridge began to speak of science, ballistics and rocketry in particular, it was then that Bill saw the real man - eloquent and erudite with a wicked sense of humour. The man also spoke of the possible advances which might be achieved from research - in any field. As he often said,

"William" –the only way he referred to Bill - research leads everywhere. All we need is the money and the time. We can do anything except fool nature. Any man who tries to do that is dangerously deluded."

Travers' immediate superior, General Bradley, had allowed him to go to France. Travers would need Patton's go-ahead to see Bill. The general listened to the Colonel's request while reading Cork's file. He immediately gave permission and granted both men one week's compassionate leave. As Travers was leaving, Patton said,

"Colonel, if that spooky bastard, Oppenheim, gives you or Major Cork any problems, refer him to me."

Pat sat in his mum's kitchen as another goodbye loomed. The death of Peter English and Amanda Bruce had hurt the Cork family deeply. Now Pat was going back to war. His parents were silent - as was his brother. Rachel was sitting next to him, her arms around his neck. Connor stood up, saying,

"Let's hope this is the last time you have to leave under these circumstances." Pat stood, and his father hugged him and walked out of the door. Christopher tried to shake his hand but then threw his arms around his brother. Rachel kissed him gently and left. Then, as he put on his coat, Mary Cork linked her son, saying,

"I'll walk down the road with you. Are you getting the bus?"

Pat managed to laugh despite his sadness.

"No, I'm not on the bus, mum. As the captain of a warship, I have a driver. I asked him to wait at the end of the road. To be frank, I'm a little embarrassed about the whole thing."

His mother looked into his eyes.

"How much more can you take, Pat?"

As usual, she had read his mind and saw her deep concern.

"I can take it as long as you and dad can. We have to beat these people, mum, and soon. I can take it until then. So please don't worry."

The navy car was waiting, and an able seaman approached them. He stood to attention and saluted Pat and then his mother. Mary Cork kissed her son and, with a demonstration of tremendous self-control, told the sailor that in future, when he collected the captain, he must come in for a cup of tea. She watched the car drive away as her thoughts went to a family across the ocean in Austin, Texas and her nephew Bill Cork.

Travers arrived in Bill's tent where he reacquainted himself with Thomas Eldridge, or, 'the long one.' Bill was surprised to see the colonel looking so grim. He was usually cheerful, if not ebullient. Travers asked the scientist to step outside for a minute.

"Please sit down, Bill. I'm afraid I have some bad news. Son, there is no way I can make this any easier for you, and God knows I've given this enough thought. Bill, your friend, Amanda Bruce, is dead. She was killed by an explosion in London five days ago. Bill, I am so sorry."

Travers watched as Bill sat in silence. He spoke after a minute or so.

"You know, in amongst all this death, I never felt it was close to me. Now I see that even in the middle of a war, you can still be hurt. How are her parents? Have they been told, colonel? I should go to them. I'm the reason she came here. If she had stayed at home, this would not have happened."

Travers waited for him to continue, but Bill just sat in silence, so Travers explained.

"Bill, I've got you one week's leave. We can get back to England. You can see her before she goes home."

HMS Longbow sailed on the morning tide. Pat Cork's orders were to rejoin the convoy escorts. There were also military personnel waiting for passage across what was the busiest piece of water anywhere in the world - and the queue was growing.

Before they left the front-line areas, Oppenheim had almost threatened both departing engineers regarding security. Travers could hardly contain his anger and disgust. Bill was in a state of shock and did not hear the ensuing row as Travers informed Oppenheim that he was on the wrong side. His behaviour would be better suited to the Nazis - not free-born men. The next day Colonel Travers and Major Cork were at the coast waiting for passage to England on the first available ship, and the prospects were not good. Patton then took a hand.

Having read Major Cork's record and being deeply impressed and aware of the bottleneck at Normandy, he contacted Admiral Hilliard, C in C Channel fleet, and requested berths for two US officers. Bill stood on the Mulberry Harbour as HMS Longbow tied up, and within an hour, he was on his way to England. In the privacy of the captain's cabin, Pat and Bill Cork hugged each other and talked of Mandy. Pat then told his cousin about the Paxtons and Barbara's engagement. Bill commented,

"Pat, you know you never mentioned Barbara very often before."

Before he could answer, Pat was called to the bridge and invited Bill. A sonar contact had been reported. The Flagship signalled HMS Longbow to investigate. Captain Cork ordered,

"depth charge crews to stand to," For an hour, Petty Officer Constantine gave a master class in tracking as Longbow stayed locked onto the submerged vessel, which, strangely, remained at fifteen fathoms and made no attempt to avoid detection. Cork considered the situation of the mystery contact. The English Channel is relatively shallow, averaging about thirty fathoms; an enemy U-boat would never attack in so little water. The target slowly increased speed, taking a course for the Solent and open water. Longbow followed four hundred yards astern. There were Royal Navy submarines assigned to escort duties, all aware of recognition procedures when detected. Enemy or friend, the captain of the target submarine, was either a complete idiot or did not regard his boat as in danger. Pat began to suspect the contact was not a U-boat boat. HMS Longbow increased speed until directly above the submarine. The deck officer reported,

"Depth charges ready to fire, sir."

As the stern of the ship passed over the target, Pat ordered.

"Hold fire."

"Aye, aye, sir."

The submerged vessel was now one hundred yards astern of Longbow and in the ideal position for a depth-charge attack. Pat confirmed,

"Depth-charge crew stand down," then added,

"Sonar, report contact position." Constantine was about to speak as Bellamy dashed to the captain's side with a signal.

'Do not attack under any circumstances. Proceed to Portsmouth'. The source was the captain of the port at Portsmouth.

Later, on the bridge, the captain of HMS Longbow was somewhat puzzled by a number of things. How did a senior officer in Portsmouth know Longbow was making an attack? Then the order to proceed to Portsmouth – by whose authority was this order given? Pat turned to Bill Cork.

"Major, there is far too much secrecy creeping into this war. It's taking all the fun out of it. The sooner we get out, the better."

Bill managed to laugh, then heard his cousin speak.

"Flags, copy all signals from Portsmouth to C in C Channel fleet. FAO Admiral Hilliard."

Within minutes, the signal to C IN C Channel was acknowledged with an attachment.

"Proceed to Portsmouth as ordered."

Pat spoke.

"Mr Bellamy, make for Portsmouth. Engine room – half ahead both."

Travers sat in the wardroom of HMS Longbow as Bill came in and joined him.

"Colonel, can I talk to you about this guy, Oppenheim?"

The colonel replied,

"Go ahead, Bill; what's on your mind."

Bill asked,

"What do you know about him and the OSS, sir?"

Travers poured another cup of tea and offered one to his comrade, who shook his head.

"Bill, this guy is a mystery. I've made a few enquiries amongst some old friends, and their advice is not to ask too many questions. It seems he has the ear of some very powerful people."

Bill posed another question.

"Sir, what if I refused to sign these secrecy papers?"

Travers put down his cup and placed his hand on the young man's shoulder.

"Major, this guy Oppenheim would probably pull your security clearance, which would mean exclusion from active service. Oppenheim would have you pushing paper in Peebles."

Bill interrupted,

"Sir, where is Peebles?"

Travers answered,

"Son, I have no idea, but it sounds pretty boring. Knowing you as I do, it's better for you to be occupied. You've just suffered a terrible loss. Bill, please bear this in mind. You and Mandy were not married, so the army will not allow you to go home. You and so many others like you are here until this war is over. Hold off signing these papers as long as you can. I'll keep an eye on you - as will others. Do as you're told and keep your head down."

Bill smiled.

"Thank you, sir. There is one more thing, sir. Would you come with me when I see Mandy?"

Travers replied with a vain attempt to lift his fellow Texan's spirits.

"Of course, I will, Bill. I told them I was going to get you home alive, so I'll be there."

HMS Longbow was alongside in Portsmouth Naval Base, where a car was placed at the disposal of the US officers. Bill and Travers did not have far to go. Amanda Bruce's body was in a mortuary in the harbour to be repatriated to the United States as soon as a suitable vessel became available. Pat Cork signalled the C in C Portsmouth that he would be away from his ship for two hours but not off base. An acknowledging signal was received with a condition. No longer than two hours.

The mortuary was as cold as it was sterile. All three men approached the remains of the beautiful young woman who had come so far to be a journalist and had died doing just that. Pat tried to think of words - any words. Travers never took his eyes off Bill Cork. The sheet covering the corpse was removed by the mortuary attendant, a kind look on his face, who Pat watched leave and, in doing so, noticed a man in a white coat standing at a discreet distance. Bill leaned over and kissed her lips, then cried uncontrollably. Travers' eyes were full of tears. Pat felt slightly guilty as he almost envied these men their emotions and thought of Bill's earlier comment about hardly having mentioned Barbara. Bill finished crying and said,

"Gentlemen, let's get back to the war and finish those bastards off for good." His companions said nothing. As Travers walked away from the remains with Bill, Pat stood for a moment. He whispered,

"Dear Mandy, thanks for making Bill happy. I just hope he gets over you. God rest you."

As the men collected their thoughts and took in some fresh air, Pat was approached by Lieutenant Bellamy, who spoke in a low voice, hoping not to intrude.

"Sir, a signal from the captain of the port. He wants to see you and me immediately."

Pat read the signal, then spoke to the US officers.

"I have to see someone urgently, then put back to sea. Bill, you and the colonel, are welcome to spend some time at my parents' house whilst you are ashore. Mum isn't pressing you, but the offer is there should you want to go. Colonel, you are more than welcome."

Bill replied,

"Pat, I'd like a little time alone, then maybe a night in a quiet hotel."

His cousin just smiled. Travers joined in.

"Lieutenant Commander, I'll look after him for the next few days. Maybe we will call on your folks, but right now, I think we Yanks need some time on our own."

"Very good, Colonel."

Then he turned to Bellamy,

"Flags, when we get back to the ship, check if there are any more signals from Admiral Hilliard on this mystery submarine business."

That afternoon, the captain of HMS Longbow, with his signals officer, Lieutenant Nigel Bellamy, stood outside the office of the captain of Portsmouth Naval Base for nearly twenty minutes before a rating asked them to follow him. The officer in question stood in silence. Beside him were two men. The slightly taller of the two spoke.

"Good afternoon, gentlemen. I am Colonel Simpson-Coyle. This gentleman is Mr Oppenheim, whom you very nearly killed earlier in the week. We would both like an explanation why you attacked an American Navy submarine."

Pat looked at the captain of the port, who was the senior naval officer present and should have intervened. Simpson-Coyle had no authority whatsoever to question naval personnel, let alone a Royal Navy ship's captain and one of his officers. Pat began to speak as the phone rang. The captain of the port, who had yet to introduce himself, answered with the words, "Port office. Port commander speaking."

Pat was certain he heard the words,

"Not for long", from the handset. The man straightened as he listened, then handed the phone to Pat, who used the time-honoured tradition of the Royal Navy for a ship's captain to identify himself,

"Longbow."

"Ahh, Cork!"

Pat recognised Admiral Hilliard's voice.

"Now listen, Pat. These men have no authority whatsoever. They seem to think they are important - well, they are not - certainly not Colonel Simpson-Coyle anyway. You are under my command, so you and young Bellamy walk straight out and get back to your ship. Is that clear?"

Pat couldn't resist a smile before replying.

"May I suggest, sir that we try to find out exactly what these gentlemen were doing with a submarine in the middle of the Normandy convoys? It might make life easier for all concerned if we explained the inherent dangers of being in that particular sea area."

There was silence for a short period then Hilliard replied,

"Good idea. Please pass this on from me. We will sink any vessel, surface or submerged, that does not identify itself immediately upon detection and challenge – and I mean, 'any vessel'. Carry on, Captain Cork."

As Travers and Bill were leaving the mortuary complex, the orderly who had assisted them earlier approached.

"Gentlemen, the chief medical officer would like to see Colonel Travers for a few minutes. Major, we have a small canteen for the relatives, it's quiet and warm, and the tea is not bad."

Bill was beyond caring; at this stage, he just wanted to sit down. Travers nodded.

"Why don't you wait in there for me, Bill?"

He followed the orderly who knocked on the door marked CMO. In the office, a medium-sized man with short black hair stood and shook Travers' hand.

"Colonel, I appreciate you coming. My name is Hallket. My rank is major, and I am the medical examiner. Please sit down."

Travers did so as the major continued.

"I am in somewhat of a quandary. Would I be correct in saying you are the major's CO?"

Travers answered,

"Yes, I am."

The MO spoke slowly.

"I am aware that as Miss Bruce and Major Cork were not married, in law their relationship has no standing. I saw how the young man cried over the deceased. These are extraordinary times in which we live, so I am going to tell you something. It is up to you to decide if Major Cork should be told."

Travers prompted,

"Please go on, doctor."

"Colonel, as Miss Bruce was a civilian, under British law I was bound to carry out a post-mortem. That examination revealed that Miss Bruce was in the early stages of pregnancy."

Travers sat in silence as the doctor moved from behind his desk.

"Colonel, I hope I have not burdened you unduly. I do not know this young man and feel that I have no right to decide whether he should be told of the young lady's condition."

Travers stood up.

"Thank you, doctor. I will decide what to do, and no, you have not burdened me."

Bill was sitting in the small canteen, staring into space. Colonel Travers stood and wondered. So far, Bill had been able to deal with the death of his girlfriend. The tears he had shed at her side had shown his ability to mourn her. At that point, Travers had thought it possible that he was accepting her death as part of the war and his life. Now the information given to him by the doctor put a completely different dimension on how Cork would deal with both Mandy's death and that of the child. Travers felt he needed to know how deeply Bill and Mandy were involved before deciding if his young Texan should be told. Bill saw his colonel, stood and walked toward the door. On the ride to the hotel, neither man spoke. Travers had no children, but right now, he regarded Bill Cork as a son. After checking in, Bill knocked on Travers' room door.

"I need a small drink and some conversation. I just need to talk about Mandy." In the bar, Travers ordered a bottle of Scotch, and then they sat in a quiet corner. For the next hour, Bill told Travers how he had met Mandy and of Big Bend and the Double B. He talked incessantly, even managing the odd smile as happy memories came to mind. He talked of how it was Mandy who found the link between Pat Cork and him. Then, as Travers was beginning to make up his mind on telling Bill of the pregnancy, he heard,

"You know, we were going to be married when this war is over. I asked her, and she said yes. We said we'd get married at home on the Double B with all the trimmings."

He paused as his eyes filled with tears.

"I'm very tired. I think I'll try to get some sleep."

With that, he left the bar. Travers sat alone, his head reeling. Right now, Bill was exhausted physically and emotionally. He was also a mature man who had borne responsibility way beyond his years. The fact that he had decided that the first thing to do after the war was to get married showed his determination to move on with Mandy by his side. Now she was gone and what might have been the start of a family was also dead.

The worrying thing for Travers was that Bill was a highly intelligent, highly educated, experienced man, trained to kill in numerous ways. The woman in his life had been his safety valve – his anchor to the humane, civilised man he really was. Now she was gone, Bill Cork could take refuge from his pain in the soldier, the commando, the killer and release his anger and grief in violence. The bomb that had killed his Mandy was made by Germans, and there were millions of these people on which Major Cork could exact revenge and, in doing so, destroy himself.

Simpson-Coyle ordered Pat and Bellamy to sit down and answer all questions put to them by Mr Oppenheim. He finished with,

"If you attempt to conceal anything, there will be dire consequences."

Pat looked at the captain of the port.

"May I have a word, sir, in private?"

The officer replied,

"I see nothing to discuss, Lieutenant Commander, other than to suggest you obey the colonel's orders."

Pat continued,

"I see. Would you be so kind as to identify yourself?"

The man stood, revealing a somewhat rotund shape.

"I am Captain Day, port commander."

Pat saw the wavy wristbands of the Royal Naval Volunteer Reserve, which explained a lot. The man was undoubtedly qualified to hold his command, possibly with a background in sea-borne freight before the war. It was obvious that he had little idea of naval etiquette. His chest ribbons confirmed he had not seen sea duty. There were other factors to consider before engaging with Simpson-Coyle or this man Oppenheim. Simpson Coyle was unaware of Pat's connections with the SOE or his direct link to Maiden Aunt. As far as he could remember, there was no time when the colonel would have heard his name mentioned in connection with Erebus or Vali. He was the type of army officer who had no interest in anything but the army.

"I have no intention of discussing any actions at sea in front of a perfect stranger, colonel, and you should know that. May I ask in what capacity Mr Oppenheim is here?"

Simpson-Coyle took the bait as he snapped,

"That, lieutenant commander, is none of your business." Pat persisted,

"Well, colonel, I'm insisting that it is because you say this gentleman was aboard a submarine which was allegedly attacked by my ship. For future reference, I have been ordered to inform you and him that any vessel, ship or submarine which does not identify itself when challenged in the English Channel will be sunk."

Simpson-Coyle was about to explode as Pat continued,

"Please allow me to finish, colonel. Any person intending to cross the Channel by whatever means would be wise to bear that in mind."

The captain of the port had gone pale, whereas Simpson-Coyle, on the other hand, was now approaching bright red. Oppenheim spoke,

"Are you threatening me, Commander Cork?"

Pat looked directly at the now puce soldier.

"Colonel, would you please explain to this gentleman that I will not answer any of his questions until he explains his role here and further what a US Navy submarine was doing in waters which are a combat zone. The Royal Navy is not playing games in the Channel, gentlemen; we will sink anything that appears to be a threat to the convoys."

Oppenheim spoke.

"Commander, I'm warning you........"

Pat cut across him with venom.

"You, Mr Oppenheim, are on a Royal Navy Base, and I am captain of one of His Majesty's ships of war. If you threaten me or any other member of His Majesty's navy again, I will have you clapped in irons. Now, are you going to tell me and Lieutenant Bellamy why you were aboard a submarine in the English

Channel?" Pat sneaked a look at Bellamy, who was clearly, hugely enjoying the whole thing but was clever enough to stay silent. Captain Day was now beginning to realise that captains of ships of the line were vastly different to the men he had been accustomed to in the volunteer reserve.

Oppenheim spat,

"I'll tell you nothing."

Pat paused as he looked at Day, who was now shaking slightly, then spoke again.

"Right, well, hear this, Mr Oppenheim. If the man who was in command of that submarine is the best you have got, then you are in trouble. There are many excellent sailors in the US Navy. I know. I've served with them. I suggest you find one before you put to sea again; otherwise, you will be sunk - literally. Come on, Flags. Let's get back to the ship. We have a war to fight. Captain Day, you will undoubtedly be hearing from an officer of the Channel Fleet before long. Good day to you all."

Bill sat and wrote to his mother. His recent letters home had an air of optimism, looking forward to the end of the war and getting home. Urging her not to worry.

This letter would be different. Bill wrote of the kindness of everybody, especially Auntie Mary, Uncle Connor and Colonel Travers. He wrote of Mandy and of the way in which she had died. There was not too much detail, just enough to let his mother know that there had been no pain - just instant peace. Bill could not recall if Mr Paxton had been mentioned in earlier letters writing of how he had died at Mandy's side. Apologising first, Bill then asked his mother to speak to the Bruces and offer his explanation of why he could not get home for the funeral. The US Army would not release him, not because he was important. No, if they did, then half of the men in Europe would be on the next boat home. Bill closed the letter with the words, 'I'll be home soon, Mum. Tell everybody I love them.' Then realised he was crying.

Travers knocked on the hotel room door. The man who opened it was still the bullet-hard US Army Engineer Travers had known since early 1942 - but was the man as resilient, as aware of danger, as sharp in all of his senses. The eyes of the man in front of him were clouded with sadness, maybe too much to allow him to risk his life again, particularly with someone as devious and callous as Oppenheim. Travers had thought long and hard about Bill. He had considered a discharge on medical grounds, but Bill was fit and able. The other option was psychological, which, if granted, would remain on Bill's file for the rest of his life. No, Travers knew that the military machine would not play along. Major Cork would have to go back into the line as soon as possible. Travers sat down as Bill closed the letter and sealed the envelope.

"I must post this before we go back to France."

Travers was aware that all personnel involved with the OSS were having mail censored and, in some cases, held.

"Give it to me, Bill; I'll get it sent out tonight from General Bradley's office. We sail for France tomorrow, Bill. There's no more to be said."

Aboard Longbow, the captain was reading a signal from the flagship. The Americans had made a formal complaint against HMS Longbow for depth charging a US Navy submarine in the English Channel. Pat looked at the times recorded by the submarine as being under attack. Having checked his log and the signals log, he replied to the signal with all the relevant information. The flagship acknowledged, and then a further signal was received from Admiral Hilliard. It read,

'Have checked all your information. Everything in order. Do not worry. Leave everything to me. Well done. Hilliard. C in C Channel Fleet.'

Simpson-Coyle and Oppenheim sat in the office allocated to them by Captain Day. The men were worried. They had not expected the captain of HMS Longbow to be so self-assured. The point of the exercise was to pressurise Lieutenant Commander Cork in such a way to force him to provide them with information on German prisoners of war being moved from the war zone to the UK. Both men had used barely legal means to advance their respective careers, and during peacetime, this had been relatively easy. Now, they were dealing with men who had seen active service and who showed little, if any, fear. Oppenheim had been given Simpson-Coyle's name by a contact in US military intelligence before he arrived in Europe. Simpson-Coyle was, at first, very cautious with the American until he explained his role and that of the OSS. The colonel saw a way of reviving his flagging career, which, due to so many complaints and transfers, was close to an inglorious end. The men agreed that there were a number of high-profile German officers in the UK under interrogation. Simpson-Coyle believed he should have been the officer commanding the Operation and was unaware of who was in command. Oppenheim was ready to use anyone to gather any and all information on British Intelligence Operations. The situation appeared to both men to be crystal clear. To the rest of the Intelligence gathering community, Simpson-Coyle and Oppenheim were dangerously deluded. Both had been under discreet observation for some time. There could be no doubting their loyalty, but their methods and motivation were now being questioned at the highest levels. Complaints were increasing about the pair's behaviour. The charges against HMS Longbow now involved high-ranking naval officers from the US and Royal Navies. If enquiries revealed that the allegations were vexatious, it would go very badly for both men. For the US High Command, the treatment of the scientists was regarded as outrageous, to say the least. Simpson-Coyle's record was now beginning to catch up with him. Oppenheim had chosen to intimidate anyone he could. They needed something big to save their careers and maybe preserve their liberty, but the end of the war was near, and both men were now becoming expendable.

— 35 —

Staying Sane

The remains of Miss Amanda Bruce finally arrived in the port of Galveston in October 1944. The town of Austin turned out to bury the young woman who had lost her life in a far distant place, doing what she loved in the company of the man she loved. Her family were dignified during the funeral as the eulogy for their daughter was given by the editor of the newspaper, which had posted her to Britain. He was not quite so dignified with an emotionally raw declaration of a personal feeling of responsibility for the death of Amanda. A glowing description of her talent and heartfelt regret at her life, full of so much promise taken so young. The funeral was one of many in the town that day, as deceased servicemen were returned to their loved ones, casualties of the wars raging in the Pacific and Europe. Somehow, the burial of Mandy Bruce seemed more poignant. Nobody expected or was prepared for the burial of a young woman. Everybody from the Double B attended; Bill Buchanan with Catherine, Thomas and Jessica Cork along with Charlie Rawlings, Bill's grandfather. All were silent, unable to speak - words wouldn't come no matter how hard they tried to think of something to say. The Bruce family finally broke down when Mrs Eleanor Roosevelt quietly slipped into the congregation and spoke to them. Bill had sent letters to Mr Bruce but was not able to say what he wanted to. Military censors were not chosen for their sensitivity. Amanda's father read the letters and in some way knew this and replied to Bill saying as much. The time for them to grieve with Bill Cork would be when he came home - when everybody came home. In his letter, Mr Bruce wished Bill the best and promised he would always be in the Bruce's family prayers. There was no legal requirement for an autopsy when the remains were returned. So, Amanda Bruce, woman, daughter, journalist and mother-to-be, was buried in the rich Texas soil. The only people who knew the full story of Amanda's time in London were Colonel Travers and a kind-hearted English doctor. Charlie Rawlings and his son-in-law sat in total silence for the entire day – both in utter despair. On the return journey to the Double B, no one spoke until the family reached the ranch, then Thomas Cork voiced what everyone had been thinking.

"Jesus! That could have been Bill's funeral, and I thank God it was not."

Nobody argued or commented. Thomas Cork's words were in some way an admission of guilt, but all of them felt better for hearing the man say them. He was speaking for all of them. The funeral took place on a Friday and, for the first time in years, there was no gathering at the Big House - everyone just went to bed, except Jessica Cork, who stayed in the lounge of the Lake House and read and re-read every one of her son's letters with tears running down her face; the same prayer running through her head over and over as she clutched his letters to her heart whispering,

"Bill, please come home. Please come home."

Major Bill Cork and Colonel Travers rejoined General George Patton's Third Army in Europe. The General asked to see Travers and, during a brief but productive meeting, proposed.

"Colonel, I need a man who has been in this war from the word go, an officer with your vast experience. I also need someone to keep an eye on this blasted OSS or whatever they are called. I fully appreciate the role of intelligence in a modern army, but these guys are just playing a different game. The role of intelligence is to support the fighting men. These people seem to think it's the other way round."

Travers accepted and was appointed to Patton's staff with a watching brief of the scientists, their minders and, in particular, Mr Oppenheim. Bill once again settled into the routine of the mission - interrogation of prisoners when captured and then the processing and moving on to the prisoner of war camps in the rear. The scientists, and John Eldridge in particular, showed huge sensitivity and no little ingenuity in keeping him busy, briefing Bill to ask questions regarding fuel shipments and specific materials. He summarised,

"William, find out anything you can to do with propulsion systems, heat-resistant materials or hazardous loads. You never know; even a lorry driver could let something slip."

With his scientific background, Bill found the list of questions from the scientist fascinating and edifying, but there was nothing out of the ordinary in the answers from the Germans. As Christmas approached, the feeling amongst all the allied servicemen was that the end was near. This mood soon disappeared when on the 16th of December 1944, 200,000 German troops, supported by 240 tanks and another 100 armoured vehicles, drove west through the Ardennes region in an attempt to capture Amsterdam and force a conditional peace with the Western Allies. Patton's Third Army marched through freezing weather and on cold food to halt the Germans' advance. Travers and Cork were part of that march which would enter the annals of American Infantry legend. The German offensive gave Bill an opportunity to return to combat. He requested a front-line position with Patton's engineers and, from late December 1944 to the 25th of January 1945, fought with a controlled ferocity against anything the Germans could throw at the Americans and him personally. At times, the fighting was hand-to-hand, and Major Cork was in the thick of it. All the time, Travers was watching Bill to see his reaction to the death of his young lady. One evening, both engineers were in an advanced observation post no more than five hundred yards from the German lines. Bill had volunteered to man the OP to guide the US Air Force onto targets when the weather cleared. Travers asked,

"Bill, how are you feeling?"

Cork replied,

"Colonel, do you remember the raid on the German destroyer?"

Travers said,

"Yes. Norway."

Bill continued.

"During that mission, I killed for the first time, and within an hour, I had killed again. I asked the man who was in command of the raid a question."

Bill then stopped talking as if reliving the moment.

Travers broke the silence.

"What was it Bill?"

Cork looked up.

"I asked him, 'When does a man know when to stop killing'?"

Travers voiced his approval.

"A very unusual question, major. What was his answer?"

Again, there was a moment's silence then Bill spoke.

"The man said, 'It's time to stop killing when you start to enjoy it.'"

He continued,

"Colonel, you asked me how I'm feeling. Maybe I can show you."

Just then, the cloud cleared, and Major Cork radioed the coordinates of the enemy positions to the circling US Air Force aircraft. Travers watched as his young Texan used the US Air Force fighter bombers to destroy the enemy with terrifying efficiency. Guiding the aeroplanes in what could only be described as a cold, calculating and utter obliteration of the German troops and their positions. Bill's face was calm and composed as he looked at his colonel and said,

"Sir, I don't know how I'm feeling. You said they won't let me go home, so right now, there's nowhere else I'd rather be but here."

In mid-channel, a signal was received aboard HMS Longbow then an officer knocked on the captain's cabin door.

"Enter."

Bellamy, having done so, announced,

"Signal from the flag, sir."

"Read it please, Flags."

Clearing his throat, the signals officer began.

"To captain, HMS Longbow. Proceed Portsmouth with all speed. Signed

Maiden Aunt. It's been copied to C in C Channel fleet, sir, and approved by flag officer."

Cork took the signal and read it again.

"Thank you, Mr Bellamy. That will be all."

Within minutes, Longbow was underway. On the bridge, it crossed the captain's mind there might be a chance to get home, then hindsight reminded him the signal was from Maiden Aunt and could result in anything. Erebus and Vali were summoned to SOE headquarters, having delivered a captured Wehrmacht Transport Command general to a safe house. While in transit, Vali had begun his debrief, which began with the general expressing anger at how he was taken prisoner.

"An order had come from the high command. A large number of technicians had to be moved to a location in Northern Germany, which had tied up badly needed vehicles. I was left behind and was captured. The unit was under the command of an officer by the name of General Von Braun."

Vali radioed the main points of the conversation to Maiden Aunt, who ordered a top priority flight to SOE headquarters. Professor Williamson continued the interrogation. Within four hours, HMS Longbow was steaming for Portsmouth.

Oppenheim was desperate to return to the front line and the scientists. But the 'Battle of the Bulge' had moved Patton's Third Army, the scientists and minders several hundred miles. Despite repeated demands and threats, Oppenheim could not discover their location. General Bradley's HQ was not being secretive when not supplying Oppenheim with the whereabouts of Major Cork's unit. They simply did not know it. Patton fought battles in his own unique but very successful way. Oppenheim contacted Colonel Simpson-Coyle, asking if he could arrange passage across the English Channel. The colonel contacted the port captain at Portsmouth to be told that no berth was available. When told, Oppenheim again tried to intimidate the chief petty officer in charge of the berth list and was informed that if Neptune himself was looking for passage to Europe, he would have to wait his turn. Both men booked into a small hotel just outside the Portsmouth base and waited. Simpson-Coyle, in the meantime, had ordered his contact - Captain Day - to report any unusual activity in the harbour.

HMS Longbow was alongside. Cork noted that Admiral Hilliard's flagship was also tied up. Within minutes, Pat and Commander Larsen were ordered to Naval Operations. The walls of the briefing room were covered with charts, all behind locked covers. Maiden Aunt, Erebus, Vali and Professor Williamson were sitting. Cork and Larsen smiled in greeting as they joined them by an exposed chart. Admiral Hilliard joined the group, introduced himself and added.

"Gentlemen, please don't identify yourselves. I am here at the request of Brigadier Davies. His is the only name I need to know."

Davies began the briefing,

"We have found Werner Von Braun; there is enough hard evidence to put men on the ground. Professor, the details, please."

The academic told the group that Werner Von Braun was in the area of Peenemunde along with nearly five hundred conscripted scientists and technicians. He raised a potential problem.

"That may mean getting about five hundred people out of enemy territory." The servicemen stirred. Hilliard spoke.

"This man Von Braun is very important, and, as for the technicians, we will get them out if we can." He concluded.

"Our primary task is to find Von Braun and his research team and extract them."

Davies took over.

"HMS Longbow, under the command of Captain Cork, will take Erebus and Vali to the coastline closest to Peenemunde, where they will go ashore and locate Von Braun and monitor him until the situation is clearer."

Pat spoke.

"May I ask a question, sir?"

Davies encouraged,

"Please do, commander."

"What do you mean by 'becomes clearer?'"

Williamson looked at Maiden Aunt and who nodded.

"It's like this, Pat. Von Braun is a 'dyed in the wool' Nazi, but he has a big mouth. In Nazi Germany, that can be very dangerous. He is outspoken in his criticism of some of the decisions being taken by the Nazi High Command. The least criticism of the leaders can result in imprisonment and, even worse, without warning. Erebus and Vali will need to let us know exactly where and how he is on a daily basis."

Davies picked up the briefing.

"That is where HMS Longbow comes in. As long as the men are ashore, your ship, Captain Cork, will need to be able to get them out at short notice. There is, of course, the real possibility that the Nazis may lose patience with him and just kill him to stop him falling into Russian hands." Admiral Hilliard then expressed a naval concern.

"Gentlemen, I must make the following clear. Peenemunde is a very isolated place to reach from land. From the sea, it is, under present conditions, virtually inaccessible. The sea areas known as Skagerrak and Kattegat, which lead to the Baltic Sea, are in German hands."

He walked to the wall chart and continued.

"With Norway and Denmark occupied, the risks to any ship entering the channel are enormous. With all due respect, gentlemen, I would submit that there is no realistic way to get anyone ashore from either sea area."

The men in the room sat in stunned silence. Pat Cork was secretly relieved - the admiral had said exactly what he was about to. The waters in that region were enemy controlled. Maiden Aunt spoke.

"Gentleman, I think you all see now why I asked the admiral to attend. Does anyone have any ideas on how to get men into the Peenemunde area?"

Williamson took up the thread.

"Please bear in mind we have little contact with the Danish resistance, and our contacts in Norway are too distant."

Erebus spoke for the first time.

"Sir, as I see it, we have two methods open to us. We parachute in, or we are taken to shore by submarine."

Vali joined in.

"There may be one more. We could be dropped on the German or Danish Coast and make our way over land."

He outlined an idea. He and Erebus would assume the identities of electrical engineers. Their work permits would show both had been working on the defences of the French Coast and had been ordered back to Germany. They might just get themselves assigned to work with Von Braun or his people. Vali reassured Maiden Aunt and the admiral,

"As long as no one actually asks us to do any work with complicated electrical equipment, we should be ok."

Erebus remained silent as he rolled his eyes to heaven. After a long and detailed discussion, Maiden Aunt finally allowed them to go.

Erebus and Vali boarded HMS Longbow, and she steamed for northern waters.

As the ship cleared the harbour, Simpson-Coyle received confirmation from Day that Longbow had sailed with two men who were not crew members. He said nothing to Oppenheim but was certain that one of them was Erebus. It did his temper no good to know that he had missed the man again and, more to the point, had not been told anything. Suddenly he seemed to lose all sense of reason and the instinct for self-preservation that had served him so well. The war was coming to an end, and he still had the problem of the 'kill' order to explain. The colonel decided that the OSS, in the person of Oppenheim, could be used to deal with Erebus and the captain of the ship - whoever he was. Later that day, Simpson-Coyle persuaded Oppenheim - who had no idea as to the importance of an admiral of the Royal Navy - to demand to see the admiral in charge of the Channel Fleet. The demand was duly received by Hilliard's staff officer, who replied with the standard answer,

"Request acknowledged."

Hilliard was aware that a formal complaint against a Royal Navy ship had been lodged. A very serious allegation - specifically, that a US Navy submarine had been depth-charged in the English Channel. What Oppenheim or Simpson-Coyle were not aware of was that any communication between Royal Navy officers and American personnel was automatically copied to a US naval flag officer. The British admiral's staff officer forwarded to Oppenheim the minimum requirements to allow the inquiry to proceed. Name and class of submarine, the names of the commanding officer and flag officer who had ordered the vessel to be in the Channel without the authorisation. The questions, when received by Oppenheim, were met with absolute silence. Hilliard went back to sea but not before instigating a discreet inquiry into the captain of the port - Captain Day. The terms of reference being his background and possible links with Simpson-Coyle. He also requested statements from two US Army officers who were somewhere in the European theatre of Operations. Hilliard had decided to take on Simpson-Coyle. Oppenheim, as an American spook, might prove slightly more difficult so, Hilliard made a number of totally untraceable phone calls to enlist support.

As Oppenheim fumed in landlocked isolation, the US Army officers in question were receiving requests for information on the matter via General Patton's Headquarters staff.

HMS Longbow steamed to the North Sea, avoiding all landfall and under cover of heavy fog, closed on a small inlet on the Dutch Coast. The weather was kind as the SOE agents were rowed ashore. Once inland, the men found a local town and asked about buses to Germany. The reply was in the form of a question.

"Why do you want to go there? If you wait, the Allies will take you with them. They'll be here fairly soon."

The public transport system in the Low Countries was non-existent as the retreating German Army commandeered vehicles to move troops. The SOE men decided walking was the only way to get to the target area and began their long trek. Along a canal towpath. Erebus saw a medium-sized enclosed barge which, at a cursory glance, seemed damaged beyond repair, but his suspicions were aroused. The barge was riding level in the water, which meant that she was not taking water. He stopped.

"Let's have a look at this," then climbed down onto the small foredeck. A tarpaulin had been placed over the full length of the deck cabin and was tied in place, then rubbish and broken agricultural machinery was laid on top.

"All in all, a pretty fair camouflage job," he said and pulled back the tarpaulin to reveal a padlocked cabin door in good condition. The lock was picked, inside the barge was in good order with signs of habitation. Traces of food and recent German newspapers and charts for the inland canals of Holland, Denmark and

Germany. The steering wheel gear allowed navigation from above or below the deck. Vali suggested.

"Let's see if the engine works." A quick search ensued, ending as Erebus raised his empty hands.

"No keys in here." Then continued.

"Let me run this by you. It looks as if someone is staying here. The barge is serviceable but has been well disguised as a wreck. To provide a hideaway or for an escape. Why don't we wait until someone comes back and find out." Vali prompted,

"Go on - you haven't finished. I know you by now. There's more to come."

The Irishman laughed.

"If what I have said is the case, this person will have a hidden store of fuel. The charts of the inland waterways aren't here by chance."

Vali agreed.

"OK, if our man does turn up, we need to surprise him. He'll probably be armed."

Erebus nodded, and they tidied up the inside. The padlock was replaced, and the tarpaulin restored. Just after midnight, the bright moon gave clear vision allowing Vali to watch as a man walked along the bank and onto the barge carrying a large fuel can. At the stern, he opened a hatch and lowered the fuel container into the body of the barge. Then went into the cabin. Vali followed him in as light from a hurricane lamp spread. The man turned, a Luger pistol in his hand as Erebus, already inside, came from behind and wrestled the gun from his hand. There was silence as Erebus, pistol in hand, spoke in German.

"What are you up to?"

The reply was in German.

"Are you the Gestapo? If you are, I can pay. I have plenty of valuables. Jewellery, works of art, sculptures, gold coins."

Vali ordered.

"Sit." Adding.

"Let's see what you've got."

The man gave a sigh of relief.

"See, I knew we could do business. We can all get out of Holland as rich men. Who else needs to know? - Just our private business deal. Come, I'll show you."

He went to the stern, followed by Vali then Erebus, opened the hatch and reached down. At that moment, Vali saw a small hole appear between the man's eyes. A second later, blood appeared on his shirt as a bullet pierced his heart. He dropped to the deck - dead. Erebus had fired twice. Vali looked at the hatch cover and saw a machine pistol stowed just inside the hinge. The dead man, whoever he was, had clearly been prepared to kill anyone who discovered his hoard. During the next hour, they uncovered a very large amount of gold coins and works of art in compartments built into the hold of the barge, which was accessible from the stern hatch only. But far more valuable to the SOE men were the hundred twenty-litre fuel cans neatly lined up – all containing diesel. Erebus estimated that at least two thousand litres of fuel was on board – enough to get them a long way from Holland and into Northern Germany. The dead man had no identity papers, but the keys to the engine were in his waistcoat. His body was weighted with some of the damaged farm machinery and lowered into the canal. The waterway was not tidal; with Holland in chaos, it would be years before the canal was dredged. Vali started the engine, which proved to be in good order. By morning the men were a good twenty-five kilometres from the original mooring and heading toward Northern Germany, Peenemunde and Werner Von Braun.

HMS Longbow's captain, Lieutenant Commander Pat Cork, was instructed to attend an official hearing to answer an allegation that his ship had depth-charged a US submarine in the English Channel. As the incident involved the US and Royal navies, Admirals from each service would hear the matter to decide if a court martial was warranted. Lieutenant Bellamy, Commander Larsen and Petty Officer Constantine were also ordered to give evidence. The Navy appointed Cork a fellow officer as a representative, in naval parlance, his, 'friend.' Pat was amazed when the 'friend' turned out to be Admiral Hilliard.

The presiding flag officers were seated at a desk which was slightly raised on a platform. The room had two more desks opposite each other with two chairs behind each. The flag officers took their seats. Admiral Spenser and US Admiral James S Burke. Immaculately dressed, with silver grey hair. Pat thought he looked like a movie star. The admiral's chest ribbons showed that he had seen convoy duty. Cork began to sense things were not too bad even at this very early stage, having feared that the hearing might be a kangaroo court. Admiral Spenser called for the evidence upon which the allegations were based. The doors of the enquiry room opened, and two men walked in. One was Oppenheim of the OSS, and the other was Colonel Simpson-Coyle, who showed some concern when seeing the Royal Navy flag officer acting as Cork's friend. Admiral Spenser spoke.

"I am informing all here that the entire proceedings held here today are top secret. Admiral Burke is from US Naval Intelligence and has agreed this category of security is appropriate."

Admiral Burke then spoke.

"Mr Oppenheim, would you begin, please."

The OSS man informed the hearing that, on a date in December 1944, a US Navy submarine had been attacked with depth charges in the English Channel. Admiral Burke opened the questioning by asking Oppenheim to name the vessel and the officer in command. The admiral was clearly annoyed when Oppenheim told him that that information was classified. Oppenheim then produced affidavits signed by the anonymous captain and first officer of the unnamed submarine, confirming the attack. Simpson-Coyle rose and confirmed that he had been in the presence of the US Navy officers when they had sworn the affidavits. He then demanded a court martial be convened. Spenser sat in silence for a moment, then asked for the officer's friend to present his evidence. Admiral Hilliard stood and said,

"Sirs, at no time did HMS Longbow deploy depth charges."

The US admiral stated.

"May we see proof of this statement." Hilliard produced the dockyard records which showed that the ship returned to port with all of the allocated depth charges aboard. Then the signal from the port captain ordering the ship to break off the attack. Oppenheim challenged the veracity of the documents saying that they could have been forged. Admiral Burke glared at his countryman but remained silent. The glare did not go unnoticed by Simpson-Coyle, who was now beginning to look decidedly uncomfortable. At this point, the lunch break was called.

The afternoon session got underway, and Hilliard continued to present his evidence. Lieutenant Bellamy told of the initial contact with the submarine and the chase, then the order to break off the attack. Again Oppenheim implied that Bellamy was lying and the signal was a fake. Hilliard remained calm. Commander Larsen was called to testify. He virtually repeated Bellamy's testimony. This time Simpson-Coyle attempted to paint a picture of a prepared plan to deceive the enquiry - a naval conspiracy. Larsen dismissed the insinuation with disdain as he demanded.

"Prove it!" Oppenheim and the Colonel did not reply.

Petty Officer Constantine then appeared. Oppenheim asked,

"How long have you known Lieutenant Commander Cork?"

PO Constantine replied,

"I have served aboard HMS Longbow with the captain, and before that, HMS Snow Eagle."

Oppenheim demanded irritably.

"I asked you how long you have known the officer."

The sailor spoke calmly.

"You said, 'Lieutenant Commander.' The captain hasn't held his current rank all of that time. I have served with him close to four years from our first commission."

Oppenheim looked at the admirals exclaiming.

"The witness is giving inaccurate answers!"

Burke replied,

"Then stop asking inaccurate questions." Then exchanged a reassuring glance with the witness.

Slightly flustered, the OSS man continued,

"Have you always been a sonar operator?"

"The equipment used in the Royal Navy is called ASDIC. The US Navy calls it Sonar, but it's all the same gear and does the same job," the Petty officer replied.

"You call me 'sir,'" Oppenheim shouted.

"Why? I don't see any uniform, and you haven't told me who or what you are." Constantine's voice was flat and controlled. Simpson-Coyle took over.

"Did you see the signal which ordered HMS Longbow to break off the attack?"

"No, sir, I did not."

Simpson-Coyle turned toward the admirals and was about to speak when Constantine continued.

"Why would I see the signal? My job was in the Asdic or Sonar cabin tracking the target. I never lost it once. The captain got us so close I could hear them pouring their coffee."

Simpson-Coyle knew his perceived advantage had gone. The faces of the flag officers confirmed this. Admiral Burke spoke.

"Thank you for your contribution, Petty Officer Constantine."

Then the captain of HMS Longbow was invited to give evidence. Pat reiterated what had been said by his shipmates, then Admiral Burke asked,

"Captain Cork, why did you wait so long before readying the ship for attack?" Pat answered,

"Sir, I have an excellent ASDIC operator in Petty Officer Constantine. He tracked the contact for just over an hour. The commander of the target never tried to escape or evade us. The man was either very stupid or had nothing to be afraid of as if he knew he was in friendly waters and clearly did not expect an attack. Every U-boat we have attacked has always tried to sink us or escape. The person in command of the target vessel never attempted either. He kept a steady course west. Any U-boat would have eventually turned northeast for the occupied coast. I judged the target not to be a threat."

Oppenheim stood and demanded,

"What qualifies you to make that judgement?"

Pat Cork replied calmly.

"Four years fighting the Battle of the Atlantic and fifteen Russian convoys." Oppenheim continued, ignoring Pat's answer, now addressing the admirals. "Gentlemen, it is obvious to me that this incident is being covered up by this ship's crew. I now demand a general court-martial."

Admiral Hilliard stood and addressed the admirals.

"Sirs, I would like to ask Mr Oppenheim a number of questions."

Both flag officers conferred, and Spenser said,

"Go ahead, please."

Oppenheim remained standing as Hilliard spoke.

"Mr Oppenheim, you are stating that a conspiracy has been hatched by the crew of HMS Longbow. Is that correct?"

The OSS man answered,

"Yes, I am."

Hilliard spoke slowly.

"May I ask why you say this?"

The answer was almost spat out.

"They're all on the same ship. They would all stick together."

Hilliard continued.

"Would you accept testimony from witnesses who are not from the crew of HMS Longbow?"

Oppenheim almost laughed.

"Yes. I would if any existed."

Admiral Hilliard picked up two pieces of paper.

"Sirs, I have here affidavits sworn by two US Army engineers who were aboard HMS Longbow at the time of the alleged depth charge attack. These officers swear that no, I repeat, no depth charges were deployed by HMS Longbow."

He approached the admirals and handed over the documents. Oppenheim shouted,

"What are those officers' names?"

Burke read the papers given him by Hilliard and spoke slowly.

"That, Mr Oppenheim, is classified."

Simpson-Coyle, now very red in the face, demanded,

"Who are those affidavits witnessed by?"

Admiral Burke looked at him with open contempt.

"Allow me to read his name." He paused.

"George S Patton. General Officer Commanding, United States Third army."

Jessica Cork sat and read Bill's letter, which described the Cork family in London. She walked over to the Big House and sat down in Catherine Buchanan's kitchen. The lady of the house came in and, as usual, smiled her welcome.

"Catherine," Jessica began.

"The funeral was one of the worst days of my life, but it helped me to reach a decision. Tom and I have never had any secrets, and I don't want to have any now. Bill says in his last letter that he will leave it to me to decide about his father being told of Connor Cork and his family in London."

Catherine said,

"Have a cup of coffee, honey."

Tom Cork sat on his horse in the middle pasture - a place where he always came in times of stress. Many years before, this pasture had been the beginning of a journey which led him to marriage and the life he now enjoyed. His mind was racked with the pain of Mandy Bruce's parents. He did not regret speaking his mind about the funeral. Now he just wanted his boy home and did not care how it was done. From his letters, it was obvious that Bill was now a highly experienced battle-hardened soldier. Tom was not worried about his son's ability to survive combat. His concern was how he would deal with the death of someone who was very special to him. Tom Cork knew about loneliness; it makes people do strange things. He and Charlie Rawlings were so worried they'd even talked about pulling strings and getting Bill sent back to the US as a training officer. Then something moved in the distance. Years on the range had sharpened his eyesight. His heart sank and terrible thoughts of Bill raced through his mind as he identified three riders approaching at full gallop. Jessica on her powerful chestnut mare and Catherine's grey range horse with Buchanan on an Appaloosa stallion. They pulled up in arrived in a flurry of grass moisture thrown up by the horse's hooves. Almost afraid to speak, Thomas Cork asked,

"What are you all doing out here? What's wrong? Is it Bill?"

His wife kissed him on the cheek and said,

"No, my darling Irishman, as far as we know, he is fine. Tom, I have a letter from Bill which I want you to read. Now please finish the letter before you say anything. Will you do that for me, Tom? Please."

The joint owner of the Double B dismounted and stood by his wife as she handed him the letter. Jessica remained in the saddle, her hand draped across her husband's shoulder, as he read of Connor and his wife and family, the business and how Bill had met his cousin in the middle of a bloody battle. It did not take long to read the letter through. Tom mounted his horse, saying,

"We should be getting home. It'll soon be dark."

On the ride back to the Ranch, Tom Cork stopped twice to read his son's letter again, as if he was going over the details or trying to absorb the meaning of the words. That evening, in the lounge of the Lake House, he began to talk about Connor. Every now and then referring to the letter as a prompter.

"Married a Kerry girl - Mary Cork. Could be problems come Munster final day."

His wife and the Buchanans just listened. Then silence until,

"Two boys and a girl, fair play to ya, Connor boy."

His wife had never heard his West Cork accent so pronounced as if Tom was talking to his brother.

"Managing director of a big building company - I knew he'd do well. Brains to burn has Connor, and he'd charm the leaves off the trees."

Then silence once more as he stood up, poured four drinks, and handing one to each of the people in the room, he raised his glass, saying,

"To my brother and his wonderful family for being so good to our Bill. Whatever happens from here on, I'll always thank them for that kindness." Jessica looked at Catherine, who said,

"Tom, they weren't being kind; they were just being family."

The sun came up over the flat land of the Dutch-German border. Erebus and Vali had made good progress. It seemed remarkable to them that the canals of the lowlands were not too badly damaged. They were, along with the Germans, unaware that the RAF pilots and navigators used the canals as night-time navigational aids, so spared them. There were no roadblocks or checkpoints, so progress for the barge was swift. On the odd occasion when they were questioned, the sight of a few gold coins worked wonders. Germany was in meltdown and it seemed that 'every man for himself was the order of the day. The canals stretched all the way into Northern Germany. As the barge neared the North Eastern Coast, the landscape became sparse and unwelcoming. Food was not as scarce as being near the sea; the agents bought fresh fish for a price with gold that also guaranteed silence amongst the civilian population. Erebus and Vali took the barge into the marshy waters of the coastal seas near the small village of Peenemunde and found an ancient mooring built into the bog banks, which had grown up over hundreds of years of peat cutting. This mooring gave great cover to the barge, which was, even at high tide, barely visible from the landward side of the marsh. The seaward side was always fog-bound. As February came to an end, the days were very short. The barge was proving to be a very good friend indeed, providing both transport and shelter. Very early one morning, the men decided to go inshore and find the nearest village but just then, from the landward side, there came a roaring sound - an ugly noise - not like the sound of a Spitfire, its Rolls Royce Merlin engine almost singing, or the raw power of the American Pratt and Whitney engines. It was an almost evil noise. To Vali and Erebus, it was an odd sound. Then they saw a rocket climbing into the sky and heading out to sea. Both men knew immediately that their search was over. Vali reached for the SOE radio and began to signal Maiden Aunt.

In Portsmouth, the enquiry was coming to an end. Admirals Spenser and Burke held discussions behind closed doors. Spenser summarised the Royal Navy's point of view.

"No loss of life has occurred, and Mr Oppenheim and Colonel Simpson-Coyle have, in my opinion, failed to prove any attack by HMS Longbow." Admiral Burke was more affected by the whole episode.

"May God help us all, admiral."

Spenser was taken aback by the words.

"I'm sorry, admiral. I don't follow."

Burke repeated his words.

"May God help us all if men such as Oppenheim and that colonel are allowed to remain in the service of their countries? All we have heard from them today is pernicious mendacity. They came here to advance nothing but their own twisted agendas. Admiral Spenser, I would like to propose that we get young Cork in here, shake his hand, promote him, and ask if he has any room aboard HMS Longbow for two tired admirals who have seen too much of the dark side of humanity."

Spenser rose and asked the lieutenant standing outside the conference room to reconvene the hearing.

"Lieutenant Commander Cork, it is clear to me and my fellow flag officer that the submarine which was in the Channel was not attacked by your ship. From the evidence given by you and your shipmates, it is obvious that the case put forward by Colonel Simpson-Coyle and Mr Oppenheim is nothing more than a tissue of lies. Captain Cork, please return to your ship and carry on with the work you have been doing. Good luck to you and your crew."

Admiral Burke then turned his glare to Oppenheim and Simpson-Coyle.

"I am speechless at the scurrilous way in which you two have attempted to cover up whatever dirty game you are playing. I have no control over your actions, Mr Oppenheim, but hear me now and hear me loud and clear. I am an admiral in the United States Navy, and I am utterly convinced that those affidavits were not sworn by US naval officers. It seems that you have a submarine at your disposal. It may be a US Navy vessel. If that submarine and her crew are lost because of your orders, we will find out, and you will be charged with multiple murders."

He paused to calm down then, looking at the other man making the allegations, added with overt contempt,

"Colonel Simpson-Coyle, Admiral Spenser will speak to you in private. This hearing is concluded."

Bill Cork was finishing his notes on yet another interrogation when his colonel entered the tent.

"Some of our pilots who were returning after a bombing raid in Germany were buzzed by a form of pilotless aircraft. It was later confirmed as a V1 flying bomb. The pilots backtracked the trajectory and calculated it came from an area near the German North Eastern Coast called Peenemunde. Bill, our orders are to go there and find Von Braun. Wherever the rockets are, he will not be far away from them."

Jessica Cork watched as her husband sat at his desk. She knew Tom always got his paperwork done early in the morning because 'It gives me the rest of the day to do the things I enjoy.' He stood and walked over to her.

"The day we buried that beautiful young woman was one of the saddest days of my life. I tried to figure out if some good could come from Mandy's death. That beautiful girl taken by a rocket explosion in the middle of a city full of civilians. These Germans are evil beyond belief. Maybe I'm wrong, but I realise now that life is too precious to bear old hatreds. I know Bill is worried about my reaction to finding out about Con. Well, I don't want him worrying about me or anything else. I want only one thing in life now - our boy home."

His wife took his hand.

"What are you going to do, Tom?"

"Jessie, this is a letter to my brother Connor. I think you know the address. I just want to say hello. All the questions that will come afterwards, I'll deal with when Bill is back on the Double B."

Jessica Cork took the envelope.

"I'll post it in the morning."

Professor John Eldridge was closing a number of files on his camp bed when Major Cork walked in.

"William, how are you this fine morning?"

Bill smiled at the eccentric genius with a heart of gold, for whom tidiness was never a strong point. There were files all over the bed. He asked,

"Are these confidential, John? You know what the security guys are like." Eldridge took some sheets of paper from Bill and leafed through them. As usual, his mind wandered as he concentrated on one piece of paper.

"Terrifying. Absolutely terrifying. Devil's weapon."

Bill asked,

"What is?"

Eldridge handed Bill the report.

"A rocket landed in a London suburb some weeks ago - killed over a hundred poor souls. A place called Dollis Hill. The man we're going to rescue from the Nazis - Herr Professor Werner Von Braun - designed that rocket."

Bill Cork remained silent. Maybe because of shock or grief he had never found out the details of Mandy's death. All Colonel Travers had said was that she had died as the result of an explosion in North London.

Colonel Simpson-Coyle stood to attention in front of Admiral Spenser in an office at Portsmouth Naval Base. His demeanour was no longer arrogant. The conclusion of the investigation was damning, and he knew he was running out of time and friends. Spenser looked at the man who had so blatantly lied, fabricated evidence and had attempted to pervert all known natural justice. His instinctive reaction was to court-martial the colonel and drum him out of the army. But he couldn't. There was still the problem of the breach of security. Who had given Erebus his code name? He spoke slowly.

"Colonel, I presume you are aware that there is now enough evidence against you for a court-martial to summarily dismiss you from the service and possibly impose a custodial sentence. Remember, I hold all of this evidence and will use it should you attempt to repeat your actions. You will return to headquarters and await further orders. Is that understood?"

"Perfectly, sir."

The relief was clear in his voice. Spenser carried on.

"Simpson-Coyle, if you do not obey all orders from now on, I will personally destroy what's left of your career. Now go."

Bill Cork and John Eldridge finished packing his papers in their tent. Bill asked a question.

"John, this guy we're after - Von Braun. Is he the only man who is qualified to make these rockets work?"

The scientist answered,

"Indeed, William. That is why we need to talk to him. There is no greater expert on these weapons."

Bill spoke slowly.

"Which means he is responsible for any deaths caused by these rockets?"

Yes, William, every single one of them."

Bill continued.

"So there is no doubt that he designed the rocket that exploded in Dollis Hill in North London."

Eldridge was adamant.

"None whatsoever, William. Absolutely no doubt at all."

As the convoy got underway, Major Bill Cork sat in a truck and felt his anger grow. Until now, the war had been impersonal - just names and faces - no one close, except, of course, for his beloved Mandy, Pat Cork and his family. Bill had even begun to come to terms with her death - an accident, a consequence of war, another casualty. Now it was different. Now he was going to come face to face with her murderer. His rage changed to cold hard hatred. Bill now realised how Irish he was and understood how his father must have felt. Now he knew of the passion, the blinding need for revenge that drives every thought and action. For Bill Cork, the war had just become very personal.

36

Operation Javelin

The report on the allegations made against the captain of HMS Longbow was circulated to senior officers of the US and Royal Navies. Admiral Burke was ordered to find the submarine. There was no proof except the testimony of HMS Longbow's crew that the boat existed. It was possible to hide a submarine in the myriad of small inlets and harbours on the British Isles coastline. What really concerned the appalled admiral was that the OSS could run a piece of equipment as potent as a submarine without authorisation from US Government services. He silently swore.

"Jesus, this guy has got his own private navy."

His thoughts were disturbed by an aide.

"A call for you, Sir. Admiral Spenser". Burke picked up the handset.

"Good afternoon, Admiral."

"Good afternoon, Admiral Burke." The Englishman was precise.

"We've checked all of our escort's logs, and apart from Longbow, there are no reports of an unidentified submarine in the channel." Spenser continued.

"May I make an observation? Burke encouraged.

"Please do, Admiral, please do." Spenser began,

"There is a US navy officer named Clinton who has worked with the Royal Navy." Burke commented.

"I've heard of him. Raised a number of vessels in Pearl after the Japanese attack." Spenser went on.

"Just a thought, but were any of the vessels raised submarines?" Burke became optimistic.

"I'll start if checking the OSS could have acquired one." Spenser asked.

"Acquired?" Burke answered.

"Just that, during the chaos." He finished with.

"We might just be getting a handle on these people."

Erebus and Vali reconnoitred the outskirts of Peenemunde. The terrain around the village was bare. The marshlands offering little succour for trees or foliage. The village itself had been forced to be a town by the influx of over five hundred personnel and was largely undamaged by the recent raid, unlike the rocket development site, which had been literally flattened and was now in the early stages of being rebuilt. The agents decided all they could do for now was report to HQ.

"It's no good having gold if there is no one to bribe. Those SS Guards are all fanatics. They wouldn't be here if they weren't. As for the technical people, we don't know any of them." Vali sat deep in thought as he sipped his tea. His comrade continued.

"How do we get recruited to the team working on the rockets without attracting the attention of the SS?" Then questioned.

"Any ideas?" His comrade replied.

"Well, we've found what looks like the launch site. We'll tie up and watch for a while." That night the camouflaged barge was moored about three kilometres from the compound. The OP was halfway between the barge and the exterior wire of the compound. For three days, they watched as a large tower was erected. Encircling, at a distance from the increasingly high structure, were a series of barrack-like huts. The site perimeter was patrolled by heavily armed SS men. All lorries and buses were rigorously searched in and out at the gates. Erebus observed.

"The scientists are billeted in town and bussed to work every morning." Vali pondered.

"So, what's in the huts inside the wire?" The answer to his question was made tragically clear as the occupants of the huts began to fill the compound in the striped uniforms of slave workers.

"Look at those poor devils," Vali whispered as both men watched the clearly distinct lower stages of a rocket surrounded by a number of men in white coats, others in overalls and the poor men in striped clothes. The missile began to take shape. Vali looked down, then heard Erebus gasp.

"My God, it's on fire." A huge explosion rocked the entire area. Vali's eyes came up to see the rocket assembly and all those near to it disappear in a ball of flame. The smoke blew away, and the full extent of the damage became clear. The tower had disappeared. The huts in the compound were ablaze, with men in flames running from them. Scientists in white coats staggering around and many more lying prone on the scorched earth. Erebus asked of no one.

"What the hell happened?" Slowly order was brought to the carnage. Ambulances entered the launch site, and the technicians were evacuated. Little help was given to casualties in striped clothes. The SOE agents returned to the barge and were silent for the rest of the day. Erebus spoke with urgency.

"We need to report this to HQ and get some orders. This waiting around will get us killed." Vali nodded his head in agreement and voiced some questions.

"Have you noticed there are no antennae or aerials in the compound? Maybe the boffins can spread a little light on that mystery?" The radio call was short as Erebus brought Maiden Aunt up to date on the explosion and the slave labour. Then described the very tight security in the compound. Davies' orders were explicit.

"Do not take any risks whatsoever. Do you understand, Boys? No risks at all. Just keep a watch on the whole bloody disgraceful carry-on; I'll see what the scientists say about the aerial question. Now, remember, no risks. Over and out." Sitting in silence in his office Maiden Aunt sighed with relief. The report on the explosion was passed on to higher authority. At least in the short term, London would get respite, which pleased Davies, as did the fact his men were safe for a while longer. The next night Erebus and Vali had some relatively good news from Prof Williamson.

"Gentlemen, we're fairly certain that the Germans are concerned that radio waves could affect the guidance systems of the long-distance rockets. Hence no radio near the compound. Just please be careful, boys. Over." Erebus asked about Von Braun.

"Do we know if the target wants to leave the nest and come to a new home," He added,

"Does he know we are here? Over," Maiden Aunt replied frankly.

"The answer to your first question is no; from the information so far, we have no idea of what he will do. The second question. Again, the answer is no. Sorry. Over and out." After the radio call, Vali summarised.

"So, Charles, all we have to do is walk into a compound crawling with Nazi fanatics and ask the second most heavily guarded man in Germany if he would like to defect to the Allies." Erebus replied with a question.

"Do you have any brothers or sisters?" Vali responded.

"I told you I have a family in Norway. Yes, I've got one brother."

"Would you do anything for him?" Erebus continued his enquiry.

"In certain circumstances, yes, I suppose I would. What are you on about, Charles?" He asked.

"Well, my friend, we cannot approach Werner Von Braun, but there is nothing stopping us talking to his little brother. Tomorrow you and I will officially report for work. In the process, we might find out if the baby rocket maker has a weakness." Vali smiled.

"And you know as well as I do everyone has a weakness."

Vali and Erebus watched the funeral services for the German fatalities; nothing was said for the dead slave workers, and they felt sheer horror as the bodies were buried in separate mass graves. That afternoon, they approached the younger Von Braun as he crossed the village square heading toward the hotel. He seemed very nervous as the men presented papers showing them to be electrical technicians who had just returned from France.

"You have arrived just in time; we had a bad accident recently." His voice unsure, despite efforts to be commanding.

"You will ask for me when you report for work tomorrow." Erebus asked.

"Where do we stay Sir?" The German snapped.

"I cannot be expected to do everything for you. You will have to find your own rooms. You are electricians; that is my only concern. After that, look after yourselves." He was unnerved, clearly not good at dealing with pressure.

Both were silently pleased. Von Braun's indecision allowed them to stay in the barge, and their hunch had been correct. Gerber Von Braun was the weakness and might just be the way to his elder brother. The next morning two new 'electrical engineers began work. The compound was under the constant scrutiny of SS men and Nazi party officials. It was clear that technicians and scientists were living and working in an atmosphere of complete terror. Vali and Erebus kept to themselves, somehow convincing other colleagues of their competence. They even became party to compound gossip about an incident at the hotel. Werner Von Braun had been dangerously loud in his criticism of the Nazi leadership, within earshot of SS officers and party officials. Later that week, the elder Von Braun was inspecting the V2 rocket, on which, amongst others, Vali and Erebus were working. As they were attempting to connect complicated wiring, Erebus whispered to Vali.

"Remember what you said about as long as we don't have to use any…." He was silenced by the elder Von Braun, who pushed him aside and, having checked their work, began shouting.

"You people are not technicians. What are you? Who are you? Are you spies or saboteurs?" As he turned to call the guards, a vehicle pulled up in the compound, and two high-ranking SS officers climbed out. They marched straight to where Vali, Erebus and von Braun were standing. One shouted at the SOE men.

"You two move away from this man immediately." Both did as ordered, but stayed close enough to hear.

"Herr Professor, we have received reports that you may have doubts about the inevitability of our victory. Please come with us." Erebus and Vali stood in silence and a mixture of utter amazement and relief. They had just been saved from certain death by the Waffen SS. Von Braun was driven away. All work was cancelled until further notice. The SOE officers walked out of the compound and returned to the barge.

Oppenheim was desperate, having promised his superior a number of leading German scientists within weeks of his posting to Britain. So far, all he had done was antagonise a number of senior officers in the US and British Navies. As for the secrecy of the OSS, he heard a report that General Patton had described the organisation as covert as 'a bull with a hard on in field of heifers.' Patton was proving to be a real problem. His popularity in the United States was immense. There were rumours that he regularly spoke to Roosevelt. Oppenheim swore.

"Jesus, I hate these fucking patrician Ivy league bastards."

Oppenheim was from a family of patricians but was a considerable disappointment to them. His father and Uncle had a very successful 'Family Law Practice' in Tennessee with an office in Washington dedicated to providing legal advice to US Government departments. They had expected young Oppenheim to qualify from Yale, practice in Tennessee, then Washington. Oppenheim soon found that both Yale and the 'law' bored him. What the college did bring out in the young man was an aptitude for finding financial, sexual or political nonconformity in people, which he ruthlessly exploited. This 'gift' helped him cheat his way through two years at the illustrious school. The academic authorities were suspicious, but his father and uncle were honoured, former students. Then Oppenheim was suspected of being a significant factor in the death of a young homosexual law student. His name being mentioned in the tragic young man's journal on an almost daily basis. The death was confirmed as suicide; the diary was suppressed at the family's wishes. All of Oppenheim's coursework was examined and found to have been completed by students he had coerced. He was given twenty-four hours to leave Yale. The expulsion left the men in the 'Family Practice' beyond words and with no idea what to do with the 'malcontent' as his father called him. Then an old friend of his Uncle in Washington took a hand. He was part of a team recruiting staff for an organisation to gather information beneficial to the US in war and then peace. The majority of recruits were Harvard and Yale graduates, but there was work for those not imbued with the righteous zeal of the Ivy League. Men who could find weaknesses and exploit them. Oppenheim was ideal and immediately signed on. Yale tried to forget all about him; the Family Firm were glad he was out of the way.

In London, Oppenheim was an increasingly worried man. Despite high-powered friends, his actions were ringing alarm bells in Washington. The men who had set up the US intelligence services were beginning to demand reasons for certain actions and statements. Particularly accusations made against an experienced Royal Navy escort officer by Oppenheim. The US and Royal Navies had, with other allied Navies, paid a very high price to deliver the convoys to Britain and Russia. Oppenheim's gross disrespect for service and rank was now raising doubts about the ability of the men who recruited him to do their jobs. A general search for a missing submarine was underway in the UK when the US Navy was stretched to the limit. Oppenheim was unofficially told one more mistake, and his career in espionage would be over. He decided someone else would have to take the blame for the allegations of an attack on a submarine and contacted Simpson-Coyle.

The German holy river. The Rhine. The last line of defence of the Fatherland was breached on the night of the 22nd of March 1945. Three thousand men of General Patton's 5th division simply rowed across. Bill Cork, the other minders and the scientists followed closely. The 'research unit,' as it was known, was ordered to find Werner Von Braun before the British and the Russians. Travers and Cork knew that Von Braun was near Peenemunde in northeastern Germany, which was still in German hands with the Russians advancing from the east. They knew nothing of Erebus and Vali.

Odin and Maiden Aunt sat in utter amazement as Erebus finished his briefing.

"Well, Sir, that's what happened. As of now, Von Braun is a prisoner of the SS and is being held in an interrogation centre. Over." Maiden Aunt signed off the signal with the words.

"Please let me have an update of the situation as soon as possible with any suggestions as to how we bring this mess to a conclusion. Just remember this. At the first sign of danger to yourselves, get out immediately. I repeat immediately. Over and out."

Davies had become accustomed to Odin's mannerisms as a commanding officer, and what came next was a total surprise.

"Jesus, those Nazis are all utterly insane. Every single fucking one of them."

Oppenheim and Simpson-Coyle agreed to meet in Piccadilly Circus. The American began.

"Colonel, we have to find something which will give us - as we say in America - a win before the end of the war."

"I agree wholeheartedly, Mr Oppenheim," Simpson-Coyle summarised the current situation,

"We must now consider a degree of damage limitation. The hunt for the submarine is gathering pace. The fact that you were never on that submarine and I never met the officers will be confirmed." Oppenheim was as furtive as ever, even in the middle of a packed city.

"I have arranged a way of bringing that investigation to an end. That's all you need to know." Simpson-Coyle nodded his head as he concluded the meeting.

"Now let's look after each other until the German surrender. We may get out with our pensions". Oppenheim's plan involved Captain Day leaving his personal office keys in his desk, where an operative of the OSS would use them to remove and destroy all incriminating evidence. Day, now a very nervous man, got his dates mixed up.

In His Majesty's naval base Portsmouth, the night shore patrol was carrying out a routine clean desk sweep of all offices. In the port captain's office, a set of keys were slightly protruding from a desk drawer. As standard procedure, the keys were confiscated. In the morning, Captain Day was ordered to the office of a Commodore who demanded an explanation as to why the keys were not secured. This he could not do. The cupboards and safe, which the keys opened, were searched and revealed a number of unusual documents. The first was an original signal sent to HMS Longbow ordering the cessation of a depth charge attack. The second was a copy of a signal from the USS Tigerfish to the Port captain's office. In which the captain of the submarine took full responsibility for his submarine being in the English Channel without the necessary authorisation and recognition signals. The reason given was two of his crew had been seriously injured when a torpedo had fallen on them during a loading drill in the forward torpedo chamber. He was making all speed to a US naval hospital ship in the Solent, which had special lifting gear to remove injured men from a submarine. The captain's actions had been authorised by the USN C in C Atlantic Submarines. There was in this new evidence two damning facts. One, the time of receipt of the Tigerfish signal by the port captain's office was ninety minutes before the alleged depth charge attack. Two. The signal had a priority cover note attachment. 'Forward to Royal Navy, C in C, Channel Fleet, Convoy Escorts. Immediately.' This instruction had not been carried out.

Captain Day was placed under close arrest and restricted to the base. Where he was now desperately regretting taking the word of Colonel Simpson-Coyle and the man Oppenheim for anything. He fervently wished he was back in Felixstowe port handling cargo ships. The documents and a report of the interview with the port captain were forwarded to Admirals Hilliard, Spenser and US Admiral Burke. Luckily for Day, the flag officers took the view that he had been set up by Oppenheim and Simpson-Coyle. His naval career as a member of the Volunteer naval reserve was finished. A court-martial was considered but it seemed very harsh to prosecute him and not the others involved. As for Simpson-Coyle and Oppenheim, the admirals took a very different position. Both would be utilised in front-line units. Colonel Travers and Bill Cork were informed that Oppenheim would be joining the research unit with one difference. Colonel Travers would have command. Simpson-Coyle's posting had not been briefed because of factors which Spenser did not reveal. The first was the unresolved security leak. The second was personal. He simply did not trust Simpson-Coyle at all. Spenser's explained to Admiral Burke. "Things were somewhat fluid."

Erebus and Vali had come to a similar conclusion about their situation and were explaining this to Maiden Aunt and Odin; unaware C was in the room.

"You see, gentlemen, we are convinced Von Braun has got to come back to Peenemunde. This is the only facility launching the V2 rocket. The scientific team is here, and we believe of greater importance is his brother. Over." Erebus asked.

"Do you have any idea where the SS have him imprisoned? Over." Vali answered.

"Not the faintest idea, Sir. Over."

"Right, well, that's fair enough. Listen, boys, sit tight for as long as you can. If he returns, try to make contact with him. Over." Another voice came on the radio.

"Gentlemen, this is 'C'. I want to stress that you only make contact with this man if there is absolutely safe to do so. We will be getting you out of there as soon as possible. There are other people looking for this man, as I am sure you are aware. To this end, the decision has been made to allow the Americans to join the Operation. You will be supplied with details which will enable you to contact the aforementioned Allies; please do so immediately and arrange to join forces. I have ensured that the soldiers involved in the American team are experienced. In fact, I think you are acquainted with one of them. Good luck to you both, and please be careful. Over and out." Once the radio link was closed, Maiden Aunt spoke.

"Gentlemen, I intend to provide the American research team with assistance when attempting to make contact with Erebus. I further intend to ask for a Special Forces unit to be placed on standby to carry out an evacuation of our men behind enemy lines if the situation demands." Odin replied.

"Permission granted on both counts. I take it you will use your collectors to deliver the Research team to Erebus. I'll request that Colonel Weir and his 62 commando be assigned to your section until further notice. I can't see any problems there; they are near the front-lines as we speak."

Simpson-Coyle stood in front of Admiral Spenser. The report from the investigators at Portsmouth on his desk.

"I see from this document that there were never any witness statements or affidavits from the officers aboard the mystery submarine. Which is, for your information, called the USS Tigerfish. Tell me something, have you completely lost the ability to tell the truth?" Simpson-Coyle was about to answer when Spenser exploded.

"I don't want an answer. It would undoubtedly be yet another falsehood. Oppenheim has been sent to the front to assist in the capture of a number of scientists. One of these men is called Werner Von Braun. You will accompany a number of British non-service personnel to interview Von Braun. You will assist these men in every way possible whilst ensuring their safety at all times. That Colonel is entirely your responsibility. The interview with Von Braun will take place under the aegis of a British forces front-line unit. What I have just told you is top secret. Should I hear anything of this mission from anybody but those authorised to know, I will hold you responsible. I also hold you responsible for keeping Oppenheim's knowledge of this mission confidential. If anything leaks, I will bury both of you. So pass that on to him. Your orders and travel permits are with the officer outside. Now get out."

Colonel Travers was called to the radio truck by a 5th division sergeant. "Colonel, there's a signal message for you from Colonel Weir of Combined

Operations." Travers read the signal and returned to the tent where Bill and John Eldridge were waiting. He closed the flap.

"Major Cork, I have just been briefed that a number of British agents are in touch with a relative of Von Braun somewhere in northern Germany. We have been ordered to join these men. Apparently, you know them personally." Bill asked.

"Do you have their call signs, Colonel?"

"No, they will make contact with us". Travers continued.

"A section of this signal is encoded. When we are contacted, they will ask us for a sequence of letters which they will decode. This guarantees they are speaking to the correct people and not the enemy." John Eldridge asked

"May I see the signal, Colonel?" Travers looked to Bill Cork, who nodded, saying.

"You're in command now, Sir" Travers smiled with real satisfaction.

"Yes, so I am." The scientist's eyes lit up as he examined the coded signal then silence, as he scribbled columns and squares made up of numbers and letters. Soon he had a base grid to work from then, in another hour, had arrived at a square made up of letters and numbers. Eldridge smiled and asked his young minder.

"William, these code squares have a theme or master word, don't they?" For the first time since they had met, Bill had the intellectual advantage and was enjoying it.

"Try Norse mythology?" Eldridge looked perplexed, then concentrated on the grid.

"Yes, there are words contained in the grid which have Norse references. If you didn't know what you were looking for, you'd never find them. Very simple but very effective." Travers asked.

"Do you know these men, Bill?" Major Cork stood as he remembered the raid in Norway, and his chest filled out.

"Yes, I know them Sir, and they are the best there is. If they are near this guy Von Braun, we are in good hands." At that moment the tent opened, and a quartermaster came in.

"Colonel, I have a radio here for your personal use. Please sign here, would you?" As the soldier left the tent, the radio was switched on and immediately crackled to life.

"Calling Operation Javelin. Please acknowledge. Over." Bill recognised the voice of his comrade in arms, Erebus. Once identities had been confirmed, Bill asked.

"Please brief current state of Operation. Over." Erebus briefed in general terms about the initial contact with the targets and referred to operating from a mobile base. He informed them that he would be their minder once behind enemy lines. Then, the Von Brauns would be contacted and persuaded to join the allies. Erebus signed off with grid references for the collection and informed Bill Cork that all transport needs would be supplied by the British.

Having shut down the radio, Erebus looked at Vali and sighed.

"Right, it's time to get this Operation going."

Gerber Von Braun was in his brother's office in the launch pad area when he heard a voice calling his name. His terror that the Gestapo had come for him was reflected in his tremulous voice.

"I'm in here." The office door opened, and two new electricians entered. The German snapped.

"I told you idiots to find your own accommodation." The reply to his rudeness came in a cultured English accent.

"Von Braun, I'm led to believe you and your brother speak very good English. Is that the case?" The German stood and inhaled to allow him to shout for guards. Erebus produced a Luger pistol.

"Please remain silent, then calm down and answer my question." His voice was flat. The scientist realised to disobey could mean death.

"Yes, it is true; I speak English, as does my brother." Erebus motioned with his firearm for the German to retake his seat and continued.

"We have come to talk about your accommodation, not ours. To discuss you and your brother's survival in the long term." Von Braun, now completely stunned, reverted to German.

"What do you mean? Who…" Erebus cut across him.

"English, please, Von Braun." He repeated the point to establish control of the situation. "From now on, English only." Then continued.

"Now, please listen. We represent a western power which can, when your brother returns, make it possible for both of you to be out of harm's way quickly and permanently" Von Braun's voice became desperate.

"What do you know of my brother? Is he safe?" Vali answered.

"We have no idea what your brother's current whereabouts or the state of his health. What do you know?"

"Nothing whatsoever," was the surly reply. Erebus encouraged.

"Let's be optimistic. In the meantime, you must carry on as you are. Do not tell anyone what we have said to you. Please bear in mind the Nazis will never allow you or your brother to live. The Russians will, but under very harsh conditions. Our principals offer freedom and good life, and protection from those seeking retribution for the rockets which have killed so many civilians." While his comrade had been talking to the German, Vali had been going through the papers on the office desk and asked the German.

"Have you read any of these documents?"

"No, I have been too worried about Werner". Von Braun retorted. Vali continued.

"The high command have allocated more materials and labour to this installation, which means your brother is coming back. When he does, you must get him to talk to us immediately. Von Braun, we are the only way in which you and your brother can get out of here." The German demanded.

"How do I know you can do what you say you can?" Erebus answered.

"We got in here without anyone knowing, and we will get out as well." The younger Von Braun dropped his head.

"What happens now?"

"You do nothing until we tell you, do you understand?" Gerber had been controlled easily. The elder brother might not be so obedient.

As Bill and Travers were making final equipment checks, John Eldridge asked a question.

"William, what happens if Von Braun doesn't speak English or will only speak to a fellow scientist?" The soldiers had no answers. Travers voiced a thought.

"Mr Eldridge, would I be correct in stating you speak fluent German?"

"Well, when I learned I was coming to this country, I thought, why not?" His voice was without a hint of pomposity. Travers was silent; Bill, who sensed the Colonel's reluctance, butted in.

"Sir. Let me say this. We do not speak German, and we may need someone with a scientific background who does." Bill paused and then went for broke,

"If I may remind you, Sir, you have the authority to assign people to Operation Javelin?" Travers gave Bill a look.

"Major, you've got the gift of the gab; of that, there is no doubt." He turned to Eldridge,

"May I call you John?" The scientist smiled.

"Of course, Colonel. Now, what did you want to know?"

"John, how long did it take you to learn the German language" Eldridge needed no prompting.

"Oh, about ten weeks, really. Then I have been listening to the people here since we arrived. That has helped no end." Travers sighed.

"Do you need any help to pack? John. If not, we leave in an hour." Just then the tent flap opened, and a sergeant of the 5th brigade asked.

"Colonel, could you step outside for a minute, please." Travers did so and re-entered the tent minutes later with the words.

"As we're all Americans here, I believe I can say. Let's saddle up. Our transport has arrived." They left the tent to be greeted by the sight of a German Army truck and two soldiers standing next to it. Travers nodded to the taller man who spoke.

"Gentlemen, my comrade and I have been asked to get where you need to be. This fine figure of a man is Sergeant Mullen, and I am Sergeant major Reilly. Please do not ask us about our methods or where the truck came from. We are codenamed the 'collectors,' and that is all you need to know."

Vali booked into the town hotel and took covert guard on the baby rocket maker. After two days, Erebus was alongside a small jetty just behind allied lines and listened to a diesel engine closing. Soon he was shaking hands with Major Bill Cork and being introduced to Colonel Travers and John Eldridge. Reilly and Mullen greeted him warmly and passed on new equipment. A very powerful compact radio and up-to-date charts of the canal system in Germany, Holland and Denmark. The barge headed toward Peenemunde and the inventor of the V2 rocket and the man responsible for the murder of Bill Cork's fiancé. The 'Collectors' set off to find 62 Commando somewhere to the west and prepare an escape route for Operation Javelin. Sergeant Mullen asked,

"Cormac, how many of these Special Forces boys will there be?"

At the HQ of the SOE Menzies, Spenser and Davies sat as Professor Williamson briefed them on the situation in Germany. Allied forces were advancing from the west. The Russians were invading Germany from the east and displaying no regard for the human cost of their troops or German civilians. Hence the speed of the advance. Latest intelligence reports led him to conclude that unless the men now on their way back to Peenemunde got out very quickly, it was likely they would be surrounded not by Germans but Russians.

Finally, Davies spoke.

"Forgive me, gentlemen, but there is a question I feel I must ask?" Spenser said. "Please do Brigadier."

"How far are we prepared to go to extract Von Braun from Germany? I ask this because I am becoming profoundly concerned for the welfare of my men." Menzies answered in an almost scolding tone of voice.

"They are our men, Maiden Aunt and whilst I empathise with your concern, Erebus and Vali are first and foremost members of the allied armed forces." Davies would not back down.

"I have considered that Sir, but are they expendable? They have delivered close to miracles for the allied cause. I will not lose them now to a gang of murdering psychopaths for the sake of a rocket scientist who is utterly amoral and unethical."

The senior officers showed little emotion as they considered the Welshman's words. Menzies stood and walked around the room.

"I think much clearer when I walk. Goes back to my days aboard ship. I used to walk the length of the foc'sle every day for at least an hour. Keeps the circulation fast. Small things, ships, when looked at in the overall span of things." Spenser and Davies sat and watched in silence as the human side of this man came through as C sat down.

"Maiden Aunt, I will ensure you have at your disposal the elements to affect the escape of all of our men from enemy territory. How you use them is up to you." He then listed the resources in detail. Davies replied.

"Thank you, Sir, that will do very nicely." Odin summarised.

"Gentlemen, we must bear in mind the entire Operation hinges on what Werner Von Braun does. If he betrays the Javelin team, they all face death in Nazi Germany or will disappear into Stalinist Russia for good."

37

Bringing Order

Connor Cork sat in his office. The war was coming to a close - just a matter of weeks if the newspaper headlines were to be believed - but when would Pat and Bill come home? The death of Peter English and the work on the Mulberry Harbours had occupied his mind. Now he had to force himself to think about something else, anything but the thought of losing Pat or Bill. Connor's natural optimism rose as he considered the future and the 'Peace'. The practicalities of which raised questions. Where would they live when the war was over? How much would it cost to rebuild the house in Dollis Hill? The business had gone well during the war; the Cork family were not without means. Mary and he had inadvertently touched on the future, then quickly changed the subject; since the death of Mandy Bruce, both silently acknowledged a ridiculous superstition that became an iron rule. They were practical and successful people - yet afraid of tempting fate. There would be no plans made until everybody was safe and sound at home. Connor began to read the business post on his desk; the majority were invoices from suppliers and government circulars. There was one unusual letter from a firm of solicitors in The Aldwych in London. He and Mary were asked to arrange an appointment as soon as possible. The letter was signed by a partner of the firm dealing with the matter at hand.

Connor looked at the empty office next door then his eye was drawn to a tender document requiring completion. The business was good, but a replacement for Peter English was badly needed. Some might call him unfeeling for filling the position so soon, but as managing director, it was his responsibility. What was needed was a highly experienced civil engineer. Cork's mind meandered through the men he had met during his time with the company. Maybe one would stand out as suitable for the job of replacing Peter English. He looked up to see the sunshine outside. Perhaps some fresh air would help.

Connor walked around the site enjoying the warm weather, subconsciously sifting names and faces of engineers who had worked with the company, and then, of course, there would be men coming home from the services looking for work. An idea began to take root in the recesses of his mind. At first, just a small inkling, but it began to grow without much effort on his part. A name came to the fore. The man was an excellent engineer, there was no doubt, and had proved himself to be flexible and adaptable - something which would be essential in a changing world. He was trustworthy and reliable. Connor, feeling good about it, put the idea to rest.

Having returned to the office, he then remembered the letter his wife had given him that morning with the words,

"Con, this came this morning. Maybe you could read it later on when things are quiet."

He walked to the coat stand in the corner of his office and found the envelope. Since the separation of his family, letters had become of vital importance. Connor knew his family members' handwriting instantly, but the address was in a longhand he did not recognise. The stamp was American. He opened the envelope and read,

'Dear Connor, after so many years apart, I thought maybe we could catch up....' He put the letter down, then picked it up again, turned to the last page and read, 'Your brother, Tom'.

He sat in his chair, heart pumping. Tom had written, after all these years. Connor could not read the letter yet. Contact with his brother was more than he could deal with right now. This was a huge issue to be dealt with. Connor felt panic rising through him; there was already enough uncertainty in his life. He needed time to think, to put his feelings in some sort of order. Tom's letter was placed in a drawer of his desk. What was needed now was to get something done, to achieve a degree of certainty. If only for today - that would do.

He dialled the number on the top of the solicitor's letter. A voice answered with the practice name. Cork identified himself and asked to speak to the partner named in the letter. Within ten minutes, an appointment had been confirmed for the Corks to go to London and meet the gentleman. The second phone call was to an army base not far from Portsmouth. Again, he was put through quickly and, as in the earlier call, he and the person to whom he was talking agreed a time and date for a chat and a spot of lunch. Connor then opened the desk drawer and began to read his brother's letter.

HMS Longbow was on escort duty; her captain stood on the bridge of his ship, looked to port, then starboard and saw a huge fleet of merchantmen all heading for France. Heen issued an order to the officer of the day.

"Mr Bellamy. Take us out to the edge of the convoy, please. I'll leave the course to you."

The reply came in a voice which brimmed with confidence.

"Aye, aye, sir."

The convoys were running nonstop to France, all loaded to the gunnels with supplies for yet another final push which would end the war - or so everybody was being told. Larsen approached.

"Captain, sir, I have two signals for you. Might I suggest you read them in private? Pat looked quizzically at his first officer and said,

"Flags, if you need me, I'll be in my cabin with the first officer."

Bellamy acknowledged,

"Very good, sir."

In the privacy of his cabin, Pat invited the first officer to sit as the captain's steward brought in two mugs of tea. Pat read the first signal, which informed him of his promotion to commander - endorsed by Royal Navy Admirals Hilliard and Spenser with congratulations from Admiral Burke of the US Navy. Pat handed the signal to Larsen and asked,

"Well, what do you think?"

Larsen began,

"Well, Pat, many congratulations on the third ring," then, looking at the endorsements, he could not resist adding,

"Christ, Pat! You really have got friends in high places."

There was no need to say more - Pat could see his friend was bursting with pride. The next signal was not so pleasant, ordering him to provision the ship from a supply vessel and make ready to steam at least a thousand miles at high speed. Lars was handed the second signal, was silent for a minute then said,

"This looks like we are once again under the orders of Odin and Maiden Aunt - hence the order to provision at sea - which is unfortunate. The boys were looking forward to some leave."

Pat replied,

"Agreed, but to put it in context, the weather has been relatively soft, the ship is in good condition, and the crew are reasonably rested. Considering the time of year, we cannot complain. This part of the Channel can be rough on men and ships."

They discussed the possibilities of where the ship would be operating. A knock came on the door and a midshipman entered with another signal which Lars decoded.

"Upon making contact with the fleet auxiliary, Sir Ivanhoe, you will take aboard three men, take station in the North Sea and await further orders."

Pat looked at his first officer.

"Right then! We'd better have a look at some charts of the Baltic and North Seas."

The men pored over the charts and the latest reports on the Allied and Russian land advances. Commander Cork spoke.

"I wonder where Erebus and Vali are now. Come to that, where are Bill Cork and his scientist? Lars, it's only an educated guess, but I think we will be ordered into the Baltic Sea to collect men from behind enemy lines. If that is the case, what concerns me, my friend, is that the only access to the German Coastline is from the North Sea and the Baltic which are both awash with Germans and Russians."

Oppenheim was standing in an empty tent, having been ignored, when demanding to know the location of Travers, Cork and Eldridge. The captain of the 5th Infantry division had obeyed his orders precisely.

"When a civilian called Oppenheim gets here, tell him to wait and tell him nothing more." Colonel Travers had warned him of the numerous threats he would be subjected to, his parting words being,

"Ignore him, Captain. I'll deal with him when we get back."

Oppenheim was learning the hard way that once the services closed ranks, no amount of covert pressure from powerful friends in Washington could do anything. He was at a base where the men had been in action since landing at Omaha Beach and were in no mood to listen to his threats. As one bullet-hard Kentuckian veteran, aged all of twenty-four, had growled,

"Things can get a little dangerous for greenhorns around here. If I were you, I just might want to remember that."

Simpson-Coyle collected his orders and travel permits. He was to proceed to Portsmouth Naval base to meet two gentlemen; then, all three men were to board a ship. Who these men were and what they did was unspecified. Simpson-Coyle was seething, having been, in his eyes, reduced to an escort officer to civilians. The train to Portsmouth was crowded, and he felt overwhelmed. As a man who had spent most of his adult life in foreign climes, he was not at ease in the country of his birth - it was just too crowded. Simpson-Coyle longed for the open spaces of Africa where there was solitude - but not a welcome - through the years, he had made a few reliable friends but many enemies. Now, as the war was coming to an end, his future was far from certain. Sometime later, the slightly calmer colonel arrived at the main gate of Portsmouth Naval Base and was escorted by the duty officer to an office where two men were waiting. Neither introduced themselves other than to say they were both engineers. Simpson-Coyle asked,

"Gentlemen, may I have your names please?"

The reply from one of the men was very much to the point.

"Colonel, we have been asked not to identify ourselves to you. This request we have agreed to."

The Royal Navy duty officer was not in the least put out by the strange conversation taking place in front of him. The manner in which his orders had been issued made it clear that this was an unusual situation.

"Get them aboard, make certain they put to sea, then forget you ever saw anything or anyone."

Admiral Spenser's voice had been deadly serious. The officer obeyed.

"Gentlemen, colonel, would you follow me please."

The barge nosed its way back to the mooring where Vali was waiting - as he had been every day. Erebus introduced him to Colonel Travers and Thomas Eldridge. He shook hands with them and then welcomed Bill Cork warmly with a handshake and a smile.

"How are you, Major Cork? Good to have you here on this job - might not be as straightforward as the Crown Jewels, though."

Bill spoke.

"Good to see you both. To be honest, I have been wondering if we are all insane. We're completely outnumbered, outgunned and miles from the nearest friendly forces."

There was silence as everyone digested the young American's cogent summary. Vali brought everyone up to speed.

"The arrest of Von Braun Senior has resulted in most of the SS officials and party members leaving. The hotel is virtually empty, so I took a room there for two reasons - firstly, to pick up any gossip and secondly, to stay close to the younger Von Braun. Nobody knows anything about the elder Von Braun. The entire scientific team is living in an atmosphere of pure terror, so nobody is saying anything."

Travers asked,

"What is the younger brother like?"

Vali continued.

"Weak and indecisive - without his brother, he will do nothing. I have been at the compound every day, and there is no evidence to suggest that Werner Von Braun is dead, so we assume that we still have a mission to complete. Now, might I suggest we lie low and possibly try to get some sleep? I will take the first watch."

Travers and Cork volunteered to relieve him. Now all they could do was wait. The morning brought good news. Vali and Erebus returned to the rocket site to learn that during the night, Werner Von Braun had been released by the SS. There had been no warning - a car simply arrived; the man got out and walked into the site office. Now, decisions had to be made. Colonel Travers took the lead.

"Gentlemen, we will have to find out if this guy will defect. If he won't, he will have to be eliminated. In either case, there is a need for us to have an escape plan which caters for everybody here. Now, any ideas on how we approach this Nazi rocket man?"

Vali proposed.

"Erebus and I will speak to him initially."

Bill Cork spoke.

"I'm a bit worried about both of you going in. If things go very wrong, we will need one of you to get us out of here and remember that the Germans, not to mention the Russians, would love to get their hands on John Eldridge."

Erebus had been watching Bill as he spoke, having noticed earlier how, at the mention of Von Braun's name, his eyes became steely cold. Professor Eldridge raised his hand in an almost apologetic fashion.

"Gentlemen, please excuse my intrusion. If I might speak?"

Bill said,

"Please go ahead, John."

Eldridge smiled.

"Thank you, William. Gentlemen, I would ask you to bear in mind that this man has been in the custody of the SS for at least two weeks. He is undoubtedly scared and profoundly distrustful of anyone remotely connected to the darker forces which have been unleashed by this war. I say this after my initial contact with a certain man called Oppenheim. Perhaps if Colonel Travers, Vali and myself spoke to either him or his brother, we could be successful in bringing both of them over to our way of thinking."

Erebus fired a question at the academic in German. His reply was word perfect. Both men smiled in acknowledgement. Erebus continued.

"Sorry about that, but I don't want anybody who can't speak German anywhere near the Von Braun's at first, so may I suggest a course of action. Vali, you speak to them and make it obvious what choices they have, which are, either come with us, or we leave them to the Russians and the SS. Then, you bring them out of the compound to meet the colonel and the professor."

There was a murmur of general agreement then Erebus continued,

"Should they agree to come with us, then they'll be told as much as they need to know. Just one more thing - we tell them nothing about this barge."

Travers realised why the missions these men had been involved in were successful. Everything was examined and dissected; every eventuality discussed before consensus was reached.

"Good morning, Herr Von Braun. How are you and your brother?"

Gerber turned to see Vali standing at the entrance to his office. The Norwegian could see he was deeply upset.

"My brother is back, but not for long. The SS want to move us all to Bavaria immediately. They are putting together a convoy now. They have even brought in drivers from the labour camps."

Vali demanded,

"When do you move out?"

"Within forty-eight hours. We have been ordered to bring all the technicians and as much equipment as possible. My brother is near breaking point. We need help, and we need it now!" he spluttered hysterically.

Vali spoke slowly.

"Will you please calm down? We have the means to get you and your brother away from here soon, but it must be timed properly. We don't need half the SS in pursuit. Do you understand?"

The German began to breathe easier as Vali said,

"Please contact your brother. Then we are all going for a walk."

Colonel Travers and Dr Eldridge stood in a quiet part of the countryside and watched three men approach. Vali was easily recognisable. The other two, both in Waffen SS uniforms, were quite different in stature. Eldridge produced a small camera and took photographs of the approaching group, ensuring that the compound was included in the frame. He advised Travers,

"The one on the right is Werner Von Braun."

The elder Von Braun was a good six inches taller than his brother and much broader and heavier build. Travers looked to see if he had been injured by his interrogators. Von Braun was unmarked. His eyes, set in a broad face topped with jet black hair, were watchful. The brothers had similar features, and both were clearly very nervous. Vali spoke.

"Gentlemen, these are the brothers Von Braun - Herr Professor Werner Von Braun and Gerber Von Braun."

He continued,

"Colonel Travers, United States Army Engineers and Dr John Eldridge of Harvard University. The elder Von Braun's face was quizzical as if he were trying to place the name as he spoke in English.

"Eldridge. I think I have read some of your work. It was - how you say - not too bad."

Travers cut in.

"We do not have much time, so let's get to the point. If you don't understand, my comrade will interpret. Gentlemen, we are here to offer you safety and a new life in the West. If you accept, you must be prepared to leave within twenty-four hours. I believe I am correct in saying that the alternatives are less than pleasant."

Eldridge then asked the Germans,

"What are you looking for if and when you leave Germany?"

Werner Von Braun answered,

"What are you offering?"

The scientist hit back.

"I am not here to trade. You will tell us your aspirations for a new life in the

West, and we will tell you what the reality will be."

Vali and Travers looked on with growing respect.

"You are a scientist - why are you being so aggressive?" the younger Von Braun asked.

"I am a scientist, and, as one, I find the work you have been doing and the regime you have embraced loathsome. I am here as a free man and as an American. As a human being and scientist, I could not care less whether you both live or die, but these brave men are here to rescue you, so I suggest you shut up and do as you are told. As has been explained to you, the alternatives are less than attractive. The choice is yours - death in Germany, living death in Russia or come with us."

The elder brother's arrogance came to the fore.

"How do you know we will die if we stay?"

Travers answered,

"Von Braun, you wear the uniform of the Waffen SS. I can assure you that all members of that organisation will be treated as war criminals by the Allies. We can arrange for you and your brother to be viewed in a different light."

Von Braun asked,

"But what about Germany?"

Eldridge spoke.

"Von Braun, in about three weeks, the Germany you know will not exist and may never return to its pre-war status." Eldridge's face was slightly red, but he was in complete control as he finished speaking. The elder Von Braun seemed to concede to the logic he was confronted with.

"The SS have given me twenty-four to forty-eight hours to prepare all of my people to move to Bavaria. What am I to do with them? The Nazis intend to kill all of them. How do I deal with that?"

Vali spoke.

"You will return to the compound where you will do just as you are ordered. We will be in touch soon. Do not speak to anyone about this matter. Remember, we are now your only way out. The Russians are advancing on Berlin and will soon overrun most of Germany. The SS has nowhere to run to. Only we can take you to safety. Keep that in mind."

Maiden Aunt was brought up to date by Erebus.

"Sir, we have confirmation that the target will come over immediately. The total number of people he wishes us to bring out is nearly five hundred. Can you please advise us as to the positions of the Allied and Russian Armies? In a nutshell, sir, how long do we have before we are overrun by invading forces and will those forces be friendly or Russian? Over."

The Sir Ivanhoe was a large vessel of about fifteen thousand tons - a Royal Fleet Auxiliary designed to supply warships at sea. Despite the bulk of the ship, it was subject to the sea motion, which had two effects upon Simpson-Coyle. One, bouts of violent seasickness and two, despite never being a remotely religious man – it caused him to promise eternal devotion to whatever deity would grant him just one hour on dry land. During a brief respite, he watched HMS Longbow, which was dwarfed by the sheer bulk of the supply ship, attach fuel lines and carry out the very tricky manoeuvre of refuelling at sea. He and his anonymous travelling companions - who were infuriatingly completely at ease on board - were advised that they would be transferred to the warship by something called a 'bosun's chair'. Simpson-Coyle watched in horror as the men were winched from the deck of Ivanhoe to the foc'sle of HMS Longbow. It was his turn, but suddenly all lines linking the ships were cast off. He watched in growing anger as signal lamps flashed between the ships. HMS Longbow moved gracefully away and headed into the quickly falling night.

Simpson Coyle demanded to see the captain and was told by an unapologetic, vastly experienced RFA captain that the weather had been worsening, so he had decided that it was too dangerous to transfer any further personnel. The colonel demanded to know what the flashing lights were about and was told that Longbow had signalled by lamp that once fully provisioned, she had been ordered to return to duty immediately. The captain finished the conversation with the words,

"Colonel, I have no idea what the captain's orders were, but I can tell you that we will be at sea for another three weeks so, if I were you, I'd make the best of it and no, you cannot use the radio. The captain of Longbow said he would inform those who needed to know of what had happened."

Commander Cork sat in his cabin alone and pondered.

'Simpson-Coyle will never believe it was the weather, then laughed. His mood became serious, having read the orders just received. 'Proceed with all speed to the Baltic Sea and take station as close as possible to Peenemunde'.

Pat's mood darkened further. The war that he'd been fighting for nearly five years would soon be over. Norway, the battle of the Atlantic, the Russian convoys – for the first time since enlisting in the military, Pat was truly afraid. Not of dying - that, if he was being honest, had never crossed his mind. What was disturbing for him was the thought of the pending peace. He did not want to die just before the whole bloody madness was over - a madness which had taken the best years of his adult life. There was so much to live for. He had done his part in defeating Hitler, and now all the captain of HMS Longbow wanted to do was go home. Having sat for a short time, he read the final part of the signal which concentrated his mind on other men in similar, if not even more hazardous, predicaments. The ship would collect two such men, both he would proudly call his friends. Erebus and Vali. The captain of HMS Longbow silently rebuked himself and began to work out a way to get into the Baltic Sea and then out again - alive.

Admiral Hilliard wrote a situation report on the orders given to Commander Cork which he copied to Admiral Burke; the original was submitted to Admiral Spenser. The American flag officer quickly summarised the difficulties facing HMS Longbow. Perhaps a little help would not go amiss. He asked his signals officer to contact the Operations room at the USN Atlantic Submarines Operations Command, then phoned Admiral Spenser and asked for a meeting, if possible, with Admiral Hilliard in attendance.

Odin and Maiden Aunt were becoming increasingly worried about the situation in and around Peenemunde. There was little intelligence coming from the advancing forces. Odin began to detest the phrase, 'fluid situation'. He spoke to Davies.

"If we have to get over five hundred Germans out of Peenemunde, it cannot be done by sea. To be frank, we will be exceedingly lucky if we get Erebus and Vali out alive." Maiden Aunt was listening even though he was concentrating on finding a possible solution.

"Sir, we know that the enemy is in virtual disarray in the West. They seem to be concentrating all of their forces against the Russians."

Odin had learned that once the Welshman began to 'adlib' a plan, the process was usually very productive. He encouraged.

"Go on please, brigadier."

"We have Reilly and Mullen in a forward position with Colonel Weir and 62 Commando. Then, there are Colonel Travers and Major Cork with our men in Peenemunde. If we keep HMS Longbow on standby as an emergency pickup, we just might be able to get everybody out using the very column the Germans intend to use to move them all to Bavaria. So we have two options. One, if all else fails, the Javelin team take Werner Von Braun out on HMS Longbow, and we write off the technicians. Two, if things go to plan, a commando column on advanced reconnaissance finds and escorts the German scientists' convoy led by the Javelin team with the Von Braun's. We get everybody out."

Odin asked,

"How long do you need to get the details of what will be needed?"

Davies, his mind now in a whirl, replied,

"Once I have the answers to certain questions, not long at all, sir."

A knock at the office door interrupted them.

"Enter!"

An officer handed Odin a signal which caused the admiral to laugh out loud.

"Maiden Aunt. Did you say that Commander Cork has Irish blood in him?" Davies's voice reflected his surprise at the question.

"Yes, sir. Both his parents are Munster people, I believe."

Odin continued to smile as he handed the signal to Davies.

"Then I see he has an Irish sense of humour. He has left Colonel Simpson-Coyle on board the Sir Ivanhoe. She'll be at sea for at least another three weeks."

Davies laughed,

"Best place for him."

Odin's smile then faded.

"Remember, we still have the issue of the security leak. I'll get him ashore on the European coast then he can go in with the advance column. I want him to keep an eye on Oppenheim as well. Right, I take it you have some people in mind to make up the advance column?"

Davies answered,

"Yes, sir - one or two people spring to mind."

Maiden Aunt was pleased and relieved to be informed that the unit he had in mind was within a few hours of the Suffolks. C had kept his word. He then called Reilly on the radio.

"Good morning, sergeant major; how are you both? Well, I trust? Over."

Reilly responded.

"In good shape, sir. Thanks for asking. Over"

"Right, sergeant major. Erebus and Vali will be in touch very soon. They require a collection to be made behind enemy lines, only this time you won't have to provide the transport – well, at least, not all of it. What I need you gentlemen to do is to get a number of Special Forces commandos as close as possible to a place called Peenemunde. The men in question are from 62 Commando Royal Marines and are en route to your current location as we speak. I will confirm the grid references for Peenemunde straight away. Do you have your maps to hand? Over."

Reilly answered,

"Just a moment, sir - I keep them in the truck. Won't be long. Over."

Maiden Aunt replied,

"Good. Let me have word with the sergeant while you collect them. Over."

Mullen came on the radio.

"Good afternoon, sir - unexpected pleasure. Over,"

Maiden Aunt laughed.

"How are you sergeant? How are the Suffolks treating you? Over."

"Not too bad sir. They're good lads - good soldiers as well."

Mullen's curiosity got the better of him as he continued,

"May I ask, sir, have we dealt with these Special Forces boys before? Over."

Reilly came into the radio tent as the brigadier answered,

"Glad you asked. Yes, we have. These Marines are commanded by Colonel Weir and Major Campion. We've done business with them - very good men. Now, as I said, Erebus will be in touch as soon as possible. Right! Get a pencil and take down these references for Peenemunde."

The location of the town was confirmed, and as the brigadier was about to conclude the briefing, Mullen asked,

"Just a thought, sir. From the transport point of view, how many men are we taking in? Over."

Davies remained silent for a few seconds, then spoke slowly.

"Good question sergeant - one hundred and twenty Royal Marine Commandos. Good luck. Over and out."

Colonel Weir of 62 Commando had received the brigadier's call with great interest. His men had been involved in the point of the advance and were unaccustomed to the relatively slow progress of an army. On numerous occasions, they had been ordered to hold positions rather than push ahead into the enemy rear areas. Now, as the mission was explained to him, it was much more the type of thing that his men had trained for. Get behind enemy lines, cause as much chaos as possible and then get out with a group of personnel or prisoners. He picked up the radio and began calling the 'collectors.'

HMS Longbow steamed at full speed to the North Sea. Intelligence reports indicated that the Luftwaffe was virtually defeated, but the U-boat fleet was not. Despite appalling losses, Admiral Raeder's men continued to fight on with fanatical intensity. The ship was heading for the Baltic Sea via the Denmark Straits, the most heavily mined water in the history of sea warfare. Captain Cork and his first officer were deep in conversation regarding the safest course into the Baltic Sea. Lars began,

"Pat, I did a good deal of my sail training around the seas off Denmark. I know the coastline well, and I believe we have two options. The first is to go round the Danish headland."

He indicated a point on the chart marked as 'The Skaw'.

"As you can see, it's the most northerly point of the Danish Coast. The only problem there is that the sea is heavily mined."

Pat joined in.

"I know and have asked naval Operations for any available information on the minefields. What's your second idea, Lars?"

Lars then gave a brief history lesson; during the year 1825, a ferocious storm had broken the natural coastline and formed a canal at a small coastal village called Thyboron. The small village soon became a fishing port and the entry point for the canal, which opened up the inland waterways for small and medium-sized vessels. Pat looked at his first officer quizzically, then went to the charts.

"Lars, are you suggesting that we make a quick dash across the inland waterways into the Kattegat?"

Pat found Thyboron and the West Coast of Denmark and tracked across the chart to the sea area known as the Kattegat on the East Coast, then commented,

"Well, on paper, it looks possible. I repeat - on paper."

Lars spoke.

"Well, it's something to consider. The route around the Skaw is 150 miles of mine-infested waters, and at ten knots will take at least 12 hours. The alternative is to try something which has never been done before and just might fool everyone."

"How do we know we will have clear water for the ship? We draw eleven and a half feet, plus the fact that the country is crawling with Germans," Pat asked. Lars was about to answer when a knock was heard on the cabin door.

"Get that please, Lars," Pat said as he looked closely at the chart.

Having read the signal, Lars whistled.

"What's in it?" Pat asked.

"Well, according to naval Operations, if we take the route by the 'Skaw', between us and the Baltic Sea is a mixture of magnetic and acoustically activated mines."

Cork asked,

"Do they give us any idea of where the minefields are?"

The reply was quick.

"No, sir, but we do have a figure for the number of mines which make up the minefields," Lars replied quietly.

Cork spoke.

"So we do not know where the minefields are but we know how many mines make up those fields."

"Yes sir. There is an approximation."

Pat asked impatiently

"Well, Lars how many?" The Norwegian answered straight-faced.

"Give or take a few hundred, eighty thousand."

The situation in Peenemunde was becoming critical. Waffen SS reinforcements appeared overnight. Erebus assessed them from the compound gate. None were front-line calibre, but obviously, fanatics and heavily armed and would use the guns on the scientists without hesitation. Vali joined him, and both watched a number of lorries being prepared for the technicians and equipment to be moved out of Peenemunde. Werner Von Braun approached them.

"It appears my comments about the state of the Reich were not as inaccurate as some would have us believe. Troops are deserting in greater numbers the closer the Allies and the Russians get. Now, what do you have planned for me and my brother? Those guns you can hear are Russian and are about four days away at the most."

Vali replied,

"Just sit tight; we will brief you soon. Is that clear?"

The German nodded and was about to ask another question when Erebus spoke.

"There are a number of civilians driving trucks. Why is that general?"

Von Braun almost spat his reply.

"Do not call me 'general'. I am a civilian and a scientist - not a soldier. Understand?"

The reply from Erebus was equally curt.

"You listen to me, Von Braun. These new guards are all brain-dead morons who will obey orders from anyone in an SS uniform. Your rank and uniform may be very important in getting us out of here. Now please answer my question."

The German looked at the prisoners who were in a physically dreadful state.

"The drivers are prisoners who have experience of driving large vehicles. They have been given a choice. Drive the fuel tankers or be shot. They do not know the rocket fuel is highly unstable."

Erebus continued to interrogate the scientist.

"I take it that the plan is to move the fuel in a separate column to the technicians."

Von Braun said testily,

"How would I know? My brother deals with all such matters. I have more important things to do. Ask Gerber for the details."

As he walked away, Vali turned to his comrade and said.

"Nice job in distracting him, but his question remains unanswered, so I'll ask it again. How are we going to get out of here, and when?"

Erebus spoke slowly.

"That's two questions, and I don't have answers for either. Let's ask Maiden Aunt. Hopefully, he'll have an idea or two."

As the men walked toward the barge, Vali broke the silence.

"Von Braun isn't that clever. Those guns aren't four days away."

Erebus nodded.

"Yes, he's no soldier. I'd say the troops advancing just behind the fall of that barrage are about two days away at the most."

On the way from Portsmouth, Connor and Mary Cork talked of many things with the ease of people dedicated to each other and their family, yet for some reason, neither mentioned the letter from America. As if to spite their fear of tempting fate, soon after arriving at the offices of Lambert and Partners in The Aldwych, they were reminded of how odd life can be. A very respectful young woman introduced them as she ushered them into the office of Mr Lambert. A relatively young man who walked with the aid of a stick and informed them, as he walked around the desk to welcome them,

"Got the limp at Tobruk with the 8th army. They shipped me home soon after that."

He returned to his seat in some discomfort.

"Now, Mr and Mrs Cork. First of all, may I apologise for taking so long to make contact. We have had the devil of a job contacting you. I can tell you. Our offices were bombed in 1941, and it has taken us since then to get our files in order. Once we had done that, we still had to get a current address. It's ironic; we did that by checking the bombed property owners' register - silver lining and all that. May I just deal with the formalities?"

The solicitor went on to confirm the identity and address of Connor and Mary Cork. Having offered them tea, he got - in his words - 'down to business.'

"Mr Cork, you were an employee and close acquaintance of a Mr Peter Wilde. Is that correct?"

Con answered,

"Yes, I worked for Peter when I came to England, and we became good friends."

The solicitor addressed Mary.

"Mrs Cork, you were also a 'dear friend'- I use his words, not mine - of the deceased. Is that correct?"

"Yes, I was. Peter, God rest his soul, was godfather to our second boy."

Lambert smiled.

"Good, now that's out of the way, I have some news for you both regarding the estate of the late Peter Wilde."

The couple sat in growing disbelief as Mr Lambert read out to them - to use the solicitor's words - an abridged version of the last will and testament of Peter Wilde. In the event of his death before reaching America, the sale of his house was to be cancelled. The property and all its contents were to be left to Connor and Mary Cork. An amount of ten thousand pounds cash was willed to Patrick William Cork. Christopher and Rachel Cork received five thousand pounds each. There were also a number of items of fine art which could not be valued until the end of the war. These were to be divided among the family. Mr Lambert asked both Corks to sign a number of documents, then handed over the keys and deeds of a three-storey, eight-bedroom house in Belgravia, London.

He finished by saying,

"I recently examined the property and am happy to report that it is undamaged from the bombing and, although a little dusty inside, it is in magnificent condition."

38

Blood is Thicker than Water

Erebus considered the situation. The Russians were getting closer. Within forty-eight hours the column must be out of Peenemunde - but how? He intended to destroy the compound using the abandoned rocket fuel, but how? Something would have to be done. Vali's voice came as a welcome distraction.

"Maiden Aunt on the radio."

Davies spoke slowly.

"Gentlemen, I can now confirm the resources which are at your disposal. In the event of the barge being used to escape, a Royal Navy ship on station in the North Sea will close to your position, wherever that may be. The second option is a convoy of Special Forces troops which will advance into enemy territory to link up with your column from Peenemunde. Both are now ready to move on your instruction. Now, have you anything for us? Over." Erebus spoke.

"Thank you, Maiden Aunt, Erebus here. It looks as if we will be able to get a column out, but I want your opinion on the following."

He explained his plan for the destruction of the compound and concluded.

"The Russians would find nothing of scientific value and would be unable to estimate how many people had left Peenemunde. Over."

Maiden aunt spoke.

"I take it you will be using a timed detonator. Over."

Erebus answered,

"We hope to, sir."

Davies closed off his radio mouthpiece and mused,

"If the Russians lose any men, the Germans will be blamed."

His voice rang clear on the radio.

"Right, go ahead, gentlemen. I am handing you over to Professor Williamson." He began with a question.

"Gentlemen, how long do you think you have before unwelcome company arrives? Over."

"I'd say about forty-eight hours at the most. Over," Vali replied.

Williamson explained that the American forces were fighting through Austria, and the British were advancing east through Germany. His words became precise.

"The Russians want Berlin. Stalin is adamant that the Red Army must take the city. This will slow their advance considerably and give you more time. When you leave Peenemunde, avoid Berlin and head west, staying as far north as possible. Give none of this information to the Von Braun's or anyone else in the column. Over."

Erebus asked,

"Why not tell them? Over."

Williams looked at Maiden Aunt, who signalled his assent.

"Gentlemen, in intelligence gathering, always assume the enemy knows what you know, if not more. If the enemy are being given information, we want them told the column is heading southwest to Austria. Not due west, and hopefully, straight into the arms of the collectors and 62 Commando."

He paused.

"There is also the fear factor. Little knowledge of the Russian advance will keep the German reliant upon you. Over."

Erebus replied,

"Understood, prof, and thanks. Over."

Travers' voice was the next heard.

"Colonel Travers here, Maiden Aunt. We need to confirm priorities."

Davies answered.

"Colonel, they are as follows. I do not want any of you to take any risks. If there is the remotest chance of any of you being taken by the Russians or captured by the Nazis, grab the Von Brauns and get out using the barge. Do not place yourselves at risk. Over."

Travers spoke again.

"Maiden Aunt, what if we are unable to extract the Von Brauns? Over."

There was silence, then Davies spoke.

"I'll leave that up to you, gentlemen. Over."

Travers continued,

"Thank you, Maiden Aunt. We'll be in touch when we have something concrete put together. Over and out."

There was silence in the barge. Every man there knew what had been left unsaid. The Von Brauns could not fall into the hands of the Russians under any circumstances. Erebus broke the silence.

"Right, we need to put together some hard plans and then get out of here as quickly as possible. Any ideas?"

The conversation was soon in full swing. Back at SOE HQ, another conversation was taking place. Professor Williamson asked the brigadier,

"What's worrying you, sir?"

The soldier in Davies replied,

"Almost everything. There's a lot that can go wrong, and I don't like having my men dependent on so many unknowns."

Davies sensed Williamson had more to say.

"What about you, Prof? Feel free to speak."

Williamson began,

"Well, maybe I can clarify some of the unknowns. We currently have exactly what the Soviets and the Nazis want – namely, the Von Brauns. We have been tasked with getting them out of Germany. Against us, we have the Soviets who want them alive."

Davies's face reflected his growing interest and concern; Williamson continued,

"The next bit is simple. The Nazis want them dead and will do anything to achieve that aim, which includes killing all of our men."

He paused.

"Now, there is only one unknown as I see it. We do not know how far the Russians are prepared to go to capture the Von Brauns or stop them coming to the West. They may in fact, want them dead rather than in our hands. If that is the case, they will kill our men as well. Of that, I have little doubt."

Davies looked at the academic. Neither spoke. The silence was thunderous but did not hide the obvious. The Allies were equally prepared to kill the German scientists rather than let the opposition - whoever it was- get them. Davies broke the spell.

"Well, we had better get everybody out as quickly as possible."

Erebus returned to the compound and, having located Gerber Von Braun, demanded,

"We need to know the makeup of the column. The number of technicians, guards and drivers - even those from the labour camp."

The smaller man turned, his face filled with disgust.

"I can supply the number of scientific personnel and SS guards. As for the prisoners from the camp, how would I know their names? What made you think I would have any interest in the names of such beings?"

Erebus felt pure loathing for the man in front of him.

"Von Braun, if we are to escape in a convoy, we need to know everything about the people in the column - the guards, the drivers, everyone. Now get me that information. We are the only way out now for you and your brother. Don't forget that."

The German snapped,

"Wait here."

He walked across the compound to the office.

Erebus waited, watched him walk to the office then saw then saw Vali and when told of Von Braun's attitude, he asked,

"Well, we've been given a number of options. What do you think we should do?"

Erebus gave a mirthless laugh.

"What should we do? Bill Cork, Colonel Travers and John Eldridge and you and me should get out and go home and leave those arrogant bastards to their fate, whatever it may be. That's what I think we should do."

Gerber von Braun returned.

"I have ordered an engineer to supply all the information you require. He will be on duty tonight. Now do not trouble me again. I am far too busy."

Von Braun stomped off as Vali asked,

"Why do you need the information?"

Erebus explained,

"The plan is for 62 Commando to take over the convoy. They need to know how many SS guards they will face. As for the fuel drivers, some might be German or even Russian agents." He paused, then added.

"We need to destroy everything of scientific value and conceal the size of the convoy."

Vali asked,

"What will you use as an explosive?"

Then saw a quizzical look on his comrade's face as he answered.

"The rocket fuel." There was a pregnant pause.

"I think."

As Vali and Erebus neared Werner Von Braun's office, loud scared voices alerted them to trouble. Vali pushed his way in. Von Braun, clearly highly agitated, signalled him to wait outside. A couple of minutes later, he joined the SOE men and was about to speak when Erebus cut across him.

"You need to calm them down and win these people's confidence." The German, though listening, showed his customary mocking arrogance.

"Go on, whatever your name is."

Erebus, remembering Moen, smiled inwardly.

Vali took over from his irate comrade.

"You will call a staff meeting and brief them on the following." He then outlined a number of points to be explained by the German.

Von Braun listened, eventually nodding a grudging approval. Erebus added one more thing.

"When you call the meeting, order all of the guards to attend. That is vitally important. Do you understand?"

An hour later, Von Braun had gathered scientists and guards in a large room adjacent to his office. Erebus counted a total of fifty SS uniforms, far too many for him and Vali to take on, even with Bill Cork. Von Braun began,

"To avoid being taken prisoner by the Russians, we have been ordered to move to Bavaria. The High Command believes that we will be better defended there from attack by the Allied air forces."

A voice asked,

"Why are they still bombing us, Herr Professor?"

Von Braun answered,

"The Allies believe that we are still capable of producing V weapons and will not rest until we are destroyed or captured." There was an audible groan from the assembled group. Von Braun added quickly.

"We can use this to our advantage," and continued.

"The move to Bavaria will be in a convoy which will travel nonstop day and night. If we are challenged by security police, I will say we are moving to avoid allied bombers. Once in Bavaria, production of V weapons will begin again. There will be no mention of escaping from the Russians." Erebus sensed the group of people were in agreement with Von Braun. He expected the German to stop talking but to his surprise, then consternation, the man continued.

"Once in Bavaria, we must surrender to the Americans or the British. My information is that the Allied forces are pushing up through Austria. So that is where we will head for. There is one more thing I am now in absolute command of the column?" A large man with the rank of SS-Standardenfuhrer spoke.

"General, we are the SS and will obey the Fuehrer until ordered to do otherwise. I support your suggestion that we move toward Bavaria. As for surrender, that is out of the question. On behalf of the Fuehrer, I expressly forbid it. I further forbid you to mention the matter again." Von Braun's riposte was quick and far from subtle.

"A large number of the SS senior officers have disappeared. The Nazi high command is deserting by the hundreds. What is to say you and your guards will not do the same when we meet the enemy? Any enemy? Rumours are rife here that the Russians are executing all SS men upon capture. Surrender to the Western Allies is the only option you and your men have. That or death at the hands of the Russians." The big SS man's face displayed his silent fury at being spoken to in such a fashion. Erebus whispered to Vali.

"Why can't that idiot just keep his mouth shut?"

Back at the barge, Erebus updated his comrades.

"As of now, we need answers to the following questions. One. How to detonate the rocket fuel? Two. What do with a senior SS officer who was provoked by Von Braun and just might turn very nasty?" John Eldridge spoke first.

"I need to examine that fuel. Then I can give you an answer." Erebus nodded gratefully. Bill Cork joined in.

"I think we need to take care of this SS guy fairly quickly. He could be suspicious and order reinforcements." he paused, then posed a question.

"Von Braun pointed out that the SS are deserting by the boat load as the

Russians get nearer. If the SS guy Von Braun upset disappeared, would his superiors assume he had deserted like so many others?" Erebus and Vali nodded their understanding. Travers asked.

"I take it everybody will be occupied tonight. What do you want me to do?"

Vali answered

"I'm going to be busy on the marsh tonight, so please stay here and cover the radio, Colonel."

That night, one of three men who had their false ID papers perfunctorily checked at the compound gatehouse noticed a number of fast escape vehicles being prepared for a quick getaway. Erebus began to feel optimistic. Von Braun's earlier taunts were starting to ring true. The more SS deserting, the better, the less to guard the convoy.

John Eldridge headed for the fifteen fuel tankers, which he assumed contained the V weapon fuel. A man in a white coat approached with a folder and clipboard, his fear confirmed by a garbled introduction.

"I am the engineer responsible for the fuel." Then he almost shouted.

"My predecessor was killed in the recent explosion."

Eldridge presumed this was the man Erebus had briefed him on - the baby rocket maker's 'gopher' and took the initiative.

"I will be taking responsibility for the fuel from now on. I need to know how much fuel is in these tankers. Please see Herr Professor Von Braun in the morning. He will confirm everything." The man's eyes showed relief, speech slowing as he raised a paper-filled clipboard.

"Here are the figures. There are approximately ten thousand litres. Highly unstable. But years ahead of anything the Americans or the British have." Ever the scientist, Eldridge probed.

"How do you know that?" The man replied.

"I am a Chemical engineer. As a student, I was awarded a Scholarship by the British Petroleum Company. I studied in Oxford, then London and New York." Then he looked around nervously.

"I loved those wonderful cities. Then Hitler came to power. So I was forced to come home and join the party. Where did you study?"

Eldridge answered with the name of a specialised and highly respected German college often mentioned in lectures at Harvard. The German scientist sounded almost ashamed.

"I wanted to attend that institute but was told there were rumours it was run by Jews. I think the Nazis closed it down just before the war started."

Any doubts John Eldridge had about the mission and the reasons for the war were dispelled by that one sentence. He asked the sad, innocent-looking man.

"What information do you have for me on the makeup of the convoy?"

The scientist gladly handed over the clipboard, saying.

"Everything is in this folder." He pointed out a page. "This is the number of guards." Whispering, he added.

"Those that haven't deserted." He flicked over the next sheet.

"The names of the tanker drivers are broken down by nationality. Each name has a capital P following denoting the man is from the labour camp and must be guarded when working." Eldridge pressed on.

"Where are the drivers kept overnight?" The engineer pointed in the direction of a cluster of huts.

"They are kept in the huts. The Guards have numbered the hut nearest the rocket site 'Thirteen'. Its where troublesome prisoners are held. The last explosion destroyed that hut and killed everybody. It was rebuilt on the same site as a deterrent to all the prisoners." Eldridge, now approaching a state of shock, tried to think of something to say. He mumbled through taut lips.

"Thank you for the folder." The man left with the words.

"Don't thank me, and don't ask me my name. First chance I get, I'm getting as far from here as possible, and you should do the same. There are some prototype weapons in the trucks and the huts. It's all in the folders. These Nazis still think we can produce wonder weapons. I tell you, they are all mad." He paused as his eyes, filled with horror, met the American's.

"How did we ever let it happen?" Eldridge watched the man walk away. He was alone in the middle of enemy territory and realised he did not have the remotest idea how to get back to the barge and suddenly felt real fear.

Erebus and Bill Cork found the elder Von Braun in his office.

"The SS man you humiliated earlier, would there be many questions should he go missing?" Erebus asked in English. Von Braun shrugged.

"As far as I know, he is just a functionary within the SS." Bill Cork pressed.

"That doesn't answer the question. Will he be missed enough to cause a replacement to be sent from Berlin" Von Braun replied.

"From what I gather, Berlin is in chaos. If someone doesn't report in within 72 hours, it is presumed he has deserted. A replacement will be sent. But be aware, if something happens to that replacement, and his body is found, everybody here will quickly die at the hands of a revenge squad." Bill queried.

"Does he have his own transport, and if so, is there a driver assigned to him?" Von Braun said impatiently.

"Yes, he has a car but does not have a driver. He likes to drive his big car through the town to show off. Though, I do recall when dignitaries are in the compound, he has a driver." Bill Cork suggested.

"So the gate guards would be used to him having a driver if there were passengers." Von Braun answered.

"Yes, they would." Bill went on to ask about the man's size and physical condition. Von Braun's answer was encouraging.

"I doubt he's ever been under fire."

Erebus ordered.

"Get him on the phone General." Von Braun snapped.

"I refuse to speak to that pig." Questioning.

"I doubt he will even take the call. What will I say?" Bill Cork butted in.

"You could try apologising; it will be a novel experience for you. We don't care what you say just get him here" The ensuing call did not take long as Von Braun finished with the words.

"Five minutes in my office. Thank you." Erebus instructed.

"When he gets here you are to say this," paused, then forcibly stressed, "and only this."

John Eldridge stood in the gap between two trucks, not having the remotest idea what to do on hearing the voices of two men, both German coming closer. He recognised Von Braun's, but the other was unknown. Suddenly he was confronted by a man in SS uniform who shouted he was under arrest and was about to blow a whistle when Bill Cork appeared and stabbed the man from behind. The point of the knife was aimed at and destroyed the lower ventricle of the target's heart. As the SS man slid to the ground, Eldridge watched the light of life leave his eyes. Ever the scientist, he measured the twenty seconds it took the German to die. Then watched his young friend focus on Von Braun. It was as if Bill was straining every sinew to restrain himself from repeating the action. His eyes were black. For some reason, Eldridge thought of the eyes of a Great White Shark he had seen in a research facility in California. Von Braun immediately left the scene with the words.

"I did what you asked and got him here. Now I am going back to my office."

A car pulled up as Bill spoke.

"John, we're going now. Get in the rear seat with the body. Keep it upright until we get through the gate." Eldridge saw Erebus at the steering wheel with Bill now wearing a Waffen SS weatherproof cape. The dead SS man's body was leaning against him, propped up on the other side by a suitcase. As the car approached the gate, the guards on duty simply lifted the barrier. There were no questions or salutes. Erebus drove to the barge where John Eldridge began to recover from his first taste of active service. Despite trying to concentrate on the folders brought out of Peenemunde, his eyes were drawn to three young men preparing to dispose of a body. Recalling earlier in the evening when all three had silently nodded, they had sentenced the SS man to death. Eldridge shuddered, realising what a terrible price each of them had paid to defeat the Nazis.

As dawn rose' under cover of fog, the barge eased away from the mooring. Within an hour, the weighted body, with all personal belongings in a suitcase, was at the bottom of a canal. Soon after the barge was tying up back at the mooring. The car was left on a main road where it was promptly stolen by fleeing Wehrmacht troops. If caught, they could explain to the SS how they came to be in possession of an SS vehicle. A task no one envied them.

The convoy was forming up. Seeing the SOE men enter the compound Werner Von Braun in a loud commanding voice, ordered Erebus, Vali, along with Bill Cork and Travers to assist him and his brother. Vali had to admit silently it was a good idea as nobody questioned them from then on.

There were a total of twenty-seven trucks. Gerber Von Braun pointed to six tankers parked in a line at the wire fence, confirming to Erebus these would be driven by prisoners. In the centre of the compound, the convoy vehicles were being loaded with files and equipment. Research personnel were sitting on wooden benches which ran the length of each lorry. Erebus and Eldridge quietly approached and inspected the abandoned tankers. Bill Cork did a quick head-count of the SS guards, estimating at least another ten had disappeared, which brought his natural optimism to the fore. He whispered to Travers.

"You know we just might get away with this." Travers was silent as he watched Erebus and Eldridge converse as they moved amongst the fuel tankers.

"Well John, what do we need to blow this lot?" Eldridge replied, ever the gentlemen.

"Please follow me, and I think I will be able to show…He paused.

"May I ask young man, what is your name? I find Erebus so theatrical." Despite the pressure, Lewis smiled.

"My name is Charles; now Sir, may we continue."

"Excellent, now Charles, we do not have too many problems here. A cursory glance of the folder has led me to conclude the fuel is highly unstable. Even the crudest propellant will cause an explosion which in turn will act as a trigger for the chain reaction." Erebus said.

"Right so we won't need anything too intricate to blow the lot up?" Eldridge nodded his head.

"That is correct Charles, but I would stress in the strongest possible terms that when the chain reaction takes place, it is best for us to be some distance away. A kilometre at the least." Erebus looked around and saw the hut nearest the tankers and asked.

"John, do you have any idea what that hut is used for?" Eldridge repeated what he had been told the night before. Erebus suggested.

"So, if any people are in the huts when the fuel explodes, they are certain to die." Eldridge, his head bowed, replied.

"Without the slightest shadow of a doubt, Charles." The men looked at each other as Erebus prompted.

"John would it be possible to devise a delayed trigger."

"Why do you say that?" The American academic asked.

"I am presuming the rest of the guards will leave soon after the column. Any people left in the compound might have time to escape." Eldridge furrowed his brow.

"Interesting thought Charles. Let's have a look at the batteries on these vehicles." Erebus pulled open the bonnet of the truck nearest to them as he said.

"Please remember we do not have long. Even with the Von Braun's covering for us, we need to work quickly." There was no reply as Eldridge began to examine the batteries.

Some distance to the west of Peenemunde, 62 Commando waited by the side of a busy road, all 'fully fed and watered' as the regimental Sergeant major reported to Colonel Weir. Major Campion was on the radio speaking to Sergeant major Reilly, who had just given him the pickup point coordinates.

"Right Major, I estimate we can get twenty men to a truck and allow another two lorries for kit and ammo and a fuel tanker. A total of nine vehicles. Is that to your satisfaction? Over." Campion enthused.

"Excellent Sergeant major. We'll be with you in an hour. Over and out." The Marines marched from the assembly point of the advanced British units to a forest just off the main road. In front of them was a large semi-circle of British army five-ton vehicles with a fuel tanker. A bus was leaving the scene with a number of Suffolks who had volunteered to deliver the Lorries. Reilly saluted the Colonel, then Major Campion.

"Maiden Aunt sends his best gentlemen; he thought perhaps we could do with a little mobility for the advance reconnaissance unit." He spoke into a radio.

"Right Sergeant Mullen, bring them out." There was a rumble of diesel engines, and two reinforced jeeps with mounted twin Vickers machine guns drove out of the head-high foliage coming to a halt beside the officers. Mullen jumped down and saluted.

"As ordered Sergeant major, with enough ammo to last a good while." He turned to the other driver with the words.

"Thanks Corporal, good luck to you." The soldier ran off to catch the bus carrying his regimental comrades. Weir looked at the equipment and said.

"Well, now all we need is someone to bump into. Any idea what's happening at Peenemunde Gentlemen?" Reilly answered.

"No sir." Weir looked at his second in command.

"Major Campion, why don't we start to reconnoitre a little further east and see what we can find." The reply was instant.

"Absolutely sir. I'll tell the lads to mount up, and we'll be on our way. I take it radio silence until further notice." Weir nodded and turned to Reilly and Mullen.

"Where would you gentlemen care to ride?" Mullen replied.

"Don't worry about us sir. We have our own transport. We like to keep very mobile if you see what I mean" Both men then walked into a small copse of trees and minutes later roared into view in a German armoured half-track with a large calibre machine mounted on the front. They came to a halt in front of the astonished Royal marine officers. Mullen was irrepressible.

"Present from General Patton, Sirs. He said it might give us an edge." Weir climbed into one of the jeeps and asked.

"Major Campion, don't we have some men who speak German?" The major replied instantly.

"Yes sir, two Norwegians who speak it like naturals learned it as youngsters."

"Good, see if they want to accompany Sergeant major Reilly and Sergeant Mullen as the advance guard." Both men volunteered without hesitation. Weir was ebullient.

"Right, let's go and find this column. Corporal, please head due east and don't stop until I tell you."

Off the coast of Denmark, HMS Longbow was awaiting further orders. Commander Cork and his first officer had examined every possible course in and out of the Baltic. In the privacy of his cabin, Pat mused.

"None seem particularly inviting, Lars, though none are impossible either. We'll just have to wait for the orders to proceed or stand down. The weather's closing: Heave to and ride out the storm." Larsen replied.

"Pat, the war will be over soon. What's left of the German Navy will be heading for home waters. We may have some fun and games getting into the Baltic, but we might have a lot more getting out with the North Sea awash with U-boats." Cork acknowledged his first officer's observation.

"Duly noted, Lars. Now how are our guests?"

"The gentlemen who came aboard from Lancelot are quite happy, sir. They found the affair with Simpson-Coyle highly amusing. Any idea where he is at the moment?"

"Not a clue number one, but rest assured, I'm certain we have not seen the last of him or Oppenheim." There was knock on the door, and a midshipman entered with a signal. Lars handed it to the captain. Having decoded the order, Cork spoke.

"We are to remain on station until further notice." Larsen acknowledged.

"Aye, aye, Sir"

In Peenemunde, the convoy would be led by two staff cars, Werner Von Braun, Erebus and Bill Cork in one. Gerber Von Braun, John Eldridge and Vali, who would drive the other. Then the trucks with technicians followed by the fuel tankers five hundred metres to the rear. The SS guards were spread amongst the column in small, fast vehicles. A short distance away, John Eldridge explained that a chemical reaction between the rocket fuel and the highly corrosive battery fluid would cause an explosion within four to six days. If the Russians arrived before then, the fuel would be too degraded to allow a formula to be derived. Erebus offered thanks, mixed with relief.

"Thanks for sorting this out, John." Eldridge acknowledged the gratitude as his companion scanned the column.

"There seems to be fewer guards than yesterday." Then paused before adding.

"Come on John, let's go and get everybody home and safe." They climbed into their respective vehicles, as the elder Von Braun signalled for the drivers to move out. As the column drove westward, John Eldridge inspected a folder, voicing his thought to no one in particular.

"According to this paperwork, the entire research papers for the V2 rocket are in truck 12." Then silence, as he repeatedly read a number of documents.

"These papers indicate there is what appears to be a revolutionary dual-purpose engine in Hut 18 back at Peenemunde. A power unit which generates enough jet propulsion for an aircraft and a rocket to cross the Atlantic." Again, more silence broken by a sudden exclamation.

"Good God! They were developing an intercontinental missile, had this weapon been mass-produced, it would have been catastrophic. It is frighteningly advanced." Then concentrated on the files again, before speaking directly to Gerber Von Braun.

"There are a number of references in this paperwork to something called the witness factor. What is that please?" Von Braun remained, shifting uneasily in his seat. Vali noticed the German's reaction.

"You seem to have struck a raw nerve, John." Eldridge checked his watch.

"We have been on the road for over six hours now at thirty kilometres an hour. That puts us 180 kilometres from the compound." Then remembering what Charles had said, demanded.

"Where are the rest of the guards?" The German remained silent as Eldridge drew his own conclusion.

"The huts were empty. In fact, there were no prisoners to be seen when we left. Prisoners mean witnesses, and if there are no survivors, there will be no witnesses." The scientist's voice sharpened.

"Von Braun, what is happening back at Peenemunde?" The small man panicked, shouting.

"It is nothing to do with me or Werner; the SS know what is going on; only they know." Vali kept driving. There was nothing that could be done for now; there were too many SS guards, but his gut instinct, fuelled by experience, screamed that something was dreadfully wrong back at the compound. Eldridge moved on to the list of prisoner drivers who were divided by nationality. The headings were from the occupied countries, French, Dutch, Danish even a Pole. Then he read a Norwegian name.

"Vali, there is one of your countrymen on this list." Bakken reached for the sheet of paper.

Eldridge offered guidance,

"Third column." Then watched the Norwegian's face turn ashen and heard a fierce despairing whisper.

"Good God, it's Moen." Vali ordered Gerber Von Braun.

"Signal your brother that you wish to stop for a short break." Gerber waved to the car in front to bring the column to a halt. Erebus looked at the list, then staring at the SS General spoke in a voice filled with menace and resolve.

"General Von Braun, you will tell the column to take a one-hour rest under cover of the forest to our left" Von Braun did so. Within minutes Erebus was on a personal radio secretly confirming with Reilly that 62 Commando were less than a hundred kilometres west.

As a result of the British and American armies launching simultaneous attacks on the Wehrmacht, the German defences were stretched across a very wide front. 62 Commando obeying Colonel Weirs' orders with Reilly and Mullen on point, avoided all contact with the enemy as they headed toward Peenemunde. Major Campion remarked to his boss pensively.

"Still no contact from the Peenemunde Column". Suddenly the German half-track veered into view. Sergeant Mullen pulled up beside Weir's jeep, and without ceremony, Reilly announced.

"Colonel Weir, the boys have been on and, by my calculations, are about a hundred kilometres ahead of us." He handed a piece of paper to the radio operator,

"These are the frequencies they are using. Remember, we cannot, I repeat, we cannot hail them under any circumstance. They must raise us."

Weir almost yelled.

"Right, let's go and get them and fast. We've been very lucky so far. Let's not push it."

Erebus and Vali talked quickly. There was no proof that the man in Peenemunde was Moen. As if to reassure himself, Erebus repeated his parting words to the big Norwegian.

"I told him no involvement with the resistance. None at all without us." Vali, as shocked as his comrade, replied with irony.

"Well, none of us can be regarded as being particularly obedient." Then added.

"Is there any way we can confirm it is him?" There was silence until Bill Cork joined them.

"What's wrong, boys? According to the baby rocket maker, the technicians are getting nervous, and some of the SS men impatient." Erebus explained about the name Moen being on the prisoner's list as a driver. Bill, though concerned, thought quickly.

"I see it this way. Gents, we are seriously outnumbered. There is nothing we can do until that changes. The best thing is to find 62 Commando.

Then we'll think about Moen." Erebus spoke.

"Listen, I'll have a go at the General about this witness factor business. Vali, you try and get something out of his idiot brother. Then the sound of engines was heard. Everyone looked to the rear of the convoy and saw a number of small, fast scout cars and two motorcycle sidecar units pass the fuel tankers. One scout car stopped by Werner Von Braun's vehicle, and an SS officer saluted. Erebus listened. The Nazi reported everything was in hand at the compound, but there was no mention of prisoners. Vali calculated with the reinforcements from Peenemunde there were now nearly fifty SS guards. Most were men with a number of Hitler youth who were on the sidecar bikes. The SS officer shouted orders, and the vehicles dispersed amongst the column. None went near the fuel tankers. In a moment of inspiration perhaps brought on by desperation Vali had an answer. He whispered excitedly to Erebus.

"The tanker drivers, they will know if it's Moen. Christ, the poor sods were all in the same hell hole." Erebus nodded as he said.

"We need a reason to talk to them." Professor Eldridge, who was within ear-shot, climbed from the staff car and approached Gerber Von Braun.

"General, I think I should inspect the fuel tankers, some may have begun to leak." The elder Von Braun displayed his customary indifference.

"If you must but hurry up." Erebus and Eldridge drove in the staff car to the rear of the column. Erebus complimented his passenger.

"Great piece of thinking back there, John." The first driver the men spoke to was too terrified to speak; the second spoke only Hungarian. The next man was slightly more talkative despite being horribly emaciated and fearful.

Erebus asked in German.

"Where are you from, and what is your name, please?" The man's face showed fear as he answered.

"Polska". Speaking Polish, Erebus tried to calm him as he continued.

"Please do not be afraid we are here to help; you will not be going to Germany. We are going to take you to the Allied forces. This will happen very soon, believe me.

I need to ask you a question; we must be quick. Do you understand?" The Pole seemed to recover slightly.

"My name is Viktor. What do you want to know, sir" Erebus asked about a big Norwegian man known as Moen. Viktor managed a smile.

"He kept calling them bastards. They could not break him." Erebus felt his heart race as he tried to speak slowly and gently.

"Where is he now, do you know."

"I do not know. They would not trust him with a tanker; he said he would blow them all to hell and back. They may have put him in hut thirteen. It was to be filled with prisoners once the convoy left. I think they meant to starve them to death." Erebus looked at John Eldridge. His face was white with shock as he reached out to touch the Polish man, desperate to let him know there was human warmth in the world.

Vali watched the staff car pull up slowly as if nothing were out of the ordinary. Eldridge walked over to the Von Braun's and reported.

"Everything is in order with the tankers." Neither Von Braun mentioned the welfare of the drivers as they nodded. Erebus whispered to Vali.

"It is Moen." The column was moving again as Erebus studied a map, then indicated a location to Werner Von Braun, saying.

"This is where we will stop for a short time to allow everyone to rest. We have made good time." The German was indifferent.

"I leave everything to you." Then Bill Cork received his orders.

"Bill, you slip ahead and contact the relief column; tell them to travel through the night and be ready to take out fifty SS men." He showed his comrade a map.

"There is one road through this part of the forest. We will wait here until 62 Commando, and you find us." Bill replied.

"Fine, but I need transport."

After dark, the Hitler youth were ordered to guard the perimeter of the camp. Two were on the very edge of the forest, where they were approached by Vali, Erebus and Bill Cork. Both stood as Erebus asked.

"How old are you people?" The bigger boy seeing the men were not in uniform, arrogantly demanded.

"I am eighteen, what's it to do with you?" Erebus struck with his right hand, and the boy fell to his knees, clutching his stomach as he vomited. His comrade spoke very quickly.

"He is sixteen, I am fifteen, and we are cousins from Peenemunde." Bill took the keys of the sidecar bike from the youth on the ground. Vali spoke.

"You both must go home before you are hurt or killed." The elder tried to stand and hit Erebus but only staggered into him before collapsing. Vali continued.

"The war is over. Germany has lost; now go home and look after your families." Bill had removed the cover of the sidecar and found some provisions and handed them to the younger boy, as Erebus said.

"As you have seen, we are in no mood to play games. Your homes are four to five days walk east of here. Now go and get rid of those uniforms." Both young men remained silent as they gathered up their belongings and started walking.

The younger boy turned and said,

"Thank you." Bill Cork started the bike and headed west. For over an hour, he had an open road which then narrowed and ran through a dense forest. Innate caution, and pending darkness caused him to slow down.

The half-track was partially hidden in heavy undergrowth with Sergeant Major Reilly and Sergeant Mullen drinking coffee when the radio came to life. Erebus briefed that Bill Cork would be coming down the single forest road. Within minutes a motorbike bike engine was heard at first at maximum revs and then slowing as it neared. Mullen, ever cautious, reached for his rifle as Reilly waited till the last minute to switch on the arc lights. The bike rider was blinded and slid into the side of the much larger machine.

Reilly trapped the driver's face in the full spotlight as Mullen shouted.

"Sorry, Major Cork, our fault. In Britain we drive on the left hand side of the road." Bill, hugely relieved, could only answer.

"Gentlemen, that coffee smells very good." Within twenty minutes, he was briefing Colonel Weir and Major Campion.

Just after midnight, the men of 62 Commando Royal Marines combined Operations began the assault with one overriding order. If any of the enemy offered the least resistance, they were to be eliminated.

The attack was swift. The convoy was spread over a distance of half a kilometre. The SS troops were camped together, with the Hitler youth still standing perimeter guard. These boys were taken without injury. Some of the SS guards, when confronted by combat troops appearing from the trees, believed the party propaganda about the 'Master Race' and chose to fight. The battle as such lasted five minutes. Colonel Weir ordered a roll call. 62 Commando had no fatalities, just a few cuts and one broken leg. Sergeant Major Reilly, Sergeant Mullen and Major Cork had accounted for eight of the thirty-two enemy killed in hand-to-hand fighting. The remainder surrendered to the Marines with great haste.

The sun rose as the Marines marshalled the convoy for the last leg of the journey to the Allied forward units. Colonel Weir and Major Campion looked worried as Erebus explained about Moen. Vali was at his side throughout the somewhat one-sided exchange, as was Major Bill Cork of the US army engineers. Colonel Travers felt he had to speak.

"Gentlemen, if I understand the situation, you intend to return to Peenemunde to rescue a man who fought by your side in Norway. Is that correct?" Erebus replied.

"Yes Colonel, that is precisely what we intend to do." Travers looked around at Erebus, Vali and Cork. All three signalled their agreement with a simple "Yes, Sir." Colonel Weir spoke.

"Gentlemen, I feel I must point out that there is no proof that this man is still alive. There is also the matter of disobeying orders; please give these points some thought." Eldridge had been studying a section of the folder given to him in the compound. He looked up.

"Gentlemen, I feel there is more in Peenemunde than this brave man. This folder has revealed that the Germans have designed a jet engine which is advanced beyond anything we or the Soviets have. I believe a prototype of this engine is in Hut 18 in Peenemunde. If it were to fall into Russian hands it would give them a huge advantage in jet propulsion." Bill Cork asked.

"What's so special about it, John?" Eldridge replied.

"If this engine works, and I think it might, it has the capability to power a plane or rocket across the Atlantic Ocean. There are plans for intercontinental bombers and ballistic missiles. The engine is coded the V4 with a range of over three thousand miles." Erebus spoke first.

"Well, we'd better go and get it before the 'Ivans' do." Major Campion raised a question.

"Do we know exactly where the prototype is in the compound?" Bill Cork answered him.

"No, but the Von Brauns do, so one of them will have to come with us." Campion commented.

"That is most unlikely to happen." Cork spoke.

"Leave it to me. I have a way with Germans." As he walked away, Bill saw and approached a familiar face. As both went to Von Braun's staff car, Bill said

"I never did get your name on the raid in Norway. Mine is Bill Cork."

"Anders Madsen, Sir. Pleased to make your acquaintance." Bill replied.

"Well, it's a pleasure to know you, Anders. Now we have another German to persuade to come round to our way of thinking." The marine replied.

"It will be a pleasure, Sir."

Amidst all the action and planning, no one noticed John Eldridge speaking to the 'collectors' as he sat in their half-track.

Von Braun was talking to his brother when he was rudely interrupted.

"General, I am Major Bill Cork of the US Army Engineers. My comrade is Corporal Anders Madsen of 62 Commando, Royal Marines and Norway. I am here to tell you, General, that there has been a change of plan. We have to return to the compound, and you are coming with us. Do you understand?" Von Braun remained silent and looked around. The main body of the convoy was forming up a hundred meters away. The demeanour of the American and his very big companion was aggressive yet controlled. The younger Von Braun spat a reply.

"Don't be ridiculous. We have no intention of going anywhere near Peene-munde ever." Cork was equally dismissive.

"If you know what's good for you, little man, you will keep quiet. Let your elders and betters do the talking." Both Von Brauns were becoming disturbed by the attitude of the US Officer.

"What would motivate me to return to the compound?" Cork's voice was steely cold.

"I'm glad you mentioned motivation. Let me explain mine in persuading you to go. Then Corporal Madsen will do the same" The blood drained from the German brothers' faces as Bill spoke of Mandy and Anders Madsen of his sister Inger. They heard words such as fiancé and V2 and rape and suicide. Finally, how both young women were now dead. Bill finally let all the pain and anger he had bottled up flow as he pressed his face close to the elder Von Braun's.

"I will guarantee before any God you would care to pray to that if you refuse to come with me, you and your brother will have fatal accidents before this convoy has travelled fifty kilometres." Pointing at Gerber Von Braun, Bill continued.

"My friend here will make certain that he dies slowly and in exquisite pain. You, I will deal with personally and later on today, I will explain how I will get away with it. Now, I do not have time."

As they watched three vehicles disappear, Colonel Weir asked his second in command.

"Any idea how we explain this to the top brass." The reply was honest.

"Not the faintest idea, Sir. All we can do is as asked and inform them that Erebus and Vali, Sergeant Major Reilly, Sergeant Mullen and Major Cork of the US Army, accompanied by two Norwegian Royal marines of 62 Commando, have returned to Peenemunde." Weir remained silent, then looked at his fellow marine and, in a laconic soft Scottish voice, asked.

"At what point do you think we should mention that they have taken Werner Von Braun with them?"

39

Drinking Water and a Bridge

The yard was silent, the working day over. Connor sat in his office, angry and disappointed. Thomas's letter contained news of his family in Texas and words of thanks for the kindness shown to his boy, which his friends, the Buchanan's said was 'just being family'. Connor silently asked, if family meant so much to his brother, what about the Cork family? There were no words on the early death of their broken-hearted mother, beloved father, estranged sisters or the family farm and birthright gone forever. Nothing for the destroyed Bagot family. Connor repeatedly read the letter trying to find a trace of regret or sorrow but was left more convinced of his brother's selfishness and lack of remorse for the murder and tragedy wreaked on so many people. Suddenly, Connor was gripped by pernicious spite, thinking of telling his nephew what had happened in Cork. Maybe then Tom could justify to his son the murder of fellow Irishmen, killed in the name of a country he had disowned. A son he had raised to hate a so-called, oppressive Empire that had lost so many of its sons and daughters, fighting to preserve the rights and freedoms that Thomas Cork had so savagely taken from innocent people in the name of Irish Freedom. Connor realised his hand was shaking, writing was impossible. Maybe later when he had cooled down a bit – much later. His thoughts went to his son, nephew and family, and he rushed home.

In Texas, a woman was sitting, reading a letter from her son many miles away in a country - it would seem - her husband had lied about for many years. Now their son was telling of a country where people of all nationalities were fighting to be free. A country that cherished culture so much that even in war, the theatres were open and concerts taking place regardless of bombings and huge tragedy. Jessica Cork reread her son's most recent letter in which he wrote of Connor Cork. Bill was greatly taken with his uncle, describing him as a strong, quiet man who was not afraid to show his emotions. An Irishman who was totally at ease with all nationalities, especially the English, and Aunty Mary, everything a mother should be, strong and completely at home in the country where, according to Jessica's husband, the Irish were ruthlessly oppressed. Jessica read on. Bill described his cousins - Pat in particular and then Christopher and Rachel. The similarities between the families were wonderfully surprising and striking. Jessica wondered how and when they would meet. Despite the uncertainties, her mind was made up; they would meet, come what may.

There were three vehicles. The first carried Erebus, Vali and Werner Von Braun; the second was transport for Bill Cork and the Norwegian Royal Marines, Madsen and Norsen. Leading the race to Peenemunde was the German half-track with the 'Collectors'. The return to the compound had been a unanimous decision except for Von Braun, who sat in the staff car in a state of sheer terror. No one else had questioned going back for Moen, a man who generated emotions which defied logic. Vali thought of the dangers ahead as the vehicle neared the compound. If they evaded capture by the Russians or Germans and escaped death, a charge of gross insubordination awaited all of them. Their orders were crystal clear. 'Get Von Braun out' - orders which they had completely disobeyed. He looked ahead to the half-track and saw three figures and, with growing horror, recognised Professor Eldridge. In the other staff car, Bill Cork raised his head from a map and, for the first time since Mandy had died, felt a moment of true joy on seeing John Eldridge, as much a man of the heart as any of them. His love was science, and that meant risking his liberty and life in the pursuit of that calling.

After four hours of hard driving, Erebus called a halt a kilometre from the outer wire. The sun was high, defining the outline of the compound on the horizon. In the distance, the sound of erratic, heavy artillery shelling could be heard as Bill and Vali approached the half-track, about to demand some answers from Eldridge. The scientist pre-empted any query by waving the drawings of the engine in his hand.

"Gentlemen, we cannot allow this prototype to fall into Soviet hands. It is simply too advanced. We must secure it for the Allies. Now, how do you propose to get me into the compound? Once I am there, you can leave the rest to me."

The scientist was utterly oblivious to danger as he prepared to go into detail as to what was in the huts. Erebus looked at the man he had come to like and chose his words carefully.

"John, we are all in serious trouble for what we have done. I'll be frank; we'll be very lucky if any of us come out of this free or alive."

Eldridge replied,

"Oh, come now, Charles, I have every confidence in you and the rest of the boys." He buried his head in the papers. Bill Cork and Cormac Reilly had high-powered binoculars trained on the compound. The Texan broke the silence.

"No signs of life or, for that matter, death. The place looks as if it was abandoned months ago – not days. The huts are all sealed, and I can't see any fresh military vehicle tracks in the area."

He looked at Erebus and asked.

"The gates are open. Well, do we go straight in?"

Reilly suggested,

"Why don't we take in the German half-track? If there are any guards in there, it might buy us enough time to get close and catch them napping."

Erebus nodded as he climbed aboard. Under protest, John Eldridge was removed and placed in one of the staff cars.

62 Commando reached an advanced base of the Allied units where the German technicians and Gerber Von Braun were detained while undergoing identity checks and interrogation. Colonel Weir and Major Campion were met by a rather concerned British colonel, who took them to a covered vehicle where they were soon being threatened by an American called Oppenheim. The Royal Marine officers ignored the attempted intimidation and told the pompous American that, within twenty-four hours, they would hand Von Braun over to him. Oppenheim, in his excitement and haste to inform his superiors, forgot to ask which Von Braun. The Royal Marine officers maintained a satisfied silence.

Vali walked into the gatehouse at Peenemunde and then to the inner wire. So far, the compound appeared abandoned. The half-track with Reilly, Mullen and Erebus was parked inside the gate. Bill Cork and the rest of the team at the staff cars saw Vali giving the signal to follow him. As they all stood in the middle of the deserted yard, Erebus carried out a silent roll call - Eldridge, the Norwegian marines and Bill Cork next to Von Braun to his left; Vali, Reilly and Mullen on his right. Madsen, the biggest of the 'boot necks,' spoke.

"Gentlemen, might I suggest we get on with finding what we are looking for and then get out of here."

This triggered Erebus into action.

"Ok, let's find Moen and the prof's rocket or whatever it is." Then cautioned. "Watch out for booby traps." Vali took over.

"Bill, you take John and Von Braun and look for the engine."

Turning to the rest, he said,

"Gentlemen, we'll check the huts for Moen and the prisoners."

Erebus, Reilly and Mullen went to hut 13. The door was locked, the windows shuttered and nailed. A quick inspection confirmed that there were no nasty surprises. The door offered little resistance to Reilly's considerable bulk, and Mullen was choked by an overwhelming stench as he entered. Another check and the window shutters were torn away, bringing in light, which revealed men tied to wooden bed frames. A glance was enough to suggest most were dead. Erebus heard a voice - weak but unmistakable.

"Laudrup or whatever your name is, over here - over here, my friend."

Erebus cut him free, and the big man managed to lever himself onto one elbow. He was in a horribly weakened condition. There was no time for first aid or re-unions; the sound of artillery shells was getting closer. Mullen checked the other prisoners and found one alive – but only just. The man managed to speak.

"Please, for the love of God, get us out of here. Please."

Mullen lifted the man in his arms while Erebus helped Moen. Reilly took a hopeful, final look at the others. A shake of the head confirmed that all were beyond help; his face reflected memories of the labour camps in Norway. Outside, Erebus sat Moen down and signalled Madsen, who had finished a search of the next hut, to bring a vehicle. Bill Cork stayed close to John Eldridge and never took his eyes off Von Braun, who was now focusing on self-preservation as he remembered what the young American said to him during the long drive.

"This is the way it is, Von Braun. Fate, or whatever you wish to call it, has given me the chance to get even for the people of London. If I stand trial for your death, I'll demand to be tried in London. I will tell them that I got the man who killed their families, how I cut the throat of the German who designed the Buzz bombs and the V2 rockets. They'll appreciate that in London. No jury of those fine people will convict me. Hell, they'll probably give me a knighthood."

The German's terror-stricken memories were interrupted by Eldridge demanding,

"Von Braun! Where is Hut 18?"

The German, his hand trembling, pointed to a long building with extra wide doors in the middle of one side wall and at both ends. Bill Cork motioned Norsen to go after the scientist who was almost at the hut. The Marine caught up with Eldridge and gently stopped him from trying to open one of the doors.

"Please, Professor Eldridge, let me check it for booby traps. We'd much prefer you alive if you don't mind."

The scientist smiled as the Norwegian inspected and then made his way through the door. Two minutes later, he had opened some shutters and called to Eldridge,

"Professor! Come ahead. Be careful, the light fittings are very low."

Eldridge walked into the hut ahead of Von Braun, with Bill Cork following. In the middle of the floor was a large object covered with a tarpaulin, which Norsen was checking for traps. The walls were covered with rows of engineering tools and equipment, which Bill Cork satisfied himself were not rigged. He signalled Eldridge that it was safe to remove the cover, which all three men did. After a period of silence, the professor spoke with reverence.

"Gentlemen, before you, you see the future."

Cork and Norsen were unsure how to react, so stayed silent until the sound of loud shelling reminded everybody that, very soon, the compound would be very much in the present. The scientist turned to Von Braun,

"How much does this engine weigh?"

Von Braun was precise.

"Seven hundred and fifty kilos."

Eldridge turned to Bill Cork and Norsen.

"William, would you signal the half-track, we'll need it to remove this engine."

The marine took over.

"I'll do it, sir. Bill, you keep an eye on our Nazi friend."

"Right, Sven."

Eldridge, now reading paperwork he had found under the tarpaulin, looked up.

"Thank you, William. I had forgotten that young man's name. I felt it would be rude to ask again. Sven - I must remember that. William, now let's see what we have here."

Then he was silent as he examined the prototype, occasionally uttering the word,

"Extraordinary."

Having signalled for the half-track, Norsen rigged lifting gear as it pulled up outside Hut 18, closely followed by one staff car. The third car was still by Hut 13 as the survivors were being made comfortable by Erebus and Vali, then joined the other vehicles. As the engine was loaded onto the half-track, Bill was struck by the concern shown by Erebus and Vali for Moen.

Maiden Aunt sat in his office, waiting for confirmation that the Von Brauns were in custody. As if to order, his desk phone rang.

"Williamson here, sir. Would you mind coming to the radio room now please. Colonel Weir and Major Campion are ready to make their report."

The communications room staff was silent as Williamson handed Maiden Aunt the radio headset.

"Commanding Officer, 62 Commando for you, sir."

"Colonel Weir here, Maiden Aunt. I have an update for you on Operation Javelin. Over."

"Excellent, colonel, please go ahead. Over," Davies replied with genuine pleasure. Weir reported, in taciturn fashion, the events of the previous two days and the current situation. Remaining calm, Davies asked,

"Are they certain that it is Moen, and that the equipment is as potentially revolutionary as Dr Eldridge outlined? Over."

Weir confirmed,

"There is no doubt in both cases, sir. Over."

There was silence, then Weir almost pleaded,

"Sir, once we hand over the technicians, we can fight our way in and get the boys out. Over."

"That is a very courageous offer, but it is not the answer. Thank you, Colonel

Weir, and congratulations on an excellent Operation. Please inform me when you have delivered the Peenemunde personnel to the appropriate units behind our lines. Good luck to you. Over and out."

Placing the headset on the desk, the Welshmen turned to the radio room supervisor.

"Put me in contact with the captain of HMS Longbow, please."

Turning to Williamson.

"Prof, please establish the whereabouts of Colonel Simpson-Coyle and the most recent update on the Red Army's positions around Peenemunde."

Odin's face was passive. Having briefed the admiral on the status of the Javelin Operation, Davies watched, waiting for a reaction. What would he do? Which way would he go? All of the men heading to Peenemunde had totally disobeyed orders and had compounded that mutinous act by taking a valuable asset back into enemy territory.

Spenser sat, quiet, his mind in conflict. Since being commissioned years ago, physical and mental self-control had been fundamental to every waking hour of his service. Now he was sorely tempted to forget all those years of self-discipline and scream at the man in front of him. Just one word at the top of his voice - a yell, a roar, a bellow - anything to ease the pressure - the one question that could never be answered. Why? But no. Davies had done all that could be expected of a CO.

"Please sit down, brigadier, and tell me how you plan to get our men out of Peenemunde," he paused,

"For the second time?"

The engine was being lashed to the rear of the half-track as the radio crackled. Vali waited.

"Operation Javelin. This is the 'Prof.' I have a question from Maiden Aunt. Over."

The word 'Prof' was satisfactory proof of the caller's identity. Vali replied,

"Operation Javelin, please go ahead, Prof. Over."

"Vali, how are you and where are you? Over."

The Norwegian made a concise report. Williamson began,

"Right, the Russians have outflanked you to the south, so the plan is to get you out by keeping your feet dry. Understood?"

To Vali, the allusion was obvious. There would be no mention of the barge or HMS Longbow in case the enemy or the Russians had active listening stations. He confirmed this.

"Understood. We will keep our feet dry."

The decision had been made. The only way out for everyone was the barge, then HMS Longbow.

Pat Cork stood on the bridge; the charts for the sea areas around Thyboron had given him an idea. If Longbow could steam into the natural lake beyond the canal, it would be much easier to collect the Javelin team and the cargo. However, some very important pieces of information would be required in order to move the idea to a finalised plan. Could the barge get to the lake? How long would it take to do so? Finally, an accurate weather forecast for the Danish East Coast was crucial. Pat instructed his signals officer,

"Mr Bellamy, ask the first officer to meet me in the radio cabin. You come along as well, please."

The radio cabin was silent apart from the Sonar operated by Petty Officer Constantine. Cork handed Bellamy a piece of paper.

"Flags, please call this radio frequency until you get a response. When you do, ask for this man."

Bellamy did as ordered. A reply was quickly forthcoming.

"This is Professor Williamson, Commander Cork. Let's make this quick, shall we? Over."

Cork explained the situation and what was required.

"We will get back to you once clearance has been given. Good luck. Over and out."

The team was ready to leave the compound. Having been displaced from the half-track, which now carried Reilly, Mullen, Professor Eldridge and the engine unit, Von Braun was now in the diligent care of the Norwegian Marines. Erebus looked at the remaining fuel tankers with trepidation. The original plan was for the fuel to explode two days hence. That would now have to be advanced somewhat.

"Dr Eldridge, what would set the fuel off as quickly as possible?" There was a pause then,

"I suggest that we immerse as many batteries as possible in the fuel. A reaction should take place soon after. An exact time I cannot give you. The use of batteries as detonators for rocket fuel is not an exact science."

He then volunteered to go with Erebus and Madsen, but the offer was politely declined.

Erebus climbed onto the first tanker and allowed the batteries to sink into the fuel. He and Marine Madsen repeated the process in six more tankers. They were moving on to the eighth when, from the East, two or possibly three Russian fighter planes appeared flying at a low level. Then a number of tanks came over the horizon and started firing at the vehicles. Why not? One was a German half-track; the other two were Wehrmacht staff cars. The men of Operation Javelin had no choice but to make a run for it. Erebus and Madsen jumped on the running gear of the staff car, which, along with the other vehicles, sped toward the perimeter wire on the marsh side of the compound and the barge four kilometres away. The tanks broke through the compound wire and, as they came abreast of the fuel tankers and huts, found their range. Von Braun was screaming,

"We must surrender. I can do a deal. I'll look after you all."

Nobody was taking too much notice of his hysteria. Suddenly, the earth literally moved. Afterwards, Erebus remembered a phrase he had once heard somewhere, which went. 'All hell broke loose.' The fuel tankers disappeared in an explosion that blew the Russian tanks onto their sides. One of the fighters above the tankers simply disappeared. The other two headed east, trailing smoke from engines and wings. The escaping vehicles, though shaken, managed to keep traction and continued on their way. Whatever research documentation and equipment had been left in the compound was now definitely beyond the reach of the Russians. As the air cleared, John Eldridge commented.

"Well, what an interesting reaction."

In an overcrowded radio cabin aboard Longbow, Larsen stated,

"Captain, we have no choice but to wait for the Javelin team to contact us. To attempt to raise them could be futile and dangerous." Captain Cork moved to the bridge with the first officer.

"Now that you've brought up 'futile and dangerous,' I've been mulling something over. Try this for futile and dangerous. Remember what you told me about Thyboron?"

Lars nodded as his captain led him to the chart table and explained the plan for a rendezvous with the Javelin team. Lars listened intently, then offered his thoughts.

"Captain, it is dangerous, but I would disagree with 'futile'. It will work, and if my memory serves me, that fjord is barely tidal, which gives us ample water. As you point out, the crucial factor is how long we have to wait on station for the barge."

'Flags' approached with a signal. Cork scanned it and spoke.

"Number one, this is permission from Maiden Aunt to contact the Javelin team. Once we've done that, we can put together some kind of time scale for the Operation; futile, dangerous or otherwise. At least we'll know where they are."

He laughed as he asked Bellamy a question.

"Now, Flags, what do you know about Pirates and Crown jewels?"

Professor Eldridge stood in awe of the strength of the young men as they had manhandled the prototype engine into the barge's rear compartment. Vali and Norsen were now at the wheel above the main cabin. Below, Reilly and Mullen tried to make Moen and his fellow patient comfortable. The big Norwegian lay on a bunk, sipping water and eating army rations while slipping in and out of delirium. The other man was desperately ill. He could just hold water, but not any solid food. Reilly advised as he looked on with deep concern,

"Slowly, my friend, slowly. A little at a time."

Erebus looked at Moen, certain that some colour was returning to his skin, and again he mumbled something about pilots, then slipped back into sleep. Reilly spoke quietly at his side.

"Charles, we need to get medical help for both of them. Moen is stronger, but the other man - I don't know. God knows what they have been through."

Lewis asked,

"Is it that bad, Cormac?"

"I'd say they haven't eaten anything decent in months, and they have lost a huge amount of weight. They keep coming around and then falling back into unconsciousness. It's the dehydration, I think. Either way, I'm very worried," came the whispered reply.

The radio came alive with the words,

"Calling Javelin. Please come in, Javelin. Please confirm identification as per Operation Crown Jewels."

Eldridge picked up the handset and responded.

"Javelin here, please hold. Over."

Erebus instructed,

"Professor, repeat after me please, 'Javelin here, confirming ID. Erebus and Vali with a number of pirates. Over."

The scientist did exactly as told, his eyes lighting up with pleasure.

Pat Cork smiled as he replied,

"Javelin, we are on station to ensure you do not get your feet wet. Propose you transmit your location and future travel plans. Over."

Erebus took the handset.

"Good to hear from you. Please let us know where you want to collect us. We are currently in transit and will use drinking water to reach you. Over." There was silence then the radio spoke again.

"Proceed on a northerly course. Suggest we make radio contact at end of every watch to ensure swift journey home. Understand you have some more crown jewels. Over."

Eldridge looked intrigued as Erebus acknowledged,

"Yes, we do. Will comply as suggested. Over and out."

Vali explained what had been agreed.

"The Royal Navy divides every twenty-four hour period into six watches – I'll leave the mental arithmetic to you. So every four hours, we will contact them with an update."

Eldridge interrupted,

"Excuse me, but those check words were not part of the grid code-word system. How do we know the message is from our friends?"

Erebus and Vali smiled as Bill Cork spoke for all three.

"Professor, there is only one man who would know of the Crown Jewels."

"And who is that William?"

"The man on the other end of that radio. Captain Pat Cork."

The captain of HMS Longbow knew that the reference to 'drinking water' confirmed the barge would be in the inland freshwater canal network - at least that much was clear. The sea was becoming increasingly rough, and there was little point in heading south until the exact course of the Javelin barge was known. Captain Cork gave the order to heave to and studied the weather forecast just received from SOE HQ.

Erebus was on the radio to Williamson, who told him that Maiden Aunt wanted a 'word'. The Irishman in him marvelled at the English facility for under-statement and prepared to speak in, what he hoped was, an apologetic tone.

"Erebus here."

There was absolute silence, so he finished the sentence with "Over." Maiden Aunt's voice was calm and controlled, but his Welsh temper was up.

"Well, Boyo, you'd better have a bloody good reason for this little detour. Over."

Vali and Cork were listening as Erebus smiled at the Celt's feigned anger and obvious relief.

"Yes, sir. We've got our man out and more Crown Jewels. All present and correct, although we have a number of men in need of medical help. Over." Davies demanded,

"Do you have wounded? Over."

"No, but our friends are very weak and possibly failing. Over."

"Have you been in touch with the exporter? Over."

Erebus remembered the escape from Bergen.

"Yes, we are in contact and are underway. Over."

Davies signed off with,

"Good, well done and good luck. Over and out."

At the wheel, Vali was reasonably sure they had left Germany. The barge was in good order and had adequate supplies. If they ran short, the gold aboard would buy more and be used for bribes. The growing problem was fuel. Dipping the voluminous fuel tank and reading very old gauges had allowed a rough calculation of enough fuel to travel six hundred kilometres at the most. Ahead were the canals of Denmark, which presented substantial challenges. The alternatives were the seas off the West Coast of Denmark or a dash up the Baltic coastline which were equally hazardous. As for the crew, he couldn't have been more confident of any group of men. On a personal note, Vali, like Erebus, was desperately worried about Moen and the other poor soul. Moen had now become delirious and occasionally called out,

"Laudrup! The pilots! The bastards killed so many pilots." Then he would fall asleep again from exhaustion.

The first check-in with HMS Longbow confirmed that the barge was in the canal system. The possible courses were outlined by Vali. Captain Cork proposed he contact SOE for an update on the positions of invading and occupying forces in the Jutland peninsula. Vali agreed and confirmed the barge's location, then signed off.

The Javelin team was briefed by Vali.

"Right, we are approximately 400 hundred kilometres from the ship which will collect us. Our current course will take us through the inland canals of Denmark. One slight problem there - Denmark is occupied by the Germans!! Alternatives are as follows. We could move up the Baltic Coast and risk the Russian Air Force and navy, or go up the West Coast of Denmark, which will leave us exposed to the Luftwaffe and the German Navy."

The only comment was from Erebus.

"Please stop being so optimistic."

He then continued,

"Do we know where the Russians are?"

Vali answered,

"It's no longer our concern - we are out of Germany. Now we need to decide what to do next."

Silence reigned until interrupted by the radio.

"Calling Javelin. Calling Javelin. Please come in Javelin. Over."

Vali answered,

"Javelin here. Go ahead. Over."

The voice he recognised instantly.

"Maiden Aunt here, Vali. Please report current location. Over."

Vali did and listened as Maiden Aunt spoke again.

"Four hundred kilometres! Right, please listen. Intelligence tells us that Denmark is rapidly filling up with German refugees fleeing the Russians. I'm afraid we will have to use this human disaster to aid your escape. Head straight through Denmark via the canals. Do not stop. The Germans are in chaos everywhere. Their occupying forces in Denmark have had it relatively easy and will want to avoid any casualties this late in the war. I'm sure they are aware that serious charges for war crimes have already been laid against numerous German officers and Nazis. Do you follow? Over."

Vali replied,

"Perfectly, will proceed immediately. Hope we didn't cause too much of a fuss going back for our friend. Over."

There was silence and then a terse reply.

"It's not me you boys have to worry about. Believe me. Over and out."

The Javelin barge was twenty to thirty kilometres inside Denmark and steamed on a northerly heading. When challenged by SS Guards or military police, Von Braun, in his Waffen SS uniform, accompanied by Erebus, dealt with the situation. In the case of ordinary Wehrmacht soldiers or their Danish allies, any questions as to where the barge was going were satisfactorily answered as gold coins bought silence and onward passage. The Third Reich was literally falling to pieces. Denmark's roads were jammed with the young, the sick and the elderly, but the waterways were clear. Within two days, the Javelin team had travelled two hundred and fifty kilometres. Aboard the barge, Moen's condition was stabilising, but Reilly was still profoundly worried about both of the former prisoners. Bergen had taught him what symptoms to look for. Though Moen seemed to be getting stronger, Reilly knew he needed proper medical care if he was to avoid developing any number of life-threatening infections. The other man was barely hanging on to life. Tragically, no one knew the man's name. His identity, like his life, had been brutally stripped from him.

HMS Longbow was hove to just out of sight of landfall at Thyboron when the signal came from the Javelin team that they were one hundred and fifty kilometres away. The fog was impenetrable as the ship edged toward the canal and access to the inland water called Limfiorden. The lake was located on the North Eastern Coast of Denmark, about 100 kilometres south of the Skaw and was part of a system of shallow lakes and canals which criss-crossed Denmark. It was suitable for light cargo vessels accessing the country inland and the Kattegat and the Baltic. Pat Cork radioed the location for the rendezvous. When Vali saw the coordinates on the map, he whistled quietly,

"Well, let's hope for the luck of the Irish because, by God, we are going to need it."

Vali checked the chart repeatedly to ensure the barge was on course. Then a thought came to mind. The current course took them through the middle of Silkeborg, a large town. Refugees congregated in such towns, as did troops to control them. Vali's instincts warned that the canal through that town was too dangerous, and an alternative route must be found. Finding the barge's current position on the chart, he followed the canal to a point ten kilometres south of Silkeborg, where it branched east through the sparsely populated agricultural countryside to a smaller fjord called Nissum. The fjord was closer to German waters and increased the barge's sailing distance by at least one hundred and fifty kilometres. He checked his watch. Four hours had passed; time to call Longbow and give her the good news.

Colonel Simpson-Coyle was on dry land. A Royal Navy frigate, refuelling at Sir Ivanhoe, was ordered to deliver the colonel to Europe. He travelled cross-country with a radio monitoring unit from the Royal Signals to the advanced areas. Simpson-Coyle rejoined Oppenheim just as the younger Von Braun was handed over to the OSS. The interrogation quickly revealed to the scientific expert present that Gerber Von Braun was a minor contributor to German rocket development. Then Gerber told of his brother, being taken by force back to Peenemunde by Erebus, Vali and the Javelin team. Oppenheim remained silent, his mind digesting this incredible news as a knock came on the interview room door. The OSS man shouted,

"We're not to be disturbed. Go away."

The door opened, and both men were ordered to a briefing where they, with other officers, were told of the death of Franklin D. Roosevelt. Minutes later, outside the interrogation room, Simpson-Coyle watched as Oppenheim showed his elation at the death of the US President almost yelling,

"Now I've got the Ivy League bastards. Patton won't be able to protect them now. Truman's a different man entirely."

Thinking out loud, he continued,

"Patton is in trouble again with General Eisenhower because of his outbursts against the Russians."

Another pause then he exclaimed,

"I'm going to contact my people and demand to be placed in command. This was always my Operation."

Simpson-Coyle was slightly more circumspect about the great man's death and, on a personal level, not surprised by Oppenheim's behaviour. The man was utterly self-centred. The colonel returned to the interview room and asked Gerber Von Braun why his brother had been taken back to Peenemunde. The answer he kept to himself and warned the prisoner to do the same. Then quickly decided he had numerous grounds to order the arrest of Erebus and Vali and, if necessary, anyone else involved in the gross insubordination. But Simpson-Coyle's instinct for survival had returned. Nagging doubts arose. The actions of the Javelin team were inexplicable. Or were they? Erebus and Vali were highly intelligent, experienced soldiers. They had disobeyed direct orders. But why? The war was nearly over. Why risk everything? Simpson-Coyle decided he needed more information on everyone involved in Operation Javelin. Leaving the interrogation area, the colonel watched as Oppenheim climbed into the rear of a US Army Communications radio truck. The soldier's long years of service had taught him, 'Trust no one.' As one war-weary intelligence officer had put it, 'Believe half of what you see and nothing of what you hear, and you just might stay alive.' He returned to the Royal Signals truck, climbed into the rear and showed his ID.

"Good afternoon, Sergeant. You know my name, rank and authority. Please carry out a routine radio sweep. I want to know if anyone is broadcasting from this base."

The sergeant was used to senior officers asking the 'signals' to gather information and passed the silent comment. 'I swear there are more spooks than soldiers in this 'bloody war,' as he replied,

"Yes, sir."

The sweep picked up a conversation between two American voices. Simpson-Coyle recognised Oppenheim's, then asked the sergeant to rig an earpiece for him and tape the transmission. He sat and listened as Oppenheim spoke to what was later revealed to be a secret OSS communications base in England. The content of the transmission reinforced Simpson-Coyle's burgeoning suspicions. Oppenheim and the OSS had no intention of sharing any information with the British or anyone else. Von Braun was to be moved to the US along with any other German scientist - Nazi or otherwise - regardless of whether or not they were wanted for war crimes. The entire Javelin team, including all of the scientists, were to be sacrificed, if necessary, to achieve this. All were expendable. There was also an aside by the second voice that the destruction of these men would solve the problem of witnesses giving evidence that the Von Braun's were Nazis. As for Oppenheim, in the event of an official investigation into his behaviour, there would be no witnesses either. Finally, the colonel heard a reference which left him in no doubt about Oppenheim and his motives.

"Yeah, I've got one Von Braun here. I'll soon have the other one."

There was a pause then,

"The Limeys? Don't worry about them. I've got one by the balls; he'll do as he's told. He thinks I'm on his side. Once I get hold of Werner Von Braun, I'll destroy him. I've got enough to hang him out to dry. I'm sick of all his superior British horseshit."

Colonel Simpson-Coyle thanked the sergeant and requested a tape of the radio call, which was delivered to him within the hour. He then contacted Maiden Aunt to report his location. All of the other information and the tape he kept to himself. From now on, Colonel Simpson-Coyle would be keeping a very close eye on Operation Javelin, Oppenheim and the OSS.

Five miles off the occupied coast of Denmark, the captain of HMS Longbow was about to brief his crew.

"Attention ship's company. This is the captain. As you will have gathered, we are currently involved in a waiting game. This will soon be over."

Pat paused.

"We will soon be underway to pick up a number of men from behind enemy lines. Please be extra vigilant during the next forty-eight hours; then, after that, hopefully, we can all go home for good. Good luck to you all. Over."

The ensuing silence was broken by a cheer.

The barge moved closer to the small bridge ten kilometres from Silkeborg and formed the crossing point of two canals. The easterly canal was the new course. The bridge was packed with refugees, but remarkably, the waterway was clear. Erebus commented,

"There are no military personnel anywhere."

Then, looking at Vali, he added,

"Do you think the Germans have surrendered?"

His hopeful question was answered when German military police began forcing a passage through the people on the bridge for a staff car, with yelled threats and shots being fired into the air. Von Braun, below deck, stiffened as he heard the machine gun. Bill Cork was at his side, a knife drawn and leaving no doubt that death would be swift and silent if any alarm was raised with the troops ashore. Moen and his fellow escapee slept. John Eldridge was busy in the rear compartment examining the engine. Madsen and Norsen were with him to assist and secretly to stop him from forgetting where he was and wandering on deck. They all felt the sensation of the barge veering to port, then an increase in the engine noise as the vessel moved away from the bridge and on toward the new pickup point. Vali put his head into the cabin announcing,

"We're through the bridge and, according to the chart, we only have a hundred kilometres to go. You know, we just might make it."

The radio aboard HMS Longbow sprung to life. Constantine's orders from the captain had been precise.

"Contact me immediately Javelin makes contact?"

The petty officer handed the radio microphone to his captain. Cork spoke.

"Javelin, do you have a location fix? Over."

Vali replied,

"We do, but there has been a slight change of collection point. Over."

Pat replied,

"Please go ahead. Over."

Vali explained the need for the change of pickup as Cork remained silent. He then spoke.

"Understood, Javelin. Please give the coordinates to my signals officer," and, turning to Bellamy, saw him nod his understanding of the situation.

Having closed the transmission with a 'good luck,' Flags delivered the coordinates to his captain. Cork, looking up from the chart table, announced.

Gentlemen, we are heading for Nissum Fjord. That's where we will pick up Javelin."

The ship headed south for a fjord perilously close to the entrance of Helgoland Bay, the sea entrance to the ports of Hamburg and Bremerhaven. Both were safe harbours for the remainder of the U-boats and the German surface fleet and, consequently, potentially fatal for a British warship.

The barge moved further northeast, and each passing hour brought a belief that they might be successful. Vali checked and doubled checked his calculations; six hours at the most before the vessel entered the southern waters of Nissum fjord. His eye was drawn to the fuel gauge. The needle level showed an eighth of a tank left, but how dependable was the gauge?

HMS Longbow contacted Admiral Hilliard with an update. Hilliard was tempted to send HMS Snow Tiger as reinforcements. He suggested this to Admiral Spenser, who courteously declined the offer. The light faded as Longbow closed on the entrance to the fjord. The for'ard lookouts peered into the darkness. Commander Larsen estimated that the ship was around one mile off the shoreline.

The barge had just entered the waters of the fjord, which were slightly choppier than expected. Vali suggested to Erebus,

"We're not due a check-in for another hour. I think we should contact Longbow now and ask if they can steam into the fjord to meet us. It would speed things up no end. This fjord is only thirty-five kilometres in length. At ten knots, we could be out in an hour and on our way home within two."

HMS Longbow closed on the entrance to Nissum Fjord. The charts showed the depth of the fjord to be between eleven and fifteen fathoms - more than enough water for the ship. The lookouts reported visibility at about two hundred yards, far from ideal. On the bridge, the captain was surprised by his signals officer Bellamy calling him.

"Captain, the barge is on the radio."

Cork replied,

"Very good, Flags."

Checking his watch, Pat observed to Larsen,

"One hour early, out of character for these men."

"Vali here. We are, by my calculations, about three kilometres from the eastern exit of the fjord. Submit you come in and get us. It would speed things up no end. Over."

The reply was,

"Will consider options and call ASAP. Over."

Cork looked from the bridge into the pitch-black night. The darkness would give cover to his ship but would also make the barge far harder to locate. Then having made the decision, he turned to his first officer.

"Lars, I need you on the bow with the lookouts. Take a two-way radio with you."

Larsen nodded his head as he pulled on his sea coat. The captain continued,

"Mr Bellamy, take us as close as possible. Please confirm the canal width and depth of water."

Bellamy moved beside the sailor on the ship's wheel as he replied,

Aye, aye, sir."

Longbow eased in toward the mouth of the canal. The sea was now slightly calmer as she edged forward into the sheltered waters of the inland lake. The land mist and fog now closing in, Larsen's voice came over the two-way radio set.

"Keep five knots, Flags. Just enough to give her headway and steady."

The darkness was almost opaque, with visibility down to under one hundred yards. Captain Cork peered through binoculars. Bellamy spoke in a low voice.

"Captain, sir. Canal width, twenty metres – depth, ten fathoms. We are about halfway through."

Pat nodded his head in thanks. Larsen's voice came over the radio again.

"I can just see a horizontal beam at about four metres above sea level. Can't quite make it out; seems to be floating in mid-air."

There was silence, then,

"Good God! It's a bridge."

One of the lookouts confirmed,

"Bridge dead ahead!"

Cork ordered,

"Half astern both."

Bellamy checked the charts, uttering, with amazement,

"Where did that bloody bridge come from?"

At that point, the radio came alive.

"Javelin here. Please come in Longbow. Over."

Pat picked up the ship's radio handset.

"Longbow here. Go ahead, Javelin. Over."

Vali's voice came on.

"Javelin here. We have run out of fuel and are at full stop. Dead in the water. Please advise. Over."

40

Hands Across the Sea

Connor nervously reread the first words to his brother in twenty years. The letter contained praise for Bill, and the delight everybody in the family felt in meeting him. Then maybe as a conciliatory gesture, Connor wrote of the shared terror of all parents whose children were at war. He asked for his brother's family and, presuming Tom knew nothing of his nieces and nephews, listed their sister's children and his own. There was a short reference to Pat's war service and Connor's business. The possibility of meeting was touched on in general terms and qualified with the difficulties of crossing the Atlantic. There was no mention of the past, Connor believing that was between them, not their families. He commented that war changes people and again assured Tom that Bill had always had a home in London. He left the letter unfinished until Mary read it. Once she had, he would close it with best wishes.

Thomas Cork sat on his horse in the middle pasture with memories of Dunmanway as clear as yesterday. Even now, he was convinced that all that happened was the fault of the British. Then wondered about Con and, for a fleeting moment, hoped he may have mellowed, then sadly knew better. His mind moved on to others, who, unlike him and his brother, had changed. His son being one. Bill's letters made that clear. Letters about the war, Europe and meeting his Uncle Connor, Aunt Mary and their family. Now riding home, Thomas Cork was increasingly worried. Bill was fighting beside and living amongst people he had been told he should hate and would ask questions about his father's facts and motive. His answers to those questions could alter their relationship forever. Worry turned to concern as he tried to assess Bill's emotions. He would be confused, though once back on the Double B would come to terms with all that had happened. Mandy's death. The influences on him in London and Europe. Tom needed someone to reassure him about his son. Jessica was in the kitchen as her husband tried to put his earlier thoughts into words.

"Jessie, this war is nearly over and then Bill will be home soon. He'll need time to settle down. I think what he's seen and done and the people he's met will have confused him, giving him strange ideas. It might be a bit much to expect him to deal with so much so quick." Tom paused, then continued nervously.

"Maybe we should put off meeting Connor and his family for a year or two after Bill comes home." Jessica Cork remained silent. Bill was alive and well but would come home a vastly changed man, and it seemed her husband was now only starting to appreciate just how different. All she wanted now was to see her son, and she didn't care where. Texas or England, it did not matter. The faces of the Bruce family as they buried their daughter were burned into her soul. Suddenly she was aware Tom had stopped talking, he had kissed her and gone back to work.

Jessica Cork picked up the phone. The conversation was short as she asked her father for a number of contact phone numbers and to exert some of his considerable influence to discover the fastest way to get across the Atlantic as soon as the war ended. She then placed a call to a gentleman in Austin who represented a major shareholder in a new company called Transworld Airlines.

Aboard HMS Longbow, all faces on the bridge turned to Lieutenant Bellamy as the captain asked in a remarkably calm voice.

"Mr Bellamy, where did that bridge come from?" Flags answered with astonished honesty.

"There is nothing on the chart, Sir. The canal is clear right through to the fjord."

Lars came onto the bridge.

"The bridge has been built by German military engineers. A temporary pontoon bridge to allow troops to move around the shoreline. An example of first-class German engineering." Pat Cork pondered.

"Well, we can't blow it out of the water, and there is no time to dismantle it." Adding quickly.

"Flags make contact with Javelin and confirm just how far away they are." Turning to Larsen, he continued.

"Number one. Please ask our non-existent civilian guests to join us. I think we need to bring them up to date." Both men stood on the bridge. The dark-haired man spoke with authority.

"Gentlemen, may I introduce myself and my colleague. My name is Roger Surtees, and this is Jeremy Wiley." Both men were about six foot tall and reasonably well built. What set them apart was Surtees' dark hair; Wiley was pure blonde. Cork began.

"Gentlemen, thank you for your patience and can I officially welcome you to HMS Longbow." Both nodded, and Surtees continued.

"Good to be here, Captain. Now, where is this engine and Von Braun? I'd like to get cracking?" Pat replied.

"There may be a slight problem there. Please allow me to explain."

When Cork had finished, Surtees took the lead.

"Captain, you say the barge ran out of fuel." Pat and Surtees walked to the chart table. The civilian continued.

"Captain, what is the distance to the barge?" Flags interrupted.

"Excuse me, Sir, I have Javelin on the radio."

Cork replied to both men.

"We will soon know Mr Surtees. Put them on please, Flags." Bellamy handed him the handset.

"Javelin, have you worked out the distance between us? Over." Vali replied.

"I make between two and three thousand yards. Is there a problem? Over."

The answer was detailed.

"Yes, we are currently the unwilling beneficiaries of German engineering efficiency. They've built a pontoon bridge across the entrance to the lake. Any ideas how we get to you. I take it from your fuel situation you are unlikely to get to us." Vali answered.

"Well, we can't abandon her here. We have two very sick people and a rather heavy crown jewel. Over." Corks remained silent, a serious look on his face before replying.

"Will get back to you, Javelin. Over and out." Then Surtees spoke.

"With your permission, captain, I have an idea how to get the barge out. May I carry on?" The captain encouraged his guest.

"Please feel free, Mr Surtees."

The plan suggested by Surtees caused great and hasty deliberation by all present. First, after a brief radio conversation, it was estimated the barge displaced between thirty-five and forty tons. The possibility of transferring all crew members and 'crown jewels' to the ships boats was mooted but quickly discarded. The physical condition of the casualties was critical, and the engine was far too heavy. Surtees spoke up.

"But the ship's boats could tow the barge." This statement opened a further debate, with everybody joining in. The distance to be rowed. At least six thousand yards. Half of which would be with a forty-ton barge in tow, which would require some exceedingly fit, experienced men. HMS Longbow always kept a minimum of twelve crew members in first-class condition to man the ship's boat at a minute's notice. In fact, throughout the Royal Navy, being a member of the 'ship's boat crew' was of great prestige. Larsen advised the men gathered on the bridge of the hard facts of rowing from experience gained at Oslo University.

"Be aware that we are intending to row three thousand yards and then tow forty-odd tonnes the same distance. It's a bloody long way. Remember, the Varsity boat race in England is over four miles in length, and those guys are experts. Allowing for the tonnage and distance involved, I think it would take a minimum of two ship's boats to tow the barge out of the fjord."

Commander Cork listened, his mind on the conversation and the positions of the ship and the barge, both in real danger. Then recalled the Admiral's orders. 'Collect Erebus and others from the enemy territory.' He announced that due to time requirements, Surtees' proposal be adopted immediately, finishing with.

"We need to find oarsmen for the second boat."

His statement triggered a unique selection process. Bellamy volunteered immediately, citing his suitability, having won school colours for rowing, and became the first crew member. Mr Surtees then spoke.

"Well, since it was my idea, I'd better go, and if I may reinforce your point, Mr Larsen, the 'boat race' is over seven thousand yards. I know the race intimately as I rowed in two." At this point, Wiley spoke.

"Well, I'm not a boat race man, but like Mr Surtees, I did some long-distance canoeing and coastal rowing, so I'd like to go as well."

Captain Cork concealed his concern. The ship had been at battle stations for twenty hours. The loss of twelve experienced crew members further depleted the lookouts. No more trained men could be spared for rowing. There were too many dangers around the ship. He had to allow the mystery guests to row. There was no alternative. Towing the barge out of the fjord was the only way. Within a short time, the ship's boats were in the water with oars at the ready. The first crewed by expert oarsmen. The second not so practised but equally committed. Without Bellamy and Larsen aboard, he would have to command the ship with CPO Baker. Petty Officer Constantine was the eyes and ears of the ship. They must stay aboard. Lieutenant Forrestal would need to adjust to a new role quickly.

"Mr Baker, please ask Mr Forrestal to report to me." The lieutenant appeared on the bridge.

"Ah! Mr Forrestal, please take the ship. At the first sign of anything out of the ordinary, let me know immediately. I mean immediately. I will be in the radio room." Forrestal, his eyes now wide open, replied nervously.

"Aye, aye, Sir."

Aboard the ship's boats, the crews were working well, and the stroke increased. The course had been set by Larsen who had a handheld radio set to contact the barge. The time of the outward trip was unknown, but as long as the stroke was steady, it was agreed twenty minutes should do it. Stowed in the prow of the volunteer boat by the for'rard gunwale was a pair of two hundred yard, one-inch diameter cables. Aboard the barge, the plan being confirmed had resulted in a flurry of action with two cast iron towing rings freed up on either side of the bow. The sense of excitement was tangible. John Eldridge telling everyone how he would join the boat's crew on the way back, as he had rowed for Harvard. The rest of the men just laughed with the man, who seemed to be enjoying every minute of the mission. Reilly tempered his optimism with a growing concern for the rapid deterioration in the condition of Moen, now convinced an infection had taken hold of his system.

Captain Cork was in contact with Maiden Aunt and had finished explaining the current situation and action. Davies sat in silence and then asked Williamson to inform Odin. In the meantime, he asked the captain of Longbow.

"Commander Cork, please confirm that Mr Surtees and Mr Wiley are part of the towing crews. Over?" The answer came.

"Yes, I can confirm both men volunteered to join the crew of the second boat." He was about to finish but felt inclined to add.

"In fact, the whole thing was Mr Surtees' idea. Over." The silence was a little disconcerting then another voice came on the air.

"Captain Cork, Odin here. Is there any possibility of Mr Surtees and Mr Wiley being captured by the enemy or the Russians whilst towing the barge? Over." Pat gave his honest opinion.

"No more than the rest of us, sir. The barge is about three thousand yards away from us in the centre of the fjord, which is nearly twenty kilometres in width. The dangerous point is the pontoon bridge. But all being well we should clear that quickly. Over."

"That is reassuring, captain. It would be better for all of us if they got back home in one piece. It's only fair I tell you more of the gentlemen. Mr Wiley is chief test pilot." Pat, astounded, stayed calm and could only think to say.

"May I ask what Mr Surtees' role is, Sir? Over."

"Of course. He is the Head of engine design." Pat just managed to ask.

"Chief test pilot and head of engine design for whom, Sir? Over." There was a pause before Odin answered.

"Oh, did I forget to mention that? Rolls Royce. So be a good chap and don't lose them, will you? Good luck. Over." Finally stuck for words, Pat Cork fell back upon naval etiquette.

"Aye, aye, Sir. Over and out."

Colonel Simpson-Coyle had made contact with SOE HQ. Maiden Aunt listened as the soldier detailed the report made by Gerber Von Braun to Oppenheim. He said nothing of the taped radio conversation. Instead asked,

"I need to know where the Javelin team is and also make contact with the man in charge. My information is that a Colonel of US army engineers is in Operational command. Is that correct? Over." Maiden Aunt regretfully began to supply information.

"I will arrange for the details to be forwarded to you in coded form via the Royal Signals unit you are travelling with. Now is there anything else you require? Over." Simpson-Coyle pressed on.

"The names of any other senior officers involved in allowing the return of a valuable asset to enemy territory by junior officers. Over." Maiden Aunt stalled.

"Please hold, over." Next to him, Professor Williamson pleaded.

"Sir, you can't tell him that; all he wants to do is to cover his tracks by hanging the boys out to dry." Davies' face was desolate.

"I know that, prof, but there's nothing I can do. The order giving him Operational command of all SOE Operations outside Norway has never been rescinded. We have no choice but to give Simpson-Coyle any details he requires." The Welshmen returned to the radio.

"Understood. I will have everything you asked for sent to you. Over and out." Simpson-Coyle was in deep thought as he approached the Royal Signals truck. Looking into the rear of the vehicle he enquired of anything for him. The answer was no, then he ordered.

"Sergeant, I am expecting a signal, have it brought to me in the officers' rest tent immediately after decoding." As he walked, Simpson-Coyle thought about the position of the men who had disobeyed orders. Erebus, Vali and whomever else was involved were in serious trouble. The charges could be at least gross insubordination. At worst, mutiny. Both were very grave offences in times of war. His situation on a personal level had improved somewhat. At least he knew what the Yanks were really up to. Now, if he could establish control of Erebus and Vali, he could find a way to advance his own position and make life harder for Oppenheim. Just then, an orderly entered the rest hut with an envelope for him. Simpson-Coyle read it, quickly noting the names and current location of the officers. He then set out to find Colonel Travers of the US army engineers and Colonel Weir of 62 Commando.

Travers had been busy while the Javelin team were out of contact. He had contacted Patton's HQ to report and assess the effect of the death of President Roosevelt on the general's position within the US political and army hierarchy. Travers knew that for men like Patton, the impending peace meant new terms of reference in which they were to operate. President Harry S Truman was a vastly different politician to his predecessor, facing hugely different problems. Travers, only concern was finding a means to nullify Oppenheim's undoubted lust for revenge on anyone who stood in the way of him and the OSS. He had no doubt that the Javelin team would get out of Germany with Von Braun. The fact that they had taken back into enemy territory was slightly more worrying and was something Oppenheim would use against Bill Cork without mercy. Just then, his thoughts were disturbed when an officer approached.

"Gentlemen, I understand you both have an Operational role in something called Operation Javelin. My name is Simpson-Coyle, and I believe we have a common interest in ensuring that everybody involved in that Operation returns safely." Weir was the first to speak.

"Colonel, may I see some identification before we go any further, if at all." Simpson-Coyle did as asked. Both Travers and Weir nodded in acceptance. Travers began.

"Tell me, Colonel, what you need to know and what do you have to offer to help the Javelin team." Colonel Weir continued.

"Colonel Simpson-Coyle, I will add that Colonel Travers and I have a similar view on this matter. Our aim is to get our men out and go home. So tell us what you know, and we'll see where we go from there." The army man seemed quite calm as he informed the officers of his position within the SOE and how the Operation was under his command. Having finally met Simpson-Coyle, Travers decided to rely upon his instincts. He had no doubt the man was ruthless but felt there might be external factors affecting his decisions regarding 'Javelin.' The British colonel was a career soldier and getting on in years; maybe he just wanted to get out with his reputation and pension intact. If this was the case, there might be a way to handle the situation. He looked at the English man and asked.

"Colonel, we need to stifle any attempts to convene courts-martial and to do this, we might have to bend the rule book or lose it completely. These boys are going home once the war is over. Do you understand me?" The reply astounded him.

"Colonel Travers there is only one rule book for a court-martial. That is Kings Regulations which does not bend or get lost."

The ship's boats were now over two thousand yards into the fjord. The lead boat manned by the volunteer crew had Larsen on the prow, his oar shipped, as he held a radio and binoculars with which he canned the lake. Ahead the visibility was poor, raising concern of possible discovery by German motor patrol boats. Then a shadow appeared, Larsen allowed the crew to row for roughly another hundred yards, but the shape was still unclear. He signalled to the oarsmen to rest, then spoke on the transmitter. The radio aboard the Javelin barge came to life as Vali heard.

"Javelin, come in, Javelin; this is exporter over." He replied instantly.

"Javelin here; please give location. Over." Lars spoke.

"I have a vessel about two hundred yards dead ahead. Please look to your starboard side. Over." Erebus ran on deck and spotted both boats. He confirmed with Vali.

"It's them. Tell Larsen to steer straight ahead." Vali relayed the instruction. Within minutes the tow lines were attached. The initial attempt to move the barge was unsuccessful, caused by tension and length in the towlines being unequal. It soon became obvious that keeping the barge hull parallel with the towing boats' course was essential. As any change in the alignment of the hulls brought huge drag on the towing boats and caused the barge to swerve maddeningly. After numerous attempts to coordinate the strokes of the oars in both boats, the vessel slowly gathered momentum, the progress painstakingly slow with the strain on the crews intense. The trio of boats began making steady headway toward the bridge and freedom. After a short time, the strain was clearly evident on the faces of Surtees and Wiley. Lars picked up on this and signalled a halt. The barge drifted alongside the stationary ships' boats. Erebus and Vali, along with - true to his word- John Eldridge, and Bill Cork switched with the Rolls Royce men and Bellamy, who took over steering of the barge. Below decks, Reilly kept an eye on Von Braun. The small flotilla again laboriously began to make way as the reinforced crews took the strain on the tow ropes. Minutes later, Mullen appeared on the barge deck and was about to volunteer to change with John Eldridge when a muffled shout went up from the ship's boat.

"Bridge dead ahead." The fog seemed to evaporate as the distance between the warship and the towing crews shortened. Aboard Longbow, the crew witnessed an extraordinary scene as the three vessels appeared out of the mist as if from a different age. Slowly the towing boats were carefully manoeuvred under the pontoon bridge. The crews boarded Longbow, and the boats were lifted to deck level and stowed. The two towing cables were attached to the eyes of the warship, the barge being about forty yards away. Captain Cork ordered.

"Slow astern both."

The barge was carefully manoeuvred between the pontoon uprights and then attached to the stern of Longbow and towed to sea out of sight of land, then finally pulled alongside Longbow and secured. With great care, Erebus and Vali, helped by the medical orderlies, carried Moen and his nameless companion to the sick bay. They returned on deck to see Surtees, Wiley and Eldridge overseeing the transfer of the engine aboard the sloop by crane and winch rigged by Longbow's engineers. Both men returned to the barge where Reilly, Mullen, Madsen and Norsen were gathering all documents taken from Peenemunde. The SOE men joined the clean-up Operation as the stolen works of art, the gold and any weapons were all to be stowed aboard HMS Longbow. Bill Cork had become Werner Von Braun's guard since the barge had been taken under tow by Longbow. Erebus informed his comrade.

"They're ready for him now, Bill." He escorted the German aboard Longbow where they were met by Commander Larsen - who had resumed his duties, relieving a grateful Forrestal – and Captain Cork, who made the scientist's status very clear.

"General Von Braun, you are now a prisoner of war aboard one of His majesty's warships. You will be escorted to quarters, where you will remain until further notice. I am placing you in the custody of this officer." Lieutenant Forrestal stepped forward, his voice firm.

"I will now inform you of regulations you must obey whilst aboard this ship. You will not converse with any member of the crew. You will not leave your quarters without my permission and under escort by your guards. Do you understand? Please answer yes or no." Werner Von Braun seemed to be looking for help and sought out John Eldridge, who was checking the prototype engine was secure on deck. Eldridge walked past him without a glance. The General nodded his head to signal his understanding. Forrestal was precise.

"Answer yes or no." Von Braun almost whispered.

"Yes." Lieutenant Forrestal remained impassive.

"Follow me. Please." Von Braun followed the young naval officer as did Major Bill Cork, who, throughout the entire briefing, remained silent, his hard gaze never leaving the Nazi general's eyes. Without further ceremony, the barge was towed out to deeper water and the bilge valves opened. She sank almost straight away.

Bellamy joined Petty Officer Constantine in the radio shack.

"Anything to report?" A calm voice replied.

"Nothing Sir, and welcome back." Bellamy was genuinely touched as he replied.

"Thank you, Petty Officer Constantine, and between you and me, after all that rowing, I'd rather you didn't mention my back." The captain came in.

"Well done Flags. Now get me Maiden Aunt, please." Bellamy got on the radio.

"Exporter calling Maiden Aunt. Over." He repeated the signal, then waited. The vibration of the engines increased as the ship picked up speed and headed out to the North Sea.

A voice came over the radio.

"Maiden Aunt to exporter, come in. Over." Cork took the handset.

"Exporter here, go ahead please. Over." Davies' voice was unmistakable.

"Right, bring me up to date. Over." Captain Cork briefed the SOE chief on the status of Operation Javelin finishing with the words.

"All men accounted for, and crown jewels recovered, over." Maiden Aunt's relief was obvious.

"Well done to all concerned." then his voice firmed.

"Right. This is a message from me and the other people who are supposed to be in charge of you lot. So, listen up. This order is to all of you. Vali, Erebus, Major Cork, Reilly and Mullen and Winston bloody Churchill, if he's there. You come straight home now, do hear me captain. Straight home. Is that understood?" The commander of HMS Longbow did not argue.

"Perfectly Sir. Over and out." As Pat was returning to the bridge, he saw Forrestal and called to him.

"Mr Forrestal, you did an excellent job while number one was away. Well done and thank you. I could not have coped without you." The lieutenant broke into a broad smile and replied.

"Thank you, Sir. It's an honour to be aboard your ship." The captain replied.

"It's not my ship Franco. She belongs to all of us, as we belong to her."

Simpson-Coyle sat in a tent and reviewed the situation. He still had serious problems as the war was ending. The matter of the kill order given some five years before was still unresolved. The only certainty was that the order was illegal. The breach in security was still unsolved. How did the top-secret code name of a senior officer in British Intelligence become known to a field operative? Both unanswered questions were directly linked to him and could ruin him. Vali and Erebus had disobeyed orders on at least three occasions. Both were regulars and subject to military law, which provided ample grounds to recommend both to face courts-martial. Their almost 'serial' disobedience might allow him to convince a court-martial they were responsible for the security breach. Simpson-Coyle located Colonels Travers and Weir and stated his position regarding Operation Javelin.

"Gentlemen, it is my duty to ensure that gross disobedience and irresponsibility is investigated and, if proven, punished." With that statement, he turned his back and walked out of the rest tent.

In London, Oppenheim informed the Colonel he had been ordered by senior OSS officials in Washington to get the Von Brauns to the US and in doing so, advance his position and that of the OSS with the US government. He then outlined how a court-martial would camouflage any wrongdoing on their part by cloaking everything in secrecy.

"Charges against the British officers and Major Cork for taking Von Braun back into enemy territory against orders will provide us with both."

Oppenheim was ebullient. Simpson-Coyle was silently far more cautious. He suspected that amongst the men involved in Operation Javelin were military and now increasingly important and influential civilian scientists who would staunchly defend the accused. He would tread very carefully.

Jessica Cork was fully aware of the situation in Europe from Catherine Buchanan, who confidently predicted a collapse of Nazi Germany sometime during May 1945. Jessica was very much in love with her husband but was tiring of his attitude to the people of Britain. Bill's letters more and more hinted that once the war was won, he would come home. But his long-term plans seemed to be based in Europe. His time spent in London had opened his mind to so much more than what Texas and, indeed, America had to offer. She laughed to herself. Maybe Bill was far more Irish than he knew. He had the Irish lust for knowledge and culture. Europe was the place to immerse himself in such things. But first, she had to make plans to either bring him home or go and find him.

Jessica Cork's son was sitting in the wardroom of HMS Longbow, his mind swirling with events of the previous days. The return to Peenemunde. The 'boat race' as the crew had nicknamed the towing Operation. The extraordinary men he had met. Suddenly Bill was overwhelmed by a longing sadness brought on by thoughts of how Mandy would have laughed at the tales of the boat race and quickly bypassed the censor to and write all about it. Then cold anger took over at the thought of the Von Braun brother.

Surtees and Eldridge were below decks with the prisoner demanding details of every aspect of the research, development and production of the V weapons. Von Braun studied his interrogators. The Englishman, who had not given his name, asked perceptive questions on the development and production of the V weapons. The German concluded this man was reasonably talented. Eldridge's questions centred on the V weapon project, with emphasis on the type and source of labour used in the testing and production of the weapons. Then, another Englishman began asking about the aerodynamics of the V1 or flying bomb and the guidance system used to deliver the V2 weapon on target. Von Braun tried to assess what each man did within the aeronautical scientific discipline. The first man was undoubtedly a research scientist and designer. Eldridge was from Harvard. The third man's questions led the German to believe he was involved in the production of aeroplanes. Von Braun began to relax, enjoying his sessions with men with intellects close to his own. But only close. There was no contact with the crew of any sort except for his guards, who remained silent at all times. The German had tried to time how long he had been aboard the warship and was feeling more secure in the knowledge that the ship was heading away from Nazi Germany and the Russians. Then his arrogance came to the fore.

"I need to shower. I have not washed properly in some time. I want to shower now; is that clear?" Lieutenant Forrestal was summoned and when the scientists signalled their agreement, said.

"Please wait here, I will make the arrangements. You will be allowed two minutes to shower."

On the bridge, Larsen confirmed the ship's position in reply to the captain.

"We are heading out of Helgoland Bay, captain. Helgoland Island is to the south of us. We should be clear of enemy waters within twenty-four hours." Cork remained silent as he motioned to Larsen to follow him to the radio room. Petty Officer Constantine was at the Radar set with Bellamy next to him. The captain asked.

"Anything on the Radar?" Constantine replied.

"One distant contact, Sir. Slightly south of our current position and between us and the open sea. At extreme range. Course indistinct but general heading is toward Helgoland Bay."

"Any ideas P.O?"

"Yes, Sir, even at that distance, it looks like a U-boat. He's on the surface probably recharging his batteries as its dark." Lars pointed out.

"He could be trouble, Sir. Some of the later U-boats have radar capability. Up to seven thousand yards range." Cork ordered.

"Right, we'll head north and then west before turning south again." Lars confirmed.

"Aye, aye, Sir." As Pat turned to leave Constantine, lifted his hand again. All three officers were silent.

"Radar contact from the north, sir and a good deal closer." Lars demanded.

"Can you confirm what it is?" Constantine's voice was calm, as usual.

"Oh yes, Sir. It is a U-boat and on a course which will intersect ours." The ensuing silence was broken by the captain.

"Well, gentlemen, it seems we are now caught in what the Army would call a pincer movement. Number One signal battle stations." He continued.

"And please ask Mr Forestall to bring our guests to the bridge. Von Braun remains where he is." Forestall did as ordered. The civilians stood on the now crowded bridge.

"Gentlemen," the captain began,

"A quick update. Dead ahead is a German offshore settlement known as Helgoland Bight, where there are long-range radar stations which work in conjunction with radar posts on the German coast. We may have been detected by these installations." He paused.

"We have encountered a number of surface contacts to the north and south, Gentlemen, we must assume the enemy is aware of our presence, and they are readying to attack us." Surtees replied.

"Captain, I think I speak for the civilians aboard when I say we have every confidence in you and your crew. Good luck."

Forrestal returned with the scientists to the interrogation cabin and stood in front of his captive.

"General, I'm afraid the shower will have to wait until we get a little further away from your glorious fatherland. So please remain here until further notice." Von Braun squealed sarcastically.

"Why have you stopped me? Is there a water shortage?" The reply came in a calm voice.

"Von Braun, if things don't work out for us, you may have more than enough water to wash in. Now do as you are told." The ship vibrated as speed was increased. The scientists decided there was nothing to be done other than continue examining the paperwork and questioning Von Braun. Who was now, to their amusement, highly agitated and a little smelly. Captain Cork was in the radio cabin with Bellamy, Constantine and Lars, where he explained his course of action.

"Gentlemen, I intend to outrun both surface contacts by steaming straight between them. We have more than enough speed to do this." He then ordered.

"Engine room full ahead both. PO Constantine, keep me informed of any changes in the positions and courses of the surface contacts." Longbow was steaming toward safety when Constantine called for the captain.

"Sir, please come to the radio room immediately." Cork listened as Constantine explained.

"Sir. Both contacts have altered course. The northern U-boat, which is closer, is now coming straight for us. The southern contact is heading for Helgoland Island to cut us off." Pat interrupted.

"We can still outrun them." Constantine continued.

"I hadn't finished Sir. There is a third submerged contact dead ahead, which is moving slowly and coming straight for us." As Larsen and Bellamy entered the radio shack, Captain Cork announced.

"Well, gentlemen, it looks like we are about to take on three U-boats," he paused and invoked an old naval blasphemy,

"For what we are about to receive, may we be truly thankful."

Oppenheim had been contacted by his superior in London, who advised him that president Truman supported the OSS but had his own ideas on the role of the agency long term. Despite strong representations from the United States military establishment, he had decided the new agency would be led by civilians after the war. To placate the military, they remained in control until that time. Oppenheim immediately requested that all OSS Operations in Europe be under his command. His superior covered his own back by telling him to go ahead without formal permission.

Aboard HMS Longbow, the situation was now much clearer. To starboard was a U-boat closing. To port was another enemy contact holding a course to intercept close to Helgoland. Dead ahead was the third boat submerged. All within a five-mile radius. Cork spoke to Larsen.

"Number one, from now on, we assume that the enemy is being advised of our position by onshore radar. We're going to continue to run for the open sea beyond Helgoland Bight." The intercom sounded. Lars answered.

"Bridge aye."

"Engine room here sir. The sea conditions are making fourteen knots impossible. We'll get twelve if we are careful. The hull is taking an awful battering." Larsen looked at his captain.

"Very well, Number one, reduce revolutions to twelve knots." Then looked out to sea and continued.

"At least the sea conditions will force the U-boats to remain submerged, which will slow them down. Which gives us a chance of escape and maybe sinking one of them in the process."

As the sun rose further, the ship ploughed into heavy seas. Below decks, Von Braun was very upset. His temper was not helped by the continuous pitching of the ship and the relentless questions. The German would not admit it, but the most annoying factor was that his inquisitors were fully aware if his answers to their questions were not accurate or relevant. Occasionally one of the men would leave and then return somewhat wetter. Von Braun got the impression that the three interrogators were working to a deadline. What he did not know was that each was checking the prototype engine specifications against the answers given by its designer. They had growing concerns that the engine may not be as revolutionary as the initial examination had implied. During discussions, all three agreed the jet engine was outstanding, but examination of the working notes repeatedly found reference to metal parts disintegrating, causing loss of power, and finally, engine failure. Wiley asked Von Braun.

"General, has the engine ever been used aboard an aircraft in flight conditions?" Von Braun hesitated, then shouted.

"The engine was rushed. Hitler demanded too much of my people. We could have perfected the power unit in time. But, no, he wanted two hundred jet powered aircraft. We had the engines almost ready, but the most modern airframe could not take the erratic power surges." Eldridge cut in.

"General, I read in your brother's personal notes that aircraft were tested with imperfect engines, some of which exploded after take-off. How were these aircraft piloted?" Von Braun cursed in German and then hissed.

"Those records are inaccurate. Gerber chose the wrong people to keep the test logs." Eldridge pressed on.

"Von Braun you must have used pilots to man the prototype aircraft; where did you get the pilots to fly these death traps?" The German seemed to shrink slightly and remained silent. Wiley, his face cold, delved further into the notes. He swore softly, then looked the German in the face.

"My god, you used allied prisoners of war. RAF, Norwegian and USAF POWs." Trying to control himself, Eldridge shouted.

"How many of our boys did you kill, you Nazi bastard?" Wiley answered the question as he stood, his voice trembling.

"According to his brother's papers, fifty-six pilot officers were forced to fly the test aircraft, that or be shot."

Captain Cork surveyed the steely grey, very rough sea. In the radio room, despite hints from Bellamy, Constantine had remained on duty for twenty-four hours glued to the ASDIC earphones awaiting the first close-quarter contact. Cork had ordered radio silence until further notice. There was no point in contacting either SOE HQ or C in C Channel fleet. There was nothing anyone could do. HMS Longbow was alone as she steamed due west with her valuable cargo and irreplaceable scientists. All the prey of three enemy submarines which were inexorably closing on her.

41

Changing Context

The men sat in silence. Colonel Simpson-Coyle of the British Army and Mr Oppenheim of the Office of Strategic Services on opposite sides of a table in a debriefing centre in Germany. The OSS man was scribbling on a sheet of paper. The colonel was bemused but not surprised. The American was a very arrogant, ambitious and careless man. Simpson-Coyle had survived by never committing anything to paper, let alone signing a document. A practice which ensured that if things went wrong, other people got the blame. The words of his Intelligence Training Officer still reverberated, 'Never leave a paper trail. All of what you do from now on never happened.'

Adhering to this practice and unknown to Oppenheim, Simpson-Coyle had initiated background checks on the men aboard HMS Longbow. Unwilling to trust the analysts at SOE, he had contacted Chief Superintendent Peters of the Royal Ulster Constabulary in Northern Ireland. The list of names supplied by Simpson-Coyle for general background checks had been distributed amongst RUC officers. One being Detective Sergeant Bagot, who had been ordered to check out Richard Lionel Surtees, Guy Jeremy Wiley, Professor John Eldridge and, once again, Commander Patrick Cork RN. The reasons for the checks had not been explained. For Peters, that was nothing new. Man management was never his strong point. Bagotsoon became aware of the sensitivity of the situation when, within hours of telephoning Belfast for subject background information, he received a phone call from an office on the mainland. The man identified himself simply as RAF Intelligence. No rank, no name – just a polite but forceful manner.

"Why, sergeant, are you asking questions about Messrs Surtees and Wiley and who requested that you do so?" All Bagotcould say was that the information requested was part of a general background check. The voice then softened and asked,

"Is it just these two men you are interested in, sergeant?"

Bagotcould see no reason not to answer and supplied the names of Eldridge and Cork. Bagotwas told there was one more question.

"May I have the name of your commanding officer, please, sergeant?"

Bagot, by now enthralled, named the man. The next morning, Superintendent Peters, who - in his eyes - was above all else a patriot, loyal to king and country, confirmed to the group captain, who had arrived at his office unannounced, that he was under the orders of a senior officer. Peters was handed a letter signed by the Chief Constable of the RUC instructing him to take the matter no further. The anonymous RAF officer ordered all those involved to say nothing more of the matter to anyone. Before leaving, he asked for the identity of the aforementioned senior officer and was given the name - Simpson-Coyle.

As President Truman began to assume the responsibilities of what was effectively the most powerful man in the world, the United States Armed forces generals and admirals under his command were adopting, in their respective theatres of Operations, the positions of pro-consuls, dealing with civilian and military issues as Germany collapsed. One such man was General Patton, who had just finished a meeting with Colonel Travers where Operation Javelin, Bill Cork, Eldridge and, in particular, Oppenheim had been discussed. Travers had briefed the general on the current situation and the whereabouts of the Javelin team. Patton spoke.

"Colonel, the priority must be to get the Javelin team to safety. The Americans involved are seconded to the Third Army and technically under my command. Therefore, I am ordering you to ensure that they report to me alone and no one else."

Travers was about to leave when Patton added,

"Colonel, from what you have told me, we have one real issue. Major Cork did disobey a direct order. That is something we cannot deny or ignore. If that OSS spook knows military law, we have a problem."

In Austin, Texas, Charlie Rawlings was deep in thought. There must be a way to get to Europe. He remembered the words of Catherine Buchanan during a recent Friday night gathering.

'The war is nearly over, and the Nazi regime is in its death throes. Once the surrender has been signed, the priorities of the Allies will change. Food supplies for the people have to be delivered quickly, or Europe will starve.'

Perhaps a call to contacts in Washington might lead to something. He phoned a friend at the Department of Agriculture and was told about a vague plan for relief to Europe being put together by the Chairman of the Joint Chiefs of Staff, General Marshall. Rawlings asked if the beef industry would be involved. His contact would call back. Charlie then phoned Elmer Riddle and asked him to enquire if anyone in the Hunt Organisation had heard of plans being put together by General Marshall. Riddle replied,

"Charlie, we have done a lot of business with the military during the war. I'll see what I can dig up."

Rawlings then spoke to a business associate with contacts in the State Department to see if any plans had been made to allow civilian companies to provide travel facilities to Europe after the German surrender.

In the North Sea, HMS Longbow steamed straight into the path of three enemy submarines. On the bridge, Captain Cork assessed the situation as part of a discussion with Lars and Erebus.

"Well, gentlemen, what would we do if we were in Norway with C squad?"

The first officer answered quickly,

"We would gather as much information as possible."

Erebus added,

"Even up the odds a little, captain."

Cork then turned to Bellamy.

"Flags, speak to Petty Officer Constantine and see if he can give me an estimate of the speed of each enemy contact."

Bellamy acknowledged.

"Aye, aye, sir."

The captain looked at his old friends.

"Ok, let's analyse the situation. We are outnumbered three to one. Currently, there are two enemy vessels on the surface and one submerged. Until the boats currently on the surface fully recharge their batteries, they can remain submerged for a short time. The crews will be tired. Due to the high seas, the conning tower lookouts will see very little. In fact, they may be running blind. Should they submerge to attack, the same conditions will make it impossible for them to get a periscope sighting unless they come to within three hundred yards of us, and then we've got them loud and clear on SONAR." Bellamy returned to hear.

"The submerged boat is dead ahead, and his current course has him coming straight for us." Cork paused, then added.

"Yes, Flags."

"Captain, Constantine has tracked all three enemy contacts. The U-boat to the north of us is running slower than the enemy vessel to the south. The U-boat dead ahead is the slowest of the three. He thinks, and I agree, they intend to intercept us simultaneously."

Cork spoke slowly.

"Flags, designate the U-boat north of us, target one. The enemy boat dead ahead, target two and the U-boat to the south of us, target three."

"Captain to radio cabin. Immediately, please."

Pat stood as Constantine pointed to the screen.

"Sir, all targets are closing on us. The German radar on Helgoland Bite must be guiding them. On our current course and speed, in about two hours, we will have target two dead ahead and blocking our westerly course. Target three will stop us from sailing south, and target one will make an escape to the north impossible."

Cork knew that before engaging the enemy, he needed the fuel status of the ship.

"Number one, calculate how far we can steam at our current speed."

As if by instinct, Pat knew Bellamy was at his elbow.

"Flags, calculate exactly where the supply ship, Sir Ivanhoe, is and then tell the first officer."

Lars returned and spoke quietly.

"The extra distance steamed to collect the Javelin team has taken its toll. We have just enough fuel to reach Sir Ivanhoe and nothing else."

Captain Cork announced,

"Okay. Target one to the north and target three to the south are out of torpedo range. We can get away from them by taking a westerly course at about twelve knots. They will not be able to keep up with us. This will leave just target two dead ahead which we will sink, and we should still have enough fuel left to reach Sir Ivanhoe."

Pat began to see a very slim chance of escape.

He reached for the intercom.

"Engine room, give me everything you've got."

After a short time, the engine room officer informed Cork,

"Captain, the sea conditions are worsening. We are not making anything like twelve knots and are in danger of sustaining severe hull damage at our current speed."

Pat asked,

"Mr Bellamy, how many knots are we making?"

Flags replied,

"Barely eight, sir."

Constantine came on the intercom.

"Captain, target one to the north and target three to the south have submerged and are currently averaging just over eight knots and closing on us."

Larsen reported in a low voice,

"Sir, at our current speed, target one and target three will be in torpedo range very soon."

In Texas, Charlie Rawlings was on the phone to the Department of Agriculture and receiving interesting news as his contact briefed him on a developing situation in Europe. The newly liberated European countries were forming provisional governments which were formulating plans for the rebuilding of their economies, part of which was the re-establishment of the devastated agriculture sectors, including their national herds. The US Livestock Association had been ordered by the US Department of Agriculture to canvas all meat producers in the US who wished to export livestock to Europe. All suppliers of beef must be willing to send experienced cattle handlers to tend the livestock during the passage. Rawlings saw his chance and, as a part owner of the Double B, immediately asked for the ranch to be registered as a supplier of Aberdeen Angus breeding stock to Europe. Buchanan, when told, readily agreed.

"The Double B would supply all the cattle needed and handlers as well. Will you tell Tom?"

Rawlings replied,

"I'll tell Jessie - she can let Tom know."

Oppenheim was brought up to date on OSS matters over the radio by an officer based in Washington. President Truman had appointed Admiral Stark, the current commander of Naval Operations in the USA, to oversee the organisation in the short term. The OSS officer continued,

"The admiral has been ordered to report to Truman on the strategic direction and activities of the OSS. The importance of Javelin has become clear to Stark who is viewing it as an opportunity to advance his standing with the President and has guaranteed that it will be quickly completed."

Oppenheim later confided in Simpson-Coyle, having confirmed his intention to prosecute all the men involved in Operation Javelin to the maximum.

"All I want from this sailor is authority over all of the US personnel involved in Javelin; then I'll run rings around him."

Simpson-Coyle's view on Oppenheim and the Americans began to harden. He would be glad to be rid of them all, but for now, he needed at least two of the 'cousins.'

At SOE HQ, Maiden Aunt and Williamson began to plan for the coming battle with the military legal system. Simpson-Coyle had made his aims clear. Any member of the Javelin team found to have disobeyed orders would be prosecuted under Kings Regulations. The Prof spoke.

"Sir, we need to know where we stand, so I've put together my understanding of the situation."

He handed the brigadier a sheet of paper with two lists. One contained the names of Dr Eldridge, Erebus, Vali, Reilly, Mullen, Madsen and Norsen. Moen's name had been pencilled in. Underneath these names and separated from them were listed the names Surtees, Wiley, Travers and Colonel Weir. Opposite this list was a second column made up of Simpson-Coyle, Oppenheim, the Von Brauns and the OSS.

"Please explain, Prof."

Williamson outlined how the column on the left contained the names of those who were likely to be charged and those who would help in their defence. The people listed in the column on the right had numerous reasons to see the servicemen convicted and the entire Javelin Operation matter closed as an official secret. Davies looked helplessly at the former 'conchie' academic who had thrown himself into the war and said,

"Thanks Prof; right now, I'd settle for the boys being alive to face a court-martial."

Some of the men on that list were in great danger on the North Sea. The interrogation of Von Braun had been halted as the ship went to battle stations. The German was in his cabin, having been shown his lifeboat station if the ship was hit. The look of sheer terror in his eyes brought pleasure to his Donegal guards, Sean Macnally and Fergus Canavan. The scientists, along with Bill Cork, were told of the situation by Larsen, who then invited them to the bridge, which was described by the captain on their arrival as 'As safe a place as any.'

HMS Longbow was now making barely seven knots, enabling the U-boats to close to nearly maximum torpedo range. Cork tried to put himself in the U-boat commander's place. The boats were returning to base after a long patrol and may only have a few if any, torpedoes left. The crews would be exhausted and maybe careless. His thoughts were interrupted by Constantine, who reported that targets two and three were still out of torpedo range, but that target one to the north was closing in at a right angle to take a beam shot at Longbow. Pat knew instantly that they had a chance. The captain of target one had rushed in for the kill and, in doing so, had made a huge error. Constantine's voice was clear.

"Target one has fired two torpedoes, at maximum range, running straight for us."

Cork ordered,

"Hard-a-starboard! Full ahead both." And whispered.

"Thank God for fanatics."

The engines screamed as the ship fought the seas to turn on to a course parallel to the torpedoes now heading to destroy her. Bellamy had joined Constantine in the radio shack and reported,

"Estimated Torpedo contact time approximately one hundred and twenty seconds."

The ship dived into the huge waves, the decks almost submerged, awash with freezing water which tore away anything not bolted down. Every crewman counted. Eighty seconds, sixty seconds, forty seconds. Longbow completed the manoeuvre and was now heading true north. Bellamy's voice was calm.

"Twenty seconds."

Aboard the ship, the waves and the wind made it impossible to see or hear the torpedoes. Five seconds and still no explosion. The silence was broken by Constantine's voice over the intercom.

"Captain, torpedoes should have made contact by now. I have a fix on target one."

Captain Cork ordered.

"Steer straight for him. We'll use the forrard and aft 'hedgehogs' to depth charge him. Run up the battle flags, Mr Bellamy."

The ship again fought through the heaving seas then Constantine shouted.

"Target one in range, sir."

Cork ordered,

"Fire all 'hedgehogs' and depth charges as they bear and keep firing."

The sonar picked up the sound of the depth charges exploding; nothing after that. The sea was too rough for oil slicks or debris to be seen. There was no confirmation of target one being destroyed. Still silence, then Constantine reported,

"I can hear cracking noises. Ammunition exploding. He's breaking up, sir. We bloody well got them."

Then just the howling of the wind and the roaring of the waves until the spell was broken by a lookout's cry.

"U-boat! Port side!"

All eyes turned to see the enemy U-boat around two hundred and fifty yards away with torpedo tube doors open, ready to fire. The captain of Target three had decided to risk a surface shot, convinced he could not miss. Longbow had no escape. Constantine's voice came over the intercom.

"Target three on the surface, sir. Target two submerged and closing portside, abeam of us, at about two hundred and fifty yards."

They all looked at the U-boat, which was preparing to sink them, when, suddenly, Constantine and Bellamy yelled almost together,

"Target two has fired torpedoes, Sir."

All eyes watched as the surfaced U-boat disappeared in an explosion caused by two direct torpedo hits just below the water line. The weather seemed to ease as Target two surfaced. The wind made voice contact impossible, but then, suddenly, a flag unfurled on the submarine's radio mast. A Stars and Stripes, confirmed by a lookout's shout.

"It's the bloody Yanks."

Radio contact followed immediately. The men aboard the British warship listened in disbelief to the loudspeakers as an American voice announced,

"Ahoy, HMS Longbow. USS Tigerfish. Captain Templeton here. Greetings, Captain Cork. Admiral Burke thought you might need a little help. Glad to oblige. We owed you for that time in the English Channel when you could have sunk us and didn't." There followed a brief pause of total silence. Then.

"Now, might I suggest we all get the hell out of here?" Lars later remarked that the cheer from Longbow's crew could be heard in Portsmouth.

The signal that HMS Longbow had successfully extracted the Javelin team was greeted with grateful satisfaction from the C in C Portsmouth, Admirals Hilliard and Burke to the clandestine world of Menzies, Odin and Maiden Aunt. Travers and Weir, although delighted, now began to prepare for the weight of military justice which could come to bear on their men, and to plan how to frustrate Simpson-Coyle.

Alone in a tent, the colonel even managed a covert smile. His self-survival instincts were now fully alert and advised extreme caution. A strategy adopted because of contact with a very senior RAF officer, who subtly implied that the civilians involved in Javelin had support from the highest authority, and Simpson-Coyle's activities were impinging on some exceedingly sensitive issues. Then, in a far more overt fashion, added that the war was coming to an end and the military would have its powers curtailed very quickly. Simpson-Coyle concluded there was nothing more to be learned at the camp and boarded a priority flight to the UK.

Oppenheim, aware of the successful conclusion of Javelin, made contact with Admiral Sparks and requested full authority over any Americans involved in the Operation. Sparks had little experience of men like Oppenheim and, believing him to be a normal human being, verbally granted the OSS man's request.

The men of HMS Longbow carried out damage assessment checks on their battered ship as she steamed toward Sir Ivanhoe four days away. The captain and the first officer paid a visit to check on the scientists who, they presumed, were continuing to debrief Von Braun. They found Reilly and Mullen with Eldridge, Surtees and Wiley, all going through Von Braun's files in great detail. The prisoner was next, who immediately demanded to know when he would be going to America. Finally, the officers visited the sick bay, where a very concerned medical orderly spoke as he watched Moen and the unknown man.

"I am extremely worried about both. We need professional medical help and soon, sir. Mr Moen is in and out of consciousness. The other gentleman has not come around at all."

All Pat could say was,

"Do the best you can, please."

Upon leaving the sick bay, he and Lars met Erebus and Vali, who spoke first.

"Well done captain; number one. I couldn't have done a better job myself."

Pat nodded his appreciation but remained silent, his face dark.

"How is Moen?" Erebus asked quietly.

"He is not good, Charles, not good at all, and we are four days from the nearest medical centre – if the weather doesn't worsen."

John Eldridge appeared; his face serious.

"Good afternoon, gentlemen."

Then speaking directly to Pat, he asked,

"Captain, would it be possible to speak to Mr Moen? Believe me; it is vitally important."

The reply was heartfelt.

"Mr Eldridge, you may, but he is a very sick man. I know you will bear that in mind." The scientist signalled his understanding then, before opening the door, suggested.

"Charles, perhaps if you were with me?" Erebus agreed.

"Why not? Maybe he'll hear me, get angry and come around just to tell me off."

Maiden Aunt was sitting in his office along with Odin and C, and Professor Williamson. The men were quietly relieved but concerned. 'C' spoke.

"Gentlemen, we have carried out a very successful extraction of valuable assets. The gentlemen from Rolls Royce will be back in the UK very soon, and we will know how much they have learned. The initial reports are very promising. I will, of course, offer every support to the remarkable young men who successfully accomplished the mission. Unfortunately, I must be seen to leave the disciplinary issues to you, Maiden Aunt and you, Odin. Brigadier, please bring us up to date." Davies summarised the military position.

"Unfortunately, it is crystal clear Erebus, Vali, Reilly, Mullen, Madsen, and Norsen have disobeyed a direct order. All were technically under the command of Colonel Simpson-Coyle at the time the insubordination took place, and he is within his legal rights to recommend that all of them face court-martial."

There was silence as Davies began to outline a possible tactic for the defence of the men he had sent into Peenemunde.

"The Professor and I have been giving this some thought, having discussed the issue with a leading expert in Military law, a Barrister by the name of Boyd. We believe there is a viable defence. Prof, please elucidate." Williamson did as asked, and when finished, the admiral nodded as he said quietly,

"Let's get our men back to the UK while you and Professor Williamson and Mr Boyd KC progress the line of defence. Please temper your deliberations with the real probability of a huge change in context. I received information earlier that the Germans will surrender in a matter of days."

Aboard Longbow, John Eldridge and Erebus sat by the cot as Moen was beginning to come round. Slowly his eyes opened and then seemed to light up a little as he recognised the man next to him.

"Laudrup, where the hell have you been? I've been looking for you. We've got more targets for those 'Dum Dum' bullets of yours. The bastards are building rockets and other shit like them."

He then began to throw up. Erebus whispered to Eldridge,

"He thinks he's back in Norway, earlier in the war. I'll get the medic. "

As he left, Moen's voice weakened to a barely audible whisper. Eldridge leaned closer.

"I saw it. I drove one of the lorries full of rocket fuel. Everything kept blowing up. They're evil bastards. They've been killing pilots testing the planes. American, Norwegian and British pilots. Forced them to fly or be shot. Same as me. Drive the rocket fuel or be shot."

At that point, he almost passed out but fought to stay awake.

"Like Mueller. Got their names. The head bastard is called Von Braun. That's the bastard we should kill him and his twisted, short-arse brother."

Eldridge wrote every word down as it was spoken. The medical orderly arrived and asked,

"Gentlemen, please allow this man some rest." Eldridge agreed.

"Of course. What I've heard so far is most helpful."

Pat Cork stood on the bridge as the weather eased, and every hour brought Longbow closer to home. His crew was safe, and the ship intact. Silently, he prayed, 'Any day now, any hour, it must be over soon - any hour now.'

Flags approached with a number of signals which Pat flicked through, then decided to read in his cabin.

"Mr Larsen, you have the ship. Mr Bellamy, should I be needed, I'll be in my cabin."

The bridge crew replied as one,

"Aye, aye, sir."

Pat concentrated on the signals. There were three. Two from Admiral Hilliard. The first words of congratulations on a job well done. The second ordered Longbow to wait for orders as to where to take Von Braun. The final signal referred to the OSS and how every effort was to be made to assist them. It ordered Pat to be ready to transfer personnel to a US Navy ship as soon as possible, along with all equipment and paperwork relating to Operation Javelin. The order was signed by an unknown admiral based in Whitehall. Cork immediately forwarded a copy of the order to Admiral Hilliard and C in C, Portsmouth.

Pat wondered if Eldridge, Surtees and Wiley might have something to say about the engine and its accompanying paperwork being taken elsewhere. A fourth signal came from Admiral Hilliard.

'Steam for Portsmouth with all possible speed, weather permitting.'

Captain Cork was now caught between two admirals. Not a good place for a ship's commander to be, but Hilliard was his flag officer, so once the ship had provisioned and refuelled at Sir Ivanhoe, Portsmouth would be the next port. There was a knock on the cabin door.

"Enter."

Chief petty officer Baker opened the door, accompanied by Petty Officers McNally and Canavan. Surprised, Pat half smiled, saying,

"Come in, gentlemen."

Baker began to speak.

"Sir, we may have a problem involving the gentlemen we picked up in Danish waters." Cork asked slowly,

"Mr Baker, please expand upon the word 'problem.'"

Petty Officer Fergus McNally cut in.

"With your permission, chief."

Baker nodded his head, a grateful look on his face.

"Well, sir, as the guards assigned to the prisoner, we take some responsibility for losing a piece of his property." Pat pressed his shipmates.

"Gentlemen, please get on with whatever you have to say."

McNally continued,

"Very good, sir. It's the equipment that was brought aboard with the men from the barge, sir. We can't find it. The engine which was lashed to the bulkhead has gone, sir. We're fairly certain it went overboard when we took on the U-boat."

Cork almost laughed out loud.

"Thank you, gentlemen. Please leave this with me."

Before Baker could leave, Pat asked,

"Chief, please ask Mr Surtees to come and see me."

At the Big Bend ranch, Charlie Rawlings and Buchanan were deep in conversation, having read the instructions for shipping cattle to Europe. The animals were to be moved in cargo ships specially built for livestock. Each ranch was to supply as many experienced hands as possible. When Buchanan queried why and how many, Rawlings answered,

"Things are pretty rough in Europe. Shortages everywhere - rumours of epidemics – typhoid, and such. There is still some Nazi resistance. Some people just don't want to go. Hell, Bill, life's good here in the US compared to what those people over there have been through."

Buchanan responded eagerly.

"That means we can take as many as we want."

Rawlings raised his hand in caution.

"The war in Europe isn't over yet, but it seems that the convoys are getting through without any trouble. Now let's find out who wants to go to Europe with the best cattle in Texas."

As HMS Longbow fuelled and provisioned, the weather worsened. To move them to the much larger vessel would have been hazardous, so Moen and his fellow patient stayed aboard. The conditions also dictated that the entire Javelin team remain aboard the warship until reaching Portsmouth. Mr Surtees gave his reaction to the loss of the engine to the captain.

"The engine was, in theory, revolutionary, but the more we looked at the data compiled by the Germans, it became clear that, as a propulsion unit, it was never viable. The materials used in the construction of the engine were too unstable. So, captain, I shouldn't worry about the loss of the unit. It was, to put it politely, a very dangerous delusion. If there are any awkward questions about the engine, I will take full responsibility for it being lost overboard."

Pat asked outright,

"Do you think it was worthwhile going back for it, Mr Surtees?" The Rolls Royce designer spoke with certainty.

"Yes, it was worth going back for the research papers alone. Captain, the information we got out of Von Braun is revolutionary, and I would be grateful if you could take as long as possible to reach Portsmouth. We need more time with him." Pat Cork relaxed and set a course for Portsmouth. In the wardroom, Erebus, Vali, Reilly, Mullen, Madsen and Norsen waited for landfall and the inevitable inquiry to decide if they were to face charges for returning to Peenemunde. Bill Cork was out on deck trying to control his emotions as he thought of Mandy in her grave and Von Braun getting closer every day to America and freedom.

Jessica Cork sat in her kitchen, having just been told of the possibility of getting to Europe as part of the support team with the Double B cattle export project. Her father explained in detail what was required and then asked her to tell Tom about the possible new business. She knew her husband would not be happy about anyone from the family going to Europe, let alone Britain or Ireland. His mind was on getting Bill home - not going to meet him over there. Tom was very busy on the spring roundup which would last at least two weeks. Jessica suggested to Buchanan and her father that she take on all of the arrangements for moving cattle and people to Europe. Both readily agreed. Her efficiency and enthusiasm soon resulted in other ranches in Texas being redirected to her by the US Stock Association. There were a total of ten Texan ranches, all shipping cattle. Jessica found herself as the focal point of the shipping process for all involved and was appointed to the position of State Coordinator. Her husband was aware that the ranch might pick up new business but was too busy to get any details. In fact, he was finding it hard to contact his wife at home; such was her commitment and workload. Jessica threw herself into the project as it helped to alleviate her constant concern about Bill. Then, one evening, she sat her husband down and explained the export project and her role in it. As he leafed through the paperwork, two questions arose.

"Jessie, where in Europe are we shipping these cattle, and how many heads will there be?"

His wife explained.

"The initial shipment is one hundred animals per ranch - seventy-five heifers and twenty-five bulls. The first port of call is England and then wherever the cattle are needed the most. Until the war ends, we will cross the Atlantic in convoy, which will take between fifteen and twenty days."

He asked a third question.

"It says here that we have to send hands with the beef. Have you asked any of our people?"

Jessica steeled herself.

"Bill and Catherine Buchanan are going and so is my father, Carlito and Chato and one each of their sons."

She paused, and then with a firm voice, stated,

"And so am I, Tom."

HMS Longbow cast off from Sir Ivanhoe and, at the unofficial request of a gentleman from Rolls Royce, steered a long and steady arc which would eventually bring her to Portsmouth harbour. Aboard, Surtees, Wiley and Eldridge never gave Von Braun a waking moment without a question. The men were both scientific interrogators and moral inquisitors. Eldridge, in particular, probed more and more about the methods employed by Von Braun, his brother and the Peenemunde research team to build the V weapons. All three would randomly throw in questions about the airborne testing of the engine. Who were the pilots? How were the test results recorded? Were the pilots volunteers from the Luftwaffe? If not, where were the pilots sourced from? The same questions were applied to the labour force. Von Braun was no fool and considered every question before giving a guarded answer, but the relentless pressure slowly wore him down, and a picture began to emerge. A picture of the use and mistreatment of slave labour and the possible murder of Allied pilots. Bill Cork would occasionally sit in but had no role to play. As he remarked to John Eldridge in the wardroom,

"If I had that bastard Von Braun, I'd have him singing like a nightingale. One way or the other."

Tom Cork sat on his horse in the middle pasture. His wife had been adamant.

'Tom, I am going with the cattle to Europe, and if I can manage it, I will find Bill and maybe meet your brother and all of our family.'

His argument from the beginning was unconvincing.

"But, Jessie, what about the kids?" Her reply was scathing.

"Our children are young adults at college and are extremely mature and sensible. The only child I can see is the one in front of me."

The argument, as such, continued with Tom trying to find reasons, ranging from pressure of work to insufficient supervision if he left the ranch, to persuade his wife not to go to Europe. All were quickly rebuffed.

"Tom, because of you and Buchanan, this ranch is one of the best run in Texas. The boys who Buchanan brought here are now men and more than capable of looking after things. The spring round-up is finished and we'll be back for the autumn. Felix and Simon can deal with any major problems, so the only question left, Thomas Cork, is whether or not you are coming with us."

Tom, as part owner of the Double B, was used to being in control. Now he clearly was not, and Jessica was crossing the Atlantic whether he liked it or not. A thought crossed his mind. Any questions asked by Bill would be answered in Britain, the country he hated and lied about. There might be explanations demanded by his boy, having seen how his Uncle Connor had done so well. Then there was the real possibility of meeting Connor and his family. As he rode back to the ranch, Tom accepted that there was no way to avoid this journey. At the back of his mind was the thought that there just might be an arrest warrant outstanding for the murder of the Bagots.

In his office, Connor Cork heard cheering, then clapping, then singing. His secretary ran in shouting,

"It's over, Mr Cork, we've won. Mr Churchill has just announced the surrender of the Nazi High Command. Now we can get on with tomorrow."

Connor reached for his jacket and asked the jubilant girl,

"Call my wife at home, please and then take the rest of the day off."

He turned on the radio and listened to the BBC, still broadcasting despite all of Hitler's threats and vows to destroy it. The phrase 'unconditional surrender' reverberated as he picked up the phone.

"Mary, have you heard? It's official. The war is over. Pat and Bill are safe. Now we can look forward to them coming home. I'm closing the plant down for the afternoon. Maybe we'll go and celebrate."

His wife could hardly speak but managed to reply.

"We'll decide when you get here. Con. Why don't you pick up Chris and Rachel on the way home?"

Connor excitedly agreed, then the phone line went dead. She had listened to the radio broadcast in silence, and now there were tears of relief and joy. Mary was a very strong woman, but occasionally she needed a moment to herself. This was one. She sat in an armchair and cried for Mandy and the Bruce family and all those people whose children would not be coming home.

The merchant ship left Galveston and headed out to sea as a radio message was received aboard. The passengers were all asked to meet in the saloon cabin. The contingent from the Double B stood together as the clearly relieved captain entered the saloon and said,

"Ladies and gentlemen, I have something to read to you."

He cleared his throat.

"At two am Greenwich meantime, this morning, at General Eisenhower's headquarters, the representatives of the German State signed the document of unconditional surrender of all German Forces on land, sea and air. The war in Europe is now over."

He paused and then added,

"The surrender of all German Forces is effective immediately. We have been advised that if we wish to do so, we can proceed independently of the convoy. This I intend to do. Our passage will now be ten to twelve days."

He paused again, walked to the porthole and looked out at a US Navy escort steaming alongside, her battle colours hoisted in celebration. A steward was offering drinks all-round. The captain took a glass, and raised it to the escort and with tears in his eyes, he spoke slowly.

"For the first time in six years, there are no U-boats out there. To the men and their ships that won the Battle of the Atlantic."

He drained the glass and exclaimed.

"Ladies and gentlemen, please enjoy your drinks!"

HMS Longbow had steamed to a position one day out from Portsmouth when the signal was received. The radio cabin was usually airtight where the security of signals was concerned. Bellamy and Constantine just about contained their emotions when the plain text signal was completed. Flags took the message to the bridge, his face a mixture of delight and pleasure as he handed it to his captain with a trembling hand. Captain Cork looked at his signals officer, who he had watched grow from an eager seventeen-year-old boy to a battle-hardened naval officer and veteran of the Battle of the Atlantic. Despite Bellamy's undoubted maturity, he still had the face of a school choirboy. Pat read Hilliard's message. 'Germany surrendered two am this morning. Congratulations to all aboard for winning the Battle of the Atlantic. Heave to and await further orders. God save the King."

Pat, now smiling, said,

"Flags, never play poker."

He called the ship on the intercom and said,

"HMS Longbow, this is the captain. At two am this morning, the Supreme Commander in Europe accepted the unconditional surrender of all German Military Forces."

The ship erupted with cheering. Pat allowed it to subside and continued.

"We have been ordered to heave to and wait for new orders, so let's just do that and hope we will all be home soon. I think we all need time to digest the news, wonderful as it is, but we are at sea, so let's keep on our toes. I'll keep you informed of developments. In the meantime, well done everyone. It looks like we made it to the end of this madness."

A further signal was then handed to him. Flags almost whispered,

"From Admiral Hilliard, sir."

The signal had been decoded.

"Prepare to disembark all non-Royal Navy personnel to ships now closing on you." The lookouts shouted as if on cue,

"Submarine surfacing port side - about three hundred yards."

The vessel looked familiar then Pat recognised the USS Tigerfish. An American destroyer appeared on the horizon and closed at speed on Longbow. Within an hour, two more warships had come alongside. One was HMS Snow Tiger, the other a Norwegian vessel. The Norwegian captain radioed for permission to come aboard with a doctor to examine Moen and the nameless man. He introduced himself with a smile on his face.

"Captain, my name is Lisgard. I am captain of the Norskall and took part in the rescue of the POWs. It is good to see you again."

Pat shook his hand, but before he could speak, the Norwegian continued,

"May I express my profound sorrow at the loss of Snow Eagle and Polar Star and the deaths of Commodore Loftus, Captain Crowley and Captain Buchan?"

Pat remained silent as the faces of so many brave men, now gone, flashed before him. Captain Lisgard went on to explain that he had been ordered to ensure that Mr Moen received the best possible treatment and, as a result, he and the other patient were to be taken aboard his ship. Commander Bakken would also be given passage to Portsmouth. The medical party appeared on deck as the Norwegian warship came alongside. The transfer of stretchers went ahead without a hitch, and the Norksall prepared to get underway. Bakken came on deck and simply shook Cork's hand. He spoke slowly as Erebus and all of the Javelin team came on deck.

"Do you know, I think I'm actually going to miss you all?"

He turned to Captain Lisgard.

"May I, sir."

His countryman said,

"Carry on, Commander Bakken."

Vali turned back and stood to attention.

"Permission to leave the ship, sir."

Every man on deck stood to attention and, with Captain Cork, returned the salute of their comrade-in-arms,

"Permission granted, commander."

As the boat from the Norskall moved away from Longbow, the USS Tigerfish was preparing a dinghy to ferry a number of men to the British ship. Captain Cork was soon shaking hands with Captain Templeton and his first officer. Bill Cork came to the bridge, and the Americans retired to the wardroom for a coffee. The civilians were about to transfer to Snow Tiger. Surtees and Wiley waited on the foredeck to say goodbye.

"Well, captain, it's all been great fun," Surtees said as Cork shook his hand, then continued,

"And we've got some first-class research data."

As Wiley stood next to him, his face darkened.

"Yes, it's remarkable what can be achieved with no legal restraints and the use of slave labour."

Then brightened.

"Captain, I will dine out on the story of the boat race for years to come. Not that many will believe me, but who cares, I was there."

Members of the crew had loaded the packaged paperwork aboard the sea boat from Snow Tiger, which departed with the gentlemen from Rolls Royce aboard. A third launch was now nearing Longbow from the US destroyer. The officer in command requested and was granted permission to come aboard. Captain Cork sent for Templeton, who, having arrived on deck, spoke to his countryman. To the surprise of the crew of Longbow on deck, the conversation soon became heated, with raised voices allowing them to hear as Templeton almost shouted.

"You cannot be serious. This is insanity."

The reply was equally clear.

"Captain, I appreciate that, but this order comes right from the top." Templeton was trying very hard to remain calm as he turned to Pat Cork.

"Captain, my fellow officer has received an order from a US admiral regarding an officer aboard your ship."

Pat thought carefully.

"Captain, how does that affect my ship?"

The answer was instant.

"Captain Cork, I am requesting your permission to allow this officer to place Major William Cork, US Army Engineers, under close arrest."

42

It's All Over

The crew of HMS Longbow stood in silence as a handcuffed American officer was taken under arrest from the ship by US naval police. An action which seemed pointless and heartless even to sailors hardened by five years of war and cynical to the point where nothing surprised them. John Eldridge stood on deck, incandescent with rage. He was approached by Captain Templeton, who nervously explained.

"The orders came from US Naval Operations command in the US, Sir." Eldridge demanded.

"With what is Major Cork being charged?" The submariner replied.

"I have not been told, Sir and have been ordered not to speak about the action off Helgoland Bight." Eldridge remained silent as the Captain of the US destroyer approached and introduced himself.

"Good afternoon, Dr Eldridge. I am Captain Carlson, I have orders to escort you and another scientist to Portsmouth." Eldridge suspected 'another scientist' meant Werner Von Braun and vented his anger by demanding.

"Tell me, Captain, do you intend to arrest and detain me as you have Major Cork?" The US officer looked a little perplexed.

"No, Sir, I have no orders to detain you. Just to get you on dry land." The scientist calmed down. He needed time to find out Williams's place of imprisonment and knew that the only way to take on Oppenheim was to be just as devious and unethical.

HMS Longbow docked in Portsmouth, and as the Javelin team disembarked, they were arrested by the Royal Military Police under orders from Colonel Simpson-Coyle and taken to SOE HQ. In Germany, Colonel Travers attempted to discover the whereabouts of Bill Cork and Dr Eldridge with little success.

Aboard the steamer crossing the Atlantic, Jessica Cork was enjoying her first sea voyage, unaware of the benefits of peacetime sailing. She asked the purser if it was possible to send a telegram to an address in Portsmouth in England. The purser delightedly explained that wartime restrictions had been lifted and it would be a pleasure. The telegram she was assured would be delivered within forty-eight hours.

Oppenheim was pleased with his work so far. Werner Von Braun was now aboard an American warship and heading for a safe base in England. Gerber Von Braun was in custody in Germany and would soon be flown to the same base, then on to the USA with his brother. The troublesome Major Cork was in detention and soon would face court-martial. Colonel Travers was in Germany and subject to military law. He would deal with him later. In his pompous self-satisfaction, Oppenheim had completely overlooked John Eldridge.

Colonel Weir was sure his men were in custody and would face a court-martial. It followed that all the men involved in Operation Javelin would be held in the same location if Oppenheim and Simpson-Coyle had their way. The Scotsman had dealt with men like them before and knew he needed to have a bargaining tool. Something or someone they wanted. Weir spoke by radio to the General in command of the Special Forces Brigade based in the UK.

"Sir, I want to discuss a security issue which has arisen at this end." His CO prompted.

"Go on please Colonel." Weir did.

"General, I believe that because of the highly sensitive nature of Operation Javelin that any prisoners taken must remain in the custody of the unit that captured them." The reply was instant.

"I agree entirely Colonel. I'll leave it to you to bring these people back to the UK. Please carry on. Over and out." Weir immediately contacted Colonel Travers and explained his thinking.

"Colonel we hold Von Braun. Oppenheim and Simpson Coyle are holding our men. We will deliver Von Braun and, in doing so, find out where are boys are being held and what charges they face." Travers agreed and called General Patton's HQ by radio. Within minutes the general replied in his usual plain language.

"Do whatever is necessary. I will back you." Travers contacted Maiden Aunt and suggested that the SOE provide the means to return the Marines and their prisoner to the UK in a secure fashion. The reply was affirmative. Colonel Weir was assured by Travers.

"Transportation to the UK has been confirmed."

Aboard HMS Longbow Captain Cork received a signal ordering him to refuel and steam for the German port of Wilhelmshaven and provide passage to Portsmouth for Colonel Travers, Colonel Weir, twenty Royal Marines and Gerber Von Braun. A return passage of eight days.

Simpson-Coyle surveyed the list of servicemen Oppenheim intended to prosecute. Major Charles Lewis - Irish Guards, Commander Bakken - Royal Norwegian Navy, Sergeant Major Reilly and Sergeant Mullen - both SOE troopers. Royal Marine Commandos Madsen and Norsen. Major William Cork - US Army engineers. The Colonel reached two conclusions. The first, the OSS man intended to silence anyone who had knowledge of Operation Javelin by ensuring that any man convicted would serve a lengthy custodial sentence. The second, that again Oppenheim had underestimated the military and especially men who had seen active service. This was confirmed as he witnessed the 'spooks' fury when US military police in Germany, trying to collect Gerber Von Braun from the processing camp, could not locate him, let alone bring him to the UK. As usual, Oppenheim demanded the commanding officer of the camp identify who had taken the German scientist. The bulletproof British officer replied.

"We have processed up to a thousand former Nazis here. Do you have any more details of this chap than just his name? Might be able to do more then." Then continued with a very pointed question.

"What was the name of the organisation you represent? Was it OSS you said or SS?" Oppenheim, now apoplectic, slammed down the radio handset. Simpson-Coyle knew at that moment that the court-martial was far from a foregone conclusion, and he should further rethink his position.

John Eldridge watched Major Cork being taken ashore. He made no attempt to speak to his young friend, remaining calm. He found a telephone box and contacted a friend and fellow academic at Balliol College, Oxford. His request for a week's room and board was willingly granted. Eldridge travelled by bus and, once settled, was soon using the college's extensive archive copying facilities to compile four packages of identical documents and develop and enlarge a number of photographs.

Commander Bakken and Moen, along with the nameless man, arrived at the Norwegian navy's main naval base in Britain. Moen and his companion were placed in the medical centre, and Bakken was taken to an office where a tall, slim, elegant dark-haired man welcomed him.

"Ah, Commander Bakken, congratulations on a good job well done. May I introduce myself. I am Commodore Strom, and at the risk of being insensitive, I must insist we discuss the circumstances which have led to you facing a court-martial. Bakken replied.

"Certainly, Sir, do you mind if we just call into the medical centre for a short time? "The commodore agreed and suggested they talk on the way. Vali spoke frankly,

"Sir, I have been in the navy for fifteen years as a career officer and am surprised I have not met you before. May I ask how long you have been in the navy?" The flag officer replied.

"I am a lawyer by profession and wartime conscript and have been ordered to prepare your defence. Now tell what you know of Colonel Simpson-Coyle and the American Oppenheim." Before answering the Admirals question, Bakken raised another potential problem.

"Sir, there are two Norwegian marines with 62 Commando; they will need a lawyer as well." The senior officer reassured.

"Believe me, all of you will be represented properly. Commander Bakken, you and Mr Moen and the Royal Marines have friends in high places. Now please tell me everything, and I will take it from there." Bakken began.

"Sir, I did disobey a direct order, but I could not leave Moen in that place. No more than I could leave any other human being." The Commodore then explained.

"Commander Bakken, I will need a complete account of your time spent with the SOE, and specifically the orders issued to you. Colonel Simpson-Coyle is demanding you face a court-martial. His reason being that you were complicit in a breach of national security." They had reached the medical centre. Strom seeing Vali's concern for the sick men, advised.

"Commander, please feel free to take as long as you want." As they approached his bed Moen, recognised Bakken, greeting him in a weak voice.

"Hello Vali, maybe now you can tell me your real name and Laudrup's or Erebus, whatever his name is. Where is he, and where am I?" Before Bakken could reply, Moen, exhausted. fell into semi-sleep. The other patient looked, even to the visitor's untrained eyes, extremely ill. Commodore Strom's concern was reflected in his question to Bakken.

"Commander, do we have any idea of his name or nationality?" Bakken, his face sad, replied.

"None whatsoever. He spoke only once or twice, then fell into this state. God help him." Strom remained silent and then, as they walked out of the medical centre, said.

"Commander, I have, in my legal haste, forgotten the fact that our home will be liberated by the British in the very near future. I suggest we have lunch and perhaps a glass of something to celebrate the defeat of the Germans." Bakken laughed as he said.

"Bastards." Strom was startled.

"I beg your pardon?" Bakken laughed again.

"Bastards, Commodore, that's all Moen ever calls the Germans. Bastards." They walked in silence until Strom said,

"I can see Mr Moen has made quite an impression on you."

In SOE headquarters, Simpson-Coyle prepared his case for a court-martial to be convened to try all those involved in the return to Peenemunde. He would have to convince five senior officers that his orders had been disobeyed and that disobedience was compounded by endangering the life of a valuable intelligence asset. The crux of the matter was to prove his authority over all SOE operations outside Norway as assigned to him by Odin. Simpson-Coyle would demand the trial be held in secrecy, alluding to the investigation into the leak of a senior officer's code name as justification. The secrecy would also enable him to bury the origin of the 'kill' order issued on Erebus. The colonel knew that he and Oppenheim had to make a joint case for all those accused to be tried in secret.

To this end, he dialled the US diplomatic office, which was a cover for the OSS control unit in London and spoke to Oppenheim. A meeting was arranged at a small pub just outside the town of Bletchley. Oppenheim began by explaining that the US Government had given orders that all American personnel who had seen active service were to be returned home as soon as possible. The US navy obliged, deploying all its ships, aircraft carriers and sloops as transports to get the boys 'Stateside' in 'Operation Magic Carpet.'

Simpson-Coyle listened as Oppenheim detailed how the mass repatriation of service personnel was not just enlisted men. Senior officers were just as anxious to see their families and were being replaced in Europe by younger less experienced men. Simpson-Coyle offered his thoughts beginning with a question.

"Mr Oppenheim, who will make the decision on the makeup of the members of the tribunal?" The American replied.

"Admiral Stark, a four-star flag officer. He will nominate the American Officers that will sit on the five-man tribunal and set the terms of reference." Simpson-Coyle saw an opportunity.

"Might I suggest that to underline the need for secrecy, you highlight the public outcry if the identities of the people you intend to move to the US should become known? It would be in the interests of Justice that all those charged appear before one tribunal made up of men with objectivity and patience. Rather those who may empathise with fellow fighting men and wish to get home as soon as possible." The Colonel paused, waiting for any comments, there were none so he continued.

"May I further suggest that you request from Admiral Stark the names of all senior officers going home and those being posted to replace them? From that second group, you submit a list of officers that you regard as suitable to hear the case because they meet the criteria mentioned earlier." Oppenheim was far less subtle.

"You mean we get the court made up of men who can be persuaded that the right verdict will help everyone, especially them." Simpson-Coyle tried very hard to conceal his disdain,

"Just as you say, Mr Oppenheim. Those officers will be subtly advised of the personal gains to be made from being favourable to secrecy and the long-term benefits of the scientists getting to America. All of which will be assisted by a finding of guilty."

Mary Cork opened the front door, and her blood ran cold. The Post office telegram messenger was just out of adolescence but being aware of what news might be conveyed in the small brown envelope, the young man's face was serious and respectful. Mary signed for the telegram and opened the envelope before the messenger could leave. His face brightened as the lady smiled. Mary Cork asked him to wait and soon returned with a freshly baked hot tea cake as thanks. The telegram was from Jessica Cork and briefly explained that she, her husband and a number of people from the Double B Ranch were in transit to Britain. There was a notional date of arrival. Mary sat and pondered what the next few weeks could bring. Her son and nephew coming home, and her husband meeting his brother. She returned to the telegram and read the details of the number of people that might be staying at her Portsmouth house, quickly concluding it was not big enough. Then she smiled, remembering the Corks now had a much bigger house in London and whispered. 'Why not.' Then her smile faded as she spoke in a slightly louder voice.

"Now all I've got to do is tell my husband."

Connor Cork entered the pub and saw his lunch guest, Colonel Morley, in civilian clothes but still every inch the military man. They shook hands and were shown to a table. Morley spoke first.

"May I say, Mr Cork, how pleased I was to hear from you? How's your son, well I trust, coming home soon. May I also express my sincere condolences on the passing of Mr English?" Connor nodded his head in appreciation and enquired about the Colonel's situation regarding the Royal Corp of Engineers and the Army in general.

"Well, Mr Cork, I'm afraid I've outlived my usefulness and have been given formal notice of retirement. So, I'll be looking for something to occupy me over the coming few years." During the next hour, Connor gradually learned more about the Colonel. A widower with one son who was in a reserved occupation at a place called Bletchley Park. At this point, Morley surprised Connor as he said.

"My boy is a bit of a mathematical specialist." And added wistfully.

"Gets his brains from his late mother; bless her." Connor encouraged the Colonel to talk about his career in the Sappers by saying.

"I take it you have seen a fair part of the world." Morley seemed to relax and told of leaving Cambridge with a civil engineering degree and like his father and grandfather, joining the Royal Engineers. In fifteen minutes, Connor knew he was dealing with a highly experienced man with knowledge of all forms of civil engineering. Morley then again surprised Connor by saying.

"Mind you, Mr Cork; nothing prepared me for the Mulberry harbour build. I freely admit it was Captain Clinton who made it possible. He and people like you and your colleagues. I was lucky that you all became involved. Damn lucky. I learned a huge amount."

Connor was coming to a decision and, having paid the bill, asked Morley to come over to the plant the next day to have a look around. The Colonel was intrigued and accepted. The cattle ship sailed on eastward. Buchanan and Tom were in the clean and very well air-conditioned livestock compartment. Chato and Carlito looked pleased as they assured both men that the cattle were well and relaxed. Now equally relaxed, Tom and Buchanan stood at the rail of the ship looking out to sea.

"Hell, Tom, I thought Texas was big, but this ocean! Heck, it goes on forever." Thomas Cork nodded as he replied.

"Yes, Bill it is wide, and this is the second time I've crossed it." Buchanan cheerfully continued.

"Tom, I tell you, Catherine and I can't wait to see Bill and then London. She hasn't stopped making plans about where we're going to visit in the city."

HMS Longbow was on course for Wilhelmshaven; her captain's orders were clear. Collect his passengers in the utmost secrecy. On a personal note, Pat was under no illusion that Bill was in trouble, and hoped he might have an opportunity to question the German POW and get something to help his cousin.

The man responsible for Bill Cork's arrest had for once listened to his British counterpart. A request to Admiral Stark's office produced a list of all those senior officers being shipped home, along with a second with the names of the men replacing them. This list Oppenheim concentrated on and quickly discarded those who were conscripts, concentrating on the career servicemen. From those names, he compiled a list of men suitable for court-martial duties and justifying the need for a single tribunal held in absolute secrecy because of the Von Brauns' work on the V weapons. Simpson-Coyle cited the interests of national security when he recommended a single tribunal to the General Officer commanding UK Land forces. The man requested the opinions of Odin and Menzies; both had no choice but to recommend the proposal be viewed favourably. Then Menzies showed why he had played the great game so well for so long. A message outlining Oppenheim's and Simpson-Coyle's proposal was sent to General Patton's HQ. Later in the US, Admiral Stark was surprised to receive a signal informing him that a number of men involved in Operation Javelin were under Patton's command. Subsequently, he was assuming equal responsibility for the selection of the members of the Tribunal and setting its terms of reference. Stark was aware of Patton's influence, and as one four-star officer to another did not object.

Gerber Von Braun sat in a jeep surrounded by Royal marines as he was driven north to the port of Wilhelmshaven. His fury was compounded by being told nothing other than he would soon be in England for a formal debriefing.

The cargo ship SS Arathusa docked at Plymouth, and all passengers were asked to report to passport control. Bill and Catherine Buchanan were the first to be interviewed by the Customs officers, who were polite and welcoming. Buchanan stressed the need to get back to the ship to oversee the unloading of the cattle. A gentleman in civilian clothes standing behind the uniformed officials stepped forward and asked.

"Mr and Mrs Buchanan, would you please be so kind as to follow me." The Americans looked at each other, and Catherine answered.

"Please lead on." Both sat in a small office and were quickly joined by Jessica and Thomas Cork. Once everyone was seated, the official began.

"My name is Fortescue, and I am a veterinary official with the Ministry of Agriculture. My colleague is Mr Wetherall, who has been dealing with your parties' passports. We will be boarding the Arathusa soon, and once satisfied as to the condition of the stock, will be transferring them to a farm outside Plymouth." Buchanan was as ebullient as ever.

"Great, when you want to go on aboard, we'll be waiting." He paused and glanced at Catherine, who, as if in deep thought, was looking at the destruction caused by the air raids. Her husband continued.

"But I can guarantee those cattle are the finest and healthiest in Texas. Hell, I should know I brought their breed stock over in 1919 from this country." The official smiled as he replied.

"Good we'll meet up with the rest of your party and complete the inspection as quickly as possible." Wetherall, who was standing, then spoke.

"Mrs Cork. We have been informed that you are the official representative of the Texas Stock association, so we will be asking you to coordinate all the paperwork generated by the allocation of the stock as it is cleared by the veterinary officers. I hope that meets with your agreement." Jessica smiled as she spoke.

"That is acceptable. We also have a number of staff from the ranch travelling with us. Will you want to see them individually? Wetherall replied, a hint of pleasantness in his voice.

"No, Mrs Cork, we will examine their papers aboard ship. Once you have vouched for them, there shouldn't be any problems. Now about the farm near Plymouth. There is fully found accommodation for six men from each ranch. I'm afraid we did not allow for couples, but I'm sure we can find suitable hotels and such for you all."

He looked straight into Thomas Cork's eyes - who had, since landing, been convinced he was about to be arrested - and handed over the Cork's passports, then the Buchanan's, with the words.

"Welcome to the United Kingdom, Mr and Mrs Cork and Mr and Mrs Buchanan, and may I say how glad we are to see you."

Colonel Weir and his men arrived in convoy at a side gate of Wilhelmshaven harbour manned by British Military police and passed through without any questions being asked or records kept. A confirmation was received by Maiden Aunt that the non-existent column was aboard the ship. If asked, the 'Redcaps' had seen nothing and were to report who was asking. The entire non-existent operation was carried out to non-existent orders. Aboard Longbow the 'boot necks' shared the PO's mess deck. Colonels Weir and Travers, along with Major Campion, enjoyed the comforts of the wardroom. PO's Canavan and McNally were given the pleasure of Gerber Von Braun's company along with Lieutenant Forrestal, who listened and watched with pure delight as Von Braun tried to decipher the Donegal men's accents.

Travers contacted Patton's HQ in Germany, reporting by radio to the General, who informed him that Admiral Stark had agreed to joint authority. They had decided upon Tribunal members and agreed on terms of reference. The Tribunal would take place in a UK base under US military law and Kings Regulations.

The British Ministry of Agriculture veterinary officers passed the cattle aboard the Arathusa as perfectly healthy and gave the go-ahead for them to be moved ashore. Buchanan, Catherine and the Cork's moved to a hotel in Plymouth. Carlos and Chato, along with their sons, settled into a small comfortable cottage on the farm and, in the evenings, got to know Plymouth and tried to understand how the British survived the climate. The Buchanans sat in the hotel restaurant with Jessica, who had the telephone number for Mary and Connor Cork's house in Portsmouth. When Tom joined them, Jessica began to shake slightly as she leaned over and said.

"Tom, when do you think we should meet your brother? Thomas Cork was still recovering from coming through customs but now felt a little more confident and began to reassert himself.

"Jessie, we'll wait because if anyone should be there when we meet C's family it should be Bill. Let's find our boy first." Then he thought of something else.

"We have business in this country; if we get it right, there could be a good deal for us with the British. So, let's concentrate on these things first." Jessica felt slightly ashamed as she said.

"Of course, Tom, whatever you say. I wasn't thinking."

Travers and Colonel Weir watched the prisoner as he sat restlessly in the wardroom. The questioning was at first calm. Then they stepped up the pressure. Demanding to know about the labour used at Peenemunde. How many people? Male or female? Age and nationality? Von Braun spat back in answer.

"Why do you need to know? They were just prisoners. They were not important in the overall scheme of things." Travers exploded.

"Not important in the scheme of things. They were human beings with families just like you and your brother. Or are all you Nazis different?"

Colonel Weir sat in silent amazement. Von Braun's attitude was astounding and terrifying. But he had to remain calm. Information was needed for the defence of Norsen and Madsen. He probed again.

"How many drivers were assigned to you from the labour camps, and how would we find their names." Von Braun sullenly answered.

"I gave a file to Eldridge with all the names of the drivers. He will know how to identify them." Weir was beginning to see the beginning of a reason for the Norwegian marines returning to Peenemunde. Then Captain Cork joined them and listened as the questioning continued, but there was not anything that would help Bill.

Having got through UK customs, Charlie Rawlings left the Double B group and began a surreptitious search for his beloved grandson. He had some contacts within the US military personnel in London, one of which gave him the name of a US Army officer who might know the location of Colonel Travers. Rawlings was told the Colonel was in transit from Europe to England and would be docking in a number of days. No, he did not know when or where. But felt sure that the security surrounding the Colonel's movements would soon lighten. Rawlings immediately moved to a hotel in London, close to the US combined command.

Connor Cork sat down with Morley after spending at least two hours showing him the plant. The engineer had remained silent for most of the time, occasionally asking a question, nothing specific, but Connor sensed the man was very interested in the work done. He waited for the Englishman to speak.

"Mr Cork, I am going to be frank. I believe I am correct in saying that you wish to fill the vacancy created by the death of Mr English with an experienced engineer. Connor replied.

"Perfectly." Morley straightened himself.

"Good. Now may I ask you to listen for a short while?" Cork nodded his head and moved forward in his seat.

"Mr Cork, I was surprised when you contacted me because of the nature of our initial meeting. That you did is to your immense credit. I thank you for the courtesy. Now, I have been giving you and your company a lot of thought since our lunch. I believe the reason that E and C is successful is because Mr English brought in the contracts, and you managed the labour force, which resulted in work being completed on time and within budget." Connor nodded as Morley continued explaining how he had received formal notice to quit the Army within three weeks. Then his voice hardened.

"Mr Cork, I believe I can in some small way replace Mr English. Even though I have been discarded by the Army, I have many friends who are still in situ in the various government ministries which will run this country now the war is over. I will use these contacts to ensure that E and C fabrications is on as many lists of preferred contractors as legally possible. I am not a corrupt man Mr Cork, but in a way, we are both outsiders. You, an Irishman, and me a career soldier, and as outsiders, we must make every opportunity count in our favour." Connor sat in silence. He was still not certain. Then Morley continued.

"Mr Cork, I need something very important from you. I have spent my life in the Army where an order is just that. I have no knowledge of civilian life, or how to handle civilians in general," and with remarkable candour added.

"As you saw during the Mulberry harbour project." Connor was impressed by the man's brutal honesty and said.

"Please continue."

"Mr Cork, I need you to teach me how to work in the civilian world. How to deal with people. How to manage, not just issue orders. In return, I am willing to use all means to assist you in the running of the company as well as providing you with engineering experience, expertise and contacts."

Connor sat back as Morley finished, his mind already made up as he spoke.

"Colonel, are you willing to join my company?" Morley raised his hand.

"Mr Cork, I would be delighted to join the company. I am a civilian now; my Christian name is Lionel. However, if you feel more at ease, please call me Mr," Connor saw a twinkle in the man's eye as he continued.

"We'll only use the Colonel if we need to," Connor was hugely pleased to have made the appointment. The details were discussed. A provisional start date was agreed, and Lionel Morley would run the yard and live in Portsmouth in the short term. Connor asked.

"When would you like to move into the office?" Again, Morley surprised him as he looked at what was Peter English's office.

"Mr Cork, I will move into that office when I have earned the right to."

The men shook hands and said goodbye.

Mary Cork read the telegram a number of times while trying to decide the best time to show it to her husband. Then still undecided, put the paper in a kitchen cupboard drawer. That evening as her family sat down to eat, Mary began a conversation.

"Con have you given any thought to moving back to London." He was not surprised by her question.

"We really should think about it. Now we have another house." Their children looked up. Rachel was the first to speak.

"What do you mean, Daddy, another house?" Connor explained about the property left to them by Peter Wilde. Christopher spoke with the fearlessness of youth.

"Well, another school would be no problem. I'll go wherever you and Mum want to go." Rachel agreed.

"Yes, if you want to live in London again, so do I." The decision had been made for Mary Cork; she left the table to retrieve the telegram. Then handed it to her husband with the words.

"Con, please read this. It arrived earlier today." His family waited in silence as Connor Cork read the telegram and then looked at his wife and children. All he ever cared for was now safe. The three people in this room and Pat, still at sea, but safe also. They had seen five years of war off together. He spoke.

"Well, the best thing to do is to go to London and see the house as soon as possible. Then we'll make a decision on where to live. Does that sound reasonable?" Christopher asked.

"What about the business Dad?" Connor explained about Lionel Morley replacing Peter English and running the yard in Portsmouth until further notice. Connor glanced at the telegram and said.

"It looks as if there may be some Americans coming to see us." There was silence so he continued.

"My brother Tom and his wife and some other people from Texas." Rachel said excitedly.

"It will be lovely to meet Bill's mum and dad." Mary watched her husband's face relax as Rachel put in a nutshell what Tom Cork was. Not the man from West Cork all those years before, but Bill's father. Con spoke.

"Why don't we go to London the day after tomorrow?"

For the first time, they all stood in the house left to them. Mary immediately felt settled and said a silent prayer for Wilde. Christopher and Rachel began opening rooms and windows, spreading light everywhere. Connor checked the building for electricity, heat and water. Mary called all of them to her.

"Con, I would like to move in here as quickly as possible. To make this beautiful house a home for all of us." Connor did not react immediately. He sat in the chair in a drawing room, feeling surprisingly at ease as the teenagers walked in.

"Chris, Rachel, now you have seen the house, how do you feel about moving back to London? Christopher answered.

"No problem Dad." His sister followed.

"There are lots of schools here Dad, and Portsmouth is not too far away."

Connor looked at his wife and two of his children and said.

"Mary, if we do meet my brother's family, I can think of no finer place than our beautiful home." He couldn't help but add.

"I used to refurbish houses like this. Now we own one." They all laughed and started making plans for the next few days. Mary occasionally looked at her husband and saw despite the activity; he was in deep thought. Then seeing her look, he said.

"Mary, we can't meet Tom and his wife and friends without Pat being here. When we meet, all of our family must be here. Let's wait for Pat. This is his home as well."

Chris heard his father and spoke.

"Then we'd better send a message to him about his new address."

HMS Longbow was underway with her top-secret human cargo. Portsmouth was only a day away, and still, Pat had gleaned nothing from Von Braun which might help Bill. Travers told him that the evidence was mounting that the Von Brauns were involved in the use of slave labour, but that alone did not help Bill. Pat had put together a number of questions for Von Braun. The first was at random.

"Tell me, have you had any dealings with the German Navy or the U-boats?" Gerber was tired and blurted an emotional answer.

"Those idiots, we asked them to transport items to South America during the war. They said they couldn't sail that far." The contempt in his voice was clear as he continued.

"Then we were told they could take us to South America if the Fuehrer gave his permission." Pat immediately began to press the prisoner.

"What do you mean 'Take you' was it just you and your brother?" Von Braun raised his voice in exasperation.

"Not alone us. The offer was made to many high-ranking officials." Pat left the cabin and immediately radioed Maiden Aunt and Admiral Hilliard. The signal was short.

'Suspect U-Boat fleet to be used as escape route for senior Nazis. Source Gerber Von Braun.' Then HMS Longbow steamed at full speed for Portsmouth.

Near Plymouth, the Aberdeen Angus were settled, and the contingent from the Double B, were taking in the sights of the south of England. Catherine Buchanan and Jessica had decided to spend a day in London. Then, as always in the lives of the people of the Double B, the cattle took over. The Ministry of Agriculture vets decided to move the Double B stock to farms in Northern Ireland. Buchanan was pleased. It was a chance to see the farmland in the UK. Catherine wanted to meet the people of the country and jumped at the chance to go with her husband. Jessica as the coordinator of the Texas Stock Association, had to go. Her husband was much quieter, secretly being terrified of setting foot on any Irish soil - still convinced there was an arrest warrant awaiting him.

HMS Longbow docked in Portsmouth and Colonel Travers, Colonel Weir and the men of 62 Commando, along with a disgruntled prisoner, clandestinely made their way in vehicles provided by Maiden Aunt to the Royal Marines Headquarters at Poole in Dorset.

The signal received from Captain Cork had added to a growing belief amongst allied intelligence agencies that senior Nazis had escaped to South American states governed by politicians sympathetic to the Nazi cause or willing to accept bribes for safe haven. Orders were issued that all U-boats were to surrender in Felixstowe on the east coast of England and in Londonderry. HMS Longbow was among a number of ships given the honour of overseeing the surrender of the defeated deadly foe. Pat Cork was returning to Londonderry, if only for a short time.

The Tribunal personnel selection was near completion. Oppenheim, via Admiral Stark, had selected two career officers, both supply experts. They were relatively young and had requested overseas postings just before the German surrender. This ensured their records showed they had seen active service in a foreign theatre of operations, which after a suitable time in the military, would not harm their political aspirations. The British officers were selected by a very senior old-fashioned officer. A man who had little time for Special Operation's regarding them as 'Out laws' who regularly ignored the rules of war. He selected the commandant of Sandhurst Military Academy, totally unaware of his many connections with the Lewis family. The second British officer was an admiral who issued the order authorising Major Cork's arrest on a British warship on the high seas. His interest in the Tribunal was the involvement of an officer from Snow Eagle, now the captain of HMS Longbow. This career officer required confirmation of the existence of any evidence linking him to convoy PQ19 and the infamous - and still secret - 'Scatter order'. The fifth officer was named by General Patton. He was General Stuart F Mallem, now Patton's second in command, who had been assistant divisional commander of the 29th Infantry Brigade on Omaha beach. When shown told the names of the accused, he was unaware that two of them were the Special Forces officers he had intended to decorate for their bravery on D-Day. A third name he did recognise. Major William Cork of the US army engineers. He simply said to General Patton.

"I'll make sure the boys get a fair hearing.

43

Trial and Ego

The port of Londonderry had witnessed many extraordinary events in its long history. The U-boats and the warships escorting them were another. Single line ahead, the defeated German vessels sailed into the harbour crewed by a small number of defeated submariners and their Royal Navy 'captors'. In the vanguard was HMS Longbow, her crew silent as memories of so many storms and convoys came to mind mixed with names and faces of absent shipmates. As the U-boats tied up, the crews were disembarked and escorted by naval police, then RUC officers to buses for transportation to a detention camp for interrogation. Captain Cork watched the prisoners and saw a familiar face supervising the operation. Detective Sergeant Bagot smiled as he approached the shore patrol on duty at the gangway of Longbow. Cork signalled his assent, and once aboard, the policeman cheerfully greeted his host.

"Good morning, captain." And queried.

"What happens to the U-boats now?" Cork returned the greeting before explaining the submarines were to be sunk at sea or used for target practice by the Royal Navy. Bagot nodded his head and began.

"Chief Superintendent Peters is, to put it mildly, a little put out he is not in charge of questioning the prisoners." As Peters' face came to mind, Pat informed his visitor.

"Sergeant, to be honest, I'm not really too bothered about men like Peters. I never was." Once in his cabin, Pat asked.

Now tell me how you are?" Bagot replied he was well and continued with a question.

"I suppose all of you boys can't wait to get home?" The reply was instant.

"Your supposition is perfectly correct. We've done our bit, and that's all they're going to get from us." The sergeant, his face pensive, continued.

"Well, since you intend to become a civilian, I can't see a problem in letting you know about some of Mr Peters' less than official investigations." Pat was told how the policeman had been ordered to carry out background checks on him and others. Cork was silent, then scoffed.

"I didn't realise I was so important," Bagot laughed as he said.

"Well, if it's any consolation, you'll be pleased to know it all blew up in Peters' face when he was told in no uncertain terms to back off." The background checks brought a question to Cork's mind.

"Tell me sergeant, how difficult is it to trace a person in Northern Ireland?" Again, the reply was upbeat.

"Commander, if you need any information, just give me a call," and handed Pat his card as they said goodbye. Bagot proceeded to the Customs area of the harbour to report to Chief Superintendent Peters, who was checking the passports of anyone that took, his less than pleasant, fancy.

Oppenheim and Simpson-Coyle were preparing the mechanics of the court-martial tribunal. Each member was issued with the charge sheets and service files of the defendants. The US Major Generals, named Gustav, and Spitzer, viewed the trial as an open and shut case. All of the defendants had disobeyed direct orders from the British Colonel. The second charge was again indefensible. Professor Von Braun was under Allied military protection and should have never been taken back to Peenemunde. Admiral Sparks of the Royal Navy was objective regarding the evidence, but still had to ensure he had enough leverage over HMS Longbow's officers to bury PQ 19 in naval records forever. The Commandant of the Sandhurst Military Academy, Colonel Roger Faraday, was initially surprised to be ordered to sit on the tribunal. He had intended to declare a conflict of interest until seeing the defendant's active service records. These men were not the average miscreants, and neither were the prosecution's motives purely objective. Experience had made him suspicious of all intelligence organisations, so the Colonel decided to wait and see. Finally, General Mallem, having been briefed by Patton on the affair and the OSS in detail, remained objective, though his natural affinity for fighting men would be a strong influence in his decisions. Mallem was a solidly built, relatively short man with a constant crew cut and flashing blue eyes, once described - not to his face - as a two-legged barrel of dynamite. Fiercely loyal to the US army, General Patton, and above all else, his fighting comrades.

Oppenheim was confident the tribunal was loaded in his favour, having drawn up the court procedure, which had been rubber-stamped by Admiral Stark. Patton had demanded certain points of law be applied, but with the right tribunal president, they would be ignored. The charge of disobeying orders would be heard first. The charges of endangering an intelligence asset were more difficult to prove, so they would be used as a last resort. Simpson-Coyle knew the American's sole aim was silencing anyone who could raise the Von Brauns' Waffen SS connection by convictions on one or both charges and the ensuing lengthy custodial sentences. The American could not have cared less about a leak in British intelligence. The Colonel began to doubt the merits of the charge of disobeying orders and decided to narrow his priorities to confirm if there was a leak in the SOE or British Intelligence and cover up his issuing an illegal order.

Oppenheim's plans began to falter as the tribunal members were about to elect a president. General Mallem saw the defendants arrive. The man never forgot a fighting soldier and instantly recognised the men from Omaha beach. In the closed session, he asserted being the senior army officer best qualified him to adjudicate on the actions of infantrymen. Colonel Faraday was more than pleased to agree, also Admiral Sparks. The US Major Generals, aware the man had the ear of Patton, acquiesced. An infuriated Oppenheim sat silently as Mallem was announced as tribunal president. He began proceedings by granting permission to defendants to select their advocates or 'friends' and adjourning the tribunal for the day. The next morning the defence counsel was confirmed. Commodore Strom stated he was the advocate for Bakken, Norsen and Madsen.

Lewis, Reilly and Mullen were represented by Thomas Boyd KC, the author of the defence's primary strategy. Professor Williamson would assist.

Bill Cork's defence was in the hands of Mr James Racq, Counsel to the US Ambassador and Harvard law professor aided by Travers and Eldridge.

General Mallem approved the defence teams and opened the proceedings for submissions. Commodore Strom was first as he requested that witnesses not directly involved in Operation Javelin be allowed to testify.

The prosecution, made up of Oppenheim, Colonel Schwartzberg, a US law officer and Colonel Simpson-Coyle with a UK Foreign Office barrister objected, citing secrecy. Strom countered that all witnesses had been vetted by SOE analysts and classified as secure, adding the defence would be calling Mr Oppenheim and Colonel Simpson Coyle with the intelligence assets as hostile witnesses.

The submissions continued as Admiral Sparkes requested that members of HMS Longbow ships Company give evidence. Mallem agreed ordering any of the crew required to testify must be available within forty-eight hours.

At the Royal Marine's home base, when told the name of the prisoner brought from Germany, the commanding general asked Colonel Weir if he knew the locations of two members of the Operation Javelin team. A Colonel Travers and Professor John Eldridge. Before Weir could answer, he was instructed.

"If you do, get them, the prisoner and Major Campion, to SOE HQ for this tribunal immediately. Certain members of the High Command want this thing over and done with." Weir, through Travers, contacted Eldridge and both Von Brauns and the now complete defence teams were in court the next morning.

Charlie Rawlings was totally frustrated in his effort to establish the where-abouts of Bill Cork and Travers, as every enquiry was met with silence. Finally, when confronting a junior officer, his patience ran out.

"The war's over remember, what's so secret about two brave men from Texas? All I want to do is say hello to my grandson and his CO. How hard can that be?" The outburst was met with absolute stone walling. Despite growing concern, Charlie was certain Bill was ok. Not even the US military machine would conceal a fatality. He decided to bypass the military and use Elmer Riddle's contacts in the Hunter Corporation UK office in central London. Square. A meeting was arranged with an executive who Rawlings asked about Hunter Corporation's business with the US Army Air force and Engineers. The contact revealed an outline plan for the Aviation division to run a rocket research unit headed by 'European' scientists. The project was to be based in the US once the men were released from protective custody. Charlie probed deeper.

"So what has this to do with the Army Airforce or Army Engineers?" The contact answered.

"Mr Rawlings, you asked about US Army contacts. The European scientists are witnesses in an investigation into Operation Javelin, which involved US Army Engineers. Who, when demobilised, may be interested in becoming employees of the Hunter Corporation. So, we needed to get their names." Rawlings went for broke.

"Can I have those names?" The man replied.

"No, you cannot, but why don't you tell me who you are looking for?" Charlie named his grandson and Colonel Travers.

The Hunter Corporation man replied cryptically.

"I cannot give you any more information, Mr Rawlings, though I am certain you have many other contacts. I suggest you ask as many questions as possible about Operation Javelin. You never know what might come out." Rawlings was intrigued and confident he was making progress, so he contacted the British Ministry of Agriculture and was given the name of the Double B Ranch people's hotel.

The steamship Arathusa eased into the port of Belfast. Thomas Cork was suddenly surrounded by British servicemen and panicked. Then realised the people wearing the uniforms he hated had no interest in him at all and were getting on with their lives. Buchanan called to him to supervise the transfer of the cattle from the ship to stock lorries.

"Tom, we'll be moving them soon to a farm just outside Belfast." And laughed as he demanded.

"This is your country. How far is it? Do you know?" Tom didn't bother to answer. Buchanan's excitement was infectious. Jessica and Catherine expectantly waited in the car until both men joined them. The Buchanans soaked up the verdant landscape of county Antrim in silence. Jessica sat next to her husband, holding his hand.

"Welcome home, Tom." Without thinking, Thomas Cork whispered.

"Oh, Jessie, you should see west Cork; that is our home. This is not my country," he paused,

"But it should be."

HMS Longbow tied up, and Cork received orders to report to the SOE base. As the captain of a Royal Navy ship Pat was entitled to an escort. The Petty Officers from Donegal, along with Chief Petty Officer Baker, quickly volunteered. Two cars left Portsmouth. The first with captain and escort, followed by Commander Larsen and Lieutenants Bellamy and Forrestal.

Oppenheim's arrogance fuelled confidence was high, unlike a certain British Colonel who became increasingly cautious as he surveyed the very astute legal minds representing the defendants.

The tribunal members sat on a slightly raised dais. Those testifying would do so from a single desk facing the tribunal chairman. Defence and prosecution counsel sat either side. Those in attendance - all witnesses - were in rows of chairs facing the tribunal. Mallem nodded, and Oppenheim read out a summary of the first charge.

"All those under indictment had deliberately disobeyed the orders of Colonel Simpson-Coyle by returning to Peenemunde." General Mallem spoke.

"The defendants will reply to the charge by rank. Those in command will testify first. Call Major Charles Lewis, Irish Guards." Lewis sat. His defence counsel Mr Boyd. K C asked.

"Major Lewis did you at any time before or during Operation Javelin receive a direct order either verbally or in writing from Colonel Simpson-Coyle?"

Erebus replied.

"No Sir, I did not." Boyd then called Reilly and Mullen, respectively and asked the same question. Both answered as Lewis had.

Simpson-Coyle was called. Boyd continued.

"Colonel, at any time did you issue direct orders in verbal or written form for Operation Javelin to Major Lewis, Sergeant Major Reilly and Sergeant Mullen."

The reply was succinct.

"No, I did not." He continued.

"I did have operational command of all SOE operations outside the Norwegian theatre. So, I was in command." Boyd carried on.

"Colonel Simpson-Coyle at what time did you become aware that Operation Javelin was underway?"

"When informed by my superiors at the SOE."

Boyd raised the legal point arrived at in discussion with Williamson and the Brigadier.

"Colonel, I put to you that it is impossible to justify charges of disobeying your orders against men engaged in an operation you had no knowledge of. An operation for which you confirm you did not issue any orders, verbal or written to any of the men on that operation?"

Simpson-Coyle knew he had to agree. Not to do so would be admitting he knew nothing of the operation until it was over, which could lead to an accusation of dereliction of duty. He looked at Oppenheim, whose face was white with rage, as he glared at the US members of the tribunal. The colonel saw in the OSS man's eyes sheer fanaticism. His mind made up, he answered.

"Yes, Mr Boyd, I have to agree with you."

Boyd turned to the tribunal.

"Members of the tribunal, I submit that the charge of Disobedience against my clients be dismissed on the grounds that the charge, such as it is, is specific to Operation Javelin. Colonel Simpson-Coyle issued no orders for the operation to any of my clients."

General Mallem turned to the other members of the tribunal.

"Gentlemen, we really have no choice as the Colonel is in agreement with Mr Boyd." He stood and addressed the assembled servicemen.

"Major Lewis. Sergeant Major Reilly and Sergeant Mullen, the charge of disobeying Colonel Simpson-Coyle's order is dismissed. Do not leave the court; there are other charges to be heard."

Commodore Strom rose.

"Mr President, I submit that the ruling just handed down applies to the charge against my clients equally. It would be wasting the court's time to call the Colonel again to face identical questions." Erebus looked up and saw Colonel Faraday's face break into the slightest smile as Mallem spoke to the tribunal members.

"Gentlemen, I am of the opinion that the Commodore's submission is correct." There followed a brief conversation, then Mallem spoke to the court.

"Commander Bakken, Royal Marines Madsen and Norsen, the charge of disobedience is dismissed." He added.

"You all face further charges, so you will remain on base." Then with the slightest look of satisfaction on his face, he adjourned the court for the day.

The evening in Antrim was settling into a long sunset, a pleasant surprise early in the year. In a small hotel, the owners of the Double B enjoyed a fresh food dinner, having settled into the comfortable compact rooms. The hotel owner had become accustomed to the American Military. Now here was somewhat of a rarity, US civilians. The man soon learned his guests owned a large ranch in Texas, which surprised him as Mr Cork's accent was far closer to home. The next day Buchanan and Jessie were busy dealing with British veterinary and Ministry of Agriculture officials. The hotel was quiet, giving Tomas some time to assess his situation. Pleasantly surprised by the goodwill extended, he still refused to allow himself to trust any British official. Then, silently admitted his distrust was an excuse for avoiding his real concern, meeting his son and Connor. From Bill's letters it was clear that Connor had not revealed anything of those terrible times in west Cork. Tom knew there were two questions that would be answered for good or bad. The first. How would his son react to knowing his father had shot two men? And second, what Connor would do after all the years? Needing a distraction, Tom joined Catherine in conversation on Northern Irish history with the Protestant landlords of the hotel. He soon lost interest as his mind was drawn back to Bill and Connor.

After a week of assessments and quality control examinations by veterinary officials, the Double B Ranch cattle were approved. A contract was signed with the British Ministry of Agriculture to supply up to five thousand head of cattle per year. Buchanan and Jessica were delighted with the deal, as was Thomas, who unexpectedly announced.

"Right, let's go to London and find Bill." Jessica looked at him, a question on her lips. He continued.

"And whatever else comes up." His wife smiled as she began to pack. Her husband had accepted they were going to meet his brother and his family. As the Double B party approached the passport control point in Belfast docks, Thomas Cork broke into a cold sweat. Standing just behind the young customs officers was a man spot-checking passports. A man burned into his memory. RIC District Officer Peters. Now a senior officer in the RUC.

The trial resumed as Oppenheim read the second indictment.

"All defendants are charged with endangering a valuable intelligence asset when taking him back into enemy territory by force." Having taken the witness stand, Werner Von Braun, prompted by Oppenheim, told of how he was forced to return under guard by the accused. Then General Mallem asked the defence counsel if they wished to cross-examine.

Commodore Strom rose first.

"Mr President, I have no questions at this time, but reserve the right to cross examine later." Oppenheim stood to object, and Colonel Schwartzberg - a man of medium build with thinning hair -, known for his even temperament told the OSS man with a rare angry tone.

"Please shut up and sit down."

The German scientist stood down, and Strom called Commander Bakken, who told how as an SOE agent he had been ordered to extract Werner Von Braun and his research team from Peenemunde. Strom asked.

"Commander, at any time during the escape from or return to Peenemunde, did you use physical violence to intimidate Wernher or Gerber Von Braun?" The answer was forceful.

"No, Sir, I did not?" Strom continued.

"Commander, why did you return to Peenemunde?"

Bakken explained that having departed Peenemunde, Dr Eldridge discovered information about a revolutionary prototype engine which, in his words.

'….must be taken into Allied hands for examination, at all costs,' and added.

"Then we discovered there were a number of Norwegian nationals being held as slave labour in appalling conditions at the camp." Strom prompted.

"So, you'll agree that you returned to Peenemunde to secure a prototype engine and rescue fellow Norwegians. Is that correct?" Before Bakken could answer, Oppenheim jumped up,

"I object. He's leading the witness, Mr President." Colonel Schwartzberg glared again at his countryman. General Mallem instructed.

"Carry on Commander."

"Yes, Sir, Von Braun had information which we required to enable us to find the engine and the prisoners." He continued.

"The Von Brauns were now on our side - or so we'd been told - so it seemed only fair to ask them for help." Strom concluded.

"I have no further questions, Mr President." Colonel Schwartzberg stood up.

"Commander, you stated that you returned to Peenemunde for two reasons. One is clear. The authorisation for the second is not." He was about to continue when Oppenheim stood and shouted.

"You had no authority or orders to go back for Norwegian nationals?" Bakken answered.

"It is a standing order issued to all Norwegian servicemen who escaped from Norway. All efforts must be made to rescue Norwegian nationals in captivity." The OSS man continued oblivious, to the warning look on Schwartzberg's face.

"I am unaware of this order, Commander." Bakken looked straight at his inquisitor.

"The order was approved by all allied commanders. If you had ever seen active service, you would know that." The fighting men on the tribunal smiled covertly as the Norwegian drove his point home.

"Mr Oppenheim, our orders were to gather as much information as possible on the V weapons and the development team and get them out. Going back in was in line with those orders. The captives still in the camp might know more about that team and what they did, or don't you want to know about that." Oppenheim snapped.

"Remember, Commander; it is not the Von Brauns who are on trial." Bakken stared at the OSS man.

"Well, not for now, Mr Oppenheim, not for now." General Mallem pressed on.

"Does the prosecution have any more questions for the Commander?" Schwartzberg answered.

"Not at this time, Mr President." Mallem nodded as he adjourned the court for the day. Outside the courtroom, Schwartzberg confronted Oppenheim with venom.

"I suggest you leave the legal issues to me. I will do my job, not you. Do you understand?" Oppenheim ignored him.

Superintendent Peters looked at the list of passengers' names to board the steamer for Liverpool. Most were servicemen, then four names with the capital letters US and 'Civilian' behind them.

"Yankee civilians, what brings them here?" and took the passports from the desk officer, then looked up at the man called Buchanan. The photograph was a good resemblance, a big man in every sense of the word. Catherine Buchanan, the man's wife, was a good-looking woman. Nothing out of the ordinary with this couple, both ranchers. The next US passport was Jessica Cork. Peters read the details, born in Texas, married to a ranch owner. He again glanced up and saw a very pretty woman. The passport beneath must be her husband's. Peters was just about to open Thomas Cork's passport when he heard a voice.

"Ah, the party from the Double B in Texas. We'll be sailing with you to Liverpool." The Superintendent demanded of the speaker.

"Who are you, may I ask?" The official was cheerful.

"Wetherall, Ministry of Agriculture, London. These people are our guests" Peters shut the passport in his hand, returned all four documents and gave the nod to the customs officers who returned them with an apologetic smile. Superintendent Peters walked away just audibly muttering.

"Can't stand either, bloody Yanks or bloody pompous English civil servants." Thomas Cork stood behind his wife and watched the man who would have readily hanged him some years earlier disappear. Then the same 'bloody yank' boarded the steamer and, once in the cabin, looked at his mirrored reflection and saw a very relaxed, well-dressed, affluent American who has a beautiful family and home. Then remembered Peters as he had seen him only minutes before. A tired greying bitter old man with more anger than common humanity. Maybe Thomas Cork had won that private war. He felt a kiss on his cheek and followed by his beloved Jessie's words.

"Come o,n let's get to the dining saloon. All this cattle trading has made me hungry." He smiled.

"Then, my darling, I am going to buy you the biggest steak on this ship."

The third day of the trial began with Royal Marine Madsen being questioned. Oppenheim demanded.

"Marine Madsen, why did you go back to Peenemunde?" The big marine looked a little perplexed.

"What do you mean go back to Peenemunde?" Oppenheim snapped.

"You know exactly what I mean." Madsen went on to explain that he had only been to Peenemunde once after having been involved in the attack that captured the SS guards and freed the scientists. General Mallem observed, his voice laden with sarcasm.

"Mr Oppenheim, I presume it is practice in the OSS to study a case file before asking questions?" Oppenheim tried to cover his error and rushed to the next question.

"Who ordered you to go to Peenemunde?" Madsen replied.

"I was not ordered. I volunteered; some of my countrymen's lives were at stake." The OSS man again pressed.

"Did you threaten either of the Von Brauns?" Madsen answered.

"I never spoke to either of them." Oppenheim demanded

"Why is that?" Madsen looked at both Von Brauns.

"I prefer Germans silent or dead. If they are silent, that's fine. If they're dead, that's even better." Oppenheim shouted at the tribunal members.

"This man is not being serious." Faraday spoke.

"On the contrary, Mr Oppenheim. The Royal Marine is deadly serious." Mallem asked.

"Marine Madsen, did you threaten either of the Von Brauns?" The reply was instant.

"No, Sir, I did not threaten them in any way. My only interest was freeing Norwegians from the slave labour camp at Peenemunde." Colonel Schwartzberg stood.

"The prosecution has no further questions for this Royal Marine. Please call Marine Norsen."

As the Texans settled into the Liverpool hotel booked for them, they were given Charlie Rawlings' London contact number.

The city and port had been a primary target for the Luftwaffe and bore the scars of that brutal, sustained assault. As Catherine walked through the city, Jessica by her side listened as her friend said in a low voice.

"We have no idea what these people have been through, no idea at all." Jessica, though sympathetic, was becoming increasingly worried for her son and pressed her husband to go to London. Thomas, was equally concerned, the war had ended in Europe some weeks ago and there was still no word from Bill, so he contacted Charlie Rawlings and asked him to arrange rooms for both couples in London.

The second marine was ready to testify. Mallem signalled to Schwartzberg to carry on.

"Marine Norsen did you at any time threaten either of the Von Brauns?" Norsen explained.

"All I said was that there were many dangers in going back to Peenemunde and I made it clear his welfare was my responsibility, Sir."

The prosecutor asked.

"What do you mean by his welfare?" Norsen spoke.

"It was my responsibility to ensure that nothing happened to him while going to Peenemunde, while we were there, and until we returned to Allied lines." The Marine paused, then added his face cold.

"That nothing unexpected happened, that he had not been warned about. I assured him he had my undivided attention at all times." General Mallem again pushed on.

"Colonel, are there any further questions?" The American sat down as he replied.

"No, Sir, no further questions on this matter for these defendants." Strom stood.

"Mr President if I may be so bold. It appears there has been a misunderstanding of the motives of the men involved in this matter. Marines Norsen and Madsen, along with Commander Bakken, were obeying orders which complimented and supported Operation Javelin."

Oppenheim jumped up, his voice raised.

"It's their word against the Von Brauns." Mallem summarised.

"The tribunal will wait to hear the evidence of the other defendants before arriving at a decision." He paused and lowered his voice speaking to the tribunal members.

"We could do with more witnesses." Then adjourned for lunch.

At the Norwegian medical centre, proper food and medication had strengthened Moen to a little of his old self. The unknown casualty's vital signs were improving almost hourly and then he woke. The medical staff were delighted and sent word to Commodore Strom, who, after the break, stood.

"Mr President, I have been informed that the men rescued from Peenemunde have regained consciousness, and I request permission of the court to interview them. I further request permission for Majors Lewis and Cork and Commander Bakken to accompany me." Oppenheim jumped up.

"They're under close arrest, you cannot let them go. They must be under escort, they could escape!" Colonel Faraday voiced an opinion.

"Mr Oppenheim, from what I have seen from these officers' service records, they could escape at any time, should they wish to." Mallem said, his face hard.

"It seems to satisfy the gentlemen from the OSS we will need an escort for these officers." From the body of the court, he heard.

"Permission to speak, Sir." The president spoke.

"Please identify yourself to the court." Admiral Sparkes looked down the room and heard.

"Commander Cork. Captain HMS Longbow." Followed by,

"I have six of my ship's company here and will provide the required escort."

Mallem spoke to the tribunal members, during which Admiral Sparkes was heard to say.

"I'll vouch for all of them." Mallem announced.

"Gentlemen, I believe interviewing these men may assist the tribunal in finding the truth." Then looked at the defendants.

"I release you on your own parole to the custody of Commander Cork and the men of HMS Longbow." Then with a slightly pleasant face said.

"Commodore, you have forty-eight hours." As the court broke up, Cork was approached by John Eldridge, who asked in his inimitable way.

"Patrick, may I accompany you to Portsmouth?" He answered with a smile, "Whatever you want, Dr Eldridge."

Connor Cork and his family moved into their new home with little fuss. The décor reflected the late Peter Wilde's taste and Mary Cork was quite happy to leave everything as it was for now. The house was big but felt warm and intimate. The address was five minutes walk from Eton square. Once settled, Connor sent a telegram to the Royal Navy family liaison department. Pat returned to Portsmouth with the escort, and CPO Baker collected personal messages from Longbow, one of which informed the captain he was now living in a very posh part of London. Within minutes Bill was told the new address. What the cousins were unaware of was that their fathers were now in the same country and possibly the same city. Strom, accompanied by Lewis, Bakken, Bill Cork and Dr Eldridge, stood in the sick bay ward as Moen woke up and welcomed all of them with the words.

"Jesus, it's good to see you all. Let's go kill some more bastards." Commodore Strom introduced himself and asked.

"Mr Moen, may I ask you some questions?" Moen laughed weakly.

"Commodore, you can ask me anything you like as long as you get a message home to my wife and children. The bastards came for me in the middle of the night about eighteen months ago. My wife hasn't heard a word since then." The other man was weaker but still managed to ask.

"Where am I?", as he pulled the blankets around him and smiled as he whispered.

"It's so warm here, so clean." Then went back to sleep.

The Norwegian flag officer waited while a doctor examined the patient.

"The intravenous feeding has worked, but he is still extremely weak." Strom apologetically asked.

"Doctor, is there any idea as to his name?" Before the medic could answer, Moen spoke.

"I know who he is. He's the only decent German I've come across, and the bastards gave him a hell of a time. But for some reason, they wouldn't kill him. God knows they shot plenty of other prisoners." The man slept on, too exhausted to stir.

Strom, accompanied by Bakken and Lewis, sat down and listened as Moen told of happenings in the research centre run by Werner and Gerber Von Braun.

Every so often, the men listening became worried they might be overtaxing him and Lewis suggested.

"Why don't you sleep now? We don't want you sick again." The reply was vintage Moen.

"I have all the time in the world to sleep. Right now, I want everyone to know, especially the bloody Von Brauns, the bastards couldn't break or kill me." Moen pointed to the German man, still in a deep sleep.

"You see that man? They couldn't break him either." He began to fall asleep as he whispered fiercely.

"We beat the bastards Laudrup; we beat them." Then as if content with his contribution, he too fell into a deep and reinvigorating sleep.

Twenty-four hours into the recess allowed by the tribunal, the news broke of the consequences of an earlier outburst by General Patton regarding the Russians. He had been ordered to return to the US for a War Bond sales drive. This was camouflage for the fact that President Truman had finally lost patience and relieved him of command of the US Third Army. Oppenheim was elated as he whispered.

"That's the end of the Patrician Wasp bastard." He contacted Major Generals Gustav and Spitzer, telling them exactly how things were going to go from now on. Orders were issued for the defendants to return to court immediately. John Eldridge saw signs of the unknown man waking and told Pat Cork he would wait to talk to him. CPO Baker volunteered to drive Eldridge to the tribunal when he was ready. As the escort left Portsmouth, Pat watched his cousin climb into his car with a small backpack carrying his personal kit.' He was deep in thought. The news about Patton had made up Bill's mind. The Von Brauns were not going to get away with killing Mandy, not if he had anything to do with it.

At the naval medical centre, John Eldridge was a constant companion to Moen and his fellow patient. The Norwegian had not stopped talking since regaining his strength. The other man though still very weak, was beginning to show signs of recovery. Moen was talking to Eldridge surprisingly in English, which was, if he spoke slowly, reasonably understandable. Eldridge asked.

"Mr Moen, where did you learn English?

Moen looked at his fellow patient, still asleep and replied.

"From him, we needed something to concentrate on to stay alive, so he taught me. He's German, the only decent one I've ever met. I was always wondering why he wasn't shot. The guards singled him out for special treatment. They called him a traitor." Just then, both heard a weak but distinct voice.

"Thank you for the compliment, Mr Moen. I hope there will be many more decent Germans now Hitler has gone." Eldridge asked.

"Tell me, Sir, are you well enough to talk to me for a while? My name is John Eldridge." He replied with a weak smile.

"Mr Eldridge, it will be a pleasure to talk to you." His name was Peter Vogt, and the next two hours were filled with tales of horror and heroism, despair and a little hope, but above all else, the strength of the human spirit. Eldridge thanked Peter Vogt and, as he left, heard Moen ask.

"Why didn't the bastards kill you?"

The answer was in a whisper.

"They knew they dare not kill me. Even those savages had to respect something."

John Eldridge phoned the Chief Petty Officer's quarters, identified himself and asked to speak to CPO Baker who asked instantly.

"Yes, professor, what can I do for you?"

"Ahh… Mr Baker, do you think it would be possible for you to arrange transport for me and the patients? We need to get back to the trial. I've had a very productive and satisfying day."

44

Peacetime and Politics

Oppenheim had been busy since the fall of Patton. He had wired a secret list of revised tribunal operating procedures to Admiral Stark. The admiral had promised the President he would deliver the scientists and technology as part of the Rocket research programme. The secrecy surrounding that programme could be used to deal with questions being asked by the joint Congressional and Senate committee investigating a number of his wartime commands, including the Pearl Harbour catastrophe. He approved the revised procedures, giving the OSS man a virtual freehand. The court reconvened with the president stating that General Patton had been reassigned and the tribunal would report to Admiral Stark. Major General Gustav spoke.

"I have received orders from Admiral Stark that all tribunal judgements and procedures be reviewed without delay."

Mallem was doubtful that Stark's orders were legal, but before he could speak, Oppenheim stood and demanded.

"All earlier rulings must be quashed and reviewed in the light of the new command structure."

Mallem tried to conceal his dislike of the man and asked the lawyers present,

"Gentlemen, are there any objections to the submission made by Mr Oppenheim?"

Commodore Strom stood.

"The issue of 'Double Jeopardy' would undoubtedly arise and certainly result in successful appeals against any convictions."

Mr Boyd KC spoke of "blatant interference in due process" and was about to continue when Major General Gustav butted in and repeated Stark's orders stressing the admiral had sole command. The UK Foreign Office barrister then stood.

"General, my name is Colonel Giles Tindall, King's Counsel. I represent the British Military Legal Services. I have serious misgivings regarding the admiral's right to assume sole command."

He then asked the president,

"Sir, would you please confirm that you are second in command of the US Third Army."

Mallem answered,

"Yes, I am," and prompted,

"Please go on, Colonel Tindall."

"Thank you, sir. I submit that until a replacement officer is appointed, you are in command of the US Third Army and hold equal authority with Admiral Stark in all matters relating to the tribunal. I question the legality of Admiral Stark's authority to issue the order under discussion."

Oppenheim blustered pointlessly,

"You are supposed to be prosecuting."

Tindall answered without emotion,

"Precisely, Mr Oppenheim, and I intend to prosecute by proper legal means."

The court was quiet while Mallem spoke to the tribunal members. The US officers supported Stark's orders without question. Despite his need to exert pressure on the officers of HMS Longbow, Admiral Sparkes voiced his concerns about the dictatorial attitude of the US admiral. Colonel Faraday whispered fiercely,

"I am not going to throw any of the SOE soldiers or the young American major to the wolves."

Mallem sat in the middle, fully aware that he needed to exercise extreme caution with the casting vote, or it could cost him dearly.

Charlie Rawlings was making telephone calls from the London office of the Hunter Corporation. Once the polite niceties were done, he got to the point. The answers were equally brief and all along similar lines.

"Charlie, I have never heard of Operation Javelin."

That evening, somewhat disheartened, he returned to the hotel. The front was ablaze with lights, giving clear sight of four familiar faces as they got out of a taxi. Rawlings felt elated. Buchanan saw him first and yelled his name. Charlie's elation faded slightly, knowing he had no news for them on Bill or Colonel Travers. Thomas Cork shook his hand. Jessica kissed him and followed with the words,

"Hello, Daddy, any news of Bill?"

He hugged his daughter and answered all of them.

"I cannot find hide or hair of Bill or Travers - but there's always tomorrow. Now I think we should all get some food and a good night's sleep."

Thomas and Jessica Cork had anything but. The Buchanans were worried and, knowing there was little they could do to help the search, decided to tour London the following day.

Connor Cork sat in his office in Portsmouth, pondering why Pat had not been in touch. Their last conversation was about what his son would do after the war. An extended stay in the Royal Navy had never been mentioned; on the contrary, he wanted to demob as soon as possible. Lionel Morley knocked on the open door.

"Good morning, Connor. There are some tenders on your desk for approval.

I'll get those off to the Ministry of Works straight away if you're happy with them. I think, on average, we should get one in five jobs we tender for."

Connor looked up.

"Lionel, please come in. I looked over the tenders, and they're fine."

Morley had been commanding men long enough to know the signs.

"Connor, if I may say, you seem rather distracted."

Connor smiled and said,

"Please sit down. I want to talk to you."

He explained his concerns. Morley listened, then asked,

"Connor, do you remember when we were discussing my joining the company, I mentioned contacts? Well, if it's alright with you, I'll call in a few favours."

The tribunal room was tense as Mallem stood to announce his decision on the new 'orders and procedure'.

"I have listened to the opinions of all learned counsel, defence and prosecution, and the less qualified pronouncements of others, who are not so interested in the course of justice. I am going to proceed with the hearings under the original terms of reference and operating procedures."

Faraday whispered to Sparkes,

'Good lord! He's ignoring the orders of a four-star admiral and risking his career. Good for him. I'm supporting the general."

The next morning saw Buchanan and his wife set out to explore a proud but battered city. Charlie Rawlings, along with Jessica and Thomas Cork, returned to the Hunter Corporation office to continue the phone calls. Lionel Morley was also making a call and had soon arranged to meet a friend in a pub near Portsmouth and called into Connor's office and suggested he attend as well.

The court resumed its deliberations with Erebus in the witness chair. Oppenheim asked,

"Did you threaten the Von Brauns at any time?"

Lewis looked at both Von Brauns.

"Mr Oppenheim, my job was to get personnel and documentation out of Peenemunde. I said and did whatever was necessary to achieve that. In answer to your question, I did at times pressurise, some might say intimidate, the Von Brauns."

Oppenheim jumped at the answer.

"So, you did threaten them."

Erebus ignored the accusation and explained to the court that Gerber Von Braun wanted to wear civilian clothes when leaving Peenemunde and was told forcefully to stay in uniform. Oppenheim pressed.

"By forcing him to wear a uniform, you were making him a target."

The defendant replied,

"The guards in the camp were fanatics and never questioned orders from someone in uniform. Von Braun had absolute power over those morons. I told him what to do and he gave the orders, which helped to get everyone out of the camp."

Oppenheim almost shouted,

"I find it hard to believe that any one man in a particular uniform could carry such weight and influence."

Erebus waited for a short time.

"It does in Nazi Germany when that man is wearing the uniform of a general of the Waffen SS." Oppenheim and Von Braun rose to speak but Mallen warned,

"Sit down, gentlemen."

Oppenheim shouted,

"I don't take orders from you!"

Schwartzberg, sensing the tribunal members were turning against the OSS man ordered,

"Sit down, you idiot."

The president announced,

"We will recess to allow certain people to calm down."

In London, Charlie Rawlings, his daughter and son-in-law were leaving the Hunter Corporation office for some fresh air when they were approached by a man in a trenchcoat who spoke in a low, precise voice.

"Mr Rawlings, Mr and Mrs Cork, would you be so kind as to accompany me and my colleague."

A large saloon car pulled up: the nearside rear passenger door was opened by the driver, who then got out. Tom Cork could only think of Belfast Port and that Peters had remembered him and contacted London demanding his arrest. He shouted,

"Who are you, and what do you want?"

The driver, now behind Jessica, demanded, in an American accent,

"Just get in the car, will you. You're not in any danger. Just do as you're told and do it now."

He tried to grab Jessica's arm, and Thomas began to struggle with him. At this moment, two London Metropolitan police officers on foot patrol saw the developing fracas and intervened. One stood in front of the car; the other demanded to know what was going on. The trench coated men refused to answer any questions and were arrested. Charlie Rawlings and Mr and Mrs Cork were asked to go to West End Central police station, where they provided proof of identity - unlike the other Americans who refused to do so and were immediately detained. Thomas began to relax a little as he and Jessica's papers, along with her father's, were quickly returned with thanks. They were then astounded as a London Metropolitan Police Detective Inspector apologised to them for not being able to walk the streets of London in peace and asked if they wanted to press charges against the two men. Tomas was unsure what to do, but the inspector was clearly angry with the American men, who he now regarded as the aggressors and asked,

"Mr Cork, do you have any idea why these men attempted to carry out what I can only describe as an attempted triple kidnap?"

He looked at Jessica and Rawlings as Thomas remained silent.

"Mr and Mrs Cork, Mr Rawlings, please understand this is something we will not tolerate on the streets of London. If you have any information, please tell me now."

Jessica was at a complete loss, and then Charlie Rawlings spoke.

"Inspector, the only connection I can make is from my activities since arriving in London."

The police officer urged,

"Please go on, sir."

Before leaving the police station, the Corks and Rawlings had signed a witness statement and told of their search for Major William Cork, and something called Operation Javelin. They were asked to give contact telephone numbers which, for all three, were the British Ministry of Agriculture and their hotel, and they were advised that they had seventy-two hours in which to press charges.

Lionel Morley and Conor Cork sat in a small pub outside Portsmouth and listened as the Royal Engineers' chief security officer explained all he had learned of a tribunal being held in camera, which was hearing charges arising from Operation Javelin.

"What's unusual about this tribunal is that it's made up of British and American officers. Now, Lionel, you asked me about Mr Cork's son. I can confirm that Commander Cork is a witness. There is another name which might interest you. Major William Cork of the US Army Engineers."

Connor asked.

"Is he a witness as well?"

"No, Mr Cork, he is a defendant. If you can give me time, I can get more detail as to the charges; something called the OSS is trying to keep the whole thing top-secret and failing miserably. They insisted on holding this tribunal, despite warnings that it is impossible to hold a joint services enquiry, let alone a multinational one, without leaks. Now the war is over, the majority of people can't wait to be demobilised and couldn't care less about security. Some full-time military people seem unable to grasp that fact, especially the Americans." He lowered his voice and added,

"Mind you; it's becoming impossible to tell the Americans anything."

Connor stood, thanked the officer and said to Morley,

"I'll get the car."

As he walked away, the security officer asked the former sapper,

"Didn't you ask for a check on an Irishman called Cork in 1943?"

Morley nodded his head.

"Yes, but that was a long time ago in a different world. Now, just one more thing. Any idea where this tribunal is being held?"

The reply was disdainful.

"As I said, leaks everywhere. A stately home come army base just outside and north of Colchester."

Morley stood.

"Thanks for your help."

The Metropolitan Police Officers were about to interview the 'kidnappers' when a Captain in the United States Navy, seconded to the US diplomatic service, arrived at West End Central Police station. The officer demanded the release of - in his words - 'the innocent American citizens' being held illegally. London-born Detective Inspector Fordyce had recently returned to police duty after four years flying Lancaster's in RAF Bomber Command, being invalided out six months before the end of the war due to severe dysentery. He was in no mood to take orders from an anonymous uniform, let alone a navy one, American or otherwise.

"Captain, the war is over. Civilians now give the orders and those two 'innocent American citizens' stay in my cells until they tell me what gives them the right to act like Chicago gangsters in my city!"

Simpson-Coyle was in deep thought. His original plan for the tribunal was now ruined. The question of how a top-secret code name became known remained unanswered, as did his problem with the kill order. Oppenheim was clearly out of control, using Stark's authority to demand guilty verdicts and determined to go to any lengths to get his way. He could not be trusted with the secrets of the SOE and British Intelligence. Stark's claim to sole command of the tribunal was now under close scrutiny at a very senior level, possibly Allied Supreme Command, and could attract serious attention. Something Simpson-Coyle did not want or could control. He called into Colonel Tindall's quarters and explained his concerns about the current situation but never mentioned the kill order. The FO barrister was already very perturbed about events and the attitude of Oppenheim but admitted he saw very little that could be done. There was a knock on the lawyer's door. Tindall was surprised to see Professor Williamson, who, on seeing Simpson-Coyle in the room, said,

"Good evening, gentlemen. It's lucky I caught you together. Brigadier Davies wants to see you both immediately."

In Maiden Aunt's office, as the men sat down, there was little time for politeness. The Welshman got to the point.

"It seems this so-called tribunal has now become an attempt at a secret lynching by an American Admiral and that lunatic Oppenheim. Now, what do you gentlemen intend to do about this increasingly dangerous farce?"

Tindall was clearly shocked. Davies noticed and commented,

"Colonel, you may seem surprised, but we are going to get this situation under our control."

He looked at Simpson-Coyle.

"Colonel, you have already had one charge thrown out. the other is equally shaky when challenged by capable counsel. I'll be frank. My only concern is that the issue of a leak or mole within British Intelligence is to be investigated in front of a man who would sell his granny to get his own way."

Tindall asked,

"What do you suggest, brigadier?"

The Welshman was ebullient.

"Now you're learning. Welcome to the world of smoke and mirrors and the dark arts. We are going to engineer a situation where Oppenheim and his two tame generals are removed from the proceedings while we get to the bottom of the leak of that code name."

He outlined the action to be taken and gave Simpson-Coyle and Colonel Tindall their orders.

The Tribunal hearings resumed. Erebus was asked by Mr Boyd,

"Major Lewis, did you at any time intend to endanger the lives of the Von Brauns?"

"No, sir, I did not. My job and that of my colleagues was to get them into Allied hands."

The barrister closed the file on his desk.

"Thank you, Major Lewis. I have no further questions."

Mallem asked the court,

"Any further questions for this officer?"

All prosecution counsel signalled they had none. Colonel Tindall stood up and spoke.

"Mr President, I submit we have heard enough evidence, and now it is time to reach a verdict on the second charge."

Oppenheim jumped up.

"I protest. I have contacted Admiral Stark, and he has repeated his orders that all previous judgements be reviewed."

Colonel Tindall, still standing, continued.

"His Majesty's government will not countenance what appears to be an American admiral demanding guilty verdicts against all defendants, despite the findings of the Tribunal members, which were reached by correct legal argument and on sound evidence."

The barrister paused and flashed a look at Davies, who nodded invisibly, then continued.

"If Admiral Stark and Mr Oppenheim continue with these demands, I will have no choice other than to give notice to withdraw all British personnel and, if they agree, allied personnel from these proceedings."

There was silence as the fundamental differences between Oppenheim, Stark, Major Generals Gustav and Spitzer, and the rest of the tribunal members and lawyers brought about an impasse. Then Oppenheim stood up shouting,

"If you people continue to disobey orders, then, under the authority of Admiral Stark, I will have all of you charged with mutiny."

He looked at Gustav and Spitzer, who promptly stood. Simpson-Coyle broke the silence.

"Mr President, as the initiator of this prosecution, I am now withdrawing the remaining charges against all members of the Operation Javelin Team." Oppenheim and the US tribunal members walked out. Sensing that the general had lost patience with the OSS man, Simpson-Coyle completed the strategy by addressing Brigadier Mallem.

"Sir, Brigadier Davies, the Commanding Officer of the Norwegian section of SOE, would like to make a statement to the tribunal."

Mallem replied,

"Please do, brigadier. Things are pretty out of the ordinary so far today anyway."

Davies stood.

"Thank you, Mr President. There is another matter which I would ask the tribunal to consider. It is an issue which is peculiar to the Special Operations Executive and involves members of what I will call C squad. General, I would be obliged if you would chair the tribunal to hear this matter."

Mallem looked intrigued.

"Brigadier, I believe there is another issue to clarify first. Do you agree with Colonel Simpson-Coyle withdrawing the remaining charges?"

Davies answered.

"Yes, sir, I do, and may I ask Colonel Tindall to give the reasons."

Mallem nodded his head. Tindall rose.

"Sir, we believe that until a decision has been arrived at on the legality of the Tribunal and the consequences of the withdrawal of two Tribunal members, no further charges should be heard."

Mallem replied immediately.

"I agree, and to establish the legality of Admiral Stark's position, I have passed a copy of his orders with my report to the Supreme Allied Commander, General Eisenhower, for a decision."

He then looked at Davies.

"Brigadier Davies, I presume that you and Colonels Tindall and Simpson-Coyle have concluded that the remaining members of this tribunal are qualified and suitable to hear the issue concerning C squad."

Davies was direct.

"We have, sir."

Mallem asked,

"Please give me a brief summary of the basis of that conclusion."

Davies looked at Tindal, then Mallem.

"Mr President, with your permission, Colonel Tindall will do so."

Mallem instructed,

"Please proceed, Colonel Tindall."

"Yes, sir. You hold joint command of Allied and US forces and, as with Colonel Faraday and Admiral Sparkes, have top-level security clearance. There is no doubt that all issues raised will remain secret. The matter to be raised involves only members of C squad, which is made up of British and Norwegian servicemen. Your impartiality is guaranteed."

Mallen looked at the British Army brigadier – his instinct screamed, 'spook', but the man had presented a solid case for the tribunal hearing the C squad issues. He breathed in and told the slightly stunned assembly.

"Until I receive a decision from the Supreme Commander on the legality of Admiral Stark's orders, and because of the withdrawal of the US officers the five-man tribunal is adjourned."

He then announced,

"We can move on with other matters. I will preside over the tribunal hearing on issues pertaining to C Squad. We will begin the hearing in the morning."

Bill Cork's lawyer, Mr Racq, stood.

"Mr President, unless Mr Oppenheim is ready to present the case for the prosecution within forty-eight hours, I will be moving to have all charges against Major William Cork dismissed."

Mallem, with an almost cheerful tone, replied,

"I hear you loud and clear, counsellor, loud and clear."

His voice still cheerful, he continued.

"In the meantime, Major Cork, you are released into the custody of Commander Cork and his men on your own parole."

The Buchanans sat in the saloon bar of the hotel in growing shock as Charlie Rawlings, and the Corks recounted the events of the day. Catherine asked,

"Tom, you are certain these men had American accents?"

Jessica answered,

"Oh yes, they were definitely Americans. There's no doubt."

The discussion carried on. Jessica asked of no one in particular,

"Why would anyone in London want to kidnap us?"

Charlie Rawlings offered a thought.

"How did they know where we were? This city is enormous."

Tom tried to apply logic.

"There's no reason for it. We're here to sell cattle and find Bill."

Buchanan raised his hand.

"That's it, Tom. It must be something to do with Bill."

He looked at Rawlings.

"Charlie, you spent a whole day calling people about Operation Javelin from one address. Where were you stopped by these men?"

Tom answered,

"We'd only just left that building."

Catherine continued her husband's train of thought.

"If we have contacts in the Hunter Corporation office, it's safe to say other people do as well."

Jessica picked up the thread.

"We haven't been able to contact Bill for some time. Maybe these men are connected with something he was involved in on active service."

There was silence until Tom spoke.

"Bill, you told me when I first came to the Double B to always use local knowledge. Well, we're in London, and I reckon that we know two men with the kind of knowledge we need. The first is Inspector Fordyce, who is definitely not afraid of anyone."

He paused.

"The second is my brother, Connor. This is his home city, and if he's anything like other Irishmen all over the world, he'll have plenty of contacts and local knowledge."

Jessica handed her husband the letter with his brother's work and home numbers. Buchanan and Charlie Rawlings had booked a taxi to take them to West End Central Police station, having just made an appointment with Inspector Fordyce. Rawlings was going to make a formal complaint and use the London

Metropolitan Police to find out the identity of the Americans in custody and, hopefully, the whereabouts of his grandson.

Conner sat in his office with the former soldier who was becoming a friend.

"So, Lionel, how do we contact Pat and Bill?"

Morley advised care.

"We have to exercise caution. The unknown people running this tribunal seem to have very powerful support in the US. Pat is a witness, so there shouldn't be a problem getting word to him. Major Cork is another matter. He is a defendant and an American serviceman. If we had someone close to him, we could use the family connection. Unfortunately, you being his uncle, won't carry too much weight. You could try and contact Pat but that may cause trouble for him. I have no contacts there at all. We will have to tread carefully."

The phone rang on Connor's desk. His secretary said,

"Sorry to bother you, Mr Cork, but it's a personal call."

Connor's heart lifted.

"That's alright, Sally. Is it my son, Pat?"

The line was silent, then,

"No, the gentleman said he is your brother, Mr Thomas Cork."

The tribunal sat with three members. The court layout was identical. Brigadier Davies stood up.

"Members of the tribunal, the aim of this hearing is to establish how the secret code name of a senior officer in British Intelligence became known to an operative on active service. I will now give a synopsis of events leading to the use of that codename in a theatre of operations."

The Brigadier gave the history of C squad up to their evacuation from Norway in 1941, finishing with the incident where the codename was used. He then stated that, as, at the time of the matter under investigation, Colonel Simpson-Coyle was in command of SOE operations, he was recusing himself from all further proceedings."

Davies finished with,

"Colonel Tindall will now lead the investigation."

Mallem nodded his approval as he said.

"Please call your first witness, colonel."

Pat Cork sat in the witness chair as Tindal asked,

"Commander Cork, please tell the tribunal of your service in Norway."

Pat recounted his military history, from landing in Norway to being shot in the leg and returning to the UK. Tindall prompted,

"Thank you, commander. Would you please tell the tribunal members who shot you."

The tribunal members' faces darkened as the answer came.

"I was shot by Major Lewis."

Tindal continued,

"After shooting you, what did the major say?"

Pat answered in a flat voice.

"He apologised to me and added, 'Tell Odin that Erebus will be in touch.'"

Mallem, clearly shocked, asked,

"Are there any questions for the commander?"

The lawyers all declined, and Pat was excused. Tindall pressed on.

"Please call Major Lewis."

Thomas Cork spoke with a slow voice.

"Hello, Con. How's things boy?"

Connor, after all the years of wondering what he would say to the man, simply replied.

"Fine Tom, how are you, and where are you?"

They decided to meet and bring only their wives - the others would understand. Just before they said goodbye, Con heard his brother say with passion.

"Con, we've got to forget what happened for the time being. I've got a feeling that my Bill could be in real trouble. He needs your help, and so do his mother and me."

Con said goodbye and looked at Morley.

"Lionel, I think we've just found our close connection."

Lewis sat as Tindall posed a question.

"Major, we know of the circumstances of your service in Norway and how much you achieved with your comrades in C Squad. This tribunal is here to establish how you learned the codename 'Odin' and from whom. Do you understand?"

Lewis was surprised that no one had raised the issue of the 'kill order'. He was about to then thought that perhaps Simpson-Coyle was not interested in having anyone jailed. All he wanted was the source of the leak. He looked at Bakken, who nodded his head.

"Sir, I was told the code name by Commander Bakken – call sign 'Vali'."

The court was silent as Tindall said quietly,

"No further questions for this witness. Please call Commander Bakken."

Again, Tindall got straight to the point.

"Commander Bakken, who revealed to you the codename 'Odin'?"

Bakken said,

"I was given the code name by my commanding officer."

The colonel hardened his voice.

"Your commanding officer is Colonel Simpson-Coyle."

The room was in silence as Vali replied,

"With all due respect, sir, he is not."

Tindall reminded the witness.

"Commander, you are aware that there could be serious consequences if you do not answer my question."

Vali answered.

"I am aware, sir, but I must have personal permission from my commanding officer."

Tindall demanded,

"Then please tell the tribunal the name of that officer."

"Bakken replied,

"With respect, colonel, I cannot do that for reasons I have just stated."

Tindall was becoming desperate as he envisaged this brave young man throwing away years of his life.

"Commander, will you please tell us the man's identity and now!"

Mallen interrupted as he spoke to Strom.

"Is there any contribution you can make here?"

Strom replied,

"May I consult with the commander?"

Mallem, his voice now slightly desperate,

"Please do so - and quickly."

The Norwegian officers conversed in low whispers until Strom spoke to the court, clearly surprised.

"Mr President, my client has asked for time to make contact with the officer in question."

Mallem addressed Bakken.

"Commander, how long do you need to get this officer's permission?"

"Twenty-four hours at the most, sir."

Nodding his head, the general asked,

"Colonel Tindall, do you have any objections."

Tindall, visibly relieved, replied,

"None at all, sir."

Connor and Mary Cork stood outside Westminster Abbey. The time agreed for the meeting was six o'clock. London's weather had not let them down, giving a clear day. A taxi pulled up, and Mary felt her husband's grip tighten in her hand. They didn't often hold hands, but Connor had taken hers without thinking. Mary saw a man emerge from the taxi and knew immediately that he was her brother-in-law. Jessica Cork had waited impatiently as her father hailed a taxi, then she waved as they drove to meet the man her husband had not spoken to in over twenty years. As the taxi came to a halt, she saw someone she could only describe as her husband's double – a handsome man with the Cork neck, a very attractive woman by his side. She wanted to run to them to thank them for all they had done for her boy. The men met. Connor was lost for words but then remembered his manners.

"Tom, this is my wife, Mary."

Tom replied,

"And this lady is my Jessica."

The men looked at each other, neither sure what to do. Finally, Tom said.

"How are ya, Con boy?"

Connor tried to smile and then put his hand out to shake his brother's. Tom took the outstretched palm as Connor said,

"You look well, Tom boy."

He turned to Jessica and hugged her. Tom did the same to Mary, and soon the women were talking. The men walked ahead silent until the women, now relaxed, called to them.

"Tom, Mary has laid on some food for us at her house. It's not far from here." The men turned, and both nodded as Connor hailed a taxi. The brothers climbed in, Connor said to his brother.

"Jesus! It's good to see you, Tom."

Tom sat in the taxi and replied,

"Take us home, Con boy, to your and this lovely lady's home."

The taxi came to a halt outside the large, terraced house in Belgravia. Rachel and Christopher were at the door to meet their uncle and aunt. The welcome was emotional, with hugs and kisses all around. Mary and Jessica quickly agreed that all the Double B party should stay in the house until Bill and Pat came home. Connor and Thomas seemed taken by the idea as the younger Cork looked at the house, saying,

"By God, Mary, there's plenty of room. Bill, Catherine and Charlie will love this house." Christopher and Rachel took over the re-location project, which involved taxis being taken to the hotel and the Buchanans and Charlie Rawlings being brought back to a highly desirable part of London. The introductions were somewhat stilted as the guests slowly recovered from the shock of seeing the incredible likeness of Tom and Connor Cork. The subject then turned to Bill and how to reach him. Connor explained about his colleague and the possibility of finding out exactly where Bill was. Before any more could be said, Mary Cork announced,

"You are all guests in our new home, and it is getting late. Can I suggest that we eat and then plan a campaign to find your son and ours and bring them home?" After dinner, they all sat in the spacious drawing room. Connor could see Catherine Buchanan was already completely at home as her eyes roamed around the room from ceiling to floor.

"Right, Tom, what do we need to do to find Bill? How much do you know about this 'trouble,' as you put it?"

His brother explained about Operation Javelin, and then Charlie Rawlings described the attempted kidnap and the reaction of the police inspector. Connor could not conceal his amazement,

"Jesus! Who the hell do they think they are?"

He saw in Tom and Jessica, a father and mother who were scared for their son, and involuntarily felt protective toward his younger brother, and tried to reassure both parents.

"Tom, Jessica, the police in this country are, on the whole, pretty good. So maybe we should wait and see what they say. If Bill is in trouble, as long as he is in England, he's fairly safe. They – whoever they are – won't be able to get him out of the country without us knowing."

By now, everybody was exhausted, and Mary suggested,

"Let's all get a good night's sleep and start the campaign in the morning,"

At no time during the evening were the Bagots or West Cork mentioned.

Inspector Fordyce had been called to see the Assistant Commissioner, Special Operations at Scotland Yard. The office was deliberately imposing, but as Fordyce entered, he laughed to himself,

'It's not as scary as the approach to the Mohne Dam.'

The AC special ops looked up; glad to see Fordyce. So many of the 'Mets' best men had gone to war and would never return.

"Inspector, please take a seat. It appears you have upset some very self-important people. Please tell me about these Americans your uniformed lads arrested, and the other people involved."

He paused and opened a file as Fordyce made himself comfortable.

"Now let's see, we have Mr Rawlings, who made the complaint, and Mr and Mrs Thomas Cork."

The Inspector began to do as asked and then saw the AC special ops was wearing an RAF tie and relaxed.

Major Lewis sat in his room at the SOE HQ, feeling slightly confused. The tribunal had found in his favour on the gross disobedience charge, and now the evidence given by Vali had cleared him of all responsibility in the code name leak. The 'Kill order' had not been mentioned at any point, which would leave a loose end as long as he and Vali were alive. Men like Colonel Simpson-Coyle did not like such things. Erebus decided to speak to the man he did trust. Brigadier Davies opened the door of his office and heard.

"May I come in, sir? I think we need to talk."

The Brigadier stood aside, saying,

"Please do – and take a seat. Now, what can I do for you?"

Erebus outlined his concerns and suspicions.

Davies suggested,

"Major, I think we should get all those concerned in here and develop a common approach."

Colonel Simpson-Coyle, along with Colonel Tindall, were summoned to the brigadier's office later that evening. They entered to see Davies, Lewis and Professor Williamson seated. Maiden Aunt began.

"Gentlemen, please sit down. We have a number of issues which need to be aired and resolved."

He then addressed Simpson-Coyle.

"Colonel, we have all been playing the same game for the last five years, namely 'smoke and mirrors and the dark arts.' So might I suggest that we now suspend these tactics which have been forced on us and speak as men?"

Simpson-Coyle seemed relieved.

"By all means."

He addressed each man.

"Maiden Aunt, Erebus, by all means."

He paused as Davies and Lewis watched and listened to the man they were convinced had given the kill order.

"My apologies, I should say, Brigadier Davies, Major Lewis. I agree it is time we cleared the air. I have seen enough in this war to know I want nothing more of this profession or whatever you may choose to call what we do. Information has come to light which has made me conclude there is only one enemy I face - and it is not you and your comrades. I have one grave problem which is the leak of a top-secret code name. Once I have resolved this potential treason, for me, the war is over."

Lewis could only think of one question.

"Colonel, what do you want in return?"

The colonial veteran looked the young Irishman in the eye and said,

"I want to grow old gracefully. To achieve this, I need you to forget about an order that may have been issued and persuade your comrades and friends to do the same. You see, young man, unlike you, I do not have many friends."

Lewis found himself feeling sorry for a man who now looked very old and very tired. Davies spoke.

"Now, gentlemen, for the last time, hopefully, we will speak off the record. Are you all in agreement?"

There is no record of the conversation that took place, but within an hour, Simpson-Coyle had agreed to make every effort to clear the Javelin team of the remaining charge. Davies and Lewis promised that all members of that team would assist in solving the mystery of the leak of the top-secret code name. Finally, Lewis asked,

"Colonel, I believe we have agreement on most points, but there is still the problem facing Vali. How do we deal with that?"

The man opposite him replied,

"Major Lewis, I believe that Vali will be cleared of all charges."

Lewis probed.

"What makes you say that?"

The FO barrister, Colonel Tindall, spoke.

"Gentlemen, I have every confidence in the Norwegians, specifically Commodore Strom, to give us the answers we need to close the matter forever. The man is very well connected."

Lewis pushed on.

"There is also Major Cork. Oppenheim is obsessed with jailing Bill."

Simpson-Coyle's eyes hardened.

"Gentlemen, please believe me. I will provide all that is needed to control our OSS friend."

The men parted without a handshake or confirmation of anything said. Lewis, Davies and Williamson were feeling slightly more at ease. Simpson-Coyle was a relaxed man, knowing he had made peace with the very talented and dangerously unpredictable young men of C squad and Operation Javelin. Now he faced only one enemy, one which he would happily destroy.

Rawlings woke in his bedroom just off Belgravia and felt at home. He had enjoyed the previous evening tremendously, and having listened to Connor Cork, he was now far more confident of finding his grandson - and quickly. Tom's brother was so like him and yet so different - a calmer man who thought things through before deciding a course of action. Charlie rose and, having eaten a good breakfast, continued his quest for Bill. He began by contacting Inspector Fordyce's office with his new temporary phone number and address.

In the office of the OSS, Oppenheim was reading a signal from Admiral Stark, which demanded to know why the Von Brauns were not in the US. The admiral had promised Truman results. The OSS man had underestimated the resolve and character of the members of the tribunal, particularly the officers who had seen active service and were adamant that justice was done. As for Mallem, despite less than subtle hints he be replaced, even Stark would not take on Eisenhower, who, in the eyes of the free world, could do no wrong.

The twenty-four hours allowed to Bakken to contact his commanding officer had expired. General Mallem began the proceedings with a caution to all present.

"These are grave matters we address today. I want all here to be fully aware that I believe that punishment must be a deterrent. There can be no further delays or deferments. Commodore, is your client prepared to answer all questions put to him by the members of this tribunal and the prosecution?"

Strom rose.

"Mr President, my client has been in contact with his superior officer who, in turn, has decided to address the court. I therefore, ask permission for this witness to do so.

Mallem looked at Brigadier Davies and Tindall, who replied,

"We have no objections, sir."

Then, surprisingly, the general looked around the court until he located Simpson-Coyle.

"Colonel, as the issue at hand is one of security, do you have any objections to the witness, whoever he may be, testifying?"

Simpson-Coyle looked hard at Strom, who slightly nodded his head.

"If Commodore Strom and Commander Bakken are prepared to guarantee the security of the witness, I have no objections, sir."

Mallem instructed,

"Very well. Commodore, please proceed."

Strom began to brief the court on the command structure of the Royal Norwegian Navy.

"Members of the tribunal, all Royal Norwegian naval officers are granted their commission by the Admiral in Chief, who remains their commander even when they are under the operational command of senior officers from Allied services."

He waited, then said.

"I call Commander Bakken."

Bakken sat down as Colonel Tindall stood.

"Commander Bakken, would you please explain to the tribunal why you revealed the code name of a senior officer of an Allied Intelligence section."

Bakken explained that if any officer was given an illegal order, he was bound to report the matter to a senior officer. When C squad were sent to Norway in 1941, Vali believed he had been given such an order. Tindall asked,

"Please detail the order for the tribunal."

Bakken paused as he remembered the words of Simpson-Coyle, then said.

"Sir, if a certain member of the expeditionary force attempted to desert, I was to kill him."

Tindall, visibly shocked, asked,

"Were you given any reason for this order?"

The reply was short,

"None, sir."

"What did you do then?"

"I reported to my commander-in-chief's office."

Mallem prompted,

"Go on, commander."

Vali told the court of the orders given to him by his Commanding Officer. Mallem interrupted,

"Commander, what was the name of the man this order referred to?"

The reply was instant.

"Major Lewis, sir."

Tindall pressed on.

"What was the name of the officer who issued this order?"

Bakken waited for a moment.

"Sir, I have been ordered not to identify the officer."

Tindall, surprisingly, snapped a reply.

"I presume your commanding officer will confirm all of your testimony."

"Yes, sir."

The barrister nodded his head slowly and looked at a clearly shocked Mallem.

"No further questions, Mr President."

Strom stood.

"Mr President, I wish to call my final witness."

Inspector Fordyce returned to West End Central relieved but inquisitive. The AC special ops had been direct.

"Inspector, with so many countries, now falling under the Soviet heel, we, in this country, are going to be inundated with asylum seekers and refugees - all with a cause to promote or revenge to be exacted. The police need to send out a strong, clear message to all of them."

Fordyce listened with growing interest as the AC continued.

"If these freedom fighters and the so-called security services trying to suppress them want to go to war, they can do so, but not in London or any other British city. Our people have had enough." His voice hardened.

"Charge our American cousins with attempted kidnap and see what comes out of the woodwork. Let's flush out this OSS man and make that clear to him and others. Understood?"

Fordyce answered,

"Perfectly, sir."

45

Red, White and Green

The man wore the uniform of a Norwegian Navy admiral. General Mallem ordered,

"Colonel Tindall, the witness, will take the oath and state his identity."

The British officer looked at the general in amazement, but when sworn in, the witness was ordered,

"Please identify yourself to the tribunal." The officer stood to attention.

"I am Commander in Chief of the Armed forces of Norway - Olav the Fifth, King of the Norwegians."

All the servicemen in the room stood to attention. Somewhat flustered, Mallem replied,

"Thank you......"

He seemed at a loss, then regained his composure.

".......sir."

Then looked down courtroom and said,

"Resume your seats, gentlemen. Commodore Strom, please proceed."

Inspector Fordyce returned from Scotland Yard and spoke to both men, who still refused to provide any identification or explanation.

"You will be formally charged with attempted kidnapping."

He paused for effect, then cautioned,

"In Britain, this is a serious offence which, on conviction, carries a minimum sentence of ten years. Believe me, gentlemen, you would not like ten years in the Wormwood Scrubs prison."

The prisoners remained silent, but as the charges were being read, one began to lose control and shouted at his companion.

"Jesus, what the hell is going on? These limeys are serious?"

The trip in a prison van to Westminster Magistrates Court was not pleasant, and the ensuing remand in custody resulted in a further loss of control and a considerable amount of information from one of the prisoners. The Inspector contacted the AC Special Ops by phone with an update on the accused.

"Sir, the men are operatives in the Office of Strategic Services, or OSS, under the command of a man named Oppenheim, who has, it appears, completely deserted them."

The AC special Ops asked,

"What did the men say about the people they accosted?"

The detective replied,

"Apparently, they were ordered by this man Oppenheim to find out why Mr Rawlings and the Corks were asking questions about an American officer, and something called Operation Javelin."

Fordyce expected a question, but there was just silence, so he continued.

"Sir, I can confirm that the officer in question is Major William Cork, US Army Engineers, who is Mr and Mrs Cork's son and Mr Rawlings' grandson."

The AC Special Ops said,

"Keep them at West End Central. I'll make a few enquiries about the OSS and this Oppenheim chap at this end. You see what you can dig up at yours. After all, we are dealing with an attempted kidnap which is a serious offence. Let's not forget that."

At the Cork house in Belgravia, the atmosphere was one of guarded optimism. Inspector Fordyce had phoned, saying he would call with an update everyone on the investigation. There were also three questions which could greatly help his enquiries.

Commodore Strom rose and asked,

"Admiral, would you please tell the tribunal when you were made aware of what we will refer to as the 'Kill' order?"

The Flag officer began.

"Immediately prior to the departure of Norwegian servicemen to Norway with the Irish Guards. My aide briefed me on the kill order, as reported by the officer who received it - Commander Bakken - who also identified the target, code named Erebus."

Strom was brief.

"What did you do, sir?"

The witness continued,

"I instructed my aide to tell Bakken to await further orders. I was forwarded the records of Erebus and conducted an in-depth investigation which involved studying the military and medical records, particularly a psychological profile of the man. Finally, Commander Bakken was ordered to make regular reports on the officer's conduct on active service in Norway."

Strom prompted,

"Please go on, admiral."

"Bakken's reports described a brave man, vastly different to his psychological profile, who was making an immense contribution as part of a team fighting the enemy. I ordered Bakken to allow Erebus to escape."

Strom, slightly aghast, asked,

"Why did you do that?"

"I have extensive experience with the British Armed forces, and as a result I am certain a 'kill order' would never have been sanctioned by any commanding officer. Erebus had to be given a chance to contact the senior command in the SOE and report the illegal order issued against him."

Strom, now clearly amazed, requested.

"Would you please enlarge upon the phrase, 'given a chance?'"

"Commander Bakken was ordered to give Erebus the top-secret call sign of a senior officer of British Intelligence, which would enable him to contact and inform that officer of his situation."

Mallem interrupted.

"I take it, therefore, that you trusted Erebus."

The admiral continued.

"I considered the security of the SOE was not at risk and had every confidence that Erebus would remain loyal to the Allied and Norwegian cause and continue the fight behind enemy lines. In both cases, I am pleased to say he proved me correct."

There was silence then Mallem asked,

"Sir, do you know the name of the officer who issued the kill order?"

Simpson-Coyle broke into a cold sweat. He had completely overlooked General Mallem, who, as president of the Tribunal, had every right to ask the question that, if answered, would ruin him. Davies's face reflected his concern. In agreeing a plan with Simpson-Coyle, he too had forgotten the straight-talking American. The witness replied,

"Mr President, with all due respect, I see no point in revealing the name of the officer, as the order was not executed. It would serve no purpose and is not fundamental to the issue we are dealing with today, but in answer to your question sir, yes, I do know the man's identity."

Mallen could not argue with the logic and looked at Strom for guidance.

"Mr President, the witness is within his rights."

The American's gaze switched to Colonel Tindall, who stood.

"Sir, please name the officer who divulged the code name and call sign 'Odin' to Commander Bakken."

The room was silent as the witness stood upright.

"I am the man who revealed that code name. As Bakken's Commander in Chief, I considered it a necessary risk to resolve a very dangerous situation."

Mallem looked at Simpson-Coyle, who, though still reeling in a landslide of emotion, managed to stand.

"Colonel, does the witness's testimony answer all of your questions?"

The SOE man stood to attention.

"Mr President, the witness's testimony is proof that there is not a security failure or double agent within the SOE or British Intelligence. The loop has been closed, and the matter is now officially concluded."

General Mallem sat in his temporary office and looked at the pile of paperwork on his desk. Despite being President of the Tribunal, he still had to attend to the duties as the commander of the Third Army. A top priority order had been issued to allied commanders instructing that all servicemen and women were to be disarmed immediately, then repatriated and demobilised as soon as possible. The peacetime Allied governments were realising just how much armed forces cost. The brigadier knew that there was very little time left to conclude the tribunal, which had so far cleared the British and Norwegian defendants of two of the three charges. The reduced tribunal had answered all Simpson-Coyle's questions and had, in his own words, 'closed the loop'. Still outstanding and now, he suspected, profoundly political, was the charge of endangering an intelligence asset. Mallem had been at a loss to know how to decide what constituted 'endangering' or how to prove intent or guilt. He had learned over the years that if you don't know something ask someone who does. He had consulted a number of legal experts, who had come up with a basis to work from in reaching a decision. They advised,

'You've got to decide who is lying and not necessarily about the matter at hand. Any proof of mendacity by any witness on any issue will weaken their credibility considerably.'

He called his admin officer and said,

"Major, I want everyone involved in the Tribunal in court tomorrow. We need to finish this thing quickly."

A slightly bemused Inspector Fordyce sat in the very elegant property in Belgravia. The owner of the house introduced himself and his wife and explained the connection between them, the Corks and Charlie Rawlings.

"Inspector, my brother, Thomas, emigrated to America some years ago and this is the first time we have met in over twenty years. He and his wife Jessica, along with Mr Rawlings and the Buchanans, will be staying in our home until further notice."

Fordyce came from a large family in East London, some of whom had emigrated and so empathised with the Cork brothers' separation. Mary Cork watched the policeman's face as he gazed around the large drawing room. He spoke to her directly.

"You have a beautiful home, Mrs Cork."

The lady of the house, still a feeling a little unaccustomed to life in Belgravia, offered an almost apologetic reply.

"Thank you, inspector. We've only just moved in, having inherited the house from my husband's late business partner, who was killed in 1942."

She silently scolded herself and took charge of her 'beautiful home.'

"Now, I understand you have something to say to us all. Please go ahead."

Fordyce stood.

"Ladies and gentlemen, I have three questions for you all. First, has anyone heard of an organisation called the OSS? Two. Does anyone have any knowledge of Operation Javelin?"

He paused.

"Finally, does anyone know of an American man called Oppenheim?"

Charlie Rawlings spoke.

"As you know, we have found out that Bill Cork, my grandson, is involved in Operation Javelin, but since then, we have learned nothing more than what we told you at the police station."

Fordyce nodded, and then Connor spoke.

"Inspector, I asked a colleague of mine, a former army colonel, if he could locate our son, Commander Pat Cork and our nephew, Major Bill Cork. He discovered that both are involved in a tribunal investigating Operation Javelin."

Fordyce asked,

"Mr Cork, what exactly do you mean by involved?"

Connor looked at his brother and sister-in-law.

"Tom, Jessica, I've only recently been told that Bill is a defendant facing charges at this tribunal and that Pat is a witness."

Catherine Buchanan instinctively went to Bill's defence.

"Do you know where this 'so-called' tribunal is being held?"

Connor looked at Tom, who nodded.

"At a military installation near Colchester."

Buchanan immediately wanted action.

"Well, the sooner we get there and find out what the hell is going on, the better." Fordyce cautioned,

"Mr Buchanan, there is an ongoing criminal investigation, so please leave this matter to the Metropolitan Police Force."

He paused and looked at Connor.

"Mr Cork, how did your colleague access this information?"

Connor summarised the words of the Royal Engineer security officer, finishing with,

"Inspector, everybody wants to go home, so security across the military is, to say the least, relaxed."

Fordyce said his goodbyes and, when he returned to the police station, sat both OSS men down in his office and said,

"Right, if you now tell me everything about Operation Javelin and this man Oppenheim, maybe you won't be visiting His Majesty's Prison Wormwood Scrubs."

The morning after the loop had been closed, Odin called on Commodore Strom and requested permission for him and one other senior officer to see the witness. He was asked to wait and then given the address of a small hotel a few minutes' drive from the SOE base.

The room was smaller than expected, supporting rumours that the Norwegian monarch lived a frugal life, believing that creature comforts were not acceptable while Norway was occupied. The occupant of the room turned to greet his visitors.

"Good morning, Odin."

He then looked at the other visitor and continued.

"Admiral Menzies, good to see you again. Now gentlemen, how may I be of assistance?"

Odin spoke.

"Good morning, sir. Thank you for seeing us."

The man they had come to see remained silent, and Spenser realised he was waiting for an answer to the earlier question. Menzies smiled as he thought. 'A man of few words and all of them relevant.' Odin got to the point.

"Sir, I'd like to know why you didn't name the man who gave the kill order."

The king smiled.

"Admiral, in a few days, I am returning to my home and people, both of which have been torn apart by the Nazis. There will be much recrimination and many allegations of collaboration and undoubtedly calls for severe punishment."

He paused and motioned his visitors to sit.

"As I testified yesterday, there is little point in naming the man as the order was never executed. There are other factors to be allowed for too. A number of character traits described in Erebus' file were misleading, and the urgent need to send men to Norway exerted undue influence and extreme pressure on the officer issuing the order."

He stood and walked toward the room door.

"Admiral, there has been enough pain in Norway. The Erebus affair ended well, and the identity of the man who issued the illegal order remains a secret along with so many others."

Menzies spoke for the first time.

"Would you have issued a similar order, sir?"

Olav smiled.

"Well, admiral, we will never know."

The British flag officers stood and saluted as Odin said,

"Thank you, sir, and good luck at home."

The man's face lit up as he replied,

"Yes, Admiral, I will soon be going home, thanks to many brave people."

There was one more question that had to be asked to finally satisfy the senior British Intelligence Officer.

"Sir, may I ask who revealed to you the code name 'Odin'?"

The King of the Norwegians paused.

"A dear friend of mine, Admiral Menzies. A dear friend by the name of Winston Churchill."

Oppenheim had attempted to reach Admiral Stark to request a written copy of the orders, which instructed Mallem to revise the judgements handed down by the tribunal. The reply was from the admiral's second in command via a transatlantic telephone link.

"Mr Oppenheim, your job is to get those scientists to America and quickly. Now get on with it, or we'll find someone who can!"

Mallen convened the hearing with Admiral Sparks and Colonel Faraday. As per orders, all concerned were in attendance. along with the senior SOE officers. As Major Cork's defence counsel rose to speak, Oppenheim and Major Generals Gustav and Spitzer entered. Mallem demanded,

"Well, gentlemen, are you prepared to resume the proceeding under my jurisdiction?"

Gustav replied,

"Mr President, after consultation with Admiral Stark, we have been instructed to complete the work of the tribunal."

Mallem studied Oppenheim, his anger blatant, but he remained silent as the general announced,

"We will hear evidence on the charge of endangering an intelligence asset by forcibly returning that asset to Peenemunde. Now, I want it clearly understood that the tribunal members will decide the case based on the evidence and testimony presented in this court. Mendacity, obfuscation, and subterfuge will, if proven, greatly damage the credibility of the witness and his case."

Gerber Von Braun was called to testify. Oppenheim began the questioning.

"Herr Von Braun were you at any time threatened by and felt in peril of your life from the defendants."

The younger brother told the court about the threats from Vali and Erebus when they first made contact and those to force the elder Von Braun to return to Peenemunde and concluded by saying,

"I felt threatened by them from the minute I met them."

Mr Racq stood.

"Herr Von Braun, was Major Cork at any time violent toward you or your brother?"

Von Braun began,

"He never stopped using threatening language."

Racq cut across him.

"Did the major at any time use physical force against you? Please answer yes or no to the question."

The German scientist was truculent.

"No, he did not at any time use force against me or Werner."

The lawyer finished with,

"Thank you, Herr Von Braun. I knew we'd get there eventually."

The day went on with Gerber Von Braun facing virtually identical questions from all of the defence lawyers. It became clear the only evidence of the defendants threatening Werner Von Braun was his brother's testimony. Oppenheim could see the tribunal members were becoming restless with the lack of any conclusive proof of guilt. He hissed at Colonel Schwartzberg,

"Do something. You're supposed to be the legal expert."

The US army lawyer replied,

"There is no evidence other than what the Von Brauns say, and it's their word against the men of Operation Javelin."

He paused before adding in a fierce whisper,

"And, for your information, they are all war heroes. Your witnesses are Nazis."

As with the US armed forces, the British were disarming all servicemen with immediate effect. To guarantee that all weapons were surrendered, the British military high command ordered the Royal Military Police to carry out unannounced searches on every base on the British mainland. The order applied to all ranks. Anyone found attempting to conceal weapons was to be prosecuted under military law.

Dr Eldridge and Moen, along with Peter Vogt, left the base in Portsmouth and made their way to the SOE HQ. CPO Baker drove slowly to ensure the comfort of his passengers. Sitting beside him was John Eldridge, concentrating on the contents of a file he had compiled from documents recovered in Peenemunde. The scientist was deep in thought only looking up to turn and give reassuring smiles to the passengers.

The tribunal reconvened after lunch, and Werner Von Braun was called to testify. Oppenheim began.

"Herr Professor, were you, at any time, threatened by any officer or Royal Marine in this room."

"I was threatened by the American major on more than one occasion," he replied. The OSS man prompted,

"Please elaborate."

Von Braun raised his voice and pointed at Bill.

"It was him. It was as if he couldn't wait to kill me. He was as bad as the SS." Schwartzberg interrupted.

"Mr President, I withdraw that remark by the witness."

Mallem looked at Major Cork, who did not seem upset by Von Braun's words. In fact, he seemed to welcome the insult.

"Herr Von Braun, can you give any specific examples of your life being threatened by the man you have just pointed out."

Von Braun said,

"Yes, I can," and went into detail of being held prisoner and how on the return to Peenemunde, the 'American' said. 'If he was charged with my murder, his trial would be held in London. The people there would not convict him, in fact…..' Von Braun, now sweating, stopped, then almost shouted,

"….the American boasted, 'For killing the man who invented the V weapons, they'd give him a knighthood.'

The court was silent as Mallem looked at his watch.

"We will continue tomorrow."

Later that evening, Pat was summoned to a telephone and heard Admiral Hilliard's voice.

"Commander Cork, we are decommissioning HMS Longbow. The armourers will be dismantling the ship's weapons first, so we won't need you or the other officers straight away. Sorry to be so abrupt, but needs must."

Pat replied,

"Very good, sir. When do you want me aboard?"

Hilliard seemed to pause as if thinking.

"It will take two weeks to make the ship safe, so when the tribunal is over, take a few days leave and let me know where you are, then check in every day for orders. I have already signed a number of demobilisation orders for your crew. As I said, Pat, sorry it's so quick, but we're at peace, and the Royal Navy has to cut its cloth accordingly."

Pat put the phone down as Petty Officers McNally and Canavan walked in and saluted.

"Sir, it seems the Royal Navy no longer requires our services. We've been told to ask you when can we leave the tribunal and return to Portsmouth."

Pat stood and shook both men's hands, saying.

"It's the same for everybody. Of course, you could enlist for ten years, otherwise you might as well head for Portsmouth and demob as soon as you can. Take one of the navy cars. On a personal note, please leave a contact address with CPO Baker or, if he's been demobbed, Lieutenant Bellamy. I won't say goodbye until we have a beer somewhere. Is that ok with you gentlemen?"

Both Irishmen nodded and saluted, leaving with the words.

"See you back at Pompey, sir."

The court sat, and Mr Racq questioned Von Braun.

"Why are you making these allegations against men who saved you and your brother's life?"

Von Braun looked surprised and blustered.

"I don't know what you mean."

The American law expert nodded his head as he said.

"You don't understand? Well, let me clarify. I put it to you that if it was not for the men of Operation Javelin, both of you would have been left to the tender mercies of the Nazis or other interested parties."

Von Braun seemed too astounded to reply. Racq pressed on mercilessly.

"I submit these charges are trumped up by you and the OSS to hide the fact that you and your brother were, and still are, fanatical Nazis and are guilty of war crimes."

Oppenheim jumped up.

"Where's your proof? Show us the proof."

Mallem cut in.

"Mr Racq, where is this line of questioning going?"

The lawyer said,

"Mr President, the OSS and the Von Brauns have charged the defendants with numerous offences purely to stop any questions being raised about their activities in Peenemunde."

He reached for a folder.

"Mr President, the defence will prove that the witnesses were members of the Nazi party and did commit war crimes."

Oppenheim screamed,

"The Von Brauns are not on trial here!"

Racq stated very clearly,

"The witnesses are not on trial, but their willingness to tell the truth is. Mr President, you stated that the charge would be judged on the veracity of the evidence given. We will prove the Von Braun's and the OSS have deliberately lied to this tribunal and, in doing so, have destroyed all credibility in any testimony they've given to support the charges against my client."

Oppenheim glared at Mallem then hissed,

"You cannot allow this to go on. Admiral Stark will hear of this."

Mallem spoke without a hint of emotion.

"Mr Oppenheim, it was you who demanded the defence prove their allegations. You and Admiral Stark must allow them the opportunity to do just that."

He then recessed for the day.

CPO Baker, Thomas Eldridge, Moen and Peter Vogt arrived at the SOE base just as Petty Officers Canavan and McNally were driving out of the gate. All were surprised to see a large contingent of Royal Military Police arrive.

The court was in session as Werner Von Braun faced Mr Racq for a second day. The German noticed that next to his American tormentor was US Colonel Travers. Racq stood.

"Now, Herr Von Braun, what do you know of the Todt Organisation?"

The reply was terse.

"They built anything we needed. That is all I know. I remember little else of them."

Racq continued,

"Allow me to enlighten you and refresh your memory."

The lawyer proceeded to give the court a summary of the Organisation Todt and its methods of using slave labour. He then asked Von Braun,

"Do you still say you have little or no knowledge of the organisation?"

Von Braun snapped,

"How many times do I have to tell you? I know virtually nothing of these people."

He then watched as Travers handed the lawyer a number of papers which he held up.

"Herr Von Braun, if you know so little about 'these people,' as you put it, how do you explain your signature on fifty requisition orders demanding the supply of lorry drivers and unskilled labour for general manual labour to support your scientists."

The courtroom was silent as the witness stared at the papers and remained silent. For the next two hours, the American lawyer produced document after document linking Werner and Gerber Von Braun to the use of slave labour in Peenemunde. At the back of the court, Pat Cork sat with Nigel Bellamy, who whispered,

"I think this is going our way, sir."

Before Pat could reply, Mr Racq announced,

"I have nothing further to say on these matters other than to request the tribunal consider the evidence presented today. Evidence of the use of forced slave labour as a result of orders and demands made by both of the Von Brauns. Something they have consistently denied, but the tribunal now knows to be true. Brigadier Mallem asked,

"Mr Racq, do you intend to present any more evidence tomorrow?"

The lawyer replied.

"No, sir, that is the defence case for Major William Cork. The allegations against him are pernicious vexatious calumnies."

Mallem looked at the British lawyers.

Mr Boyd KC stood,

"We will begin the defence case for Major Lewis, Sergeant Major Reilly and Sergeant Mullen as directed."

Mallem replied.

"First thing tomorrow morning Mr Boyd." then adjourned the court.

The next day was a repeat of the previous except that Werner Von Braun was answering questions from Mr Boyd KC, who queried in general terms the methods used to research and produce the V weapons. The British barrister then switched to a singular line of questions.

"Herr Von Braun, when testing the V weapons, specifically the V1 or Doodlebug as it is known in many British cities, were any trials carried out with manned prototypes?"

Von Braun did not answer immediately, then said.

"I don't understand the question."

Boyd's face was cold though his eyes were glowing with anger.

"Right, I'll explain to you. Did you or your brother force Allied Airforce prisoners of war, under threat of death, to pilot the V1 prototypes to test their airworthiness? Does that make it clear enough?"

Von Braun shouted at Oppenheim,

"What is going on here? You said we would be in America by now. This stops now, Oppenheim, or you get nothing from me. No rockets. Nothing! Do you hear me?"

Oppenheim remained silent and seated as the President of the tribunal looked at the OSS man and then asked Colonel Schwartzberg,

"Does the prosecution have anything to say on the witness's rather curious answer to a perfectly valid question from defence counsel?"

Colonel Schwartzberg stood.

"Mr President, may we ask for a recess until the morning."

Mallem replied,

"If the defence has no objection...."

He scanned the defence teams and was greeted with a number of assent signs which barely concealed the real feeling of elation amongst them. The entire courtroom knew Oppenheim had to destroy the veracity of the evidence being submitted or face having the charges dismissed. Mallem announced,

"We will recess until tomorrow morning."

Pat picked up the conversation with Bellamy.

"Nigel, I need to talk to you. Let's grab a cup of tea."

"Flags, I had a telephone call from Admiral Hilliard giving me new orders which affect you and our shipmates. Longbow is being decommissioned over the next few weeks. A number of the boys have already been told and are on their way back to Portsmouth. I've been given some leave when this tribunal is ended, and then I report back to complete the mothballing."

He paused, looking into the young man's face he asked,

"Have you given any thought as to what you want to do, now the war's over?" Bellamy replied,

"I haven't got a clue, but I'll get by. First thing is to go home and see my parents and family."

He added as an afterthought,

"I was wondering why the watchers said goodbye as they were leaving the base."

Pat spoke.

"Nigel, you can stay until the tribunal ends or head for Portsmouth now. I'll leave it up to you."

Flags answered,

"I'll wait here, sir, until this thing is over. Then Franco Forrestal and I will go back together."

Oppenheim was beside himself with anger. The evidence being presented to the court was damning, and there was nothing he could do about it. It looked as if the Tribunal was about to throw out all of the remaining charges, which meant that he had no control over anyone remotely connected with Operation Javelin. They could say and do what they wanted and publish what they liked. He needed something to regain control of the situation. The 'so-called' legal expert from the US Army was proving to be more interested in the law being administered properly than getting the Von Brauns into America.

Pat had met Lewis, and both went to see Bill in the small room which had been allocated to him since the tribunal had begun.

"Looks like it won't be long before we'll be going home. Longbow's being mothballed. I'll get my demob orders soon."

Bill looked up but remained silent. Lewis tried to lighten his mood as he said to Pat,

"That makes the world a far safer place - if you're not sailing the seven seas picking fights with perfectly innocent sailors."

At that moment, there was a knock on the door, and Colonel Travers entered, now completely at ease with the Corks and Lewis.

"Sorry to disturb you, my friends. Bill, just a quick word. The general demobilisation order has come, so get ready to go stateside once we sort out Oppenheim and the OSS."

Pat watched his cousin's face, which showed no emotion at the news.

Bill replied,

"Thank you, sir, that's great news."

As Travers was leaving, he added,

"Bill, all weapons are to be surrendered immediately. You don't have anything with you, do you?"

Bill replied,

"No, colonel, my side arms were confiscated when I was arrested aboard HMS Longbow."

Travers' anger showed as he thought of Bill in handcuffs.

"That was a disgrace. Still, it will all soon be over."

Lewis picked up on Travers' theme and tried once again to lighten his comrade's mood.

"The tribunal's going well. We'll all be out of here in no time."

Bill's eyes were cold as he replied,

"Yeah, all of us. Including the Von Brauns."

The following morning, the tribunal sat, but the Von Brauns were absent. General Mallem demanded, with heavy sarcasm,

"Does anyone know the whereabouts of the alleged victim and the chief prosecution witness?"

Colonel Schwartzberg stood.

"Sir, we have received notification that the Von Braun's will not answer any more questions on their involvement in the research and development work at Peenemunde."

Mallem remained silent for a minute, then decided to push matters on.

"Would the defence counsels please prepare their closing submissions, which will be heard as soon as possible?"

There was a stunned silence in the courtroom as the tribunal members left.

Davies asked Professor Williamson to locate Colonel Travers, Commodore Strom and Mr Boyd as soon as possible. The meeting which ensued was in many ways a council of war, where it was decided to take Oppenheim head on. He and Colonel Schwartzberg were asked to attend a meeting in the tribunal room. Oppenheim remained seated as the three senior officers and the barrister walked in. Colonel Schwartzberg showed far more respect and stood to greet the men.

Maiden Aunt began.

"Gentlemen, it appears the time has come for a discussion." He paused as his eyes centred on the OSS man, then Boyd, Strom and Travers. The words left no doubt.

"Our objectives are as follows. We want to get our men cleared of all charges and back into civilian life and home."

Colonel Schwartzberg looked at Oppenheim who said nothing. The colonel, with an apologetic look on his face, spoke.

"Please tell us what you have in mind which will resolve this matter and close the tribunal."

Commodore Strom answered,

"It's quite simple, colonel. The OSS and Mr Oppenheim drop all charges, and our men walk out of here free and clear."

Oppenheim snapped,

"That's no good to me."

Boyd snapped back at him,

"Then tell us what *is* good for you?"

The OSS man listed his basic requirements. All evidence presented to the tribunal thus far by the defence must be handed over to the OSS. He then produced a number of documents which were to be signed by everyone remotely connected to Operation Javelin, which swore the signatories to secrecy on all matters relating to the OSS, the Von Brauns, and the tribunal. Finally, he demanded that the American citizens involved in the tribunal keep the OSS informed of their whereabouts until further notice. The demands were met with astonished silence. Travers said later that he would have would have laughed, if he had not been ashamed that an American government official could propose such preposterous and oppressive conditions. Mr Boyd replied,

"Mr Oppenheim, we are offering you the following and nothing else. You will tell us exactly what your orders are. After which you and your organisation will cease using secrecy, fear and intimidation against our clients. Do you understand?" Oppenheim remained silent.

Colonel Schwartzberg progressed the matter.

"Gentlemen, we will discuss the issues and will be in court tomorrow morning with or without the Von Braun's. If I might suggest that you make your submissions to have all charges dropped. He looked at Oppenheim, who was increasingly sullen and continued in a firm voice.

"There will be no objections."

The next morning, Mr Boyd KC rose to speak on behalf of Major Lewis and his army comrades.

"Mr President, members of the tribunal. The fact that the defendants risked their lives to bring the Von Brauns to safety would make the charges brought by the prosecution ridiculous if the potential consequences for my clients were not so serious. We all fully understood the president's words regarding the veracity of evidence given during this tribunal. The witnesses, by refusing to face any further cross-examination, have demonstrated that there is no proof of the allegations. I submit that my clients have no case to answer and respectfully request that all charges be dismissed."

Mallem looked to his left - the US officers were poker-faced - then to his right, where Faraday could hardly conceal his pleasure. Next to him, Sparkes was nodding his head slowly. The president asked,

"Colonel Schwartzberg, may we have your reply to the submission made by the defence?"

The reply was succinct.

"Sir, the prosecution has no issue with the submission being granted."

Mallem stood, as did the defendants.

"Major Lewis, Sergeant Major Reilly and Sergeant Mullen, you are acquitted of all charges and are free to go."

Commodore Strom stood and made a similar submission. The result was identical as Mallem pronounced.

"Commander Bakken, Royal Marines, Madsen and Norsen, you are acquitted of all charges and are free to go."

At that moment, a colonel of the Royal Military Police entered the room and approached the President.

Pat was in Bill's room trying to cheer his cousin up or at least figure out what was going on inside his head. The court was already in session and Pat knew that Mr Racq was ready to make a submission to dismiss all charges against Bill. There was a knock on the door and a sergeant major of the RMP entered.

"Excuse us, gentlemen, we are under orders to search this room."

Pat answered,

"Please carry on, sergeant major."

He looked at, Bill who remained silent, his face impassive as one military policeman stretched under the single bunk, and with difficulty retrieved a combat rucksack. The redcap's face whitened as he opened the flap to see three grenades, a small lump of plastic explosive, six detonators and a Smith and Weston 357 short-barrelled pistol with forty rounds of ammunition. Bill reassured the soldier,

"Relax, sergeant major; you're quite safe. The guns not loaded, or the weapons primed."

The sergeant major drew his sidearm and ordered,

"Gentlemen, stay exactly where you are until my commanding officer arrives." He turned to the other redcap and hissed,

"Jesus, Tom, find the colonel - now."

Bill seemed to wake up as he said,

"Sergeant, this has nothing to do with the commander."

The door opened, and a colonel of the Royal Military Police entered.

"Sergeant major, please report."

Having been told by the soldier what had happened, the colonel spoke to Pat and Bill.

"Gentlemen, as of now, you are both under close arrest and will remain so until further notice."

Mallem saw the Military Police colonel enter the court and signalled him to approach. They held a quick discussion, and then the brigadier general stood. The courtroom was silent.

"Gentlemen, I have to inform you that this tribunal is suspended until a certain matter has been dealt with."

46

Where to from Here?

nspector Fordyce had completed his report to the Assistant Commissioner, Special Operations and was now in possession of a warrant for the arrest of Mr Oppenheim of the OSS. On charges of conspiracy to kidnap and attempted illegal imprisonment. Fordyce queried,

"Sir, won't the gentleman claim diplomatic immunity?"

The AC Special Ops replied,

"Good question, inspector, but discreet enquiries have revealed that sections of US Military High Command in the UK have no love for Mr Oppenheim. We've been unofficially told to go ahead."

Mary Cork rose early to prepare breakfast. Jessica joined her, and as they sat in the spacious kitchen, she asked,

"How do you think things will work out between Con and Tom?"

Jessica sighed.

"Tom is deeply sorry for the damage done to the Cork family, but whether he regrets what happened in Dunmanway is another thing. The years in Texas have allowed him to become convinced that the British can be blamed for everything."

She sipped her tea and continued.

"For years, Tom told us all how much the Irish were downtrodden by the British. Now our son has seen what your lives are like here and knows that most of what his father told him about England is blatantly untrue."

Jessica said pensively.

"Bill has seen and done so much and is so different to when he left home." She paused.

"Now Tom's terrified how Bill will react." Then in a tremulous voice, admitted.

"And so am I, Mary, so am I."

Her sister-in-law tried to cheer her up.

"The waiting is not helping anyone. Our husbands will relax when the boys get here. Once they're home, we'll all see things differently."

Jessica replied,

"Mary, you don't seem too worried about Bill and your son."

Mary answered,

"Jessica, I've seen those men together, and I have an idea of some of what they've experienced. Believe me, if they put their minds to it, there is nothing they can't deal with."

Sir Geoffrey and Lady Lewis were driving to Aldershot. Colonel Faraday had phoned earlier in the day to tell them the outcome of the tribunal. Now they were going to surprise their son, celebrate the end of the war with him and hopefully meet some of the young men he had fought alongside - men who had brought about such a wonderful change in Charles. Unknown to Lady Felicity, Sir Geoffrey also had news from Kilkenny to share with his boy.

Colonel Simpson-Coyle had been preparing for the final day of the tribunal when he was asked by a Military Policeman to go immediately to the tribunal president's office. The colonel was escorted in by an armed redcap and saw Brigadiers Davies and General Mallem alongside a colonel of the Royal Military Police. Simpson-Coyle sensed an atmosphere of shock in the office and quickly realised why as his eyes came upon Commander Cork and Major Cork in handcuffs. General Mallem announced,

"Colonel, as the officer with responsibility for security, I now appoint you to investigate the matter of these officers being found in possession of illegal weapons and ordnance."

Simpson-Coyle did not try to hide his astonishment as he instructed the RMP officer,

"Colonel, please have these gentlemen escorted to their rooms and detained there. I will interview them later."

As the officers were led out, Simpson-Coyle surprised everyone as he almost shouted at the military police,

"And remove those bloody handcuffs. Now!"

Charlie Rawlings was on the phone, his voice becoming calmer as he wrote down details being dictated to him by a policeman at West End Central Police Station. The American was a little confused.

"Sergeant, I don't see why the inspector would give me this address."

The officer replied,

"Mr Fordyce said to tell you that after tomorrow you can collect your relatives at this location."

Charlie went into the living room and exclaimed to all present,

"That was Inspector Fordyce's sergeant. We can go and get Bill and Pat tomorrow, and that's official."

Simpson-Coyle spoke to Mallem.

"Sir, may I ask what the terms of reference are for the investigation."

Mallem was about to answer when the 'redcap' outside knocked on his office door. The general responded with,

"Enter."

The soldier announced,

"A Mr Oppenheim for you, sir."

The other officers began to leave. Mallem suggested,

"Gentlemen, please remain. It might be expeditious if we all hear what this man has to say."

Oppenheim burst in, his face alight with satisfaction.

"I told you these guys were out to kill the Von Brauns. Now I am going to charge them with conspiracy to murder."

Bill and Catherine Buchanan sat with Charlie Rawlings in a small bar in the West End of London. Charlie asked,

"Well, what do you think of Connor Cork?"

Bill answered,

"Well, all I will say is that he deals with problems well. Hell! That is one beautiful house, and those children are great young people. Mary is someone special. She is the bedrock of the family, and they all adore her."

Rawlings commented,

"It's not hard to see why."

Buchanan spoke to his wife.

"Honey, you're very quiet."

She looked at both men and replied,

"Connor is different to Tom. He's a more controlled, logical person - a man who always plans ahead no matter what he is doing."

Again there was a pause. It seemed as if she was hesitant to say more. Her husband prompted,

"Go on, Catherine."

She did as asked.

"I think Connor is still very angry with his brother about what happened in Dunmanway and wants an explanation. Tom may feel he does not owe Connor anything. Bill, Charlie, we are dealing with two secure family men. Independent, strong men who have built highly successful lives on separate sides of an ocean without help from each other."

She chose her next words with great care.

"I'm not sure either of them sees any reason to forgive and forget. Why should they?"

Oppenheim officially informed Brigadier Mallem that he was compiling a case to prosecute Major Cork and Commander Cork. The general knew that under military law there was nothing he could do to stop him. The OSS man returned to his office and summoned Schwartzberg.

"I am preparing a case against Cork and the Limey, and you are going to help me."

In his excitement, he did not see the look of contempt on the face of the US legal expert as he ordered.

"You make certain both men are kept here."

Schwartzberg, like Mallem, knew he had no choice.

"I will ensure that they remain on the base for the next forty-eight hours. Now, what do you need for your case?"

Oppenheim demanded the lawyer secure the US military record of Major William Cork along with the Royal Navy file of Commander Pat Cork. The colonel returned within the hour with Bill Cork's file and told Oppenheim he had arranged an appointment with Admiral Sparkes.

Oppenheim discovered that the major had been the subject of a security check while on leave in London. The officer carrying out the investigation was satisfied that Cork's relationship with an American female journalist did not compromise security. The personal file on Amanda Bruce attached to Cork's record described her as a close personal friend and was stamped 'subject deceased'. Cause of death was an explosion caused by a V2 rocket. Oppenheim was satisfied - he was beginning to see a motive.

Colonel Schwartzberg sat in Admiral Sparkes' office.

"Sir, I have been ordered to ask you for Commander Cork's personal file and his military service record."

The file was in the SOE HQ because of the commander's involvement with C squad and Operation Javelin. Sparkes was silent. Cork had been in the room when the weapons and explosives were found, so the Royal Navy had to comply. The file was duly handed over.

From that file, Oppenheim quickly confirmed that the defendants were first cousins. The men were found together with concealed armaments after the general order to disarm had been issued. Oppenheim concluded that he had enough to prosecute both men – the evidence was substantial, their motives were clear.

Major Cork blamed the Von Brauns for the death of his lover and intended to use the grenades and plastic explosive to exact revenge. Commander Cork had volunteered as the escort, knowing his rank would deter any vehicle searches, allowing the weapons and ordnance to be smuggled onto the base. Oppenheim was satisfied that the charges were valid under existing wartime legislation.

Theawyerrs, who, twenty-four hours earlier, were elated at virtually forcing Oppenheim to drop all charges against Major Cork, were now at a loss to know how to defend him and Commander Cork. The finding of weapons and explosives made the situation for both men very serious.

Pat sat in the room, which was now his cell, and answered the questions put by Mr Boyd KC.

"Commander, please tell me what you know of these events?"

Pat answered Boyd's question quickly. He knew nothing about the grenades and explosives found in Major Cork's room and explained the familial link with Bill Cork. The King's Counsel's reaction was not encouraging.

"Commander, we all know what Oppenheim is capable of. He is going to use the fact that you and Bill are related as the basis to prove a conspiracy to murder the Von Brauns."

At this point, there was a knock on the door, and Admiral Sparkes entered.

"May I have a word with the commander, please?"

Boyd agreed and left as the admiral began.

"Commander, I will come straight to the point. It is my opinion that Oppenheim wants to convict just Major Cork. I think I can persuade him to drop the charges against you by offering your testimony that Major Cork was acting alone and that you knew nothing of the intended attack."

Pat asked,

"Why would he do that?"

Sparkes replied,

"Because I will tell him that he will have great difficulty in proving conspiracy against a British officer."

He went on,

"I'll also remind him that he's crossed swords with you before, during the investigation of the alleged depth charging of a submarine in the English Channel, and that it would be wise not to take you on again."

For some reason, Pat felt he should ask,

"Why are you doing this for me.....?"

Then instinctively demanded,

"......and what do you want?

Sparkes looked a little surprised but answered,

"There is a certain action which you were involved in which I would prefer to be forgotten."

Inspiration came to Pat in a flash.

"You mean PQ19,"...... and continued,

"I've always wondered what brought you to this tribunal."

The admiral nodded his appreciation.

"I always said Loftus had a gift for finding talent."

Then, with a steely look in his eyes, he sat down in front of Cork.

"Commander, during the 'clearing the air' meeting aboard Snow Eagle, you referred to a dinosaur."

There was a pause before the flag officer continued.

"Well, Mr Cork, I am that dinosaur. I issued the 'scatter' order. Now, understand, that fact, or I being in any way connected with the convoy will never be made public. Do I make myself clear? If you agree to forget all about PQ19, all charges against you will be dropped."

Again he paused.

"As for your cousin, I am afraid he is not part of the arrangement and is on his own. Do you agree?"

Pat decided to play for time by making Sparkes think he'd won, as he asked,

"When does the hearing begin?"

The admiral's reply was more than he'd hoped for.

"I'll take that as a yes. Oppenheim is pushing to have a hearing tomorrow. From now on, you will speak to no one but Forrestal. He will be our liaison."

Within minutes of Sparkes leaving, Forrestal was in Cork's room expressing his thoughts on 'the whole bloody mess.'

"Sir, this is all wrong. Admiral Sparkes should be on your side. He's got no right to do this to you," adding.

"I mean, the man has never seen a convoy, let alone escorted one."

Pat cautioned his young shipmate.

"Be careful, Franco, that's a very ambitious flag officer you're talking about." Forrestal replied in an exasperated tone,

"It's not alone me, sir. Before I joined Longbow, I worked for an officer of equal rank to him at the Admiralty in Whitehall. There was always gossip about how Sparkes had made flag rank, as the only sea duty he'd ever seen was on HMS Renown in 1920 on a world tour with the former king."

Cork mused,

"That could explain the rapid promotion."

He decided to tell Forrestal what had been put to him.

"Franco, this is my problem."

Forrestal listened and when PQ19 was mentioned Pat saw the young man's face harden as he said,

"I can help you. I think we can beat him at his own game."

Pat began to hope that there may be a way out as he said,

"Ok, what tell me you have in mind," then cautioned.

"...but I don't want you taking any risks, Franco. You don't owe me anything -you've done more than enough."

Forrestal's voice was clear.

"It's not about owing anything. I want to help you, and I'll tell you why."

Pat remained silent as his shipmate continued.

"Sir, when I came aboard Longbow, I let everyone think I was obsessed with the security of the ship. To be honest, I was scared stiff, alone in a ship full of vastly experienced sailors. Thanks to you and my shipmates, I was made welcome even if I was watching everyone. Sir, that night we picked up the Javelin team, you said to me that during the boat race, you could not have commanded Longbow without me. That meant a huge amount to me."

A greatly humbled commander nodded his head.

"Ok, Franco, what do you intend to do?"

The young lieutenant was energised.

"Sir, the first thing is to get to the Admiralty as soon as possible. All we need is there."

Having been told to go ahead, Forrestal looked for Bellamy.

"Flags, I need to talk to you."

The conversation did not take long and, within minutes the officers were heading for London.

Doctor Eldridge sat in his room, head in his hands. It was now obvious that William, because of anger or grief or fatigue, had played into Oppenheim's hands. Being found in possession of the explosives was something not even the OSS would try to frame Bill Cork with. There was a knock on the door, and Travers walked in and sat. Both men remained silent for several minutes until the colonel spoke.

"Well, Prof, it looks as if we need to fight dirty to get Bill out of this."

Eldridge looked u,p nodding his head.

"Colonel, we need to speak to the following people and soon."

Brigadier Mallem discovered he was first on the list when Travers and Eldridge walked into his office. Maiden Aunt found out he was second when his phone rang, and a familiar American voice asked,

"Mallem here. Could you spare me a moment, please, brigadier?"

Having joined them, there began an unofficial, totally deniable meeting which finished with Mallem saying,

"Two o'clock in the tribunal room. I'll have everybody we need there." Bellamy sat in the car outside the Admiralty in Whitehall, heart beating. Forrestal hadn't explained what he was going to do, other than to say,

"Nigel, if we get caught, we could be in real trouble."

Flags replied,

"There are degrees of trouble. There's trouble ashore, and there's trouble in the Atlantic and the Baltic."

Both young men laughed as Forrestal left the car. Bellamy counted the minutes until he saw Forrestal run down the steps and, as the car door closed, he asked,

"Well, have we got any trouble?"

The answer was illuminating.

"Nigel, the thing about people like Sparkes is that when they practice illicit secrecy, it makes them vulnerable."

Flags requested,

"Explain please?"

Forrestal did.

"The thing about this particular illicit secrecy is that no one else is aware that the documents Sparkes is hiding are of any importance. I just walked into the records admin section and asked to see records and orders for convoy PQ19. They simply handed them over."

Bellamy pressed.

"Did anyone ask why just PQ19."

"No, they're all land-based officers. They would not know one convoy from the other. The escorts and convoys were run from Liverpool and Londonderry, which is why Sparkes had certain files moved to Admiralty records here." Bellamy laughed.

"Hide in plain sight doesn't always work."

Forrestal maintained the good spirits.

"Flags, I think we have enough to give the captain the upper hand in dealing with Sparkes."

He showed Bellamy a small telegram size piece of paper which was stamped in red, 'records copy'. The signals officer read the paper and, as he drove away, exclaimed.

"Full ahead, both!"

A seething Oppenheim and the Von Brauns approached the tribunal room, having been ordered there by Brigadier Mallem. His initial reaction was to refuse, but then, recalling Admiral Stark's waning support and ensuing ultimatum, decided to comply. Awaiting them were a number of people. Colonel Schwartzberg was seated. The OSS man realised the gathering was not formal as other seats were occupied by Davies, Simpson-Coyle, Colonel Tindall and one man unknown to him. Mr Racq was present as were Mr Boyd KC, Colonel Travers and, beside him, Dr Eldridge. Two armchairs from a mess were in the room. The tribunal members were also present - US Major Generals Gustav and Spitzer and Colonel Faraday. Only Admiral Sparkes was absent. The former defendants were standing to one side. Lewis, Reilly, Mullen and Bakken - all in uniform. There was no sign of either Major Cork or Commander Cork.

Eldridge began.

"Mr Oppenheim, we are all here to bring this matter to a close and quickly." Oppenheim scoffed,

"The only conclusion I can see is Major Cork doing twenty years in Fort Leavenworth military prison."

Eldridge, who had a folder under his arm, began to speak in a forthright tone as he stood up.

"Mr Oppenheim, we need to explain that the point of this gathering is not to negotiate with you. It is to present a number of facts and potential actions over which you have no control. We are here to give you an ultimatum."

The door to the tribunal room opened, and two men in wheelchairs were brought in by CPO Baker and Commodore Strom – Moen in one, Peter Vogt in the other. When the Von Brauns saw Vogt, the colour drained from their faces. Eldridge continued as both patients were made comfortable in the armchairs.

"Oppenheim, we are here to listen to the evidence of Peter Vogt, design engineer and former Luftwaffe fighter pilot, who was decorated for bravery during many missions over Britain and then the Eastern Front. The man was a national hero in Germany until he refused to work with you developing the V weapons."

Eldridge turned to the man in question.

"Herr Vogt, would you please carry on."

The German air ace stayed seated as he spoke.

"You will forgive me, gentlemen, if I do not rise. I was a guest of the SS at Peenemunde for some time, and, as you can see, their methods are effective." Vogt explained that, after having been wounded in air combat, he was appointed commandant of a Stalag run by the Luftwaffe for allied air force POWs. From there he had been ordered to 'supply' prisoners as test pilots for a secret project. At this point, he managed to stand.

"I refused to even consider such an order unless I was given details of the project. For this disobedience, I was relieved of command and sent to Peenemunde as a test pilot on the V1 Doodlebug flying bombs, where I was soon joined by allied pilots that my successor at the Stalag willingly provided."

The room remained silent as he sat down again. Eldridge asked,

"Herr Vogt, would you like a rest?"

The German rose again, bowing his head in thanks and continued his account.

"I realised what a terrible weapon the V1s were and decided the Allies must be told of them."

Again, he paused then said,

"At the early stages of development, the fuel for the V1 prototypes was so volatile that the German ground crews refused to fuel the aircraft. The test pilots did this under armed supervision but loaded only enough fuel for the particular test."

Again, the man sat down, his skin now pale. Eldridge moved toward Vogt who quickly waved him away.

"Pilots are fliers first and foremost. I had formed friendships with two fliers. One RAF and one Norwegian. The Norwegian had links with resistance groups in Norway. We decided that if the opportunity arose, we should somehow steal enough fuel to fly a V1 to Norway, where the resistance would try to get it to England."

The room was silent as Vogt seemed to be gaining in strength.

"Our chance finally came during an air raid warning. While the guards hid in the shelters, we filled a prototype with fuel, and the Norwegian pilot took off in what the Nazis thought was another test flight. When he didn't return, it was presumed the aircraft had blown up over the North Sea. The pilot made it to Norway only to be betrayed by an informer in a resistance group. We heard nothing until the SS arrested me. The Nazis couldn't try or execute me as I was well known in Germany. It was the only time I was grateful for being photographed with Hitler."

Then, looking at Von Braun with a piercing stare, he said,

"Instead, during a living death, I went from pilot to truck driver and the pilots were still forced to test those flying death traps."

There was silence as Vogt sat down. Eldridge asked,

"Her Vogt, who was in overall command at Peenemunde?"

The reply was instant.

"SS General Wernher Von Braun and SS Oberführer Gerber Von Braun." Oppenheim jumped up to speak but was shut up by Eldridge.

"I repeat - this is not a tribunal, Oppenheim. You are here to listen."

Moen stood up, and although weak, his voice was clear.

"The bastards made me drive the fuel trucks. I wasn't supposed to survive either, but I saw the pilots being forced at gunpoint to fly those things."

His voice became louder and angrier.

"Now I know why I was arrested in Norway. I was part of the plan to get the prototype to the British."

Moen looked at Lewis and shouted,

"You can tell me off later on, Laudrup."

Lewis managed a smile as the big man continued - his voice weaker.

"I saw SS officers signal other SS bastards to force the pilots into those rockets or whatever they were."

Moen's voice broke with emotion.

"And I saw all those brave boys fly away, and some never came back."

He pointed at the Von Brauns and shouted,

"They were the ones giving the orders - both of them in SS uniforms!"

Oppenheim shouted as he waved his arm at the men in the armchairs.

"None of this can be disclosed. It's their word against the Von Brauns.

It's just hearsay. You have no proof of the Von Brauns being in the Waffen SS. None at all."

Eldridge walked over to where Moen and Vogt were sitting.

"Thank you, gentlemen."

He turned to the OSS man and the Von Brauns who were now all standing.

"So, your rebuttal is that there is no concrete evidence which can be published. No proof that the Von Brauns were in the Waffen SS."

The scientist opened the folder under his arm.

"Oppenheim, I have here a number of photographs taken during Operation Javelin."

He raised an eight by four-inch photograph.

"When you examine the photo in detail, you will see two men wearing the uniform of the Waffen SS. In the background is the compound of Peenemunde. The enlarged photograph shows beyond doubt that the men are the Von Brauns." Eldridge stopped for a moment, his face dark as he stared into the image.

"Clearly visible are a number of people in striped clothes."

Again, he paused, then almost spat out the words as he spoke directly at Oppenheim and the Von Brauns.

"Yes, I said 'people'. Human beings in rags worn by slave labour."

Both Von Brauns sat down as if defeated. Oppenheim was not.

"There is no connection to these so-called pilots."

Colonel Tindall spoke.

"Mr Oppenheim, Peenemunde was under the command of the Von Brauns. They were in charge of the entire V weapons project and will be held responsible for all that happened there – forever."

Oppenheim reverted to what he knew best.

"I'm warning you not to publish those photographs. Its treason against the US government. I will have anyone who does jailed for twenty years."

Eldridge savoured the moment.

"Oppenheim, whilst you were busy arresting Major Cork, I was in a university in England where I copied these images and distributed them to numerous academic contacts in the US and the UK."

There was a thunderous silence as his gaze settled on the US major generals.

"They will publish if anything untoward should happen to William Cork or me. You will not find any of them – let alone charge them with treason."

The scientist then looked at the men in the armchairs.

"You cannot silence Herr Vogt or Mr Moen."

He paused and laughed.

"I can assure you, Oppenheim, that no one can silence Mr Moen."

Mallem called a break. Outside the tribunal room he said to Colonel Faraday,

"Well, let's get Oppenheim alone and finish this farce."

In Pat Cork's room, another meeting was taking place. Bellamy and Forrestal had returned and were briefing their captain on what they had brought with them. Cork spoke.

"Gentlemen, I'd say this document is secret and could get you into all sorts of trouble."

Both the younger men smiled as Forrestal replied,

"Not really, Captain. We have both received our demob notices. Sparkes cannot touch us - we are civilians again."

Pat remained silent, digesting the paper in front of him and the news that his crew were going home safe and sound. Forrestal continued,

"The Royal Navy is a huge organisation which runs on paperwork. Convoy operations regulations state that there must be at least five copies of all orders issued. What we have given you is a standard administration copy."

Flags joined in.

"Sparkes will never dare to admit where it came from or try to prove how it got here."

Cork cleared his mind and asked,

"Well, if either of you civilians don't mind taking an order, can someone get Sparkes in here please?"

Forrestal almost shouted,

"Aye, aye, sir."

Inspector Fordyce was on the phone to Superintendent Spence of Hampshire Constabulary, who had agreed to execute the warrant to arrest a Mr Oppenheim at a location just outside Aldershot.

"Good afternoon, sir. Do you know anything about this man Oppenheim or the organisation he works for?"

Spence had spent half the war dealing with enquiries about the activities of clandestine organisations operating from the many military bases around the Portsmouth naval ports. He replied,

"Inspector, let's just arrest this man and then try to find out who he really is and what he really does."

Oppenheim had been ordered by Gustav not to take any action until he had briefed Admiral Stark's second in command. Unknown to all involved in Operation Javelin, decisions had been made which were to alter the situation in SOE HQ for good. In Washington, things were changing rapidly as the Truman Administration appointed a new tranche of officials to push through fresh policies. One of which was the civilianisation of the many government agencies. Among them were the Intelligence Services, which would be gathering intelligence on the economic, political, commercial and military status of America's enemies and friends. The policymakers in Washington believed military men lacked the sophistication to supply all that was needed in a vastly changed world, which was, on the surface, at peace. The USA was about to establish a new intelligence organisation. The Office of Strategic Services would cease to exist and be replaced by the Central Intelligence Agency, which immediately adopted a policy of ignoring the indigenous laws of the countries in which it operated - friendly or otherwise.

In the SOE base outside Aldershot, the case of Major Cork and Commander Cork was coming to a close.

Admiral Sparkes was approached by Lieutenant Forestall and told,

"Commander Cork would like to see you, sir, if that is convenient."

The admiral confirmed,

"I'll be in his room in one hour."

During that hour, the officers of HMS Longbow prepared to deal with the admiral who had never seen a U-boat or convoy.

In London, Jessica, her father and the Buchanans had, even, in a short time, grown very close to Connor, Mary and the young people. Now, as they got ready to meet Bill and Pat, the excitement felt by everyone was tempered with the knowledge that once the boys were home, Connor and Thomas would have to air if not settle their differences, one way or the other.

Maiden Aunt was in his office when the phone rang. The caller was an Inspector from the Metropolitan police, enquiring if a Mr Oppenheim was currently at the base and, if so, how much longer would he be there. Davies asked what the Police wanted with Oppenheim. The answer initially shocked him, then, while replying, he laughed inwardly.

"I see, Inspector Fordyce. If I heard you correctly, you have a warrant for the arrest of Mr Oppenheim on serious charges."

The reply was a simple,

"Yes, brigadier – very serious."

Davies informed the police officer that, as far as he knew, Oppenheim would be on the base for at least another forty-eight hours.

In Pat Cork's room, Bellamy, Forrestal, Larsen and Mr Boyd KC waited for the admiral, who entered exactly on time. Sparkes' voice was smug as he surveyed the officers of Longbow in front of him.

"Good, all of you are here. I take it you have all agreed to my proposition."

Pat cut across him.

"Admiral, please sit down. There is something you should see." Larsen handed the paper which Forrestal had recovered from the Admiralty. Sparkes immediately went on the offensive.

"This is top secret. Where did you get this from?"

Forrestal looked at his captain, who nodded his assent and began.

"Admiral, that document is not top secret. It could, at worst, be described as politically disastrous - but only to the man who signed it."

Sparkes was now starting to raise his voice.

"I will have you all arrested."

Mr Boyd KC's voice was firm.

"I am becoming increasingly tired of senior officers who have never got their heads, hands or feet wet threatening experienced sailors."

Sparkes was about to reply when Lars raised his hand.

"Admiral, if you look carefully, you will see your signature and initials at the bottom right-hand corner just above the typed order, 'Scatter, Repeat, Scatter'. It is proof of the order you issued to the merchantmen of convoy PQ19 and which you have been trying to suppress."

The admiral remained silent.

Lars continued,

"We have all seen this copy, and there are others secured should you try to blackmail any of us in future."

The admiral asked,

"What do you want?"

Cork stood.

"What we want is to go home and take Major Cork with us. There will be no deal with Oppenheim or anyone else. The situation is really in deadlock. Bill Cork cannot give a reason for the weapons being in his room, but no one can prove that he intended to kill anyone."

Pat allowed a minute for his words to sink in.

"Sparkes, you will go to Oppenheim and tell him that you will not support him in the charges against Major Cork and me. You, admiral, will now stop Oppenheim dead in his tracks. Do you understand? It's Major Cork's freedom or your career. It's as simple as that."

Sparkes just managed to say,

"You had better all swear that PQ19 will never be made public by any of you - or else."

Pat raised his voice.

"Jesus Christ! We joined up to fight the Nazis, not to be subjected to empty threats from the likes of you, Sparkes. We have all appeared in front of Royal Navy boards of enquiry and know what the Royal Navy can do if it turns against us. But we also know it is commanded by fair-minded men. You! You're a bloody disgrace. Your only thought is what is good for you."

Cork paused, his chest heaving with temper.

"You really don't know us at all."

He then spoke slowly.

"Loftus knew us, Crowley and Campbell and Buchan, they knew us."

Then took a second as if paying respect to the men he named.

"Sparkes, we won't talk about convoy PQ19 ever again, and I'll tell you why. Every man of the convoy escorts will spend the rest of their lives trying to forget the men who died screaming in the water because of the no-stopping order. They'll always be trying to forget about convoy PQ19 and all the other ships that they couldn't protect from the U-boats."

Sparkes remained silent, then stood and looked at all the officers of HMS Longbow.

"I really have no choice, do I?"

His question was answered with cold stares and silence.

The British flag officer located Oppenheim and told him the position he was taking on the pending conspiracy charges but did not mention the ultimatum from the officers of HMS Longbow. Sparkes had seen enough of the OSS man to know better than reveal any compromising information. He finished the one-sided conversation with the words,

"You're on your own, Oppenheim, and if you take my advice, you'll stay well away from the men of HMS Longbow."

Oppenheim, now seething and desperate, returned to his office just as the phone rang. He answered and was told by the switchboard operator there was a call from Washington. For twenty minutes, he listened. Oppenheim finally broke his silence when the call finished by saying,

"Yes, sir, I fully understood. I will have everything organised. We will be ready to move at any time."

Due to his excitement, he didn't hear the slightest of clicks on the line as he put down the phone.

Mallem called the meeting to informal order. As he did, Admiral Sparkes and the officers from Longbow entered the room along with Major Cork and Mr Racq.

Oppenheim and the Von Brauns came in and were promptly told by Mallem to sit down. The Brigadier continued.

"Mr Oppenheim, we were all brought here to try a number of men charged by you with serious offences. Those matters have now been concluded."

He paused, expecting a reaction from the OSS man, who remained silent. Mallem continued.

"Now, we find ourselves forced to try another two defendants on charges, again brought by you. Well, Mr Oppenheim, there will be no further trials. We are now going to explain why."

Eldridge stood and recounted the evidence presented by Moen, Vogt and all the others. He finished with the words,

"Oppenheim, you may cross our paths in the future but be warned, all of us have documents secreted in safe places, which can and will destroy you and your scientists' reputations, should you take any action against any man in this room." Again, to everyone's surprise, Oppenheim remained silent. He stood and walked out of the room, accompanied by Werner and Gerber Von Braun and followed by Major Generals Gustav and Spitzer.

Colonel Tindall stood.

"Gentlemen, one of the very few benefits of the Official Secrets Act is that it occasionally allows matters to be classified as secret for the good of all concerned. I have now applied an official secret seal on all matters that occurred here during the tribunal."

He looked at Mallem.

"Sir, you have the floor.

The US general rose and announced.

"Gentlemen, you are all free to go. Please carry on with the rest of your lives, and good luck to each and every one of you."

The men departed in silence as Maiden Aunt approached Mallem.

"General, I have to tell you that Metropolitan Police officers are on the way to execute an arrest warrant for Oppenheim."

Mallem replied, as he smiled very slightly,

"Well, we yanks cannot interfere with the London Metropolitan Police, now can we?"

The following morning, as Pat Cork was packing his kit bag, Colonel Simpson-Coyle called to his room.

"Commander, may I have a word?"

Cork turned in surprise.

"Please come in, colonel."

The British officer did so and closed the door.

"Commander Cork, Oppenheim has gone, so have the scientists, I presume, to America. He is now joining a new organisation called the Central Intelligence Agency or the CIA. I know this because we British are not quite as stupid as certain people would believe."

Cork just listened.

"Commander, Oppenheim is a very dangerous, unbalanced individual. I believe the man will be even more dangerous on US soil. Major Cork is at liberty and remains a threat to his ambitions. Please pass on to the Major that there are steps being taken which will neutralise Oppenheim for good." He remained silent, as did Pat, then spoke again.

"I think it is better that I say no more. The least known about this matter the better. I'm sure you understand. Commander, you can leave Oppenheim to me."

Simpson-Coyle stood to attention and saluted. The young Anglo-Irish Commander returned the salute as the English man said,

"Goodbye and good luck to you, Commander Cork."

Bill walked into Pat's room as he finished packing and began to speak.

"Pat, I owe you an apology and an explanation why those weapons were in my kit bag."

Pat replied, with a hint of anger in his voice,

"Too bloody right you do! But leave it for now. The guards on the gate have just told me that your mum and dad are outside with your grandad and the Buchanans and, from the sound of it, half of Texas."

He watched his cousin's face light up as he continued,

"How long has it been since you saw them?"

Bill had to think, then began to murmur before he exclaimed!

"1942 to… Hell, Pat, it's been over three years."

Remembering his reunion, Pat advised,

"You go and see them and forget about everything else. Don't try to tell them everything at once, and maybe we should say nothing of this tribunal until after we've talked. Now go and enjoy yourself."

Bill began to leave, then stopped and looked at his cousin.

"Pat, they're desperate to meet you."

The reply was to the point.

"Yes, and they will, but later on. You all have a lot of catching up to do. Now go before somebody tries to charge us with something else."

Connor Cork and his family, along with his brother and wife and friends, drove into the former SOE HQ, now slowly returning to a pre-war country house and estate. Thomas Cork gasped when he saw his son and then his nephew as they walked down the steps into the morning sunshine.

Bill and Catherine Buchanan stood in awe at the men in front of them. The resemblance between Bill and his cousin was as strong as their fathers. The cousins separated as Bill went to meet his parents and family. The Buchanans watched as Jessica walked to her son, and both felt the pain of the childless couple like never before. Though overjoyed to see the Corks reunited with their son, Buchanans first thought was for his wife and he reached out and took her hand. She squeezed his and linked his arm as they both watched Jessica and Tom embrace their boy. Bill Cork felt tears come to his eyes. His mother just kissed him as she had when he left Texas, luxuriating in the knowledge that her son was no longer in danger. Tom Cork looked at his boy, whose appearance confirmed his earlier thoughts. Bill was as hard as steel, his body like a coiled spring, his eyes alert and clear even though filling with tears. They all stood together hugging until Bill looked toward his grandfather and then saw the Buchanans. He walked to the three most important people in his life after his parents and hugged them. Buchanan was now openly crying, as was Rawlings. Catherine Buchanan hugged Bill and then her eyes caught his cousin, Commander Pat Cork who was talking to his mother and father. She noticed how Mary had linked her husband and son as she walked with them toward Tom and his family. Thomas Cork walked to greet his nephew for the first time. Catherine Buchanan whispered to her husband,

"Look at Con and Mary's boy. In that uniform, he couldn't be more British." Tom stood as if in a daze as Pat walked toward him. Both remained silent. Then Bill broke the silence.

"Mum, Dad, say hello to Commander Pat Cork, Royal Navy and my first cousin."

Tom hugged his nephew and said to his wife,

"Jessie, I never had a photograph to show you. But this man is the nearest I've ever seen to him."

He turned to his brother, his Cork accent now strong and clear.

"Con boy, he's the image of daddy."

The Buchanans and Charlie Rawlings were introduced then they all got into the cars and headed for home.

Off to one side, Erebus saw his parents and decided they could meet the Corks another time. For the first time in years, Charles Lewis wanted his mother and father all to himself.

Elsewhere, a discussion was taking place which involved some very angry policemen and a group of reticent army-cum-intelligence officers. Superintendent Spence demanded,

"Well, gentlemen, where is this man, Oppenheim? My colleague and I have a number of questions for him and the small matter of a warrant for his arrest."

Davies looked at Simpson-Coyle, who in turn looked at Admiral Menzies, who had attended the ultimatum meetings. He spoke.

"Gentlemen, I cannot identify myself; however, I have briefed Colonel Simpson-Coyle, who will answer as many of your questions as possible."

Spence signalled to Fordyce to go ahead.

"Colonel, do you know where this man Oppenheim is at this moment in time?" The soldier asked everyone to sit down and began.

"Gentlemen, now the war was over, the OSS, the organisation which Oppenheim worked for, has been dissolved. All personnel have been transferred to a new body called the Central Intelligence Agency. All offences allegedly committed by OSS staff, other than those of violence, are now expunged."

Fordyce pressed.

"What about the attempted kidnap of American citizens?"

Simpson-Coyle carried on.

"I am reliably informed that, as the incident you refer to concerns only US citizens, it is a matter for the American authorities to pursue when the alleged victims and perpetrators return to the US."

Spence asked,

"What do you know about the CIA, colonel?"

The SOE man answered with startling honesty.

"Superintendent, I know enough to know that I do not want to know any more."

Menzies stood and said,

"Gentlemen, a decision has been taken at the highest level, which has resulted in the following order. We are all to forget about Operation Javelin and everyone involved in it."

He stood and, before leaving, announced,

"The war is over - now let's get on with the peace."

47

Finding Roots

Pat watched Mary and Jessica Cork talking as if they'd known each other for years. It was obvious the Buchanans and Charlie Rawlings were totally devoted to Jessica and her family and delighted to be part of the united Cork family. Then, as his gaze wandered to where his father and uncle were talking, a question came to mind. If they had had their way, none of the people in the room would have ever met. Surprisingly, he felt angry with them, which then became a sense of guilt. Pat forced himself to think of other people. The men he had fought beside and those who were lost. The women who had come into his life. The fighting in which he had killed strangers without a second thought. There was no regret or sorrow for words or deeds. Now, feeling more at ease, positives came to mind. Beginning with the people who would remain friends and the extraordinary people who had not survived but would always influence him. Best of all was the family coming together. His thoughts were broken by a familiar voice.

"You look miles away, commander. Dreaming of being back at sea with everyone calling you sir?"

Pat's reply reflected some of his train of thought.

"To be honest, Bill, I'm thinking that if it wasn't for the war, none of us would have met."

Then he posed a question.

"Bill, after what we've seen and done in the past five years of our lives, just how bad can what happened in a small village in Ireland be?"

After a pause, in a slightly angry tone, he stated,

"They had no right to keep the family apart."

Bill revealed a similar frame of mind.

"Well, let's push for answers. We'll ask them what happened."

A further brief silence followed until Bill added, more assuredly,

"If they won't tell us, we'll find out for ourselves. Ireland, West Cork and Dunmanway aren't that far away."

The party continued until midnight, when everybody went to bed. The next morning at breakfast, Buchanan announced.

"I want to thank Connor and Mary for their hospitality and kindness."

Then, looking at Charlie Rawlings, he continued,

"We have a ranch to run at home, and it's time we got back to doing just that." Tom Cork joined in with,

"You're right, Bill. I'll get started on booking passage home for everybody." Rawlings added,

"Make it as quick as possible."

He looked at Connor and then Mary.

"It's been great to meet everyone, but the vacation is over."

Connor agreed.

"Yes, we've had a good time, but, as you say, it's time to go back to work."

Pat and Bill sat in silence, both beginning to think their conversation the night before may be coming to fact.

Admiral Spenser's tone was brisk.

"Gentlemen, I have been ordered to disband the SOE with immediate effect." Simpson-Coyle opened a folder.

"There are a number of operatives who are subject to legally binding contracts. I need your permission to release them from all obligations."

Davies requested,

"Names, please, colonel."

Simpson-Coyle read out a short list finishing with,

"Erebus and Vali."

He took two sheets of paper from a folder and handed them to Odin who promptly tore up the contracts. Spenser went on,

"Gentlemen, I leave it to you to inform and demobilise the men under your command. Thank you; that will be all. Please carry on."

Lionel Morley sat at his desk in the E and C yard in Portsmouth, feeling both anxious and optimistic as he put down the phone. The company had been short-listed for a very large contract in London. The final decision would be made within twenty-four hours.

Davies called Sergeant Major Reilly and Sergeant Mullen to his office.

"Gentlemen, I have received orders. The SOE is to be shut down, so, any ideas what you are going to do?"

Reilly answered,

"Well, sir, as we discussed when I joined up, the reception in Ireland for men who deserted the Irish Army will not be too warm."

Mullen joined in.

"Same for me, so we've decided to stay in England for a while, then slip home and see how the land lies."

Davies handed both men their release papers, concluding the meeting with,

"Right, sign those, please and I'll keep an ear out for any likely work."

Since his arrival in the UK an officer from the RAF liaison department had been trying to address Peter Vogt's deep concerns.

"Wing commander, please tell me. Where is my family? Has my home been destroyed?"

The officer had some details of the man's wife and family along with the barest background information. Vogt provided a little more.

"My family have been resident in the same city for the last four hundred years."

The RAF officer's face turned pale when told that the family's home was in Dresden. He promised to make every effort to trace them.

Moen, too was preoccupied with getting home, desperately missing his family and Norway. Both were trying to rest as Commodore Strom approached and sat down in between the men's beds.

"Gentlemen, I have been ordered to bring you up to date on 'Operation Javelin.'"

Moen butted in.

"This sounds like one of those official announcements which turn out to be either warnings or orders."

Strom laughed weakly, then told them of the decision to shut down the SOE and eradicate Operation Javelin from any official records.

Moen demanded,

"What the hell does that mean?"

Strom was about to answer when Peter Vogt raised his hand.

"If I may, commodore?"

Strom didn't try to conceal his relief.

"Please do, sir."

The German raised himself on one elbow.

"My dear friend, what it means is that the operation to rescue us never happened, and that, in turn, means that the Von Brauns will never be investigated for their activities in Peenemunde."

He paused and, seeing Strom nodding, he continued.

"As they will not be investigated, they will be allowed into America where they will continue the work on rocket development."

All three men were silent as Moen and Vogt lay back until the big man raised himself on one elbow.

"Well, it was fun apart from the last bit. I've made some good friends and helped to kill a good few bastards."

Looking straight at Strom, he continued.

"But now I have to go home and support my family. It's the same for you, Peter. The Nazis could have taken everything I have for being in the resistance; burned down my house. God knows where my family is."

As his voice trailed off, Strom heard desperation and despair and started to worry that the big man might finally be overwhelmed by exhaustion and depression. At a loss about what to do, he decided to contact Bakken.

Vali was completing his report on the Norwegian involvement in C squad, SOE operations when he received Strom's message to call him. The lawyer quickly explained his concerns for Moen, and Bakken decided to contact Erebus. Leading on from the earlier meeting, Colonel Simpson-Coyle sent a message to Erebus asking him to report to the SOE HQ within forty-eight hours. Bakken contacted Simpson-Coyle and asked for a contact number for Lewis without explaining his concerns about Moen's welfare. The colonel used this opportunity to ask Bakken to attend the same meeting he had arranged with Erebus. Now both men sat in Simpson-Coyle's office. The colonel handed them both a glass of whiskey.

"Gentlemen, I now officially inform you that you are both demobilised with immediate effect and the SOE closed down. It falls to me, therefore, to thank you both for your tremendous contributions and officially release you from your military contracts."

He handed each man a sheet of paper which they duly signed. The colonel continued, almost pleasantly,

"Well, that's it. Good luck and goodbye to you both."

Erebus spoke up.

"Colonel, we may have problem, with our friend, Moen."

Simpson-Coyle's face showed concern as he prompted,

"Please explain, Mr Lewis."

The big man's state of mind was quickly outlined. Simpson-Coyle stood up and walked to a portrait hanging on the office wall, which, when removed, revealed a small wall safe. There was silence as the safe was opened, and a medium-sized velvet bag was placed on the desk between the three men.

"Gentlemen, we.....," he paused.

"....and I include Mr Moen in that 'we', have been involved in many covert operations – the most recent being Operation Javelin. There were a number of untraceable items which have come into our possession as a result of Javelin."

He tipped the bag upside down, and a substantial amount of solid gold coins poured onto the desk. Bakken and Lewis would swear later they saw the SOE colonel smile as he continued.

"These were taken from the enemy, so it seems only fair that, as Mr Moen's current situation is due to the activities of that enemy, he benefits from them." He gathered up the coins and handed them to Lewis, saying,

"On the precious metals market, these were valued at about twenty thousand pounds sterling. Tell Mr Moen he won't have to smuggle them into Norway as I believe he'll be travelling home with the Norwegian Navy."

As the men left, Simpson-Coyle opened a civil service internal mail envelope. The documents within came from the London Metropolitan Police and requested a recommendation and, if applicable, a positive reference for RUC Chief Superintendent Peters' application to join Special Branch. Simpson-Coyle reached a decision quickly and wrote that he considered the applicant unsuitable for Special Branch. The reasons being his handling of the Hartmann incident and general xenophobia, which made him utterly unable to objectively assess terrorist threats. Simpson-Coyle wrote declining to support Peters' application or give a favourable reference and was about to return the document endorsed with an SOE stamp - surnames were never used - when he recalled the name of a young detective sergeant who had impressed him immensely. The way Peters relied upon the officer was enough for Simpson-Coyle to suggest to the recruitment officer he consider RUC Detective Sergeant Graham Bagotfor transfer to the Metropolitan Police Force.

Davies watched Professor Williamson read a document which - once signed - would bind him to total secrecy about every day of the last three and half years of his life. In fact, to the 'profs' amazement, the exact number of days was stated. His liberal instincts came to the fore but so did realism. So much for being the 'conchie'? He had thrown himself into the war and had willingly planned and abetted the death of more than one human being. The thought made him shiver, but he assuaged his badly battered conscience by assuring himself that all operations that C squad and the SOE carried out were absolutely necessary. As an academic, he had learned a huge amount, and as he re-read the paper he was about to sign, he knew he could never disclose or publish any of it. As a man, he had made some tremendous friends and learned one or two dirty tricks. Davies spoke.

"Sorry about the secrecy, but some people in high places were both impressed and worried by the accuracy and perception of your reports on the political situations in the occupied countries."

The 'prof' signed the Official Secrets Act Addendum and shook Davies' hand.

"Brigadier, I'm going back to University College, London, where I belong." Professors Williamson's voice concealed his relief at returning to academic life. In his final days at SOE, he had begun to estimate the numbers of lives lost in Europe based on confidential data, and the figures were beyond comprehension. Now he just wanted to forget.

Having contacted Portsmouth, Pat was ordered to report to Admiral Hilliard within twenty-four hours. He was sitting on a train, making the journey for maybe the last time. The carriage was quiet as he pondered his future. There were no doubts about leaving the Royal Navy. Being arrested with Bill had convinced him that he'd had enough of military life. The idea of practising law was becoming more attractive. Maybe the 'prof' could help in getting him into a good college? As for the McBurney's' little boy, he had written two letters. The first to Dr Trimble asking him to pass the second on to the boy's guardians. It was an introduction and a brief history of his meeting with the boy's parents. There was no mention of his possible paternity claim. Pat decided he would also keep in touch with Sergeant Bagot. Then the immediate problem. The events in Dunmanway all those years ago. Still no explanation. That could not go on. Portsmouth came quickly, and Hilliard was polite but very business-like.

"Well, commander, it looks as if we're going to lose you rather more quickly than I had hoped."

He paused, then opened a file on his desk.

"I can have your demobilisation papers completed within four hours. The majority of Longbow's crew have already gone. Most couldn't get away quick enough."

Pat defended his shipmates.

"They were always civilians at heart. Now the war's over, they have lives to get on with."

Hilliard smiled.

"Just as you have, I imagine. Well, this time tomorrow, you will be Mr Pat Cork."

Again there was a short silence before Pat heard,

"There are a few of the ship's crew left aboard. Why don't you go and say goodbye?"

Within the hour, he was speaking with the redoubtable Constantine.

"Any ideas what you are going to do?"

The reply was, as usual, optimistically to the point.

"I'm thinking of starting a radio and electronic repair business, sir." Pat said.

"If you're in London, please call me at home. We'll have a drink." He handed Constantine a small slip of paper as they shook hands.

Then came Grimaldi, who, with great delight, told his captain about securing a position in a top London Hotel as concierge. Petty Officers Canavan and McNally were next. Sean Canavan's Donegal accent was as strong as ever when Pat asked him the same question.

"We'll be going home straight away. See how the fishing goes, and if it doesn't pay, we'll be back in London."

Pat found himself insisting,

"Please take my home phone number. Call if you think I can help."

McNally spoke.

"Righto, sir, will do,"

Then finally, Baker, and as they shook hands, Pat said,

"Good luck to you, chief, and thanks for all your help."

The urbane, tough cockney took his captain's hand and replied,

"Sir, if you're ever around Romford, give me a call. Maybe we could go to an Arsenal match."

Suddenly, apart from the shore patrol and Naval Police, Longbow, which had always been a throbbing, heaving, living entity, was empty and silent. Pat felt a shiver run down his spine and headed ashore. As he left the ship, Flags Bellamy waved, and both men headed for the officers' quarters and the bar. In the morning, Mr Pat Cork handed over his home phone number to Mr Nigel Bellamy at Portsmouth station as he said goodbye with the words,

"Keep in touch, Nigel, and whenever you are in London, give me a call."

The young man replied.

"Aye, aye, sir."

Both men laughed, and as the train pulled out of the station, the former naval commander headed for London and civilian life, knowing he would not miss the military life one bit.

All the reasons for fighting, which, after Norway, he had never questioned, were now gone. The men he had fought beside would get on with their lives without his help. Those who had died - well - there was nothing he could do for them. An entirely new set of priorities were now in his mind.

Back in London, the Cork house was buzzing with the news that the Texas side of the family would be going home in twelve days. Thomas Cork had booked passage for everyone. Bill Cork listened, slightly put out, as he was still a member of the US Army, which might have other ideas. Bill phoned Travers who, when told, contacted General Bradley's staff in London. Within an hour, he called Bill.

"Major, we are now under General Mallem's command and are to report to his office in London at nine o'clock tomorrow morning. I'll pick you up at eight."

The second piece of news came later in the day, when Connor announced that the company had secured a substantial contract with the Ministry of Public Works. Morley was delighted as he told Connor the news.

"Connor, we are going to need at least another thirty tradesmen and over one hundred general labourers.'"

Connor replied,

"Right, I'll start looking at this end and you use your military contacts. There's bound to be plenty of demobbed men looking for work now."

Pat walked in the door to be told of both events and decided to say nothing about being demobbed.

Moen and Peter Vogt were growing in strength and pleased to see Major Lewis and Strom walk into the ward. Once the matter of the gold was explained, Moen looked at his comrade and queried,

"Let me get this straight. This gold used to belong to the bastards?"

He turned to Vogt and added,

"Sorry, Peter."

Then Strom told Moen he would be going home within five days. The big man stood up and hugged Erebus, who, when he saw an RAF officer enter the ward, suggested,

"Why don't you get some fresh air, my friend?"

Strom, standing nearby, took the hint. He persuaded Moen to sit in a wheel-chair and pushed him out onto the grass. They left as the RAF officer spoke to Peter Vogt.

"Herr Vogt, despite extensive enquiries, we have been unable to locate any of your family in or around the city of Dresden."

He then gently pressed,

"I'm sorry to cause you further distress, but is there anywhere else in Germany they could have moved to?"

Vogt answered uncertainly,

"My mother had a brother in Bavaria - a small town named Wallgau, near the Austrian border. They may have moved there when I was arrested."

Again, the officer probed,

"Are you certain that is the name of the village, Her Vogt?"

Now clearly distressed, he answered,

"My memory is not what it used to be. The Nazis gave me a hard time."

The Wing Commander tried to calm Vogt.

"We have something to work on now, sir. Please rest, and we'll make enquiries." Once he and the RAF officer were out of Vogt's earshot, Charles Lewis quietly enquired.

"Why is it so difficult to find his family?"

The answer was delivered in a quiet clear voice.

"Major, the city of Dresden was subjected to an air raid comprising nearly one thousand bomber aircraft."

He paused, looking back at Vogt, and almost whispered,

"We have no idea how many civilians died - and no way of knowing who survived."

Travers and Bill Cork, as ordered, reported to General Bradley's office. Bradley's liaison officer for the US military repatriation programme in the UK, codenamed 'Magic Carpet', told them,

"Colonel Travers, Major Cork, I have orders to ship you both out on the first available transport."

Travers interrupted.

"Why so quickly?"

The reply was terse.

"Colonel, there are over one and a half million men trying to get home. It is simply first come, first served."

Bill asked,

"What sort of transport are we on?"

Again, the reply was short as the officer impatiently flicked through a clipboard.

"USS Arlington. Aircraft carrier."

He looked up and continued,

"You and six thousand other GIs. You sail the day after tomorrow."

Both engineers were clearly taken unawares, and Travers demanded.

"What options are there?"

The transportation officer's reply reflected his growing annoyance.

"If you're looking for options, speak to the general."

Bill answered for both.

"Please arrange that immediately."

Mallem kept them waiting about half an hour, then agreed to both men leaving the US Army within twenty-four hours. His final words being,

"Gentlemen, thank you for the immense contribution made to the war effort and good luck to you both."

He paused, then whispered fiercely,

"And keep an eye out for that son of a bitch, Oppenheim."

As they left the general's office, Bill asked,

"What do we do now?"

Travers answered as he hailed a taxi.

"We'll have a drink, and I know the perfect place."

Bill sat in the taxi, still confused but, in a way, relieved. At least one decision had been taken. The cab stopped at the Café Royale. As the waiter served the drinks, Travers asked,

"Bill, do you remember the last time we were here?"

He answered indirectly,

"We've been through an awful lot since."

Travers picked up on the point.

"Bill, the war is over. We've made it. How do you feel?"

Bill was perplexed by the question and said so.

"I feel there are more questions than answers."

Travers prompted,

"Go on, major, tell me what's on your mind."

Cork scoffed,

"Ranks don't count anymore. We're civilians now."

Travers retorted jovially,

"Yes, we are, no more 'colonel', so please stick to plain Travers."

Bill pressed,

"It sounds like you have something to hide."

Travers laughed.

"Maybe, Bill, maybe."

Cork returned to his original thought.

"What about you? Don't you have any questions or doubts about the War?"

Travers suggested,

"Bill, I believe anyone with a conscience will have questions about the war, and it will take time to find answers."

He suddenly became serious.

"But I think we have a more immediate concern. Remember what the general said about Oppenheim. He is not going to forget what we did to his little plan or what we know. If I were you, I'd stay on my toes in Texas or anywhere else in the US."

Bill became more positive.

"You're right, colonel. Let's deal with one problem at a time. There's nothing we can do about Oppenheim while we're over here."

He carried on with increasing assertiveness.

"I can't bring Mandy back or find out where the Von Brauns are."

Travers noticed Bill's eyes seem to brighten slightly as he finished in a firm voice.

"There is one question I can get an answer to, though. What happened between My dad and Uncle Con. If they won't tell me, I'll go to Dunmanway and find out."

Bill ordered another round of drinks and, for the first time in weeks, joined in a conversation about his future. The men left the café with Bill asking,

"Colonel, I'd be grateful if you didn't mention us being civilians for now. Is that Ok?"

Travers merely nodded his head. They returned to a celebratory atmosphere, just in time to hear an ebullient Connor suggest to his wife.

"Mary, Tom's family and friends will be going home soon. I think we should invite everyone who helped the boys and us during the war to a small party here before they all go their own way."

His wife readily agreed, as did all of the people from the Double B. Pat looked at Bill, who remained silent. Later they had a quiet word and agreed to say nothing of their demobilisation. In the living room, Jessica spoke.

"Tom, I want to see where Amanda died."

Looking at her husband and son, she continued,

"Bill, we owe at least that to her parents."

Bill quietly agreed,

"You're right Mum. We'll do that tomorrow."

Tom nodded his head, his face reflecting the sadness her death had brought. In their room later, Jessica asked,

"Tom, what will you do if Bill wants to know why you won't say what happened in Ireland."

Her husband's face showed his concern.

"I don't know Jessie. I really don't know."

His wife continued,

"He is going to ask sooner or later."

Thomas Cork remained silent.

Bill took his parents to see the places where he and Mandy had spent time together. In the park at Dollis Hill, Jessica and Tom stared open-mouthed at the devastation caused by the V2 rocket. The silence was unbroken as they walked past the debris of the Paxton's shop, now cordoned off with the rest of the bombed street. 'Danger' notices in vivid red had been nailed to the fence. Suddenly, Bill spoke.

"You asked to see where they died. Mandy and Mr Paxton."

They walked toward a fence surrounding an enormous crater. Bill continued,

"The last time I saw her was here. We spent my leave together, and then I went back to war and......," He paused again, drawing in fresh air before adding,

"....D-day. During which time, I discovered I had another family. I learned something else too. I'm not a loner. The first thing Mandy and I decided ...,"

He paused, staring at the bomb crater, then turned and spoke in a soft but firm voice.

"......was that we were going to get married when the war was over. On the Double B."

Jessica was now crying quietly as Tom asked,

"Where were you when she was killed?"

"I was on active service in Europe - just behind the front lines. Colonel Travers told me she was dead."

Then, in a matter-of-fact tone, he added,

"I went to see her before she was taken back home, then I went back to war."

At this point, his father suggested,

"Bill, I think it's time we all had something to eat. Your mother needs a break." Bill agreed.

"Yes, dad, you're right. Let's go into the West End. It's on the way to Aunty Mary's house."

Miraculously, a taxi appeared, and soon they were in a welcoming restaurant where his parents listened to Bill talk freely about Mandy and the war. As the day came to a close, Jessica and Tom felt better for having seen some of where Mandy had spent the last year of her life. Both were more at ease that when they spoke to her parents, they could say with honesty she had been happy and fulfilled. They all got back in time for dinner and were told the party was to be the following night. After dinner, Bill and Pat had a quiet word.

"Anything said about Ireland?"

Bill shook his head. Pat continued.

"Me neither."

The doorbell rang as Tom Cork sat in the front room of his brother's house and watched another group of servicemen appear. Two were introduced as officers in the Norwegian Navy. The others, who were of all nationalities, quickly filled the house with many accents. The lady of the house, assisted by her daughter and sister-in-law, made sure that everyone felt completely at home. Colonel Travers was in conversation with Catherine, expounding the many virtues of London as a centre of culture. Bill told everyone that the brandy had come from Churchill's personal store. Nigel Bellamy arrived with Franco, Forrestal, Sean Canavan and Fergus McNally, and they were soon followed by Cormac Reilly and Tomas Mullen, with Maiden Aunt and Professor Williamson. Buchanan entertained everybody with tales of the ranch in Texas. Tom watched in silence as Con mixed with all of these people with ease and was surprised and delighted to hear so many Irish accents. He watched and listened as his son approached the man who had been his mentor and CO for the previous three and a half years.

"Colonel, may I ask you a question?"

Travers nodded his head as he took another glass of red wine. Bill began.

"Colonel, something you said yesterday made me think. We've been through a lot together and so I think I can ask you this. I've always called you sir or colonel."

The other men involved in Operation Javelin quietened as Bill continued.

"On your dog tags, you have your name and just one initial, which is 'A'."

Travers replied,

"Well, Bill, I think you've earned the right to know. My daddy was from Texas, and my family is related to Colonel Travers, who died at The Alamo."

Bill butted in.

"No, sir, he couldn't have done that to you, surely?"

Travers replied,

"Yes, he did, Bill boy. He called me Alamo Travers."

He then laughed out loud, and everyone joined in.

Thomas's eye caught Pat Cork, in whom he saw so many reminders of his father. The straight back, same mannerisms and the easy way he mixed - as he was now doing with two men. Tom knew the taller man was called John Eldridge, as Bill had earlier spoken of him with great affection. The other - everyone just called 'Prof'. He moved a little closer to hear Pat say,

"I'd like to study law but don't have the formal academic qualifications to get into university, at least not this year, and I'm not getting any younger."

Eldridge replied encouragingly,

"My dear Patrick, I think commanding a Royal Navy warship is more than enough."

Williamson was slightly more downbeat as he took a business card out of his top pocket.

"I'm going back to UCL next week. Why don't you contact the master's office? They'll pass on a message."

He sipped his drink, then declared,

"Actually, Pat, I'll start an application for you at UCL."

Eldridge offered more support.

"Patrick, I will be at Balliol for the next month. Call me if you think I can help."

Tom left Pat and began mixing freely, at first with Cormac Reilly, until they were joined by Tomas Mullen and soon after, Sean Canavan and Fergus McNally. For the first time in years, Thomas Cork was surrounded by Irishmen and was thoroughly enjoying the experience. Bill appeared by his father's side and introduced Sir Geoffrey, Lady Lewis and their son Charles. The doorbell chimed again as Lionel Morley and his son arrived, along with Colonel Weir and Major Campion. The Scotsman announced he hoped that he would not upset anyone, but he had brought some real whisky in the form of a Scottish Single Malt. Selby Constantine had arrived with his girlfriend and offered to adjudicate in a taste test.

Lionel Morley met Cormac Reilly and Tomas Mullen and soon realised he was talking to men who were ideal for the new contract. Within twenty minutes, interviews were arranged. Morley later made a point of finding Connor and quietly said,

"I think I've found two very good supervisors for the new contract."

Connor questioned.

"How can you tell so quickly?"

Morley replied confidently,

"These men are regular army. I know their backgrounds, and they know mine. Believe me; they are ideal."

Connor nodded his agreement. The party went on well into the night then everybody said their goodbyes, leaving just the immediate family. Tom said to his brother,

"I don't know about you, Con, but I'm tired from talking. I'm off to bed. I could sleep for a week."

As he finished, his son and nephew approached. Bill began.

"Dad, Uncle Con. Pat and I have been talking."

Pat continued.

"Basically, we want to know what happened in Dunmanway, which made you split the family."

Connor's eyes bore into his brother's face, his words terse.

"Well, do we tell these men?"

Tom Cork stood and, as he started to leave, replied,

"What's the point? It was a long time ago. It's best forgotten."

Pat looked at his father.

"Well, dad, will you tell us?"

Connor asked.

"Why do you want to know? The family's together now."

Bill explained.

"Uncle Con, we've fought a war - a world war. Nothing that happened in Ireland can be as bad as the tragedy all of us have lived through."

He paused as Pat continued.

"Bill wants to know why he didn't meet his uncle and Aunty Mary for years, and so do I, and we think we have a right to know."

The rest of the family was now gathered in the drawing room. Rachel and Christopher stood transfixed as Jessica and Mary sat together on the sofa, both very calm. The Buchanans and Charlie Rawlings stood in silence. Pat sensed his father wanted to say more but was holding back, his look directed at his brother was clear, demanding an answer, but none came. Then Connor broke the silence.

"There's no point in telling anyone what happened. All you need to know is that Tom and I can never go back. Our land, our birthright, has gone because of what happened. We are not welcome in West Cork and never will be."

It was clear he was trying hard to control his temper.

"We're all together now, and that's all that matters. What happened between your Uncle Tom and me is our business and nobody else's."

Pat fired back,

"But it is our business because Bill, me and the family have a right to know why. If the war hadn't broken out, none of us would have known anything about each other."

Bill joined in.

"Neither of you will justify why you kept us apart for all this time." Pat kept up the pressure.

"You say you can never go back to West Cork - we want to know why."

Connor spoke.

"Pat, we were men of means with land and stock. Our family was highly respected in West Cork."

He seemed to be thinking back.

"Lads, the land had been in our family for many years since the end of the penal laws. Land is precious to Irish people since we've had to fight so hard to win back and keep what was always ours."

Tom moved toward his brother as he spoke.

"Pat, Bill, there were things done in Ireland at that time which were for freedom or just pure madness."

Pat demanded.

"Dad, why won't you go back? Why can't you go home?"

Connor answered reluctantly.

"What happened hurt a lot of people, some innocent, and caused terrible trouble for those left in Dunmanway and West Cork."

Tom carried on.

"Boys, we had to get out of Cork quickly, so we don't know how the people still there would treat us now. We just can't go back after more than twenty years." Connor then spoke.

"Bill, Pat, there are many more reasons for us to stay away than go back."

His voice seemed to quiver as he added,

"There is nothing for us to go back to. No land, no family, no respect, no friends. All gone because of one act of madness by……."

His voice trailed off as he sat down. There was silence for a short time then Mary Cork spoke.

"I think it's time we all got some sleep."

The morning after the party had been quiet, then Bill and Pat told everyone at breakfast they had been ordered back to SOE HQ for a final debrief. This was a lie, as they had decided to go to Dunmanway. Each was packing a small suitcase as Pat noticed his mother, aunt and Catherine coming upstairs. Almost simultaneously, he and Bill were gently confronted by the women. Mary began,

"Pat, where are you really going?"

Jessica repeated the question to Bill. The men looked at each other, and then Pat explained.

"We're going to Dunmanway to get the answers which we couldn't get last night."
Jessica continued her query.
"Are you going to tell your fathers?"
Pat answered,
"No, it's best they don't know for now."
Bill was slightly more aggressive.
"We'll tell them as much as they told us."
Mary kissed her son and nephew goodbye with the words.
"Have a good trip."
Jessica, having kissed both men, added,
"Enjoy Ireland but be careful."
Both men left quickly and quietly.
Jessica asked,
"Will they be alright?"
Catherine replied with confidence.
"Those two are scared of nothing."
Mary added assertively,
"No one is going to hurt those men in Ireland. It's their home."
Catherine probed.
"What are you going to say to your husbands?"
Mary spoke firmly.
"Nothing unless they ask."
Jessica nodded her head in agreement.

Detective Sergeant George Bagotsat thinking. During the war, he had been exempt from conscription due to the security needs of the convoy escort ships in Londonderry. His superior officer was convinced that all 'Taigs' were a threat to the war effort, and, as Derry had a large Catholic population, the need for good loyalist police officers was greater than sending fit men to war. He had spent five years listening to the loathsome rantings of Chief Superintendent Peters, and now that the war was over, he had had more than enough. Bago began to consider his future. As a single man, there was nothing keeping him in Ulster. He was a police officer first, and after, that an Irishman who had no time for fanatics on either side of the religious or political divide. Maybe a transfer to the Metropolitan Police in London or one of the Commonwealth countries, or maybe even New York. Then his phone rang, and he was soon on his way to Belfast for a meeting with the Assistant Chief Constable.

As the cousins walked toward the underground, Pat spoke.
"We need some information on Ireland, and there's a man I know who can supply it."

Charles Lewis took the phone call at home and suggested,

"Why don't you both come to my father's house and plan the trip properly? You could be on a ferry tomorrow and in Dunmanway the following day."

Pat agreed. He then called Sergeant Bagot, who, when told of the trip to Dunmanway, said,

"When you get to Dublin, give me a call."

In the Assistant Chief Constable's office, Sergeant Bagot assessed the man opposite. He was about fifty years of age, with a careworn lined face - ample proof that he was an experienced policeman.

"Well, Bagot, it would appear you have impressed someone with your work in Londonderry."

The young detective decided silence was the best policy as the ACC continued.

"We've had a request for you to be interviewed for a possible transfer to the Metropolitan Police, London."

The senior officer then gave more details of the transfer and promotion prospects. He finished with,

"You have ten days to make up your mind."

Bagot left the RUC HQ and headed for his family home in Belfast. The Bagots had moved to Ulster as part of the first plantation and now regarded themselves as Irish as anyone south of the border. Although Protestant, his parents had always believed that religion was an individual matter and had raised their family to follow a faith if they wanted to. Graham Bagot had two brothers and two sisters, all professional people who had all moved to the UK before the war and had flourished. This and other factors made the offer of a transfer more attractive by the hour. Pat Cork crossed his mind as he posed a question.

"Dad, do we have any relatives in the South?"

His father, a solicitor, replied,

"Well, my boy, we had a branch of the family that lived in Cork many years ago, but we haven't kept in touch. It all ended badly. They moved out in 1919. Philip Bagot, I believe, was his name, and his son, George. Both were shot by the IRA in a place called Bandon, or close to it."

He paused as he looked at his son.

"Why do you ask?"

The younger Bagot replied with a question.

"Nothing really, dad. Were they close to us?"

"Philip Bagot was my first cousin. Once he died, no one in the family raised the matter again."

There was no reply as he handed his son a glass of Bushmills with the words, "Please understand, those were terrifying times all over Ireland."

Both men remained silent until Bagot senior asked,

"Now, my boy, how long will you be staying? Your mother and I don't see anywhere near enough of you."

The visit did not last long as Bagot, his curiosity aroused, was back at his desk in Londonderry within two days. Peters, who was absent, had left orders for him to 'organise' a number of files and documents which were on the superintendent's desk. The phone rang, and when the sergeant answered, he was told there was a call for him from a Mr Pat Cork. When finished, Bagot knew Pat Cork's plan and the reason why he was heading for West Cork. The Ulsterman began to look through Superintendent Peters' files and was surprised to find a number headed 'Royal Irish Constabulary,' which were secured with a wax seal.

The ferry docked, and Pat and Bill were dropped off by Charles Lewis at the garage near the docks, where a car - from the man who had provided a vehicle for Operation Prodigal- was waiting. The advice from Geoffrey Lewis had been succinct.

"Buy petrol when you get the chance, and take your time driving to Cork. You'll both be surprised at how much people will welcome you and remember - you're both going home."

Pat had asked about hotels in Dunmanway.

"There are plenty of hotels in West Cork - you won't have any problems." Charles had been listening and decided to go to Kilkenny and the house which his beloved Uncle Peter had left him

"Don't worry, gentlemen. I'll get you to the ferry to Dublin, and my father will arrange transport after that." All had gone to plan as they were now driving south with ten days left before Bill sailed for America. Charles was on his way to Kilkenny. Pat turned to Bill and said,

"Bill, I've just realised how little I know about this country."

His cousin agreed.

"That makes two of us."

Pat pulled into a hotel car park, saying,

"I need to make a phone call, and then we can get something to eat."

Bill grabbed a map replying,

"I'll work out a route and mileage."

Sergeant Bagot's phone rang as he was looking at the cover of a file marked West Cork 1914 to 1921. Bagot listened as Pat explained their current location. In reply, he asked Pat to clarify a point made in the earlier call.

"Pat, you did say you were going to Dunmanway in West Cork?"

The reply confirmed this. Bagot told him,

"Pat, I'm looking at some of Superintendent Peters' files now. One covers West Cork."

He paused, trying to think.

"Listen, Pat, this file might be of help to you. I'll see if I can get a look at it, but you know what Peters is like. Call me here tomorrow."

At the yard in Portsmouth, Lionel Morley had finished the day's paperwork and was looking forward to interviewing Cormac Reilly and Tomas Mullen. Both men were on time, as was Connor Cork, who had travelled from London. The interview was held in what was the late Peter English's office. The conversation was to the point as Morley fleshed out the details he had gathered at the recent party. Connor sat silently as the former military men conversed in a relaxed informed manner. He heard enough to know that the two men were highly knowledgeable and experienced in all aspects of labour management.

Finally, Morley asked the two former soldiers to wait outside for a minute.

"Well, Connor, what do you think?"

Connor was very pleased with what he had heard and said so, adding,

"See if they are happy to accept what we are offering. If so, there's no reason not to go ahead."

Reilly was called in and made an offer which he accepted immediately. Tomas Mullen was equally quick to accept, and within an hour, terms and conditions had been finalised. The new employees were given a start date and then left. Connor looked Morley in the eye as he stated,

"You said to me once you would only move into Peter's office when you earned the right to." Then shook his hand, saying.

"Well, you just have."

Lionel Morley went home a very satisfied man.

The Cork household had become accustomed to Tomas Cork and his family going home. Connor was very busy with the new contract, and Thomas was helping Charlie Rawlings with the detail of the cattle contract. Despite all being occupied, everyone sat down to evening dinner. Mary and Jessica Cork, along with Catherine Buchanan, had kept their secret but knew it was just a matter of time. Suddenly Tom looked up from his plate.

"It's been two days. I'm no soldier, but even I know debriefing can't take that long."

The women had agreed that if a question was asked, they would tell their husbands everything. Mary explained where the boys were and why.

Connor's face was worried and resigned as he said,

"I'm not surprised. We should know the men we raised."

Tom asked in a desperate voice.

"What do we do now?"

His brother's face lightened as he said.

"We go after them."

Buchanan spoke.

"I'll go with you."

Catherine Buchanan added.

"No, Bill. We'll go. I've heard so much about Cork I want to see it."

Connor was on the phone to Morley, asking him to call in some favours. The former colonel called back in an hour, saying,

"The quickest ferry to Belfast is tomorrow from Liverpool/Birkenhead, and I can arrange passage for a car and four people."

Connor replied,

"Please book the passage now, Lionel."

He returned to the living room and said,

"Tom, Bill and Catherine, pack a bag. We're leaving for Liverpool now."

The trip to Liverpool was interesting for the Buchanans as Connor and Thomas began to talk about Dunmanway. The ferry journey was pleasant, the vessel having an excellent restaurant. Tom was openly concerned about his son, yet Catherine and her husband saw that Connor was increasingly relaxed. In a moment when Tom had been elsewhere, she asked Connor,

"Connor, you don't seem too worried about the boys."

Connor replied,

"Catherine, no one's going to say anything to the lads. All those people in Dunmanway will see are two sons of Irishmen coming home. *We* made trouble for so many people - not them. Once people find out who they are, they'll be welcomed with open arms."

In no time, the car was leaving Belfast docks, each passenger having shown their passports. As per standard practice, the names of all non-Irish resident passengers entering Northern Ireland ports were collected and delivered to Chief Superintendent Peters' office in Derry. The cards arrived just as Peters, not a happy man, had returned to his office. His application for a transfer to the Metropolitan Police Force, Special Branch had been forwarded weeks earlier, but there was no reply when he left Belfast. He was unaware that the Assistant Chief Constable had received the documentation from Colonel Simpson-Coyle and was now considering if Peters had any future as a policeman in Ulster, let alone London. The ACC couldn't ignore the report of a senior British Intelligence Officer, even one he had never heard of or met.

Now in Derry, in the operations office, Peters looked through the names on the entry cards. Three stood out, and his temper rose as he read the details of Thomas Cork and William and Catherine Buchanan. The fourth passenger was a man with both British and Irish nationality. His name was Connor Cork, and he owned the expensive car in which all four people were travelling. Peters knew the ferry sailing times by heart. The men would be in his jurisdiction for some time, he yelled for Bagot. The sergeant was told to order all units to find and arrest the men in the British-registered car owned by Connor Cork. Bagot made up his mind there and then to accept the move to the 'Met.' He then called the Assistant Chief Constable in Belfast. Bagot was brief, and when finished, the ACC ordered,

"Sergeant, get me all the information you can on the passengers in that car and do nothing until I get to Londonderry.

They were heading out of Dublin as Bill, his head in a map and compass in hand, asked,

"What are the road signs like here?"

Pat was beginning to feel at home and replied,

"Listen, forget your route and mileage plan."

Bill looked surprised.

"So, how do we find Dunmanway?"

Pat laughed.

"We'll just ask. That's how normal people do it."

48

Yesterday and Today

Pat drove further south and, becoming more relaxed, voiced a thought. "Any doubts about what we're doing?"

There was silence for a moment.

"Well, we're in Ireland, so there's no turning back. So, we'll see it through to the end - whatever that might bring."

Pat was going to ask Bill about the tribunal until he heard,

"Pat, this country is so beautiful."

He decided, 'maybe another time.'

Peters became agitated when told by an officer that the Assistant Chief Constable had been in the RUC Londonderry HQ for some time. He began to lose control when, having ordered the same constable to find Sergeant Bagot, was told that he was briefing the ACC. A few minutes later, Bagot appeared and informed Peters that the Assistant Chief Constable wanted him in his office immediately, where he was ordered to sit. Bagot was told to remain and silently surveyed the scene. Peters was highly agitated and irascible. The ACC, the younger of the two senior officers with dark brown hair and a heavier build, spoke with calm authority.

"Chief Superintendent, I have been informed that you have issued an order for a number of men to be arrested. Sergeant Bagot has supplied me with the individuals' names and backgrounds."

Peters glowered at Bagot. He was about to reply, but the ACC cut across him.

"The first man is Mr William Buchanan and owner of the Double B Ranch - one the biggest ranches in Texas. He is accompanied by his wife, Catherine, both US citizens. The second suspect is Mr Thomas Cork. He is also a US citizen and a substantial shareholder in the same ranch which has been contracted to supply top quality breeding stock to the UK and Europe."

Peters tried to speak but was told forcibly,

"Please be silent."

The ACC continued.

"Now the third suspected criminal, Mr Connor Cork, is the holder of joint Irish and British citizenship. He is the owner of a large and successful UK construction company. The gentleman has full clearance from the British Security Services, having been involved in secret war work."

Peters' face was now blood red as he spluttered,

"I suspect two of these men of committing murder."

The senior officer demanded,

"Where and when did this alleged crime take place?"

Peters got halfway through the history of the murders of Philip and George Bagot when the ACC raised a hand, his face reflecting growing anger.

"Mr Peters, I've heard enough. You have ordered the arrest of a number of highly respectable, successful people because you suspect them of possible involvement in a crime committed in 1919 in an independent state where you have no jurisdiction."

With eyes fixed on Peters, the ACC did not notice the sergeant's face harden, having heard some more of the details of the Bagots' murder. The ACC carried on.

"Now, Mr Peters, listen very carefully. I've heard from London. Your application to join the Special Branch has been refused."

Peters' eyes were a mixture of outrage and disbelief as he demanded,

"I want to speak to the Commissioner of the Metropolitan Police - now."

The answer was blunt.

"That's impossible - and don't demand an explanation because none will be given."

The RUC Assistant Chief Constable was now facing a near-hysterical Chief Superintendent Peters as he continued.

"There are other matters. Detective Sergeant Bagot has been asked to attend a selection board. I have given him my support and will recommend that he be transferred to the London Metropolitan Police Force."

There was silence for a few seconds, and then Peters stormed out of the room. The ACC looked at Bagot.

"Sergeant, please gather up all of Mr Peters' files. Those that are pertinent to ongoing RUC cases pass to my staff officer. Anything else, please throw away."

He paused.

"But first, find Mr Peters and tell him I have not finished the meeting."

Before Bagot could obey, there was a knock on the office door.

"Yes, sergeant."

The man's tone was urgent.

"Sir, I think you should come with me straight away. Mr Peters is not too well." All three men went to an interview room where Chief Superintendent Peters was lying on the floor. Saliva just beginning to dribble from the left-hand side of his mouth. The policemen, all experienced first aiders, recognised the first signs of a stroke. An ambulance was called, and after Peters was taken to hospital, the ACC summed up.

"There's nothing more to be done for Mr Peters until we get the hospital report. Sergeant, carry on, please."

Bagot did so. All files relevant to the RUC were given to the ACC's aide. The rest he put into his car and examined them at home later.

A cursory examination revealed the majority were records of RIC activity in Munster from 1914 to 1921. The one mentioned earlier to Pat Cork, he read carefully. The file related to West Cork specifically and covered matters pertinent to his family and the Corks. The ACC had told him to throw the files away but hadn't said where or when. Next morning, he returned to the police station and spoke to the ACC by phone to request five days leave. This was granted and Bagot was updated on the condition of his boss.

"Sergeant, Mr Peters will be retired on medical grounds. He has suffered a major stroke which has paralysed the left-hand side of his body. The prognosis is 'no prospect of recovery.'"

Then came an interesting aside from the ACC.

"I always had my doubts about some of these former RIC men from the South. They take everything so personally. Have a good leave, sergeant."

Bagot wondered how Peters would react to being referred to as 'a man from the South.'

Graham Bagot located Dunmanway on a map of Ireland and headed south to see the scene of his relatives' murder. As the RUC officer drove through the Free State, Mr Peters was moved to a nursing home to receive twenty-four hour care. His mind was functioning, but his bodily functions and speech were irretrievably impaired.

Connor and Thomas Cork, along with the Buchanans, went through the border crossing posts after a cursory passport and vehicle check. The brothers were unaware of the existence or current condition of the man who, a few hours before, had ordered their arrests and many years ago had intended to hang both of them. Connor increased speed toward Dublin, then Cork, Bandon and finally Dunmanway - and Bill and Pat.

Oppenheim sat, fuming, in the CIA HQ at Langley. He had delivered the Von Brauns, or the 'Browns' as they were now known. Now they had been moved to a secret location. He had not been briefed where, and every enquiry made was greeted with silence. All around him, younger men were being promoted and transferred to strategic stations all over the world, while he was being fobbed off with one dead-end job after another. His angry bitterness grew until, once again, he began to lose all reason and instinct of self-preservation. He forgot all he had experienced when dealing with the military and the British Intelligence Services.

The newly confirmed Director of the CIA looked in horror at a small news item on page four of the Washington Post. The one-line title read, 'Rumours of Nazi rocket scientists working in the US.'

He immediately sent his assistant to find Oppenheim.

"Well, do you have any ideas as to where this might have come from?" Oppenheim answered the director.

"No, but give me some time, and I'll find out."

The director reluctantly agreed. Oppenheim went away pleased. He had no idea where the article originated and didn't care. This was his opportunity to show he was the only one who could keep the Von Brauns under wraps. Within two days, Oppenheim produced a report placing the blame firmly on the British Intelligences Services' lack of security in the UK. Citing his ability to spirit the Von Brauns out of the base as a prime example. Further, he stated that the origin of the article was Major William Cork, who, with the assistance of his cousin Commander Patrick Cork, had sent information on the Von Brauns to his family in Texas. They, in turn, passed the information on to local journalists - the motivation being revenge for the death of Major Cork's girlfriend caused by a V2 weapon. The director found the case put forward by Oppenheim feasible, if not wholly convincing, and ordered the Justice Department to draw up subpoenas for the Corks to appear before a grand jury. US Marshalls were also instructed to apply for arrest warrants for the Corks. Both documents to be served immediately upon their return to the US. The director, however, was a cautious man and forwarded Oppenheim's report to the CIA station chief in London with orders to contact the British for their views.

Admiral Menzies and Spenser, along with Brigadier Davies, sat with Colonel Simpson-Coyle. He sensed an air of urgency amongst the men.

"Well, colonel, it seems we have not heard the last of our friend Oppenheim." Simpson-Coyle listened as the allegations made by the CIA man were explained. Spenser continued,

"Now, the allegation that our security is not airtight is possibly very damaging. This and the accusations against former British Servicemen must be investigated."

Menzies then took over.

"Colonel, we need to deal with this man once and for all. Can you do this?" Simpson-Coyle decided to bargain.

"Sirs, I will deal with Oppenheim, as you say, 'once and for all.'"

Then, surprising everyone, he raised his voice.

"There is a way, sir, but please understand then I am out."

Menzies spoke up.

"Colonel, you have my word that you will be granted retirement as soon as this issue is dealt with satisfactorily."

Simpson-Coyle glanced at Davies, a man he had come to respect, who confirmed the admiral's statement with an imperceptible nod. Assured he spoke.

"Gentlemen, it will be."

Now in the 'Free State,' Connor and his companions were nearing Dublin, where they would spend the night. The Buchanans watched as the brothers talked for a while; then, as a landmark or feature stirred a memory, both would fall silent. The conversation would then start again, both becoming increasingly relaxed and talkative. Catherine noticed how their Irish accents became increasingly marked.

After taking Pat and Bill to Dublin, Charles Lewis headed for his home in Kilkenny. Sir Geoffrey and lady Felicity were quietly pleased that their son was reacquainting himself with what they regarded as one of the most beautiful places on earth. Sir Geoffrey, however, was aware that feelings against the British still ran high in certain sections of Irish society and sent a message to Pearse Brogan about Charles' presence, also mentioning the trip being made by the Corks.

The new landlord had just arrived when the doorbell rang. Brogan instantly recognised the man from Operation Prodigal but said nothing other than to introduce himself. Lewis asked him in. The men chatted until Brogan got to the point.

"Well, Mr Lewis, it is good to see you here and safe and sound after the war. Are you here for long?"

Lewis replied.

"Please call me Charles. I believe you and my father have been acquaintances for some time."

Brogan laughed inwardly, thinking,

'He's as good as his father at saying all the right things and giving away nothing.'

He probed,

"Yes, indeed, some considerable time. Your father let me know about the other men who are in Cork."

Lewis replied with candour as he explained the purpose of the Corks' trip and their tight schedule. He was surprised as Brogan tensed slightly.

"Is there something wrong, Mr Brogan?"

Brogan replied,

"Please call me Pearse. I am a Cork man - maybe I could help your friends get answers quickly."

Lewis mused,

"Well, they'd need someone to introduce them, and I've never been that far southwest."

Brogan's face lightened as he enquired,

"Charles, how do you fancy a few days in West Cork?"

Lewis, though surprised, readily agreed.

"Well, this house needs to be opened up, but that can wait a little longer."

He looked at the man opposite and laughed.

"We'll take my car."

Pat and Bill drove through Cork City and headed for Bandon and the truth about their fathers' past lives. The men in question, with Bill and Catherine Buchanan, were now leaving Dublin and driving southwest to Cork to open a floodgate of memories.

Donal Carthy had spent most of his life in West Cork, but time in London and New York on legal business had considerably broadened his outlook on life. Approaching his seventieth year, his once thick jet-black hair, now thinner and grey at the edges brought a dignified air to his body, which was slightly stooped and rather lighter than in his youth. Carthy's eyes were still shining bright, reflecting a mind as sharp as the day he qualified as a solicitor forty-five years earlier.

He watched as two young men walked into the Parkway Hotel in Dunmanway, his acute hearing picking up both English and American accents.

Pat Cork had driven all the way from Dublin, Bill finding the roads in Ireland too narrow for his liking. Cork City, then Bandon and suddenly Dunmanway had appeared out of nowhere. The square was small, and after one question, a man gently directed them to the Parkway Hotel. Soon after, the car was parked and having checked in. The receptionist told them there was dinner available all day. As Donal Carthy sat and listened, his mind returned to 1919. He remembered a terrible incident which had forced two brothers to leave the country. Now, with every fibre of his being, he was convinced these men were connected to those brothers and that incident. Sons perhaps? His heart rate increased. The names given were partial confirmation. Patrick Cork and William Cork. One English, one American. The essence of Irish emigration. For one fleeting second, he was about to call out, to draw back the years, to shout their names in a joyous welcome home. Then his innate legal caution regained control, and he sat to wait for his daily pot of tea and a scone. He decided to say nothing for now, just wait and watch. Both young men began to eat and did so heartily. A father himself, it was good to see young people eat well. He knew their faces and now their names, as he had known their fathers in the good times and those terrible days after the killing of Philip and George Bagot. He'd warned Michael Collins that no amount of lawyers would guarantee the Corks - especially Thomas - a fair trial. The decision was made. Thomas Cork, an impulsive passionate man - and

Carthy's client when trading fine horses and prime cattle - had to run for his life. His brother was different, cooler, more collected. Carthy's chest filled with pride, recalling standing by Connor's side when he challenged the RIC in Bandon to charge him. Then looking after his mother until the sale of the farm – and the sadness at the final goodbye to Connor, his mother and sisters. The Corks gone from their home forever - or so he had thought, but now things seemed to be different. He sat and watched the future of the family in front of him and silently rejoiced. Then emotion took over.

The young men were clearly enjoying their meals as Carthy approached their table.

"Good day, gentlemen. Forgive me for eavesdropping, but I heard your names. Would I be correct in saying I am addressing two men of the Cork family?"

Bill looked a little surprised. Pat simply smiled as he stood up and shook the solicitor's hand.

"You are correct, sir."

He introduced himself, and then Bill stood and did the same. Pat said, "please join us if you wish."

Carthy nodded as he sat and began talking about the town and then broached the subject uppermost on his mind.

"May I ask what brings you to Dunmanway?"

Pat answered,

"We've come here to find out more about our family, who originally came from Dunmanway."

Carthy asked right out,

"Would I be right in saying your fathers are Connor and Thomas Cork?"

Pat looked at Bill, who nodded.

"Yes, Connor is my father."

Bill spoke.

"Thomas Cork is my father."

Carthy raised his hand.

"Gentlemen, would you be offended if I offered you both a drink?"

Bill, now half smiling, replied,

"Not at all."

The solicitor motioned to the lady behind the bar, who nodded. He asked passionately,

"How are your fathers?"

As three whiskeys arrived, Pat told Carthy of his father and mother and a little of their life in London. As Bill began to recount the story of his side of the family, Pat signalled for three more whiskeys, and they sat and talked for what seemed a short time. But it was actually over two hours, during which the whiskey kept coming. Finally, Pat asked about the Cork farm. The solicitor looked at his watch, then suggested,

"Gentlemen, I have a few things to do first thing tomorrow. I'll see you here about ten o'clock and show you all I can."

In London, Lionel Morley with Cormac Reilly and Tomas Mullen, were recruiting for the new contract. When Connor had announced that he was going to Ireland, Morley's reaction was one of astonished trepidation until he watched his two new supervisors take the news in their stride. They drew up a plan for the recruitment of men reinforced by a cogent comment from Tomas Mullen.

"That's why the man took us on, to find the best labour. It's our job, not his."

After that, Morley relaxed, and so far, things were going well as Reilly and Mullen used their contacts in the military and the GAA in London to employ quality men.

Their absent employer, meanwhile, was booking into the Munster Arms Hotel in Bandon, West Cork. He had driven hard all day, and as the sun went down, he was looking forward to a good meal and then a walk around the town. In the morning, they would go to Dunmanway and home. Fifteen minutes after the Corks and Buchanans had gone to their rooms, the phone in the hotel reception rang. The conversation was short. Ten minutes after that, a young RUC Officer was quietly booked into the hotel. Graham Bagot had notified the Gardaí in Bandon that he was in the area on leave. Initially, the local police were apprehensive; there were still a few idiots around with daft and dangerous ideas. Once Bagot identified himself and the reason for his visit, everyone relaxed. One Gardaí even welcomed him and added,

"Jesus, we all do the same dirty job."

The Royal Norwegian Navy ship, Norskall, steamed on a northerly heading toward Oslo. Moen, standing next to Strom, Larsen and Bakken, tried to control his emotions. Arrangements had been made to bring his family to the harbour, so it was just a matter of hours before they were reunited. He tried to remain calm. There was so much to look forward to. Moen thought of the gold given to him, which would make life so much easier. No more fear, no more occupation, no more anger and no more 'bastards.' For him, it was over. Larsen, trying not to feel guilty for being alive and unscathed, was overjoyed at the prospect of going home. For how long - he did not know. His technical responsibilities and experience with the Royal Navy had made him a leading man in the field of electronics. During the brief period spent in London after the German surrender, he had received many offers of work all over Britain and Europe. Bakken was looking forward to seeing his parents. His ex-wife had sent a message through them wishing him well. Maybe he should make contact with her. Now that the war was over, things might be different, but first, he had to give evidence at the trial of a man named Quisling. After that - who knew?

Strom stood and observed all the men who had seen active service. During the tribunal, he learned of some of that action and found it hard not to be effuse in his praise of them all. Now, a civilian lawyer again, he had just received his first peacetime brief - to defend Quisling, who had been charged with High Treason against the people of Norway. Strom had told Bakken and Larsen of the brief. Both had voiced their opinions. Lars almost ordered,

"He must get a fair trial."

Bakken was equally clear.

"We are a civilised people. We will not descend to the level of the Nazis. You must do your best."

Strom, now standing with his countrymen, had never felt so privileged or proud. The ship sailed on as the sun sank, and all of the men returned to their cabins.

The Parkway Hotel in Dunmanway had two men in the bar who had progressed from Whiskey to Guinness, which was being drunk very slowly. Donal Carthy had left. A question came to Pat's mind.

"Bill, there's one thing I need to know now."

Bill, still peering into his pint glass, said,

"Go ahead."

Pat did so in a fierce whisper.

"What the hell were you playing at with the weapons and hand grenades at SOE HQ?"

He waited for a moment before continuing, his voice angry and incredulous.

"That nearly got us twenty years."

Bill's voice was non-committal.

"I've given that a lot of thought."

Pat fired back,

"Well, please enlighten me with the product of all that effort."

His cousin leaned back in his chair and began.

"Pat, I was so angry and bitter when I realised the Von Brauns were going to get away with, not alone killing Mandy, but everything else. Christ, I had to do something to stay sane."

He paused.

"I am a trained covert operations expert, so I thought, why not use it to my advantage? I could still do them some damage."

He was about to speak when Pat butted in.

"What the hell do you mean by damage?"

Bill leaned forward.

"The first thing I wanted to do was to kill them and Oppenheim, but there was no way of getting away with murder – not on the SOE base anyway."

Pat began to see the real Bill Cork again as he urged,

"Go on."

"I'd watched both of them from when we took them out of Peenemunde. The older brother is as hard as nails, but the baby rocket-maker is a total two-legged invertebrate."

He paused again.

"I thought I'd terrify him. Every time the little bastard opened his luggage or briefcase or desk drawer: even his laundry, he'd find a bullet or a hand grenade or dummy bomb. When he went for a walk in the grounds, there would be an explosion near him. My plan was to push the twisted little bastard over the edge, cause a nervous breakdown or heart attack or, better yet, suicide."

Pat decided to let Bill talk.

"I wanted him to know that he could be got at - even in America, he was never going to be safe."

Bill paused then, in a steely voice, added,

"Never!"

He continued.

"As for getting caught, how could they pin it on me? That base was full of men and women trained just as well as me."

Pat was now inquisitive.

"So what went wrong?"

Bill spoke in a matter-of-fact manner.

"I never expected you bloody Brits to be so efficient. Jesus, the Redcaps searched every military base in the country in three days."

His cousin's face relaxed.

"Well, I suppose it all worked out for the best in the end." He paused and recalled General Mallem's parting words.

"Except for our mutual friend Oppenheim."

They were silent until another officer's words prompted Pat to say.

"Bill, I shouldn't worry about Oppenheim. I have it on good authority that he will be dealt with."

Pat and Bill finished a solid breakfast just before Donal Carthy arrived and joined them for a cup of tea. The conversation quickly turned to the history of the Cork family. Carthy made his position clear.

"Gentlemen, I believe the best way forward is to show you where your fathers were born and raised. Any questions you may have after that, I will try to answer."

The cousins nodded their agreement, and all three headed for the car park.

Connor, Tom and the Buchanans had left Bandon early and were very close to Dunmanway, the journey bringing back memories for both brothers. Tom remained silent for the whole trip. The town was soon in sight, and within minutes they were on the road to what used to be their home. Buchanan spoke to his wife quietly.

"Catherine, I can see why men and women would fight for this land. It is surely beautiful and rich. Look at the green countryside."

Catherine just nodded. She watched the road ahead and saw three men get out of a car.

Donal Carthy explained,

"This is the farm where your fathers were born. As you can see, it has not been worked for a while."

He continued in a sad voice.

"It was sold by Connor Cork to a farmer who then sold it on to a Protestant family, who were never very happy here, and moved away from the land after what we call the 'Civil War.'"

Neither Pat nor Bill spoke as they looked at the fields in front of them. The rushes had overgrown the grass, the ditches and hedges were unkempt and briar ridden. The rancher in Bill came to the fore.

"Those fields would need to be cleaned up if you want to run cattle."

Pat asked,

"Mr Carthy, can you tell us why our family left?"

The solicitor's face darkened. He was about to answer when, suddenly, the sound of a car engine caused him to look toward the road from town. Carthy mused.

"Unusual to see English number plates around here."

Bill, still gazing into the fields, remarked,

"I think I can see the remnants of a cottage and a bigger house off to the left and further back from the road."

Pat, now standing beside the solicitor, recognised his father's car instantly.

"Well, Mr Carthy, if you can't tell us, someone in that car will."

Connor's heart was racing. Tom was deep in thought; neither spoke. Catherine Buchanan, looking straight ahead, broke the silence as she whispered in her husband's ear.

"Bill, it's the boys."

Buchanan, whose eyes, trained for years on the vast expanses of the Double B, were as acute as his wife's, replied,

"Yes, honey, it is them, and I guess now we're all going to find out what happened."

The English car came to a halt, and Donal Carthy immediately recognised the men who stepped from it. He slowly walked toward them.

Charles Lewis and Pearse Brogan stopped briefly in Bandon for petrol. The journey had passed quickly after Brogan had told Charles of his involvement in Operation Prodigal. Both men had then relaxed and talked freely about their backgrounds and what had brought them both to this point in their lives. Lewis asked,

"The men who were arrested, Pearse? What happened to them?"

Brogan answered,

"Both men were convicted of offences against the Irish State and under emergency legislation were sentenced to death."

Lewis remembered his Uncle Peter and asked,

"Will the sentences be carried out?"

The general replied,

"I am a soldier, not a politician. What happens to them is now out of my hands." There was silence for a while then Brogan continued.

"The war is over now, and that emergency legislation will soon be repealed. Since the context has changed, I hope the sentences will be commuted, but, I repeat, it's out of my hands."

Lewis suddenly thought of a question.

"Do those men have much support in the country, Pearse?"

Brogan smiled.

"Charles, there are a few fanatics who will always be looking to cause trouble. They will back the men who are under sentence regardless of the damage done." Charles knew enough about personal vendettas to leave the matter there. As the car pulled out of Bandon and onto the Dunmanway road, a phone call was made back at the garage.

"Hello."

The caller spoke.

"Your man who arrested Doyle is heading for Dunmanway. He'll be there in about an hour."

The recipient questioned.

"How many men does he have with him?"

The reply was as terse as it was inaccurate.

"There is no escort, just some English fella."

There was silence then the caller added,

"Driving an English car. Looked and sounded like a tourist."

The man on the other end of the line said,

"We'll find out how long Brogan's in Dunmanway."

Again there was silence until,

"Let the boys know what's happening."

The line went dead. The caller spoke under his breath.

"Let the boys know. Who's he kidding; there's only three of us. Once the Allies won the war, the rest of them gave up."

He spat out the end of the sentence.

"Jesus, you can't rely on the Germans for anything."

Mary and Jessica Cork were in Dollis Hill looking at the wreckage of the Corks' home. Both were fighting back tears as Mary recalled so much happiness. Jessica - who had become profoundly fond of her sister-in-law - shared her pain and listened as Mary announced in a quiet, firm voice,

"When the boys come back, I'll tell Con I want to rebuild the house."

Jessica put her arm around Mary and added,

"They have eight days before we sail."

Mary replied,

"I wonder how things are going."

Connor stepped down from the car, then opened the door to allow Catherine and Buchanan to join him. Tom came round from the passenger side, and all four walked over to Bill and Pat. As Donal Carthy stood and watched the men approaching, he heard, in an English accent,

"Well, Mr Carthy, would you like me to introduce you to my father and uncle?"

The offer was unnecessary. Connor walked straight to Carthy, who greeted the brothers with the words,

"Welcome home, gentlemen, and, if I may say so, you both look none the worse for wear."

Connor's eyes glowed as he replied,

"Tell me, my friend, are there any warrants out for me or my brother?"

Carthy drew himself to his full height of just over six feet and replied with defiant joviality,

"Well, Connor Cork, if there are, we'll fight them in the highest court in the land."

The old man couldn't resist an urge to hug both men, and having embraced Connor, he greeted Thomas with an equal show of affection, then continued,

"To answer your earlier question in detail...."

He gazed into Tom's face.

"....there is nothing but a welcome for you here now."

Thomas squeezed Carthy's hand fiercely.

"Does that mean what I think it does?"

Carthy placed both hands on Tom's shoulders.

"'Tom, this was and is your home. Here you are a free man and always will be."

Tomas Cork looked for his son.

"Bill, come and meet an Irish gentleman."

Bill walked toward both men saying,

"Pat and I met Donal last night, dad."

And, in a slightly strained voice added,

"He wouldn't tell us anything either."

Tom looked at his brother.

"It's time, Con, come what may, these men have a right to know."

Connor and Thomas Cork walked with their sons and Catherine and Bill Buchanan across the land where they had been born and raised. As they approached the ramshackle cottage, Connor, with anger in his voice, demanded,

"Donal, I sold this property as a going concern to people who swore they would work it. What happened?"

Carthy lifted his head.

"Con, things got very bad here for certain families during the war of independence and afterwards. There were murders here and all over West Cork...."

He paused before finishing the sentence.

"There was a lot of violence toward some people."

Tom asked,

"By some people, do you mean the British and Irish Protestants?"

The old man nodded his head.

"Yes, Thomas Cork, after 1921, things became very hard for everyone in West Cork."

He looked at Connor.

"The people who still own the farm also bought the Bagot's land. They moved out in 1926."

Then, switching his gaze to the fields next to the Corks,

"Now, as you can see, both are growing wild."

Pat, who had been deep in thought, was about to speak when his father said,

"There's one thing that must be done before anything else."

Turning to Bill and Pat, he continued,

"Lads, follow me back to Dunmanway. Donal, would you come with me and Tom?"

Charles Lewis and Pearse Brogan enquired at the Parkway Hotel as to where Pat and Bill Cork might be found and, when told, decided to wait for them to return. Graham Bagot was in Dunmanway and, having stopped, asked a man who was walking by,

"Excuse me, but I'm looking for the property that used to be owned by the Bagot family."

The local man pointed to the far end of the town square as he replied in a slightly stilted manner,

"Go straight ahead, then turn left and head out the road for nearly a mile. You'll know when you see fields that aren't worked."

He paused, looking at the car and Graham Bagot, then added…..

"And the ruins of two houses, one a cottage, the other a bigger house."

On the other side of town, Pat and Bill watched as their fathers came out of the farmers supply shop with a shovel, briar hook and a rake. Catherine Buchanan then appeared from the general store next door with her husband, both carrying boxes of flowers and potted plants.

The reason for these purchases was soon obvious as the cars stopped outside the Dunmanway Catholic Burial Ground near the Parish Church. Connor and Thomas walked straight to a badly overgrown grave and began to clean the weeds and briars from it. The Buchanans stood a little away. Bill and Pat ran to their father's side and began to help them clean and tidy the grave of their grandfather, William Cork. After half an hour of clearing weeds and briars, Connor and Tom pronounced themselves happy with 'Daddy's' grave. Then, along with their sons and Catherine Buchanan, they planted a flower for every one of William Cork's grandchildren. A priest had been watching from the nearby church and went to Donal Carthy, who had been standing with Buchanan. Carthy spoke to the young curate, who then approached the people around the grave and, looking directly at the brothers, said,

"I hope I am not intruding. Mr Carthy has explained the situation, and I am led to believe that neither of you are particularly religious."

Connor and Thomas remained silent as the man continued.

"May I just say this, God bless you all and welcome home."

The young priest then blessed the grave of William Cork without objection from two generations of his family, who then stood in silence for some time. Whether any prayers were said will never be known, but anyone passing would have witnessed a very private and yet, for the people involved, profoundly moving event. Connor broke the silence.

"Catherine, Bill, thank you for the way that you have helped my brother and have supported us. I am glad you shared this with us."

Catherine's eyes filled with tears. The big Texan just looked at his godson and slowly nodded his head. Bill suggested quietly,

"Maybe we should get something to eat. It's been a long day for all of us."

Catherine took over the organisation of the meal and arranged a private dining room. Just before they sat down to eat, Lewis and Pearse Brogan introduced themselves. Pat, delighted to see Charles, invited both to join the meal.

Graham Bagot had followed the directions to the letter and arrived at the land which had once belonged to his family. On the drive down, he had tried to imagine his emotions at this moment but now felt as he did earlier. These were just fields and stirred no emotion. His branch of the Bagot family were not farmers or builders. Graham Bagot was a policeman first and foremost and had always wanted to be and was going to join the 'Met.' This part of Ireland was beautiful, but it was not home. Ulster was just as beautiful, and that was home. He decided to drive back to Dunmanway, find Pat Cork and see if the 'Peters files', as he had labelled them, were of any help to him.

In London, Jessica Cork had told all of the ranch people when they would be going home. Charlie Rawlings was a very satisfied man as he enthused about the profits from the cattle supply contract and the excellent contacts made in London. Drinking a gin and tonic with his daughter,

"You know, Jessie, I could get used to London Town."

He sipped again and added,

"But I guess we have to go home."

His daughter replied in an exasperated voice,

"Dad, we are all set to go home now. All we need is my husband and son and the Buchanans to go with us."

The private room was quiet as everyone enjoyed their meals. Graham Bagot slowly opened the door and was seen by Pat Cork, who, having shaken his hand, introduced him.

Connor stood, as did Tom, and greeted the young Ulsterman with handshakes. Then listened as Pat told them of Graham's involvement in Dunmanway.

"Graham's surname is Bagot, and his father is first cousin to the family who used to live next to you."

Connor glanced at his brother and saw the blood drain from his face. Also aware of the change in his uncle, Pat continued,

"I met Graham when we were alongside in Derry. He is a Detective Sergeant in the RUC and has discovered some RIC files which relate to Dunmanway from 1914 to 1921."

Bill was now greeting Bagot and noticed how his Uncle Con's face had suddenly gone very pale.

49

True Colours

Tom Cork's face reflected pure fear. For twenty years, he kept the secret of why he had left Dunmanway from his son. Now there were no more excuses. He stood; his eyes glued to Bill.

"It's been too long. Now we are home, let's get the whole story out in the open."

In the small hotel, a man who had been in and out all day, silently watching one of the Cork party, left to use the town's only public phone.

Tom told of being in the IRB with Con and the arrest of the men bringing guns to Dunmanway. Then, looking at Con, he added,

"I saw Philip Bagot's face. He knew Con, as sure as God he knew."

His words were met by silence. So Tom told of watching the Bagots find rifles on the Cork farm. Suddenly he stopped, again looking at his son. Connor demanded,

"Go on, Tom, finish, for God's sake, finish."

Tom continued.

"I had a pistol, got up close and shot Philip and George Bagot…." His voice trailed off. Con spoke.

"I'll take it from here. Peters went mad, looking for a reason to hang anyone in any way connected with the IRB."

Donal Carthy supported Con.

"God help us, that RIC District Officer, Peters, was a terrible man. No one had ever seen him so demented and obsessed."

Tom walked toward Graham Bagot, his hand outstretched.

"All I can do is say sorry for what happened."

Bagot, now standing, replied,

"Mr Cork, I have no feelings either way regarding what happened. What Philip Bagot did was his choice, as what you did was yours. I have no interest in what happened years ago."

He spoke to the room.

"I worked for Peters during the war and know that bigoted tyrant well enough."

A phone rang in a small bar a short drive from Dunmanway.

"He'll be here for the rest of the evening. There's only a few tourists and some Irish back on holiday with him."

The line went dead, the man who had answered turned and spoke to three other men.

"He has no bodyguards; he'll never know what hit him. We'll wait in the car park and do the job there."

They climbed into a car and headed to Dunmanway to take revenge for the pending execution of two IRA volunteers by shooting Pearse Brogan.

Tom sat beside his son.

"Well, Bill, now you know. I killed two men."

Bill's face was as calm as his voice.

"Dad, you were in the middle of your war just the same as I was when I killed. As Bagot said, It's all a long time ago."

Then added,

"Who wouldn't fight for this land?"

Connor watched his brother react as if a huge weight had been lifted from his shoulders. Bagot spoke up.

"I have documents that may help you answer some questions about events around that time. They cover RIC operations in West Cork from 1914 to 1921."

Tom Cork asked,

"Sergeant, you are an RUC officer. Why are you giving us these papers?" Bagot answered sharply,

"The papers have no operational value to the RUC."

Then in a firm voice stated.

"And I am not an RUC officer. I will soon be joining London's Metropolitan Police Force."

Pat interrupted.

"Graham, I take it the documents are in the car. Come on, I need some fresh air."

Lewis stood.

"I'll go as well."

As the three men left, Pearse Brogan and Donal Carthy sat and told the Cork brothers and Bill about their involvement in the 'War of Independence' and the Civil War.

In fading light, as they walked toward the hotel, Lewis posed a question.

"Why would three men spend an hour or more sitting in a car park in Dunmanway? Any ideas?"

Pat chipped in,

"Make it four, Charles. The same question goes for the man by the lamp post."

Lewis continued.

"Maybe we should mention it to General Brogan."

Bagot's voice was questioning.

"General? Pearse Brogan is a general?"

Lewis gave both a quick history of the man.

Pat suggested,

"Let's get back inside. One thing at a time."

Pat and Graham Bagot put a small number of files on a desk and the policeman got to the point.

"These papers were compiled by Peters."

Picking up one file, Bagot continued as he looked at Tom Cork.

"This describes how Philip Bagot and others reported to Peters on IRB activities throughout Cork, so it is possible he knew about the arrests."

Brogan, having joined them, was looking through the other files as Bagot carried on.

"Peters had 'sources' in every town who were protected from possible IRB reprisals by the following standing order, 'In the event of large-scale rebel action, all known IRB men are to be arrested and held until the situation becomes clear. All 'sources' are to be given escorts until further notice.'"

Pat spoke as he handed some sheets of paper to Brogan.

"These papers seem to be two lists. I'd say the names in one are IRB men, the other, informers or sources. Philip Bagot is on the second list."

Brogan read the papers and commented,

"We had our suspicions about informers in the IRB. Sometimes the British and the RIC were ready for attacks and raids. Mind you, it could have been just bad luck. The Middleton men's capture could have been either."

The Corks, fathers and sons, sat in silence as Brogan handed Con the 'list,

He gasped as he handed it to his brother.

"Tom, this is the same as the papers we stole from Peters' office."

Pat Cork was reading another document and pointed to some writing in red ink.

"This may explain Peters' behaviour. It says, 'Only two copies of the attached list were made. One is now missing.'"

Graham Bagot suggested,

"He presumed you'd read the missing list and, having seen Philip Bagot's name, shoot him." Tom exclaimed,

"Jesus! We didn't have a clue what that bloody list meant."

The room was quiet until Connor looked at his son and nephew and asked,

"Well, did you get what you were looking for?"

There were silent signals of assent from both,

"Tom, we need to talk alone and maybe sort out a few things."

They moved to the deserted hotel bar.

"Tom, you were right all along."

"I was only guessing - and look where it got us."

In the dining room, Pearse Brogan stood.

"I need some fresh air."

Charles Lewis was at his side quickly.

"Wait a moment general. We think you may have some unwanted company."

Brogan's face was quizzical.

"Go on, Charles."

All four men went to the windows overlooking the car park. Pat asked,

"Mr Brogan, do you recognise the man leaning against the lamp post?"

The answer was in a voice laced with contempt.

"Yes, he's one of the self-appointed freedom fighters."

Then Brogan quietly demanded,

"Alright, gentlemen, what's going on?"

Lewis told him. Brogan seemed to be thinking out loud.

"They could be part of the same group as the two men recently sentenced." He paused to think.

"The Gardaí only have one man on duty in town, and he could be on patrol around the area. I'll phone Bandon Gardaí for reinforcements – but that could take a while."

Bill suggested,

"There is a way to force them to show their hand."

Brogan warned,

"Jesus, lads, they could be armed."

Then seeing no reaction said,

"Tell me what you have in mind."

Buchanan concluded the ensuing plan with,

"Leave the lookout to me."

On seeing Pearse Brogan walking toward the end of the car park, the waiting men got out of the car. In their haste to catch him, the IRA men ignored three drunken revellers, staggering toward them in fits of laughter, followed by a much bigger man who called out in an American accent,

"Ok, I'll get the car you, drunken bums. Hey! The car's over here, you jackasses!"

Brogan walked briskly. The three merry tourists were now very close to the unknown men. Within seconds Bill Cork had knocked the first man unconscious. The second was lying on the floor semi-stunned, his attacker, Pat Cork, frisking him for a weapon. The third had produced a pistol from his coat which he aimed at Brogan. A rabbit punch from Lewis knocked the pistol to the ground. A solid crack was heard from under the lamppost as Buchanan felled the lookout with a classic straight right jab. Pearse Brogan looked at the men on the ground and, seeing the gun, ordered,

"Right, gentlemen, when the Gardaí arrive, leave the talking to me."

Con and Tom were sitting in the bar, trying to come to terms with what Graham Bagot had told them, when Pearse Brogan came in and made a phone call. He left as quickly as he entered, assured by Bandon Gardaí that enough men and vehicles to arrest and transport four prisoners had been dispatched to Dunmanway. Oblivious to all this, Connor looked at his brother and said.

"Tom, I don't know what to say."

His brother replied,

"Jesus, Con boy, you're not the only one."

Carthy, seeing their utterly confused faces, joined the brothers and asked,

"Gentlemen, as someone who watched you grow up so young, may I offer some advice?"

They nodded. Carthy began,

"All I can say is that what has happened cannot be changed. You must both accept that. You alone know how you both feel."

The brothers remained silent as the elderly man spoke passionately.

"There has been too much time lost by you both; don't waste any more. Forgive each other and be proud of your families and the lives you have built for them."

Connor looked at his brother.

"I think Donal's right. I was wrong to blame you for everything, and now I know how much I missed you. We can't change anything, and I'm sorry Tom boy." He gently probed,

"What do you think?"

Tom had tears in his eyes.

"Jesus, Con boy, I need time to think this all through, but I will say this - and I mean it."

He touched his brother's hand.

"Apologies don't come easy to me, but I'm saying sorry for all the trouble I caused. I never meant to hurt anyone in the family."

Carthy hoped the Corks were finally forgiving each other and cautiously tested their mood.

"Well, two Cork men admitting they were wrong, that must be a first in Irish history."

The ensuing laughter proved that no more words were needed. At that moment, several Gardaí marched the four, worse for wear, would-be assassins into reception, where an inspector demanded,

"Does anyone know what happened here?"

Carthy watched as Pat, Bill, Lewis, and Buchanan came in accompanied by three officers. He immediately took charge and walked over, stood by the four visitors and announced,

"Inspector, these gentlemen are my clients and will remain silent until I have consulted with them."

The brothers stood as Tom exclaimed,

"Jesus, Con, here we go again!"

Brogan appeared and spoke to the inspector, who announced,

"Mr Carthy, your clients will not be facing any charges. As for the other men here, charges, if any, will be made later. They will be detained overnight for further questioning."

As the Gardaí and prisoners left, Bagot, who had been working through all the Peters files, called,

"Mr Brogan, these files are yours if you want them?"

For the next two hours, Pearse Brogan pored over the papers. The information in the documents was, even twenty-five years after the events, politically explosive and potentially very damaging for a number of people both in and opposed to the ruling establishment of the Free State.

There were a number of goodbyes outside Bandon Gardaí barracks as the town clocks chimed noon. Donal Carthy was sad to see the Cork brothers leave and after he had praised their sons, remarked of Tom's friend,

"So, Texans are that big and tough."

As Connor was packing the car, he noticed Pat in deep conversation with the solicitor. Then the two-car convoy headed towards Dublin and the ferry. They had five days left. As Connor drove along the road to Cork City, he relived the events leading up to the night the Bagot's were killed. Suddenly, he said to his brother,

"Tom, that's why Peters beat me up. He was certain we had the bloody list."

There was silence for a moment then Tom asked nervously,

"Do you still keep in touch with Cora and Josie?"

"Regularly, by letter," Con replied. Tom's voice was plaintive.

"Connor, I've always blamed myself for mammy dying so young, but after what we heard last night, I'm not sure it was all my fault."

He faced his brother.

"I need to see where mammy is buried and.............. Maybe try to explain the whole desperate mess to our sisters," he added hopefully.

Con was increasingly conciliatory.

"Well, Tom, I think you've earned the right to explain, but it's not just your mess - it's just as much my fault. We'll do it together."

The car, followed by an increasingly confused Pat Cork, reached a major crossroads and turned north towards the midlands. Bill noticed Pat's puzzled look.

"What's up?"

The reply was ambiguous.

"I don't know where we're going, but it certainly isn't Dublin."

In the car ahead, Connor said to his brother,

"We'll head for Tipperary and then Leitrim and call in on our sisters."

In Bandon, Pearse Brogan interrogated the men who wanted to kill him. Two had just turned twenty, the others were older, and all were on the fringes of the IRA. The general could hardly contain his anger as the two younger men stood in front of him and the Station Superintendent.

"When are you stupid little boys going to grow up?"

There was silence, each prisoner looking at the floor. The superintendent posed another question.

"Are you aware that you could be charged with attempted murder?"

Then, in a ruthless tone, added,

"Upon conviction - that's fifteen years in jail, and I'd make sure you do every day!"

Brogan stared at both prisoners.

"Right, I have no intention of making you two martyrs. You will be released, and if I ever hear of you being involved in anything like this again, it will be leaked that you gave us names and locations of arms dumps."

He saw, from the terror on the young men's faces, they fully understood the consequences of such rumours. Brogan then shouted,

"Now, get out and never let me see you again."

The superintendent asked,

"Will they listen?"

The reply was heavy with contempt.

"If they have any sense, they will."

The Garda continued,

"What about the gunman and the lookout? What the hell was the point?"

Brogan answered,

"I think the attempt to kill me was motivated by revenge and their way of getting into the hard-line IRA."

He paused.

"Thankfully, they're no bloody good."

And continuing scornfully,

"The idiot with the gun wouldn't hit the side of a barn from the inside. As for the lookout, he might as well have carried a placard!"

The superintendent agreed.

"Well, now they've lost their private war."

Brogan picked up a file, and both went into the bare room which held the prisoners. He had decided to test the men's loyalty to the cause.

"My information is that the IRA has not sanctioned any attacks - which means that you two have serious problems - whatever we decide to do."

He then demanded sarcastically,

"So, what was that bloody stupid carry-on about?"

The man who had carried the pistol spat a reply.

"Doyle will hang because of you."

Brogan opened one of the Peters files and showed it to both prisoners.

"Look at this."

The gunman pulled his head away, but his comrade began to read. Brogan almost taunted,

"Go on, read about your bloody hero and then do something that might just save you both wasting your lives."

The lookout had been reading for a few minutes then said to his 'comrade'.

"You'd want to take a look at this."

Grudgingly, the gunman did. Pearse Brogan maintained the pressure.

"Take a good look, that's how much of a hero he really was."

The man reading retorted venomously,

"That's all lies! You made this up."

Brogan answered,

"That file comes from the RIC and the British. Look at the date."

He added,

"When that was written, I was on the run."

A flash of anger came across his face as he posed a question.

"You think about it. How did certain men always escape unhurt from any raids or ambushes by the RIC or British army?"

The gunman remained silent as the 'lookout' asked.

"What do you want?"

The general gave them little choice.

"If you don't want to be locked up for life, you will stay away from all politics."

After some silence, both men, now confused, asked for time alone. The superintendent barked.

"Five minutes only."

Standing outside the room, they listened to the prisoners argue vehemently. The superintendent asked,

"What's the point of this - we have enough to convict both?"

Listening to the row, Brogan replied,

"If we go to trial, our prosecution witnesses will be allied special forces officers. Two British and one American. How do you think certain people in Dublin will react when the defence asks about their involvement in the arrests?"

The Garda's eyes reflected his understanding as Brogan continued.

"And if he then demands to know if that involvement is deliberate collusion with the Allies and a direct contravention of Ireland's neutral status."

Brogan stressed the next point.

"Those same witnesses are all of Irish descent. I'm not having them, or their families drawn into this bloody nonsense."

Then pensively commented.

"Michael Collins once said to me, 'We can learn from everyone, including the British. They are the masters of divide and conquer.'"

The row was now a shouting match. He added as he opened the door,

"Let's see if the 'The Big Fella' was right."

The gunman was silent and surly as the lookout spoke.

"It seems you're right. Ok, it's over for us. We're out."

Brogan swore the Gardaí superintendent to secrecy and left the barracks to be greeted by Lewis with the words,

"I'm heading toward Kilkenny. May I offer you a lift?"

Brogan replied,

"I can be a risky man to be around."

Lewis laughed.

"That makes two of us."

Brogan sat in the passenger seat.

Josephine Maloney watched as two new cars pulled into the yard in front of her house. Her husband was working, and their children were on their way home from school. The man who stepped out of the first car brought a scream from her.

"Connor! Oh Connor."

A second man then walked around the vehicle; his face shrouded in a worried, half-scared look. She ran to her brother Tomas. The years disappeared in an instant as she hugged him, both now in tears. Then Con was in her arms – big, reliable, tough Con. The introductions were made as she hurried everyone into the house, embracing Pat and Bill and fussing over the Buchanans. Josie's children arrived home to find their mother in tears of joy as she introduced them to their uncles and cousins. Her husband was not far behind them and made everyone equally welcome. Con explained that they did not have much time, and then he and Tom told of what they had learned in the previous twenty-four hours. As evening came, Josie's husband drove into the nearest town of Clonmel and arranged hotel rooms. Then they listened as Tom tried to tell them about the last twenty-five years in just three hours. Josie Maloney made it abundantly clear that her brother, Thomas Cork, was welcome now and forevermore. They left late into the night with a sincere promise of more visits.

The next morning, as they checked out, Connor said to his brother,
"Now we have to see Cora; that could be a very different reunion."

As Lewis drove to Kilkenny, his passenger asked,
"Charles, would I be right in saying that you're close to your father?"
Lewis answered with silent pride,
"Yes."
Brogan continued.
"The information contained in the Peters files has given me some leverage over certain people."
Charles prompted,
"Please go on."
As they neared Kilkenny, the general had detailed his plan. Lewis replied,
"My father would agree with you, as I do."
Brogan smiled.
"Thank you, Charles."

Cora and her husband had guarded their family against politics. When the children asked questions about the War of Independence and the Civil War, their parents spoke about that period of Irish history in general terms. Occasionally, their father thought of two fine young men with sorrow and disappointment that the children would never meet their uncles. Dan Flaherty was a successful builder and had built a fine house for his family. When doing so, he had laid out a large area at the front where maybe, one day, his children would park their fine cars. Two such cars swung into the yard as he parked his small lorry. An unmistakable man got out of one, followed by another he thought he would never see again. The second car contained two young men and a beautiful woman accompanied by a big man. Dan walked towards his brothers-in-law, unsure what to say or do. Connor broke the silence,
"Tell me, Mr Flaherty, is there any chance of a cup of tea for weary travellers?"
Dan replied with pleasure,
"Welcome to my home."
He shook Connor's hand, then turned with hand outstretched.
"Welcome home, Tomas Cork."
The introductions were swift, Dan instantly recognising Bill and Pat and warmly greeting the Buchanans. Once inside the house, he explained that Cora was in town, shopping, adding,
"She has her own car, so she'll be home soon."

In the living room were photographs Cora and her mother had brought from the house in Dunmanway. Connor and Thomas were soon pointing out images of their youth. An engine noise was heard. Dan went out. A woman appeared at the door, the anger on her face obvious as she looked round the room. When Cora saw Bill and Pat, her face changed to a huge smile as she embraced both, followed by her big brother Connor. Tom stood alone as if waiting for judgement. Mrs Cora Delaney took her brother by the arm and said,

"Tom, we need to talk."

They went down the yard into a field just beside the house and walked and talked. Suddenly Cora threw her arms around her brother and, linking him, returned to the house. Cora looked round the room and said quietly,

"I think it's time we all went to see mammy."

The graveyard was a short drive, and they all watched Thomas Cork mourn his mother for the first time. He cried as he had so long ago above the high pasture. But now there was no despair, just tears of relief and joy that he was home and with all his family. Finally, Mary Cork's sons and grandsons planted flowers on her grave.

Back at the house, Cora served dinner to her visitors all the time asking questions about their families and homes. She sat between her nephews, just looking at them as her husband Dan asked about their war service. He had always been bitterly opposed to Ireland's neutrality - his face reflecting an attempt to understand their experiences. The evening flew by as the children asked everyone questions about Texas and London. Finally, Tom said,

"We need to find hotels for the night."

Cora was adamant.

"Tomas and Connor Cork, you and your guests will stay in my house tonight." Connor didn't press Tom about what was said by him and Cora in the field, silently delighted that the family was together. The morning came, and the Corks parted once more, except this time, their sadness was tempered with optimistic intent to visit at the first opportunity. As the cars drove away, Tom, still in tears, whispered,

"God, I wish Jessie had been here."

Then said exultantly,

"But she will be because I'll bring her and our children."

Connor drove on to Dublin with just four days left. Pat returned the car in Dublin. In Liverpool, a car was hired for the run to London. The phone at the Cork house rang and Mary's face made it clear to Jessica that all was well with the travellers. Tom spoke to his wife, as did her son, and both were hurried back to London with the words,

"Get here soon. We are running out of time."

The RAF officer approached Peter Vogt, who seemed to be asleep, and gently touched his hand. Vogt moved, his face lightening as he woke up.

"Well, wing commander, do you have anything for me?"

The officer's face broke into a smile.

"Herr Vogt, we have found your wife and family - but not in Wallgau. We checked all the large cities and found them with a family in Munich. They are shaken - but alive."

Vogt said, through tears,

"Munich? Who does my wife know there? Still, that's not important. When can we go home to Dresden?"

The wing commander straightened as he replied,

"Herr Vogt, Dresden is now in the hands of the Russians and is likely to be so for some time to come."

He paused.

"It is unlikely that you will ever be allowed to return to your home."

Vogt's face darkened.

"We have nothing. The Nazis took everything."

The RAF man cautiously enquired,

"Herr Vogt, there are some people here to see you. Are you feeling strong enough?"

The German looked up and nodded as the RAF officer waved his hand. Two civilians walked in, and one explained in detail the situation in Dresden. The former Luftwaffe pilot advised,

"I fully appreciate the effect of mass bombing and know a little of the Russians."

He then listened with growing relief as the second gentleman invited the Vogt family to settle in Britain. Though confused, Vogt was able to ask,

"Where will I find work?"

The man introduced himself as Mr Surtees from Rolls Royce and assured the research engineer and pilot how delighted they would be if he joined their jet-engine development programme. Peter Vogt did not take very long to accept.

As they organised the departure, Mary and Jessica Cork noticed how Con and Tom were utterly at ease with each other. The Buchanans and Charlie Rawlings were soon ready. Bill Cork, like all servicemen, travelled light. Earlier, he and Pat had found an hour to say goodbye in a small pub in Bayswater.

"Well, Bill Cork, it's all been very interesting."

His cousin fired back,

"Stop trying to sound like Churchill."

Pat laughed as he asked,

"How are you feeling about going home?"

Bill spoke slowly.

"First, I must see Mandy's parents, then I'll go to the ranch for a while and get my bearings. Then head for New York to find work. After London, I've begun to like big cities. Honestly, Pat, after that, who knows?"

He looked up.

"What about you, commander?"

Pat's reply surprised him.

"Frankly, Bill, I need a bit of stability. Maybe that's why I'm studying law. I need to do something productive and have some time to think about how I'm going to handle the possibility of being a father."

His face was perplexed as he continued.

"I've been wondering if I should tell my family. What do you think?"

They were silent until,

"Pat, I'd say stick to the original plan. Wait until you are qualified and then establish where you stand with the boy."

Again there was silence then Bill spoke.

"Forgive me for changing the subject...."

He paused as Pat faced him.

".....with a stupid question."

A short silence ensued until,

"Was it all worth it?"

Pat sipped his beer and replied,

"Bill, we helped beat a maniac called Adolph Hitler and brought our family together. The people who died - Mandy, the Paxtons and all the men we served with - I have no answers for that. But I know we can't blame ourselves just because we came through it in one piece."

Lifting his leg, he laughed.

"Well - almost."

Bill's voice was demanding.

"Jesus, Pat, where do we go from here? Christ! Every day for the last five years was an adrenalin rush. I'm getting bored already."

Pat advised,

"Well then, cousin, if that's how you feel, from what I've been told by the US Navy, New York is the place for you!"

Simpson-Coyle completed the reply to the allegations made by Oppenheim with great care. The document was read by the Director of the CIA with growing anger. UK passport records showed William Cork's parents entering the UK seven days before the Von Brauns left for the US, thus making it impossible for the Corks to have contacted anyone in the US, let alone Texas. The allegations against Major Cork and Commander Cork were groundless. Both officers had been under close arrest at a secure base. Then, having been demobilised had gone to Ireland, where they were now with their families. During this period, neither could have contacted anyone in the United States. Simpson-Coyle assured the director that the British Intelligence facility, at which the Browns and the officers had been held, was fully secure with all communications monitored and enclosed a document to prove it - the transcript of a telephone conversation involving the director himself.

Finally, Simpson-Coyle suggested a possible source of the leak by pointing out that the Von Brauns were well known throughout the worldwide scientific community. Any US academic could have recognised their work and, out of jealousy or greed, leaked their suspicions to the press. He then proposed that in the future, in the interests of secrecy between the US and UK, a forum for sharing intelligence be established between the CIA and MI6. Simpson-Coyle then ended his career in counterintelligence by, for the first time in over thirty years, committing his name, rank and signature to an intelligence document seen by someone outside the British Secret Intelligence Services.

In Dublin, Pearse Brogan stood in the office of the Secretary General of the Department of Justice and listened to the senior civil servant reply to his forthright proposal that the death sentences handed down to Doyle and his companion be commuted to life in prison.

"That's all very well, general, but I think I should make you aware that the Department of Justice is not in the habit of changing its mind based on proposals from you or anyone else."

Brogan smiled inside as he relished his reply.

"Well, you had better change your habits."

He then handed over a number of papers taken from the Peters files and continued,

"As you will clearly see, if these documents reached the public domain, there are a number of current government officials, TDs and senators who would have difficulty proving that the freedom-fighting records they claim are genuine."

He then spoke very slowly.

"It would appear that some of them were not quite as dedicated to the Republican cause, as early in the struggle, as they would have us believe. In fact, some did not become involved until the outcome had been decided."

The official simply replied,

"I'll see what I can do," then demanded,

"Where did you get these documents?"

Brogan couldn't resist,

"That is not the business of a civil servant. These papers are not the property of the Irish State. How I acquired them is not your concern. They are all genuine, and I have many more, all relating to the period 1914 to 1921."

Pearse Brogan was later informed through reliable, though unofficial channels, that both sentences had been commuted. Official confirmation was announced a week later. Brogan whispered to himself as he thought of his younger brother and Peter Lewis, 'There's been enough killing'.

Oppenheim was summoned to the office of the Director of the Central Intelligence Agency.

"Mr Oppenheim, you submitted a report to me which accused a number of American and British citizens and servicemen of serious breaches of security both in the US and the UK. I raised the issues in your report with the relevant personnel in British Intelligence, who have now replied."

The director summarised the evidence presented in the British document, which completely disproved Oppenheim's allegations. He then read the British assurance that the facility where the Von Brauns had stayed was completely secure. Oppenheim, now becoming angry, shouted,

"If it's so secure, how did I get the Von Brauns out from under their noses? I ran rings around them."

The director almost goaded,

"So you completely fooled them?"

Oppenheim spat,

"I made bloody fools of those upper-class clowns."

The director continued,

"Then perhaps you could explain how attached to this report, there is an exact transcription of the telephone conversation describing how the scientists were to be taken to the USA."

He paused then, with deliberate slowness, continued.

"The British had Werner Von Braun aboard one of their warships for at least five days. During which time he was interrogated by their top rocket engine experts, who got all the information they required from him. That is why you were allowed to remove the Von Brauns. The British had no further use for them. The upper-class clowns ran rings around you." The OSS man screamed,

"Let me see the report. I'm entitled to see it and know who wrote it."

The director stood and leaned toward Oppenheim to emphasize the next point.

"Mr Oppenheim, there will be no more said about the British report or who compiled it. As for rights, since you have told a tissue of lies, you have none."

He paused, trying to control his anger.

"I have now cancelled all warrants and subpoenas issued as a result of your scurrilous accusations against loyal and brave servicemen and honest upstanding United States citizens."

He spoke into the desk intercom. A man entered, and he was issued with orders.

"You will brief Mr Oppenheim on his new appointment as Station Officer in Cambodia."

Oppenheim demanded,

"Cambodia? Where the hell is that?"

He then showed growing appreciation of his situation by asking in a quieter voice,

"Do I have a choice?"

The reply was instant.

"Yes. Take this posting, or tomorrow morning this officer will ensure that you sign your official resignation from the Central Intelligence Agency."

Two weeks after receiving Simpson-Coyle's report, the director ordered the CIA station chief in London to propose a permanent weekly meeting between CIA and MI6 officers to share information of mutual interest. The proposal was quickly approved by the British Foreign and Commonwealth Office and the US Department of State. Colonel Simpson-Coyle held one more meeting with Odin, 'C' and Maiden Aunt, at which he was secretly promoted to brigadier and immediately retired with full pension and the top-secret grateful thanks of His Majesty's Government. After Simpson-Coyle had left, Menzies asked his colleagues a general question.

"He has mellowed considerably. What do you think changed him so much?" Spenser looked at Davies.

"Maiden Aunt, you worked with him closely."

The Welshman eased back in his seat.

"He finally realised we couldn't win the war without the amateurs and part-timers, and I think he actually began to like people." Davies paused.

"He said something else." Both men noticed Maiden Aunt's face become serious.

"That he recently realised he'd spent his whole life fighting other men's wars."

All three men paused uneasily to think. Then closed the file of Brigadier Simpson-Coyle (retired).

The former colonial soldier and counterintelligence officer cleared his desk feeling great satisfaction. Always a man of frugal personal tastes, a brigadier's pension would make life very comfortable.

Unknown to him, at MI6 HQ, three spymasters each held a glass of scotch as C said,

"Gentlemen. To the 'Great Game.'"

He paused as all three raised their glasses.

"To smoke and mirrors and the dark arts."

Then added in a weary voice,

"May God help us all?"

John Eldridge sat in Balliol College. He had never hurt a human being in his life. He felt no guilt whatsoever about being in concert with Colonel Simpson-Coyle in destroying Oppenheim. The rumour started at his request by a fellow academic in a US mid-west college had resulted in the article being published in the media.

The station officer's post in Cambodia was of no strategic importance to the CIA, and everybody knew it. Despite the people being welcoming and friendly, within six months, Oppenheim had discovered the opium-smoking houses. Boredom and isolation led him to inevitably experimenting with cocaine and heroin. He was finally listed as killed in action. There was no star placed on the wall at the CIA's HQ at Langley.

Pat sat with his mother and father in the drawing room. Beside him were Bill and his parents. Christopher and Rachel were pouring tea and drinks. Mary asked,

"Where are the Buchanans and Charlie?"

Jessica answered,

"They thought we needed a few moments; just for the Corks."

Connor raised his glass to his nephew and son.

"Well, gentlemen, you have both fought and won a war and know why your fathers left home. How do you both feel?"

Pat answered,

"Well, as far as I'm concerned, the war's behind me, as I hope it is for all of us who fought. Did it change me? I don't know. But I am certain of this. I feel equally at home in England and Ireland."

He looked at his cousin.

"Bill, what do you think?"

The reply came slowly.

"I agree with Pat, but I'll go one further. Only those who were in the fighting will know when it's over for them. No one else."

Pat was nodding his head slowly. Bill continued with a question.

"Where is home? Well, I'm a Texan, and yet I felt completely at ease in England and Ireland too. So much so, it wouldn't bother me where I lived or worked."

His parents began to see how much their son had changed and what his future plans might be. Pat spoke again.

"As for why you and Uncle Tom left - that's a very important part of our history too, so I'm glad it's out in the open."

He sipped his drink as Bill commented,

"Same for me."

Pat then spoke.

"I have to tell you something which may affect all of you in the long term." He paused.

"It's a secret I've been keeping." His cousin's face was a mixture of surprise and confusion.

Pat faced his father and uncle.

"I've been lucky enough to know two extraordinary Englishmen. They left me a substantial amount of money which I felt I didn't deserve and really didn't know what to do with."

He sipped his drink and continued.

"When we were in Dunmanway, I saw how much the farm meant to you and Uncle Tom. As I said, I felt at home in Ireland, and so did Bill."

He sat forward.

"So I bought the land that was your farm."

His father's and uncle's eyes were glued to him as he continued.

"I also bought the Bagot's farm. It seemed the right thing to do - after so much pain and suffering - to bring the land together."

There was silence for a moment before he continued.

"So it's there. A home for the Corks of whatever generation or nationality, and it's in Ireland and it belongs to all of us."

Pat Cork raised his glass.

"To Peter English and Peter Wilde, wherever they are."

Connor Cork's eyes were like saucers. Mary Cork just smiled. Tomas Cork held his wife's hand, a deeply peaceful look on his face. For the first time in living memory, two generations of the Cork family had nothing to fear from the past or the future.

Southampton was cold and windy as the Corks began to say goodbye. There was little point in trying to organise the farewell. Everyone just went around hugging everyone else over and over. Finally, the time came for all to say farewell. The Buchanans were already aboard and, with the ranch hands looked down on the dockside, where Connor and Tomas stood with Pat and Bill by the gang-plank. Charlie Rawlings linked Jessica, who linked Mary, Rachel and Chris as they listened to Connor say.

"Goodbye, Tom, and we'll see you in the Double B soon, maybe within a year." His brother replied,

"Connor, come as soon as you can. You'd love the Big Bend country and Texas would welcome a man like you."

Rawlings sensed his son-in-law had more to say.

"Connor, maybe the sons our beautiful wives gave us brought us together, maybe it was daddy and mammy, I don't know but I have never been happier than I am now. Let's live with the past and enjoy the future." Then the brothers embraced. Aboard, Buchanan looked on.

"That's the way it should be with family. There's nothing more important honey."

Catherine squeezed her husband's hand as she replied,

"I know, Bill, and this is our family on both sides of the ocean. Mary told me so."

The big man replied,

"Well, it doesn't get any better than that."

Dockside Connor spoke.

"The Cork family has three homes now. One in the US. One in the UK." Pat continued

"And one in Ireland." Bill joked.

"We'll need our own flag." His father spoke proudly.

"Yes, made up of the colours of Ireland and America and Britain. Our flag will be Red, White and Green."

Acknowledgements

With thanks to my friends Jim Gornall, Frank McNerney and Dr John Halkett who offered great encouragement and had the patience to read the very rough early drafts of the novel.

Thanks to Billy Keane for telling me, 'You can write, now go and do it!'

Thanks to Breeda Mullen for being a good friend.

Joe Lane, Listowel November 2022.

About the Author

Joseph Lane was born in North West London to Irish parents in 1955. Upon leaving school he furthered his education by vocational training providing expertise for employment in management positions in the security, logistics and financial services sectors in the public and private sector. Including a number of years at Lloyds of London.

Having moved to Ireland in 2000 Joseph worked in logistics and distribution for a variety of large Irish companies, including Kerry Group Plc and Dunnes Stores. While working in Bandon he became a close friend of the late Liam Deasy, whose uncle fought in the War of Independence, before becoming a leading figure in the anti-treaty movement in Cork. Being the son of a Cork man his interest was aroused as Liam told of many incidents from the Civil War related to him by Liam Deasey. Added to this during a Writer's Week event in Listowel an actor from Fermanagh spoke of how his uncles had fought for the Allies in WW2. These events and people inspired the idea of the novel *Red White and Green*.

www.ingramcontent.com/pod-product-compliance
Lightning Source LLC
Chambersburg PA
CBHW050840210726
48290CB00004B/1013